I0758042

Hunted by Fate

A Gown of Leather and Bone
Volume One

Aurora Steinhart

Copyright © 2025 by Aurora Steinhart

All rights reserved.

No part of this publication may be reproduced, distributed, or transmitted in any form or by any means, including photocopying, recording, or other electronic or mechanical methods, without the prior written permission of the publisher, except as permitted by U.S. copyright law. For permission requests, contact Aurora Steinhart at aurora.steinhart@gmail.com.

The story, all names, characters, and incidents portrayed in this production are fictitious. No identification with actual persons (living or deceased), places, buildings, and products is intended or should be inferred.

No generative artificial intelligence (AI) was used in the writing of this work. Without in any way limiting the author's exclusive rights under copyright, any use of this publication to "train" generative artificial intelligence technologies to generate text is expressly prohibited.

First edition: 2025

Cover Design by Dragana; Graphicsoulart

Printed in the United States of America

ISBN – 979-8-9914855-2-4

Hunted by Fate

*A Gown
of Leather
and Bone
Volume One*

AURORA STEINHART

*To my book besties that wanted a
smutty, dark romantasy,*

this one, is for you.

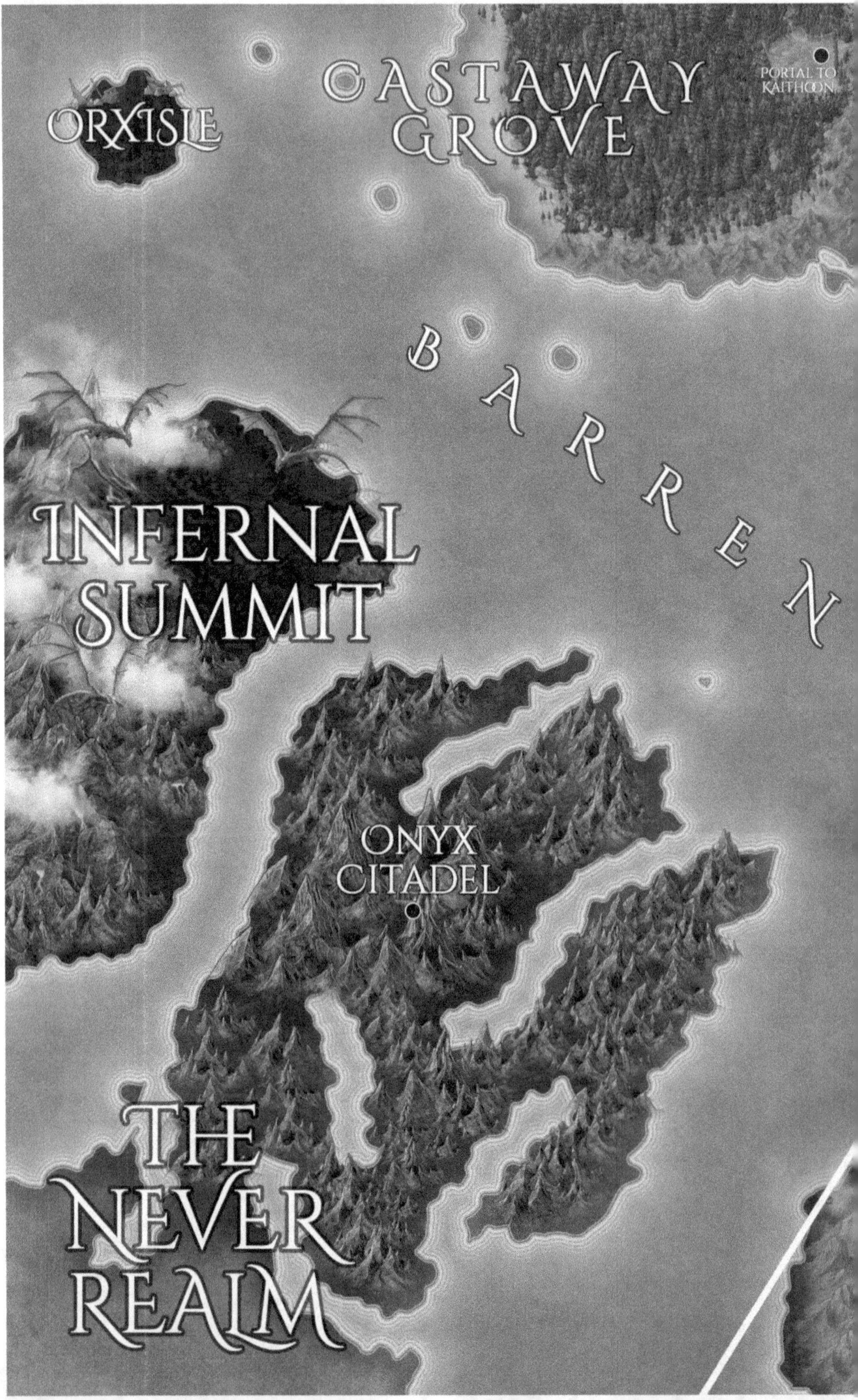

ORXISLE
CASTAWAY GROVE
PORTAL TO KAITHOON
BARREN
INFERNAL SUMMIT
ONYX CITADEL
THE NEVER REALM

TANTALIA
THE NEVER REALM PORTAL
THE FARMLANDS
CELESTIAL KEEP
THE CATACOMBS
THE BARRACKS
DEMON'S COVE
THE PITS
THE ANCIENT WISTERIA
KAITHOON PORTAL
WARD LINE
WEST TERRITORY RAVENSONG TREETOPS
NORTH TERRITORY BLOODREIGN ESTATE
TANTALIA PORTAL
EAST TERRITORY SHADOWFANG HIDEOUT
CITY CENTER
BLACKWOOD BUNKER
VESPERHOLM
GULF
WARD LINE
KAITHOON REALM OF MAGES
TANTALIA PORTAL
FORGE CASTLE
TOWN CENTER
PORTAL TO CASTAWAY GROVE

Index

People

- Seraphina - sair-uh-fee-nuh

- Velaria - veh-lar-ee-uh

- Learra - lee-are-uh

- Orona - or-oo-nuh

- Zephyra - ze-fur-uh

- Zyrella - zeer-ella

- Reasha - ree-ahh-sha

- Xeneera - ze-near-uh

- Bruthar - brew-thar

- Psylax - sigh-lax

- Kyraxes - kai-rax-eez

- Vizzuu - veez-oo

- Xykes - zai-kess

- Vylai - vai-lie

<u>Places and Things</u>

- Lapis Crpytus – Stone Crypt

- Lapis Amoretstra – Stone of Love and Chaos

- Knogdagh – nog-dag

Hymns
for
the Wicked

The list of songs I used while writing this book, were far too long for a paper list. So, I have provided a code for your use instead. Merely point your looking glass at the labyrinth below, and tap the small portal that appears.
(point your camera at it, and tap the link)

Or, You can look up the playlist "Hunted by Fate" by Aurora Steinhart on Spotify.

Cock Docket

For those of you that are not so interested in
the spicy bits and pieces.
I have provided a docket of sorts to skip.
Or… to turn to if it so tickles your fancy.
Happy reading, Darlings.

Chapter
4
Chapter
20
Chapter
23
Chapter
28
Chapter
31

Chapter
35
Chapter
38
Chapter
48
Chapter
49
Chapter
56
Chapter
61

Disclaimer
Please Read

This is a succubus story.

What is a succubus?

Merriam-Webster defines a succubus as:

"a demon assuming female form to have sexual intercourse with men in their sleep."

The FMC in this book draws her power and strength from sexual intercourse. She also uses it as a way to work through her emotions. (Toxic and unhealthy, I am well aware, but this is fiction and she is a demon. Demon's aren't exactly... non-toxic.)

That being said, there are scenes in this book that may be seen as gratuitous, and deemed unnecessary.

This is for two reasons.

1. I wanted to write more smut.

2. Because they're succubus.

Also, seed and cunt are used profusely. So.

Listen, it's like medieval, olden times, alright, I'm trying to stay time period accurate.

Jizz and cum is not period accurate.

We listen and we don't judge.

TRIGGER WARNINGS
READ AT YOUR OWN RISK

While I don't usually provide trigger warnings; I find it imperative for this book, as the subject matter can turn dark, rather quickly.

Therefore, if there are any instances in which you may find your mental health to be compromised; please, take a step back, put the book down, have a cup of tea, and find your peace.

Because there is a chance you will not find it in this story.

Happy reading, my dear friends.

- Depictions of death

- Blood/War

- Graphic sex scenes

- Consensual nonconsent

- Aggressive/angry sexual intercourse

- Forced/non-consensual breeding

- Many instances of choking

- Near-death experiences

- Dealing with loss and grief of a loved one

- Panic

- Feelings of inadequacy

- Depictions of male/female rage

- Men in captivity

- Family drama

- On page description of decapitation

Hunters are equipped with the ability to resist the succubus. And I **have** to do this if I have any chance of survival. If my **people** have any chance at survival.

Prologue
The Alley

Asher Blackwood
Five years ago

Congealed muck squelches under my boots as quick breaths escape me. My eyes drop to the ground below, connecting with the dying heap of limbs and wings.

The pungent stench of supernatural death adheres to my clothes and burrows into my nostrils as drips of a mystery liquid fall from my frazzled hair.

My onyx cloak is heavy and gore-soaked, causing the metal clasp securing it to press against my throat. Stray red splatter on the alley walls tell the tale of the slaughter that took place here.

That demon put up a good fight. Even if it was an almost backward game of cat and mouse.

Usually, they attempt a diversion, some method of their little tricks.

The mist. Their song. *Something.*

She did none of the above. She came to me willingly; said she had been looking for me. And while she put up a fight, I didn't expect a demon with horns of that size to be taken down so easily.

A jagged slit runs from one side of her neck to the other. And under it, a necklace.

Clotted blood pools in the space between the gem that adorns the thick chain and her wound. It's of considerable size and it pulses a bright

1

purple. The pulse slows until the light fades and eventually blinks into the darkness.

I nudge her shoulder with my boot.

She doesn't move. She no longer breathes.

"Vesperholm thanks you for your sacrifice," I murmur to the dead demon. Crouching down, the fabric of my breeches soaks up the sludge that runs through the spaces of the cobblestone. I press her eyes closed with my blood-dampened leather glove.

The once vibrant magenta orbs have clouded, and her silver hair has lost its luster. But the massive black horns on her head look stark as ever against her now pale blue skin.

Leathery wings lay in tragic disarray on the ground, covered in more of the carnage. The tapered, sharpened wingtips leak green fluid that causes small drips to sound off in the silent alley. A small puddle of the liquid collects in a pit formed in the stone.

Poison.

I'm not a killer by nature. But my ancestry demands it, as do the skills that have been ingrained in me since birth.

Hunters are equipped with the ability to resist the succubus. And I *have* to do this if I have any chance of survival. If my *people* have any chance at survival.

I fish a hand into my pocket, retrieving a tattered cloth and wiping my dagger clean before I sheath it on my thigh. The worn fabric swipes over my brow, ridding it of the sweat before it finds its home back on my side.

My thick leather boots carry me through the puddles of gore on the cobblestone, toward the opening of the alley. When suddenly, I'm blown back against the stained brick. The impact against the stone empties my lungs as my body drops onto the ground and I struggle to breathe. Pain shoots through me as I attempt to lift my head to spot the source of the blast. Sharp breaths prick at my ribs as I try to inhale. Slowly, I make to my feet, all the while groaning in agony. Drops of liquid fly from the strands of my hair as I shake my head and face the threat that tossed me like a fucking ragdoll.

Massive wings beat powerfully in the small alley, kicking up more of the debris around us. Generous curved horns silhouette against the fired lamps on the street behind her, as silvery-white hair gleams and violet eyes pin into me.

A *new* demon coming to block my only exit home.

"LILITH!!!" her distorted voice wails. Iridescent tears shimmer against her pale skin as they streak down her face. Her hair begins to stand on end as it engulfs her horns and lightning crackles fervently around us, its vibrant hue illuminating the space where she has me cornered.

A thick, spaded tail articulates violently behind her as the massive, membranous wings bat once more, causing the air to twist with vengeance.

"YOU KILLED *MY* LILITH!!!" she screeches again. The dangerously high pitch causes my eardrums to wobble in pain, forcing my hands to clap over my ears.

Her cries spear through the sleeping town as she collapses next to the dead succubus. Debris drops from the air as the wind and lightning surrounding her slows and eventually dies. Defeat pulls her head, wings and tail to a droop as she grieves her fallen friend. They encircle her and her companion's body with the grace of a demonically stitched ball gown.

My chest heaves slowly, deliberately, as I observe her. Clawed hands tremble with grief as she removes the necklace from her fallen friend, bringing it close to her chest. The gem slowly pulses to life against her. It illuminates her features in a sickeningly purple hue.

Sharp, elongated ears peak from under her hair as starkly magenta eyes seem to glow against her pale skin. Full lips curve elegantly against one another, stretching maliciously up to her carved cheekbones. Her nose is softened to a small, rounded point. With a delicate chin and seductively tilted eyelids, she is reminiscent of a vixen.

She would be a breathtaking sight to behold... if I didn't have to end her life.

Unfortunate.

Rooting my feet into the cobblestone, I turn to her. My hand twitches above the handle of my dagger as I pin her with a glare. "You don't belong here. Leave! Before you end up like her," I warn sternly, my graveled voice scrapes against the dull air as I await her response.

The weeping ceases, and her head slowly lifts to meet my gaze. Her eyes narrow in warning as they connect with mine. Her armored bodice glints in the light of the moon as she stands. Metal scrapes against leather as the stacked plates on her shoulders move. The sound of the clasp along her large chest rattles against the scales armoring her torso while two sliver hilted handles protrude from behind her head, alluding to the fearsome weapons strapped at her spine.

Muscled legs are wrapped in the same onyx leather that binds her torso. With her feet sheathed in thick boots, she takes cat-like strides toward me. The tail attached to the back of her thick hips makes slow, irritated flicks. Her elaborate display casts sickening shadows along the ground as she advances. The massive wings at her back flare wide in the small alley to further block my escape. Moonlight filters through the thin, tough membrane that connects to the delicate bones, showcasing the haphazard lines that run through them like chaotic webbing. The sharp points of her expertly crafted armor that braces her forearms refract some of the night's light, signifying their intimidating curvature.

"You're quite the *strong man,* aren't you?" she mocks low and angered, her voice seeps with melodic tones. Her words sing a dangerously ethereal song.

"I'm a Blackwood, your powers have no use here," I retort.

"Oh, but don't they?" she responds as her booted foot splashes into the pooled blood on the ground.

"Did you not hear me, demon?! I'm a Blackwood!" I call again as my hand lays against my dagger. The edges of its ornamental handle bite into my palm and send my adrenaline running as my fingers wrap around the hilt.

Her steps are slow and precise as she comes within inches of my face. Ravenous eyes glide up and down my form before her long, clawed finger glides along my jaw. The sharp talon superficially sinks into my flesh as I peer into her eyes, the brilliant purple gleaming fervently with lust.

And the spell within them tugs viciously on my soul, pressing me deep against her being with the urge to take all that I can from her.

Succubus scents is always so strong and repulsive, usually it's some kind of disgustingly floral, musky odor.

But *her* scent is… decadent and rich. As if just the smell of her promises everything I could have ever wished for.

I can't help it when I hear her speak. I *want* to be closer to her. I want to be in her skin. I want to hear what she sounds like under my touch. I want to make her *shudder*.

"Did she scream?" she asks softly.

"They all do," I respond, though my throat betrays my confidence and my voice wobbles.

"Hm…" She ponders for a moment before she leans in. Her full lips part and soft, sultry tones pour from them as her breath grazes my ear.

Succubus Song.

"Your methods… don't… wo-" I attempt to respond.

But I can't. My voice fades as my body slowly melts against her. Her delicious scent increases and the restraint I've attempted to hold dear snaps under her influence.

She's enchanting. Mesmerizing…*Tantalizing.*

Her song tugs me deeper and deeper with pure need and desire. My gloved hand wraps around her jaw as I lean into her trap.

I need to taste her. I need to be *in* her.

I need… *need…*

The lustful haze lifts for the barest moment and it's all I need to grab hold of my restraint before yanking it with all my might.

Rough stone abrades my cloak as I step back, giving me enough space to thrust my boot into her generous chest. Her distorted screech echoes through the night as she stumbles and her wing lifts just enough to allow me exit.

I dip under the lifted appendage before my feet beat rapidly against the stone, racing to the end of the alley. I round the corner, onto the street where my horse, Gnox, is secured to a fired lamp post. My fingers grip at the free end of his tether, making quick work of the knot before I fling my leg over him and place myself sturdy in the saddle. My boot strikes into his side, kicking him into gear as we sprint toward the bunker at breakneck speed.

A tornado consumes my mind; thoughts and emotions swirl in a frenzy of confusion as I think of what came over me. The lust I just experienced. The desire I had acquired in the few seconds in her grasp.

I couldn't… block her entirely. She… she *broke through*.

That wasn't supposed to happen. It's the entire reason for my gifts. It's never happened.

It *can't* happen.

The Hunter Houses in Vesperholm are the only reason we have survived this plague as long as we have.

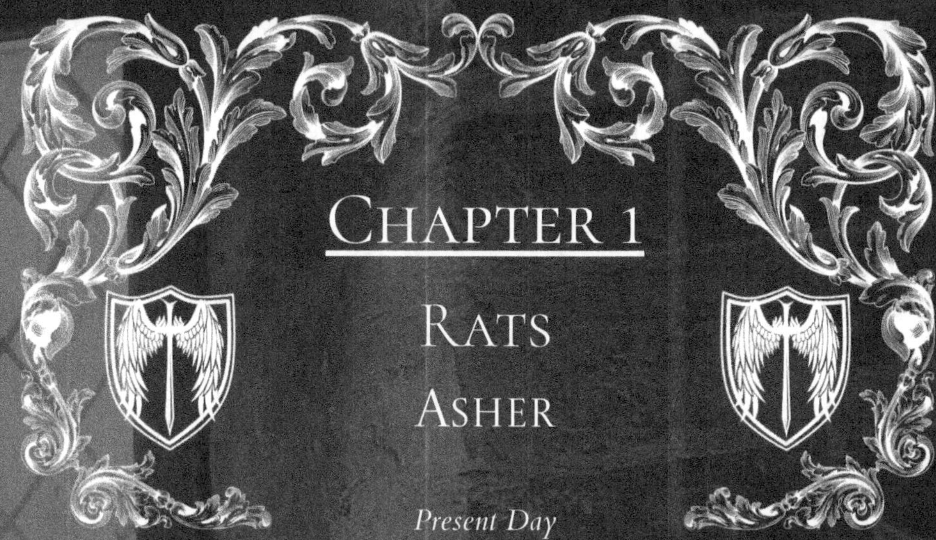

Chapter 1

Rats

Asher

Present Day

Gnox's heavy trot thumps against the rugged cobblestone in the abandoned South Territory of Vesperholm. Buildings that line the long main street of City Center sit in dilapidated chaos from the humans that raided their wares years ago. Window frames are decorated in jagged shards of glass from being broken, or are completely cordoned off by long planks of rotted wood. The once bustling area now feels like a ghost town.

But even ghost town would feel a tad generous for Vesperholm.

Pressure bears down on my windpipe from the small metal insignia that clasps my cloak around my shoulders as the wind tugs at its ends. I keep my eyes and ears open for any small animal to kill for dinner as Gnox and I march through the desolate town.

A rat, a squirrel. *Anything.*

The succubi that have continuously picked off our men has left us without farmers for meat and grocers for markets.

Tonight was my night to find dinner. If I wanted, I could go out to East Territory and hunt for a deer.

Maybe. Even that is not guaranteed.

Gnox moves along the road steadily, taking softer trots to not alert any wayward rodents. Broken glass from the shattered windows glints in the hazed and dulled setting sun where it rests on the sidewalk.

Blazed wood from the burning succubus bodies have clouded the air in City Center with stagnant smoke of floral death, like a bed of roses was set ablaze on an unmarked, rotted mass grave.

The few shops without their windows boarded have been left in shambles, with forgotten heirlooms and wares strewn about the floors covered in dust, webs, and age.

A gentle sigh escapes me as I remember how busy Vesperholm used to be. Merchants calling along the streets hawking their hard work, or women selling baked goods, handmade trinkets and clothing.

A *proper* city.

Most townsfolk have retreated to the forests -- what little of them were left.

The pitter patter of furred feet catches my ear, and I pull Gnox to a gentle stop. My head snaps to see a small rat chewing at a piece of rotted meat that festers along the dilapidated stone. The leather reins slide through my gloves as I slowly rest them at Gnox's neck.

I lock onto the rodent, moving at a snail's pace and try not scare it off.

Not too small. But big enough for at least one of us.

My foot swings quietly from Gnox and I creep against the cobblestone toward the little being. My hand twitches as it slides to the dagger sheathed on my thigh. In one swift movement, I grip the end of the handle between my forefinger and thumb, flicking it into the rat from where I stand.

Small squeaks replace the silence as I walk to retrieve my meager dinner. Eventually, the squeaking halts and the animal's breathing slows until it rests motionless on the ground.

I breath a relieved, yet annoyed sigh as I wrap my hand around the dagger, pulling the rat along with it. I slide the blade from the dead creature before opening the small bag I have strapped to my waist and dropping my dinner in it.

One down.

An hour or two later, I've collected a few more rats, and I feel like I can finally go home.

The sky has darkened into inky blackness and the moon is invisible from the clouds that surround our land.

The click of my tongue echoes through the town as I come up to the outside of an abandoned shop, causing Gnox to slow to the entrance of a deteriorating stable beside it. I swing my leg from my saddle and jump to the ground.

Leading Gnox inside I remove his lead and hang it next to his tacking gear. Gnox stands idly by his companions — my brother and father's horses — as I take long strokes of his thick, onyx mane. Some bits of dried blood and dirt flake from the strands as I run my gloves through it. The coarse fur of his face scratches into my forehead as I press it to his nose in goodbye.

The hay crunches under my boots as I exit the stable and enter the abandoned shop it's attached to.

The shop used to belong to us; a forging family we once were. We supplied armor and weapons to the town to fight off the threat, until it was discovered that there wasn't much that could be done anymore.

The windows have aged and some of the glass panels are shattered. The tables inside have been overturned, and it looks as if no one has been here in centuries. Webs and dust cover every small surface of the abandoned shop. Rusted knives, daggers and dulled axe heads litter the floor in a harsh array of disorder. The air is thick and damp with the scent of earthy mold.

The wooden floorboards creak under my weight as I make my way to a small door at the back of the shop. Amongst the dust, it sticks out because it's the only thing in here not rotted or covered by time.

The hinges creak as I pull the door open. Behind it, a closet, no bigger than a pantry. The only thing inside is a wooden hatch in the dirt floor.

Blackwood Bunker.

I lift the hatch and jump into the small hole at the bottom. A dirt tunnel, just barely tall enough for a full-grown man, leads into a long passageway of more dirt laden walls. Wood beams are erected every few feet to keep the tunnel from collapsing.

Dead ahead, a dull orange firelight wavers in the dark against the tunnel's walls. Once through the passage, I find my father and brother in the main living area, both deep in thought as they sharpen their weapons. They've waited for me to return with dinner.

Along the left wall is a wooden bench littered with more weapons, resting next to the main dinner table which seems to heave under the weight of the daggers and swords that also lay on top of it.

To the other side of the living area is a hearth that sits in front of worn leather armchairs. The large fireplace leads to a chimney on the outside, which keeps the smoke from killing us down here.

Our family crest sits above the dirt mantle. Large wings hide behind a version of the same dagger I now carry, signifying our strong familial power. We are the strongest hunter house in Vesperholm, even if we are the smallest. There is only me, my brother Cedric, my father Rowan, and my mother Ophelia.

There was my brother, Alden.

Was.

"Rats," I tell them softly. Unlatching the bag from around my waist, I drop it on the dinner table, causing the weapons to clatter around it. Four large rats fall from the bag and my brother and father to look at me with annoyed expressions.

"All I could get," I shrug as I grab a rat of my own. Reaching for one of the several daggers strewn about the table, I skin and gut the creature, preparing it to roast over the fireplace.

My brother and father sigh in unison as they each grab a rat, mirroring my movements.

"Who's gonna make mother's rat?" Cedric asks. A soft *riiiip* sounds from his hands as he rids the rat of its coat.

No one answers. Not even my father.

I sigh. "I'll do it," I say gently.

There is silence as we all settle into the daily routine.

Skin, gut, roast, eat.

The same thing, every day. I would barely quantify it as survival.

What I wouldn't give for a nice venison.

I prepare my rat and finish my meager meal before I begin on my mother's.

I left the largest one for her as she is with child. Another warrior to add to our small group of Blackwoods. There aren't many of us left. My father's brothers were picked off by the succubus. And soon after, their sons. The other houses were able to secure their lineages a bit longer with their decision to relocate to the forests. Ravensong and Shadowfang now live amongst the trees, while House Bloodreign can keep intact by hoarding themselves in their fortress they call a mansion.

Eventually, I prepare Mother's dinner. Standing from the hearth, I walk to the door that rests in the back of the living area, which leads to another tunnel, dimly lit by small piles of melted wax on the floor, with two doors on each side to signify our rooms.

My room, Cedric's room, my mother and father's room… and Alden's. I walk slowly past his door as I make my way to my mother, knocking softly against the wood before I enter. "Dinner," I whisper.

My mother looks up from her bed, giving me a tired smile. Her long brown hair is sprinkled with strands of grey, and the skin around her eyes has been creased by time. Having to bear children at her age has been hard on her, so she spends most of her days sleeping.

Her hand rests against her swollen stomach as she settles under her rough blankets. I have no idea how long she has left with this one, but it feels like it drags on, the more children she must bear. While Alden was the last, there have been numerous others.

They had not survived birth.

I bring the metal plate to the hardened mound of dirt next to their bed, leaving it there in case she decides to eat.

She exhales an exhausted moan as she drifts back to sleep. I give her a gentle smile as I retreat quietly from the room, closing the small door behind me.

I make my way back down the corridor, returning to my father and brother.

"Bloodreign has wares for pickup. And a sister to bed," my father grunts bluntly as I enter the living area.

I peer at Cedric cautiously, who rolls his jade-colored eyes. You'd think a man would be excited to fuck anyone he was allowed to. He surely wouldn't have any trouble finding a woman of his own. If our circumstances were different, of course.

His jaw is shrouded in a layer of short hairs. Something he usually keeps shaved down. With a prominent brow, dark green eyes, and high set cheekbones. His nose is like mine; sharp and strong, straight down his face. And a subtlety dimpled chin, just as all the Blackwoods have.

His mid-length brown hair is usually pressed back. Alluding to the number of times he runs his hands through it in frustration. He is only a few inches taller than me, with a similar build. Though, he has less tone than me. He isn't hunting as much these days, what with being made a bed brother.

But I think he *would* rather be out on the hunts. The eldest brothers of the Hunter Houses were never excited to bed the sisters. At least from what I've been told.

The Hunter Houses have hidden the women in secure hovels to sustain our population. After the men had been picked off one by one by one…

Vesperholm had no choice.

The Hunter Houses in Vesperholm are the only reason we have survived this plague as long as we have.

Only the top men of the houses are allowed to procreate with sisters of separate houses. Their powers of resistance are far stronger than any of the younger brood — my own included — which allows for better viability and greater strength in the spawn to come. Middle and younger brothers are trained in the hunter's gifts and used as weapons. Being able to combine the powers of the houses allows for the babies to be born with more than just one area of resistance.

If only to secure the stability of our town. We can't allow our future generations to be without the powers of the Houses. The brothers are not allowed to take wives, merely bed sisters of other houses. We can't risk the loss for them to fight over each other. From what I've heard when making rounds to the houses, the brothers just wanted someone of their own.

Our plight didn't allow that.

Even still… The new heirs are babies and therefore useless for another fifteen years.

Our lineages have become of the utmost importance.

House Blackwood, my own house, has what they've referred to as "*immunitas completum*," or complete immunity. We are immune to any succubus advances. Their mist, their songs, their movements, their seduction.

But I alone carry the relic to slay them where they stand. A dagger made from an obsidian blade. A metal black as the night itself. The handle and hilt are made of unique swirls and patterns, with a red ruby set within its hilt.

Other hunters have to aim for their heart with iron to kill a succ. I can slice one anywhere with the Blackwood Dagger and they fall where they stand. This dagger has been handed down through the generations. From Broward Blackwood, the founding member of our house.

"Why can't Asher do it?" Cedric groans as he crosses his arm against his chest in defiance. His eyes dart to the dirt floor beside the dinner.

Though he's thirty, he acts like he's twelve.

"Asher is a warrior, he needs to strengthen his own abilities. He has no time for breeding," my father retorts, not sparing either of us a glance.

Cedric scoffs as he stands from his chair. The wooden legs scratch into the dirt as he reaches for his black cloak that hangs on the wall near the exit tunnel.

I sigh a soft breath as I follow Cedric out of the bunker's main tunnel, accompanied by angry mutters that claw at the dirt walls. Climbing out of the hatch, we stalk through the shop and onto the street.

The two of us creep quietly through the night as to not alert any succs that may be skulking about. Cedric and I make our way to the stable, where the horses spook slightly at our arrival.

Cedric's booted feet crunch in the stable as he walks to the tall white horse that is grazing on a small bale of hay. He reaches down to tighten its saddle and check the bridle before he climbs on and exits the stable gates. I retrieve Gnox's reins and attach it to his bridle before I mount the saddle, giving a soft stroke to his mane before I click. He follows Cedric's horse out onto the street. Where the sound of our horse's hooves echoes through the cold, dark night.

Cedric has not said anything or even spared me a glance as we've meandered our way through the quiet city streets. The sound of our horses' hooves claps against the stone, until eventually they give way to dirt as we reach the edge of the city. Our path is now a dirt road all the way to the Bloodreign Estate.

The ancient mansion has sat high in North Territory of Vesperholm for hundreds of years, having been passed down from the founding member of House Bloodreign. A once wealthy family, they fell into peril just like the rest of us.

House Bloodreign are the only group of Hunters that are resistant to poison.

"Venenum resistentia."

They also create a poison that can slow the succ down enough to subdue them. But getting close enough to them without being stolen can be difficult. At least for the normal townsfolk that don't have any resistance capabilities. Getting struck by a poisonous wingtip can be lethal. The venom seeps through the veins and clots the blood, the victim then slowly is overtaken by their magic until it devours the body, leaving you to die as a rigid cask of meat.

Bloodreigns antidotes for such instances have come in handy more times than I can count.

The road to the estate is a long one, surrounded by dying trees that speckle against the landscape in a backdrop of rotted stems and drying branches. Paired with the lands of Vesperholm being unnaturally quiet at night, eventually, it gets to me.

"Do you think we'll ever have our land back?" I finally ask Cedric.

There is nothing but the sound of hooves against the dirt as we continue along our path. No birds, no scurrying critters. They have gone deep… deep into the woods.

"I don't know, Asher…" Cedric responds after a long moment, his voice low and irritated.

I sigh. "I wish there was a way we could end this plague."

"We've tried since we could hold a sword, I think this is just how things are," Cedric responds tersely.

The way he goes through the motions of our insufferable day to day sends fury through my veins.

He has no urgency to change our circumstance. No one here does. They all just want to keep the threat at bay. At least from the outside, that's how it feels. As the strongest warrior amongst them all, it feels as though I'm the only one who truly cares about going back to a normal life. The number of succs I can kill any given week rivals that of any of the other hunters. And I abhor it. I don't want to kill these demons. I just want them to go away. I've always been under the impression that an eye for an eye will leave our world blind.

But trying to convince anyone here to hold onto a demon for information is a futile attempt at salvation.

Everyone else gave up when they hid in the woods. But even I have no idea what to do. No matter how badly I want to change it, I can't do it alone.

"But you can't just give in to the idea of this life that easily, can you? What about our people?" I push. He has to feel some kind of anger to all of this. He *must* if he hates being subjected to *this* part of our reality.

"We have no choice, Asher, we have done what we could for centuries," Cedric says, his voice tenses higher as his frustrations increase.

"But we have the key to holding them back. Why can't we restrain one and get answers from them? Maybe there's a reason," I argue.

"They don't have a reason. They just fuck men and eat them. There's nothing we can do but fight back."

I sigh as I realize I'm tugging on a broken lead. The conversation falls from my thoughts, almost as quickly as it began. At this time of night, it's not worth the energy.

Other memories, however, are pushed to the forefront as the dark night presses in around us.

With the dark comes the memory of that succubus. The one in the alley…

Her impact has not been forgotten.

After all, even to this day, she was the only one I was not able to resist.

Every succubus since then has not had the same effect. They've sung me their song and blown their mist, and my heart has stayed true. Not nary a waver in my gifts when facing the other demons.

Every time I must kill one, I think of her. Why did she break through my fortress? How?

Was it a moment of weakness? Was I not developed enough in my power to resist her?

None of it makes sense, and every time it crosses my mind, anger pounds through my soul. I normally push it away and focus on the task at hand.

Any other option would result in blinding rage.

I shake my head of the pricking thoughts as we come across a row of dancing fired lamps that sit at the bottom of the hill. The Bloodreign Estate comes into view, and we begin the steep climb to the front of the mansion.

At one point, this house was the pinnacle of status in the land. The siding was a pristine ivory, and the windows were so clear you could swear glass wasn't there to begin with. Marbled columns stood around the house like solid, silent sentinels.

The lands were surrounded by bright green grass and an array of well-kept flowerbeds, their colors vivid against the luxurious exterior of the house.

That is no longer the reality for Bloodreign Estate. The grass has overgrown until it died and laid along the property in heaps of crisp blades. The flowerbeds hold thick weeds and memories of time where color existed.

The normally white siding is brown from the lack of upkeep. The once proud stone guardians are crumbling and consumed by vining plants. Rusted nails pierce through rotted planks of wood into the siding of the house. No one can see anything from the outside.

Cedric leads his horse into a large paddock that rests to the side of the house. He climbs down and ties his horse to a post inside and then takes the courtesy of tying Gnox up for me as well. Climbing off Gnox, I walk to Cedric, where we both amble the long path to the front door. Pebbles of wear chip off the steps as we make the hardened walk to the large oak doors. Cedric and I look at each other with a nod before he lifts a hand to knock.

The door opens, causing Cedric's fist to damn-near land on the chest of our gracious host.

Lothaire Bloodreign stands tall, proud, and regal in the doorway. His piercing blue eyes glance between both of us and he nods once before he turns around to lead us into the large foyer. The high-ceilinged entry chamber is in a state of disrepair so consuming that you might be fooled into believing that no one lives here.

Large white sheets cover all of what I'm assuming are heirlooms. Furniture, chairs, and other large objects have been sheathed in splotched, white fabric.

The chandelier is covered by haphazard webs and dust. Its once shimmering gems have dulled, and the air of the house is thick with the scent of decay and ancient textbooks.

Lothaire turns back around to us, offering a grimace to Cedric before he replaces it with a fake smile, "Emery will be down in a moment," he says curtly as he waits by the misshapen staircase. The wooden steps have been warped by what I can only assume is water damage. The roof and ceiling don't seem to be particularly secure.

Cedric rolls his eyes as we wait silently in the entry room.

"I hear from Shadowfangs that a portal has risen in the East Territory," Lothaire says to us matter-of-factly. His voice drips with regality, causing letters to roll off his tongue with ease.

While he is a rather tall member of the Bloodreign House, he is spindly. Not much for muscle, considering his contributions to Vesperholm are spent in a lab of sorts.

His short blond hair is neatly combed back with a sharp and narrow bone structure making up his features. The members of Bloodreign are usually cloaked in luxurious crimson cloaks.

Tonight appears to be no exception for Lothaire.

My brow furrows as I peer at Cedric from the corner of my eye in confusion. Cedric's eyes meet mine to return the sentiment.

Turning back my attention to Lothaire, "A portal?" I ask cautiously.

"It appears so. Though, it *is* Shadowfang. They're known for their tall tales," Lothaire shrugs.

I glance to Cedric again, to see him peek at me. I offer a nod to him, and he returns it as we turn our attention on Lothaire. We know that the Bloodreigns find themselves to be the height of our society. They tend to look down on the rest of us hunters. What with being holed up in a mansion, they are still under the impression they are better than us.

I don't believe they have accepted that they are just as fucked as the rest of us. The one thing Cedric and I tend to agree on is the audacity of the Bloodreigns at times.

But they continue to provide us antidotes and poisons, so we have it within our right minds to keep our mouths shut.

"So, this pick-up? Is it more antidotes?" I ask Lothaire.

"Antidotes, poisons. A new weapon of my own creation," Lothaire responds with a devilish smile.

I quirk an eyebrow in curiosity before my attention is brought to the sound of squeaking hinges and a door closing softly from upstairs.

The floorboards of the upper-level creak under the weight of light footsteps as a young woman comes around the corner.

Long, blonde hair frames her slender, pale face, and icy-blue eyes lock onto Cedric in apprehension. Her body, draped in a white, silk nightgown, mirrors the state of the other heirlooms in the house.

From my understanding, Emery Bloodreign is about twenty-five. Five years younger than Cedric.

She's given Bloodreign three heirs so far. One from Shadowfang, and two from Ravensong. Blackwood has none.

Blackwood has none from *any* of the houses.

Cedric eyes Emery cautiously before he climbs the steps, and the two disappear from whence the girl came.

Lothaire nods to me as he turns on a heel, leading me deeper into the mansion.

Cloth draped furniture feels like it takes up every corner of the house, and we pass numerous pieces until we reach a large door. Crimson light oozes from the space between the wood and the door jam, lending an eerie glow to the walls that surround it.

The door squeals as Lothaire presses it open and a flood of red smoke seeps into the hallway, giving way to the inside of the room.

Beakers and vials are hooked to a variety of glass and rubber tubing. Liquid drips and the sound of bubbling liquid fills the dark space.

I've been to The Antidote Room before, but the smoke is new. The shelves in the cramped room are crowded with small glass vials and bottles of various shades of liquids.

A buckled shelf rests along the opposite wall, its wood panels contorted under the weight of fraying leather tomes. In the middle rests a large wooden worktable that has been stained by Lothaire's creations.

Lothaire has been Vesperholm's top alchemist, providing antidotes and poisons to the hunters of our town from the moment he was old enough to mix them together.

There were times we've had to collect some of the succubus blood for his work. It proved to be a gruesome trial, but if it helped the good of our people, I was more than happy to oblige.

"So, what is this new creation?" I ask as we pass a distillation set up of dark red goo. The drips take forever to fall as they cling to the surface of the bulbous glass above it.

"Smoke bombs," Lothaire responds plainly.

My face contorts in confusion, "Smoke… bombs?"

Lothaire bends over beside his worktable, coming to a stand with a small wooden chest in his arms. He places the chest gingerly on the table before lifting the lid.

My normal pick-up of small glass vials is corked and glisten with red fluid. Some house green liquid that is a tad thicker. Alongside our normal pick-up are small black orbs that fill the empty space.

"These not only hide you for escape, but they also incapacitate a succ long enough for you to flee," he tells me as he picks up one of the balls. Its shiny surface reflects in the red glowing light of the laboratory. I watch as he moves the ball around in his fingers.

It seems unassuming and I imagine carrying some wouldn't be difficult.

But at the same time…

"I appreciate it, but why do you think Blackwoods need these?" I ask him.

Lothaire raises an eyebrow and gives me a small smirk as a scoff escapes him. "Better to have it and not need it, than need it and not have it," he responds as he places the ball back in the chest, closing and locking it securely.

"Fair enough," I tell him as I pull the chest from the table, holding it tight against me.

Heading back into the hallway, I turn to Lothaire. "Can you tell Cedric I'll be waiting for him at the paddock? I have to go secure this."

Lothaire gives me a slow nod as I make my way to the front door, his tall form falls in step behind me.

I turn around and give him a nod in thanks before he returns it and closes the door behind me.

I make my way to the horses, entering the paddock to walk up to Gnox. I press my forehead to his scratchy nose when I approach him. "Hey buddy, we have a package. I hope you don't mind," I tell him with a gentle smile.

Gnox huffs and I laugh at him in response. "Oh, come on, you don't mind."

I come to Gnox's rear, stealing a soft pat to his hindquarters before I retrieve a rope from my waist-bag, securing the small chest to his rump behind my saddle. Gnox's tail flicks back and forth before swatting at me as I secure the chest. I give him a soft laugh as I pat his rump. "Don't do that to me! You know this is part of our job."

Gnox huffs as his head bobs up and down. I come to the front and scratch at his mane as I smile. "See that's what I thought." I chuckle.

Small murmurs and a door opening break through the quiet night, the silence interrupted once more by the sound of the door closing. Booted steps grow louder as Cedric comes around the corner.

"Have fun?" I ask with a grin.

Cedric rolls his eyes, "Shut up," he responds tersely as he begins untying the horses from the paddock fence.

"Come on, don't you think it's fun to fuck one of your oldest best-friend's sister?" I tease as I reach for the horn of the saddle, shoving my boot into the stirrup and swinging a leg over. Settling into my seat I turn around to make sure the chest is secure before I turn to face Cedric.

He has yet to respond as he climbs his own horse, Rosey, and clicks her out of the paddock.

"It's not fucking funny, Asher," he grumbles as I follow him down the dirt road.

"Well maybe if we tried to take a different approach to getting rid of the succs, you wouldn't have to," I respond as Gnox takes a gentle trot to come up beside Cedric's horse.

"Enough, Asher! We can't fucking do anything! We're stuck in this purgatory until we're both dead, rotted and feeding the worms," Cedric yells as his head snaps in my direction. A blue vein bulges against his reddening forehead as his frustrations increase. Fury tugs against his furrowed brow and his lips damn near lift in a snarl.

"It's that kind of mindset that keeps us stuck in this purgatory! How can you stand by and watch our people die! Be taken from us?!" I yell back. We've pulled our horses to a stop along the dirt road. Their large bodies shimmy back and forth against the ground as we hold them, hooves pawing the sand as they get anxious from the halt.

"Because I'm done, Asher! I can't do this shit anymore! You wanna know why Blackwood hasn't had any heirs? Because I can't finish!"

My brow contorts in confusion. "What the fuck are you talking about?"

"I get up there, I fuck the sister and can't finish because I don't give a shit about any of these women!"

"So then do something about it! Help me change this place," I plead, for any ounce of evidence that shows he gives a damn about Vesperholm.

Cedric's eyes drift away to gaze at the ground below us. "I… can't."

"You fucking can! We all can!"

"If we couldn't save Alden, what makes you think we can save this whole fucking town?!" he yells as his watery gaze comes back up to me, the irritation in his voice has peaked and I can tell he's reaching his limit.

"I can't do this…" he mutters almost inaudibly.

"HYA!" he cries into the night with a sharp kick to his horse's side, sending them down the dirt road and off into the night.

I watch as the dust kicks up behind him and the sound of gallops fade into nothing.

A sigh escapes me before I click at Gnox. A smooth jolt tugs at my torso as Gnox begins to mosey forward and we ride home in the dark all by ourselves.

My eyes meet my father's in a plea.

A desperate plea in an attempt to save our people from extinction.

A final plea.

CHAPTER 2
THE PORTAL
ASHER

The next morning, I roll out of my bed. Quite literally.

The night had attacked me with visions of trying to save Cedric from a succubus. He had thrashed and fought but she pinned him with a poisonous talon, and he had no antidote. I tried to reach for him. To throw him a single vial. But I couldn't.

The dream caused me to scream, and I awoke to my body shuffling in the dirt below my bed. My tattered blankets are in a rumpled pile of fabric on the floor next to me.

Coming back to the real world, I take a deep breath before convincing myself to stand and face the day. My ribs prick with pain from the fall, and I groan as my body rises to full height. My hands brush down my night clothes to rid them of the dust before I take a wide stretch in my cramped room. As I reach for my tunic and breeches along the wall, I push the dream out of my thoughts.

I secure the leather belt of my waist pack before grabbing my cloak, throwing it over my shoulders and securing it around my neck with the metal insignia. I reach to the hardened mound of dirt beside my bed where my menagerie of daggers lay. One by one, I secure them to the holsters on my thighs, ribs, and chest – including the important one.

I usually carry six to ten daggers. You never know how many you can lose, and I don't want to dull the only one worth using.

After several minutes of convincing myself to leave my room and be the hunter I'm supposed to be, I make my way to the living area.

Grinding metal fills the space as my father sharpens an axe over a strip of leather on his thigh.

He has always been an early riser, so it's no surprise that he's out here this early.

What *is* surprising, however...

"Where's Cedric?" I ask as my eyes survey the main living chambers. The hearth burns a soft red glow from the lack of fire, brightened only by the dying embers. My boots drag along the dirt floor as I make my way over to grab a few logs from the stack of wood beside the fireplace. One by one, throwing them onto the weakening flame. I pick up the long sword next to the mantle and poke at the hot ashes to get the fire started again.

Slowly, the blaze glows brighter as the flames engulf the dry tinder. Standing from the hearth, I turn to the table, dusting my knees and hands off as I come to sit with my father.

"He never came home last night," my father grunts.

My face tightens in curiosity. "Well, maybe he got a jump on the hunt and decided to get us some venison for dinner," I say lightheartedly.

My father huffs in disagreement as the rusted rasp in his thick hands continues to scrape at the ax head.

Soon, three knocks wrap at the door of the hatch, breaking the concentration I had on my father's chore.

Ravensong.

I walk down the small tunnel to open the hatch, allowing Darian Ravensong to jump in.

"Morning, Asher," the black-haired mountain of a man says nonchalantly as he walks past me to the living area.

"Rowan," Darian says to my father as he enters the space.

My father sends him a grunt without breaking the focus on his task.

"What are you doing here? Did you get a jump on your hunt with Cedric?" I ask jokingly as I follow him down the tunnel, sliding the chair next to the table out to sit down in it.

I take the lull to survey the wall that holds our cloaks, noticing that Cedric's is still gone. Which means he really *didn't* come back last night. A knot of fear begins to weave itself tight in my stomach as I think back to my dream.

Shaking my head of the thought, my hand slides to my thigh. I grasp the handle of my dagger and its swirling edges bite into my palm as I pull it from its sheath. Swinging the handle in my fingers, I toy with its weight for a moment before I flick it above me. A loud *thunk* sounds off as it lodges into the rotted wooden beams that support the ceiling of the bunker. My palm stays open as I wait for it to come back down. Eventually the blade separates from above, flipping a few times before the handle lands in my palm for me to spin as I look to Darian.

"Shadowfang brings word of a portal," Darian says casually as he reaches to his back, fisting a long iron staff to pull in front of him. He presses his weight onto it as he sits in the leather armchair by the fire.

"Yeah, Lothaire told Cedric and I about it last night, but he brushed it off because it's Shadowfang," I tell him.

Darian smirks, "Lothaire…" he sighs as he shakes his head, the long, jet-black strands wave in his face.

Darian is the eldest brother of House Ravensong, which means he is their bed brother and messenger. They have taken refuge in the West Territory, hiding in well-crafted little treehouses in treetops.

They're staff wielders, so they use their weapon of choice to get from tree to tree with small wires that are connected between the branches. It seems like an ingenious little idea. They also possess, *"fumo resistentia,"* or resistance to fumes. Because they're close combat hunters, they need to be able to resist something like the succubus mist. That doesn't shield them from song, so they wear earmuffs made of deer pelts to protect their ears.

They are usually signified with deep green cloaks. With similarly muscular builds, they have honeyed skin and softened brows and cheekbones. Their heads are usually covered with stark, pin straight onyx hair.

"He needs to learn to take them more seriously," Darian adds. His hazel eyes come to connect with mine as he flashes me a smile, "I've seen the portal myself."

The metal of my father's sharpening stops, and I turn to look at him. He eyes me for a moment in disbelief and I return the sentiment, my eyes wide as we both look back at Darian.

"It's real?" I ask cautiously.

Darian nods, "A glowing purple thing. Looks like a nest gone sideways if you ask me."

My father and I connect gazes again, in question before we both face Darian once more.

"On the external boundaries of East Territory. Right outside the woods of Shadowfang Hideout, Gideon has been scouting the area. He followed one the other day, stayed in the dark as he watched her. He had no arrows to take her down, so he watched from a distance and found the twisted place she came from," Darian continues.

"Is there anyone guarding it?" I ask, my hand holding the dagger pauses as I absorb the reality of his words.

Shadowfang was right.

There hasn't been a portal in Vesperholm for as long as I've been hunting succs. We have never been able to find anything like it. Granted, with these lot, I imagine they may not have looked too hard and, in all honesty, we didn't know where they were coming from.

But why weren't we told about it earlier? And how long have they known about it?

"As of right now, no. They think a guard would allow for a portal to pop up elsewhere. We can't risk losing the one portal we know to exist," Darian responds as his eyes scan the metal of his iron staff, using the sleeve of his beige tunic to shine part of it.

"Did Shadowfang at least place an archer near it?" my father asks. The grinding metal resumes, however, more aggressive than it was previously.

"They have… But with their supply of arrows dwindling, they can't risk killing them all. The smaller succubus, they've let in for the sheer fact they're easier to kill on the ground in close combat. But for Shadowfang to engage in close combat fighting with them means more men gone," Darian sighs.

Great.

I thoroughly wish these people would do anything to find out more about these demons other than senseless killing.

But people of Vesperholm don't want answers, they want blood. They've *always* wanted blood.

My mind spins with the news. The fact that this is the one chance I have where I can do something to save my people.

I'm the only warrior with full immunity, the only one with the strongest weapon, and the only one not being used for carrying the lineage. The chair I'm sitting in scrapes against the dirt floor as I rise, my eyes pinned into my father, "Let me go," I tell him.

He stops his task once more as his eyes connect to mine in shock, "Asher, you may be strong, but you can't guard a portal. Who knows how many can come out at once."

"I'm the only one who can. And I've not let one get away from me yet," I tell him confidently.

All except the one in the alley.

"Asher…" My father sighs, his brow furrowing as he tries to think of a reason I shouldn't. "You can scout it. But you come back. No guarding. See this thing for yourself and then come back."

I nod with a smile, "Will do."

Armed with my daggers and my trusty steed, we speed through City Center to the edge of the tall woods in the distance. Soon, we reach the outskirts of the city, the assault on my rear end halting as Gnox slows to a trot. The massive trees look like a large barricade of haphazard twigs, sticks and branches.

The terrain in Vesperholm lends nothing to the imagination. It merely reminds you of your reality. Thick clouds drape the sky, allowing barely any sun to come through. It doesn't allow for proper growth or general life to succeed here. The bleak guardians have covered Vesperholm for as long as I can remember.

From my understanding, they came with the succubus and never left. Some days they thin and we get a glimpse of a sun beyond them. But most of the time, the clouds are grey and plentiful.

Previously green bushes have become balls of dried twigs as they pop up every so often along the infertile, muddy ground.

My father would tell me stories of when the succubus first started coming centuries ago. He said the tale had been passed down for years. Small appearances here and there. Men had their seeds taken from their beds. But were still able to go about their life. Until they started taking the men, and the hunters had learned of their own gifts, using them to train the broods of years ahead.

My father became reclusive when we lost his brothers and nephews to the winged plague.

He tries to do what he can for at least our family, by continuing to give us heirs. But with Alden gone, and my mother not doing well with carrying more, I have no idea what may come next for us.

Especially if Cedric has not been able to procure an heir for us.

And as much as I tease Cedric, I can't imagine I would want to do it either. Especially when I too would enjoy having someone of my own. What is the point of having someone if you must share them?

I shake my head as the sky around me deepens into darkness, causing Gnox to slow even more outside of the thick, dense brush ahead of us.

The forests outside of Shadowfang hideout are a tangled web of dark, black trees. House Shadowfang don't have any discernible housing. They've mostly hidden in the trunks of the dead trees, or under the ground in their root systems. The trees that house them are some of the largest I think I've ever seen, with their trunks as big as a small shop in some cases. They stretch high into the sky, piercing through the clouds and capping their tops with menacing grey crowns.

Sneaky little group of hunters.

Gnox whinnies as I pull him closer to the menacing thicket, "Hey, it's alright, it's just trees. We have a portal to find," I tell him softly.

Gnox takes cautious steps through the dark branches, and I keep my eyes peeled for any kind of glowing circle.

Hooves lump over roots in the uneven ground until I hear the *thunk* of splitting wood as an arrow whizzes past my head.

I grip the reins in my hands and pull my torso upright as Gnox brays and rears at the intrusion. His hooves swat at the dull air as his cries of fear grow louder. I press him back into the ground, leaning forward to stroke his mane and settle him down before I'm able to lead the massive creature to the impaled tree and swing off. I stroke the black hair on his face in calm as I reach for a throwaway dagger on my side, piercing the wood and attaching his lead to it. "It's alright, I'll do the rest on foot," I whisper to him while I pat his neck.

My boot plants into a thick root at the base of the tree, yanking the arrow from the bark as I take a deep sigh. I scan the dark foliage around me to see if I can spot anyone. But I already know who would've sent this kind of warning shot.

"YOU'RE WASTING RESOURCES, GIDEON!" I call into the thicket.

The ground shakes as a thump of boots land behind me.

"Can't be too sure nowadays," a muffled and thick voice responds. The giant man in a dark blue cloak towers over me. Blue eyes darken as he looks down at me. It's the only thing I can see with his hood over his head and a cowl covering his nose and mouth. His brown hair shakes free as he pushes his hood from the top of his head, allowing it to rest in a bundle around the back of his neck. Gideon himself is a rather intimidating hunter. His brow is robust with a thick jaw and cheekbones. His torso is built of wide, broad shoulders and massive limbs. He looks like he could kill you without lifting his pinky.

The truth is, Gideon is just a large teddy bear. He means no harm if you aren't a succubus. Almost everything seems less serious than it is to him.

I turn around to stare boringly at Gideon, "There's not another way you could have announced your arrival?" I ask with a roll of my eyes. I flick the arrow at his boots, the sharp point burrowing into the ground in front of him.

"Hello is dull," Gideon responds as he bends down to pick up the arrow to shove it in the quiver at his back.

Gideon Shadowfang is the middle brother of House Shadowfang; he's their hunter brother. Good for them, because the man is huge. He has enormous arms and towers above most of us. He has solid height on me, *and* muscle. But I suppose you must have muscle for archery. His cloak hides how big he truly is.

House Shadowfang are known for being skilled archers. Their house was given, *"canticum resistentia,"* Resistance to Song. With their ability to be targeted from a distance, it's perfect for them. But because they aren't resistant to mist, they wear a thick cowl in the same shade as their cloaks around their nose and mouth.

"You're dull," I huff as I make my way through the forest. Vines of varying lengths and thickness hang from the branches, and I have to pull out a dagger to cut through some of them as we advance deeper.

"I find myself to be the least dull of all of us," Gideon laughs, pulling the dark blue fabric from around his nose to rest under his chin.

My eyes roll, the action allowing me to spot a glowing light up ahead, nestled in a small clearing in the middle of the trees.

Stepping through the dense foliage, we advance closer. Fierce lightning crackles in a wall of purple, framed with a circle of rotted sticks and twigs. It's built into the foundation of the Earth like an upright nest.

Just like Darian said.

The ground outside and around the portal is blanketed in lush grass and wildflowers, which is an odd contrast to the dismal display outside of the little bubble it created here.

What the hell?

"How long has this been here?" I ask Gideon as I step onto the grass that has taken refuge in this forgotten corner of the forest. The air feels like it changes as I get closer to the portal. It feels... *clearer.*

"I can't say. I only found it recently," Gideon responds gruffly, he comes to stand next to me as he looks around. He steps to the portal and pokes at some of the twigs that make up the entry.

"Hmm..." I think out loud as I crouch to touch the grass. It's... warm. And it feels like it hums.

"Have you seen any demons come from it?"

"Other than the one I watched go back into it? No. Scouts have stated younger demons come in and out of it. Their horns are too small to be anyone of importance," he responds.

"What a shame. I surely think I'm important enough," a thick, sultry voice muses from behind the portal. The tones of its musings feel like they warp the space around us. A winged shape warbles against the air as her form becomes clearer.

Gideon and I look for the source, backing up as we are spooked by the noise. Black wings splay wide as she places herself in front of the portal.

The demon was hiding behind it, waiting for a hunter to snag.

No wonder no one was here to guard it; they would have been nabbed without a trace.

"Stay the *fuck* back!" Gideon bellows as he reaches into the quiver on his back to retrieve an arrow and knock it into his bow.

The handle of my dagger feels like home as I wrench it from its sheath. My arm snaps up, guarding my face as I flip the handle of my dagger to line the blade against my forearm.

The demon seems unperturbed by our presence as she steps closer. Her bare foot sinks into the grass as her milky skin shimmers against the purple light of the portal. The bottom talons of her wings leave small trails in the grass where they drag behind her.

Her vibrant red eyes flicker with vile hunger as she sizes us up.

"My, my, *my*. A treat for me, today. How The Fates shine down upon me," she muses as she looks between the two of us. Her fanged teeth show her appeasement as her lips curl in a devouring smile.

"I said, STAY THE *FUCK* BACK!" Gideon calls again. His wooden bow creaks as he pulls back on the string, aiming straight for the demon's chest.

For a moment, she's disappeared. Her entire body gone, until her wing whacks at my body from behind, causing me to tumble forward into the grass. I turn quickly against the humming ground, trying everything I can to keep my eye on this leather-bound threat. Her arm wraps around Gideon's throat in a crushing chokehold.

She's wrapped herself around Gideon's back, and he attempts to fling her in the process. As he tries to release her, he releases the grip on his bowstring, causing his arrow to spear through the sky.

"A shame, really. You seem so sure of yourself. It's always nice to play with my meals. Tell me, do you have any special *proclivities*?" she asks

Gideon as her wings envelop him in a crushing grip. Her mouth falls open, and with it a thick torrent of purple smoke escapes.

The mist.

Gods damnit, he's fucked.

Gideon's tense body relaxes, and his lids lower as her mist takes its hold on him, turning him into a horny mush for her to eat.

"You hunters are always so delightful to toy with. But it appears you aren't a Blackwood," she murmurs against the shell of Gideon's ear. Her tongue falls from her mouth to show two long halves that she runs up the flesh of his neck.

"No. But I am," I tell her as I rise from the ground, reaching for the dagger that can stop her.

I must be careful. If I make a wrong move, Gideon is done for. And we *can't* lose Gideon.

"Ahhhhhh. A famous *Blackwood.* Your kin sends his regards," she says softly with a devilish nod. A crazed tightness pulls at her eyes as her gaze connects with mine.

I freeze. "Alden," I whisper. My arm begins to move with the dagger in hand, charging at her, but her tail whips from behind her, swatting the dagger from my hand to land in the grass several feet away. Before I'm able to realize her agility, one of her wings bats at my body, causing me to fall back against the grass once more. A frustrated growl escapes me as I stand and scan the grass for my dagger, unable to find it.

"Is that his name? I wouldn't know. I merely know he's a Blackwood, he wouldn't stop *screaming* about it," she goes on, her hand flips against the air as she turns her attention back to Gideon.

As she loses herself to her distraction, I search the sky for the arrow. I spot a bright red feather as it comes barreling to the ground. My eyes lock onto its trajectory, and I open my palm, waiting for it to fall.

Come on, come on, come on. Faster damn you!

When I feel the slender shaft of the wood, I spin in place, winding up the shot before catapulting it through the succs shoulder.

Her screech distorts the air as it fills the dead space of the woods.

Her grip on Gideon wavers for the barest of moments, but she steadies herself. A feral grin contorts her lips and her cackle echoes through the sky as she reaches up, pulling the bloodied arrow from her flesh and chucking it to the ground.

I watch her in paralyzed fear as she throws Gideon on her shoulder. Blood pours from her wound as it continues to close, her body stitching itself back together as she settles Gideon's weight onto her.

The blood drains from my face as I realize she has him in her grasp.

There is only so much I can do with her holding Gideon. There are so many things that can go wrong, and Gideon ending up dead is the conclusion to any of the scenarios.

Retrieving one more dagger, just one more attempt, I charge at her. My boot barely makes contact with the ground before her free hand shoots out a lightning bolt into my chest. The force tosses my body into the trunk of a large tree outside of the portal's vibrant circle, knocking the air and my thoughts from me.

I struggle against the ground when I notice the Blackwood Dagger just out of reach. I groan as I try to regain the air that has escaped my lungs, crawling toward it to at least try to flick at her. But the force from the knockback has me moving like sap.

"Ah, ah, ah. Enough play for one day. We need hunters. This one shall do nicely. Just as your kin has. Such glorious offspring he's produced," she heckles. An evil, distorted giggle comes from her as she walks to the portal, even though she's carrying a fucking horse of a man. But one word sticks out.

Offspring?

I groan as I try to make sense of what she's saying, but having the air knocked out of me is making it hard to register her words.

Offspring… The fuck does she mean, *offspring?*

"Ta-ta! I'll be seeing you, Little Blackwood," she calls as she takes elegant strides into the portal, her body disappearing with the massive

Gideon in tow. By the time I gain enough strength to stand, she's disappeared. I scramble through the rugged brush, running straight at the swirling curtain. The action slaps me like a brick wall as I slam into it. The grass behind me catches my fall as I land in front of the solid wall.

I groan in pain as I catch my breath on the ground, attempting to level myself from the repetitive instances of being thrown around.

"Fuck," I mumble as I stare at the sputtering, sparked portal. The purple glares at me in humor as I try to comprehend the series of events that just took place.

My eyes bolt back and forth around the portal in a desperate attempt to rectify this mess when I catch a swath of black fabric. Quickly, I crawl through the grass on my hands and knees, gripping it. The cloth shreds as it's wrenched out of the sticks that make up the portal, leaving a small piece behind.

Black…

I frantically move the fabric around to find the insignia.

"Cedric…" I murmur as I realize whose cloak I'm holding.

Gnox gallops at full speed through the empty streets of North Territory in Vesperholm.

"Fuck, come on Gnox, come on. We've got to get back," I grunt as I try and hold my seat. Gnox is going as fast as he can, but it feels like it's not enough. His hooves beat hard against the cobblestone, the sound is deafening against the rapid pounding in my chest.

We finally reach the bunker, and I swing my leg off my steed to slide against the ground.

I rush to the inside of the shop, throwing the closet door open. I peel off the hatch before I jump down into the hovel, running down the tunnel as fast as I can.

"Gideon! They took Gideon!" I pant as I reach the living area. My hands brace on my knees as I breathe fire through my sore lungs.

Darian stands from the armchair and my father stands from the table as they stare at me in confusion.

"The fuck do you mean 'they took Gideon'?!" My father exclaims.

"They took him! I went to go see the portal. Gideon was scouting but a succ was hiding. She took him! He fell right into her fucking arms!" I explain as I try to catch my breath.

My father stands, "Is he alive?"

"The fuck if I know! I can't enter the portal! It's like some kind of protection is placed on it."

Darian ponders from his spot, "That tracks... We've seen them come in and out, but since we have no idea where this portal leads, we've not sent men in. They've approached it and thrown things at it. But they always bounce back at us."

"You could have, oh, I don't fucking know, WARNED ME?!" I yell at Darian.

He shrugs, "We were shit out of luck no matter what we did. I figured if you wanted to be the guinea pig, be the guinea pig."

I throw my arms up in defeat before I hunch over to take deep breaths again, "She mentioned... She mentioned Alden," I pant through my exasperation.

My father looks at me, "What?"

"She said... She said he makes good offspring."

My father's face pales, "Offspring? What does she mean offspring?!"

"I don't fucking *KNOW*! I don't have the gods-damned answers! And I found this!" I tell my father as I throw the tattered black cloak to the ground at his feet.

My father rounds the dining table to pick up the cloth, his face seems to tighten as he realizes what it is. "Cedric…"

"Yes! They might even have Cedric! We can't continue to lose our people! We can't continue this life we live!" I plead with them. My voice pitches and wavers as I beg with the only people that have the ability to help.

"Asher, it's…" my father sighs as he tugs his beard. "It's not safe. We've already lost Alden. And now you're telling me we've lost Cedric."

"We don't even know if we lost them! If she said he's making offspring, he has to be alive, isn't he?! Cedric might be fucking off in the forest, but we won't know a damn thing if we don't TRY!" My eyes beg for mercy from this hell we have forced ourselves to endure. The urgency of the matter is now so strong that my eyes water. We have decayed here for too long, and this was the last straw.

Father thinks for a moment; his aged green eyes linger off onto a wall on the other end of the bunker.

"Send *me*. I'm the strongest we have. And the most experienced. I can't continue to let our people fucking die to this plague. Let *me* go," I tell him softly, though I can see his heartbreaking under what I ask.

"I… Asher…" he sighs.

"I have to do this. I'm the only one who can," I say.

"I can gather huntsman from Ravensong. They can watch the ground, and I can send word to Shadowfang when I get to East Territory," Darian adds from behind me.

My eyes meet my father's in a plea. A desperate plea to save our people from extinction.

A *final* plea.

"If Alden and Cedric are still alive, I have to try. I can't leave them there."

My father sighs, "Fine. But gather proper reinforcements. You can't go alone against them."

"I'll be alright. I promise."

Chapter 3

Tantalia

Seraphina Moonsong

Mistress of Bloodshed and General of the Nights Legions

Metal clashes, pebbles fly, and dust tornados in small brown funnels along the ground. The heavy beats of wings are a symphony against the grunts of halflings.

Lightning cracks in a purple web overhead as I lose my patience once again. The warriors in this large dirt floored arena freeze in their places and drop to a knee before me.

"Never drop your FUCKING GUARD! Wings are your friends! Not your *FUCKING* enemies! Get it together!" My distorted voice bellows over the numerous winged fighters.

Human hybrids of varying hair colors and sizes. Halflings; the spawn of demon and human. Used for fortifying our ranks and fueling our Legions.

The Warriors of Tantalia. The Nights Legions.

Solis. Lunae. Stella… and these ones…

Their breath is heavy from the intense training session I have subjected them to. But Cometas Legion… they're young. The youngest ones out of the four. They haven't had the time to get used to the giant limbs of leather and bone strapped to their spine. Halflings don't get their wings until adolescence. These ones have just barely gotten them, making this lot the worst ones to train. But the faster we can get them in, the more protection we have.

As the Mistress of Bloodshed, I must make sure the legions are ready to fight at a moment's notice, especially with the wards on our portals destabilizing so quickly. More Drannars creep in the longer we fuck around figuring out why our magic is so unstable.

Stella is our all-star legion. The strongest and most accomplished warriors, even if they are the smallest group of only about seventy-five strong. They spend less time in the pits, and more time guarding the things worth guarding. Though are called to action when breaches occur.

Which has been more often, as of late.

Lunae, the second strongest of the legions. They are a larger group than Stella, still immensely powerful, but not as powerful as Stella.

Solis, the middle-aged legion. Warriors on the rise, but not quite ready for the big conflicts that are expected from legions like Stella and Lunae. Still, a legion of three hundred fighters, nonetheless.

And Cometas. The babies of the legions. But also, the largest group. As halflings are transferred from The Pods, and sprout their wings, a sword is thrust upon them, where they learn the ways of our people.

In turn, I learn how many different ways *our* people can be completely oblivious to the movement of their own bodies.

Today is no exception.

Dust slowly settles as the warriors catch their breaths. The strong scent of halfling sweat lingers in the unnaturally damp air. I look over them all with disgust; they couldn't have done *worse* today.

"Get out of my face," I groan as I wave them off.

"Yes General," the menagerie of voices call back as they all stand and retreat to their living quarters. Murmurs and voices reverberate as they drag their feet along the ground.

A tense hand comes to pinch at my brow as I wait for them all to vacate my proximity.

I only want bloodshed for those who dare to harm us. Everything else is just collateral.

"Come on, they're Cometas. Give them a break," a voice says from behind me.

I tilt my head toward the noise with annoyance.

I don't have the patience for this today.

"Selene, you train them then," I retort as I face her.

Selene Nightshade; Lilith's eldest daughter. A fine warrior herself but made for politics. For now, she is the Mistress of Law.

While she bears the normal leather corset we all do, hers is fitted with a flowing black skirt. A long slit up the thigh shows her tanned skin. Large, black horns protrude from her skull, with knee length white hair that flows behind her just as her skirt does. Her eyes are a vibrant purple, like her mother's. Her features are sharp and angular, with high cheekbones and a pointed chin.

"Not my job," she says with an evil grin.

I roll my eyes as my feet carry me from the training grounds -- a large arena at the South End of the main Tantalia grounds. Not the type of arena you'd sit in and watch challenges in. I suppose more like a giant stone corral.

The Pits.

I hear crunching dirt from behind as Selene comes to fall in step beside me.

"Then shut your mouth," I respond as I round the exit onto the main grounds. The lush green grass is abundant in the large courtyards. Wildflowers grow with ease and the gentle fragrance of violet wisteria trees drift in the air as their branches sway in the warm Tantalia winds. A large fountain sits in the middle of the grounds, burbling with jets of water. Succubus will take breaks from their duties to sit and read or just relax in the warm sun.

I take a left when I reach the main walkway around the field. The thick training boots I wear pound against the bright white stone below me as I make my way to The Nursery.

"Care to walk with me?" I ask Selene sarcastically.

"Can't, there's a meeting. And it'd behoove you to be seen there as well," she responds.

I roll my eyes again as I send a wave over my shoulder, "We'll see."

Selene laughs and the whirling wind marking her departure kicks up my hair as the unmistakable sound of wings beat into the air.

The path to The Nursery is short. But the location it's held in is cloaked. Or glamoured is the magical term for it. We can't risk losing our spawns if there is to be another attack on Tantalia.

At the end of the long stone walkway is a large meadow. Buzzing bees and butterflies float along the varying shades of velvety color that peak from the tall grasses. It's a gorgeous day in Tantalia. Most are, with the bright and warming sun beaming down across the lands. The wisteria tree that sits in the middle of the field is much larger – and far more ancient – than the rest of the trees that surround the grounds.

There has always been something here for me. A connection unlike anything I've felt elsewhere in Tantalia. Then again, we're all born and raised within The Ancient Wisteria. It would make sense that this is something so inherently familiar to all of us.

Stepping through the grasses, I approach the tree. Pressing my hand against a worn space on the bark, the exterior warbles as my hand is sucked through, pulling my body into the trunk.

On the other side of the hidden entry is a large metal room. Distorted shrieks and cries come from within as I enter a nursery lined with hundreds of cradles. Baby halflings and succubus of varying ages are in the small beds and being cared for by a plethora of older succubus in long periwinkle cloaks.

The Nursery; an overarching area of rooms that births, and cares for all our spawn, halfling and succubus alike. This chamber is specifically the Daycare. Succubus don't typically care for their own young. Being "blessed" with magical affinities gives you the option to carry the babes yourself to term, or to place them within pods for incubation.

Most demon choose the latter.

The Pods, where the spawn are incubated, is deeper within. But entering the tree, you walk into a room of tiny cribs with demons walking to and fro.

There's one demon I've come for that is much younger than the other caregiving succubus, and I hear her before I see her.

"Sera!" a high-pitched voice rings from the other end of the large space.

My first smile of the day tugs at my cheeks as I spot Velaria. "Velly," I sigh gently.

The Mistress of Kin approaches me with a small bundle of black cloth. Her lavender eyes are gentle and seeping with adoration as she greets me. Her silvery-white hair is in a slim bob that shimmers around her jaw as she walks to me with slow but excited steps so as not to wake the bundle in her arms.

"This one just came from the pods today," she says softly. Velaria tilts the halfling gently toward me.

Brown of hair. Pale of skin.

A Blackwood.

I hmmph as I look down at it. "*Grand,*" I say with a grimace.

"Oh, don't be that way! A new warrior with exceptional abilities," she says cheerfully, her arms rocking the small being.

It's hard to stay mad when her excitement is so infectious.

Velaria is my youngest sister. And the youngest so far of House Moonsong. She keeps me sane most days. Especially after infuriating training sessions like today.

She has such a deep love for our people, even the human halflings. I personally can't understand her love for them. Especially considering the one Blackwood I have yet to find is the one that took our Lilith.

The bastard. The *scum.*

I will relish in the way he screams when I finally get the chance to torture him.

To heal him, only to torture him again.

In Tantalia, it is illegal to kill unless attacked. But there is nothing in the laws that say we can't torture.

And I will enjoy *every* minute of his pained screams.

Velaria must notice my thoughts and gently places the spawn in an empty, nearby cradle. "Come, we have to get to The Court," she says gently.

Her words pull me out of my reverie, and I nod softly as my eyes come to meet hers. She leads the way out of The Nursery, our bodies melting through the trunk as we exit. The grasses brush against our thighs as we make our way to the main walkway.

"How was training?" Velaria asks sweetly as she takes a deep inhale of the potent Tantalia air. Her wings flare wide at her back, and she shakes them out as we enter an open space. "Ah, feels *so* good!" she giggles as she spins next to me.

I smile at her, "Cometas were in today. It was… something," I tell her with a sigh.

"Give them a chance! You were new once!" She says with a gentle shove to my arm. "I did my best to prepare them for you, ya know. I made sure they knew you were tough but fair." She nods triumphantly with a proud smile.

My own smile widens as I listen to her. Part of her job is to raise the young until they're thrust into the barracks and onto the battlefield. So, knowing that they at least have *some* level of preparation for my methods, is very much appreciated.

Splashing waters floods my conscious as we pass the large water fountain in the middle of the courtyard, its bubbling centerpiece filling the air around us with its song.

"I didn't have nearly as rough of a time as they are," I respond.

"Liar! You came back to The Keep every day covered in mud!" Velaria laughs in my direction.

The memories of Lilith working me into the ground, one on one, comes to the forefront of my mind along with a series of confusing emotions.

Happiness for the memory. Sadness for her death. Anger for the way she worked me.

Grateful for how she molded me.

Velaria grasps my hand and swings it between us, "You've done right by her, ya know," she says softly.

I turn to her with a solemn smile, "I'm trying to."

"You're the Mistress of Bloodshed! You couldn't have gotten there without the things you've done for Lilith," she responds.

I peer down at Velaria, her head barely reaches my chest. She's a tiny little thing, but she's *my* tiny little thing, regardless.

My gaze connects with hers, and I can see how much of my light I hold in her eyes.

I give her a soft kiss on the forehead as I stroke the back of her head, "Thanks Velly," I murmur. "Come on, we have a meeting."

Velaria nods excitedly before she bolts for the air. The fine dust on the ground spins in small tornados as her wings splay wide and billow against the weight of her body in the sky. She shoots through the clouds, leaving misty trails of fluff in her wake.

A chuckle escapes me before I follow suit. Expanding my wings, I lunge into the air. The wind rings through my ears as the thin, leathered skin of my wings tighten against the fragrant breeze.

The feeling is so freeing that I can't help when I barrel roll into a hard leaning bank to the magnificently spired fortress in the distance. Straightening back out on the winds, I open my eyes, searching for the short bob of Velaria. She's several feet in front of me, and my competitive side starts to rear its ugly head as my wings tighten against my back and I dive toward her.

She's not beating me today.

The colossal spires of The Keep come into view as the speed rips through my hair and small water droplets beat against my face. Staircases wrap along the exterior, with splotches of black wings bobbing along its ascensions. Purple bundles of wisteria trees with their fragrant bloomed flowers coil around monumental columns of ivory stone, integrating into its foundation like they have become one entity. The palace is built into an enormous mountain of blinding milky rock, as if it was carved directly from it. White clouds wrap around portions of the massive castle, cloaking it in a majestic fluffy cape.

Celestial Keep. The home to The Courts and their Houses, as well as the main structure of Tantalia.

Home.

A smile pulls against my face as the balconied courtyard at the very top floor of The Keep approaches at an alarming speed. Flaring my wings wide, the air catches them, causing the space between the bones to stretch taut against the current. I swing my feet in front of me to break my landing, my heels sliding through the lush grass of the courtyard balcony to pull me to a graceful stop. I shake my wings out to loosen their tension as I turn around to see Velaria diving to the veranda at breakneck speed. But her wings don't flare until the last second and she barrels into the grass beside me. She blasts through the large patch of greenery like a tiny falling star, sending small bits of dirt and grass flying around her.

A hearty laugh creeps from my belly as I watch her tumble. Barely able to catch my breath, I double over as the hilarity consumes me. Velaria groans from her mangled position.

"Help," a tiny squeak comes from under her wings.

I laugh a second longer before I bend over to fling her wing from her face. Her cheek squishes against the grass and a muffled groan sounds from her once more.

"Come on, crazy. You're supposed to open your wings much earlier," I tell her as I press my hands into her armpits to pull her to a stand.

I dust off her now green-stained cloak and some of the grass and dirt from her face.

"I just wanted to get here first! Ugh, I'll never beat you!" she groans frustratedly as she shakes out her wings and body. Her tail scrapes some of the grass from her leather breeches. Straightening herself up, Velaria marches with a pout into The Court. Another laugh escapes me as I fall in step behind her.

This room sits on one of the highest levels of Celestial Keep. It houses a long table made of ebony stone. White veins creep through its surface, and it's polished to a glossy finish. Cages of candles reflect off the table as they hang from the ceiling on chains. White brick makes up the floor and gleams a brilliant gloss as well.

Tall columns of Elder Succubus, carved from the same stone, take residence in the space and lift the high, vaulted ceilings with enormous open windows that overlook the entire land. Singular statues of important succubus are placed on the window balconies as menacing gargoyles to watch our people.

Succs lost to hunters or Drannars.

Lilith's sits the highest, and the brightest.

The newest.

The Court of Mistresses is just the room. And while it is important, the people that frequent it are more so.

The Ladies of The Court. The mistresses that lead different aspects of our people.

My own mother, Orona Moonsong — the Mistress of Justice — sits next to Selene.

Mistress of Agriculture, Learra Nightshade, stands next to the Mistress of Bloods, Zephyra Lunarflame.

Mistress of Consequence, Zyrella Lunarflame, stands to the opposite on the table, next to the Mistress of Sword, my cousin, Reasha Moonsong.

All these women lead different aspects of our land, and their work is of the utmost importance.

At the head of the table, standing where Lilith's throne once sat, is Mistress Kalinda and her small handmaid, Rialla. She was Lilith's advisor once upon a time, alongside her official title as Mistress of the Keep. She essentially is in charge of the succubus that run the smaller sectors inside The Keep. Kitchens, foods, clothing, the things that aren't seen as large and important as the other sectors.

Rialla has been next to Kalinda for as long as I can remember, but she's small, quiet. She merely follows Kalinda around and takes orders from her. I do feel bad for the little demon, to be honest. I couldn't imagine having to be around Kalinda more than I have to.

Kalinda's presence, however, has always irked me. And I never understood why Lilith was so keen on keeping her so close when she serves no other purpose than to irritate the Mistresses. I find her to be useless. She doesn't fight, she doesn't train the warriors or grow crops. She does nothing for weapons, interrogations; her presence is absent in The Infirmary and The Nursery. I'd pay to see her even contemplate the forge. She doesn't inherently *do* anything. She seems to just be here to command things inside The Keep. Other than that, she's nowhere to be found.

How can one be the Mistress of the Keep and so *worthless?*

My body falls into the chair at the other end of the table, and Velaria comes to sit next to me.

Other leading houses sit at the table as well. Though, they hold no titles, they are merely nobility. Sisters, daughters, and aunts bred all from Lilith. In some ways, we are all Lilith's daughters. But as time went on, the lines blurred, and our lineages separated as we came to be. The ancestral lines span from the Drannars at the beginning. Eventually, the humans were introduced, and the tree becomes a forest. But now, as The Pods have grown and we have grown our society, the females are born as succubus. While the male seeds become halflings and feed our army and ranks.

We all may be Lilith's daughters in a sense, but we have different mothers. As more succubi were born, they wandered to Vesperholm, and we were born under those demons and men, leaving *them* to be our mothers.

Selene was the last direct descendant of Lilith's.

The last of Lilith's true daughters. The ones born from other men in Vesperholm were killed in the massacre.

But Selene lived a sheltered upbringing. She was taught to fight, she was taught to read and learn the same as I was, but she had to learn the rules and the laws.

Most of our demon are too busy in their lives to carry the babes, so they are thrown into the pods and raised by the givers, taught and grown within the ancient wisteria tree.

"Glad to see you could make it, Phinney," Selene muses from her seat.

My eyes roll as my arms cross over my chest. Slinging a leg over the arm of my chair, the meeting begins.

"We can no longer lead without a Queen," Mistress Kalinda's voice breaks over the murmurs that move around the table. The group of horned mistresses look to the standing succ in shock.

I pick at the bits of blood under my claws as I listen, not sparing her a glance.

Yeah, over my dead fucking body will we have a new Queen.

"The instability of *Lapis Amoretstra* is causing the wards to waver in their strength. Drannars have been spotted near portals on more than one occasion," Kalinda says gently. She and Rialla are the only succs covered entirely in white cloaks. Her long, silvery hair lays against her chest as it flows around her. Wide sleeves hide her hands as they fold into each other against her chest.

"What's fucking new, Kalinda?" I sigh from my seat as I wave a hand in the air.

"Without a Queen, *Lapis Amoretstra* is incapable of dealing with the influx of magic from the new brood of younglings. The portals are losing their protection the longer we go without a ruler," Kalinda responds softly.

I scoff as I listen to her. She sits in her position yet does nothing to remedy the situation.

Laughable, if you ask me.

"Zyrella returned today with a human. She informed me that there were two there, surveying the portal. Which means we've lost the glamours cloaking them. It bares our entry to anyone who dare to look for it," Mistress Kalinda continues.

Tension tugs between my brows as I look up at Zyrella. Her red eyes connect to mine as she nods, "The one with him was not able to follow. I watched from the other side to make sure he couldn't. The wards are still in place, but I fear there is not much time until they fall too."

Zyrella is one of our larger succubus. Tall, with broad shoulders and thick hips. I find her to be perfect for scouting the portal. Learning now that the humans have found it brings me mixed emotions. On one hand, perhaps it will lure the Blackwood into my grasp. On the other, my people become exposed.

Do I sacrifice vengeance for mercy? Do I trade my pursuits for protection?

I huff in annoyance as I fix my gaze on Kalinda.

"Then *you* do it! What is the hold up?" I growl.

So intent on fixing the wards and magic, but with no *urgency* to step up and claim the crown.

"I am not a warrior. I have no wish to rule," she responds plainly.

"Cry me a fucking river," I scoff.

"Sera…" Velaria says softly from next to me.

My focus has been laid on Kalinda as I give in to my growing fury. Until my gaze roams over all the Ladies of the Court, where I notice all the eyes in the room are on me.

"What?" I say as I quirk a brow in confusion.

"Seraphina… You…" My mother sighs.

"No… no, you all can't *possibly* be serious!" I say. My chair squeals against the white tile of The Court as I stand. The cold black stone sears into my hands as they press into the table. My eyes peer at all of them, surveying the expressions that hold different sentiments.

Hope. Sadness. *Fear.*

"Lilith trained *you*. There is no one better to lead our people," Selene says softly.

"Have you all gone absolutely mad?! I have not the makings of a Queen!" I respond. The anger courses through my veins like hot ice as I digest what they're asking of me.

The responsibility they expect me to take on and the burden they are forcing me to carry, without a consideration of carrying it themselves.

Not to mention, this is Lilith's throne. It should *stay* Lilith's, even in her death. There is no one better to take her place.

Especially not me.

Lilith loved her people, and she essentially died for them. She loved the hybrids, the demons, *all* our people. She worked day in and day out for them in all facets of our society. I don't have that level of compassion. I don't *care* to have that level of love.

I only want bloodshed for those who dare to harm us. Everything else is just collateral.

"Sera! You are the Mistress of Bloodshed! How can you think that?!" My mother yells as she too stands from her seat.

"Because I'M NOT FUCKING LILITH! I cannot do what Lilith had done! I will NOT do what Lilith had done!" I yell at her. The tension in my face burns as a scowl tugs at my features. The large limbs of leather and bone splay wide at my spine, tugging tightly at the delicate calcifications between the tough skin as they eat up the space in the room.

Silence descends upon The Court. Eyes of the mistresses avert from my outrage to meet the table in submission.

All but Mistress Kalinda.

"You are to be Queen, Sera. This is not up for discussion. The decision is final," she states in frigid disregard.

Fire burns my irises as I stare at her, "Over. My. Dead. Fucking. Body." I grit through bared teeth as a snarl pulls at my lips in challenge.

Kalinda's icy gaze holds steady. Her silence is blaringly loud as she meets my defiance with cool indifference.

"You are to begin induction in two weeks' time. I suspect you'll be ready to take the throne by then," Kalinda states.

"You've all gone fucking mad. I'm not doing this!" I shout to the Mistresses. Turning around, my fingers splay to the chair I was sitting in. Darkness pricks against my palm as the air in the room charges. Within an instant, purple snaps fervently through the space as I blow a lightning bolt at it. The stone room echoes with vengeance as the chair slams into the wall in a burst of flames and purple sparks. Heavy, booted steps dripping with vitriol pound against stone as I make my way to the grassy veranda.

My wings open wide, preparing to take off, when I feel delicate fingers tug on my wrist. I whip around to glare at the being who even dare to disrupt my anger.

Velaria.

Her lavender gaze is watery as she looks up at me, "Please… Please just consider it… Sera," she begs. Strain contorts her voice as it attempts to make its way from her throat, but her eyes show how much she is really asking. A droop pulls at my wings as I hear her.

I hear her. But I'm unable to listen. Not now.

Not this way.

The burning intensity of my anger cools slightly as a sigh escapes me, "Maybe, Vel..." I tell her as I gently unwrap her fingers from my wrist.

My wings expand once more as I take a step onto the balcony. I look down at the cliff below before I turn back to Velaria.

Silver tears run down her cheeks as she nods softly.

A tilt of my head returns her ask, and I face the edge of the cliff, falling forward.

The wind catches me, and soon I drift on the fragrant skies of Tantalia.

A growl echoes through the room as the pressure in my tailbone climbs the deeper he goes, before I decide I need to really feel him. And get my mind off of The Court.

CHAPTER 4

RESISTANCE

SERAPHINA

Splinters fly from my boot as I kick the door to the barracks wide open.

The large slab of wood is rendered useless as it slams against the wall beside it.

The conversing warriors freeze where they stand as they all turn to look at me. Long lines of bunk beds fill the space, and the thick voices of winged men silence as I enter.

My gaze roams over the men as I size them up to take my pick.

Seething fury from The Court courses through me, and I only have one thought in mind to dull the rabid pounding within my skull.

A massive, brown-haired beauty stands front and center. Thick muscles bulge under his tight skin, and he furrows his brow as he looks at me. Large wingtips rise high above his head.

He's a *proper* warrior, with sculpted pectorals and bulk padding every inch of his arms and legs. Red eyes curiously gaze at me as he waits for my next words.

The tips of my fangs bare as my lips curl into a deadly smile. "You… You're coming with me," I muse softly.

My arm cocks back to whip a bolt of lightning through my wrist and around his neck; purple sparks bring him to heel as he crashes to his knees.

Callous grunts come from him as he attempts to pry the collar from his throat. And as I tug at the power restraining him, his body slowly slides to me. He looks up at me with curious eyes, "What do you need from me, Mistress?"

My smile widens, "Your cock," I lilt seductively as I kneel in front of him, taking his strong jaw in my claws. Pressing his cheeks together, my head tilts in feral amusement.

He grins with a delighted nod as the red of his eyes bleed with desire.

"Oh… Oh yes, you shall do just nicely," I whisper as I rise. Spinning on a heel, I tug at the purple lead to guide my new toy to a private place.

I continue leading him to an empty, single barracks room down the hall, flicking a hand at the door to open it. His grunts are quiet as he follows me.

I fling his large body into the room by his restraint, kicking the door closed behind me. I meet his gaze as he kneels on the floor in front of me.

In here there is but a singular bed and a table in the corner. The space reserved for higher ranking warriors of Stella Legion.

I grin as I approach him, his eyes lidding half-way as he anticipates our tryst.

"Tell me… your tongue. Is it forked?" I ask as I grip his chin in my hands, pressing his head up for me to search his crimson irises.

He grins as he slacks his jaw, his tongue falling from his mouth; a split through the middle divides it into two parts. He twists the halves around each other as he awaits my command.

"Divine," I muse seductively as I latch onto his mouth. Our tongues dance around each other's with lust before I pull away. I saunter to the bed, looking back over my shoulder to connect gazes with him. I lean against the footboard as the snap of my fingers echoes in the desolate room and my leather corset shimmers before it leaves my body. The warrior's jaw falls as he devours my curves with his eyes. As I position myself on the top of the footboard, I spread my legs, and cool air hits my heated cunt. The warrior's eyes widen as he catches sight, and a delighted grin pulls at the corners of my lips.

"Eat," I tell him as I take a gentle tug of the lavender sparks that wrap around his neck.

He crawls on his hands and knees to me before his thick hands grip the soft flesh of my thighs, pressing them open. His tongue dips into my core, and I allow a groan to escape me from the sensation. Gripping his brown hair in my claws, I bring him in deeper. His forked tongue dips half inside of me, while the other swirls around my swollen clit.

My toes curl as I descend into the feeling of the divided muscle in my center when a quiet voice muses through my thoughts.

To be Queen.

I groan as I attempt to bring my focus back to the task at hand. The tones that pour from my throat turn ethereal as he laps up every drip of my need and his taloned claws pierce the meat of my thighs, pressing them open farther.

Drips of warm blood trickle across my skin, sending shivers of lust through my body as his tongue drives deeper and deeper.

In two weeks' time.

A growl echoes through the room as the pressure in my tailbone climbs the deeper he goes, before I decide I need to *really* feel him.

And get my mind off The Court.

Cresting my head above the waves of pleasure, I tug back at his lead, wrenching him from my soaked center. His crimson eyes beam in that dark space as they come to meet mine. His chin shines from my lust, with his tongue slipping from his mouth to lap the sheen from his face. My eyes slowly travel down his sculpted frame before they reach his groin. The thick bulge threatens to rip the fabric of his breeches as his cock presses hard against it.

"Fuck me with it," I tell him with a fanged grin.

"Yes Mistress," he rasps in a husky, pleasure filled growl as he stands. The large hands on my thighs leave to tug the band of his pants down, allowing his cock to spring free. Human hybrids always have such delicious cocks. It's thick and pulsing for me to take.

My body falls back onto the soft bed, my wings splaying at my spine to catch the fall.

I open my legs wide for him. My cunt grips around nothing as cool air hits it again and causes a shudder to roll through me. His eyes lock onto my core as he climbs over the footboard to kneel in front of me. His hand wrapped around his cock as he strokes it, admiring my dripping cunt that he intends to take.

He leans forward, his hands coming to rest on either side of my head before he reaches down, gripping his cock to guide the head of himself into me. A hiss escapes him as he takes in the way I wrap around him.

My throat releases a distorted moan as the hardened flesh of his back splits under my claws. He groans as he sits himself balls deep into me.

I can barely think with the pressure of his girth, the way he stretches me. He leans up, his eyes locked onto where he enters me. Strong hands grip my hips, pulling me onto him in violent strokes.

Using me for his pleasure.

His groans mix with my moans as he continues pounding into me. His thrusts lose precision as he approaches the edge of ecstasy. The pressure from his cock and the force of his thrusts causes my orgasm to spill over and I let out an ethereal screech as my cunt clenches around him. Jagged groans fill the space around us before he pulls out and spills himself all over my stomach, the fluid pooling on my belly in jets of silver.

I'm still panting as my eyes come to meet his face, the poor soul's attention still drawn to his work of art splattered against my stomach.

The realization of what I did creeps in.

Gave my body to a *halfling* as a source of relief. To distract myself. Willingly.

A grimace contorts my lips and brow as my eyes roam over the Blackwood looking warrior, "Get out of my sight," I growl.

His grin disappears before he nods, "Yes Mistress," he says softly as he climbs off the bed. He leans to the floor to grab his breeches and pulls them on before he exits the room.

The soft pillow catches my head as it falls, and I'm left staring at the ceiling.

I think about life before the chaos, before Lilith taught me of my purpose.

Before I was the Mistress of Bloodshed.

When life was just that...
Living.

CHAPTER 5

FIGHT OR FLIGHT

SERAPHINA

Long after I've blown off my anger with that disgusting human-hybrid, I make my way back to my bedroom, trying as hard as I can to avoid anyone and everyone that I can.

I thought fucking one of the warriors would help my anger and bide my time for reflection.

It did not.

It only made me more hostile.

The idea of having to lead these people, while also needing to train them, makes bile rise in my throat. There is no way I can take up Lilith's grand throne.

Lilith was hundreds of years my elder. She led with fervor, but she cared for her people. Even the halflings, which is why we have them at all.

But it's the same reason we still don't have a queen.

I can't be the reason these people fall. I wouldn't be able to live with myself if I was the catalyst for their destruction.

A soft knock at my bedroom door breaks my concentration from the stars I'm watching, and the thoughts consuming me.

I turn from the balcony of my wide-open window along the back wall of my room, wrapping my lilac silk night robe tighter around my waist and I sigh. My feet barely make a noise as I take soft steps to my bedroom door.

I glare at the being for a moment before my expression softens, realizing who it is.

"Hey, Sera," the meek voice squeaks. Velaria's eyes glisten with hope as she looks at me. "Can I come in?" she asks.

I sigh as I nod, stepping aside to allow her in. Her steps are cautious as she enters, padding softly over to my bed to sit on the plush white comforter. She releases a sigh of relief.

"What brings you here?" I ask. Though I have a feeling, I already know what it is.

Velaria's cheeks heat, her face contorted in apprehension as she leans back into her hands. Her feet kick lazily at the edge of my bed from where she sits.

"The Court wanted me to talk to you," she admits nervously.

I roll my eyes as I close the door to my bedroom and take irritated steps back to the balcony window, leaning against the frame as I watch the night sky once more.

The moon is exceptionally bright tonight; it's the same brightness as the night that Lilith died. The stars sprinkle against the black, blue, purple and green backdrop, twinkling softly in the distance. They don't have to worry about destabilizing wards and magic. They don't have to save the other stars in the sky. They just exist in the deep ebony blanket of the ages.

My eyes slide down the mountain, where it lands on the courtyard. No one is out, only massive Stella warriors that guard the lands as the rest of us sleep. The wisteria trees sway in the gentle breeze, wafting their fragrance into the air.

"Of course they did..." I mumble as I cross my arms against my chest.

"But I came because I also wanted to talk to you," she adds sheepishly.

I turn to face her; the ends of her hair curl around her talons as she nervously fidgets on the bed, her eyes locked onto her swaying feet.

"Velly... I don't want to do it."

"I know. But you're the only one who *can.* There's no one that can lead our people. You're the strongest of us, and Lilith trained *you,* Sera. Not Selene, not me, not even Mistress Kalinda. She. Trained. *You.*"

I'm silent as I turn back to the open window, my eyes locking onto the dancing colors in the sky.

"Velaria…" I sigh softly, my head falling in defeat.

"I know you don't want to. I wouldn't ask this of you if I didn't think you could do it. But our realm needs a ruler. It needs *you,*" Velaria says gently, her voice wavers as she tries to hold herself together.

I imagine her pushing this issue comes from her love of the kin. She cares for the tiny beings so much that she just wants to ensure their safety.

I can't blame her, she does so much for them. It would be hard to see tragedy befall them.

But even still.

"I could never be what Lilith was. No matter how hard I were to try, I could never be Lilith."

"You're right, you won't be Lilith. You'll be Sera; *Queen* of Bloodshed."

I turn to her, connecting to her lavender gaze. They hold so much conviction in what she says. They beg. They plead. They lament for our people.

Slow steps eat the distance from the window to the bed before I come to sit next to her. My wing expands to wrap around her shoulders, as I wrap my arms around her waist in a hug. "I just don't know, Velly," I sigh.

"But I do. I know you're the only person for this job. The only one that has the ferocity to keep us safe. To fix the Stone." Her voice is watery as she buries her head in my chest, hugging me tightly. My tail comes up to rub gently against her back with the flat spade.

"I have to think about it," I tell her.

"There is no one I would rather see sit the throne than you. You've put your soul into our people even if you don't know it," she responds.

The gem of my necklace pulses in a purple glow; its illumination bright against the darkened room that wraps the both of us in comfort.

A tug pulls my eyebrow to my forehead as I observe the curious crystal.

"How about we go out for a flight?" I ask softly.

If there is anything that will get me out of this feeling, it's flying with Velaria. Just like we used to.

She looks to me with a smile and an excited nod, jumping from the bed and running at my open window to get a head start. The long silk of her black nightgown flows behind her as she makes for the baluster. Before she runs into it, she grafts the small distance between the metal bars and the air. As if it was not even there to begin with, her wings flay wide against the gentle night breeze as her arms extend and she floats on the night sky.

A soft laugh rumbles from my chest as I follow her. Running toward the ledge, I lunge for the sky with a mighty beat of my wings and let the winds catch between the leather. I see her in the distance against the curtains of color, and I take a wide sweep of air into my wings to catch up with her.

I relish in the way the wind blows through every strand of my hair and caresses the skin of my scalp.

My arms tuck tight as I spear in her direction, corkscrewing through the air as I let everything melt away. There's nothing quite as freeing as flying. No quarrels about being a queen. No need to fix a magical stone. *Nothing* matters in the sky.

Velaria's childlike laugh breaks through the darkness. My head turns to see her up ahead, beating her wings in wide, sweeping waves as she hovers above the meadow. As I catch up to her, her wings tighten and she spins, falling to the grass below in a loud thud as her feet make contact.

I follow suit, tucking my wings and allowing my weight to pull me to the ground. My hair flies around my horns as I descend faster and faster before the grass slams into the soles of my feet.

Velaria runs through the flowers that have opened with the moon, enjoying the calm that the night brings, sprinting until she reaches the hill beyond the ancient wisteria that looks over the large valley below. The river that runs through the middle of it sparkles in a vibrant teal, as if lit from within.

She pauses as she looks at the dashing blue specks of light that whiz past us. Other specks join the first one and swirl around each other in a dance before they soar through the sky.

"Willows are out in full force tonight," I say gently as I come up beside her.

"They are," she whispers as she holds her hand out. A few land in her palm, spinning in a circle before jetting off again.

A smile tugs at my lips in content as I come to sit in the grass, patting it as she looks down at me. She plops down next to me, leaning back on her hands as her feet flop back and forth against each other.

I pull my knees to my chest as I gaze out over the valley. Tantalia's sky is always so brilliant at night. The black is painted with splashes of blue, purple, and greens that swirl and dance around each other. The sparkling gems of the stars twinkle throughout. It's reminiscent of a beaded train for a long gown.

A gown elegant enough for a Queen.

The thought begins to sink into me the longer I gaze at the barrage of colored curtains and release a sigh as my chin plops against my arms that I have crossed upon my knees.

Velaria's hand rubs my shoulder in tender comfort, "Remember when we would sneak out at the end of the day to come catch willows?"

A smile tugs at my lips as I recall our misadventures. My head tilts to lay against my arms as I look to her. "Kalinda would always reem us when she caught us." The memory brings about warm feelings of a time where life was simpler. Easier.

At least comparably.

"I was always so upset when she would make us release them! I just wanted a little blue lamp!" Velaria laughs in response.

The look of Kalinda's sneer flashing in my mind causes me to split at the seams and I fall back in the grass holding my stomach as my laughs pour out of me.

"Remember when mother would sneak some willows in for you? She made sure you got your willow lamp," I remind her. My hands clasp behind my head as I continue to gaze up at the stars.

This is why I love coming out here with Velaria. I haven't been able to do it in a while. Not since I've been looking for that hunter. I've been so consumed with exacting my revenge on him. If I were to ever find him again. He is much harder to find than I previously expected.

But sometimes it's nice to get away from the rage that urges me forth and bring myself to moments like this where it's just this.

Staring at the sky with my dear sister in the middle of the night.

Being sisters, we grew up next to each other in the pods. I was only a few years older than Velaria. But with how the pods work, we ended up in the daycare together as well. We never know our fathers. None of us really do with how the nursery works. We just know our mothers, and we know that we come from the same seed.

It fosters a closeness with your kin when you share a lineage. And I surely feel it with Velaria.

I always have.

Being so close in age allowed us to get into so much trouble when we were allowed to venture out on our own.

We would go down to the barracks and play pranks on the warriors, replacing all the silver swords in the arena with wooden sticks. It would take so long, but Lilith made them work so much harder for it.

My head shifts in the grass to watch Velaria, who has also laid down, peering up at the beyond as she reaches her hand out every so often to touch a willow that floats past.

"Do you ever think Lilith's magic is in the willows?" she asks quietly.

I watch as a willow spins and swirls in front of us, dancing in the sky like it has nowhere to be.

That's probably because it doesn't.

"I hope so," I respond softly as I watch it whiz away.

Velaria turns her head to me and offers me a sweet smile, "I really do think you'd make a great Queen, Phinney."

I give her a sad smile in return, "I wish I thought the same."

"It is hard. And if there was anyone else that I thought was better for the job, I wouldn't push it on you. But..." Velaria sighs.

"It's a big ask," I remind her.

"I know... I know it is. But the younglings... You know how much magic they take as they grow. I've noticed how much slower they've grown as the years go on and the stone's power decreases."

I sigh as I look back at the sky, "I just... I can't sit where she sat. She was larger than life, you know that. I could never measure up to her. It would be a mockery to even attempt to parade around as something as large as Lilith."

"I don't see it that way. You aren't replacing Lilith. No one can. You're stepping into your own rule."

The stars continue their twinkling, the night around us sings with the hoots of owls in the trees, and the breeze that whispers through the branches. Small bugs titter with their chirps.

Velaria goes silent as we lay in the grass and watch the night together.

I think about life before the chaos, before Lilith taught me of my purpose.

Before I was the Mistress of Bloodshed.

When life was just that...

Living.

"You're all cowards... Every. Last. One of you."

CHAPTER 6
PUPPET
SERAPHINA

Eventually, Velaria and I flew back to my room, where I gave her a hug good night and sent her on her way.

The night in the meadow calmed me enough to go to bed with a peace I hadn't experienced in a long time.

Probably since I started hunting that murderer.

Those moments with Velaria were needed. So needed in fact, that I was blissfully unaware of their necessity.

I go to see her in the Nursery every day, but I'd never taken the time to reminisce on our upbringing. The times when life was simple.

It was nice to experience that, even if it was for a little while.

The next morning, I started my day a little more level-headed than the night before. Time with Velaria is always renewing, but last night was more so.

More so enough that I wanted to take the time today to address The Legions.

Cometas, and their several hundred warriors line the back of the arena. Solis, standing three hundred strong are ahead of them, with Lunae and Stella leading the way. The arena is packed in neat little rows with every warrior that is not essential to guarding the portals and other important areas.

The men watch as I pace the front of the arena. Their arms behind their backs and their wings tightened at their spine as they wait for me to speak.

My gaze focuses on the small pebbles that roll across the ground as I kick the dirt in front of me. Dust floats into the air as I think of what I want to say and how to say it.

Leading The Legions was always meant for me; it's the thing I didn't mind being thrust into when Lilith placed me here.

War. Bloodshed. *Death* to those who'd lay their ill intentions upon us. It was something I craved. Fighting, leading, *teaching* – even if some days became unbearable – it's what my heart yearns for.

Sings for.

But the prospect of leading all Tantalia; every wing, horn and tail in this kingdom --*that* is not what I long for. That was for Lilith. And Lilith only.

"Legions!" I call out to the men, their attention snapping and all eyes coming to me as I continue my pacing. "The Mistresses have deemed me important… as we all know," I joke.

A few deep chuckles sound within the ranks.

"But… They have deemed me so important, in fact, that they wish for *me,* your general… to rule all Tantalia. How bizarre!" I say as I stop my movements, turning toward the hoard of men and gesturing in disbelief.

The warriors exchange glances with each other in curiosity.

Brutus, commander of Stella Legion steps forward, the harsh lines of his elaborate armor shimmering in the light of the day. "There is no better option, General!"

My lip curls in annoyance. "That is what the others have stated as well," I grumble. My arms cross over my chest as I lean on a hip and glance away.

"Then what is the issue?"

"I have no *wish* to rule!" I shout as I throw my arms out.

"Then why did you bring us here?" A stray warrior calls out.

I roll my eyes as I come to pinch the space between my eyebrows, "Because I've canceled trainings today to mull over this rather IM-PORTANT decision! If there is an issue with such, I can surely subject everyone to more training, if that's what you'd like!" I groan.

Quick murmurs and shakes of heads are heard and seen amongst the soldiers.

"That's what I thought," I murmur.

My pacing continues, the line of my boot prints in the sand begins wearing a path where I've trodden.

"If I am to become Queen… No matter what, my heart is within The Legions. They are always of the utmost importance, and my position here will not be going anywhere. No matter how badly they want me to sit a chair. I am the MISTRESS OF BLOODSHED! The Angel of Death! Above all else. And I will stay that until my dying breath," I say as I face them again.

Wingtips rise and twitch as I speak, with varying levels of tension flicking through tails behind their knees. I'm sure they expected some-one to take over my position if I were to become Queen.

But the arena is where I'll stay.

"Yes, General!" the warriors call out in agreement.

"I take my leave but know that there are changes coming. Whether I am Queen or not, someone is being chosen for the throne. You're all dismissed," I call out.

The soldiers bow, "To Tantalia," they murmur in low unison.

"To Tantalia." I respond, and the soldiers rise. Their ranks break and boots scrape against dirt as they retreat to the exit.

My arms cross as I watch them all file out. All the while, my thoughts run, work, and grip me by my throat. But there is no clear path. There are no clear words.

Just a jumble of emotions, if anything. And those emotions run deeper with every thought, threatening to seal off my air entirely.

"Heartwarming, I'd say, Phinney," Selene's voice sounds from behind me.

A groan works its way out of me, as my previously *somewhat* peaceful mood is absconded from my grasp.

Turning to face her, my head tilts in annoyance, "Says the one who won't step up to take her mother's crown."

"I am not a ruler. Mother never trained me as such." Selene shrugs.

My eyes roll and I look toward the sky, in the direction of the Wisteria in the meadow.

"Velly came to see me last night," I admit.

"I'm aware."

"Were you a part of this discussion?" I ask as I turn my gaze on her and my eyes narrow in accusation.

Selene's eyes drift to the side of the arena as she breathes a sigh, her hands clasped behind her back as her feet lazily kick the dirt in my direction, "I was."

"So, we have discussions without the patron in question?"

"You left so suddenly, what were we to do? The wards keep wavering. Guards killed another four Drannars this morning. Something has to give, Seraphina." Selene sighs as her eyes come to land on me.

"Why does it have to be me? Why am *I* the one that has to give?"

"Because you're the only one who can! What part of that are you not understanding?"

I groan as my arms unfold in agitation, gesturing to the arena, to the world, to *anyone* who cares enough to listen, "I don't see it that way, Selene! There are much more worthy people for this! Why must it be me?! And how can you all be so keen to place anyone on the throne at all? Did your mother's rule mean nothing to you all? Must you squander her memory with a puppet!?"

"That's the thing, Sera. No one could puppeteer you! That's *why* you're the one for this!"

I scoff, brushing off her backhanded compliment, "I have rounds to do."

The sand kicks out in front of me as I stalk to the exit. I head to the meadow when Selene's voice breaks through my anger. "Mother wanted this for *you,* Seraphina. Not me, not Orona, not Velaria, not even Kalinda. *You.* At the end of the day, Mother chose you, before everyone else."

My steps halt, my mind working over her words and what they could implicate in the overarching scheme of this situation.

But I don't want to think about it… I can't. Not right now.

The sound of the dirt crunching under my feet carries me out of the arena and into the grassy meadow beyond.

After retrieving Velaria from the nursery, we walked in silence to the farmland, checking on Learra and the crops. Everything there seemed to be going well, and we continued our trek through the land, only speaking when we needed to check on the mistresses.

Our cousin, Reasha was busy in the forges, sharpening and honing the weapons for the warriors -- especially after the skirmish this morning at the Drannar portal. As the Mistress of Sword, she is the one who keeps all our weapons intact, and in the process, I drop my swords with her for balancing.

Soon after, we headed to the infirmary to visit Mistress of Bloods, Zephyra. Some of the guards were wounded and I wanted to make sure they were okay. Luckily, they were from Lunae Legion and had their wits about them enough to not die by Drannar hands.

But as Velaria and I climb the stairs to return to The Court of Mistresses, she turns to me, "Can't you see what you're doing?" her voice soft and kind against the light taps of our boots against the marble steps.

"It's my duty. The warriors and the people here are important."

"But that's the point, Sera. No one else does this much work every day. You're the only mistress that comes and checks on me in the nursery, and I can't remember the last time anyone spoke to Reasha. They merely drop their weapons off and leave."

I roll my eyes, "Just because everyone else lacks common decency doesn't make me the right person for the job. If that was the case, they'd throw you on the throne."

I peer at Velaria, her features nervous as her eyes drift away.

She should know by now that I would never be angry with her. But I imagine with the way she sees me go at everyone else, she'd be next on the chopping block.

No other words are spoken as we approach the stone doors to The Court. The large rocky panels rumble against the floor to alert the other mistresses standing around the table of our arrival.

Kalinda's wings come into view, which sends my pulse thrumming violently. I know what words will come from all of these demons' mouths next. I *know* what I'm walking into.

Velaria and I join the rest of the mistresses, silence falling upon The Court as they look at me.

"The elves breeching our defenses this morning should prove only one thing to you, General," Mistress Kalinda starts as she peers at me with her normally indifferent gaze.

I hold my gaze steady against her, though challenging as she tempts her life with such idle threats. "It proves you're wasting your time trying to convince me of a useless endeavor."

"It is *not* useless if it affects the wellbeing of the people."

"Again Kalinda, why aren't *you* stepping up to *do* something about it? Surely, with your age you know something about the stone that we do not."

Mistress Kalinda's eyes narrow on me, the dig at her age not settling well.

As it should.

"I was not made privy to the invocation of the stone when its wards were placed. But surely with your *wisdom* and magical prowess, you can figure something out."

My eyes narrow on her, my hands press into the stone table and my nails squeal against it as they clench into fists. I lean forward, furthering my challenge. "There are other ways to fix the stone than a on a throne."

"Unfortunately, what I do know… as stated yesterday… is the stone needs the queen."

My brow furrows. This damn thing she keeps echoing about the stone needing a queen… It's insanity.

But, as if the gem on my necklace hears the squabble, it vibrates a simple pulse against my chest.

My eyes flick to the amulet for a moment before they return to Kalinda. "Is there another reason you brought me here?" I grit through a rabid sneer.

"Other than the proverbial stone in the room? No. Your time is ticking, Seraphina. It would be within your best interest to see this through."

A snarl pulls at my lips, and I glance to the women around the table who continue holding their tongues over my *proverbial* execution.

To be a Queen means to die in your people's stead.

How can you lead if you are to die?

My spine straightens, my brow and lip pulling tight in a disgusted grimace as I look over the trembling dogs that decorate the edges of the table with their malfeasance, "You're all cowards… Every. Last. One of you."

"Seraphina!" My mother speaks up.

"So now your teeth release your tongue!? In *this* instance when your position is challenged? Not when your *daughter* is forced to take a throne she can't sit?" I growl as my eyes meet hers.

Her gaze drifts away at my accusations, her head bowing as she remembers her place here.

"What is your aversion to all of this?" Learra asks, her face furrows in concern and is speckled in dirt from her duties of the day.

"What aren't you all understanding!? You'd rather sit someone in Lilith's throne than see its legacy through?!"

"Seraphina, you *are* the throne's legacy," Selene says softly.

"If legacy was in question, then *you'd* be on its seat," I growl in response as I whip my head to glare at her. Selene's head drops as the message sends an arrow through her. "You can throw your weak ideologies in my face all day, of legacies, and *suitability*. But there is no better demon to sit the throne than the one who created it."

My eyes slide beside me, to peer at Velaria, whose cheeks are streaked with tears. Her face is stoic, and her spine is rigid as she tries to hold everything together.

She is such a gentle being, I know she doesn't like seeing us at odds with each other.

And I do love her. More than anyone knows.

But I love the memory of Lilith more.

"Lilith is not to be replaced. And for you all to disregard *her* legacy, to throw someone in her stead, is to admit your lack of loyalty to the one who gave you all the chance at breathing. *She* gave you the chance to throw me here in the first place. And I surely will not be the one to replace her," I murmur as I round the meeting table, and through the doors of the court.

The rumbling stone marks my exit as I stomp back to my room.

Suddenly, the fear I wasn't having blasts through my chest as I face the one thing I wasn't thinking about.

Chapter 7

The Final Plea

Asher

One by one, I secure numerous daggers to every part of my body that I can. I also take a few extra minutes to sharpen the Blackwood Dagger. With our familial roots in forging, there are always daggers for me to take. I rotate the hoard I carry as father sharpens and takes care of them.

But the Blackwood Dagger stays with me, considering I'm the only one that *would* use it.

My hands pat each of my sheathes, making sure each one is tight against me. Taking a deep breath, I look to my father, who eyes me cautiously. "Bring them back," he says gruffly.

I give him a half smile as I look back at him, "I will, father."

He gives me a slight nod before he latches onto my shoulder with a strong handed grip.

My eyes track to Darian, who nods to my father in goodbye before we make our way out of the bunker. His fawny steed sits outside of the shop, grazing on some of the hay with Gnox and the other horses.

Cedric's horse, Rosey, has returned.

But a horse without its rider is never a good sign. Especially one that returned home on its own.

Air fills my chest as I take a deep breath, shaking my head of the thought as I climb Gnox, clicking him out of the paddock to follow Darian.

Cedric is fine. He's fine.

Darian's click and whip of his reigns sends his horse flying, and I follow suit.

The rapid pounding of hooves against stone mimics the pounding in my heart. My vision tunnels as I lock into the hunt. The prospect of *finally* doing something about this disease that has raided our lands and left it barren sends my thoughts into overdrive. And the smallest sliver of hope begins to break through the rabble. I can finally do something, do anything to save my people. But I hate that this is the result.

I should be scared. I should be nervous.

I am scared *for* Cedric and Gideon.

But I am ready to face this plague.

Eventually, the stone below the pounding hooves gives way to rough grass as we head to the west. My weapons clink against the metal buckles and leather straps that secure them to my body as we slowly approach the massive trees of Ravensong territory.

The lines and ropes that web from tree to tree come into view from the ground. Large wooden balconies rest along the deep green leaves and thick branches.

A few men and women walk along the boards as they carry out their daily duties.

Ravensong has done moderately well for themselves, all things considered.

Because the animals drifted more toward this neck of the woods, they seem to always have more furs and meat. Though, because only a select few are allowed to roam at one time, they never have enough meat to spare for the rest of us. Their cloaks are decorated with large pelts of deer fur around the cowl along with pads of fur they use to guard their ears from the demon's song.

Some children go back and forth between their lines, bounding from tree to tree with their smaller staffs of iron.

"Asher!" a voice calls from a tree above.

Peering up at the vegetative canopy, I spot the spindly frame of the warrior brother, Phineas, his staff in hand as he looks over the railing of the main Ravensong treehouse. His staff is a peculiarly crafted weapon. The top of it is twisted in a loose corkscrew with a hook at the top. I remember my father complaining about the specifications Phineas had wanted for this staff. But Phineas had insisted.

His black hair is pulled into a bun at the top of his head, and he waves down at me in excitement.

I would like to smile, but addressing the houses is always difficult. Even more so now that we intend to ambush a portal we know very little about.

A singular rope leads from the top of the treehouse to the ground, and Phineas bounds over the railing, whipping his staff at it. The rope corkscrews into the channels bent into the weapon and rough fibers rain from the sky as it snakes through it, zipping furiously as he descends to the ground with a pounding thud. He looks to the top of the rope and swings his staff free before replacing it on his back. "What brings you to the west?" he asks with a smile as he approaches me.

I've fought alongside Phineas on a few occasions. A moderately sized Ravensong middle brother, and a fine warrior. He's lightweight and thin, but what he lacks in muscle, he surely makes up for in speed. Amber eyes and tawny skin, he always seems to be more laidback and merely realizes his place in the grand scheme of things. He does what needs to be done and returns home. He doesn't ever seem to be concerned about the circumstance, just embraces it.

To an extent, I envy him. I wish I could live in willful ignorance in this way.

I imagine it is more peaceful.

"I wish I came on lighter terms. But we need any hunters you can spare." I sigh softly.

The dulled spike of the end of my dagger handle keeps me calm as I fiddle with it against my thigh.

Phineas' face contorts in confusion as he gaze lands on me, then at Darian at my side, "This isn't about the portal, is it?"

I sigh as I nod, "Gideon was taken this morning by a succ, and Cedric is missing… I found his cloak in the sticks."

His golden-brown eyes look to me in concern, and he glances to Darian, who nods solemnly.

"We're planning an ambush, and I need reinforcements." I inform him.

Phineas nods slowly, his thoughts seem to run as he weighs what we've asked of him. Darian nods up to the main treehouse, "Tell father to send the boys, and gather the surrounding hunters. Asher and I are going to Shadowfang, and we'll converge outside of the portal."

Phineas nods once more before he runs off into the trees. Releasing his staff from his back, he clanks it against the trees as he runs past. Phineas calls a loud ululating noise that echoes through the leaves as he alerts the rest of House Ravensong.

I turn to Darian as I blow out a heavy breath, and his hand comes to my shoulder, shaking me slowly in solidarity. "I'll go to Bloodreign for poisons; go tell Shadowfang," he says gently.

I nod before I make to run for Gnox, mounting him and racing to East Territory at unparalleled speed. The nerves running through me grip me by my throat as the visions of the skirmish play through my head.

How many will come out? An army? A few?

There is a plethora of questions, with no real answers.

It eats into me, and I kick Gnox to speed him up. Pressing through my heels into my stirrups, I make to stand and let my hands hold loose against the reigns as I bring them to his neck. I let Gnox take the lead as we rush to the darkened trees in the distance, through the cobblestoned area of City Center and onto the decayed landscape surrounding the east.

Eventually, we reach the narrow paths that have been laid in the forest floor to mark the areas of space that Shadowfangs inhabit. I lead Gnox in circles around the largest main tree that rests among the smaller ones, making it a point to pound his hooves against the earth. I pull heavy on his reigns to rear him up and make him whinny, alerting anyone that I can.

With the Shadowfangs so close to the portals, even if they don't bring all of their warriors, they need to be on alert now that their hunter is gone.

Slowly, members of Shadowfang come from tops of the trees, leaning out of the branches to look down at me.

"Asher! What is this?!" Lord Riald shouts from the top branch.

The Father of Shadowfang.

Gideon's father.

Suddenly, the fear I wasn't having blasts through my chest as I face the one thing I wasn't thinking about.

"It's Gideon…! He's… he's been taken," I pant as I look up at him. Gnox stomps back and forth against the ground as I hold him in place, my face contorted in apology.

"W-What?" Riald responds as his tanned skin begins to bleach.

Other members of Shadowfang come from the trunks of the trees.

Loud thuds sound off from different areas of the forest as barked doors are removed; curious eyes and faces coming to look at the ruckus.

A thud sounds behind me as the ground quakes. I turn to see Finnley, Gideon's eldest brother towering over me from where he vacated his own tree.

If you thought Gideon was large, Finnley has him beat.

He looks down at me with dark brown eyes, as if it's my fault, "What do you mean, 'he's been taken'?" he growls.

I pant, trying desperately to gain my bearings from the ride here, "He… a succ… She came and took him… I tried to fight her off, but he removed his cowl. She seduced him," I explain. I feel the contortions in my face as I plea for forgiveness. "Darian and I are gathering huntsman to go to the portal. We're planning an ambush."

Finnley's brow furrows as he looks up at his father, "We have to get him."

Lord Riald nods slowly, still in shock from the fact his strongest warrior has been nabbed.

Our house lost a bed brother. Shadowfang lost their strongest warrior.

If these weren't dire enough consequences to get everybody moving, I don't know what would be. But at least I have their backing.

Finnley's eyes meet mine and he nods once in agreement, "You better be right about this, Asher."

"Me too," I respond softly.

The usually white fluffy guardians that bathe the spire in its magnificence have darkened in a bleak omen, causing my gut to twist in apprehension as Celestial Keep closes in.

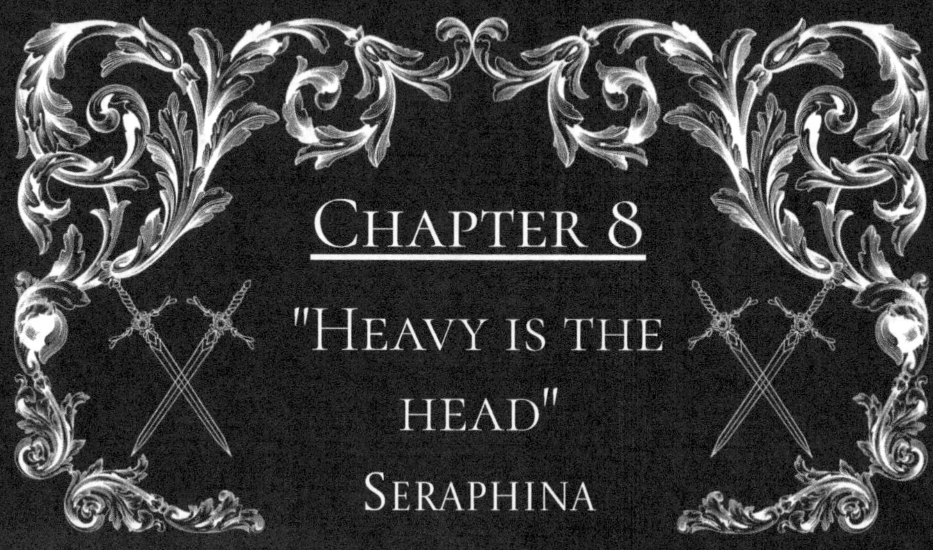

Chapter 8

"Heavy is the head"

Seraphina

Rays of the bright Tantalia sun shock me awake. Streaming in from my open balcony window, the light slaps me in the face, and I respond at it with an irritated groan. Using my pillow to cover my head, I try to stave the duties of my day away a bit longer.

A soft rap shakes my bedroom door, and another loud groan echoes in the warm air around me as it escapes me.

"Come on, Sera!! It's time for training; the warriors are waiting!" I hear Selene call from the door.

My fingers pinch at the corner of a stray pillow on my bed, whirling it at the large wooden barrier like a fluffy purple throwing star.

It hits the wood with a thud and Selene laughs from outside. "TICK-TOCK, GENERAL!" she calls.

Her heavy boot falls fade down the hall as I flip over in my bed. The sheer canopy stares back at me, reminding me of the conversation I had with Velaria a few nights ago.

The urgency of the request only makes me want to resist it more. You can't ask this of me and only give me two weeks to come into the idea of ruling an entire hoard of magical beings.

The thoughts propel me to anger, and I throw my sheets back. Slamming my feet against the cool marble, I snap once. My nightgown shimmers off my skin and my body fills in my black leather training corset and armor. My feet grow heavy as they become sheathed in thick boots. Weight settles on my spine as my swords find their home, and straps of leather and metal clasp around my chest. Venomous steps carry me from my room to the Training Grounds to make every single one of those shits suffer under my hand.

"I SWEAR TO THE GODS IF YOU CAN'T GET YOUR WINGS IN ORDER, I'LL CUT THEM OFF MY FUCKING SELF! TUCK FOR FUCK'S SAKE! ALL OF YOU, LET'S GO!" I bellow amongst the depleted warriors.

For the past two hours, I have worked them into the ground. I've made them all piles of mush with the maneuvers I've forced upon them, just as Lilith did to me. They can barely stand, with the talons at the bottom of their wings pinning into the ground behind them to hold them up straight. The Pits are filled with the sounds of groans and heavy pants from another group of Cometas.

"Get out of my face. Now," I wave them off. A collective sigh of relief comes from them as they are finally released from my torture.

I wait for them all to vacate the arena before I take my leave, with heavy steps pounding on the walkway that leads to The Nursery.

The stone below feels sturdy, grounding my rapidly growing anger.

Until a flurry of wind ruffles my hair from behind. Thick boots slap the path as pants emanate from my new visitor. I turn lazily toward the scene to see Selene bent over her knees, panting. Her features are contorted in panic as her long hair sticks haphazardly around her armor. "The Keep, we must get to The Keep," she manages to gasp through her deep breaths.

Irritation pricks into the meat of my brow.

Again, with this Queen shit.

I turn back to the path, "I'm busy," I say as I take a few steps forward.

My neck constricts as emerald sparks crackle in the edge of my vision. I turn toward Selene to see a bright jade bolt of lightning shooting from her wrist, its length leading straight to my throat. My talons grip for purchase against it, clawing at the rabid sparks. "YOU DARE ATTEMPT TO DEFILE ME?!" I bellow as I bat my wings to try to escape. Wisteria petals and blades of grass twist around as the tension against my windpipe causes my air to deplete rapidly. My efforts halt as I settle against her restraint, panting in anger.

"Now, Sera." Selene's voice levels me. Her tone is calm, but her eyes show fear. *Something.* Something familiar but unplaceable.

Though… it's not at me.

The expression catches me off guard and I raise my hands in submission.

Her hand whips back and the air returns to my lungs as the collar is released from me.

"*Now*," she says once more.

I return her demand with an understanding nod.

Selene crouches as she shoots into the air with a powerful blast, soaring toward Celestial Keep at lightning speed.

I follow suit. The climb into the sky is deafening as the wind rips against my eardrums and my hair tangles in a fury behind me.

The usually white fluffy guardians that bathe the spire in its magnificence have darkened in a bleak omen, causing my gut to twist in apprehension as Celestial Keep closes in.

Flinging out my feet as I approach the balcony of The Court, my heels scrape the green grass of the courtyard. Thudded steps alert the mistress of my arrival as I enter the vaulted meeting room.

"What is the meaning of this?!" I call amongst the ladies already standing around the table. The scene is a vision of mourning; faces of contorted sadness and solemn sincerity. Selene goes to stand at the table next to my mother, bowing her head in solidarity.

The actions of The Court make the twisting knot of fear wring tighter against my insides. There has never been a moment like this since the day I came back to announce the loss of Lilith.

All have bowed their heads. All except for Mistress Kalinda, her hands hidden in her long sleeves as her hood rests against the top of her tiny horns and her face locks into grave sobriety.

"You must… take the position," she says calmly. Her eyes cold as she pins them into me.

I knew it.

"Get fucked, Kalinda. Find a new queen," I snarl at her. My hands slap into the cold stone table as I lean forward, the air of The Court charges rapidly with my climbing fury.

"Your time for decision is done. You are to be Queen. Tantalia is out of time," she says.

"Says fucking who. Suddenly, we go from two weeks to now. What is your malfunction?" I growl defiantly.

"Rialla," Mistress Kalinda calls softly as her eyes stay locked onto me.

Mistress Kalinda's handmaid brings a small brown sack to the table, nodding with a bow as she hands the bag to Kalinda. Solemnly, she retreats to the doors.

Eyes shift around the table to land on me as Kalinda places the sack against the onyx meeting space. The rough fabric sobs a crimson stream as it settles against the stone.

My confusion increases the longer they don't speak. The longer *no one* speaks, and this *gift* is placed before us.

Kalinda begins to untie the bag, allowing its opening to fall around the object inside.

Small black horns are seen first, flaked with dried blood; silver hair is matted and stained with the dark fluid.

My eyes widen as I realize what is in the bag.

A head…?

My heart begins to thrash violently against the bones in my chest, the thumping echoes against my eardrums as the bag continues to fall from around the face. Fear tightens my throat in a gripping chokehold. It feels as if my breathing stops altogether.

Clouded eyes are lifeless, the mouth agape as the severed head stares back at me.

"She came bearing a message," Kalinda says as she pulls the head from the bag, placing it on the table.

My mother wails as she takes sight of the gruesome display. Her wings wrap tight around her body as her claws grip for purchase against the edge of the table to keep herself standing.

Velaria…

My sweet… Velaria…

Rage pulses in my veins with an unheard velocity as my eyes lock on the sight of my no longer breathing sister. My eyes dart around the head, mentally grasping for anything to keep me standing.

She… my… my Velaria…

The nights in the meadow. Chasing the willows and visiting The Nursery...

Gone. With the strike of a blade.

Sparks sound off against the cries of my mother as purple lightning wraps tightly around my feet, my hands. My hair begins to stand on end as my wings flare. The tension of the membrane in between the bones feels like my wings will snap, but I'm not here. I'll never see her light again. I'll never seek her warmth for solace.

And with the loss of her, I've lost myself.

I've lost control.

Heat broils the surface of my skin while drips of tears roll down my cheeks. The gem on my necklace glows brightly below my vision. So much so, that it begins to burn against my chest. The ever-growing lightning has begun to swirl around me. The sparks build and crackle as my eyes meet Kalinda's. The air thins from the increased charge of the rage pulsing through me. The tears on my face whip away with the swirling wind, floating in small drips against the sparks to create a horrific display of solemn rage.

"WHO?! WHO DID THIS?!" My voice booms through The Court like thunder, shaking the columns of stone and causing the window-panes to tremble.

Kalinda's face mimics the stony mountain The Keep is carved into as she speaks, "Hunters."

The alley demon...

It's her.

CHAPTER 9

POISONED

ASHER

Cloaks of blue and green have obscured themselves in the rough foliage that surround the portal.

Wooden bows creak through the dense thicket from above and the soft ting of metal comes from behind me as warriors of Ravenwood and Shadowfang hide in the woods, preparing for a slaughter.

House Bloodreign has supplied Shadowfang with arrows tipped in poison and have set a trap around the bright green grass with small needles dipped in their concoctions.

With only *me* to speak for House Blackwood.

During the tense trek here, I learned the portal has been sparking and crackling with rage. Nothing has come out or gone into it. So, the strange reaction regarding the flaming circle is unknown.

My muscles twitch in waiting as I stand front and center. The brilliant lights of the portal sear into my eyes as I lock onto it. Silence causes the air to grow thick with tension as we all sit and wait.

Watching.

Soon, the portal begins to crackle and spark violently. The center of the entry begins to spin as it gears up for the immense power from the other side.

Whatever the fuck is going to come out, is *mad*. Sickeningly so.

Harsh winds whip at the branches as the already dark sky descends into inky blackness. Purple lightning cracks from above as thunder booms around me, and the air carries a nauseating floral odor as the winds heave with our visitor.

The grounds around the portal have dulled to nothing as darkness blankets the woods into a void.

The portal stands like a menacing entity of its own as I realize it's the only thing I'm able to see anymore. The trees have disappeared, the sounds of birds in the forest have silenced. I can't see any of my cloaked brethren.

A heavy, booted-foot steps out from the portal, pressing softly into the grass as the portal warbles with their arrival.

A long leg follows, and soon, the wide hips and slim waist exit. Followed by a long, thick spaded tail that flicks with rabid anger. A tight, black leather corset grips around the curves and large breasts of a demon. Her silver hair seems to float around her long black horns as she peers at me. Her smile is wide in contempt as she sizes me up. Her bright violet eyes almost twinkle in relief as she registers who I am.

The alley demon… *It's her.*

Expanded wings of ebony leather and delicate bones emerge from the portal, reaching incredible lengths as her entire body exits and she splays them wide. The thin skin that covers them damn near shimmer in the light of her magical entry point, marked with thin lines that run through the webbing.

The demon's head tilts in curiosity, like she's found a precious relic she's looked eons for.

"You," she lilts. That ethereal voice fills the air and shakes the ground. As if the portal listens to her, it sparks with her timbre.

"Me?" I ask curiously.

"I've been looking for you," she coos, a crazed tone in her voice echoes through the forest as she watches me.

Elegant steps slowly eat the distance between me and her.

An arrow whizzes past my head, striking the ground in front of her foot.

Her advance halts as her head drops to look at the weapon, tilting her head at it in amusement before her gaze connects with mine again.

"This certainly won't do," she says. Clawed hands rise beside her and toward the sky, with it, a dome of violet film, barricading me into a secured enclosure with her... and the portal.

Fuck.

The silence in the dome is broken by the pinging of arrows as they bounce off the cage she's placed around us. Bangs and metal clashing cause the forcefield to reverberate as she steps closer to me, her eyes locked onto me like a deadly apex predator. Her booted foot crushes the arrow with a deafening crack, snapping it in half as the smoke bombs from Bloodreign pelt the dome, to no avail. Men's voices muffle against the power caging me in.

"You... are coming with me," she says with a devilish grin as she points a bloodied talon at me.

"Like Hells I am," I growl at her. With a quick flick of my hands and a turn, my daggers are secured in my palms, flipping them so the blades line my forearms. I charge at her, but she sidesteps and spins. I make a swift turn, and my arm extends to swipe at her side. The blade makes contact, and I feel the grind of bone as it slips through her skin. A screech consumes the compressed air in the dome as her wings jolt, and a taloned wing wraps along my back. A poisoned wingtip tears at the flesh along my ribs, and I fall past her. Hitting the humming grass I grip my side, groaning in agony at the burning that seeps through the cut.

Poison.

Dropping the daggers in my hand, I scramble to reach for my waist pack, fiddling with the closure to grab an antidote. The small clasp refuses to budge under my efforts, and her footsteps on my hand, halting my progress. The bones in my hand crunch as my screams ring through the air of the dome.

The demon breathes heavily as her hand swipes along the split in her armor. It cries a red river against the onyx leather bodice sheathing her. She brings the blood covered fingers to her face and her eyes narrow on them in curiosity. A malicious grin tugs on her lips as her eyes slide to me in taunt. She swipes her fingers across her split tongue, cleaning the blood from them. "Pity. I thought this would be harder, considering you took my Lilith *and* Velaria with such ease," she muses. Her grip is crushing around the back of my neck, pulling me to a stand with supernatural strength.

Lilith? Velaria?

My breaths quicken and thin as I try to fight the hold the poison is taking on me. The wound in my side pulses with fire and my blood carries through my veins like thick mud. With what little strength I have, I punt her in the head with my skull before I swipe at her legs. Her grip around my neck releases as she falls to the ground behind me, her wings opening against the grass.

My hand deftly scrambles for the Blackwood Dagger, but my strength comes up short. My movements are sluggish as I amble toward her and pulsing consumes my head.

My vision blurs and all I see is the stark outline of her horns as they tilt. The fuzzy mass of her body becomes a blob of black against the green grass.

"My… my… my… you sure made this easy for me, human." I hear her voice. It wavers in and out of my ears. My head begins to lighten as my pulse quickens and my breaths heave. The heat inside of the dome rises and my skin dampens with sweat.

My lungs fight for air, and my muscles grow weak. The last thing I remember is the richly intoxicating scent of succubus and the harsh scrape of leather against my skin, as a tender voice whispers.

"You're mine now, Little Blackwood."

Black wipes across my mind as I ease into the void I've threatened to escape.

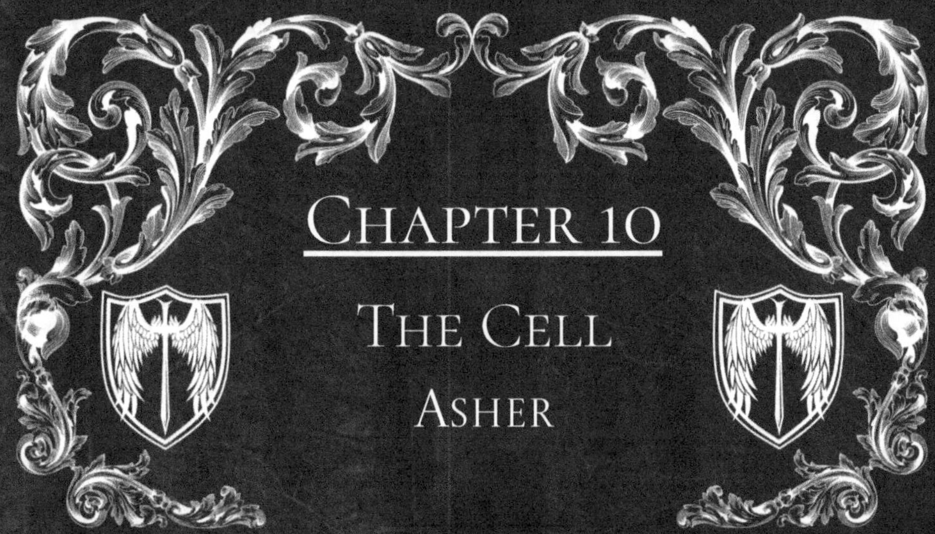

Chapter 10

The Cell

Asher

*D**rip, drip, drip.*

"Ugh, fuck…" my groan pings against what sounds like brick walls. Blinking, I groggily survey my new surroundings, pausing when I realize my hands are secured above my head. A pained sigh escapes me as I try to tug my arms against my restraints.

Iron cuffs, I surmise as they clang in the dimly lit space.

Usually these wouldn't be an issue for me, but it feels like my blood is made of sand. My head pulses with every move I make. I can't help groaning again as my body droops against the wall.

Where the fuck am I?

The low ceiling causes the room to feel entirely too claustrophobic, even by my standards. A small lantern hangs in the middle of it, flickering with little blue bugs that hit the side of the glass in their own futile attempt to escape. A chill runs through my spine as cold drips of *something* run from the brick and soak my tunic and cloak. The contrast of the burning heat of my skin against the coolness of the liquid causes an agonizing shiver to run through me.

Directly across from me, on the other wall, is a heavy metal door. No window, no peephole; the only light in the room is from the small lantern.

I have no idea how I got here. Or even *where* I am. The last thing I remember is falling into that succ's arms.

I never thought I would see her again. And when I finally did, amongst the rabble of our fight, there was something strange stirring. Perhaps it was the rage her kind had imbued within me, but there was something *strong* fighting inside of me. Something I couldn't decipher.

But the pain coursing through me doesn't give me time to pick apart the feeling. Not when the *current* feeling is eating me alive. Panting, I look down to my side, where the pulsing seems to be the strongest. A tear through my tunic allows me to peek at the wound that begins to fester with dark liquid against my ribcage. Small lines of black branch out as they climb through my skin and up my body.

I look up at the metal shackles, attempting once more to rage against them, but my depleting strength will not allow me.

The sweat that would normally cool me seems to be just as hot as my blood as it runs down my face, only further contributing to the agony of this poison.

I've been under the influence of succubus poison before, but never for this long. I was always able to procure an antidote in time. But this is a fresh type of Hell I pray I never experience again if I make it out of here alive.

I feel as if I'm going in and out of consciousness until loud clanking echoes in my small cell, allowing the door to slowly open. My breathing speeds up as my eyes drift to the entry in delayed curiosity. My head wobbles against the weakening muscles in my neck. As the door opens, light from the hallway silhouettes a pair of large wings that rise high above a set of curved horns. Glowing eyes peer into my being as the alley demon enters. The gem around her throat feels almost blinding as it glimmers against her chest, lending a soft magenta illumination to the cramped chamber as the door slams behind her.

Breathing feels like a chore as I attempt to gain what little bearings I can, and the effort it takes to look feels monumental.

The features that pull at her brows and eyes are viscerally intimidating as she glares at me. Fury untold seems to prick at the muscles in her face as she observes me in silence.

Her thick steps bounce off the surrounding walls as she gets closer, the light of the lantern reflects off her intense armor as it pings off the harsh edges.

"Tell me... Did you enjoy it?" she asks after a long moment of silence.

I quirk an eyebrow at her as I try to make sense of her words, but with the poison, I'm having a difficult time.

"What?" I pant softly. My hair falls around my forehead in wet strands as sweat continues to pour from my body.

"My dear... Velaria... Did you enjoy taking her head?" she asks as she takes a few more steps into the cell.

I can't understand her. *Who is Velaria? And what fucking head?*

As she enters the middle of the chamber, the lantern casts a sickeningly azure glow on her features. It contorts her cheekbones and jaw in a terrifying display of prowess. One I don't remember from the alley.

Granted, I don't think I can remember much right now.

"I don't... know... what you're talking about," I pant in desperation.

In the blink of an eye, she's in front of me, a strong hand of sharpened claws grips my cheeks as she peers into my face. The sparkling irises search mine; they twinkle with a rageful amusement. At least that's what I can surmise from my altered mental state.

"THE GIRL! DID YOU ENJOY HER DEATH!? DID YOU ENJOY THE WAY HER HEAD SEPARATED FROM HER BODY!?" she bellows, her tone causes my ears to throb and my head to pound in agony, pushing me further from the realm of knowing.

My eyes blink open as I look closely at her face once more. Her features have blurred against the vision that dares to fade in and out as my mind continues to slip.

Streaks of silver come alive through the blur, canvassed on her cheeks.

"Please... I... I have no idea... what you're talking about..." I respond through shallow breaths.

The fading blur tilts, my eyes closing and darkness falling around me as I give in to my demise.

The next thing I feel is warmth against my lips, and a gust of hot air running down my throat. A heaving gasp courses through me as I inhale deeply. The feeling is...

Renewing... Revitalizing...

A groan eases from my throat as I continue absorbing *whatever* is happening right now.

Black wipes across my mind as I ease into the void I've threatened to escape.

Air fills my lungs with renewing vitality as I gasp awake; frantically surveying my surroundings once more.

The throbbing in my head from earlier is replaced by clarity.

Strength.

As I move around, I notice the clanking from my earlier cuffs is gone, but I'm still restrained. Peering above me, a vibrant purple lightning crackles around my wrists, revealing a new set of magic cuffs securing me in this blasted prison.

I may be a Blackwood, but I'm no god.

I look down to where she had scratched my ribs. There's nothing. The skin has healed and there is but a small pink mark from where she sliced me. But the blood in my arms has vacated, leaving them feeling heavier than they would usually be otherwise.

My now clarified gaze tracks the floor to the door of the cell, my thoughts begin to run wild.

Did she heal me? If so, why? Maybe they like their meals without the decay already set in.

Regardless, I'm alive. I'll take that.

But she keeps spouting off about a Velaria. I don't know fuckall about a Velaria.

Soon, muffled voices and footsteps sound off outside my cell door. Bracing my spine against the wall, I try to be on my guard. At least in the best way that I can with my hands above my head.

The lock clanks before the door opens, and in walks the alley demon herself. The black leather of her corset bodice glints in the dull blue lighting of the makeshift lantern and her silvery-white hair shines from the light outside of the cell as her tail flicks irritatedly behind her.

The purple of her eyes is piercing as they meet mine.

They show no emotion. No hatred, no fear, nothing. It's oddly unnerving.

The door closes behind her, and she walks further into the light of the small cell.

Her eyes don't search me. They don't wander, they stay on my face, steady.

"The girl," she says. Her voice is commanding behind those vocal cords as she stares me down.

I roll my eyes. *This again.* "What fucking girl?" I ask in annoyed defiance.

"The girl you brutally murdered. My dear sister. Did you enjoy her death?" she asks again.

I groan in frustration as I charge against my cuffs, their power unmoving. "I don't know anything about a girl!"

"My…" she says once.

Crushing tension wraps at my throat as she appears in front of me in nary a blink. The sharp point of her fangs gleam in the light of my cuffs from her crazed grin and her eyes flare in feral anger as she meets me with her heavy power. A prick of *something* is felt in my chest as I connect eyes with her.

Fear? Anger? The feeling is unknown, and I can't place it. It's the same feeling as the one outside of the portal.

Her features relax as she strokes my cheek with her other hand, her voice soft, "My dear sister was beheaded this morning and her precious skull ended up on our doorstep. Now, I don't know exactly *who* did it. But I *do* know it was one of you *sick* hunters," she muses with a lethal depravity.

"We don't behead succs. And we surely don't know how to get a head through a portal. We can't even enter them," I choke against her, a sneer twisting at my lips as I glare back at her.

Her eyebrow quirks as she weighs my statement and her purple irises volley back and forth against mine. Suddenly, air floods my system as her hand releases my throat and she's backed up to the center of the room. She swipes her hands back and forth against her leather breeches, as if she's trying to remove me from her skin.

I cough to get extra air in my lungs, eyeing the demon from where I'm pinned.

"Your name," she says gently.

I quirk an eyebrow in curiosity as I take another deep breath, "I'm sorry?"

"Your name. What is your name?" she asks again.

I look at her in confusion, "Give me one good reason why I should give you that information," I snap in defiance.

"Because your people are in danger if you don't," she responds curtly.

"Yeah, by you and your sick kind," I spit at her feet.

Her eyes drag lazily to where I've spat, her head tilting in amusement as she comes to look at me again.

She takes slow, elegant steps toward me, coming within inches of my face.

I'm expecting to be hit by that classic succubus scent as she gets close.

But it never comes… something else has replaced it.

Most other succubus scents are disgustingly floral. Like a dead body wrapped in roses. But she… her scent is like a meadow of lavender, calming in the scariest possible way.

Her taloned finger slides against my jaw.

"I gave you the chance to do this the easy way," she muses before the melodic tones start to distort her voice. The claw drags down my chin, down my throat. The action causes a shiver of lust to tremble up my spine. I feel my body soften as her song lulls me into submission.

Her scent… her voice… take me deeper. I'm begging.

I can't resist the thoughts swirling within. I can't resist the way I wish she would take me right here, right now.

Show me the way it feels to be inside of you. Please… Please.

"You… you can't…" I try to say as I attempt to fight the feeling of her seduction. But I *can't.* And it eats me alive in fleeting bursts as I realize how much I can't. I tug on that restraint, but it appears to have disappeared entirely.

Her spired tail slides against my leg as it drags up my body. My abdomen. My chest. Until its sharp point pokes the hollow of my throat softly. The velvety living rope slithers around my neck until it begins to tighten and the flat spade end lays against my cheek in a gentle caress.

"Oh, but I can… And I will," she coos softly. The tones pick up, the pitch heightens, and the distortions come in and out as she speaks.

The pitches cause my body to melt against her and I can't hold myself up against the cuffs pinning me to the wall.

"P-Please…" I murmur as I sink further into her web. The idea of being inside her is all-consuming. The need. The urgency. The thought of her demon cunt wrapping around me causes blood to rush straight to my cock.

The grip of her tail around my throat tightens as her eyes glance down and a wide grin spreads across her face, revealing her gleaming fangs again. She gets sight of me hardened against the fabric of my breeches and I groan as her intoxicating rhythm lulls me into a sense of pure desire. With the urge to fuck her *and* kill her warring deep within, and the lack of air, my head spins and my thoughts scramble for purchase.

Until they grip onto the only thing I have left.

"B-Blackwood! Asher… Blackwood! My name…! Is Asher Black-wood," I pant to rid myself of this overwhelming sensation.

Her smile widens and she lingers on my face for a moment. Her hand reaches down, and the heel of her palm presses deeply against the aching bulge.

"Not yet…" she seems to whisper to herself. Her eyes drift down to where her hand is, before they trail back up to my face. Mischief cloaks her features as her head tilts once more. "Queenslayer… Yes, I think that name should do quite nicely… It has a ring to it, don't you think?" she muses as she watches me. My air depletes rapidly as her tail continues to tighten.

Queenslayer? What Queen did I slay?

The question throws me off guard, and it pulls me from my resistance before I bring my attention to my lack of air.

Her eyes sparkle with amusement as I continue to suffocate, until her tail unwraps from my neck and the seductive pull she has on me is instantly lifted. My cock begins to soften as she turns around and takes steps away from me, turning around when she reaches the door.

I groan as the life-altering seduction fades away. I've never been under a succubus' influence in my life and it's unnerving to be filled with an overwhelming lust you can't control.

Fucking hells, why can't I resist her? This is madness!

"That wasn't so hard… for me, at least," she cackles as she knocks against the cell door and the lock clanks as the door opens. Her eyes glance at my groin before she waves a hand behind her, bidding me farewell.

His chest continues to heave as his gaze burrows into mine. The intensity of it pricks into my chest and **settles** there.

CHAPTER 11

THE TRIALS

SERAPHINA

*I*f this little pissant doesn't know what happened to Velaria... then who does?

The thoughts rush through me as I pace back and forth along the black stone of my bedroom.

I came here to think; to plan what I'll do next with The Queenslayer. But even my room has not provided an ounce of solace from the war inside.

Kalinda said it was the humans, but the sick fuck that killed Lilith didn't kill Velaria. If there is anything a succ can extract, it's the truth, at least from humans. Succubi have walls in place for mind extraction.

But just because he didn't doesn't mean another hunter didn't.

He had also mentioned not being able to enter the portal. And while what he said was true... we don't know which of them *do* have the capabilities to enter. And with the wards on our portals wavering, there's no telling who could have come or gone when given the chance.

The possibilities eat at me the longer I pace the floor of my room.

The hunter is important. More important than I could have even thought possible. I didn't want to face that fact when I met him in the alley; there was no way I could deal with that information when faced with the death of my mentor.

It's even harder to resist now when I had the chance to look at him up-close. I find myself disgustingly attracted to him. In a way I'd never looked at a halfling before.

His eyes, even though they'd pulsed with fury, hid a kindness behind them. A will to live unlike any other. A hope twinkled in the deep greens that mixed with the small turquoise ring that lined his pupil.

Up close, he was devastating. Even thinking about it now causes my heart to race. Surely, I hadn't been gifted this beast for his looks alone.

The large muscles that pulled tautly against his cuffs as I watched him slump into his healing sleep left me dazed. They sent my insides fluttering. The small nicks along his flesh alluded to his prowess. Raised bumps of pink flesh, no doubt inflicted by past demons.

There's no way I can find myself attracted to The Queenslayer. He doesn't deserve that level of prestige. Perhaps The Fates speak to me in a different sense. They are known for their riddles. They don't outwardly tell you the things you should know. They merely allude to what they could mean.

A fickle thing, The Fates.

But now, with him in my grasp, finally after all these years of searching, I have to take advantage of what I know to be true.

As much as I would like to deny it.

The Fates have other plans. And who am *I* to deny the fates? Even if I would very much *love* to deny them.

The Fates know what is good for us.

I take a step onto the fence of the balcony outside of my window, flaring my wings as I fall forward. The dive down to the courtyards is quick and my booted steps enter my conscious as I land to march my way toward the cells.

Grafting is *obviously* easier. But sometimes I like to take the time that walking gives me to plan my next moves.

A shudder of air blasts against my face as Selene lands in front of me.

She has been dealing with a human hunter that was captured by Zyrella yesterday. From my understanding, he was the other human that was with The Queenslayer.

Grand leverage for me.

"May I help you?" I ask in annoyance as she blocks my path.

"The hunter you captured. Is he…?" she asks softly.

My eyebrow quirks in question as I look at her, "He is a Blackwood."

"No, did he kill her?" she asks.

I sigh with a deepening sadness at the memory of my departed sister. A tear threatens to appear, but I take a deep breath and steel my spine, forcing it away. I bring my gaze to Selene as I don a stone face. "No… No, it appears he didn't."

"The one brought in yesterday also has no idea what we're talking about," she sighs in exasperation.

Perhaps they don't know what happened to Velaria.

But…

"Go to your human captive and bring him to The Pits," I say quickly as an idea forms.

Selene nods with a curious expression before her wings bolt her through the air.

I continue toward the cell of my own human captive.

My plan for him is resolute.

The Cells is a large black building. It rests behind the barracks, where our warriors sleep. And entering the building, you greet some large Lunae warriors stationed there.

Held within, are hallways of thick metal doors. Some have windows to feed the humans kept there for information. I had The Queenslayer held at the very back of the holding space. And I've stationed massive Stella warriors outside of his door.

A necessary precaution.

Approaching the cell once more, the guards open the door for me. Allowing me sight of this human that now has to be tethered to my side.

His wet, brown hair rests against his forehead as he kicks his boot back and forth against the ground. His face doesn't meet mine as I enter, choosing instead to ignore me. The large door closes behind me as I peer at him. Even with what I know now, the rage from Lilith's death continues to rage in my skull.

The urge to torture him is so strong… but no…

The Fates decided.

Whether or not their decision was in earnest, is yet to be seen.

"I have a trial for you. That is, if you think you deserve to live," I muse.

While killing humans is forbidden in Tantalia, he surely doesn't know how to call my bluff on that.

Green eyes meet mine in confusion as he finally looks up at me. "Why would I do *anything* for you?" he asks with a disgusted grimace.

"Because you are restrained. And quite frankly, your other options are undesirable," I tell him plainly.

He huffs an annoyed breath as his eyes search mine, as if thinking he has a chance out of here, "What are my 'other' options?"

I flare my hand as I turn my attention to my claws in the dim light of the lantern above. "Fight my legions. Prove you deserve to live, and I will grant you your freedom. Or don't, and you die," I shrug as I come to cross my arms against my chest, waiting with a chilly indifference.

Drips echo in the chamber as he mulls over my words, and I peer at him from my spot. His eyes and brows stitch in irritation as he weighs the idea.

"My freedom? Just like that? I fight your little friends, and I get to walk away?" he asks skeptically.

"Precisely. If you prove to be worth the fight, I will let you have your freedom," I lilt playfully as I wave a hand through the air.

The human's face tenses at his brows, his gaze searching my own, as if seeing how genuine I am. And even now I *am* genuine. If he lives, he'll earn his freedom. It's simple really. If he is the big, *strong* Blackwood he claims to be, then the decision should be easy.

"What about my friend? My brother? Will they have their freedom as well?" he asks.

A small smirk forms against my lips, "If you prove yourself worthy enough. I shall grant freedom to your friend and… brother."

He takes a deep breath before he gives me a confident nod, "Alright."

"Splendid!" I grin with a wide, fanged smile and bring my hands together in a clap. The pop that rings through the cell echoes for the barest of moments, before the sound travels even farther and the sun blasts against us.

The clap brings the human and I to The Pits.

His eyes spin as he steadies himself. His body wobbles as his legs spread apart against the dirt to gain his bearings.

"Gods, what the fuck was that?" he groans as he finally holds true to his position.

Another groan escapes him as his arm comes up to shield his eyes from the bright sun, and his blue-cloaked friend appears next to him. The air from Selene's grafting ruffles my hair around my head and horns as she takes her spot beside me.

The two of them look to each other in relief, and the larger human slaps the murderer on the back in greeting.

"Good day, murderers! Glad to see you could make it!" I muse to the two of them. My voice carries through the arena and bounces off of the stone walls.

The humans look to me in confusion. "You fucking brought us here!" the Queenslayer calls in annoyance.

"Did I? Hm… Anyway! These are The Pits!" I shout as I gesture to the large arena surrounding us.

The mountainous man beside the Blackwood looks around the space, as *he* keeps his gaze steady on me. His arms cross over his chest as he eyes me with a look of pure disdain. It's as if his life isn't hanging by a thread.

"This is where we train The Night's Legions. A group of warriors tasked with securing the realm from outside threats," I explain.

This gets the human's attention and his eyebrow rises in curiosity, but he stays quiet.

"The Night's Legions are comprised of four different tiers," I start.

I bring my fingers to my mouth, clasping my thumb and forefinger together before I blow through them. A loud whistle sounds from between them and carries through the air. "Cometas!" I call.

Four younger warriors, nary bigger than the humans, strike into the dirt behind me. Dust tornados on the ground as the brush of air from their wings tangle my hair.

"Solis!" I call again.

Four warriors, around the same size as the humans, join the younger Cometas warriors.

"LUNAE!" I call again, louder this time. My voice begins to boom through the arena.

Four more warriors, larger than the humans, join.

"AND STELLA!" My voice rings through the arena one last time, before the ground quakes and four massive warriors of wing and glinted leather land before me.

I step out from behind one of the towering hybrids, looking to the Queenslayer and his friend in amusement. His face stays steady, body frozen, while his eyes glance over the sixteen warriors that him and his friend must survive.

"Each legion increases in strength, and power. The two of you, will fight four warriors from each legion. If you live to succeed through each tier of legions, and make it to the end, I will grant you your freedom.

Do you agree with the terms, Queenslayer?" I ask. My arms cross over my chest as I await his answer.

"What marks their end?" he returns. His eyes narrow in determination as his brow furrows.

My lips pull in a devious, half-smile. "Smart question. I will imbue your weapons with a shield of sorts. It will weaken them at the same rate a real weapon would. They will become depleted, but they will not be killed. My apologies over the lack of bloodshed. But I must protect my warriors."

"Do we get to choose our weapons?"

"So curious. I wonder if this curiosity was present during Lilith's demise."

"Get on with it, demon!" he growls.

"Tut, tut!" I wave a hand in his direction. His frustration causes a rush of giddiness to shiver through me. Ever the angry human. It's a *splendid* reaction.

A large sword lands at his feet and shimmers of purple glow brush over it in streaks.

"I don't use swords," he scoffs as he kicks the weapon away.

"That surely is a conundrum, Queenslayer. Too bad I don't care."

He rolls his eyes before he leans over and grabs the handle. He looks over it for a moment, sliding his thumb along the blade to check its sharpness. He swings the sword around his arm, feeling the weight of it before he plants the tip into the ground and leans on it. "Fine," he grumbles.

Another sword appears, and I kick it to the larger human. He doesn't put up as much of a fight as The Queenslayer as he bends over to pick up the weapon.

"Do you accept the terms, Queenslayer?" I ask again, terser this time.

"I accept. *Demon*," he says with a sneer.

"Terrific! Let the trials begin!" I call with a loud popping clap.

Twelve of the sixteen warriors disappear in a cloud of purple smoke, leaving only four Cometas soldiers.

They waste no time. A blond Cometas halfling charges The Queenslayer. Swinging their sword down on his head, he quickly plants his feet into the ground. Queenslayer blocks the chop as he brings his sword overhead, and the clash of their hilts reverberates off the stone walls.

Queenslayer kicks the warrior in the stomach, disarming him just enough for him to spin and block a bolt of lightning from the other warrior that attacks from a distance. He lines his body with the sword vertically, lifting his elbow to peek through the hole he creates. He deflects the blast, and it ricochets to knock back into the warrior's chest. Effectively knocking him on his ass.

"On your left!" The larger human calls to him as one of the warriors beats into the air. He flips and lands beside Queenslayer before he bats a wing hard against his back.

The Blackwood human rolls to the ground before he slides against the dirt in a three-point stance, surveying his new position. His hair falls against his dark brow as he glares at the warrior with a feral intensity. As I watch, I'm hit with a pang of lustful hunger.

My... Such a divine warrior would be a delicious meal... Would he fuck just as well as he fights? Would he fill me as well as the hybrid did?

My fangs catch my lower lip as I watch him move and find my face contorting in shock as I realize my thoughts.

No. No we don't lust for the Queenslayer. He is not to be fucked.

I shake the pleasured thoughts from my skull as I come back to focus.

His lip lifts in a snarl as he watches the other warriors stand off against him. His green eyes volley around the fray, calculating the best area of approach.

Dust kicks up around his feet as he charges the warrior that knocked him over. The warrior thrusts his sword through the air in an undercut swing as the Queenslayer approaches. But he sidesteps, avoiding the chop. As he sidesteps, he brings his sword through the middle of the warrior.

The imbued weapon merely swipes through the warrior, whose eyes go wide, and he falls to the ground. The halfling poofs away in a cloud of yellow smoke, and The Queenslayer stands shocked as he sees magic at work.

"One down, Queenslayer!" I cackle above the smoke.

He snaps into action when another warrior tries to whip his tail around his wrist. This seems to anger the human, and a growl rumbles from his chest. He twists his restrained hand, and in the process, the weapon moves with it, swiping through the warrior's tail. The halfling lets out a screech as part of his tail poofs away into a bright orange smoke. Turning around, the warrior meets The Queenslayer's satisfied grin. Rage pricks at the features of the soldier's face before he charges.

Stupid fucking Cometas.

Whatever confidence he gained from the last downed warrior, sends his sword through the belly of this one. His form is obscured in the bright orange smoke that replaces him, and for a moment, I lose the human.

The other two warriors are facing off against Queenslayer's companion, clashing their weapons one against the other. Only one of the Cometas warriors I've chosen, have enough magical knowledge to work with their lightning.

Queenslayer has already brought him down.

By the time they finish with the Cometas warriors, the two humans are sweaty, and panting with depleted breaths.

"Terrific work, Queenslayer!" I call to him.

He groans, "Quit calling me that! I killed no Queen!"

I *hmph* in annoyance.

So, he is unaware of his actions. I'll make him aware.

My lips curve in a tight grin. "SOLIS!" I call out.

Solis soldiers of equal size to the humans' blast onto the ground; marking the beginning of the next trial.

The Blackwood shows an agility I was unaware of. He spins and swirls against his opponents with a grace I'd find myself perplexed by on the field.

Where was this when I found him outside of the portal? Why does he show his prowess now? To him, his life held in the balance then, did he mean to be brought down so easily?

His bright jade eyes swivel as he strikes and blocks the winged men that come for him. At some point, he rids himself of his cloak by tossing it to the ground. Soon after, he does the unthinkable.

He rips his tunic from his chest, and his skin glistens under the sun with a sheen of warm sweat. A bold decision to rid yourself of protection during a fight with a demon. Even if that protection would have shredded in the process.

I continue to find myself positively annoyed at the build of him. A towering specimen of corded muscle and etched strength. Brown hair that falls in tousled clumps around his forehead and ears. It's been swept back by his movements, and curves in a mess of elegant chaos. His jaw has the hint of short stubble and carved by strength. With the high cheekbones and strong brow of a man unsure of his place in the world, decorated with a precise point of his nose.

A beautiful beast. But I cannot allow myself the pleasantries of gawking. I remind myself.

A beast is still a beast.

His muscles writhe as he tilts and swings the sword against the warriors, slowly knocking them down, one by one by one.

Eventually, we move onto Lunae. And while he has become depleted in his fight, he surges forth. The stamina of this beast, against the larger warriors, is impressive. He knows his way around a pair of wings, and tail. It alludes to the amount of blood he has truly shed.

By the end of the Lunae trial, his chest heaves. The hand gripping his sword slumps. The knuckles he's encased the handle with are whitened by his grasp and his skin glows pink from his exertion. Strands of his brown hair are darkened with sweat while drips of brine pelt the sandy ground, creating a small puddle before him.

"Your skills are magnificent, Queenslayer. I can see how you brought Lilith down with such ease," I praise with a small grin.

His chest rises and falls as he pants through a confused tilt of his head, "I don't fucking know these demon you keep naming! On with the next men!" he growls. He throws his hands to the air, beckoning the next challenge with the promise of bloodshed.

Or what he would think is bloodshed if his weapons were not spelled.

"As you wish," I say with a soft bow.

I hope he regrets his decision.

Stella Legion is the largest, strongest, and wisest of our halflings. They are massive beasts of wing and muscle, and we rarely lose a Stella warrior. They know their way around a battlefield, and they are elite in their magical handling.

The Queenslayer does not stand a chance.

The sun has begun to set, and the sky melts into a dusky pink and purple against the darkening backdrop. I raise a hand, and snap once into the cooling air. The ring of its crack carries into the night that quickly descends upon The Pits.

Without warning, metal clashes, and The Queenslayer stumbles into the dirt. Towering warriors arrive and he merely growls at their presence.

His lips move, but with the ting of their metal colliding, I can't hear him.

Over and over, he pushes onward. Him and his companion work in tandem, spinning around each other. They push one another toward the threats. The fight lasts until the moon rises high in the sky and the final Stella warrior poofs away in a puff of crimson smoke.

When the last warrior dissipates, The Queenslayer crashes to his knees.

The smoke of the dissolved warrior clings to the steam that seeps from his skin. The cool night air carries the smoke away, leaving only the man in its wake.

His breaths are heavy, and his head hangs in utter depletion. The grip on his sword has loosened as his arms fall limp at his sides. One by one, his fingers release, and the sword falls into dirt beside him with a metallic scrape.

With the hours of fighting, his veins throb under his skin. His muscles have been pumped larger from his efforts and his skin is stained in splotchy patches of dirt. Adhered to him by his sweat.

The Queenslayer fought for his freedom. And he fought off my largest, most skilled warriors.

A fine royal guard, he shall be.

"Phenomenal display of prowess, Queenslayer!" I call to him with glee.

He doesn't respond. He holds his head down as drips of sweat continue falling from his brow and his shoulders rise and fall with each calculating breath he takes.

"I must say, I thought you were for naught when Lunae made their appearance. But you held your own. Impressive."

"Let me go," he mumbles.

It's barely a whisper, but I can't help playing with him.

"What was that, Queenslayer?" I ask with a taunting grin.

"Let. Me. Go." His voice rises just enough, but it's still quiet.

If he is to be my guard, surely he cannot be so feeble.

"One more time, darling!" I call in a sing-song tone.

"LET ME GO!" he bellows. His head snaps up and his eyes are a blazing fury of emerald green.

His hair sticks to his dirtied, damp forehead and he bares his teeth in a snarl. His chest continues to heave as his gaze burrows into mine.

The intensity of it pricks into my chest and *settles* there.

The alley… I remind myself reluctantly.

The subsequent tugging against my heart unnerves me. It catches me off guard, and my amusement fades. "I offer you a deal," I say sternly.

The human stays, against my better judgement. The Fates have spoken, and I am to respect what I would like to deny.

My plan has always been to offer him a deal, he was never to walk away from here. Whether The Fates had cast their judgement or not. But they were never to be weighted in his favor. I needed to see what he's truly capable of.

I had to make sure The Fates had truly decided in earnest. I would like to reject what they have laid bare for me. But I can't.

Not when they're so blaringly loud.

He throws his hands up in desperation, "A deal!? I fought your men! I played your games, demon! I want to go home!"

The anger of this little beast is admirable.

"I promised you your freedom. And I shall grant it. The freedom of choice that is."

His face contorts in anger, "What?!"

"I never said what kind of freedom. I merely promised you freedom. And now, here, you have the freedom to choose between my royal guard, or the cells to rot and eventually die."

His brows tense, and for a moment, he looks as if I'll be the next demon to go. But he merely breathes, he watches me closely. "I want my brother released, and I want Gideon by my side. Only then I will be your royal guard," he growls.

Even in depths of his circumstance, he fights for those important to him.

Curious.

"You have a deal, Queenslayer," I say with a wild grin.

Everything seems like delusions of grandeur, until I spot a human who seems to be fighting alongside them, next to a succ that has rather enormous wings, and even larger horns. But her face and necklace, I vividly remember.

The one I killed in the alley. Where I met Seraphina...

CHAPTER 12

THE LIBRARY

ASHER

"I thought when they offered our freedom, that meant we were going home. Not… whatever the fuck this is." Gideon's voice is tight with annoyance.

The two of us have been decorated in black leather armor, adorned with glistening black scales that protect our torsos, and our forearms sheathed in gauntlets of the same material.

Our biceps are bared, and we are allowed to keep our weapons we brought with us. However…

"And this collar. How did we walk into this one?" Gideon groans as he tugs at the sparks of green lightning around his neck. My own new accessory crackles in purple.

While we do have our weapons, we are unable to use them against the succs. Which is the purpose of the collars; we've been turned into mere lap dogs.

But I'll play the game if it means I can get to the bottom of these wretches and end them from the inside.

After the deal I struck with Seraphina, – I had learned her name when I was released, but I'm supposed to call her Mistress when addressing her – we were given this dark garb and restrained by these collars. She had handed our weapons to us with an evil grin, only to explain they'd be useless. The last thing I had asked for was the small metal disk of my insignia that secured my Blackwood cloak. As I stand here guarding the door, I flip the small object in my fingers. We were provided a small meal in return before we were moved from one place to the next in the blink of an eye. The process is jarring and nauseating. I haven't been able to see any of this place during my time here so far.

My brother, I had learned, was sent to The Pits to be trained as a warrior. I'll take it if they don't kill him. I'll need his help for the next steps of whatever it is I plan to do.

I only took her deal because I have the opportunity to do the one thing I have begged my own people to do for far too long.

Gain any and every bit of information I can to stop their reign against the humans.

Being her royal guard is less than desirable, as I sincerely do not want to spend any more time around her than I have to. But fine, I'll do it, if this is what it comes down to.

"Listen, Gideon. We need to keep our eyes and ears open at ALL times. We need to learn as much about them as we can so that when we escape, we can bring the rest of us and take them all down from inside. Learn their weaknesses, learn their soft points, and then we'll go from there," I whisper to him from my post. I slide my thumb over the raised metal lines of my insignia, reminding myself of my purpose here and partially to ground me.

We stand against massive pillars of white stone in front of a glistening set of doors. A large group of demons had entered a while ago, including the mistress that now holds Gideon in her little claws. She also happened to be the one standing next to Mistress Seraphina when we faced our trial in The Pits. She looks eerily similar to my new "master", but with a smile instead of a sneer.

Gideon leans over as I speak, offering his ear to me, "Okay, but… what am I supposed to do about it?"

I sigh, "Nothing, just remember it. Log it in some weird book in your head."

Gideon shrugs as he leans back up against the column beside the door.

It's a weak plan. But it's all I have and now that I can learn about them, I can at least do something for my people instead of exposing them to mindless death. I've only killed them because there was no way Vesperholm would let me hold one hostage. And even thinking about it now, I doubt there is anything the succubus would offer as respite, even as a prisoner of ours. And with their ability to move from place to place in the blink of an eye...

I shake my head of the thoughts and go back to standing guard.

Seraphina had called this place, "The Court of Mistresses." I don't care what that means, but hopefully, I'll get closer to their ruler. Or whoever calls the shots in this gods' forsaken place.

"I'll try. But this Selene demon is intense. I don't know how I'm gonna be able to learn anything from her," he says as he itches at the collar again.

Soon, the large doors rumble open, shaking the floor where we stand. I quickly slip the disk back into a pocket on my side as Gideon and I turn stiff as boards. A rather tall demon in a long white cloak exits with a smaller demon draped in the same fabric. They pay us no mind as they turn the corner to make their way down the stairs outside of The Court. Smaller succs exit behind them, all with varying degrees of personality; rough and rugged, refined and elegant, calm and composed.

But they are all the same energy.

Powerful, *powerful* beings.

Their strong varying scents nauseate me until Seraphina and Selene exit.

Selene's scent mixes against Seraphina's in a weird concoction of calm and repulsion and my mind has no idea how to work through it.

So, I don't.

"Come Queenslayer, we have work to do," Seraphina murmurs annoyedly as she passes me. Her head doesn't even turn as her fingers splay in my direction and a beam of light shoots from her wrist, attaching to my collar to drag me harshly behind her.

This gods' damned nickname of hers.

"Agh, fuck. I'm coming, do you have to do that?" I ask as I stumble against the disarming force. My feet clamber one over the other until I gain just enough slack on my lead to not be choked.

"Yes," she responds curtly.

I groan as I follow her down the large set of steps the previous succubus descended.

"Where are we going?" I ask as my eyes roam around this massive castle. Tapestries of demons depict an ancient battle against some kind of dark creature. Pointed ears, gray-blue skin and bright red eyes decorate the walls in large panels of cloth. Bodies of dead succs litter the scene, portraying a grisly and brutal loss.

Everything seems like delusions of grandeur, until I spot a human who seems to be fighting alongside them, next to a succ that has rather enormous wings, and even larger horns. But her face and necklace, those I vividly remember.

The one I killed in the alley.

Where I met Seraphina…

I realize this tapestry demon is the one I killed, and my stomach drops. It creates a burning pit in my stomach as I continue to follow her. She leads us through the white stone corridors but has yet to answer my previous question. She pays me no mind at all as we continue down more sets of stairs. More tapestries hang, telling the tale of their people, the way they farm off the land and the harmony they all exist in here. In this set of tapestries, is a more peaceful scene. It's void of the pale blue-gray creatures and tells a tale of their ways. Demons of differing cloak colors move along fields and go about menial tasks. More panels of the colored cloth show a large group of the human-hybrids I fought for Gideon and my trial. There is also an enormous tree, decorated in purple flowers, depicted with succubus holding tiny bundles of cloth around it.

The images stir in my head and try to craft a bigger picture. Even with it presented right in front of me, I'm having a difficult time processing all that I'm learning. I didn't think everything here ran this way.

This *well.*

Pillars of tall, ivory stone have been carved into giant demons of old. Their curvy forms jut against the high ceilings of the open spaces as we cross — what Seraphina called "Celestial Keep" — through large atriums. Succs of different cloak colors scurry to and fro. Some carry baskets of food. Others carry weapons, clothes, and armor. It appears that everyone has a job, and everyone has a purpose here.

Quite a little civilized society. More so than what we even have back home.

But I suppose they would be when they've taken all our men.

Which also reminds me…

I don't have time to linger on the thought when we arrive at a pair of massive oak doors. The panels of wood creak on their hinges as they open, and the smell of old parchment rises around me. The floral bloom that we walked through was now replaced by the scent of smoke and leather.

A library.

Walking into the tall, domed atrium, small balls of flame follow some of the succubus cloaked in pale green fabric. They scurry along the aisles as the following balls of fire light their way into the depths to the back wall of the massive chamber. Lines and lines of bookcases delve deep into the castle, with hundreds of thousands of books sitting on their shelves. Small wooden tables sit in the middle of the large space, with tall shelving on either side of the wall. Metal chandeliers lit by candles hang from the ceiling on shining silver chains. Little hoods bob as they make quick work of the stray books on the tables, their faces pinched in focus as they stare at the covers before they flick the books in separate directions. The large bundles of leather and pages fly through the air as they send the volumes back to their rightful places. I feel my eyes widen and my jaw gape as I watch them; truly in awe.

My attention is pulled away when Seraphina tugs on my lead to bring me to a table. "Sit," she commands as she strikes her hand at a wooden table leg.

My lead pulls gently against my throat as it attaches to the post, my eyes sliding down to it in angst as I groan. I take a seat in a wooden chair at one of the tables and damn-near pout at how ridiculous this deal is that I made.

I truly feel like a human dog, and I can't say I enjoy it. But I'm in a library. And what better way to get information than where they keep it?

Silly succubus.

Seraphina doesn't skip a beat as she continues her trek into a darker part of the library. A ball of fire whizzes past my head and singes the ends of my hair as it quickly follows Seraphina to catch up with her. The scent of scorched hair fills the air before the smell is replaced by the leather-bound books again.

Before long, her form disappears, and the orange glow of the fireball dulls into blackness as she delves further into the aisles.

When she's out of sight, I frantically search the spines of the books in my general proximity. Most, if not all, aren't even titled. I am incapable of reading the ones that are. It's some ancient script I don't recognize.

How the fuck am I supposed to find what I'm looking for here? And *WHY* are there no titles?! How do they even find what they're looking for without their labels? What kind of bullshit is this?

I groan as I face the table and my eyes catch on a pair of demons eyeing me. Across the way, their taloned fingers point at me as they whisper to each other. I roll my eyes as the two of them begin walking away when a loud pound and an aggressive shake from the table averts my attention.

A large stack of books takes residence in front of me, but Seraphina is nowhere to be found. I look around to see if perhaps she had dropped them and run off, but there's nothing to allude to such an instance.

I take another peek around to see if the coast is clear before peering at the book on top of the stack. The cover has the image of a portal on it, and it has to be at least 1200 pages long with how thick it is. The pages look like dried skin; thin and brittle, with a leather cover that is scratched, dented, and well-loved, if I were to put a name to it.

"What the fuck…" I murmur to myself as I lift the top cover slowly.

A quick hand slaps the cover shut and I jump in response at the sudden intrusion.

"No," Seraphina reprimands me as she appears before my eyes.

"Good gods! What is wrong with you?!" I gasp as I grip my chest.

Seraphina rolls her eyes as she takes a seat across from me. She grabs the large book from the pile and places it in front of her, flipping it open.

As I catch my breath from her spooking me, I take a moment to peer at the pages, trying to make sense of any of the scribbles on the page.

That is all for naught, as the book is not only upside down; it's in the same weird script that some of the random books with titles are labeled in.

As my eyes trail from the page, they track up to the generous cleavage compressed in the bodice of her leather corset. I am reminded of how breathtaking these demons are.

I don't like it.

The reaction I have to the sight of her is an unwelcome one. So are the thoughts that trickle through my skull as I visually dissect the taut curvature of her throat, her neck. As my gaze travels up her throat, it lands on her lips.

How would her throat sing as I shoved every inch of myself into her? Gods, the way her lips would look wrapped around my c–

I clear my throat to wipe the thoughts away.

Stupid fucking cock. Stop thinking for me, this is not your place. I never think like this, what the fuck is wrong with me?

I attempt to turn my attention back to her task. "What are we doing here?" I ask.

"Studying," she says as her fingers flip through the pages, her eyes quickly scanning as she stops flipping every so often.

"For what? Aren't you people born knowing these things?" I ask.

"I'm trying to *save* my people," she says gently, the sound of pages turning fills the silence between us.

My eyes widen as I register her words.

Join the guild… Wait. What? Save her people? From what?

"What could you possibly need to save your people from? Aren't you lot the worst in the realm?" I ask.

Seraphina's eyes boringly come back to mine as she turns her attention to me with an annoyed tilt of her head. "I understand you humans may be stupid. But there are worse things out there than succubus," she responds.

I roll my eyes as I cross my arms over my chest and lean back in my chair. "Like what?"

"Drannars. Orcs. Mages. *Queenslayers*. Take your pick."

I'll ignore the last comment. I didn't kill any fucking Queen.

But… I'm sorry… What?

"Drannars?"

"Correct."

"What are… Drannars?"

Seraphina sighs as she closes her book. Her hand comes to her face to pinch the space between her brows, "Dark elves. The same ones that slaughtered my people millennia ago, and the reason we have portals."

The tapestries… that happened?

My eyes widen as I listen to her. "Dark… elves…?"

Seraphina nods as she levels her gaze with mine, her features are deadly serious if not a bit bored.

"That still doesn't explain what you're doing here," I retort.

"You worry about guarding me, and I won't have to explain anything," she responds as she attempts to go back to flipping through the tome.

"Do *you* even know what you're doing here?"

Seraphina freezes, her brow twitching as she stares at me. The lead that was originally strapped to the table is now in her hand as she stands and begins to drag me from the table, leaving the books behind.

"Gods dammit!" I grunt, following the harsh tug as she leads me out of The Library. "Do you have to fucking pull so hard?!" I groan as I catch up to her.

"Silence, Queenslayer," she murmurs. Seraphina is silent as we make the long climb back up Celestial Keep. It seems like there are over a million stairs in this place with how many we must climb.

Eventually, she leads me to a set of large white doors. Her free hand waves at them and they open before her.

As we enter, there's a cool breeze. A floral, earthy scent wafts in from the open window along the back wall. With lilac curtains that sway against the large glass panes. Without warning, however, the large doors close behind us.

A four-poster bed rests against the left wall as we enter, covered with a massive sheer canopy and a large mattress.

These guys have it made here. I wouldn't mind sleeping on something soft, considering I've just been resting on a hardened mound of dirt for the past ten years.

She tugs me over to the other side of bed, where a small cot sits on the ground. I hadn't seen it when we entered because it was obscured by her elegant sleeping arrangements.

My head tilts at the small "bed" in disbelief, "You're kidding."

"I don't kid, darling," she muses with an evil grin. Her purple eyes beam with mischief as she shoves me to the small cot. The lead in her hand snaps to the four feet of the small cot before they coil around my ankles and wrists, pinning me to it.

"Sleep well," she giggles before she leaves the room.

The doors close behind her and I'm left restrained against the cot, gawking at the ceiling above.

Fuck.

"Whatever hellscape you have retreated to, needs to be escaped. Because you cannot lead, if you cannot yield."

CHAPTER 13

"YIELD."

SERAPHINA

The human was more distracting than helpful. With night drawing quickly upon us, I imagine I'm safe to peruse The Library without the tainted voice of my captive drawing attention away from where I need it most.

I hurry back down to the books I left on the table. My mind runs with what I should be searching for to fix this damn stone.

Lilith was the only one who really knew the inner workings of the magic in Tantalia. The rest of us were just taught how to wield it.

Lilith would tell me every single day about how one day my place would be here in The Library. I didn't understand, then, what she meant. I'm a fighter; I was always going to lead our armies. What use would I have buried in ancient parchment? She never got the chance to tell me. It was something she didn't think I was ready for and in return, I *was* thankful for that. I didn't want to spend my days with my head in the sand while our people fought on the front lines, killing Drannar intrusions and guarding the important things in Tantalia. But with our Queen gone, I'm forced to face what I thought would never come.

Before I was rudely interrupted by the murderer, I had found a book on portals. It was of no use, as it only showed the available portals to the realms and some of their origins.

Useless.

The Never Realm portal, the one that we guard heavily, lays to the north of Celestial Keep, right outside of the farmlands and deep in the woods. So, at least when the Drannars break back through, – as they occasionally do – they'd have to fight to get here.

The Vesperholm Portal. The one near the bottom of The Keep where we can lead our human captives straight to The Cells.

The book said more about a third realm, called The Realm of Mages. And even a fourth, but the ink was blurred, and I couldn't read all of it.

This feels useless and I have no idea what I'm even looking for. Lilith kept the secrets of our magic and its workings closely guarded, she had reason considering the massacre. But who could possibly know the infor-

"Looking for something?" A cool voice sounds off from in front of me.

But by the smooth roll of her vowels, I already know who it is.

The pure white cloak and shining eyes of Mistress Kalinda are illuminated in the fired balls of light that float around us.

"No," I respond as I glance up at Kalinda before returning my attention to the book.

"You know, I have been here as long as Lilith had. I do happen to have a wealth of knowledge," she muses with an icy indifference.

"Then please tell me why am I being set to lead, Kalinda? Why is it *I* that must take the throne? And why aren't you giving me the information I *do* seek?" I ask with a fraying hold on my temper, the words on the pages don't even register as I flip through them faster.

"I am no fighter. A Queen must be able to fight for her people, to sacrifice her freedom for her people. Furthermore, there is only some of our history that I know. Like the Realm of Mages, you seemed to blaze past in your frantic search," Kalinda says.

"You have no fervor to fall on your sword? Then why are you so bent to make me?" I growl as my hands clasp the book shut. My eyes trail up her cloak as my body rises from the table, rooting my palms into its surface. Leveling her neutral gaze with the fire of my own, I growl. "And what of this *Realm of Mages?*"

"A realm of magical humans. Perhaps they would be privy to helping you repair the stone. Though, with the treaty, I imagine it may take some… convincing."

So, mages *do* still exist… And there is an entire realm of them? Why didn't Lilith reach out to them?

"What treaty?" I ask cautiously.

"Many, many years ago, before the wards were placed, there was an imbalance in the magic of the world. Humans fought demon; demon fought elves. So on and so forth," she explains with a wave of her hand in dismissal. "Lilith had gone to this small land of humans, who had learned how to wield magic in her frequent travels to strike a peace with them. Their only stipulation was to be shrouded from the rest of the world. So, in the process, Lilith created their secluded realm, and we got to keep our area of land to ourselves. They wanted nothing to do with us after that, and we weren't allowed into their little… place. And thus, it was lost to time."

My eyes lock onto her during her impromptu story time, my lips parting as my mind works over her words and the weight they hold.

A realm of magicians… all with a wealth of knowledge that I could possibly use.

I need to find a map. And quickly.

But my mind comes back to the actual annoyance I have with Kalinda, "And so, why can't you do it? You danced around the main question with your flowery story, so why is it you can't step up and do this with all the history you know?"

"Because this is what Lilith asked," she responds softly, completely unphased by my challenge.

My heart freezes and my skin tightens with gooseflesh as a chill runs through me. The rush of blood in my ears is the only thing I'm able to hear as I weigh her statement. But a vibrating pulse shimmers against my chest as the usually dull gem beats with light.

Kalinda's eyes flick down and catch the gems action, and a prick of her eyebrow is all that is seen as her eyes return to my face.

"What do you mean *'Lilith asked'*?"

"She said you are to be Queen. Who am I to deny our Queen's final wishes?" Kalinda says softly.

I stare at her in disbelief.

Final wishes? What would she know? Lilith was killed by the hunter that day, no one could have possibly known. I lean forward to speak, but Kalinda's gliding form begins to retreat from the table, leaving me with the crater she blasted through my chest.

"Tick-tock, General," Kalinda says as she leaves The Library. Her cloak flows behind her as she disappears into the night.

I found my time in The Library to be useless. After Kalinda paid me her unnecessary visit, my mind spun with her words.

The pressure of taking this spot and the sacrifice involved spurs me to retaliation.

Against The Court, against the throne that means to enslave me, against it all.

And at the end of it all, is Lilith. She sought to mold me and make me the one to rise when she had fallen. And for what?

The thoughts churn my anger more and more the longer I sit with them.

I'd fucked the warrior. That did nothing to satiate the fear and rage inside of me.

The fear of not living up to what Lilith had expected of me. She told me day after day of my purpose. And I never enjoyed hearing the words leave her throat. They were grating, they were something I tried so hard to deny.

And now I will attempt to deny them once more. By doing the only thing that truly silences the doubt and frustration of my circumstance.

"General, is there a reason I've been pulled from my post?" the thick voice of the Stella warrior I've chosen for this task asks.

I watch him carefully; I've picked him for the simple fact he looks just like the Queenslayer. Before I came down here, I conjured my weapons and attached them at my spine.

The weight of the crossed blades carries a burden I was not expecting.

"I'm challenging you to a duel," I murmur as I flick my hand in his direction.

A sword appears at his feet, and he raises an eyebrow as he leans down to grab it.

"A duel, General?" he asks curiously. "For what purpose?"

"Do you always ask so many questions, Krolta?" I growl as I stand to face him.

"I've just never seen you duel anyone. There has to be a reason."

His words fuel a fire inside of me, one I have no intentions of putting out.

"There does usually have to be one, doesn't there?" I murmur in annoyance.

His words are harmless. To the right person they usually would be.

But for me, in this moment, they are charged with promise. It only pushes me deeper into the realm of fiery rage.

I rip my swords from their scabbards, and the blades sing with delight. As if excited to have their chance in The Pits.

In a flash, I charge against the warrior. I swipe the blades one over the other like a pair of giant shears. Krolta jumps back before he throws a lightning bolt at my chest, and my swords come across in an X to block it. The charged, burnt air rocks against my senses, with Lilith and her teachings coming to the forefront.

A growl rips through my throat as I prowl around Krolta, my eyes glued to him as I spin with my blades, a sideways whirlwind in his direction that he blocks with his own weapon. He uses my momentum to rock the end of his handle into my skull. Fuzz blankets the inside of my brain as I shake my head clear. Rage urges me forth and I release a frustrated noise. I make for him, my arms flung back with my weapons before he juts his foot out to kick me in the chest. The force of his defense throws me back, but my wings catch at the last moment and air slows down the fall as it billows against the webbing.

As my frustration increases, my moves become less calculated, less precise.

How am I to lead if I can't defeat a Stella Warrior?

The fear of failure begins to bear down on my shoulders and spurs me into reactive fighting.

Krolta approaches in a pounding sprint, and I lunge to swing for his neck. He spins sideways from my path to knock into my wrist with the handle of his sword and throw me off balance, sending me crashing into the dirt. "General, this is pathetic." Krolta laughs.

"Feet planted, Seraphina, strike again." Lilith's voice breaks through my thoughts and throws me off kilter.

"You trained me for this, Mistress," I growl as I glare at the warrior. I come to my feet, stalking him in a circle as I line up my next attack.

Krolta's face contorts in confusion, "General?"

"Learn from this Sera. Your enemies will not be so forthcoming when they've wasted their resources for your crown." Lilith's voice comes through me again.

With an angered cry, I bring my hand up, pulling at the sky with all my might to bring a strike of lightning down in front of the warrior.

He grafts away from the blast, appearing beside me to kick my feet out from under me. As I fall into the dirt, he aims his sword into my throat, and I eye him for the barest of moments before I drop my weapons. I clap my hands together, slowly pulling them apart. I conjure a solid stream of crackling purple lightning. Flinging the power out, it expands in a semicircular loop to wrap around his back. I cross my arms one over the other to lock him into the lasso. As his arms are compressed together, I kick his weapon from his hand before I throw him over my head and into the dirt with one mighty pull.

The might of his crashing form pulls my arms above my head, and I spin against the ground to lay flat on my stomach. I release the lightning to press my hands into the dirt. Another charge of lightning rocks the earth as I use the force to blast me to my feet, allowing my wings to catch my force. I eye my dropped weapons and reach my power outward to conjure them into my hands.

As the swords seat into my palms, Krolta appears in front of me. A step into my space throws his skull into mine.

The clack of our horns echoes through the night, and the darkness closes in as the feeling of failure creeps in with it.

Inadequacy sits itself deep in my belly and my eyes well as my frustrations increase.

"YOUR SURROUNDINGS, SERAPHINA! Pay attention! Be alert! You cannot lead if you don't choose to yield when the odds are against you. You will bring them all down with you." Lilith's voice is harsh, stern.

You left me here to fight this battle on my own… I will bring them all down with me… It will be my fault, Lilith. Can't you see that?

"I don't want to fall. It is not my place to sit in your stead," I say out loud as I shake my head clear of the knock, and Krolta's face contorts with more confusion as he continues to watch me.

Krolta throws his sword to the ground before he puts his fists up.

"Weapon," I remind him.

Krolta pitifully shakes his head, "Not here, Seraphina."

Another growl courses through me. "Fight me! Fight *me!*" I plead as heated tears streak down my face. Confusion of my own tugs at my chest, at my being. How could she fall so easily? Her teachings, her words and just the mere presence of Lilith is something I have tried for years to push away. But with her voice echoing through me so clearly now, it's hard to deny the grief of her absence.

Why am I the one to warm your seat now? Why didn't you fight him, Lilith? Why did you let him bring you down? Surely you could have felled The Queenslayer...

But she didn't.

The thoughts swirl in my head, and the only thing I can focus on now is that she left me here. Lilith *abandoned* me. She brought me there that day. She let herself be absconded of her breath by a mere *human.*

Why didn't you live, Lilith? Why couldn't you live?

"I don't think it is I that you are fighting, General." Krolta's voice is low and concerned.

His words pull me from the thoughts that continually disarm me. The mentality that pulls me into the trenches of despair.

I see red at his blatant insult, and the wind sweeps my hair back as I swing a sword down on his head.

He knocks the blade off its trajectory before a jab is sent through my stomach. I come around with another slice at him, only for him to graft behind me and wrap an arm around my neck in a chokehold. "Yield," he urges.

My air depletes the tighter he holds on, and I use the moment to swing an arm down and ram the handle of my blade right into his cock.

His grip falters as he groans and he crashes to the ground gripping his groin.

I spin and pant as I try to catch my breath, watching him for a moment before I point the blade in his face.

He looks up at me with taunting eyes before his hand splays and he sends a bolt of blue lightning at my chest. The action knocks me back and I land with a thud against the sand. My wings bat against the ground to press me onto my feet and I level the warrior with a feral gaze.

Within seconds, the warrior appears in front of me to chop at my throat with the side of his hand, before a kick is sent through my stomach, sending me flying back. I slide against the ground, my claws burrowing deep into the dirt to slow me as my feet take the brunt of the shove.

"YIELD!" he shouts.

Why is it me, Lilith? How could it be me? It can't be. I can't be what you want me to be.

Over and over, we go through a game of cat and mouse, back and forth, until I have depleted my reserves, mentally and emotionally.

The ground crashes into my knees, while heavy breaths press in and out of my chest as I stare down at the sand.

Back in the place Lilith had molded me in. Back in the place I had sought refuge in, becomes a prison of my mentor's making.

A sharp point presses deep into the hollow of my throat, forcing my head up. "Yield, General," Krolta growls.

My gaze tracks up his boots, up his body, to land on his face. He secured my weapon and used it against me.

His bright red eyes show anger… but also pity.

"Whatever hellscape you have retreated to, needs to be escaped. Because you cannot lead, if you cannot yield." He presses the tip deeper. Heat begins to crawl down my chest from the cut in my throat, seeping into the light tunic under my armor. Searing pain rips against my neck as I lean in just enough to feel the burn of the blade.

Take me to eternity. It is the only place for me now.

"You must yield, if you are to save the ones you love. There is no other option." But this voice… this isn't a memory. This isn't Lilith's.

This is The Fates.

My spine stiffens and I lean away from the weapon.

"Yield." The voice whispers again.

My chest throbs, and my throat tightens as I fix my gaze on Krolta. The realization of my position coming to the forefront. *I* threw myself off my power. *I* threw myself out of my head, and *I* am the reason I kneel.

And I *don't* kneel. Not to the terrors within, or the terrors outside of these wards.

I can't kneel. Not while the ones I love still breathe.

As if The Fates speak through the warrior before me, his voice is deep as he echoes the command they've laid bare for me. "Yield," Krolta grits through his teeth. His brow is clenched and muscles tug at his cheeks to flare his nostrils wide. Heavy, calculated breaths expand his chest as he waits for my surrender.

I stare at him for a moment longer as tears heat the dusty surface of my skin.

I don't want to yield. Not to him, not to the others, not for the throne, and not even for Lilith.

But I must.

"I yield," I murmur softly.

The sword clatters against the ground as Krolta releases it. My eyes stuck to the blade as I hear his footsteps retreat.

The words escape my throat as more tears stream down my face and fear paralyzes every muscle in my body.

I can't do this. I can't be given the opportunity to let Lilith, and my people fall. I will take them down with me, and I don't want to be the reason for their failure.

But Lilith made sure I knew of what my purpose was. She made sure I was to be here…

And through it all, I can't come to grips with the crushing belief that she was wrong.

"I *yield*."

I COULD LET THE WORLD
FLOW BEFORE ME AND
THERE ISN'T A LINGERING
FEAR OF THE THINGS THAT
NEED TO BE DONE, OR
THAT I'M IN THE WRONG
PLACE.

CHAPTER 14

ROUNDS

ASHER

Finally… you have arrived in Tantalia.

Right.

As all things should be.

A rough voice sounds through the black void of my slumber, echoing through my mind until a clearer, smoother voice replaces it.

"Good morning, Queenslayer," the silky voice muses.

I groan as my eyes blink open. Glowing purple irises peer down at me in delightful mischief as silver hair curtains around long black horns. It's the only thing I'm able to register in a sleep fogged mental state. The rest of the figure is silhouetted by the beaming light at her back that comes from the balcony window.

The sharp points of Seraphina's wings rise above her head as she hunches over my body where it lays on the cot.

I groan again as I try to bring an arm up to guard my eyes in annoyance.

But am frustrated to learn that I can't.

I reluctantly remember that I've been secured to this stupid bed.

A sigh crawls from my chest as I glare at her, mumbling, "Good morning, Mistress."

"Come, we have rounds," she says as she straightens to stand.

From this vantage point, she looks larger than life and inherently powerful. With the almost perfect curvature of her breasts cresting against her chest, the elegant tapers of her body in this nightgown have my heart pounding against my own will. If she was any closer, I'd be able to see right up the silky material… right at her c–

My cheeks heat as blood fills my cock and hardens in my light breeches. I wasn't wearing these when I went to sleep, and I have no idea how I've been put in them.

Her brow rises and she grins at me before her eyes glance down at the rounded, rigid mound against my groin. Her lips then tilting in a small smirk.

My pulse climbs as I register the look on her face and what it could mean for me in the vulnerable state I'm in.

Fuck, fuck, fuck, I need to get out of here.

I can't understand the bullshit reaction I keep having to her. It's madness, it's infuriating. Because I shouldn't *be able* to react to her this way. My gifts have failed me in a time where I need them most and it's terrifying.

Her hands come together with a loud pop. The ringing of her clap loosens my restraints, and I'm finally released. I quickly crawl off the cot and away from this situation before I stand. Taking deep breaths to push away the overwhelming lust, I tilt my head from side to side, allowing the bones to crackle inside my flesh. Flexing my wrists and ankles of their tension, I take a big stretch. "What are rounds?" I ask with a gentle cough to rid my body of the heat coursing through me. But it fails.

I peek at her from the corner of my eye, taking in the way she looks bound in that sheer scrap of clothing she calls a nightgown. The pert tension of her nipples that press against the fabric and the way it clings to her tight waist. Her tail flicks in thought and lifts the back of her nightgown high enough to see the bottom of her ass.

A gulp tightens my throat, and I find myself staring. Against all sanity.

Madness. It's madness. This is her playing tricks, it's just her magic. This isn't rational.

Seraphina's voice breaks through my gawking. She sends a sly peek from under her long eyelashes as she glances at me. "For someone so keen on destroying our people, you seem more intent on fucking us, human."

She's playing more games, and I don't intend on letting her win this one.

"You have no idea what my intentions are, demon," I retort. My body stiffens and I go unnaturally rigid. In more places than one.

As if her gaze itself does something to me, my heart drums violently in my chest and I take settling breaths to keep my composure.

Seraphina turns to me, her hands on her hips as her eyes half-lid. Her elegant steps eat the distance between us before she places her hands gingerly on my chest.

Her claws prick against the soft fabric of my sleep tunic and a rush of need courses through me. Purple blazes in the hazy passion that swirls in her irises. "And even if I did, you would crumble inside of me." Her voice is thickened by seduction and my resistance flays faster than I anticipated.

"Perhaps that's what my intentions are," I respond.

She leans in slowly. My heart continues to beat like a war drum and her eyes slide down my face to land on her hands pressed against the tight muscles of my chest. Slowly, her scent strengthens as she stands on her toes to brush her lips against my ear. The action sends shivers through the entirety of my spine. Her breath grazes my ear as she speaks, causing my muscles to liquefy under her influence. "I would rather have my dead body picked clean by orcs than be *fucked* by a Queenslayer."

The admission pulls me from my lust-induced haze and my face contorts in surprise before she shoves me away with brute strength.

The lust is replaced by confusion and the previously rabid need is replaced by questions.

Sick fucking games this demon plays.

"What the f-" I murmur as I shake my head.

"Quiet. We're late," she says quickly. Her fingers snap, and suddenly we both have been clothed in leather armor from head to toe. A long violet cloak tugs at my neck as it flows around me. This armor feels lighter to move in. A necessary upgrade, even if it's one I don't welcome. It feels far more protective, and I imagine my agility is increased with it.

Fuck.

Leather bracers guard my forearms as my biceps lay bare. I drag my hands over my thighs, where I feel my dagger sheathed on the side of my long leather breeches and my feet are protected in thick black boots. I survey my weapons some more, finding other daggers not of my own realm, making their home in other spots of my body. Some attached at my ribs, and some more attached in other parts of my legs.

Nice. Even if I can't fucking use them.

I don't particularly like how much better this outfit is than the one I have back in my realm. It gives me feelings of gratefulness for the beings I *certainly* shouldn't be grateful for. I skim my hand over my pockets, grazing over the circular mound to make sure my insignia is still with me. I breathe a small sigh of relief as the feel of it brings me back down to earth.

It's all for Vesperholm. It's all for Vesperholm. We don't fuck the succubus just because our gift doesn't work. We're saving the people. We're ending this plague.

The thoughts run through my head on a loop to remind me of the reason I've agreed to any of this. Until Seraphina's armored body catches my attention.

She has also been changed from her flowing black nightgown to being wrapped in a tight leather fighting corset, with similar black plates that mine is armored with. My eyes widen as I take in her luscious curves and wide hips. Her breasts sit high on her chest, with a small slit in the middle of her ensemble to highlight her abundant cleavage. The rest of the bodice latches around her neck, like a collar of her own with that same brightly glowing gem in the center; it pulses with color as I stare at her.

I want to be able to resist and look at her in disgust. Especially after she toys with me like a mere plaything.

But my cock swells once more at the sight of her.

Fucking no. Go down, you dumb bastard.

Seraphina grins a devilish fanged smile. Her hand sparks momentarily before it conjures my lead, tugging me toward her.

Fuck, please, no more games, I can't do this.

My body falls against her and her potent lavender and jasmine scent overloads my senses. My control on my resistance flays and calm washes over me.

I want so badly to resist this. I don't want to melt against her like this.

But it also feels *so* good to fall into this level of need.

It causes a silent rage to clash against the calm she's invoked against me.

She lifts an eyebrow in hungry curiosity as her face comes within inches of mine. "You don't know what you want, Queenslayer. But I know what you *need*," she muses. Her clawed hand wraps around my jaw and presses my cheeks together as she searches my eyes. "You need a little bit of *cunt* to satisfy you, don't you?"

Her sultry voice and the feeling of her touch magnifies my lust for her the longer she lingers in front of me. My cock begins to ache where it's cramped itself in my tight leather breeches.

Soon, I've lost all control of my better judgement. My resistance is a fleeting memory, and I lean into her. "Y-yes Mistress. I need… you,"

I murmur. My liquified body leans into hers, relishing in the way she feels against me. Such a strong body, such taut curves and dips. My lips brush gently against hers, causing lava to pour through my entire body, burning with desire for my captor.

The words spill from me, and whatever sane being that would be able to step away from this power, has vacated my skull.

Right now, there is *only* Seraphina.

"You do, don't you, darling?" Her voice is like silk against my ears as she nods encouragingly. My hands roam to her hips, and I pull her against me. The feel of her body under my fingers is transcendent and soon my breath comes in shallow bursts.

Need her. Need all of her. Now.

I nod in agreement as her hand comes to cup the bulge in my breeches and she eyes me with a heated gaze.

Her caress does nothing to dull the ache, and I lean my hips into her as a tortured groan escapes my throat in a breathless plea for more.

"Do you remember my earlier words, Asher?" she whispers as the heel of her hand grinds against me.

The sound of my name on her tongue sends hot pulses through my veins and deep into my bones.

Please just fuck me. Take every ounce of my control. Make me your plaything and show me what it's like to be under you.

And I don't remember. There is nothing before now, only Seraphina.

"N-no Mistress," I respond softly. Soft breaths bleed into the space between us as I descend into her palm like a rock in the ocean.

Her lips brush against my neck, pressing delicate kisses into the sliver of flesh not blocked by my collar as the sharp points of her fangs graze the skin.

"Picked apart by orcs, darling. I don't fuck Queenslayers," she whispers and shoves me away.

The consuming lust falls away and my thoughts clear. A shake of my head lifts the haze, and I inhale a deep, *deep* breath. The desire and need evaporates and the only thing in its wake is the unbridled annoyance of losing control.

"Gods fucking damnit," I growl.

The tug on my lead is even stronger as she pulls my body toward the door.

"Enough fun. We have work to do," she cackles as she hauls me out of the room.

I remember The Pits from my trials with Gideon. But nothing could have prepared me for the sheer volume of halflings this place holds. We had only seen sixteen of them. But now, there are hundreds of giant men. Blond, brown, or black hair with different shades of eye color.

Horns, tails, and fucking *wings.* I couldn't believe what I was seeing when we came down here.

How do they procure these men? Do they take the men from Vesperholm and change them? I don't really recognize any of them. They all look somewhat similar to the different houses. Some I could pick out as Shadowfang with their dark hair, some of the Bloodreign warriors with blond.

But none of them could I point to and say I know them.

The idea is terrifying and part of me can't linger on it right now, I'll figure those things out later.

For now...

"So, have you learned anything yet?" I whisper to Gideon as I watch a winged warrior fly through the air. His massive body crashes into the sand in front of us, kicking up tornados of dirt as his wings bat to throw him back into the fray.

"Selene took me to this… place in the forest. It was heavily guarded, though, I wasn't allowed inside, and she didn't tell me what was there," Gideon responds quietly. He's been dressed in the same kind of leather armor I wear, except his cape is a dark green.

My eyes catch on the one man I've been searching for since we arrived at this giant arena.

Cedric.

"There," I whisper to Gideon as I nod to the annoyed human in the back.

"Hmm… Something he needs, honestly," Gideon nods.

I roll my eyes, "Well at least we know he's alive. But how are we going to talk to him?" I ask.

"Fuck if I know. But Asher, I've got to be entirely honest… I don't hate it here," Gideon says nervously.

I turn to him in shock, "What?!" I whisper at him. My eyes glance around the arena to see if anyone heard us.

But I imagine even if they did it wouldn't change anything.

"Yeah, I mean… The food here is incredible. Even better than when Vesperholm was at its peak. And Mistress Selene is kind of…" Gideon trails off as his eyes roam to the female succubus that stands next to an angry Seraphina barking orders. Her large wings twitch in irritation as she loses what little cool she has.

Gods, this asshole is getting food.

"No… Gideon she's a fucking succ! You're just under her influence!" I remind him.

"No, I promise, she hasn't tried anything like that with me. I've been under a demon's influence, and I haven't had an ounce of that from her. I just… I don't know. She treats me nice. I can't remember the last time I was able to have a girl all to myself," Gideon says softly as he rubs at his collar.

"You've got to be fucking kidding me…" I groan as my hand comes to pinch at the flesh between my brows.

"I kind of wish I was. But she feeds me, and she tucks me in at night," Gideon sighs dreamily into the air as his gaze lingers on *his* mistress.

"You get one second of female contact and all of a sudden you think they're our saviors!?"

"Who is to say they aren't? Last night she was telling me about their rules. She said they don't kill men. They're forbidden. And the only eating they do is that of the flesh. But not... literally. They just fuck them. Any man they bring back are to be used for whatever purposes they may need."

"You couldn't have led with that shit earlier!?" I groan.

"I'm sorry, I just... I didn't know how to tell you that... I think I may be falling for her."

Oh my gods. Our people are so fucked.

"I need you to shut up before I stick a dagger through you."

"I also don't think we're going to be getting out of here anytime soon. Mistress Selene talked with some of the guards in the forest and they were saying how heavily guarded the portals are. With our collars, there's not a chance in any of the hells that we're getting out of here," Gideon says.

"Gideon, there is always something we can do. You just have to know where to look," I sigh.

"But... What if... What if I want to stay here?" His lips thin nervously as he glances at me.

He should be nervous.

My gaze turns incredulous as I look at him in shock. "You've really fallen that far down the hole *already?!*"

"I'll help you if you want to get back home. And I won't stop you if you try to stop them. But I'm fairly confident you won't be able to. There's too many of them, and not enough of us."

I groan in annoyance as I listen to him. He's not wrong. But I don't want to accept what he's telling me, not when we have barely found a surface to scratch at. There's *always* something that can be done. And these things… these beings, have destroyed our realm. How could he just fall into their arms so easily?

My gaze lands on the warriors that clash against each other. Long swords hit at the hilt as one blocks another. Grunts sound off as they spin and blast with their powers. The colors of their lightning vary in size and strength.

If there is anything I can learn right *now*, it's their style of fighting.

I've fought and killed hundreds. And I defeated the small group of them for my trials. But it's different when you get to watch them at work, and you aren't fighting for your survival.

This defense looks more elegant. Less depraved and more precise than their female counterparts. Then again, the females are using more than blood and metal for their fights.

That doesn't seem to be good enough for Seraphina though, as she barks at them all again. The hoard of people drops to their knees as she addresses them. Her wings tense at her back and her tail flicks in anger as her voice booms through the arena like thunder.

She's fucking terrifying. I can see why she leads their trainings.

I see her hair sway as she shakes her head in disgust. Taloned hands flick at the air as she shoos them all off and watches them exit.

Cedric eyes me from where he merges with the rest of the crowd. His eyes flare with anger as he glares at me. His thumb comes across his throat in warning as he follows the hoard out.

At least you're not fucking dead, asshole.

I roll my eyes as my arms cross my chest and wait. Mistress Selene and Seraphina turn around to walk toward us, the dust kicking up around their feet as they approach. I peer at Gideon from the corner of my eye, who seems to tense with excitement the closer Selene gets.

Selene approaches him, pressing her body against his and gripping his chin softly in her hands, "Are you ready for the rest of our tour, pet?" she purrs to him.

Gideon nods quickly as his eyes meet hers.

"Good boy. Come," she says as she lazily leads him with his bright green lightning tether over her shoulder.

"Yes, Mistress," he responds dreamily as he follows closely behind her.

Give me a fucking break.

I turn my attention to Seraphina, and while she may be mighty, her head barely comes to my chest.

A pip squeak, if you ask me.

Her eyes narrow on me, "Are *you* ready for the rest of our tour, Queenslayer?" she asks with an irritated sneer.

"No."

"Too bad."

Her purple lead appears in her hand as it snaps to my collar, and she turns on a heel to drag me behind her. A grunt comes from me as I follow close behind, so as to not be choked by her strength.

We walk out of the arena and onto a white-stoned path. The path doesn't seem long, and it doesn't appear to be much when we reach a large meadow. I haven't seen this much green grass in ages.

I'm envious. Blaringly so.

The wildflowers here are strong with their scent, and small bees and butterflies flitter to and fro amongst their blooms.

As we trudge through the tall grasses and flowers, an ancient wisteria tree with bundles of long, purple flowers sways in the wind. It must be hundreds of years old with the size of it. It breaks through the white puffy clouds that paint the sky. Thick, ropey vines sway around the trunk from where they hang in the branches.

Seraphina's wings begin to tighten at her back as we approach the tree. Her once confident stride turns rigid as we get closer. She looks up and down the massive trunk before she lets out a pained sigh and her hand opens to the ground beside it, tethering me to the earth.

She takes slow, calculated steps up to it, staring at a blurred patch in the bark for a long moment. Her body is eerily still until her hand presses against the patch, and she melts through the trunk.

My eyes widen as I watch her disappear. "What the fuck was that?!" I whisper out loud.

But of course, there is no response. I'm completely alone.

I take a moment to look at the empty space where she stood for a moment longer before I sit in the grass. My mind runs with the amount of magic I've seen around here. I don't even understand how any of it works. How can *they*? Are they born with it? Do they learn how to wield this magic or is this something they inherently know how to do?

There is so much about these beings that I don't know and the more I learn, the more my mission here really *does* feel in vain.

I would sell my soul to save my people. But I can't do it by myself. The only person I have contact with is seconds away from shoving his cock in a demon. And the other, I can't even talk to.

Not to mention, I really… *really* miss Gnox.

I look to the path we came from, following the trail with my eyes until my gaze tracks to a majestic white castle, rooted into the side of the largest mountain in the area.

"Celestial Keep…" I murmur as I take it in. I hadn't had the chance to step back and look at this place I've been shackled to. But it's an incredible sight to behold. Seraphina had merely blinked us from one place to the next, and even that was an insane concept, in and of itself. One moment we were in the castle, the next we were in the arena. It made my head spin, and I had to take a second to get my bearings so I didn't spew all over the ground.

I shake my head of the recent memory and come to look back at the fortress in the mountain. Its spires are shrouded in clouds and bits of blooming flowers, the same as the tree I sit next to, giving the palace a look of calm and peace. The mountain looks as if it one day decided to swallow the castle and regurgitate it back slowly. The beautifully blue sky behind Celestial Keep is a welcome sight after my years in Vesperholm. I feel like I haven't seen a clear sky in ages.

But no matter how pretty this place is, or how well Gideon might think he has it, I have to stay the course. I have to figure out how to breach their defenses. There has to be something here I can use against them. But it's going to be a pain in the ass to do anything while I'm essentially shackled to this she-witch.

My hand reaches into my pocket, pulling the small metal insignia from within and holding it above my head. The bruised metal looks even more beat up when it's placed against the sky. The wings juxtaposed behind the dagger strikes through me harder than ever. But… there is a sense.

A small, nagging sense that tells me it isn't right.

The sight of the small crest that has brought me peace for so long, even in the darkest of days, suddenly feels so small in the grand scheme of things. I miss home, and I miss Vesperholm. My mother, my father, and my huntsman friends. My hand falls to my side as I place the metal disk back into my pocket and move my hands to rest behind my head.

Something about being here, laying in this field while I look up at the blanket of brilliant blue, causes a feeling of ease to wash over me as the grass hums against my body and the sun warms my face. Even though I am placed in unfortunate circumstance, I can't help how it feels to lay here without the fear of being snatched.

Calm, relaxed… at *peace.*

There has been a hole in my soul for as long as I can remember. Even growing up in Vesperholm, before the succubus really settled into taking our people like they are now, I felt… misplaced.

I didn't enjoy taking their lives, it felt wrong. But I did want the stealing to stop. I *do* want them to stop.

I just didn't want to take *their* lives in the process.

It was merely what I was raised to do. What do you do when you want to change the world, but the world has no intentions of changing?

I didn't enjoy playing with the others, I buried myself in my fighting to get a grip on the feeling that I didn't belong there. I thought that if I fought hard enough and was well versed enough in my gifts that I could feel like I belonged with the rest of them. The ones that relished in the slayings and cheered for the demons' deaths.

But I didn't cheer in the streets when one was caught. I didn't celebrate in their expirations. My gifts grew and so did my need to change something. Anything. A world where we could live together in peace.

But as I lay here staring at the sky above, for the first time in forever, my little lay in the grass is peaceful, belonging. I don't have to worry for once about a succ coming to take me. It's already happened.

I could let the world flow before me and there isn't a lingering fear of the things that need to be done, or that I'm in the wrong place.

For the first time, in a really long time, I feel like I'm right where I need to be.

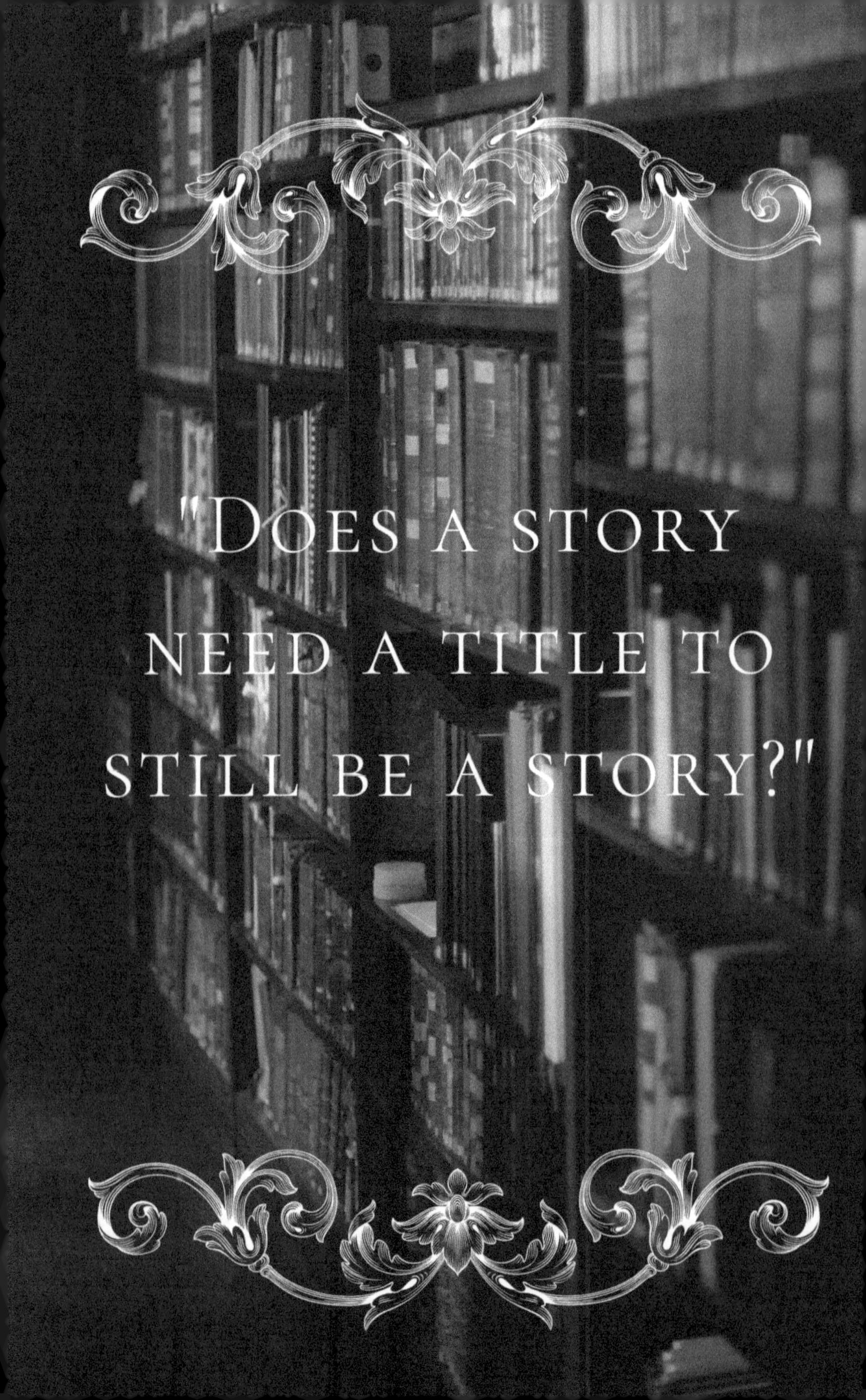

"Does a story need a title to still be a story?"

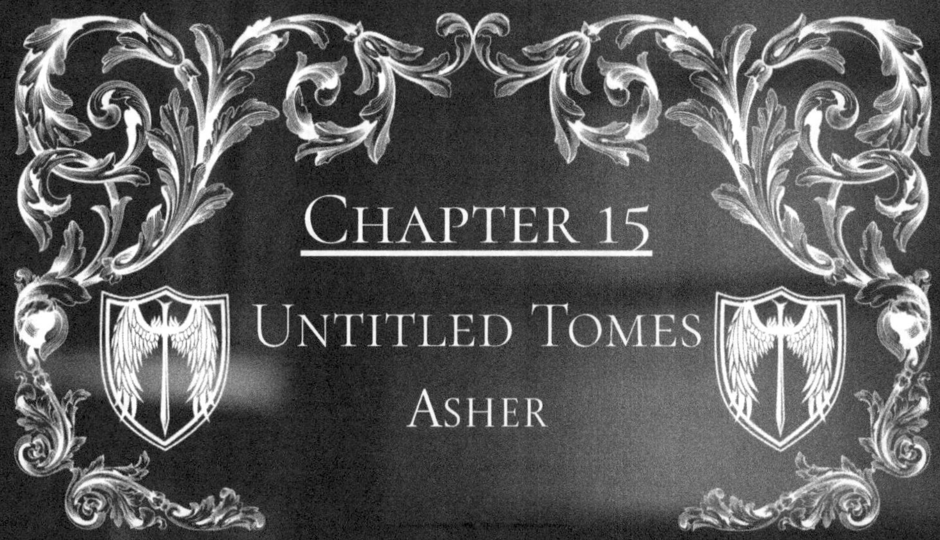

Chapter 15

Untitled Tomes

Asher

R *ight. So right.*

I had fallen asleep in the grass until the next thing I know, I'm being choked damn near to death as I'm being dragged through the meadow by my lead.

I kick at the ground as Seraphina pulls and I scratch at the collar to detach it. My cape snags on stray twigs in the grass, further contributing to my strangulation.

Until suddenly, the tugging stops.

"Oh good, you're awake," Seraphina says with a boring turn of her head.

I groan as I get to my feet, dusting off my leathers of the green reeds that stick to it. Seraphina's teeth gleam in a mischievous grin as I glare at her.

"You couldn't have woken me up?" I grit through my teeth in annoyance.

"You were so peaceful, why would I have done that?" she laughs as she tugs once on my lead, continuing her trek through the meadow with me in tow.

I grunt as I follow her. I hope this isn't what Gnox feels when he's behind me. This has me feeling bad for the poor creature.

I'm going to give him so many carrots when I see him again.

"Where are we going now?" I ask as I take in more of the sights. A large, well-kept courtyard comes into view as we finally exit the meadow, and we return to a stoned path. A massive fountain in the middle of the courtyard sparkles from the water that spurts from its center.

There are demons of various cloak colors that scurry along the paths. They seem to be doing their own daily chores. They carry weapons, baskets of fruit and vegetables or meat, bundles of clothes. Exactly like it was depicted on the tapestries.

And while I only saw the halflings in The Pits, it seems as though there are only succs that take care of the upkeep here. The grass is perfectly manicured and there doesn't seem to be a single stray twig protruding from any of the bushes.

Whatever they do here, they do well. They care for the land in a way that Vesperholm never could. While us humans were all just surviving on our land, it seems the demons of Tantalia value their realm far more than we ever did.

I don't know what I expected of this place. But it isn't anything that I've learned thus far.

Not to mention, Gideon's information about the stolen men. If they don't kill any of them then where are they? I haven't seen a single human here apart from the halflings. And even if they're half-human, they still have wings, tails, and supernatural strength.

Everything assaults my thoughts in a web of cluttered information. In the process, I lose sense of where we are.

Seraphina has led us to a large portion of farmland on the outskirts of the courtyard. Beige cloaked succubus are doing their duties, planting crops, tending to a variety of chickens, cows, sheep, and some pigs. My brow furrows as I look over them all. Some are planting seeds while a succ comes behind them to wave her hands over the recovered mounds of dirt, forcing them to sprout, flower, and fruit all within a few seconds. The sight is jarring, and it causes my head to spin.

How is this all even possible? This is the most maddening thing I think I've ever seen.

Seraphina approaches a taller demon who is overlooking the other demons that do the work in the dirt.

While most of these demons don't age, this one looks particularly scary. Her features are sharply set in her pale, dirt flecked skin, and she looks like she doesn't take any kind of shit from anyone. Her cloak doesn't flow around her like it does with the other succubus, it seems as though she wears hers more as a tag than a protection. It's attached at her neck but has been bundled behind her shoulders to allow her arms to be free. The blade of her scythe rests against the ground where her muddy boot props in its curve, and she leans against the handle. Her white hair is speckled with dirt and wrapped around her tall horns in protection.

"Learra, a pleasure," Seraphina muses as we approach her.

"Sera. Good to see you, dear." Learra nods softly.

Her red eyes flick to me with a quirked brow, her gaze returning to Seraphina as she tilts her head in question.

"Ah, this is The Queenslayer," Seraphina says as she tugs once at my lead, pulling me forward to stand next to her.

I stumble to stand next to her before I fix myself and look over her. A growl eases from between my teeth as I roll my eyes.

Stupid fucking nickname.

"Ahhh… So, it was *you* that caused mother's expiration," Learra says with an up and down glance over me.

My stomach drops and my heart pounds a little harder.

Mother? What is going on?

"A guard of mine, if you will," Seraphina muses.

Learra's eyebrows jump in amusement, "Interesting tactic, General."

My features pull in fear as I look between the two demons laughing over my misfortunes.

"You know the saying. Keep your friends close, and your enemies closer," Seraphina says with a grin and a flip of her hand.

"You surely are adhering to it."

Seraphina's taunting grin fades as she looks over the fields.

"The crops, how do they do with the magic?" Seraphina asks as she nods at the succubus tilling the fields.

"They…" she pauses as she tracks Seraphina's gaze. Her head shakes gently as she looks to the fields, then turns to lay her attention back on Seraphina. "Slowly. Unfortunately. The women need more breaks, and their magic becomes weaker much faster. We're trying to keep up with demand, but we really need the magic secured…" Learra sighs.

Seraphina nods, "Understood," she responds gently.

Far more gently than I've ever heard her speak.

"Mother would have wanted you to take the throne. We all know it," Learra says as she places a dirtied hand on Seraphina's shoulder.

The throne? What the fuck are they saying?

Seraphina sighs before she nods, "I'm aware."

"I know. I'm not gonna push you. I know how that fairs for most. But it is imperative."

"I'm working on it," Seraphina responds. Her voice turns tense, and her body goes eerily rigid.

"We know you will," Learra says before she pats Seraphina's shoulder.

Seraphina gives her a forced, half-smile as her eyes gaze away and she seems to retreat into her thoughts. Her focus comes back to Learra, taking a deep breath before she steels her spine with a tense nod. "We must get going, I needed to get my new pet used to rounds so he's not questioning me at every turn."

A confused pinch picks at my brow as I look between them.

Bizarre interaction.

"I'll see you in The Court, Sera," Learra says as Seraphina tugs my lead once more, lugging me back to the stone path.

I don't know if I can handle the amount of information that keeps getting thrown at me here.

They have farms? They grow crops? They have a massive library? Everything here runs like a well-oiled cart. Not to mention, everyone seems to bow down to Seraphina. And the throne... does somewhat not sit it? I guess that would explain the Queenslayer nickname. But I don't know what Queen I would have slayed. Was... their mother...? Their Queen? I have killed far too many Succubi to know who it could have been. Their faces blur the longer you have to watch the life drain from their eyes.

And if so, why do they want *her* on it?

It doesn't make sense, because she looks as though she would rather die every time they mention something like this. I've heard it a few times. Once in passing, and now. Everytime she waves off the comment.

But they seem to flock to her. And she leads their army.

Seraphina can't be... their queen, can she? There's no way she could be. If she is, what the fuck am I doing under her? What use could she have with me that she couldn't get elsewhere?

Everything here seems more and more confusing, and I can't get a grip on the information I learn.

Of course, I wanted to learn stuff but not this much, this fast! And not any of *this* information. It doesn't feel like anything imperative for me to know if I want to do something about saving my people. Give me a soft spot, give me an in. Anything but this shit.

The constant push and pull of these revelations have pulled me deep into my skull, but I'm forcefully pulled out of them as my body jolts from where we have blinked into Celestial Keep.

"Gods, what is that!? And why do you keep doing it!?" I groan in annoyance, my stomach beginning to churn as the cool air of the day is replaced by some of the lighter heat inside of the castle.

Seraphina doesn't spare me a glance as she continues guiding me up a set of stairs, "It's called grafting."

My brow furrows, "What?"

"I can move us from one place to the next, if I wish to do so."

My face contorts in a grimace as I watch her hair sway from where she leads me, "Well, could I get a warning next time? I'm not entirely well-versed in this method of travel and it makes me sick."

"Cry harder, Queenslayer. I imagine it'll make you feel better."

I roll my eyes with a groan as I continue walking.

Grafting. What absolute nonsense. Just fly, you have wings.

Eventually, she leads us down a corridor I do recognize.

The Library.

Thank Gods, I can try to get *something* out of her.

The large doors open for us as we approach them, that familiar scent of parchment hits me as we make our way to the table we sat at yesterday.

There are many more succs here during the day. They're organizing the books, while others grab tomes for what I imagine are their own research purposes.

My lead tethers me to the table as Seraphina retreats back into the depths of The Library. Her wings bounce and her hair sways behind her as she walks through the aisles.

When she disappears into the darkness, I turn to the table, looking around at any other books on the shelves that I may have missed last time. Again, a few more books slap on the wooden surface. These are different from what she grabbed yesterday, and I don't touch them in fear of summoning her. I glance around me for Seraphina before I peer at their spines.

Nothing.

No words, no symbols.

I tilt my head as I scan the sides. These books must be centuries old. I can't imagine what's inside of them.

A moment later, Seraphina appears in the chair across from me as if she's been sitting there the whole time.

Her instantaneous arrival startles me, and I jump in my chair as I hiss a breath, grasping at my chest. "Why…!? Must you *do that*?!" I groan to her.

Seraphina ignores me as she moves the first book from the stack, opening the cover. She flips through the pages. Her face pinches in focus as she begins looking through it, lingering for only a few seconds before she proceeds to the next page.

I give her a few moments of silence before I speak, "How do you know what book to look for? None of these have titles," I ask softly.

Seraphina continues flipping through the pages, her brows scrunch in concentration as her eyes run over the symbols, "Does a story need a title to still be a story?" she murmurs.

Her question catches me off-guard. "I… I guess not?"

"These books here all have their own souls. They talk to us, you just have to be willing to listen to them," she says as she continues scanning each page.

My brow raises as I listen to her.

What a peculiar concept.

I turn around at one of the large shelves behind me. My eyes run over some of the books, looking for a nameless one. Concentrating on its spine, I try to zero in on it.

At first, there's nothing. Not a peep.

The longer I stare, the more hopeless this seems.

Until a small whisper enters my mind, but it's unintelligible. Ramblings of words tripping over one another. My eyes widen as I continue staring at the worn brown leather of the book's spine. The voices get louder the longer I focus on it, the sensation is overwhelming as the words trip and run around each other in an indecipherable mesh of syllables and letters. Quickly, I disconnect my gaze, focusing my attention back on Seraphina.

She pays me no mind as I focus on her and silence washes over my thoughts.

"It… it talked to me," I whisper softly.

"Congratulations," Seraphina responds boringly as she flips the page.

"But I couldn't understand it," I sigh.

"Good."

I roll my eyes before I lean back and cross my arms over my chest, looking over a variety of the book spines to not conjure another one of their ramblings.

If I can figure out a way to find out what's in these books just by looking at them, then perhaps I just need to train that part of myself to learn *just* that.

Seraphina's head drops to the table in frustration. Her silver hair flows around the open book as she takes a few deep breaths. Her shoulders and wings droop completely, wrapping her in a black, leathery blanket.

"This feels impossible," she murmurs against the page.

My brow quirks as I watch her.

You're telling me. I'm stuck in a strange demon land with no escape.

Her head lifts and she peers into my eyes, quirking an eyebrow. "What do you know about magic?" she asks curiously.

My brows rise against my forehead. Why would she ask *me* if I know anything?

"Nothing, really… Humans don't really have magic," I respond.

"Wizards. Mages. Witches. All humans with magical affinities," she retorts as she brings a hand up to pinch her chin in thought.

"We don't have those where I come from," I tell her.

"You just haven't looked hard enough," she murmurs as her gaze trails back down to the page.

Her eyes freeze as she stares off into space, lost in thought before she looks up at me with a twisted smile. "I think we have to pay some friends a little visit."

Fuck.

I JUST CAN'T FACE THE
IDEA OF SITTING
WHERE SHE SAT. IT
DOESN'T FEEL RIGHT.
NO MATTER HOW
MUCH I MAY WANT TO
PROTECT OUR REALM.

Chapter 16

Swallowed

Seraphina

Though the human may be stupid, at least his presence gave me a stroke of confidence.

Who better to ask about magic than the magicians themselves?

I had spent some nights in the library while the human slept, in search of a map of any kind. I had tabled the idea while I dealt with more pressing matters, but with the idea finally gripping me, I had to do it. I had to at least *try*.

Lilith used to speak of such a thing; a realm untouched by the rest of the world that she had once visited. Though, she had never alluded to it being a realm of magicians. That would have been nice information to know.

However, with wizards and witches residing there, I imagine their wards are strong. Their magic is not attached to ours, since they pull from a different source. But Lilith taught me at least enough to figure out how to get through tough wards. It may just take some brute force.

The only information I could find was of an entrance that existed deep in a cave on the outskirts of Tantalia. It took some more digging to find a map, but I think I know where we need to go.

The human had complained the entire morning as we packed our supplies for the journey. His grating voice irked me until I muzzled him, and silence could finally find me.

We have taken the better half of the morning trekking through tall grasses and climbing boulders stained with dirt and earth until we finally come to a large, dark hole in the side of a stray mountain, far outside of Tantalia.

I look at the human with a large grin, his eyes glaring the same shade as the shining swath of purple cloth which binds his mouth shut.

I flick a hand at him to release his muzzle and he lets out a long gasp, hunching over his knees as he takes deep breaths.

"THANK YOU," he pants as I allow him to finally speak. "You have no idea how hard it is to climb boulders without breathing through your mouth," he says as he catches his breath.

I roll my eyes and tug on his lead to guide him into the dark tunnel.

He lunges forth and trips over his feet before he catches himself. "What are we doing here?" he asks.

I didn't tell the human what we were doing, I merely dragged him along. I could have kept him in the cells to suffer, but I have no idea what powers exist in the Realm of Mages. And he is a skilled fighter; I imagine I'll need his help.

"We are going to the Realm of Mages," I tell him as I lump myself over a large boulder and into a puddle on the other side.

"Oh, look at that, I get an actual answer. Perhaps you could release me next," he retorts.

"Over your dead body," I respond.

Our voices bounce off the moist cave walls. The darkness creeps in on us the farther we get, the only light able to guide us is the illumination from the human's lead and the glow of Lilith's amulet around my neck.

The smell of dank, stale earth closes in around us, accompanying the echoed sound of our movements and the drips moving around the cavern.

I peer over my shoulder at the human, his eyes stay the course as we continue forward.

I smirk as we proceed farther and farther until a dull blue glow catches my vision from the end of the tunnel. My heart begins to pound violently in my chest, and the prospect of having to talk to these magical humans makes my palms clammy.

Have we actually found it? Why hadn't Lilith ever taken me here? Couldn't she have come here to ask for their help with the stone if the powers were wavering that much?

My old mentor's face comes into the forefront of my mind. *She would* want me to take the throne. She had trained me as such. No matter how much I didn't want it. I just can't face the idea of sitting where she sat. It doesn't feel right.

But now, I don't think I have much of a choice anymore. Not after Velaria's death. Even if she didn't realize it, it was *her* dying wish.

I have to do it at least for her.

I let out a long sigh as our boots trudge over stray rocks.

"Are you okay?" the human asks gently from behind me.

My brows furrow and I turn around to look at him. His chin is chiseled in the dull glow of his collar and the small dimple set within it becomes exaggerated as I peer at him.

"Why do you ask?" I ask cautiously.

"That sigh. It seemed… sad. I wasn't sure you lot were capable of those emotions," he says gently.

My face contorts in question, "Why would you think we wouldn't be capable of that?" I ask as I turn to face the tunnel, continuing to lead the way.

"Well, where I come from, the stories of your people are different. They say you take men and you fuck them and eat them afterwards," he responds.

"Hmph," I scoff at him.

Silly humans.

"We are very emotional creatures. We laugh. We cry. We can be angry. We can be happy. We *can* be sad. We can love. Though we may seem heartless, I like to believe my kind have the biggest heart of them all."

The human silences for a long while, the sounds of our steps the only thing to keep us company as we proceed further.

"Then, why do you take my people?" he asks gently.

I halt, my boots planting into the wet cave floor.

The silence feels deafening as I weigh his words.

I shake my head of the memories as I continue walking, "That is a story for another day," I respond softly.

More silence comes as the glow at the end of the tunnel beams even brighter, consuming the small domed space it rests in.

An arch of bricks has been erected against the wall, the entire ensemble has been placed on a small marble platform above the main cavern floor. And where a curtain of color should be with a portal, there is only more stone. The bricks have chipped and are webbed with dirt and the reminders of when some small legged creatures once lived here.

In front of the archway are circles of runes in a script I have never seen before. And the runes, they pulse slowly with the blue glow we followed here. The magic in the air is thick here… Very thick… *Too* thick.

I tether my human to a boulder that rests beside the small ledge of the entry.

He stands cautiously by as I step closer. Kneeling onto the hard floor of the cavern, my hands graze the etched lines in the stone.

"Do you know what they mean?" he asks.

I study them for a moment, "No… no I don't," I admit. I sigh as I place both of my hands against the floor, murmuring an ancient slew of spells, throwing anything at the wall to see if it sticks.

Nothing.

Not even a hum.

I groan in frustration as my head hangs, and my leg comes out from under me as I sit against the ground in angst. Small pebbles scrape against my tail as it flicks the cave floor in annoyance.

There's no way I can be Queen if I can't even break the kind of magic that exists here. Sure, they may be strong wards, but I'm not a weak demon.

Soon, the glow of my necklace burns bright against my black leather corset; I stare down at it as it begins to pulse against my chest. The archway brightens in a swirl of crimson red. The center of its vortex begins bending into the brick, and with it, stones and pebbles begin flying into its center; from *behind* me. My booted foot gets caught in its path as the suction grows.

"Fuck!" I yell as I turn on my stomach, using the claws of my wings to pin into the stone and keep me from being sucked in.

My talons grip for purchase against the slippery cave floor, but they can't. They scratch against the ground in a sickening squeal as the archway begins pulling me deeper, latching onto my other foot.

Asher's eyes widen as he pulls against his lead to reach for my hand. But he's too far, he can't reach me. My hand flicks out to release his lead and he falls forward, scrambling quickly to grasp at my wrists. He tugs with all his might to get me out of the arch, and I feel like a rope being pulled between a dragon and an orc.

An ethereal screech releases from my throat as I feel my body stretch against the vortex, my pinned wings bury against the stone to help pull me out. The pressure against their light bones feels incomprehensible before my body fully releases and I'm thrown across the cave, landing several feet in front of the platform. I pant as I look up to find Asher unconscious and unmoving against the boulder I had tethered him to. He had fallen back from the force of the pull and directly into the rock.

"Fuck, fuck, fuck," I groan as I crawl over to him. The swirling archway builds in its conquest to devour, sucking more of the debris of the cave into it. Including Asher.

"Gods dammit!" I yell as I grab his arm and pull him toward me. Coming to a stand, I throw his body on my back before securing his chest against the base of my wings with his tether. Shooting forward, I bat my wings with enormous power against the force threatening to suck both of us in and bolt through the dark cavern.

Ducking and bobbing in the small space, my wings propel me toward the moonlight outside of the tunnel until we crash in a heap at the cave exit. My body crumples into the ground as Asher's weight is released and his tether no longer constricts my chest. The sound of a rolling thud happens in the distance.

A groan escapes me as the situation settles. And I take a few breaths before steadying myself. Rolling over, my breaths heaving, I look around for my human captive. His body lay unmoving a few feet from me, and I scramble through the grass over to his limp body, frantically surveying the damage.

He's *mostly* uninjured.

Aside from the large bleeding gash in the back of his skull.

My thoughts scramble. My chest aches. My heart pounds viciously against my ribs as my breaths pick up speed and my hands tremble uncontrollably.

I can't let him die; he saved my life. He could have let me get sucked into that vortex, but he saved me.

I can't let him die. Fuck!

I huff another breath as I search his body again.

His chest shallowly rises and falls as I assess his condition.

Still alive, at least.

I grasp his head in my hands as I latch my mouth to his, exhaling a large gust of mist into his throat.

I lean back to watch him, his state the same as it was before.

Come on, human. You can't be that fucking fragile.

His chest rises a few more times before he inhales a large gasp of air. His green eyes are a haze as they bolt open, and he frantically looks around.

"What the fuck, where am I?!" he says quickly before groaning in pain. His sharp movements cause him to grip the mark on his head. "What the fu-" he groans as he looks at his bloodied fingers.

His eyes widen in shock, "What did you do to me!?"

"I saved your life, asshole!"

His thoughts are slow as looks at me, blinking a few times before he speaks, "Why would you do that…? Again?"

I sigh, "Because you saved my life. You had no reason to. You could have let me die, but you… you saved me," I admit softly.

Asher blinks a few more times, almost dumbfounded by my reasoning, "Well if you died, I'd be stuck in the middle of nowhere with a fuck ton of magic I know nothing about."

I quirk a small smile, "Either way. Thank you."

His face softens, "Thanks… for saving mine."

Looking in his eyes, I see he's genuine. Along with a hint of something else.

My brow scrunches as I look at him.

Something… Something… Something. The same thing I saw in the alley… The cell. The arena. The very reason I've granted him a singular mercy.

"We must go," I tell him as I stand. Quickly, I brush my leathers off and whip his lead to his collar.

Asher's howl of agony echoes through the dark night as I tug a little too harshly.

Gods damn fragile humans.

"My head," he groans as he swipes his hand over the gash.

I sigh as I press his body up from the grass slowly, looking over his wound.

The bleeding has stopped, and the wound closes slowly. So *very* slowly.

I roll my eyes with an annoyed sigh. "I hope you like flying," I grunt as I step in front of him, squatting down to throw his arms over my shoulders and haul him onto my back like a giant human pack.

His tether wraps around his body and mine until he's secure.

"What do you mean fl-" is the last thing I hear from him as we burst into the night sky.

If I wanted peace in the first place, I have to save them both.

And there's a portion of my soul that feels like that may just be enough for me.

CHAPTER 17

THE QUEENSLAYER

ASHER

Mmmm… This is so soft.

My thoughts wake me as I nuzzle into my warm cloak. The ground below feels like clouds as I turn into the soft grass.

Except…

Blinking softly, my surroundings become clearer, the trees I sought to find were walls of white and black bedroom furniture.

Soft fabric slips through my fingers as I grip at the thing wrapped around me.

A white blanket.

My spine stiffens as I realize where I am, and a soft hiss presses through my teeth as the residual pain from my head twinges from my movements. "What the fuck…" I murmur softly.

I'm in Seraphina's bedroom… in… her bed??

Seraphina is nowhere to be found, but the purple crackling lightning that secures my collar snakes through the blankets to attach to a post on her bed; with many feet of slack in between.

How sweet of her.

Bright sun mixes with the familiar scent of the Tantalia breeze as the joining forces dance into the room from the open window.

I hate to say that this prison is the best way I've woken up in decades; plus, I abhor the way this place is growing on me.

I stretch carefully before I gently shake the sleep from my bones, taking care not to tweak the pain in my head. Black fabric bathes my body from head to toe, and I realize I've been changed into silky night clothes. Even as I move, the bed itself feels like it's heated.

What in the world even happened yesterday? I don't remember much after the cave. I sort of remember Seraphina thanking me for saving her life.

But that just seemed like it was the decent thing to do. At least in the circumstance we were in. Plus, I do *not* know my way around here, and even if I were to find the portal back home, not only would it have been guarded, but I would also have had a massive target on my back. And getting past those guards would prove to be my demise. I may have fought them off once, but with my collar intact, my weapons are still useless.

Not to mention, she already saved my life once.

I would say my debt is repaid but then she went and saved my life *again*, which just puts me back at square one.

There was a strange feeling when she looked into my eyes last night, almost like a tug against my soul. But it was hard to register with how hard my head was throbbing.

I must have blacked out after that because I remember nothing.

Though, I'm not complaining, it's *very* comfy.

A gentle squeak comes from the other side of the room as Seraphina's bedroom door opens. A small, hooded figure in a bright yellow cloak walks in, holding a silver tray.

My brow furrows in confusion as I look to what she's holding.

"Mistress asked me to bring this to you," she says softly as she places the tray on my lap, her head rising to look at me. She's young and her horns barely peak from her skull.

My attention shifts to the spread she's brought me. Fragrant, succulent chicken rests on a bed of potatoes and other small vegetables and my mouth waters from the sight as my eyes grow wide.

Fuck, I haven't eaten anything like this in ages...

I peer at the small demon apprehensively; her pastel purple eyes are innocent as she blinks and waits for me to release her.

"Uh... Thank you," I tell her gently with a nod.

Her head dips in a nod as she turns and retreats from the room.

My eyes turn back to the spread in front of me, hesitant to touch it.

Picking up one of the small eating utensils next to the plate, I poke gently at the chicken. It *looks* harmless enough. But with the magic that fuels this place, there's no saying what kind of curse that could come over me if I eat this.

Then again...

At this point, I don't think I have anything to lose, and I can't remember the last time I had a good meal, let alone chicken.

I take a small sliver of the meat from the plate, slipping it into my mouth.

A soft hum escapes me as I melt into the juicy, tender delight. I'm not sure if it's because I've only eaten rats as of late, but this is the greatest thing I've ever tasted.

Whoever made this needs their mouth kissed.

I lose control of myself as I devour the plate of food. Not even when Vesperholm was at its peak was the food this good. My mom was not the best cook, but she made do with what she had.

The whole time I've been here, Seraphina has given me small rations of things to barely keep me alive. It was amazing I even made the trek out to the cave.

Perhaps this is why Gideon is in such a tizzy over his new overlord. I suppose I might be too if she tucked me into bed and gave me food.

My eyes slowly drift from my thoughts before they come back to focus, roaming over the bed and the tray before settling on the room around me.

Fuck.

Putting the tray to the side, I throw the blankets back and stand. I can't fall into whatever trap she may be laying for me. I don't know exactly what they do to men here, but perhaps this is just part of their sick game. Their little plan to get men to stay here and give them little succs.

But as I leave the bed, I realize I've been washed. As I run my hand through my hair, it feels smooth and free of dirt or blood. My skin doesn't scratch with grit or rough cloth.

I don't like how I'm feeling about this place. Not at all.

My eyes survey the room for my armor, and when my eyes catch the swath of black leather, I rush to it. Rifling through the pockets, I find the little trinket that has kept me focused on my mission here.

But as I gaze at the little clasp in my hands, suddenly, it feels like it weighs so much less. Its meaning feels skewed. Deep breaths run through me as I hold it tight in my palm and I remind myself to stay the course and not get distracted.

This is all for Vesperholm. All of this is for Vesperholm.

The door squeaks once more to alert me of another visitor, causing me to swing in its direction. The large wingtips of my captor enter my view. Her body is sheathed in her normal leather armor and her boots make soft pats against the floor as she eases further into the room, shutting the large door behind her.

"Ah, you're awake," Seraphina says gently, her eyes almost grateful that I'm up and moving.

A jarring sight, best believe.

"Hello," I say nervously.

"How's your head?" she asks.

"Hurts."

Smooth move, dumbass.

Her eyebrow quirks as she looks at me.

"Sorry, uhm," I respond as I scratch at the collar around my neck. "You gave me food?" I ask softly.

"Well, yes. You saved my life. It was the right thing to do. Good deeds are rewarded, no matter the reason."

I watch her carefully; ve*ry* carefully. Her face is sincere enough, with a softness to her purple eyes and a small smile of gratitude gracing her lips. But there is so much to consider with all that I've learned the past few days.

The war inside of me wages.

I want to help my family survive, but this demon that I saved somehow has just thrown her gratitude at me.

I don't know why my propulsion for this comes from a place of care. Perhaps because I can relate. Even if it feels as though that shouldn't be enough.

But seeing the tapestries… seeing the way their people were slaughtered and then having her care for me after just saving her life.

It piques my curiosity and the urge to know more grows the longer I go without the full story.

I find myself leaning toward the idea of her plight.

I imagine if I wanted change in the first place, I have to do the things I'm not entirely comfortable with to start.

Worth a shot.

I take a deep breath as we connect gazes. "Your people," I start, my voice soft as I broach the subject.

Gentle pressure scrunches at her brows as she listens.

"Why do you need to save them?" I ask.

The normally bright purple hue of her gaze turns dark as it shifts to the floor. The tips of her wings lower as her shoulders droop. Her thick boots thump against the stone floors as she moves to sit on the bed. I take gentle steps to meet her and sit in the chair in front of her. The vibrant lavender and jasmine scent of her body lulls my heart rate, and I sink into calm at her proximity.

"Centuries ago, there was peace here in Tantalia. Peace amongst all our realms, at least the magical ones. The succubus would go to feed on human pleasure, but that was it. We wouldn't bring them back here. We had enough magic at the time to sustain our kingdom," she starts. Her eyes shift from the floor to her fingers as she begins picking at her claws.

"Then there was a war. The Jilted Massacre. Our mistresses were slain in the thousands by the Drannars, leaving us weak and vulnerable. Our portals were locked and warded to ensure our safety. But our population began to dwindle, and we had not enough to sustain the kingdom. So, we had to take the seeds of human men. A few at first. Over time, the strength of the halflings proved to be a hearty addition to our ranks and… and we needed more. Succubus could move freely through the realms as the magic belonged to us. But over time, the wards weakened, allowing *other* magical beings to come in." Her eyes have glazed over and her tone blanks as she recounts their history.

"Lilith worked every day to fix the stone. She couldn't hack it, she said there was something she had been missing. Drannars slowly began sending spies, taking more of our people and slaughtering them as a message. We needed more men, more guards, we couldn't allow the same history to befall us again. Soon, we had lost control of how many Succubi were taking men as we tried to pump as many soldiers out as we could,"

The tapestries… those events. They hang them in their halls, so they never forget why they fight every single day.

Their past is disheartening. These demons were just doing what they could to survive. Just as we were. But they don't kill the men they take. At least, not from what I've learned so far. Perhaps the men taken were turned into halflings and then died. I don't know the lifespan of a halfling.

Regret for my actions over the past ten years of my life weigh on me. How do you accept that the thing you thought was right, has been entirely wrong?

"The day I found Lilith in the alley, she said we were going on a mission to find a piece of the stone that could restore its power." Her hand drifts to the amulet around her neck, squeezing the pulsing purple gem in her palm.

A silver tear drips and runs down her cheek as her chest heaves in a thick sigh.

My own chest twists with remorse as I remember the day in the alley.

"Lilith… Lilith was?" I ask softly.

"She was our Queen," she responds gently.

I… Queenslayer…

It… I am the Queenslayer.

Heated bile burns the back of my throat as my heart falls into my stomach. As I realize the meaning behind her reaction and the irritating moniker.

At the time, I had never had a demon hit me with so much anger before. It was usually always lust.

But her anger, her *fury* that day.

It wasn't because she was a demon… I had truly slayed their Queen. *Their* big bad.

My eyes widen as I stare off at a point behind her.

Guilt courses through me. Guilt *becomes* me.

All of what I knew about these beings has been misplaced. We have done far worse to their people than they have ever done to us.

My realm fell apart because our people gave up.

Their realm only grew; fueled by the love of their people and their Queen.

The feeling is admirable. It's… encouraging. I don't know if I'll be able to save my people… But there is a chance I can save theirs. I can still try to save mine and perhaps saving theirs is what I need to do.

If I wanted peace in the first place, I have to save them both.

And there's a portion of my soul that feels like that may just be enough for me.

I press myself from the chair and the hard stone presses into my knees as I kneel on the ground before her, hanging my head, "I'm sorry for the turmoil we've caused amongst your people. We were merely trying to protect ourselves. We were misguided. *I* was misguided," I tell her softly. I raise my head to offer her an apologetic gaze.

"Your people killed my sister. Our dear Lilith," she responds tersely, her lips thin and her features tight as she continues living through the traumas of my people's doing. Her eyes connect to mine with silent flames of fury.

"I may have killed Lilith. That is true. I realize now your moniker for me. And for that, I am sorry. I had no idea who she was to you all, and I was only doing what I was raised to do. But your sister… we do not behead the succubus. They are burned in City Center. I don't know what happened to her. But I would like to help you find out."

Her silence is deafening, and her eyes sparkle with silver brine as she looks at me, but her face remains stoic. "They want *me* to be Queen. They want me on her throne. I can't bring myself to sit where Lilith sat," she admits in a bare whisper.

My brows furrow as I weigh her statement. "I don't know about your power structure here. But I made a deal to be your royal guard." My mouth tips up in a small smile as I watch her.

Her face twitches and pricks in thought as her gaze drifts behind me. The emotions in her eyes swirl with confusion, pain, anger, a myriad of emotions I'm learning these women are able to feel. And feel *intensely.*

Her eyes come back to mine, and she nods once, assuredly in fact, "I have to save my people," she whispers softly.

"And we will," I respond as I bow my head.

"To Seraphina Moonsong, General to the Night's Legions, Mistress of Bloodshed, Angel of Death and the Queen of Tantalia."

CHAPTER 18

THE QUEEN
SERAPHINA

I was not expecting the human to appreciate my kindness for his acts of heroism. Nor was I expecting him to bend the knee.

In Tantalia, those who do good deeds are rewarded for such. And I didn't expect anything in return. Perhaps some resistance, but nothing close to what he offered.

And I have to say, I don't know if I expected him to save me or not.

If I had been in his predicament, there's a chance I wouldn't have. Especially given his body count, which includes my departed mentor.

He not only saved me, but he also gave himself to me in complete service; granting me a deep admiration in his heart and his ability to serve those who have taken from him.

I could learn a thing or two from him.

Mmmm… Probably not.

Aside from his kindness, it is jarring not having such an overwhelming hatred for the beings that have slaughtered our people for decades. But he has the drive to help my people, and having a human on my side can be beneficial. Not only for me, but for our realm.

And as much as I want to resist the idea of being Queen, I can't stand by any longer.

Velaria made the idea more urgent.

But the human made the idea more tangible. Along with the small pull of hope he offers when we lock eyes.

I keep dancing around the task The Fates have laid bare for me.

Something I don't have the slightest clue how to approach in the grand scheme of things.

This is not something I can just approach the human and tell him.

This is something he himself must feel from The Fates. I don't know much about who the humans listen to, but they must listen to something to guide them, don't they? Surely, he sees what I see.

But how do I go about it for myself? How does a Queen serve her people, while also serving the ones who speak for them? There are too many things to consider. Especially now, when I have finally wrought the courage to do the one thing my people have asked me to do for so long.

This morning, I told Asher of my plans with The Court, and we summoned the mistresses bright and early for my announcement.

And now, here I stand, looking over the varying shades of purple and red eyes that all connect to me as they surround the large meeting table in The Court of Mistresses. Silence fills the void as I look to each one of them.

Selene seems to hold her breath as my gaze connects with hers, and she offers me a small nod. I glance to my mother, who stares down at the table in silence.

The ladies around the table seem nervous as they await my words. Mistress Kalinda stands tall at the other end with Rialla beside her, her face indifferent as she watches me. The long fabric panels of her robe shield her hands from view as she folds them into each other at her chest.

I swallow the lump in my throat that threatens to suffocate me, steeling my spine and holding my chin high. "I have given our plight much thought and I have weighed our options. While I have no wish to rule, I have the heart to save our people. I will accept the status of Queen, while upholding my position as Mistress of Bloodshed. The training will fall on me and I will delegate the external necessities to those I see fit. And I will, fix the stone, bringing peace to our people once more, just as Lilith sought to do."

Mistress Kalinda's eyes almost twinkle with excitement and her lips curl into a fierce grin as she nods deeply, "There is no better demon in this realm to be Queen, Seraphina Moonsong."

Mistress Kalinda bows in deep servitude and the other ladies of The Court follow suit.

My eyes roam over the varying horn sizes of each mistress. The steady nature of their bows, and the relaxed slump of their wings as they collectively almost breathe a sigh of relief.

"To Seraphina Moonsong, General to the Night's Legions, Mistress of Bloodshed, Angel of Death and the Queen of Tantalia," Mistress Kalinda calls amongst the other winged Mistresses as she rises from her bow, her eyes coming to meet mine in a swirl of emotions.

Too many emotions.

"To the Queen of Tantalia," the mistresses echo in their bows.

Mistress Kalinda's hands come from her sleeves, placing her palms up toward the ceiling. Light shimmers against her skin as a crown constructs itself in her hands. A large opal stone rests in its center, surrounded by obsidian spikes that refract light in the bright sun that streams in from the open windows of The Court.

The crown glows, almost blinding me and the other mistresses before it disappears from Kalinda's hands.

I feel the gem of my necklace pulse against my chest; its purple light illuminates as the crown appears on my head, melding into my hair and becoming part of my horns.

The Mistresses bow once more before they rise to meet me.

Eyes of hope, joy, and elation all ring true through them, as they accept me, Seraphina Moonsong, as their new Queen of Tantalia.

As the large white doors of The Court rumble open, Selene's massive guard-dog titters with glee as she exits with me.

Selene almost floats as she comes to press her body against his, taking his massive jaw in her delicate claws.

If he had a tail, it'd be wagging.

I scoff in amusement before I turn to my own guard-dog, who looks down at me with a small smile. "So?" There's a small hint of that insufferable *something* behind his jade eyes.

A strong beat of my heart pulls me back to the present, facing the real occasion before us.

"Queen of Tantalia," I respond with a soft smile.

Saying it out loud to Asher feels just as terrifying as I thought it could be.

I don't feel ready to take on this challenge.

And in all honesty, I don't *want* to take on this challenge.

But I must.

"Yield." The memory of that voice echoes through my head and a shiver crawls up my spine as I take a steeling breath.

Asher looks to me with a wide smile and he bows deeply, "Congratulations," he says sincerely. A small tug in my chest catches my breath and I turn quickly to the staircase beside us. "Come, Qu–" I pause for a moment as my hand extends in his direction, "pet." I catch myself. "We have work to do," I say softly as I gently lower my hand to my side, forgoing the lead altogether.

He flinches as he awaits my tug. When it doesn't come, he opens his eyes and breathes a sigh of relief.

I nod toward the staircase.

Asher's tense body softens as he follows, and he takes smooth steps to walk beside me.

"Maybe I can lose the collar next," he jokes.

"Fat chance, human," I laugh with a coy smile as we descend the staircase.

"Worth a shot," he mumbles.

The activity in The Keep today is bustling with the news of my ascension. Word travels fast here, with Mistresses of their sectors able to graft to their underlings and spread the word.

Eventually, I will have to go through each area and make sure everyone knows what I expect of them.

For a while, the different jobs have been running, but not very well. We had no leader, which also led the head mistresses to instruct their sections as they saw fit. But that didn't allow us to work in unity.

An unfortunate circumstance I now have the *pleasure* of fixing.

Asher and I make our way through the halls until his voice breaks my concentration, "Your Grace?" he asks softly. The sound of his voice as he murmurs the new moniker causes my heart to sputter uncontrollably. It's oddly seductive the way it rolls off of his tongue, and the idea of hearing him whimper those words with him under me causes heat to rush through me. But as I spot his forlorn expression, I'm pulled from my lust. I peer curiously at him as his heavy steps pause. We've stopped in front of the large tapestry that hangs in the main hall.

His eyes seem to stay stuck to the cloth as he speaks, "This is… The Jilted Massacre… right?" he asks quietly.

I come to stand beside him, looking over the history myself. "It is," I respond.

"Were you there?"

"No. This happened before me. I've merely heard tales, the stories. They do not forget, and we teach the younglings, so they understand what we fight for."

He's silent as he continues dissecting the colored threads that make up our realm's history.

"The human… Why is he there?"

My eyes glance to the human on the tapestry that fights alongside Lilith. His face has been torn from the fabric, leaving a body with a gaping hole as a head.

"Lilith forbade the realm of mentioning him, he was to be forgotten. And thus, he was," I explain.

Asher's brow furrows as he listens; something about that bothers him.

"Come. The books have words for us," I say gently.

Asher's face doesn't meet mine as he nods, turning toward the hallway to continue our trek.

Our time in The Library was useless. And the one option I sought to exploit feels like a dead end. It's not off the table, but it is not plausible right now.

I keep trying to find something, anything that can lead me in the right direction, but I am coming up empty. With every book I open, every page I scan, and every word I attempt to decipher -- nothing feels like it rings a bell, and I wish more than ever Lilith was here.

But if Lilith couldn't fix the stone, how can I even think I could accomplish such a feat? Lilith created Tantalia, she ruled it for hundreds upon hundreds of years. Yet, she herself had also come up empty.

The idea of not being able to fix our power etches its way into my core. I shake the thoughts from my head as I come to meet Asher's lost face at the dinner table. Asher had been quiet as he let me read today, he seemed to be immersed in thoughts of his own.

A room off the main kitchen, specifically for the Queen and her companions, is where we are dining tonight, and probably in the nights to follow.

It's a humble chamber, with only a wooden dining table and some chairs, plus a few small serving tables against the wall. Not a grand dining room like the one we would eat in as a troupe. But I enjoy the modesty.

Small demons in yellow cloaks bring plates of food to Asher and me. A large roasted chicken, a variety of small treats and vegetables. His eyes roam over the spread in excitement, until he reaches the carrots. His features dampen under the rooted vegetable, and he sighs as he loads his plate with food. His excitement slowly dissipates the longer he eats.

"Is there something wrong? Is the food not to your liking?" I ask.

Asher startles slightly as I pull him from his thoughts, "No, uh… Sorry. I was thinking about something," he says gently as he pushes the carrots on his plate to the side.

"Do you not like carrots?"

"No, no, it's not that," he laughs softly. "I just… back home, I have a best friend. He loves carrots." He sighs.

"Ah. This friend likes carrots…?" I ask curiously.

What an odd statement to make.

"He does. And head scratches and kisses on the nose," Asher says with a soft smile at his carrots.

Peculiar.

"This friend. Does he have a name?"

"Gnox… he's my horse," Asher says with a small melancholy smile.

Ah, the carrots and head scratches make sense now.

A pang of empathy jolts through my heart as he remembers his friend. Velaria was *my* best friend, and I would do anything to have her back.

"I really miss him. He's the only one that didn't complain about our work. And he was always ready to go when I needed him."

Interesting. It *is* endearing to see these humans love. Their souls have always been so interesting when I've had a taste of them.

Some were dirty and tainted. You could taste their evil.

Some… some had *pure* souls. *Pure* hearts. They were a delight to indulge in. They were always my favorite.

I have, of course, had my fair share of the flesh of men. I've tasted thousands over my years.

But I've never had the chance to witness a love for something so… different.

My heart softens, "I am very sorry about the loss of your companion. That is a difficult elixir to partake."

Asher's eyes connect with mine in a genuine smile, "Thank you. I just hope that wherever he is, he's well taken care of."

My brow furrows in thought as we continue to eat our meal in silence.

"Ha! You little sucker! She brings you a pack mammal and now all of a sudden Vesperholm is for naught!"

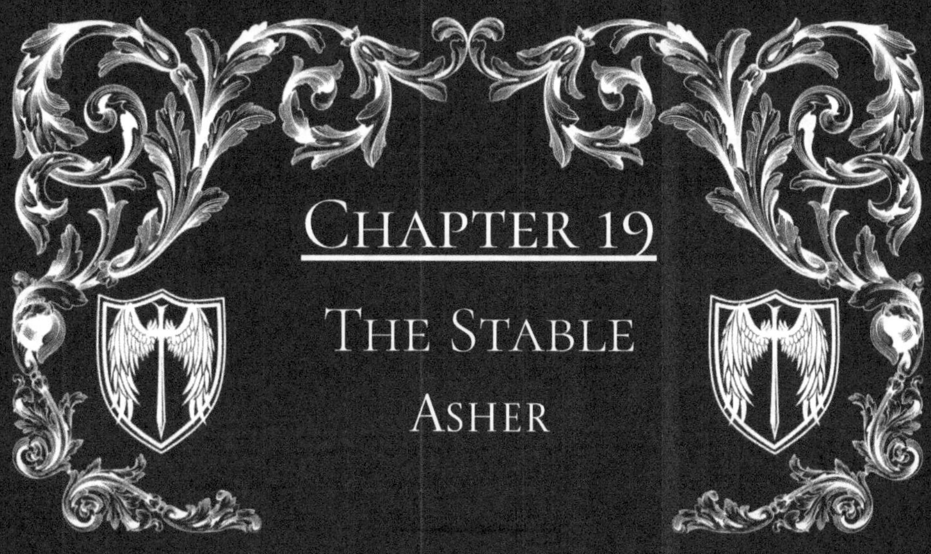

CHAPTER 19

THE STABLE

ASHER

The morning is quiet as Seraphina and I get ready for our rounds. We have settled into a routine of sorts. While my cot has been upgraded to a small bed following my acts of heroism, I still have my collar.

Seraphina transformed our sleeping clothes to our leather armor. With a few modifications, silver cuffs adorn my biceps, and my cape flows behind me in rich ebony silk, informing everyone that I am now the Queen's Commander.

I can't help feeling a sense of accomplishment. I was never shown this level of prestige in Vesperholm, and I spent every single day risking my life for the people I love. They groaned and bitched at me for trying to do right by them because they all gave up. And while I don't believe I have really done all that much to earn this title, I'll take it. Anything to feel like something I'm doing is making an impact to someone.

I wish it didn't have to be Seraphina. I still struggle with the thought of serving her and the demons. It feels as if it goes against everything I have ever known. Mortal enemies for centuries. There has never been someone from home that has ever spoken in good faith for the succubus.

And now I find myself allying with the very people responsible for my realm's downfall. How does one cope with that?

On the other hand… I hate the idea that Gideon may have been right about this place. Learning about their history, learning their motivations, it's changed the way I view Tantalia and the succubus.

It leaves a bitter taste in my mouth about Vesperholm. And while I would still love to help my people, I find myself leaning more toward the succubus for the sheer fact they want to make a difference.

But perhaps, I can save both.

Killing two birds with one stone gives everyone enough food to eat.

I haven't been here long, but I'm getting a feel for the land. In the mornings, we get ready to go down and train in The Pits, then we go to the meadow with the large tree. She still hasn't told me about what the tree is. But I imagine I'll find out eventually.

Some days we go down to the farmlands to see if there is anything we could possibly do to help. Most of the times, it's a solid no. But we still check anyway.

When Seraphina and I walk to the Pits this morning, she takes a small detour, choosing instead to walk past the training grounds to the bundle of buildings that sit at its back.

It seems like a group of shelters, with a variety of soldiers hanging out as they wait for training. This is usually the direction the winged soldiers go after training, but I've never actually seen this area.

"Where are we?" I ask.

"These are the Barracks. This is where our warriors live and sleep," Seraphina responds.

"Interesting," I murmur. But we continue to walk past the barracks, to a stable around the side.

"I didn't know you had horses," I tell her as I look over its high wooden roof. Pristine panels of white wood make up the building's exterior. Though it seems like it would be too small to fit the number of horses they would need.

"We don't," she responds.

My brow rises in question as we walk up to the stable and I see the familiar black mane of a horse grazing on a large bale of hay.

"Gnox," I whisper softly.

My horse is *here,* in Tantalia, in this stable fit for a king. My heart can barely take it as I jump the white fence and run to him. Grasping him around his large furry neck and inhaling his horse scent that I've missed so much.

Gnox huffs as he nuzzles into my shoulder.

"Hey, buddy. Hey. I'm so sorry. I didn't mean to leave you behind," I say softly as tears start to run down my cheeks. I lean back to look in his eyes.

I rest my forehead against his gently and he does the same in return before he bucks his head up and down in joy.

"I know, I know. Listen, I had stuff I had to do, alright? But they have so many carrots here! And look at this new home! You have it all to yourself," I tell him as I rub the fur on his face.

The scratchy, short fur of his nose itches at my lips as I press a kiss to it and take a step back to look around his new stable.

He has tons of room and so much hay to lay down in, with a trough of fresh water all to himself.

Next to the wall, when you enter, is an area with all his tacking gear.

A brand new, shiny, black leather saddle with sharp points of armor and braided leather reins that rest on top of it, along with an elaborately crafted halter and shiny new bit.

I turn to Seraphina with a grateful smile and watery eyes, "You brought my horse," I say softly.

"I would give anything in the world to have my best friend again. So, I figured I would do the same for you. We built the stable last night, and I sent a small succ into Vesperholm to find your steed. At first, she was a little lost, but she found him. Managed to get past your group of hunters," Seraphina responds with a gentle smile.

"You didn't have to do this," I tell her as I hop over the fence to meet her.

"No, I didn't. But I did. Can't be a Queen's Commander without a steed." She winks at me.

There is a thick feeling in the air as my gratitude for her kindness pulses through me, tugging once more at this thing in my chest. She has continued to show me this kindness even after I saved her life. And I can't tell her how much it means to me to bring my horse all the way here.

I can't help myself when I bring my arms around her in a tight hug. Though her head barely comes up to my chest, her horns knock me in the cheek as I hold her.

In all honesty, I never thought I would be doing anything like this in a million years. Especially not to a succ. I've also never really had the chance to be this close to a woman considering how I was raised.

And in all fairness, I didn't really care to have a woman. At least not in the way I've inadvertently started to care for Seraphina.

Her scent that fills my nostrils causes them to flare. Strong, and so irresistible as her body melts into mine. My cock hardens against my leather breeches, and soon, a sharp poke comes at my ribs as her tail stabs at my side in order to release me.

Seraphina's eyes widen and she clears her throat. "To the Pits, training is about to begin," she says quickly as she turns back to the arena.

My cheeks feel like they heat as the embarrassment washes over me. "Yes Mistress," I murmur.

"I need you to be entirely calm when I tell you what I'm about to tell you," I say to Gideon as we stand together in The Pits, watching the winged warriors fight. I've pulled out the small metal disk again, and my eyes lock onto it as I flip it back and forth in my fingers. The crest feels as if it curses me as I graze my eyes over it.

Am I failing them? Am I abandoning them? Am I being selfish for taking something for myself for once?

I have spent so much time caring for the people of my realm that I forgot what it's like to be taken care of.

And part of me, *really* likes the care I've received here.

I take a deep breath as I find the words to tell Gideon where my head is at.

Gideon has his arms crossed against his chest, with an unnaturally large air of confidence about him as he turns to me with the start of a smug grin.

"Don't start, Gideon, I swear to the gods," I groan.

Gideon looks at me with a large cheeky smile, "It's pretty great, right?"

I roll my eyes as I sigh, "She brought my horse back…"

"Ha! You little sucker! She brings you a pack mammal and now suddenly Vesperholm is for naught!" Gideon laughs as he grabs my shoulders and shakes me in congratulations.

I shove him away from me as I press a finger over my lips. "Shhh, keep your fucking voice down," I warn him as I knock into his shoulder, looking around to see if anyone heard his declaration. When I find no one paying us any attention, I take a deep breath. "We went to look for some sort of pocket realm, and I ended up saving her life. But I fucked up my head in the process. She healed me, brought me back and cleaned me up. I slept in her bed and the next morning she brought me the greatest chicken I think I've ever had in my life," I explain.

As my eyes connect with the insignia again, I find myself unable to look at it anymore. I shake my head in annoyance as I shove it in my pocket and fold my arms over my chest. The arena catches my attention when a large warrior is flung into one of the stone walls and falls to the ground with a callous grunt.

"I told you, Asher… This place is amazing. Selene fucks me damn near every night and I've never experienced anything like it." He nods proudly.

My cheeks heat as I think about it. I still haven't ever had the chance to fuck *anyone*. But maybe Seraphina could teach me?

I shake my head of the thought.

What the fuck am I thinking? Why the hell would I ever want that?

Gideon has had his fair share, I imagine. He's older than me and was popular with the ladies back home. He would sneak around with some of the women before they were forced into the positions they're all in now.

I never got the chance. I was too busy training; too busy learning how to fight. Blackwoods are such an important lineage, I had to be ready, not in the other territories fucking sisters.

Aside from that fact, there was never really any women in Vesperholm that caught my eye. Not that I saw many to begin with.

"Why does she fuck you every night?" I ask.

"Because I want to. She doesn't try any of her little tricks. I just love being inside of her," Gideon sighs dreamily as his gaze drifts to Selene.

I roll my eyes again as I follow his gaze. Selene stands next to Seraphina, who goes through a series of movements as she trains the new group of soldiers. Cedric isn't in this one from what I've seen.

It would be nice if he got moved up due to my own promotion. But that, of course, is something I know nothing about.

My eyes drift to Seraphina.

I'd be stupid to say the succubus weren't gorgeously shaped creatures. Even if I had despised them, I'm able to at least say the truth for what it is.

But these last few days have me thinking about Seraphina on a more physical level. A physical level that isn't due to her seduction tactics.

Wide hips frame her structure, perfect for grabbing. Her waist tapers as I look up the expanse of her and is made even more curvy in her leather corset. Not to mention, she does sport a generous chest.

Her large wings protrude from her back and give her an air of superiority that I must admit is an attractive quality. Her tail flicks behind her with seductive elegance.

She's also the Queen of this land and her people love her. Even the soldiers love her with how much torture she puts them through. That in and of itself is attractive. I love a good leader.

I'm still not able to believe the things I'm thinking right now.

Fucking a succubus of my own volition. It sounds absolutely mad. It sounds *insane* even. It was different when she would taunt me with her powers and seduce me into her arms.

But right now, these are all my own thoughts. My own propulsions…

It's madness. It's one of the most insane thoughts to ever pass through my skull.

But… I've done crazier things.

Seraphina and I bid Selene and Gideon farewell as training ends, and we leave The Pits to branch off to our separate tasks. We visit the meadow again, then Seraphina checks in on some of the leading Mistresses in their sectors to speak about the changes coming in the next few weeks with her finally taking charge; telling them what she expects and what she would like to see.

I still would like to know what that place was that Gideon spoke of.

For now, I have another thing on my mind.

I was able to bathe myself before our dinner, and it felt incredibly nice to be clean.

My heart feels like it pounds out of my chest as I think of how to ask this.

I'm just a man looking for an experience. She just happens to be the closest one around. That's all. Just an experience. There're no emotions here anyway and this is what their kind does, isn't it?

If I'm in a place where I can experiment with the unknown, who better to experiment with than her?

Gods, I have true and fully well lost it.

"Mistress?" I ask Seraphina quietly as she leans back in her chair at our table. The chair she sits in only goes up to her lower back, allowing her wings to pin into the stone behind her to hold her upper body up. Her feet are kicked onto the surface of the table as she picks at her claws.

"Hmm?" She hums softly in response as she flares her fingers out in front of her, tilting her head in observation as she looks them over.

"Your powers… How do they work, exactly?" I ask her as I push my finished dinner plate to the side.

Her eyebrow quirks as she removes her feet from the table to sit straight in her chair, her face tugs with a curious excitement. Her hands clasp under her chin as her purple eyes gleam with delight. "It's all about intentions, pet," she coos to me.

Confusion pricks at the muscles in my brow as I connect gazes with her, "In… tentions?" I ask curiously.

She nods, "Our mist, our song. Can be used for whatever we please. The intention behind it is the most important part."

My thoughts mull over her words. "So, when you breathed the mist to heal me… It wasn't to seduce me. You can differentiate their purposes?"

"Precisely. If I want to seduce you, I relay my intentions through the mist, through the song. Poison is the only thing we have no control of. Poison is just that –poison," she shrugs.

"So, both of those times you breathed the mist, there was no seduction behind it?" I ask softly.

"Not those times, no. But the night in the alley, when I sang to you, it was to seduce. I was surely surprised to see you fall victim to it. We know about the Blackwoods. Immunity, resistance. Yada, yada." She flicks her hand through the air in dismissal. "We know… so when your cock hardened under my palm, I was surely delighted," she continues. The soft *tink* of her wing tips hit the stone as she leans back in her chair, and she throws her feet back on to the table.

"When my tail wrapped around your throat in the cell and you melted under me, I would have reaped your soul right then and there. But you disgusted me in both instances, I couldn't allow you the pleasure of such delights," she finishes as she resumes looking over her nails.

"Those times in the bedroom, when you flayed apart at my mere proximity. It was a delicious experience to watch a famous *Blackwood* crumble beneath me. To see the way your eyes begged for my cunt…" She shakes her head with a smug grin. "Your brother had no such reaction. In fact, he hadn't even flinched."

My eyes widen as she recalls the events. Blood rushes to my cock as I take a deep gulp. The way she talks about it makes my heart race and my blood turn to lava.

The thought that she would have fucked me within an inch of my life is… tantalizing and horribly terrifying all at once.

Seraphina is staring off at something as she flips her hand through the air when her nostrils flare and she turns to me with a devilish grin. Her talons scratch against the wooden table as she leans against it, tilting her head in rabid hunger.

My eyes widen and I look at her with confusion.

Why is she looking at me like that?

"You… I can *smell* you… your *excitement,*" she muses softly.

Fuck.

As if a dog being called to heel, he seems to salivate at the opportunity placed in front of him.

CHAPTER 20

DEMON ANATOMY

SERAPHINA

The human's arousal awakens every ounce of strength I have.

Which, unfortunately for him, is a lot.

Of course I can smell a human's arousal.

But Asher's… Asher is *irresistible*. Even through my previous disgust I wanted to devour him. I wanted to take every last bit of his soul for my own.

Such a strong, pure energy would be a meal for the ages.

But something about taking it from him without his consent was wrong. Usually, a succubus can seduce men, and they fall into our arms.

Seducing Asher never felt like something I was allowed to do. It was the thing The Fates continuously warned me about. I had done it before for fun, but without the intentions of giving in to him. Not until he offered himself to me.

"He must yield, the same as you." A reminder of the voice had rocked through my head in the moments I toyed with him.

I had to retreat. And against my nature as a sex demon, I did.

The only time in my life that I ever had.

But he comes to me now of his own bare curiosity, his own volition, to have a taste of *demon*. The thought causes my center to pulse with urgency.

I have let his lead go as of late. But if I'm going to take care of my pet, he surely needs to be tethered.

Especially for what I intend to do with him.

My hand flicks at his collar, the purple sparks shimmering as it shoots from my wrist to attach to it. I yank him to me, and his large upper body leans over the table as I meet him in the middle.

I look over his green eyes with interest; his pupils are wide with a sense of fear, excitement, and… *nervousness?*

Peculiar little pet.

I tilt my head, delighted with my newfound observation. "You've never done this before, have you?" I purr softly as his jaw melts into my palm with the gentle caress I make of his flesh.

Asher's throat bobs in trepidation as he shakes his head slowly.

Spectacular.

My eyes widen and my lips curl with malicious desire I as inhale more of his intense, aroused scent. It's like a clash of metal, wood smoke, and human passion.

His lips collide with mine as I bring him to me. I slip my long-forked tongue into his mouth, parting within his cheeks to taste all of him. The halves of my tongue dance around his to extract every bit of his essence that I can.

Such a delicious beast. I wish I could bottle him for later pleasantries.

I pull from him, letting my tongue slither from the inside of his mouth before I look at him. "Pet, would like a lesson in demon anatomy?" I ask softly as I run a sharp claw down the skin of his neck.

Asher nods meekly as his heavy, desired eyes trail down to my exposed cleavage that peeks from the top of my black silk nightgown. My tail flicks behind me in excitement as I register his answer.

I lean back, and Asher does the same. My foot rises above my head before I bring it down on the middle of the table, splitting it in half.

"Come, darling. Mistress has lessons," I tell him as I tug at his lead.

Asher eyes the table as he steps over the splintered wood, "Was that necessary?" he asks softly as he follows me from the private kitchen.

I laugh in amusement as I lead him to our bedroom. The urge to feed from him is so inherently strong that I can't help how quick my steps are.

Traversing the stairs, we make quick work of the distance between the kitchen and my room.

When we enter, I press his body toward the bed as my tail flicks the door closed behind us.

"Kneel. On the bed," I tell him as I nod at the end of the plush platform. My wings flare out wide behind me as my tail swishes with excitement. The pounding in my chest causes my body to heat and my center to pool in anticipation.

Asher moves slowly, but he nods before perching himself on the foot of the bed, facing the headboard.

I climb onto the comforter in front of him, reaching for one of his hard, muscled arms and slowly pulling the sleeve down to his elbow. My tongue falls from my mouth to drag up the flesh. I relish deeply in the taste of his skin. His pores seep with fear and desire, further strengthening the lust that courses through me.

As my hand trails along the tense muscles, his lead follows behind, slithering around his arm like a snake as it comes to secure his wrist to the post of the bed. Soon, I do the same to his other arm. My claws drag along the hardened muscles of his chest, leaving him shivering under my touch.

His eyes are wide as he allows me to move and contort his body as I see fit, watching curiously as I carry out my lesson.

He sits on his feet as I back away from him. My eyes trail down his body to see the hard bulge pressed firmly against the fabric of his night pants.

I wave a hand over his body, his clothes shimmering in a purple glow as they evaporate from his body. They leave his rippled skin gleaming in the light of the moon that shines in from the window.

The rigid cording of his muscles writhe under his skin as his body tightens and he realizes he's entirely nude in front of me. His biceps bulge as he pulls gently against his restraints, his body shivering from the lack of fabric. Gooseflesh tightens against his skin as he adjusts to the new temperature.

My eyes drift down to his cock now that it has been freed.

My… My… MY.

So thick, long and achingly ready for me.

"You've never used this beautiful thing? Such a shame," I smirk at him.

He gulps softly as he shakes his head in fear… or excitement.

Doesn't matter, either one is fine with me.

I drag a finger gently along the top side of his pulsing cock, pressing it down when I reach the tip. I let it go to allow it to bounce against its own rigid nature. The weight and thickness of it causes it to bob slowly.

A grin tugs at my lips as I lay back on the bed, opening my legs wide for him. Even though I'm still entirely clothed, my hand grazes the center of my chest, swiping down my body to relieve me of the fabric draping my bodice.

Asher stills as he watches my naked body appear in front of him, his soft lips parting as his eyes slowly drink in my features, and his cock pulsing with need as he gets harder.

"This…" I moan ethereally as my hand reaches in between my open legs, swiping through the moisture pooled there, "is the cunt," I tell him.

He nods as he watches me, "Y–yes Mistress," he responds, though his voice is barely audible with the way he's been sucked into my display.

The feeling causes my center to throb as I press my fingers against my clit, rubbing in small circles. Another moan leaks into the air as the pleasure washes over me.

My eyes drift to his cock; it twitches with pure desire, and I grin a fanged smile in response.

"This, darling," I pant softly as I rub gently into the tender bundle of nerves that ache for him, "is the clit. *Very* important."

Asher nods again and his body begins to lean in, leaving his arms to pull back against his cuffs as he watches me pleasure myself.

As if a dog being called to heel, he seems to salivate at the opportunity placed in front of him.

"This dear… this is where you'll put your cock." My fingers press me apart, slipping a finger inside and my head tosses back. I clench my eyes shut as my hand comes to grip at my nipple. Soft pants escape me, the thought of him watching me do this makes me slicker with every second that passes.

"Fuck…" I hear him groan. My eyes open and I glance at him from my position. His cock drips with precum and his green eyes swirl with need unbound.

Gorgeous… *gorgeous* beast. The sight of him has me catching my lower lip in my teeth, nipping on it as I enjoy the sight of him nude before me.

With a wide grin, I sit up, pressing myself onto my knees. I crawl toward him before I rise. The lower talons of my wings press gently into the bed, raising me up just enough to hover my cunt on the topside of his cock. I rock my hips back and forth slowly.

Asher's gasp breaks through the nearly silent night as he takes in the sensation of my slick warmth against him.

"M–Mistress," he groans quietly. His hands pull at his restraints in an attempt to touch me.

When his lips part and he falls into the feel of me, I press my slick fingers into his mouth, allowing him to taste me. "Tsk tsk, no talking sweetheart," I whisper softly. My other hand comes to grasp the side of his neck, holding him in place while I continue grinding against him. His warm, hard length moves against every sensitive part of me. My heart races as I siphon his pleasure from him, allowing it to course through my veins in a beam of bright crimson flame. His tongue swirls around my fingers and he moans against them, his eyes rolling back at the pleasure.

Soon, his eyes press shut, trying to process the feel of me against him. Until, my tail snakes up the side of his body to stroke his cheek with the spade end. The point drags along his jaw before it pokes into the underside of his chin, pressing his head up softly to look me in the eyes. "Eyes here, darling. I need to see you fall apart for me."

The rush of his pleasure pulses through me, it's delicious. Feeding from this beast is the greatest meal I've ever consumed and he's not even inside of me.

His eyes open slowly, half-lidding in a mindless trance as he stares deep into my being. He is a beautiful sight to see untethered like this. The way he implodes at the feel of me sends a bone deep feeling of accomplishment through my veins.

I've felled the Queenslayer.

I allow his cock to slide in between the lips of my cunt with such ease, and the way his perfect cock feels against my clit drives me mad.

I slide my fingers from his mouth, moving my hand down to his hip to hold him. "Your turn, dear," I lilt softly before my tongue ejects from my mouth to slide against the side of his neck.

He shivers with pleasure as his hips begin to piston slowly, using me for his own pleasure. I guide his thrusts, feeling his strength as his muscles move and pull under my fingertips.

"Fuck… Se- M-Mis… fuck," he groans in frustration. His head tosses back as he soaks in the feeling of my wet core. The damp strands of his brown hair flying back as he does. The poor soul hasn't even been inside of me yet and he's flaying at the seams. Drops of sweat run down his skin from his hairline and along his jaw.

How spectacular.

"Shhhhh… Just feel. Don't think, darling, just feel," I whisper.

His groans pick up as his hips piston in a steady rhythm. Soft pants escape him as the muscles of his arms writhe in frustration against the cuffs, trying so hard to grip me to gain any kind of leverage.

I laugh a hearty chuckle as my wings take steps backward on the bed and my knees press back into the comforter. As his cock leaves my center, I look down at the mess I've wrought. His cock twitches as it gleams, shimmering with my lust.

I bring my hand up to his chin, surveying the depth of passion in his eyes before it slides down his chin… his neck… his chest. His muscles shiver with anticipation and Asher meets my eyes with bright emerald flames, panting as he awaits my next move. "You're a very good listener, Queenslayer."

He pants softly, those lost eyes glued to mine as his voice, heavy and husky, says, "Only for you, Mistress."

My brows rise and a nip catches my lip in glee. I beam an evil grin as I fall back onto the bed. My wings tighten to allow me to flip over onto my hands and knees and my back arches as I bring myself within inches of his delicious cock. I line him up with my entrance, pressing the head in just enough for him to take over. I toss my hair over my shoulder, looking behind me to see his gaze locked onto where he enters me.

Asher hisses as he presses in further, before he groans; low and tortured.

His thickness stretches me wide filling me with his impressive girth. The power coursing through me feels as though it'll eat me whole, and my wings begin to stretch in response. The bright red energy flows through my brain as I lock onto the feeling of his pleasure.

So strong, so potent… So *absolutely* decadent.

I've never tasted such a thing in all my years.

My hips lean in until he has filled me entirely and he pants as he continues watching where we're joined. His eyes almost glaze over as he focuses on himself inside of me, his cock twitching against my walls.

The pointed tip of my tail drags up his skin before wrapping the length of it around his neck, applying gentle pressure to his throat as my wings stretch back. I gently wrap the talons around his lower spine to push him in deeper.

He moves slowly at first, getting a feel for the movements, and I use my wings to give him a gentle urge forth. Flexing and pressing him back and forth in me until he takes over and his thrusts take control.

The sounds of our lust fill the wide chamber, mixing in a wondrous symphony of divine pleasure.

His hips thrust back and forth, and his groans are like music to my ears as he fucks me, strong and heavy with desire. The tones of my call escape from my throat as my moans continue to crawl their way into the night. His groans turn crazed as his thrusts move faster, lending to a more feral rhythm as he enters me in shallower strokes.

I slide myself forward, pulling his cock from inside of me. My tail loosens from his throat and my wings come to meet my back once more as I spin quickly to grip his throat in my palm. Allowing his skin to meld into mine as I press my body tight against his, "Lesson number six, pet... Always. Go. Deep," I whisper in his ear before I slide my tongue up his neck.

The taste of his sweat causes my insides to flare with excitement, feasting on every ounce of his soul that he has bared to me in this moment. His desire is so rich. Combined with his pure soul and his unbound pleasure, he tastes like a Heaven I'd never witness.

Asher pants softly, "Y–Yes Mistress... Deep... Go deep," he nods in mindless understanding.

"Good boy, darling," I whisper again as I pat his cheek softly.

My hands flick to his restraints, removing them. He shakes out his wrists as they come to rest on either side of him, his eyes hungry as he watches me move. I lean back on the bed again; my wings open wide against the comforter as my legs spread for him. My center pulses and aches from the lack of him, and he can tell as his eyes fixate on where he begs to be inside of.

Like a panther hunting his prey, he crawls toward me, climbing the length of my body until he reaches my face. Placing his hands on either side of my head, he moves a hand back down to line himself up with me; his thickness stretching me around him once more.

A groan echoes in the room as I take every pulsing inch, my back bowing as I relish the feeling.

"I can't believe I'm doing this," he pants softly as he slowly presses himself balls deep into me.

"No talking, just thrust," I tell him.

He lets go a tortured groan as his hips begin to move again, driving himself deep into me.

Moans flow from me as I continue siphoning his pleasure from him, the power and intensity of it so strong that it causes my lightning to crackle in the air, making my hair stand on its ends.

My hands come to grab at his face as he continues his thrusts. Looking in his face; the sweat drips from his brow and his eyes travel down to where he enters me, watching himself move inside of me.

"Mistress, y-your cunt… I.. It…" His eyes clench as his pleasure eats him from the inside out.

My hand slides down to his throat, gripping it tightly as I speak, "Look at me, pet. Be a good boy and come for me," I pant softly as I begin approaching that light at the end of the cave.

Green eyes glazed with lust open to meet mine, his thoughts have departed, and he does exactly what I tell him because at this point, he can barely remember how to breathe. His thrusts pick up, ramming deep into me with such power in every single stroke, it causes my breasts to bounce against my chest in response.

The tension in the room climbs as I feel myself reach my limit and my orgasm shudders through me. Purple lightning snaps through the air in a deafening crack and he lets out a visceral groan as his cock twitches and pulses from where he spills into me. He fills me to the brim, and I feel it leak from where he's compressed himself. Our cries of pleasure swirl through the room, dancing with the charged air and the heat of our desire. Hard waves rock through my core as I ride the waves of my release. My nails pinned into his taut muscles as my hips grind hard against him. Soon, the waves settle and heavy breaths pulse through my chest as I gaze at him. Calm washes over me, and ease fills every one of my previously tense muscles. He braces himself on his hands on either side of me, his head hung as he takes steady breaths

I stroke his cheek as his body continues to shudder, "That's it, pet. You've done so well," I whisper softly to him, allowing the lightning to slowly die down as our orgasms dance around each other. His head tilts up and he gives me an exhausted chuckle through his shy half-smile. The air turns heavy with pants as he collapses on top of me, and his cock softens from where it's still pressed into me. His hot skin sticks to mine, bringing my calm higher and higher and my eyelids grow heavy as the breaths that course through me turn renewing.

"M-Mistress… That was…" he pants softly.

"Yes?" I whisper.

"Astounding," he finishes.

I let out a soft laugh at his languished response. My chest begins to settle and the intensity of the energy in the room rolls down a hill into bliss.

For some reason, this power exchange… This feeling of him inside of me and the way he has filled me, brings a level of strength I've never experienced before. I can't stop myself when my hand comes to stroke his hair, or when my lips lean press soft kisses to his damp skin.

A purple glow begins humming against my chest, and I feel the soft pulse of the gem from where it's pressed between us.

I coil a lock of his hair around my claw as he melts against me, his breathing evening out and his skin meshing into my own.

That tug in my chest makes soft twitches as he lays with me. Any other time, I would try to push it away, I would try to deny it. But this time, I let it tug, and I let it ease through me. Soon, I try to shift out from under him, nudging his head softly with my shoulder, when I realize he's fallen asleep.

I *could* move him. I have more than enough strength to do so. Plenty more, now that I have devoured him whole.

But I leave him there to rest on me.

"Mistress? What are The Catacombs?"

I'm not sure what I was expecting when I fucked Seraphina.

But it was *nothing* I could have ever imagined. Not even in my wildest dreams.

And to be completely honest, I don't think there is ever a way I could fuck a human. That is if the opportunity presented itself.

Even if I was under her influence, with whatever I experienced last night, I don't think I care.

There was an awakening in my soul. A thread that weaved into the tattered fibers of my being, as terrifying as that sounds.

Because it is.

The scent of her skin as she approached the edge, the way her body seemed to illuminate under me. The way she commanded my every move. I can see why Gideon begs to be inside Selene.

I probably would too.

But there is something that gives me pause…

Well, two things.

The first, is the pace at which I am falling into this realm.

Shocking. Jarring. Mind-bending. Too many thoughts.

The idea of being thrust head first into this realm of beings I sought to exterminate, only to voluntarily offer my servitude – of sound body and mind – makes me feel as though I may not be so sound of mind after all.

For years, the wings and horns of these demons felt like they appeared in every corner of my vision. I was constantly on my guard to eradicate them, even if I hadn't wanted to.

Terrified.

Now… Now I live for the way it makes me feel to be here.

Safe.

As unwelcome as my mind wants to perceive the idea.

My heart *feels* safe here.

And the second thought.

The way that she held me after I finished… was a feeling of bliss I don't think I'd ever feel again.

Her claws that gingerly brushed through the strands of my hair and the way my body settled against her as I drifted to sleep. Something I've never experienced in my life before.

A feeling of fullness.

Happiness.

I don't exactly know what kind of things happen when you fuck a succubus, considering they are viciously magical beings. Most of what I do know, is their seduction.

But can a succubus make you feel the things I'm feeling now?

Like life would never be able to continue without her? Like I could never leave this place to live my life of struggle back in Vesperholm? It makes no sense; it's almost madness to face. I just met this demon, I had plans of just figuring out how to bring them apart.

But how do you forge a better world when you find out *your* people are the villains of the story?

I do miss my family. I miss my mother and my father, and my brethren hunters.

But part of me – a very deep, aching part of me – feels like this is where I belong. That *here* is where I need to be, whether I mentally want to be here or not.

It's a shock to the system, to say the least.

And even still, I wouldn't say I love Seraphina. I barely know her. And in all honesty, I don't even think I know what love feels like. I've never really been able to love anyone aside from my family.

But there is something wild in my feelings toward her. Primal even. I try to push it out of my thoughts. I try my best to ignore it when the feeling comes around. It has to just be due to my general proximity with her. Maybe she's pumping off some sort of seduction without thinking about it.

But… the lightning that crackled around us, I didn't just feel it in the air, I felt it *inside* of me. I felt it course through my veins. It was strong. But I imagine it's just part of how they fuck.

Through the entire session we've stood at the arena, I have retreated deep, deep into my thoughts, barely able to hear what Gideon says. So deep that I'm not even aware I've been watching Seraphina this entire time. Gideon apparently doing the same to Selene as I finally turn my attention on him.

Our women.

Maybe I really have lost it.

"Asher?" I hear Gideon say, his voice finally breaking through the fortress of confusion that has held my mind hostage.

"Hmm?" I mumble absently, as my eyes flick back to Seraphina. They trail up her backside to focus on her tapered waist.

The thought of her under me pulses through my vision as I watch her pin a winged warrior to the ground, holding her sword to his throat to get him to fight back.

The warrior vanishes and appears behind her with his own sword pressed to the delicate flesh of her neck.

A harsh ping of protectiveness courses through me, my muscles tensing as I almost jump to action.

But I still, as she ducks from the sword against her throat and stabs the warrior in the gut with her tail. He howls in pain as he stumbles back and she spins to throw a lightning bolt into his chest, blowing him back into the dirt. My brow furrows as my reaction registers.

The fuck was that? I don't need to protect her.

I shake my head of the fierce urge to protect her and settle myself as she throws the sword down at the warriors feet.

"Use the appendages you've been given, Liayk. You've not the density for these mistakes," Seraphina growls as the warrior groans against the ground, gripping his stomach.

Impressive. I surmise.

I can't help but appreciate her elegance in her fighting. I would be blind not to.

"You're completely gone, are you alright?" Gideon asks, pulling my attention away once more.

Ignoring his question, I peer down at my metal insignia I've flicked around between my fingers. "Gideon?" I ask. "When you're in Selene… is there… a pull?"

Gideon huffs for a moment, "So, he's come around."

I turn to glare boringly at him as I pocket it, "I was curious about their powers. So, I asked her how they work, and one thing led to another," I sigh softly.

Gideon hmphs in satisfaction, as if *he* was the one to push me into her to begin with. "There is pleasure, yes. There is a release. But a pull? I've not had that yet. Lucky dog," he says with a laugh and a slap to my back.

My body jolts forward from the impact of his brutish strength and I shake my shoulders as I readjust, "There was something that happened last night. It was like lightning had pierced through my soul and taken residence there," I admit. Hearing it out loud feels just as insane as it did in my head.

"Can't say I feel that. I like being *in* her. But I don't think the being has taken residence there," Gideon says as his eyes lock onto his Mistress across the way. He says that, but the way he looks at her seems like if I even got within inches of her, he'd rip my throat out.

I don't know if this is just what it's like to be in these demons' proximity or if it's something more. It *feels* like something more.

There is a dormant power that courses through me now, that didn't exist before. It's raw, it's visceral. It's a feral level of strength and power I'm not even sure what to do with. It pricks at the underside of my skin with an urge to burst at a moment's notice.

I try to shake my head of all the thoughts. The more they run around in my brain, the longer I lose my grip on everything.

I look over the warriors to see if I can spot the tall, broad frame of my brother. A soft patter of my heart drums against my chest when I finally lay my eyes on him.

Cedric is in The Pits today, and while he doesn't look *entirely* pissed to be here, he seems to be doing better learning their ways.

I still must find a way to talk to him. I need to see where his head is at. At least to see if I could convince him to help Gideon and me.

Perhaps with Seraphina and I becoming closer, she may trust me enough to let me have a few words with him.

Gideon and I watch the crew go through a few more movements, winged soldiers being thrown or pinned. Lightning of different colors flash every so often. All the while, I keep my eye on Cedric. He seems to be fighting with the same warrior he fought with last time. And even a few times I see him smile and laugh when the giant blond-haired warrior pins him into the dirt. Eventually, Seraphina calls them to heel and sends them to The Barracks.

But before they all get too far, I rush to Seraphina's side.

"Mistress?" I ask softly. Seraphina's hair flares behind her like a long, flowing gown as she turns to me with a gentle smile. One I don't think I've ever seen in The Pits, and even today she wasn't as rowdy as she usually is when she's training The Legions.

"Yes, pet?" she coos softly to me, her purple eyes glistening in the bright sun of the day.

"Do you think I could talk to my brother before you send him to The Barracks?"

Lines appear against the skin of her forehead as her brow furrows; as if weighing my question.

She takes a long moment before her gaze turns sympathetic and she nods once, "Make it quick. We have rounds to do," she says as she nods toward my brother.

A smile tugs at my lips as I bow in thanks. Running past her, I jog to the center of the arena, catching Cedric in the group of warriors as Seraphina walks to the exit.

"Cedric!" I call after him. He's locked in a conversation with several winged men.

He turns to me with a fowl grimace, nodding at his companions to go without him.

I nod at the warriors in hello. The blond one he was fighting with gives me a disgusted look as he turns to follow the other soldiers.

My brow contorts in confusion as I turn to Cedric, "What was that about?"

Cedric crosses his arms as he looks down at me. He's always been the larger brother, but he's put on muscle. His leather training armor is similar to mine and Gideon's. It just seems more like hand-me-downs than the new ones we were given. His arms are bare to show the increased mass of his biceps.

"What do you want, Asher?" he mumbles with a disgruntled twitch to his lip.

"How are you doing here?" I ask softly. I try to approach him with some level of kindness as I can't imagine it's easy to be here. It's not been easy for me, and I know I'm in a much better position than he is.

He gives me a bored sigh before he shrugs, "It's fine," he admits.

"Listen, I'll cut to the chase… I… I kind of like it here," I tell him quietly.

Cedric's face stays rock solid as he glares at me. His features unmoving as his familiar green eyes pin into me. "I… do too," he grunts.

The admission is shocking to say the least and it produces a puzzled expression on my face. "Then, why are you so mad at me?"

"Because you get to live it up in the castle while I rot down here with everyone else."

My brow quirks in confusion, "That's what you're mad about? I have about as much power here as a fucking worm."

"Apparently not, since you're the Queen's new whore," Cedric sneers as his chest puffs in anger, his green eyes twinkle as he prods me.

"The fuck did you call me?" I retort as I level with him. I may not anger at much, but I'll be damned if they think I'm here just because I've fucked her. They shouldn't even *know* anything. The rumor I'm her *whore* sets my blood on fire. Paired with this rage that sits just beneath the surface, I feel as if I'd rip him in half at such an implication.

"You heard me. *Whore,*" Cedric's large arms uncross from his chest as he steps to me in a show of dominance.

I knock into his chest as he continues taunting me, "You're part of the reason our town fucking decayed, Cedric. You had no urgency to save them. And now you want to be in the elite ranks of Tantalia because of what? Because you can't handle seeing me be rewarded for my efforts? Because you lack the willpower to fucking do something about your circumstance? Just like you did in Vesperholm?" I grit through my teeth. The clench of my jaw is so hard I swear I could break a tooth.

Cedric's nostrils flare as he bumps at my chest to push me back, "You're nothing but a cock to ride, Asher. If you think for one *singular* fucking second she wouldn't devour you whole, you have a whole new thing coming."

"Fuck you, you deserve to die here," I tell him as I turn to leave the arena. The anger that courses through me is all consuming. The nerve of him to even utter such bullshit.

The Queen's whore. What would he know anyway?

Gravel crunches under my boots as I approach the exit to the meadow, when I hear Cedric from behind me.

"Ask her about The Catacombs, Asher. We'll see how precious her cunt is after you learn what happened to Alden," Cedric calls.

My steps halt, my body freezes, and the world turns to black as my heart pounds against my ribcage, hearing Cedric mention our long-lost brother…

"What do you know?" I ask as I peek over my shoulder at him. The coward stands there like he has all the power.

"More than you," he says with a sly smirk and a cross of his arms.

"And yet you stay here and suffer instead of doing something about it," I call back.

Cedric turns strangely quiet as I chastise his cowardice.

"Old habits die hard, brother. I pray you find your backbone," I call over my shoulder.

I hear the crunch of boots as Cedric retreats to the other side of the arena to The Barracks.

With that, my steps continue forward out of the arena and onto the marbled path to the meadow.

Cedric knows something that I don't… And here I thought I may have had the upper hand. At least in this squabble.

Or that I could even gain his cooperation, considering the way he apparently feels about everything. But he just so happens to stay stuck in his ways. The bastard deserves to wither away amongst the ranks. How can he be here as long as I have, if not longer, and still feel the same way about keeping things just the way they are? He feels like a lost cause.

But Alden. The Catacombs. If he's alive... he could be of use to us.

I wonder if it's the underground area Gideon keeps speaking of.

Seraphina goes through her rounds, the courage to ask her about something like this continues to eat through me as I wait in the tall grasses of the meadow for her return. She doesn't say much of anything to me as she leads me to the next stop on our daily route.

Knock the arrow.

As we pass the large fountain in the middle of Tantalia, I come to walk beside her. "Mistress? What are The Catacombs?" I ask softly.

Let it fly.

Seraphina's steps halt against the walkway, her body stills, and her breathing slows but there is a twitch that comes from the base of her wings as they tighten apprehensively. She turns to me slowly, a cautious veil covering her purple eyes, "I don't know if you're ready for that, Asher," she responds.

A twitch pricks at my eyebrow as it quirks in confusion. "Seraphina, if I'm to be your guard, I have to know I can trust you. I can't help you or your realm if I don't know everything," I respond tersely as I step up to her, looking down into her eyes.

They meet mine with fury and even more apprehension, volleying back and forth against my gaze. She understands what I'm telling her, but she doesn't want to.

"I will show you. But if you get out of hand, I will restrain you. That is a promise, pet," she threatens with a flare to her nostrils.

I nod in compliance.

Seraphina tightens her wings as she passes me to walk down the path opposite of our usual route. A long trail leads us away from the main courtyard and through a series of darkened trees on the outskirts of the central hub. Their trunks are thick, with bare, jagged branches that tangle above us like a web of despair. Almost ashen in look, they are black as charcoal.

The trail feels as if it goes on forever until we reach an eerie structure. The air in this part of the forest is dense and thrums with a heavy sense of foreboding. It makes my palms sweat.

Onyx brick rises from the earth in the shape of a square in the middle of the woods, with one open side that faces the trail. Green vines grip against the stone like thick vegetative veins, creeping into open crevices to rip apart some of the facade. The blackened grass crunches under our boots as we step closer. It seems void of any life; as if whatever this place is holding, has to take the energy that surrounds it.

Stone obelisks are erect on either side of the entry, with a port carved in their fronts. Towers of wax have taken vacancy in their spaces from years of melted candles. Soon the crunching of dead grass gives way to the soft thump of brick as we descend the wide ebony steps to what appears to be the entrance of an underground bunker, where two large, winged soldiers stand guard. Their long brown hair is pulled into ponytails at the back of their necks.

Like pillars of meat, they stand on either side of the metal door. Long silver halberds cross each other to protect whatever is held inside. They bear a striking resemblance to my uncle; one taken many years ago by the succs.

I eye the two dogs in confusion as Seraphina and I meet them. They tower a solid number of inches above me and their muscles seem to be made of stone.

Stellas. I surmise.

Their eyes meet mine before they meet each other's and end up on Seraphina, who nods at them. They return her nod with a bow before they part their weapons from the door, allowing it to open at the flick of her wrist.

Seraphina's steps echo in the darkened chamber as she leads the way in. I take cautious steps behind her, my eyes roaming the grim interior.

Darkness closes in on us as we enter a long hallway, save the light that comes from the sconces on the walls that glow with crimson fire and the door at the end. Metal grinds against stone in a loud squeal as the door closes behind us with a surprising shake.

Emerald light pulses from the open doorway ahead, and a hum seems to vibrate the very walls surrounding us as we push forward.

It causes a horrible feeling to wash over me.

Seraphina takes confident steps toward the light; the rectangular frame of its entry feels like a portal to another realm.

As we approach the end of the hallway, shiny glass pricks at my eyes. And nothing could prepare me for the thing I had sought answers to.

Massive vessels line the walls, accompanied by an even louder hum as we finally enter the room. The sickeningly green glow comes from the liquid that is held in these large glass vats.

The sight is shocking. But not as shocking as what I realize the fluid holds.

Men… *Human men. Hundreds* of human men, suspended in these vats.

My heart beats wildly in my chest, threatening to burst as the realization washes over me. My mind tries desperately to process the sight I'm beholding.

And ultimately *fails.*

Their chests rise and fall, and they don't move except for the sway of their limbs against the liquid as they float up and down. They've been sustained only by masks on their face, and an apparatus attached at their groin. A small space rests at the bottom of their containers, with golden plaques meshed into the stone the vats sit on.

Names of the hunter houses signify where the men came from.

"Seraphina… What is this?" I ask nervously as I step deeper into the room and my eyes slowly roam over the men kept here.

"These… are the catacombs," she responds.

Slow, precise steps carry me as I walk down the line of tubes, looking over every name.

Ravensong. Ravensong. Shadowfang. Bloodreign. Bloodreign. Unnamed. Shadowfang. Ravensong. Unnamed.

Blackwood.

My head tilts to survey the body of the namesake I share.

And my eyes come face to face with my brother.

"Alden…" I murmur.

He looks… fine. Healthy even.

But that doesn't stop the anger that begins to take over my soul.

"Seraphina! What IS this fucking place?!" I beg as I turn to her in desperation. The fear this place has speared me with grips me by my throat, and I feel like I'm suffocating. The air has turned thin, and I beg for an answer to try to gain what little oxygen I can.

Seraphina shows no remorse, no regret. Her face is stoic as her eyes connect with mine, "The Catacombs, Asher," she repeats.

"No, explain it! Now!" I cry; the handle of my dagger feels painful in my palm when I retrieve it with a crushing grip. I move without thought and the blade comes to meet her throat. The weapon is sheathed in a purple glow, unable to make contact with her skin. My threat is useless, but that doesn't stop me.

Her eyes slide to the hand that threatens her before they come to meet mine, "When a man is stolen from Vesperholm. They are to be protected. Whether they are to provide information to us in the cells… or here, in The Catacombs to fortify our ranks. Studs to produce the halflings. Tantalia law forbids the killing of humans. So, this is where they come. The humans without powers are used for information. The hunters… are used for providing offspring."

Tears cloud my vision as I look at her. Her horns contort and her face warbles as the tears overflow and run down my cheeks, as I realize where my brother has been the past four years. *Used.* This is what that succubus meant by offspring.

The words she tells me make sense. But I don't want them to. I don't want to believe this is what they do.

I don't want to believe she could think this is right. Not after everything we've been through.

The tension against my throat threatens to cut off my air entirely, and the thrum of the vats has dulled to nothing. All I can hear is the rage in my skull and the rapid thumping of my heart.

"Tantalia needed men. The Catacombs were created for the growth of our people," she responds, unmoved by my threat.

"When were you going to tell me about this!?" I beg her. For anything, for a sign she feels regret. For a sign that she may have thought this was cruel.

Anything.

I'm unable to handle the emotion that pumps through my veins.

All our men. Here. Alive, safe. But *here.*

Wasted potential. Placed in vats for studding.

Husbands, fathers, brothers, uncles; gone.

Generations; *squandered.*

Families; *broken.*

"Eventually. But it's not an easy thing to admit," Seraphina says as her chin tilts and she looks up at me in warning.

Her expression is stony as she glares at me, her body frozen as she stands her ground.

"Tell me why I shouldn't end you right here, right now, Seraphina. Give me one good fucking reason," I grit through my teeth. The muscles in my face threaten to snap at how tense they are. Tightened from the soul-crushing pain of finding out my brother is nothing more than a pawn in their sick fucking hierarchy.

An unconscious pawn. A *wasted* pawn.

I may feel something for her. But… I can't control the emotions that course through me.

"Please…" I plead through my teeth as the tears cool down the heat that has furiously risen to my cheeks in unchecked rage. The weapon presses deeper against her skin, to no avail.

To no end. It makes no mark; it cuts no flesh.

Though, how I wish it would… Just in this one moment, how I wish more than *anything* it could.

"Aside from the obvious…" she says softly. Her eyes track to my wrist, watching carefully. "Your men are doing a good deal of service to the strength of our realm."

"You can't possibly believe that. You can't tell me this is the right thing to do, Seraphina," I growl.

This anger threatens to snap me in half. It pulses through me. I want nothing more than to blare through here with a sword, destroying every last vessel to bring my men home, where they truly belong.

"What is best, is not always what is right. This is what is *best* for my people."

"You people and your gods damned riddles!" I yell.

I press the blade deeper, but she stays her course.

"You are not in a position to threaten me, Queenslayer. You are more than welcome to join your brethren if you find your anger too much to bear."

That *fucking* nickname. My lips lift in a snarl as I listen to her, my eyes volleying back and forth against hers as I search them.

"And if I wanted to solidify that moniker amongst your people? What would stop you from stopping me?" My voice has deepened, scraping and crawling out of my chest like a bag of rocks.

Her eyes narrow on me, "You made me a deal, Asher. I assumed you were a man of your word. Are you not?"

"I want to save my people," I grit. More tears come alive against my vision and the heated streams seep down my throat to run down my chest.

"And we will. But they will have to wait. We have matters of more importance."

The normally dull purple glow, that sits outside of my vision, glows brighter as it tightens around my neck; reminding me of not only my duty, but my circumstance. I glance down at the hands that have stayed near her sides. One of her palms tighten against the air as if she's holding an invisible ball.

I pant as I try to reel in my rage, watching her hand until her fingers loosen and the restraint on my windpipe lifts. Snatching my dagger from her throat, I pocket it as I glare at her, "Why should I believe you?" I ask as my nostrils flare. My mouth feels strange. My teeth feel like they have lengthened and prick at my bottom lip. My tongue has become two sides of one coin. The humming returns with a blaringly loud and incessant hum, and the bright glow of the vats is almost blinding as the green liquid within turns vivid.

Seraphina's eyes seem to narrow in curiosity as they connect with mine. A sharp fanged grin rises against her cheeks as she tilts her head in amusement. "Because you have no other option," she taunts.

Her words sear into my being, they bring my mind back to focus.

I *really* don't have any other option. If I were to run through here with a sword and release them, there is no way I'd be able to get them out of Tantalia. And the second I were to raise a sword to them; I imagine my time on this earth would come to an abrupt halt.

Everything and all my plans would be for naught.

I must listen to her… against my better judgement.

I glare at her a moment longer before I walk past her, my boots thumping with venom against the stone of this sick holding cell. "Finish the rounds yourself," I murmur as I exit The Catacombs.

"I have no control of that. I can seduce; I can persuade. But I can't give you power."

CHAPTER 22

THE BEAUTY AND THE BEAST

SERAPHINA

Showing the human where I'd taken his people… wasn't easy. I knew it wouldn't be. I took the risk, anyway, however calculated it may have been.

But he was right in what he said. If I'm going to use his help, I need his trust. And while I didn't know the outcome of such risks, he is not able to do anything about it.

Though, I don't blame him for his reaction.

I'd have the same one if it was my own kin. In all honesty, I wouldn't have allowed him the pleasure of living, if I was in his shoes.

I spent a few more moments staring at the Blackwood he mourned over.

When we were collecting the hunters, the thought hadn't crossed my mind that they had belonged to someone; just as Velaria had belonged to me.

They were merely a means to an end, fueled by my hatred for them, and their barbaric practices; I couldn't feel anything for them.

But as Asher broke at the sight of his people, I too, broke alongside him.

His anger, his sadness, his grief, it all flowed through me. It was visceral, painful. *So* very painful.

While I couldn't connect directly with the people he missed, I did connect with him.

If he proves to be useful in our journey ahead, they deserve to have their people back. They have given a lot. And while they have taken from us, we have taken from them.

A blind world, I imagine.

After I leave The Catacombs, I make my way to the farmlands, checking in on Learra and the crops before I spend some more time in The Library.

When night descends and the moon paints the sky in its silvery glow, I head back to my bedroom.

I'm not sure whether I expect to see Asher in there when I arrive. But it doesn't shock me when I don't find him in there.

The idea I need to talk to him is one I mull over for a long while, all through my tasks and chores for the day. Weighing my options, I decide to home in on his collar.

Another wonderful application of such accessory.

Locking into the magic imbued into the collar, I get a sense of where he may be…

Barracks. Fence. Hay. Stable.

He's with his steed.

As the Mistress of Bloodshed, I not only need to be deadly, I need to be strategic. Tactful. Which is how I begin mulling over my options for reconciliation. With the change that has come over him and the anger he possesses, I *have* to be strategic now.

Popping in unannounced could have lethal consequences.

For him.

Flying would show dominance.

Grafting would cause him to startle, and I face having to subdue him permanently.

I find my best option is merely to walk.

Unfortunate.

Grafting, I obviously find to be much easier but is limited. I must have been to the location before and envision the place to get to where I need to be. I can't traverse large distances; it's too much magical energy that Tantalia is incapable of sharing. Not to mention, it's not always best practice to graft so far away; in case you arrive on something that could cause your demise.

Perhaps I can conjure my next course of action as I go down to the stable.

Bringing his steed was a vital move, one necessary if I were to gain his trust. There is also no harm in him having his companion, he did seem to miss the creature. It is a horse after all, and it should prove to be essential, I imagine, in the days to come.

Taking steps into the silent, domed greeting hall of The Keep, I make my way to the exit, taking gentle steps down the tall ivory staircase.

Almost at the exit, I pause when I hear a voice.

"General," the voice calls softly.

I stop and turn to look toward the source, where Mistress Kalinda stands at the top of the stairs.

"What do you want, Kalinda?" I ask curtly.

"Time is running out. The stone jolts, a surge even. But it continues to destabilize," she calls to me. Her gaze is steady as she glares down at me from her post at the top of the stairs.

"And why pray-tell aren't you attempting to fix it? Aren't you the Mistress of the Keep? That should be your job," I sneer in annoyance.

Kalinda begs for the power of The Stone to be fixed. She begged Lilith, and here she begs me now. But her lack of intervention makes my blood boil.

"The power comes from the Queen. Not The Keep, or its Keeper," Mistress Kalinda responds.

My brow quirks, "Keeper?" I murmur quietly to myself.

"Tick… Tock… General," Kalinda says as she glides along the stone and out of my sight.

I roll my eyes as I take my steps out of Celestial Keep, approaching the large landing platform outside of the main entry doors. I stretch my wings and give them a shake before I flare them. Walking to the edge, I fall forward onto the clouds, allowing the wind to catch the leathered webbing of my accessory limbs.

I drift on the calm, night winds until I float to the main courtyard. The air carries me to the fountain, where my boots land in the damp grass and I can continue my journey to Gnox's stable on foot.

The land tonight is quiet, save for a few massive guards that patrol the grounds, and the small hoots of owls from swaying wisteria trees nearby.

I eventually reach the stable, taking gentle steps up to the front gate. Peering over the tall fence, I see Asher laying down against his horse.

The sight is endearing. He really does love his little friend.

I take a short graft inside to avoid opening the gate and take deliberate steps toward his horse before I come to sit against the wall next to them. Sharp points poke through my clothing as I settle myself into the hay.

Quietly, I observe my human captive.

Gnox seems unphased by my presence as he lifts his head to meet my eyes. He chuffs a heated breath into the cold air as he lowers his snout softly back to the ground.

The human is still as he rests; his chest rising and falling in even rhythm.

There is something that eats at me the longer I spend time around him, especially when my mind wanders to last night.

Most humans disgust me, if not all. They represent the death of our people.

But Asher... *This* human. This annoying little *ant* seems to continue crawling his way into my being. Last night only intensified that.

I didn't want this to be the reason for our connection. I wanted to deny it for as long as I could. But at some point, The Fates have their own words. They have their own methods. And we are merely at the mercy of them.

Asher is mine, now, until the end of time. And there is nothing even *I* can do about that.

The human rests well into the night, waking only when he's been startled by a dream he may have been having.

Asher had been twitching and turning for a while now, but I let him rest. I imagine being greeted by a demon with large wings and horns is not something he would fancy, so I left him to his own devices.

His hazy jade eyes blink open as he looks around the stable. Confusion contorts the muscles in his face as his nostrils flare and his eyes reach me. He turns over against his steed, facing his back to me.

"Go away, Seraphina," he mumbles as he pulls his cloak around his shoulders for warmth.

"I came to make peace, Asher," I respond softly.

"I don't want to make peace. I want to save your people and release my men."

I sigh, "I understand why you're upset. I don't think I would take very kindly to seeing my people in the same state."

There is silence in the stable as I await his answer.

"But if we are to work together, we need to make peace. We can't save either of us if we can't be peaceful." I try my best to broach the subject as lightly as I can.

"What gives you the right to declare such a statement?" Asher responds.

"The fact that you are mine, whether you want to be or not."

Asher is silent once more, a few seconds go by before he finally speaks, "It's just another one of your tricks. I may be powerless to your magic, but I'm not stupid."

"I have no say in what The Fates decide. I must only heed their warnings."

"What do you know about fate?" Asher mumbles.

"The fact that you know exactly of what I speak and that you're angry for their doings."

Asher stills for a long few moments, the silence between us grows the longer he doesn't move.

Until he sits up and looks at me, "I don't know what The Fates are, and I don't know what any of that means," he sighs softly.

I roll my eyes as I listen to him.

"All I do know is that last night, after you… finished… there was lightning, there was *power* and it's all that courses through me right now. I don't know what the fuck it is, and I just want it to stop."

"I have no control of that. I can seduce; I can persuade. But I can't *give* you power," I tell him gently.

"Then why does it feel like I can't live without you ever again? Why do I feel like I would harm anyone that would dare harm you? Why does rage eat at my being every second of the day? I don't even know if I like you, let alone sacrifice myself for you."

"Because that is what The Fates have decided."

His eyes narrow on me, "What are you saying?"

"You'll have to come to that conclusion on your own. I will have no influence on what your mind decides to decipher."

"Damnit, Seraphina! How are we to make peace if you just fucking taunt me with bullshit riddles?!" he shouts as he stands from the hay. Strands of wheat stick to my clothes as I make to stand as well. My wings tighten against my back as I cross my arms over my chest, pinning him with a violet gaze.

"I have done no such thing. I've always told you the truth. How you perceive it is your burden."

Asher groans, turning to walk to the gate of the stables with a flourish of his cloak.

I strike my hand at his throat, the bright purple glow of his lead flashes through the dark night as it attaches to his collar and the sound of its sparks crackle in the air.

"I will not influence a realization that is to be made on your own, Asher. Until you face the mercy of The Fates, you *will* be left confused and angry," I warn.

"It can't be ANY DIFFERENT THAN WHAT I'VE EXPERI-ENCED THE LAST TEN YEARS SERAPHINA!" he yells as he turns to face me.

The bright jade color of his eyes swirl into pools of violet, the same one I saw in The Catacombs. His canines lengthen into points as his fury increases.

"You have TAKEN and kept my people for far too long, and I have been the only one left behind to give a damn about all of those ungrateful wretches that *dare* inhabit my realm!" The tone of his voice warps. It bellows through the night and awakens the stars.

He doesn't even seem to realize his transformation as he approaches me. His steps are predatory, and a new scent replaces the wood and metal I've acquainted myself with. His hand bolts to my throat, grip-ping into the flesh as he glares down at me. The purple hue continues to eat at the green of his irises until all that is left is a darkened violet gaze.

"Your realm, Asher?" I taunt through the crushing grip of his palm with a devilish grin.

"*My*. Fucking. Realm." He growls as his lips curl in a snarl to further display his new fangs.

The way he falls into this version of himself has my heart pounding and my core pulsing.

"Asher, darling," I say softly, lilting ethereal tones through my throat to soothe him.

I *must* taste this version. I must devour the beast that has come over him.

His nostrils flare as my arousal heightens and his pupils dilate as he absorbs my scent. "You're playing tricks," he growls again.

"No tricks, dear. The Fates taunt you. They await your compliance," I say through a cunning grin.

I look at his groin, where his cock swells against his leather breeches.

His eyes volley back and forth in frantic rage as his grip tightens. Suddenly, he pulls my mouth to his as his newly forked tongue slips between my lips, roaming around my cheeks just as I had done to him last night.

He pulls my body against him, and it feels like his muscles harden under my touch. His towering form encapsulates me in a cloud of heated lust as our temperatures rise. A low growl rumbles from his chest as he dives deeper into my mouth.

An echo pings through the night as I snap my fingers, grafting both of us to the comfort of our bedroom.

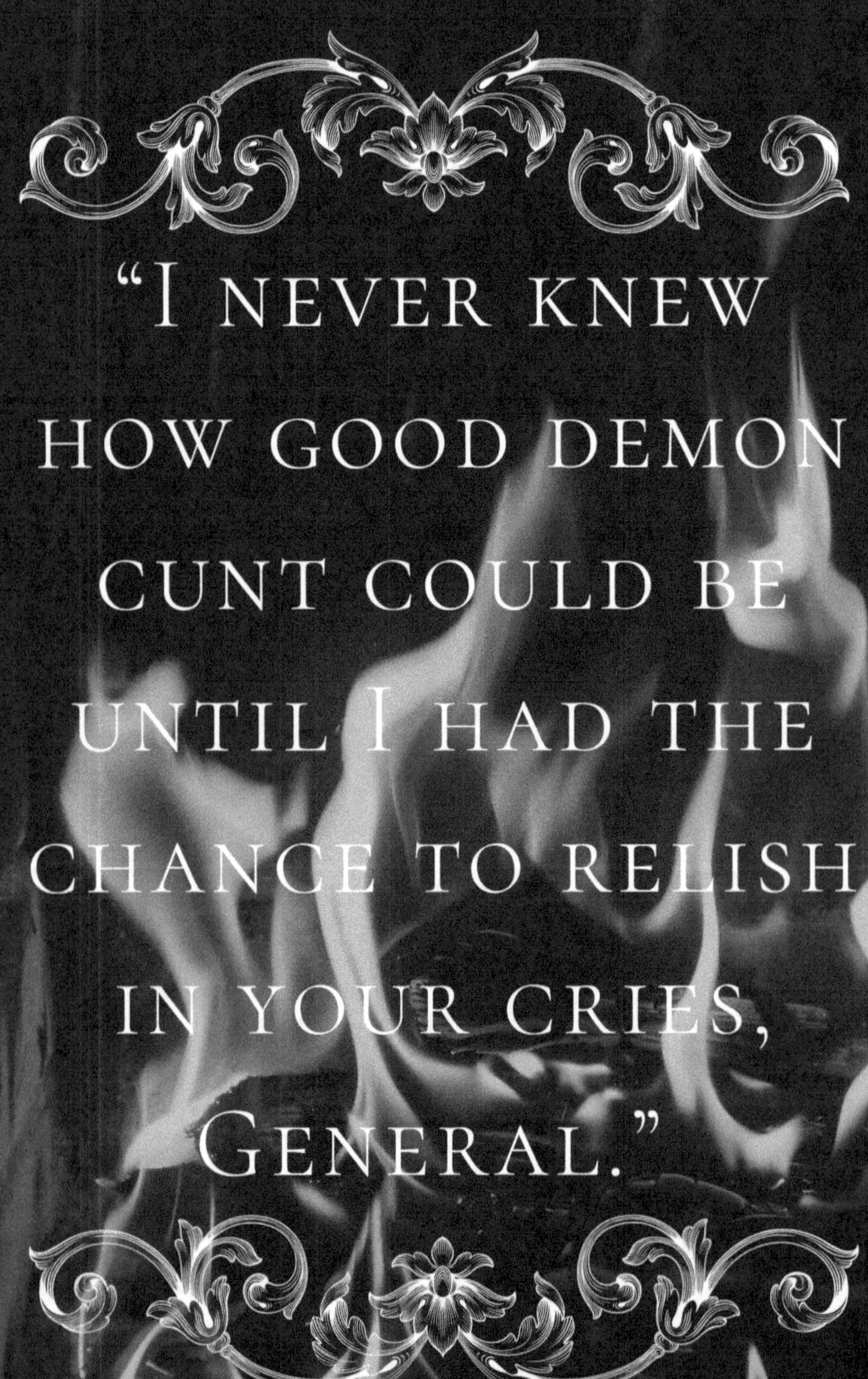
"I never knew how good demon cunt could be until I had the chance to relish in your cries, General."

CHAPTER 23

THE CLAIM
ASHER

I have no idea what is consuming me right now, what monster is coursing through my body. If I wasn't so blindingly angry, I'd assume she was controlling me. But this isn't her doing… I *know* this isn't her. But it isn't me either.

My mind blares with one thing. Over and over.

Mark. Claim. Mark her. CLAIM HER. CLAIM HER. She is YOURS for the taking. Take her. TAKE HER.

I have no desire to make her mine. I have no desire to even be *hers*.

But it's the only tangible thought I can muster in this moment.

Fuck her within an inch of her life. Devour her whole. Feast on her anger. Her rage. Her *pleasure.*

The emotions that eat into my being are not of my species. This is some new beast entirely.

The previously unstable floor transforms into sturdy stone as Seraphina grafts us to her room. The warmth of her quarters envelops us in its calm and the scent of horse and hay is replaced by the gentle floral fragrance that wafts in from the window.

Seraphina's hand waves over our bodies and the fabrics shimmer as they lift from our skin.

Her throat melts into my palm as I grip my fingers around her neck, pressing her backward onto the bed. My cock throbs as it begs to be inside her, as if it has a mind of its own.

What I'm doing doesn't even make sense, I'm seething with anger and the only response I can muster is to be inside of her. It's as if the human side of me has been locked away and is banging at the doors of my mind, begging to be let go.

But I can't. I must have her. To feel the warmth of her decadent cunt wrapped around my cock.

Seraphina complies as the back of her knees hit the edge of the bed and she descends onto the comforter. Her large wings splay out behind her as she settles. Her creamy skin almost shimmers against the moonlight as she looks up at me with wanton desire. Her breasts shake against her chest as I move her, causing my already hard cock to pulse with need.

I press her deeper into the mattress as I lean over her. Strong legs part under me, and I smell her arousal. It drives me wild with urgency as I release her throat and slide my hands down her body, relishing in the way her skin feels like a part of me. The flesh of her plush thighs melts into my hands as I grip them, pressing them open with restrained strength.

My tongue slides from my mouth, but it feels… different. Slender, but halved. Like it did in The Catacombs. The two ends twist around each other as I get a feel for the change I've been subjected to.

I would like to linger on this… But I can't. Not now.

Pressing her legs apart farther, her bare cunt gleams back at me with lust.

My pulse charges through me, urging me to dive deep into her center. My tongue explores every part of her as I extract as much of her pleasure as I can. Ethereal moans break through the darkness and contort the air around us as her claws tug at my scalp.

The forked muscle presses farther into her core, snaking against her walls to dance around inside of her. The halves separate to massage the velvety muscles of her, lapping against the top of her insides as my nose buries into her clit.

Her moans and gasps get louder until her cunt tightens around my tongue and I retreat, leaving her to approach the edge, but not take the fall.

Seraphina growls as her violet eyes connect with mine, glimmering with anger. The soft comforter falls from my sweat dripped chest as I rise above her.

I take in her perfectly carved body. Her tapered waist and her luscious tits that move like water against her chest. Barely able to contain my desire, I grip the wide frame of her hips as my eyes drink in her form, landing on her gleaming pussy. Plump, red and soaked for me to take.

I survey the mess I've made, taking pride in how I've wrecked her, before lining my cock up with her entrance. A hiss escapes me as I soak in the feeling of her, my sight glued to her tight cunt that wraps around every inch of me.

"General..." I groan as the beast gnaws incessantly at the bars inside of me.

Her supple hips give way under my fingers as I grip harder and pull her onto me with a punishing force, using her like a demonic little plaything. "A perfect fucking toy, you are." My voice vibrates the inside of my chest with a timbre I've never experienced.

"I never knew how good demon cunt could be until I had the chance to relish in your cries, General," I groan. The sensation of her wrapped around me causes my blood to pump at an accelerated rate, fueling my feral desire for her in a way I don't think I could ever satiate.

"They are all yours, Queenslayer," she moans back.

The sound of the nickname sends rage pulsing behind my eyes, and I grip tighter at her hips.

I can't help the way I begin using her. The way I don't fuck into her, I just drag her body onto me, moving her back and forth as I continue to take from her and feast on her with an incomprehensible hunger.

"Stop!" I bottom out into her with a powerful thrust. "Calling!" Another one. "ME THAT!" I growl.

I spear her repeatedly with punishing strokes, watching as her tits bounce and she takes every ounce of power I give her. Her skin leaks from between my fingers from the grasp I have on her hips.

Her eyes shine with lust as she continues to feed off my pleasure, while her taloned hands come to grab her luscious tits. She doesn't seem at all phased by my rage. If anything, it seems to fuel her own lust even more. I can feel it as it charges her power higher and higher.

The push and pull of this exchange volleys between us with every thrust I take.

She takes. I take. She takes. I take. The power between all of it so mind numbingly intense.

I let go of her hips to grip her throat once more. Leaning down to drag my tongue along her jaw, I savor her rich taste. A flavor so sinful I'd commit atrocities to experience it for the rest of my life.

"Even through my rage you find a way send my lust through the clouds. What tricks do you play with me, demon? Do you taunt me with your seduction?" I groan as I bury myself balls deep into her, filling every inch of space she has to offer.

"Only The Fates control your lust, Queenslayer. I am merely a pawn in their games, the same as you."

"You lie, General," I growl as I tighten my grip on her throat.

"I don't lie, darling. Your lust is just within your grasp. It's not my fault if you have lost your hold on it." The soft, breathy tone of her voice is like music to my ears, even against my anger. It pulls at the human Asher for merely a moment before the beast throws him back into the brig.

A feral noise exits my chest as I begin pounding into her again. The touch of her power is just out of reach, and with every thrust I just barely grasp it. It fuels me to mindless strokes as I race to abscond it from her.

Her moans continue to eat the air around us as she nods mindlessly, "Deeper, pet, please, *deeper*" she moans with a fanged grin, her voice sultry and deep as she gives into me.

I groan in intense pleasure as the power I've chased courses through me harder, my skin thrumming with energy unbound. My thrusts gain even more power behind them, and it causes her to damn near cry in response as she takes every inch of me.

Soon, she shudders through her orgasm, letting an ethereal screech out into the night as her cunt tightens around my length.

A hearty groans rumbles from my chest as I spill into her, filling her cunt with every ounce of myself that I can offer.

I flip her onto her stomach, gripping her waist in my hands as I press her into the mattress, punishing her further.

It isn't enough, I've marked her, I've claimed her. It isn't enough. It isn't enough. *I need more; I need MORE.*

"I need it all, Mistress. All of *you*," I grunt as I lean down, pressing my chest into her back. Her skin feels like silk against me, just her mere touch is like my insides have blown apart in a frantic plea for everything she is.

"You have all of me, *Queenslayer*," she muses breathlessly.

I know she's brandishing the name as a weapon for more. And it *works.*

Rage consumes my thrusts and as if my thoughts could conjure, I feel my cock thicken inside of her, expanding her more as I settle myself deep, keeping my seed in her.

She groans in response and flashes a devilish grin at me from over her shoulder. The walls of her cunt compress around my thickened length as waves ripple against it, milking me for all I have.

"You're playing with fire, pet," she moans as her leg flips over me. She wraps her legs around my waist, pinning my hips to flip me onto my back.

Her wings expand slowly, the action causing her presence to command the small space. Her chest rises before she grinds against me, taking control of me once again.

Even through my anger, I can't help admiring her beauty. Her hair flows around her as she gives in, wrapping and swaying around her gorgeous curves. The muscles of her face melt as she lets go of everything and sinks into the feeling of me inside of her. Her body feels as if it vibrates as she feeds from me. Lightning charges through the air, causing it to thin as she leans over, gripping my cheeks in her taloned fingers.

"You can come again, pet, I know you're not done, give it all to me," she hisses softly. Her eyes are half lidded in an endless plane of pure passion.

One last groan escapes my throat as I come once more and the beast retreats. The power shifts and she steals every last ounce of pleasure my body has to offer. My cock throbs inside of her as I fill her. A beautiful, fanged smile gleams against the light of the moon as it rises on her face.

Seraphina's body begins to glow, and my eyes widen as a flash of memories I've never had course through me. Visions of war, visions of a life I've never lived pass me by as the fabric of my soul slowly stitches anew.

A voice passes through my skull, one I don't recognize. As visions of a fire accompany it.

"Take it, you must protect it. Pass it through the generations and guard it with your life, brother."

"W-where are you going?!"

"Away. Protect the dagger."

The vision and voices fade away and the black warmth of the room closes in on me.

The power that coursed through me slowly dies as my orgasm finishes. Exhaustion pulls at my skin as I come down from this high and my body lies limp against the mattress in a puddle of sweat. An incredible drain has taken hold of me as the power leaves, and my tongue tightens into one unit again.

Seraphina collapses next to me on the bed, and I use the available energy I have to gaze at her. She pants with a satisfied grin and satiated eyes.

"What… what was that?" I ask softly as I try to catch my breath.

"It was The Fates, dear Asher," she responds.

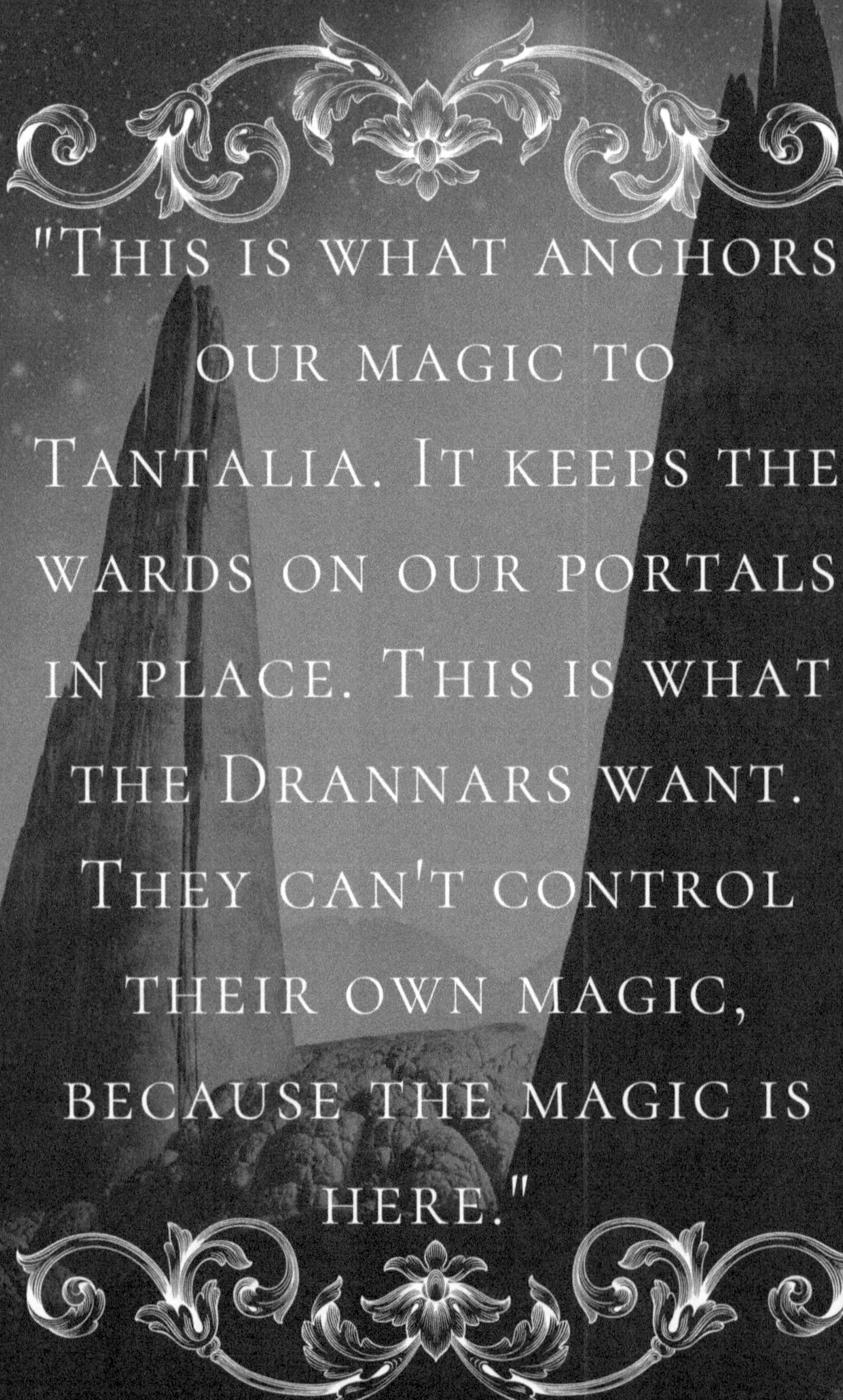

"THIS IS WHAT ANCHORS OUR MAGIC TO TANTALIA. IT KEEPS THE WARDS ON OUR PORTALS IN PLACE. THIS IS WHAT THE DRANNARS WANT. THEY CAN'T CONTROL THEIR OWN MAGIC, BECAUSE THE MAGIC IS HERE."

Chapter 24

Lapis Amoretstra Asher

The Pits are ablaze with strapping young lads today.

More specifically, Solis Legion.

Which means a more *inexperienced* group of halflings.

But I can barely care because I'm not able to stop thinking about what happened to me last night and the feeling that I was not able to overcome. The anger, the *beast*, the monster that seems to grip at me from the inside, begging to be let out. The rage that causes me to take everything I can from the Mistress that essentially took everything from me.

Not to mention, handling everything that happened in The Catacombs. Vesperholm's men are safe and alive, but still…

There isn't much I can do until I save Tantalia.

Which leads me to the next issue.

Seraphina's words on fate. What does she mean by fates? Am I fated to save this realm? Am I fated to be here in Tantalia forever? Has my own fate been reduced to a mere plaything for her pleasure?

And what could she possibly know that I don't already know myself? I don't understand any of the feelings that I experienced. The strength, the anger, the way my tongue morphed into something not even of myself. I could smell better, see better. There felt like there was no explanation for anything.

Nothing made sense and as I learn more, it feels like my time and mission here has been squandered.

The men that are being kept for their use, the damned stone she keeps talking about. *Why* is the stone deteriorating? *That* doesn't even make sense. It's a STONE!

In all honesty, I need to get away. Of course I can't, but I would like to. Even if she were to let me traverse the land and send a succ to follow me.

At this point, I know I'm stuck here. There is no escape, especially while being locked by her collar.

My attention is pulled from my thoughts as a stray warrior lands at Gideon's and my feet. The poor being was knocked back by Seraphina's rage.

She always seems to get a bit more hostile with the younger ones. Probably because they're horrible and Seraphina doesn't take anything less than perfection.

Gods, what the fuck am I even thinking? I barely know this demon and suddenly, I feel like I've known her for centuries.

It makes no fucking sense, and I get angrier the longer I think about it.

I huff an annoyed breath as I watch over the soldiers, waiting for Seraphina to get angry enough to release these weak excuses for warriors.

Gideon turns to me, "What is your issue today?" he asks gently.

"Nothing," I grunt as I peer at him from the corner of my eye.

Gideon's eyebrow raises as he looks me up and down, "Have you put on muscle?" he asks.

Confusion pricks at my brows as I turn to look at him, "What the fuck are you talking about? We've barely been here a month. How could I have put on muscle in that much time?"

"I don't know, but you look… stronger," Gideon says as he shrugs and turns back to the soldiers.

I *hmph* in his direction as Seraphina finally loses her patience. Her voice echoes through the giant stone arena at the winged warriors before she finally shoos them away.

As they vacate the arena in sweaty heaps of skin, bone and wings, Selene and Seraphina approach us. Their wings tense as the dust kicks up around their thick boots.

Selene's eyebrow raises as her eyes scan me up and down, her head tilting curiously before she turns to Seraphina with a questioning expression.

Seraphina nods in response.

"What is going on here?" I ask. The control I have on my patience frays every single second I spend around them with no answers. It feels like more questions seem to keep popping up with no resolve.

Selene laughs, "Poor boy," she says softly.

"Are you ready, dear?" Selene coos to Gideon. Gideon seems to salivate as he wraps his arms around her waist, pulling her close to him. He looks down into her eyes and his hand comes up to wrap around the back of her neck, pulling her in for a kiss.

My eyes volley between them in rabid confusion.

What in the fuck is going on here today? I can't handle everything being thrown around.

My gaze lands on Seraphina and she shrugs, "You humans are so easily swayed."

"Hush, Sera, the only sway here is in his breeches," Selene giggles as she turns to Gideon again.

He has completely given into her, and it even looks like his collar is a little duller today.

My patience snaps as I decide I can't be in this space anymore.

My cloak tugs at my throat from the way it flares behind me as I turn to the exit of The Pits. The crunch of Seraphina's boots alert me of her presence as she follows close behind. My steps are brutal against the stone as I lead the way for the rest of the rounds.

"Ornery today, are we?" she cackles as she falls in step beside me.

"Rounds, let's go," I mumble as I turn to the path for the meadow.

"Interesting. We get a little *cunt* in our system and all of a sudden we grow a spine. How wonderful," Seraphina taunts.

I growl as I turn to face her, my hand wrapping around her windpipe as I glare at her, "You're playing a dangerous game, *Mistress.*"

"A game I'm sure to win," Seraphina responds with an evil grin.

"I'm not playing."

"You don't have a choice," she muses in a sultry tone as her hands come to caress my jaw.

Lust consumes me for all but a moment before it's replaced by *rage.*

I shove her back, "Don't you think I know that!? I don't understand anything about this land, and I feel like the longer I stay here, the more insane everything is!"

Seraphina crosses her arms and leans on a hip as she watches me, her face bored.

I begin pacing back and forth in the grass as I rehash my strife, "This anger, this *rage.* I don't know what it is, and I don't know what has come over me. I have no control of my emotions, and nothing makes sense here!"

"And you won't until you accept what The Fates have laid bare for you."

"Will you shut it with The Fates bullshit!? I don't know what any of it means and at this point, I don't even think I want to know."

Seraphina's eyebrow raises as she continues her observation.

My feet make a path in the grass as the thoughts continue to run through me.

"The fucking men, this stupid fucking stone you keep talking about, everything! Now, Gideon is apparently in *love* with Mistress Selene!"

Seraphina's brow furrows in thought and annoyance, her gaze fierce as she splays her hand at my throat and the lead escapes her wrist. The tug is punishing against my neck as she hauls me behind her.

Confident strides drag me along the path to Celestial Keep. I grunt as I try to pull back against her. "Stop! You can't keep doing this shit!" I growl.

Seraphina continues to lead me through the grounds in silence. We pass the main courtyard and continue walking to The Keep. She hasn't looked back at me, and she refuses to acknowledge my gripes as she takes me to a stone staircase that wraps down and around the mountain Celestial Keep rests on.

Carefully, she steps down each of the porcelain platforms to the very bottom, where nothing but a tall archway has been carved into the base of the mountain guarded by four massive, winged men. The biggest ones I've seen thus far, they all bear striking resemblances to Gideon and the rest of the Shadowfangs.

They have to be Stella warriors. What could possibly be in here that would need Stellas? What in the fuck is this?

The winged men step aside, and their wings unfold as they turn around to face the entry, pressing their hands against the hardened gate. Stone grinds against the walls of the mountain as the space in the archway begins to rise, shaking the very ground we stand on.

Inside seems unassuming, soft light flickers against ancient brick from the fired sconces that line the walls of a very tall descending staircase, leading straight into the earth.

My complaints halt, and my body calms as I study the new area we've unlocked on this confounded map. The space is an enormous underground structure that exists right under Celestial Keep.

Seraphina leads the way, descending the ancient steps.

The air cools and silence closes in on us as we take what feels like five-hundred steps underground. The air in this underground cavern feels damp, and the passage is strong with the scent of moist earth and stone. Every so often, wings flap against the ceiling as we continue our descent.

A singular platform rests at the bottom, but it seems like it levitates when a stray pebble knocks into one of our boots and off the edge. Looking over the ledge, I look into the black abyss that lay beneath the floating rock. I wait for what feels like whole minutes until a splash finally bounces off the walls.

Long fall.

Across the floating platform is a set of massive, marbled doors. On the front are two carved beings -- their departed queen on one door and a human in a cloak on the other.

Confusion contorts my features as I study the figure on the door. The face has been scratched from the stone and all that remains is the body.

The same as the face on the tapestry.

Seraphina approaches the doors, placing her hands on two worn spots on either side where the handles would be. Her voice is low as she murmurs a slew of words in a language I've never heard. The silver strands of her hair begin to stand on end as lightning charges the air around her.

Thunder booms in the echoed chamber as the doors rumble open. Pebbles fall and dust swirls in the air as the doors grind against the ground.

A loud hum comes from inside. The warbled noise consumes the colossal domed structure as the doors grind shut behind us with a deafening thud.

Inside the large room is a monstrous, black stone. It stands at an impassible height and is shaped in a jagged shard that essentially sticks out of the earth.

Runes are etched into the ground in concentric circles, almost like the ones around the portal for the mages.

The grand rock pulses in uneven bursts of blue glow but crackles every so often.

"You want clarity? This, is *Lapis Amoretstra,*" Seraphina says as she turns to me. "*This* is what anchors our magic to Tantalia. It keeps the wards on our portals in place. *This* is what the Drannars want. They can't control their own magic, because the magic is here" She rests a hand on her hip as she gestures to the large fixture, her face pinched in annoyance.

My eyes are locked on The Stone as we approach it. Taking slow steps through the chamber, I investigate this source of power they aim to fix.

Succubus lore in Vesperholm is extremely limited and I had no idea this was part of them.

I was under the impression they just *are* magic. I didn't think it came from anything.

The runes flicker against the ground, flashing sporadically. The air in this room is heavy. It's similar to the feeling in the cave, but it's unsteady. It goes in and out like a wave cresting the shoreline.

"Why has it wavered?" I ask Seraphina as I step up to it.

On the front is a large slit, as if something is to be placed there. My brow furrows as I contemplate what could fit in something like this.

It's uneven, and the inside is covered in cobwebs. It's as if whatever is missing has been gone for far longer than they think.

"That's what I'm trying to figure out. Lilith was trying to find something in Vesperholm when you killed her. She believes it may have been the other piece to fix The Stone," Seraphina says softly.

"And you have no idea what is supposed to fit in here?" I ask as I press my finger into the hole.

A surge of power jolts through my finger and courses through my body like lightning to a rod. I'm blown back by the force and my bones take the impact of my body as I land on the ground several feet away.

I groan as I attempt to take a deep inhale, "Fuck," I grunt as I brace my hands on the ground. Coughing a few times, I try to get my breath back as I stand back up.

The air in the room thins and the humming dulls to a buzz before it silences completely, as if it were wind to a flame. An eerie stillness consumes the interior chamber as Seraphina and I look at each other.

The sensation lasts a few beats before loud trumpets begin sounding off above ground.

Seraphina's eyes widen and her wings droop, the talons clinking against the floor. She stands, frozen, staring off at the door behind me.

My brow furrows in concern as I try to make sense of the new noise.

More trumpets fill the silence as I stare at her. Her violet eyes glaze over as she blanks off into space.

"What is that?" I ask cautiously.

Seraphina blinks as her eyes connect to mine, "Drannars," she whispers.

"If only you knew, Your Majesty."

CHAPTER 25

DRANNARS
SERAPHINA

"**Q**uick! We must get to The Keep!" I call to Asher as my training kicks in. I grab his hand, throwing him onto my back as my feet pound into the stone. As I race to the colossal doors that guard The Lapis Cryptus, his tether wraps tight around my body to secure him. Brick against brick echoes through the chamber as the doors scrape open to allow us exit and I wave my hand at the air behind me to secure it.

The increased weight of Asher on my back has my wings take a wide breadth of air as they bat, propelling us to the top of the massive staircase. The torches in the dark space shiver against the torrent of wind I create as we speed toward the exit.

My throat releases a demonic caw as we approach the guarded doors, and I hear the muffled shouts of guards become clearer as the stone doors begin to rumble open for us to continue our flight path.

"NO ONE ENTERS!" I call down to the large guards as we climb through the air. Several hard wing beats carry me to The Keep at breakneck speeds, the weight of Asher's body causing my wings to work harder. Taking a hard bank, I aim for the balconied courtyard that rests outside of the Court of Mistresses.

"Tuck and roll, human," I grunt as we make our approach. I flick my shoulder to the side to unravel Asher's tether and throw him from my back. He rolls onto the grass of the balcony before my feet swing forward to land. My boots pound against the stone floor as I snap, my bodice shimmering as I arm Asher and me in hardened leather gear. Plates of glittering black scales sheath our chests, arms and legs as I approach the ebony table of The Court. My two silver short swords, secured in their scabbards, have become attached to my armor at the base of my wings in preparation for this ill-timed invasion.

"The wards!" I yell to the few Mistresses that have come to my aid. My mother, Selene and her guard-dog, Mistress Kalinda and a few other ladies take post along the table side.

"They're down, the Drannars have entered through the portal in the north," my mother relays.

The mistresses in the room have all donned their own leathers and weapons, ready for battle. All except one.

I steel my spine as I look to the end of the table, where Mistress Kalinda stands proud across from me. Her white cloak steady where it drapes her body, her arms shoved into the sleeves to show her lack of intervention.

"Time is ticking, General. What will you do?" Kalinda says with a stone face.

My lips curl in a snarl as I glare at her. I set my attention on Selene, "Guard The Pods, make sure you have the biggest warriors from Stella there, but glamour them. We can't draw attention to it."

Selene nods, before she and her dog disappear.

"Send Solis and Cometas to The Portal, and the rest of Lunae to The Keep. Increase Stellas in The Catacombs and send more men to The Crypt," I tell my mother.

She nods once before she disappears.

"Learra, take your women and secure the area outside the portal, no Drannars get into the main court," I say as I turn to Learra.

"Yes, Your Grace." She nods in compliance as her body shimmers from the space.

I glare back at Mistress Kalinda, "And what will *you* do, Kalinda?" I growl.

"As I have always done. Command The Keep."

My eyes bore into her in unchecked rage.

She doesn't budge.

She has no right to stand, if she chooses not to fall.

My hair whips behind me as my fingers bite into the hardened muscles of Asher's wrist and I graft us down to Gnox's stable.

Gnox's whinnies pierce the air as hay replaces stone under our boots, "Whoa! Whoa! Hey! Come on. It's alright, we have to go, buddy," Asher quickly remarks as he approaches Gnox with raised hands to calm his steed.

Gnox rolls his head around in a repeated, irritated nod before he takes soft trots around his stable.

"I hope he doesn't mind," I say softly before I wave my hand over him. Purple glow engulfs Gnox as his new leather armor and tack sheaths his massive body. Gnox paws at the hay as his bit begins clanking against the metal of his bridle.

Asher slings his leg over Gnox quickly before his strong arm wraps around my waist to haul my body behind his own. I blast a lightning bolt at the gate and the metal door swings wide to allow us exit as Gnox rears against the air. "HYA!" Asher calls as he kicks into Gnox's side.

Gnox breaks into a gallop through the gate. Winged warriors shout as they run through the grass, some of their forms shimmering against the air as they graft to the site. The sound of wings beat around us as they make way to their recalled positions.

Gnox's hooves pound against stone and grass as we make our way across the courtyard, closing in quickly on the edge of the woods where The Portal hides deep within its belly.

Learra's women have begun setting up fortifications around the farmlands.

More trumpets sound off in the courtyard valley behind us as we speed through the grass and into the forest. Shouts shake the leaves surrounding us as Gnox bobs between branches and foliage, the creature bounding over stray roots and boulders with ease.

Asher whips at Gnox's reins as we burrow deeper into the fray. More winged warriors appear around us as flashes of lightning break through the spaces in the dense forest.

Beyond the tree line, I see *them.* Thin figures of gray-blue skin and bone step through a now red portal. This portal would usually be purple, meaning the wards are in place.

With them being completely void of the familiar color, the protective wards have fallen entirely.

Menacing crimson eyes peer through the brush as the Drannar look for their next kill. Long, pointed ears peek from their locks of straight ivory hair. Clashes of lightning echo back and forth as the warriors that normally guard The Portal attempt to push back the threat. This area is usually heavily guarded for this exact reason.

But with the wards useless, there are too many Drannar, and not enough halflings.

My wings flare to catch the wind as Gnox continues his gallop, allowing my body to vacate the saddle so I can continue on foot.

The roots pound under my boots as I duck through the dense trees. I zero in on the opening where the Drannars continue to exit the glowing portal. Shouts sound off in the meadow ahead as warriors rain hellfire on the Drannars that continue to file out, the hoard of them armored with staffs of silver.

They don't have enough strength in their magic to wield with hands alone. So, their staffs serve as conduits for what little magic they can siphon from us.

I approach the clearing where The Portal is and survey the damage. Bodies of deceased warriors litter the previously lush grass with rivers of blood. Their wings lay in twisted heaps of gore and the grass shivers as their magic seeps back into the ground.

A stray Drannar approaches me with a large, fanged grin. "Seraphina Moonsong. Black looks good on you," he snarls. His hand reaches for the staff on his back to challenge me.

"Death will look good on you," I growl back.

"If only you knew, Your Majesty."

Your majesty?

The thought passes through me for the barest of moments, before silver flashes in my vision as he whips his staff toward me. Blue fire blasts into the ground before me as I bound up and away from its impact. Landing beside the elf, I plant my foot firm into the ground as my other leg swings around to clock him in the jaw. My boot roots back to the ground as I complete the spin.

He growls as he strikes his staff low, knocking into the back of my knees, taking them out for me to crash onto my wings in the grass. The pointed end of his staff presses into my throat as he hovers over me, his beady red eyes glistening with murderous intent.

My lips lift in a snarl as my wings tighten. Pressing through the base of my spine, I bring my knees to my chest and throw my feet into the middle of his. Knocking him back before I bat my wings into the air. I hover just above him to get a better look at the meadow below. I whip a bolt of lightning at the Drannar below and restrain him in purple webbing. With a grand pull, I lasso the Drannar from the ground before I swing him above my head. As his body rounds one last time, I retract the lightning and throw him into the ravine beyond.

When I hear the loud thud of a body making impact on the rocks in the distance, I turn my attention to the field to watch the skirmish.

More slender bodies of blue ease from the portal with staffs in hand, their eyes locked on the warriors that approach from the forest. The halflings wings flare wide as they exit the brush with swords in hand and their cries echoing through the valley.

A growl escapes me as I ascend higher, tucking my wings to corkscrew into the sky. My wings open at the top, allowing me to float for a moment before I free fall into a dive. Zooming headfirst into the ground, I let a lightning bolt fly from my wrists right before I make contact, to blast the hoard of elves through the middle of their ranks. Spindly bodies fly through the tall grasses, along with small chunks of dirt and rock. Tucking my head, I allow my hips to roll for my feet take the impact into the crater in a three-point stance.

I pop out of the hole I've blasted into the ground, looking around the battlefield to find Asher on foot, his dagger in his palm as he slices through throats of the Drannars. Blood sprays like waves and lightning sounds off around us as warriors continue proceeding through the thicket, mowing down the elves that escaped. The sickening scent of blood, magic and Drannar smoke seeps into the grasses and writhe through the air.

Asher spins and whirls toward the dark elves with laser precision and I find myself sincerely grateful to have him on my side in this moment.

Whilst distracted by Asher, a strong grasp clamps onto the base of my wings. Sharp claws pierce through the sensitive leather as two Drannars press me to my knees in the crater. Searing pain wracks through my body as my mind blanks on evasive maneuvers.

Mistress of Bloodshed, Sera. Come on, Mistress of Bloodshed. Think, damn you!

I howl in pain as I try to grasp a way out. My wings attempt to bat out of their hands, to no avail. Their strength is an unmoving force as they restrain the strongest joints of my body. I grunt as I push past the pain and into the depths of my training.

Dome. Dome. Dome.

A feral growl escapes me as the claws dig deeper. The pointed tips burrow into the meat and brush against the delicate bones within. The fabric beneath my leathered armor turns damp as warm blood leaks down my back. I throw my hands out and up toward the sky and a shield of violet follows. It encases us in a dome to lock the few Drannar in my proximity in with me.

I pant as I look for Asher, only to find him a few feet away. He pauses in his bloodshed for only a moment, and his face pales from outside of my protective bubble. A Drannar rushes him, and his focus is pulled back as he spears the Drannar through the gut. Bringing his blade up from navel to neck, he splits the disgusting creature in half, allowing the guts and innards to spill on the ground before it falls in a lifeless slump. Elf blood flies through the air as he spins at another that comes for him. Slicing through another throat, he sidesteps the dead being to make quick work of the distance separating us before standing helplessly against the dome.

My mouth opens to release a scream in the enclosed space I've locked around me. The tones are deafening as they devour the confined space, causing the Drannars to clap their hands over their pointed ears.

All but the ones at my wings. They seem to have a death wish.

Crossing my arms over my chest and reaching behind me, I grab the handles of the swords strapped to my spine. Unsheathing them causes a metallic song to ring through the air. And as the blades are released, metal meets bone. The hands of the elves restraining me become severed from their bodies.

The tension on my wings frees and I shake them out to rid myself of the still connected hands. Small drops of blood paint the inside of the dome as I regain my bearings.

Taking the chance while I have it, I spin against the ground with my wings splayed, allowing the talons to sink through their soft bellies. The vile scent of organ meat and innards consumes the inside of the dome as they all slump lifelessly against the walls. The forcefield slowly retreats from above me to sink into the earth, allowing the dead bodies to fall with it. Metal pings sound off around me as their staffs hit the ground beside them.

My breath comes out in quick bursts as my knees drop to the ground. I reach back to slide my blades into their scabbards as I look to Asher, who eyes me in paralyzed fear. His pale skin is damp with blood, dirt, and sweat as he surveys me. Purple tugs at his green irises for a moment before it retreats.

Good boy, Asher-darling.

I look into the dark trees of the forest behind him, where more colored lightning and flashes of fire break through the dense foliage. Drannars have breached the tree line, only to be mowed down by the influx of warriors that have made their way to The Portal.

Drops of blue gore drip from his hair as his chest heaves. His fearful gaze connect with mine as his lips curl in a soft smile and he releases a relieved sigh.

Such a good boy, I remind myself.

But soon, power pricks against my skin, causing the hairs on my neck to rise.

Wrong. Something is wrong. All wrong.

"Bruthar sends his regards," a graveled voice brushes against my ear from behind me. A violent thrum vibrates the delicate bones of my wings as I register the words.

But that's the last thing I remember.

That and the silver staff that was thrust through my chest.

But the feeling of being without her, even in those few moments, felt like my soul was collapsing. As if the very fabric of my universe was being torn to shreds in front of me.

Chapter 26

The Infirmary

Asher

Two Weeks Later

I haven't left her side since I brought her to The Keep.

The elf… Drannar… Whatever the fuck those monsters were, glamoured themselves just long enough to stay out of my sight. By the time I realized what happened, it was too late.

The few moments of sleep that have taken over me these weeks have been wracked with visions of that day. The sound of her flesh ripping. The blood that snaked in crimson rivers down her armor. The confused contortion of her features. The slack of her jaw as she registered what happened. The slow tilt of her head as her sight connected with the weapon impaling her.

The gurgled chokes that gripped at her throat.

Her body… her strong, unmoving frame tumbling into the dirt before me.

The crushing agony that consumed my own chest.

Seraphina had fallen on her sword, so to speak.

Before I could even conjure tangible thought, I had moved. The heft of my dagger in my palm and the pound of my boots in the grass as I charged the being with a fury unlike anything I'd ever experienced. The sound of his own gurgled chokes as I struck my blade across his throat with no more than a glance, my gaze had been glued to the unconscious Sera. He fell to the ground in a crumpled heap of blood before my resolve crumpled beside him; beside *her*.

I still remember the flaps of wings around me as birds left their trees, shaken from the branches by my screams.

Her body was so light, but carrying her back to Gnox, she felt so heavy.

I ran as fast as I could, then we charged through the woods at a speed I didn't know Gnox was capable of; but I sensed he felt my pain.

I dropped her at the foot of The Keep, screaming for help from the guards protecting it. They rushed her in because I couldn't fly up to the entry.

I failed. I fucking failed again. I let my guard down. I let Sera down.

The words were on replay as they hauled her away.

But those elves. Their rabid eyes and the way they cut down anything in their path, especially the succs.

Whatever souls they may have possessed left long ago. You could see it in the way they fought. They were hungry for one thing and one thing only.

Power. Unrelenting power.

Selene passed me on my way out of the forest, and I was informed later she had secured The Portal with a dome.

It wouldn't be able to hold for long, so in Seraphina's stead, she placed a massive number of guards and extra protective seals in the area, at least until The Stone stabilized enough for the wards to come up. They were only down for a little while, but that was still far too much time.

It only further proved why I need to stay here.

If they could knock down these powerful succs with ease, who is to say Vesperholm isn't next? Our people are already weakened. The hunters wouldn't stand a chance against these beings. They don't even *know* these things fucking exist.

The damage to Tantalia was minimal, only losing the guards around The Portal.

But it only heightened the threat.

I had no idea what rage took over me in the moments that rushed by when Gnox and I approached Celestial Keep.

My only thought was to save her.

Save her. She can't die. Save her! SAVE HER!

My heart had been pounding with an urgency I'd never experienced. The fear of losing her so great, I don't remember what happened after they took her away, my mind was a flurry of my own misgivings.

I have been here with her in The Infirmary, waiting for her to wake up. I can't bear to leave her side.

I've brushed her hair every day and I've made sure she's clean as she heals. I've helped the nurses change her dressings.

The nurses have brought me food, and I've told Seraphina stories of my childhood. How I grew up learning how to fight and hunt in the forest, how to hold a blade.

I remember bringing my dagger out to tell her about it and how it came into my possession. How, when I was old enough, my father saw something in me and entrusted me to carry it. The ruby set within its hilt would shimmer against my line of sight every so often, and the gem on her neck would pulse in response.

A peculiar thing, considering I had never seen it glow like that before.

The mistresses say the magic imbued in the Drannar's staffs is strong, causing her wounds to heal slower than she normally would. But she would make it. He had miscalculated his stab, missing her heart entirely.

I don't even *understand* this reaction; why this paralyzing fear overcame every bit of my being.

I don't love Seraphina. I don't even know if I entirely like her.

But the feeling of being without her, even in those few moments, felt like my soul was collapsing. As if the very fabric of my universe was being torn to shreds in front of me.

An implosion that sucked the air out of the world, in its entirety.

I've sat here for weeks, contemplating the reaction, looking through any and every reason why that could even be a possibility.

And every time, I come up empty.

But I can't leave her. Even if I try, even if I don't want to be in this stupid room watching her heal, I can't leave.

Something is keeping me here to make sure she wakes up.

Now, here, she rests.

She has been rousing more, as of late.

But still, she sleeps. She heals.

Asher from weeks prior would be thrilled. This is the perfect time to leave. My collar has been rendered useless by her lack of consciousness, and I am *technically* free.

But I can't... I must stay with her.

I watch her chest rise and fall slowly, as the bright sun shines through the window to reflect off the dagger I spin in my hand when a voice pulls me back to the cold stoned walls I've holed myself in. Purple begins to glow from the outside of my vision as tension begins to wrap around my throat.

"Asher," Seraphina says softly. It's meek, small.

Not at all like the Seraphina I know.

My hand sheaths my dagger to my thigh as I scramble to the edge of the bed. My drumming heart pounds against my chest as I breathe the biggest sigh of relief knowing she's awake.

Seraphina. Sera. Mistress.

"Hey, it's alright, I'm here," I whisper softly as I take her hand into mine. I rub my thumb softly across her knuckles as I peer at her face. Her features contort in a grimace as she stirs.

Seraphina groans as her head slowly turns toward me.

Her eyes blink slowly as she wakes more, offering a small smile. "They stabbed me," she says gently. Her voice is crackled, I imagine from not speaking for so long.

"Yeah, yeah they did," I respond.

"Did you kill them?"

"With pleasure."

She smiles weakly, "That's my good boy."

My eyes widen as my cock jerks to life.

Not now, asshole.

I glance around the room to distract me, my gaze landing on the small glass of water beside her. Grasping the cup, I bring it to her lips, letting her take a renewing sip. I clear my throat as I shake my head and place the cup back down, "How do you feel?"

She swallows the water with a small wince before she takes a deep breath, "My chest hurts. But I think I'll be okay. How long have I been out?" Her voice is less raspy now.

"Uhm… It's been about a fortnight…" I say gently.

She gives me a sideways smile, "I could use the rest."

I smile at her quick wit. Since I've known her, she's always been fast on the draw. But my heart sinks as I remember the reason she's here in the first place.

I look down at her hands, stroking the soft, delicate skin, "The wards… is it my fault they fell?"

Seraphina eyes my action amidst her flesh before her head turns to look out the window. "There's no way to tell," she whispers.

My brow furrows as my head drops against the bed in defeat, "I'm so sorry," I respond.

"Even if it was your fault, there's no way you could have known that would happen. I surely don't blame you. You would have died before we left The Crypt."

I give a soft chuckle. "Mistress Kalinda has been running things in your stead. But… The Court isn't happy. At least from the information I've been getting from Gideon."

"You haven't gone to The Pits?" she asks as her eyes come to meet mine in confusion.

A lightness eases through my soul at her reaction. She would be concerned about The Legion's even through her pain.

A smile tugs at my lips as I watch her, "I'm the Queen's Commander. I'm here to protect you," I respond.

I would have been here whether I wanted to or not. But I can't let her know that I couldn't bear to leave.

I smile, bringing her hand to my lips to press a kiss to the top of it.

The scent of her skin awakens me, stitching me anew. My heart slowly fills at the sound of her voice, damaged as it may be.

Seraphina is quiet as she watches me, "I dreamed."

"About what?"

"Lilith… She told me things. I don't remember. She spoke of… Caelestia. And a compendium."

My brow furrows as I listen to her, "Is she saying there's a book in The Keep that could help us?"

"I don't know. There are grimoires I've read, of course. Textbooks and history tomes I've been forced to indulge in. But I've never heard of this compendium. Lilith never mentioned such a thing."

As much as I would like to be of use, I'm about as helpful as a dry rag in an orgy.

Seraphina looks back at the window. A sparkling silver tear rolls down her cheek.

My brow furrows as the drops turn to streams, "What's wrong?" I ask softly, leaning closer to her.

"I can't be Queen, Asher," Seraphina murmurs.

"Why do you think that?"

"The Drannar came in… Lapis Amoretstra went down. I can't reach the Realm of Mages. All of it. I have failed at every single turn. I don't know what else I can do. This is why I didn't want to step up in the first place. Lilith would have never let this happen," she says. Her voice drips with the same sentiment her tears do. Her neck tightens as she attempts to hold her ground against her own worst enemy.

Herself.

Since I've arrived here, she's echoed this fear. But I couldn't disagree more.

My hand tightens around hers as I listen, and soft sniffles come from her as her tears continue to streak down her face, running down her throat to soak the front of her gown.

"Seraphina… I don't know anything about Lilith. I don't know how she ruled Tantalia. But you are the only one here I've seen that leads with true grit. If you were in Vesperholm, I'd have you lead my people. You train the soldiers every day, and you can't blame yourself for The Stone. But we will fix it," I say gently.

Maybe a month or so ago, I would have told her these words to get her to treat me better; to get on her good side so I could take her down.

But, with the arrival of the Drannar and seeing first-hand what they're capable of, Seraphina had been right this entire time.

I have no choice.

I have to save their people if I have any chance of saving mine.

Their might is far too much to handle without the succubus. If there is a threat that they could come into Vesperholm, what little people left would perish. My mother, my father, my unborn sibling, all of them.

Seraphina continues to stare out the window, "We will surely try."

"The Caelestial Compendium is a tome from ages past. It recounts the meaning of the stone and how it works."

CHAPTER 27

THE CAELESTIAL COMPENDIUM

SERAPHINA

One Week Later

Bright light tugs at my eyelids as I awake in this bed once again. It's been seven days since I had first awoken from whatever dreamlike state I was in, but every day here is a day farther away from saving Tantalia.

I've tried on numerous occasions to convince the nurses I was fit to go back to my post, but they declined, instead saying I needed "to rest" and "to heal."

Ridiculous.

Asher has not left my side, except to use the bathroom every so often. There isn't much we say to each other. Most of the time he appears to be in his head, mulling over one thing or the next. Sometimes he flips a small coin in his fingers, or he stares at it in contemplation before he pushes it back into his pocket.

But here he sits, even now, asleep in the small leather armchair with his cloak draped over his body to keep him warm.

I must admit, the sight is endearing. And fulfilling.

I have asked him to leave several times, to experience the air outside for me. He too, refused my requests.

What's the point of being Queen if no one follows my orders?

I do wonder if I should point him in the right direction for the reason I imagine causes his grief. But if he hasn't come to that conclusion on his own, I mustn't push him, as much as I would like to.

I, myself, am getting impatient at his lack of awareness, but I imagine most human men are like that.

Two Weeks Later

Healing took much longer than I would have liked, and coming back to *my* kingdom was rage inducing.

Kalinda had done absolutely nothing, and the soldiers were off kilter in my absence. Selene did the best she could, but they got sloppy.

An absolute pity. Their wings became their enemies. Their tails caused their downfall. All of it.

Especially Cometa Legion.

Selene is a fighter, but she's no warrior, and she certainly can't lead them the way I do.

Standing here, I feel a hint of trepidation. My people look to me as a strong and steadfast leader. But inside I'm flaying at the seams with the weight of this task.

I may *not* be fit to rule. Letting the Drannar breach our portals felt as though I had brought the blade down on Lilith myself.

The inadequacy of my failures hurt more than the wound in my chest. I sat for a long time in that bed, looking out the window, listening to Asher and my breathing, mulling over my own options.

I reluctantly accepted the sentiment I had echoed to Asher several times over.

I had no choice but to truly step into my rule. I had made the decision to be Queen. But I haven't yielded to the idea I am fit enough for it.

That decision was only made more apparent when Asher and I came down to The Pits today to see my strongest warriors out of sync. Their movements sloppy, their strikes lazy.

They had gotten lax in the time I was gone. But that ends today.

They will all grovel under my boot.

Even if I don't feel like a Queen, I need to act like one, at least to imbue confidence in the people around me.

With security increased at the portal, the Drannars fell back and we were able to keep them at bay.

For now.

The small hoard of them proved to have dire consequence. What happened if fifty came in? A hundred of them? A thousand?

They're just seeing what we have, waiting for the perfect time to strike.

They don't realize the being that sits on the throne now.

Lilith ruled with her heart.

But my rage moves me forward every single day, and I'll be damned two times over if I were to let them slaughter my people once more.

Eventually, Asher and I go to the The Court of Mistresses, bringing all of the noble house leaders to discuss what I wanted to ask.

"General. Such a quaint surprise to hear you calling for us," Kalinda muses from her spot at the end of the table.

I seethe with anger as I look at her.

So quick to place a Queen, yet so quick to let our people fall in my absence.

I stand tall against the ladies that sit around the table, my wings held high to command their attention, "What is the Compendium?" I ask no one in particular.

The ladies of The Court all look to one another, their eyes questioning as no one speaks.

"The Caelestial Compendium?" Kalinda asks.

My brow furrows as I peer at her, "Whatever Compendium you may know to exist, what is it?" I respond.

"The Caelestial Compendium is a tome from ages past. It recounts the meaning of The Stone and how it works," Kalinda states plainly.

That fucking bitch.

I lean against the table, challenging her with an irked glare. "Is there a reason you didn't want to come forth with this information prior, Mistress?" I grit through my teeth.

"It was lost to the Drannars during the massacre, retrieving it meant peril for whomever were to seek it. I imagined in Lilith's stead you would take the throne and find a method on your own," Kalinda retorts.

My lips curl in a snarl as I listen to her.

"Why hadn't Lilith gone to retrieve it? Surely, she would have had the might to breach their defenses?" I grit. My eyes pin into her in anger as I realize her inability to help.

"Why would she? Lilith composed The Compendium," Mistress Kalinda states matter-of-factly.

My eyes widen and my body stills against the table. My heart pounds an unsteady rhythm in my chest.

Lilith did reach out to me in my dream… It was really her.

"Lilith didn't need The Compendium. She knew how The Stone worked. She was the one who anchored The Stone and invoked it's wards all those years ago," Kalinda explains.

My mind starts to run as Kalinda goes on.

"She had kept it guarded, duly so. Something as powerful as The Compendium would need to be. Once she invoked the wards and anchored it, she hid it for safekeeping. However, there was a piece to The Stone that only Lilith knew about and only she was capable of finding. She kept it close to her, not revealing it to even me. She just needed to find it," she continues.

I sit back in the tall black throne, my body slumping into its contours as my mind continues to run… and *run.*

She wrote The Compendium? She knew what she needed and yet couldn't find it? Why didn't she tell anyone what needed to be found? Why didn't she tell anyone about The Compendium? Why didn't she tell me about it?

My eyes drift to the table as I absorb the news thrown at me.

Asher stands next to the exit of The Court, and I connect with his gaze from across the room.

He looks at me curiously, his head tilting with a questioning expression, as if to ask what the matter is.

I shake my head, and he nods in understanding.

"I have to find The Compendium," I murmur to myself.

"Seraphina, you cannot! The Compendium is in The Never Realm. It'd be a suicide mission," my mother says as she stands from her chair to place her hands against the table.

"What choice do I have, mother? There is no one I can send that could get through there and survive. And we need The Compendium if *we* are to survive," I tell her.

"Seraphina, I FORBID it!" she growls.

"Mother, you lost your say when you sacrificed your child for the kingdom. You ALL lost your say when none of you decided to step up to the challenge and threw me on the sword to die in your stead," I tell the rest of The Court as I stand again.

I survey the ladies, their heads bowed in submission as they heed my words.

"Seraphina. This mission has not been approved by The Court. Find a new avenue."

"Shove it, Kalinda," I tell her as I round the table toward the large, white doors where Asher stands.

He leans to the handle, pressing it open for me to exit. I see him give a small nod to Selene's lapdog as he follows me into the hallway.

Thick steps echo off the tall ceilings as I make my way down the staircase, heading straight for The Library.

"So, The Compendium..." Asher says quietly.

"It's real. And we are going to find it," I respond as we hit the bottom of the stairs, taking another long hallway.

"Seraphina, they said you couldn't. You are still healing, and who knows what more the Drannars have done since their attack? What if they have more guards at their portal? How do you think we're ever going to get through?" Asher asks.

"I have an idea. But we are going to need Selene and her dog," I tell him quickly.

The doors to The Library come into view but are blocked as Asher's large body halts in front of me. My face contorts in annoyance as I tilt my head up to look at him.

"Sera…" he sighs as he stops me. A frustrated, tortured pinch pulls at his brow as he takes a deep breath and gazes off beside him. As if he's finding the words to say to me.

My eyebrow arches in curiosity.

He's never called me that before.

"I don't know what we're walking in to, and I know I said I would be your guard. But I can't…" he sighs in frustration, "I don't know if I can lose you again."

Intrigue tugs at my eyebrows as I listen to his admission.

"When you were stabbed… I felt like the fabric of my universe fell into the depths of the sea. Like everything I had ever known was set ablaze in front of me. I… I can't do that again," he says nervously as his eyes fall to the floor beside me.

My head tilts as I watch him, "Are you in love with me?"

Asher's green eyes connect with mine in quizzical confusion, "I can hardly say that I love you. I'm not even entirely sure what that feels like. But whatever happened at The Portal, it needs to never happen again."

His eyes almost plead with me, and I can see how genuinely the instance hurt him.

The poor soul.

I smile, caressing his cheek with a loving thumb, "Dear Asher," I sigh tenderly.

Asher melts against my palm, giving me a sweet smile in return as he nuzzles into my skin.

I shove his head to move him from my path and his body stumbles to the side as I continue on my mission, walking into the leather scented room ahead.

"Gods damnit, Seraphina," I hear Asher grumble from behind me as his steps echo with vigor to catch up with me.

The smoke from the fired balls attacks my senses as I descend into The Library and Asher takes his normal seat.

He knows what to do by now, and his compliance makes my heart sing.

As I make my way to the darkened inner shelves, looking over the spines, voices start talking around me.

The *books* are calling to me.

I look when I hear Drannars mentioned amongst the rabble.

Turning toward the shelf, my eyes roam the spines.

Queenskinhusksportalrealmlivediehalfhumandeadpower.

Drannar. Drannar. Elf. Elf. Dark. Never. Portal.

My eyes lock onto a large black tome that speaks of the knowledge I seek, bound in a thick leather case. My eyebrow pricks with curiosity as I snap, the tome disappearing, leaving an open space along the shelf.

Another voice rambles through my mind as I turn to the shelf below it.

Portalrealmpocketmageportalwizardpockettimefartreatyresistancegone.

I decide to take that tome with me as well.

With a smooth jolt, I am sitting in the chair across from Asher, and he lets out a sharp hiss as he startles.

"Fuck, stop with that, will you!?" he groans as he runs a hand through his thick brown hair in angst.

Oh wah.

I roll my eyes as I grab the large black book from under the tome about mages.

Lifting the cover and turning to the first few pages, I scan over the text. The script is one I have to concentrate on to understand. From our knowledge, there is only the one portal to The Never Realm. And that is also what this book says.

However --

"What is it?" Asher asks as he watches me.

He must notice my confused expression as I look at him, and I note the concerned furrow of his brow.

"We have to go to The Realm of Mages again…" I sigh softly.

"We tried that already. It was a dead end," he responds.

"There is tale of the mages having access to the other realms, by use of their own magic," I explain.

I set my gaze on him, and he tilts his head in question.

I sigh, "Mages in general, aren't magical beings, they are only well versed in the use of it. Spells and the like. Succubus, elves, *we* have magic. We *are* magic. Mages merely study and wield it."

Asher looks down at the book with a frustrated brow.

The scent of aged parchment assaults my senses as my head drops to the page below.

I can't fucking do this.

It feels like one instance after another, and it wears on me. It eats at me that I keep thrusting myself into perilous situations, only for The Fates to fuck with me. Every time I try to go by the book, it bites me in the ass.

How could Lilith possibly think that burying my head in books would help me be Queen for a reality I never sought to make real?

"Asher…" I sigh softly.

It's silent for a few moments before he speaks, "What was Lilith like?"

I look up at him in confusion, peering into his eyes, "Why do you ask?"

"I'm not entirely sure. She came to mind, and I was curious about her," he responds gently.

Peculiar.

"Lilith was… everything. She ruled for hundreds of years, and we loved her. She was *our* everything. She brought us back from The Jilted Massacre. She trained us all and never did it for anyone but her people," I say softly as visions of Lilith dance around my head.

"Sera. Come on, one more time. Root your feet, face me. Hips tight." I hear her voice in the background of the vision. The dirt of the pit scratched under my boots as we went through another defensive maneuver. The same one we've practiced for several weeks.

My arms hurt, my legs hurt, my wings are bruised and if I had to pivot one more time I would have lost it.

"Lilith, this is stupid. Why do I have to keep doing this?" my voice rings through the memory.

"Because I will not always be here to guard you. I will not always be here to lead you. You have to be willing to lead yourself, Seraphina. The same as you would our people," Lilith responded.

I hmphed in return, "Lilith, you'll always be Queen. Who do you think would sit your throne, if not you?" I asked as I squared my hips again, planting my feet firm in the worn spots of ground.

Lilith gave me a gentle smile, a remorseful look contorted her features, "You, dear Sera. You shall sit the throne," she had responded.

I scoffed, "There's no way I'd ever usurp you. I can't lead the people," I told her as I adjusted my wings, pinning them tight to keep my balance in check.

Lilith smiled once more before she carried on with the lesson.

I come back to focus, staring down at the inked pages of this ancient book, and I realize now what she had been trying to say. She wouldn't always be here. I was too young and naive to see it.

Too blind.

Too narrow sighted to see what she meant.

Lilith had always meant for me to rule. That has to count for something. That, out of all the succubus in Tantalia, I was the one she chose to pick up her crown when it had fallen.

A silver tear drips down my cheek, and I wipe it away as I come to look at Asher.

So, I let her feed from me. My own pleasure comes from watching her enjoy herself.

CHAPTER 28

CARE
ASHER

My heart pounds as I listen to Seraphina, but it also breaks bit by bit. I know what it's like to have the world on your shoulders with everyone around you getting in the way.

She tries so hard, all the time, to show her strength to these demons, and they decline her with every chance she takes. Even though they were the ones to put her there in the first place.

It's not fair.

It wasn't fair for me, and it certainly isn't fair to her.

I may not know what it's like to be forced to be Queen of an entire people, but I know what it's like to want to save them on my own. To be the strongest there is and everyone around you, either has no drive to help, or stop you when you want to do something about it.

It's… frustrating, and I find myself connecting with her more now than I have in my entire time here thus far.

Her stress causes my own emotions to sink, and I lean in to place my hand against her neck. Slowly, I thread my fingers back farther, tangling into her hair and pulling her in for a deep kiss. She lets out a soft moan as she complies, melting into the kiss with me.

Her taste is sweet, decadent.

Sinful.

I pull back for a moment, looking in her gorgeous purple eyes, searching them. This tug in my chest pulls fervently against my soul,

309

urging me into her orbit. "Let me take care of you," I rasp. The skin of her jaw is soft from where my thumb rubs against it.

"How?" she asks in a low tone.

"Take us to your room," I whisper.

She smiles as she leans in, giving in deeper to our kiss. Her fingers snap, echoing in The Library for a quick moment, before the scent of smoke and leather is replaced by the floral breeze of her bedroom.

I lean back from the kiss to look in her eyes once again, they shine with promise, with trust.

I take her hand as I back up to the bed, climbing on and pulling her into my lap. Her smile tilts as she settles onto me, wrapping her strong legs around my hips.

I sink into the luxurious fabric as my arms snake around her, pressing her firmly against me. The comfort of her touch, and the security of her weight as she settles into my lap, causes my soul to ascend to bliss. My heart slows and her taste echoes through my being as I swipe my tongue across hers.

The leather of her breeches against mine gives way to her velvety skin as our clothes shimmer from our bodies in a hazy purple glow. Her skin glides under my fingers as I come around to stroke at her back, making sure not to graze her wings.

Her generous breasts squish into my chest and her nipples harden against me. It causes blood to rush directly to my cock, swelling and throbbing under her.

The solid length presses against her cunt as her tongue dives deeper into my mouth. Her clawed hands graze the hard muscles of my back gently as she melts into my embrace.

Leathery skin spooks me as my fingers graze the base of her wings and she shudders softly. "Ah, I'm so sorry," I apologize quickly as my hands drift to her lower back.

Seraphina pulls away to smile at me, "Shhh, I'll show you," she whispers. Her arms snake from around my neck to reach for my hands.

Bringing them up, her wings flare behind her, displaying their massive width.

Ever so gently, she brings my hand to the cresting bones that make up their length, sliding them along the delicate webbing. I pay careful attention to the pressure as I stroke over them and a deep moan leaks into the air; her body trembling in pleasure against me.

Her pleasure causes my cock to harden more, pulsing with urgency as I feel her cunt warm and soaked against it.

I remove my hand from her wings to bring it down to my shaft, moving it just enough to tease her entrance. The head presses into her core, and she lets out another moan as her hands grip at my shoulders. The sharp points pierce my skin in an exciting combination of pain and pleasure.

"Asher," she breathes into the air as she slowly lowers herself onto me.

I groan in response as I grasp her hips, peering up at her face. The muscles relax and her head falls back as she soaks in the feeling of me inside of her.

"There you go angel, use me," I rasp, my gaze unable to break away as she loses herself.

I don't know where angel came from. All I know is that it's exactly what she looks like in this moment.

Seraphina seemed so distraught about her predicament, and I just want to take her worries away in the only way I know how. At least when it comes to succubus.

So, I let her feed from me. My own pleasure comes from watching her enjoy herself.

Her warm, tight cunt grips my length as she takes all of me, my concentration on her starting to fray as I drown in the sensation.

The moonlight bathes her in an even more ethereal glow as her body shimmers with pleasure and calm.

Her hips move up and down on me, taking slow, deliberate strokes as she feasts.

The way she looks in this moment, letting go of her worries, giving in to her wants and renewing herself with me, causes my pulse to echo in my ears and I groan in pure passion as I watch her.

Her skin glistens with beads of iridescent sweat as she takes every ounce of my pleasure that I can offer, anything I can to make her feel good.

I've never seen her glow like this. This feeling of being fed from is usually so draining, but this feels revitalizing. Like an exchange more than a siphon.

The fullness in my chest causes me to spill into her without warning, filling her with my lust before I even have a moment to think. She presses all of me into her, all the way to the hilt as she feels me trembling against her walls. Her fanged grin shines as she pants, relishing in the speed at which I'd finished in her. The way she destroyed me so quickly. I search her eyes before I wrap my hand around the back of her neck, pulling her mouth onto mine and pressing her back onto the bed.

"Asher, wh-" she tries to say, but I cut off her question with a deep kiss. Her moan is muffled as she melts into the bed.

"I'm taking care of you, Sera," I whisper as I kiss her again, pressing my lips down her jaw and chin. I trail the kisses down her neck, to her collarbone, they continue down her chest until I reach one of her perfect tits. Bringing one into my mouth, I flick my tongue over a hardened nipple. There's no split this time as I gently tug and suck at the flesh, taking my time to savor the taste of her skin.

My other hand comes up to grip at her other breast, palming it as I continue with the one in my mouth. Her moans continue to ring through the room as I release her nipple with a soft *pop*, and kiss down the rest of her body.

Seraphina's skin feels like heaven against my lips, as I press them against her tight stomach, and down her hips, slowly making my way to her center with a trail of little kisses.

I linger on the sight of her perfect cunt, and the way that it drips with the both of us. Seeing it drives me mad with need, but I try to contain myself, so I press more kisses to the bare patch of skin above her core. Kissing around it and down the inside of her thighs, I slither down her body to rest myself in between her legs. Taking the back of her knees into my palms, I press her legs up and out, opening her cunt for me.

Pulsing, sore and aching for a release, my tongue dips into her. Relishing in the taste of our mixed lust, I drag my tongue up to her clit and press slow circles around it. Her back bows as her moans get louder and bounce off of the stone walls surrounding us with a vengeance. Desperate claws grip for purchase against my scalp, bringing me deeper. Our taste consumes my mind as I lap and devour her core like it's my last night alive.

Soon, her tail writhes beside me, poking me in the ribs, and I jolt as I look up at her.

Her eyes connect with me in half-lidded, hazy lust and she pants, "Show me your cock."

My eyebrow arches as I continue licking at her core, but I comply. Curling my body, I bring my lower half up just enough to relieve it from the bed, baring my cock to her.

The sharp, spaded tip of her tail drags along my side, down my body before the length of it wraps around my cock, tugging softly.

Ooooooh fuck.

The pleasure that courses through me as she pumps me with her tail causes me to harden with a rapid fury. My tongue delves deeper into her center, and I can't help the moans I lick into her.

Her tail moves faster around my length. And my eyes roll back at the sensation, trying so hard to focus on her cunt. I bring myself to her clit, sucking it into my lips and swirling my tongue around it.

I feel the pressure building again as she continues, her body begin-ning to tense as she gets closer. I release one of her legs to press my fingers into her soaked core, pumping them in and out.

Feeling her cunt tighten against me, I hear her ethereal cry into the night as she jumps off the cliff and into the sea of pleasure. My own groans, as I spill myself over her sheets, dance against her cunt. Her body vibrates and shudders against me with a vibrant glow as she continues to feed, feasting to her heart's content on my own excitement for her pleasure.

She writhes as she comes up for air, riding out the waves against my face. Slowly, the waves settle, and her body relaxes. I take long, languished laps at her core, cleaning her with every stroke of my tongue.

I gently stroke the soft skin of her thighs and stomach as my head falls against her leg, my own breathing slows as I relax against her.

I look up at her with not an ounce of energy, watching her come down.

Sera stares at the ceiling above as she regains herself before a moment later, she looks down at me with a satisfied grin.

I slither back up her body, resting beside her with my arm around her waist as she strokes my hair. I settle into the feeling of her flesh melding with my own. The way she makes my heartbeat slow, and the way the world around me fades into nothing with her.

All this with the succubus I aimed to kill only months ago. The way I've descended into this realm is jarring. The way I've fallen into her arms of my own volition, even more so. But I would trade everything to feel this level of peace and bliss for the rest of my life, with her.

Even with all the emotions coursing through me, I can't say I love her. That would be presumptuous.

But… I do feel a little bit more complete.

It's a risk. A huge, massive risk, with a menagerie of repercussions.

CHAPTER 29

THE NEVER REALM

SERAPHINA

"Sera, are you out of your fucking mind!?" Selene whispers aggressively at me as she attempts to stay quiet in the confines of my room.

I have called Selene and her guard into my room to discuss my plans.

After Asher and I spent the night enjoying each other, I was renewed with clarity and confidence. I knew now what I needed to do, no matter how perilous it may seem.

I'm tired of going by the book, I'm tired of tiptoeing around the mistresses.

I'm going to break into the fucking Never Realm. Sure, the Realm of Mages may have access to other portals, but *we* have one and I can go in and out of it as I please.

So, I will.

Unfortunately, I can't do it with Asher and myself alone.

Selene's lapdog and Asher sit on my bed, damn-near in a wrestling match as they shove and grab at each other like baby halflings.

Our full sacks lay against my bed where they await our retrieval.

My armored forearms scrape against my scaled chest plate as my arms cross and I pin Selene with a violet glare, "I can't tell The Court of my adventures, and I need backup in case things go south. Not to mention, there are too many guards at the portal, I need a distraction."

"This is a suicide mission. I don't side with The Court on much but *that* is true," Selene responds.

"I'm the Queen. The position that you all so desperately forced upon me. So, I'm going to be the Queen," I tell her with a shrug. Turning around, I grab a small leather bag that lays against my pack, I secure it around my waist before I take the extra leather band and wrap it around my thigh.

Asher stands after shoving Gideon from him, leaning over to grab his pack from the floor and haul it on his back. He takes the time to adjust its straps as the weight settles on him.

"And you?! You're just letting this happen?" Selene asks Asher as she throws her arms out in defeat.

Asher straightens up after situating his bag and looks at Selene with a quizzical expression, "Since when do I have a say in what she does?"

Selene's gaze comes to connect with mine, and I nod in understanding.

"When will you finally get your head out of your ass, boy?" Selene sighs as she shakes her head.

Asher's face twists in confusion as he registers her words, "I'm still lost," he mumbles.

"You will be until you accept your reality," Selene shrugs.

Asher's eyes roll and he groans in annoyance, "You crazy demons and your fucking bullshit," he mumbles almost inaudibly as he strides to the door with heavy steps.

Selene's little pet scurries over to her as Asher makes to leave, wrapping his arms around her waist and nuzzling her neck softly.

"Let's go, we're going to graft to the outskirts, then I'll have you distract the guards while Asher and I sneak in through the front of the portal," I tell Selene as I follow Asher out the door.

"Well, what the fuck do we tell The Court?! What if you're gone for too long or captured?" she asks.

"First things first, you don't tell The Court *anything*. Secondly," I hand Selene a small amethyst, "I've connected my magic and this stone to each other, if for some reason I'm in trouble, I'll send a little glow."

Selene flips the rock in her hand as she looks it, her gaze coming back to connect with mine in sheer disbelief, "You've got to be fucking kidding me."

"But alas," I laugh.

Selene grabs Gideon's arm with an annoyed roll of her eyes, before I grab Asher's and the four of us blink. Instantly, we've grafted to the forest outside of The Never Realm portal. We slink down in the trees as we watch a plethora of winged warriors stand guard outside of the now purple portal.

"Seraphina, I can't let you do this," Selene begs.

"*It's been decided,*" I echo The Court's words in a mocking tone as I watch the guards. The massive meat pillars pace the grass outside of The Portal, sometimes engaging in some kind of play fighting as they protect the space. "Okay, I'm sending you first. Once you hear the warble from the portal, I'll be in."

I peer at Asher from the corner of my eye, who cautiously scans the meadow.

His intense, green gaze comes to connect with mine, and he gives me a smile before he nods in determination.

Selene and her dog exit the woods to chat with the warriors, their attention all turns to her as they approach.

"Okay, now's our chance," I whisper to Asher, and grip his muscled forearm. A blink, and we've grafted behind the warriors, taking quiet, careful steps up to the portal.

My boot lands on a small twig outside of the portal. The sound is unnaturally loud as it snaps and alerts the guards. A soldier in the group turns around to stare at Asher and me with wide eyes. "General?!" the warrior asks.

But I don't hear the commotion that happens next, as Asher and I step through the glowing purple curtain.

"You good?" Asher's voice is hushed in the small chamber. His chest heaves in short bursts as he surveys the mess we've had to make.

His face is speckled with blue blood, and the bodies of two Drannars lay dead at our feet.

While I expected there to be guards on the other side of the portal, I didn't expect for there to only be two.

Asher and I made quick work of them, subduing them and then eventually silencing them.

I crouch to raid their bodies for anything of value, including their uniforms. I relieve the elves of their clothing, throwing one of the coats at Asher for him to put on and grab one for myself.

"Yes, I'm good," I pant in return as I shrug on one of their jackets. Taking a deep breath, I run my hands over my body, and the air shudders as my wings shrink into my spine. I look down at my hands and they begin to darken to an ashen blue-gray as my claws slowly retract into my fingers. I shake out my body as my figure thins, finally completing my transformation.

I've glamoured myself as a Drannar for the time being, but with the magic here being so unstable, I don't have as much time to get this job done as I would like.

I grab Asher's shoulders and spin him around to fish out a bundle of cloth from the sack on his back.

I turn him around and shove the cloth into his hands, "Put this on, quick."

"What is this?" he asks as he looks over it.

"Last night, I took your commander's cloak and imbued it with glamour," I tell him as I continue raiding the limp bodies for weapons or other tell-tale Drannar memorabilia.

He shakes the cloak out and throws it around his shoulders, securing it with the metal clasp. As he surveys the metal clasp with a face of longing, his body morphs and his limbs lengthen. His body slims and he stretches in height as the cloak glamours him. Ruby red eyes peer at me as his own transformation finishes.

"We don't have much time, the magic here is thin. I can feel the grip on this form wavering the longer we stay here. We have to find the Compendium and leave," I tell him as we ascend the steep brick staircase. The only light is the dim flickering fire that comes from a small space in the door at the top of the stairs.

The portal to The Never Realm is apparently in their main castle -- Onyx Citadel.

I've never been to The Never Realm. I don't know much about it other than what I have learned from Lilith. She used to frequent here often.

But from what I was able to gather in my studies on this realm, The Onyx Citadel is where their nobles live, same as in Celestial Keep.

Though instead of sharing what magic they possess, they keep it for the elves in higher standing, teaching what they know to only the ones rich enough for it. That has always been the case for the Drannars.

This land is heavy with the scent of decay. The air is damp and thick as we ascend the steps. Our boots echo as they bounce off the narrow walls of the staircase until we reach a metal door at the top, bars through the small window in the center allow us to see through to the other side.

Peering in, a menagerie of guards walk to and fro in their regalia, parading around their hovel as if they hadn't murdered my people so recently.

The sight elicits an annoyed growl from me before I look at Asher. I startle when I forget he's glamoured, but his brow raises, and I breathe a sigh of calm before I nod.

I press open the heavy door as we walk into a large main atrium. It mirrors Celestial Keep, except bathed in ebony stone and deterioration. Chains hang from the ceiling with fired lamps and towers of melted candle wax are placed around the space every few feet. Dust seems to cover everything and any sort of decoration they have is frayed, tattered, or just broken. Statues of elves are cracked or splintered, with whole sections of faces missing, and some are barely held together by haphazard lines of material in an effort to fill in the missing pieces.

We take slow steps through the area, so as to not appear suspicious. Asher steels his spine next to me as he walks, taking confident steps through the palace.

My eyes continue roaming, looking for anything that could give us any indication of where this book could be.

Guards pass by us without a second glance as we continue through the space.

Smaller elves, in tattered beige clothing, scrub at the floors around us, attempting to renew its life, to no avail. Their feet are shackled to the ground where they sit and as guards pass by, they take their rugged brushes and scrape against the stone, to clean their path. They are bone thin, and their cheeks are sunken in. They look as if they haven't real food in a *very* long time.

A snarl curls at my lips as we walk, making sure not to step in the path of the cleaning elves, so they don't have more work to do.

We pass the cleaning elves, and down a tunnel that rests across the atrium, where I look through each separate hallway. Some lead to kitchens with more elves shackled to the ground. Everywhere, there are elves shackled to their places, cleaning things, and some can walk around, but they carry a large metal ball behind them as they move back and forth. The weight of the object screeches against the stone as they walk.

The rage I feel pricks violently against my skin. If I could save these beings, I would…

One realm at a time, Sera.

We wander the halls for a long while before we come across *another* hallway, at its end is a large wooden door. An elf walks toward it, carrying a tall stack of books, and my hand flies out to stop Asher next to me. I nod at the elf in question.

Our steps are precise and calculated as we walk down the hallway, following the small elf into the room.

Tall bookcases raise against the high-vaulted ceilings and the scent of decay is even thicker in here, mixed with dense smoke and rotting leather. The beams lifting the roof are deteriorated and appear only moments from destruction.

The elf has no idea we're following it as it pushes deeper into the library. The shelves don't have nearly as many tomes as Tantalia does, and some of the shelves are completely bare. There are a generous number of books that just lay open on the floor, forgotten by whoever picked them up in the first place.

The elf rounds a corner, into an aisle, out of view from the rest of the beings in the chamber.

Approaching the elf from behind, I grip its neck, holding it in place. It drops the large stack of books at its feet, lifting its hands in submission, "I'm sorry, I was told to bring these here!" the elf whisper-squeaks.

My brow furrows as I turn the little creature around.

It's a girl.

Her eyes are bright red just as the others, but she's frail. Tiny, and barely an adult. At least over a hundred years old but still too young to suffer this way.

My heart sinks for her and I release the grip on her slowly but allow Asher to come beside me to block her exit.

"Your name?" I murmur lowly.

"My name? Uhm… 27835," she responds.

My stomach drops as I realize these poor creatures don't even get names… they are merely a *statistic.*

My mind works as I figure out how to approach this situation. "We aren't here to hurt you," I whisper.

Her frantic brow appears to soften, and her body relaxes a bit. "Is there something that needs to be done? I've done the washing," she responds softly.

My eyes glance to Asher in remorse, whose red eyes are wide with the same sentiment, and he nods in approval.

I return my gaze to hers, "Do you enjoy life here?" I ask.

Her brow furrows as she looks down at her fingers, picking nervously at her small nails, "Oh, yes, very much. Bruthar is a wonderful leader," she nods quickly, her eyes twitch back and forth in fear as she speaks.

I take a deep breath as I wave my hand over my face, a purple glow veils over my eyes as I feel my face contort back into my own, "I am Seraphina Moonsong, Queen of Tantalia and General to the Night's Legions."

The little one's eyes open wide and her mouth gapes in an attempt to scream, but Asher quickly comes up behind her, wrapping an arm around her front and a hand around her mouth, covering it. His eyes go wide as he clamps his lips together between his teeth. A plea for speed dances across his face as he looks behind me to the chamber beyond.

My hand rises against my face, and I feel it contort back into Drannar form. "I need your help. Whatever you've been told about us, isn't true, and I can make your help worthwhile," I tell her quickly.

Her panicked eyes continue to swipe back and forth, from me to the open area at my back, her body tense as Asher restrains her. But her brows seem to soften the longer she looks at us and she nods slowly.

"I am looking for an ancient text. Something called 'The Caelestial Compendium'," I say slowly.

Her brow tenses in confusion, and I shift my sights to Asher. His eyes begin to show a hint of panic, as he continues to survey the length of the aisle behind me.

I nod in his direction, and he moves his arm from around her chest to hold her shoulders.

Her chest expands as she takes a deep breath to settle herself before she looks at me, "Y-you can help me? Why would you want to help me?" she asks quietly.

"You do not deserve to suffer here, just because of your cruel leader."

Her features continue to soften as she listens to me, looking between Asher and I before she breathes a deep sigh. "I don't know anything about The Compendium; merely that it exists. The last I heard, it was given to The Orcs long ago," she responds.

Fuck. Another fucking dead-end.

I look over her. Her skin is more ashen than the rest, and her hair is in knots where it rests at her neck. She seems like whatever they're feeding her is barely enough to sustain her.

But if I can't save them all…

"Come back with me to Tantalia," I tell her.

It's a risk. A huge, massive risk, with a menagerie of repercussions.

But I can't allow this little elf to suffer here, and she could be of great use to us.

Her eyes drop to the floor, scanning slowly before she nods.

"The mistresses will end up taking you. But I will assure your safety, and you will not suffer anymore. I promise."

"Why would you help me?" she asks quietly.

I give her a small smile. She doesn't have any reason to come with me, and I can imagine her apprehension. But…

"I would like to give you a better chance at life. I see something in you. Something that can't be nurtured here. I would like to nurture it… if you'd let me?"

Because it's true. She has kind eyes, sad as they may be. But she deserves a better chance to live. If I can't save them all, at least I could try and save one.

She contemplates for a long moment before she nods again. "Okay… Okay, yes I will come with you," she says with a small smile.

I wave my hand over her, rendering her invisible.

Asher reaches for the girl's shoulders in the air, leaning down to cradle the invisible being in his arms. He adjusts her to cling to his body like a little tree-hugging creature before he nods in readiness. I lead the way out of the aisle, searching the ends for elves.

When the coast is clear, I make quick work of the distance between us and the door of the library. Peeking my head out, I scan the floors and the hallways we traverse. Drannars continue doing their work, paying us no singular mind.

We make our way quickly through the hallways, heading back to the metal door that leads to The Portal Room. Two new guards stand down by the portal entrance, prompting me to swing my head to Asher in annoyance and release a heavy sigh.

You would think there would be more of an issue with the first dead ones just for them to replace them with no distress. But The Portal from the Drannars side shocks and kills the ones who touch it. That is, when the wards are working the way they're supposed to.

Asher nods with a sigh before he looks down at the invisible bundle in his arms, "Close your eyes," he says softly as he turns away.

A snap sounds against the brick walls, alerting Asher of my completion.

He turns back around as I wipe some of the blood from my face, flicking it to the floor.

The uniform jacket is torn from where my wings have ripped through the fabric, so I tear it the rest of the way off, throwing it to the dead elf guards on the ground. I wave my hand over Asher's arms and the air warbles as the elf comes back into view.

Asher places her feet down on the ground before he unwraps his cloak from his neck, and he too, morphs slowly back into his human form.

He hands the cloak to me as he turns around to let me put it into his pack. I take notice of the gawking stare the small elf makes of Asher as she looks over him.

Her eyes are wide with wonder. "A human?"

Asher adjusts his pack before he looks down at her with a curious expression and nods.

I turn to The Portal and reach for Asher. He wraps his calloused hand around mine as he reaches for the elf, and I lead the way through the bright purple curtain.

As the fragrant Tantalia air replaces the musty dampness of the elf lands, the sharpened, metal tip of a sword is pressed to my face.

I peer down the shining silver object to find it attached to the hand of a guard, along with several others.

The ones at the back of the group divide, parting to let a white cloaked figure step through the grass.

Her eyes meet mine in fury, "Your Majesty," Kalinda's annoyed voice grits as she looks between the three of us.

"You wanted me to be Queen. And now I am. No longer shall I be under the thumb of The Court."

CHAPTER 30

CONSEQUENCES

ASHER

"**Y**ou went against the terms of The Court! What were we to do if we were to lose a Queen, so soon after induction!? Have you not thought of your people!?" Mistress Kalinda chides from her post at the end of the table, her brow pinches in anger as she glares daggers into Seraphina.

My knees ache as they rest in the stone where I'm restrained. I try to adjust my wrists from where sparks crackle against them at my back, as Seraphina stands at the table in front of us. Gideon and the small elf have also been restrained beside me. Selene stands next to Seraphina as they take their punishment.

This conversation feels like it has gone on for *far* too long.

After they secured us at The Portal, they grafted us up here. Selene and Gideon had also been restrained, yet Selene was released when we reached The Court. Seraphina's face has been pinched in fury the entire time we've had to endure this.

A bit of overkill, if you ask me, but I suppose *everything* they do is overkill.

I don't understand their hierarchy. If Seraphina is the Queen, how is she to be reprimanded? Especially if she was only doing what she could for her people. It doesn't make sense… But that's not for me to say.

I had no idea what Seraphina's thoughts were when she brought the elf here, I imagined it would be met with resistance. But I agreed, there was no way we could leave that poor girl there. It wasn't right, especially someone so young.

I glance to the small elf girl beside us. She trembles as her chest moves in quick bursts and her nostrils flare in fear. Her mouth is bound with a swath of black cloth, and her arms are restrained behind her.

I can feel the heavy charge of Seraphina's anger in the thinning air, and I return my gaze to the women at the table.

"Kalinda, what gives you the right to capture me!? Restrain my commander and my compatriots?! The Queen!?" Seraphina challenges as I hear her claws scrape into the table. The tension in the base of her wings is crushing as her tail flicks violently.

"I am the Mistress of The Keep, all orders go through me," Kalinda sneers at Seraphina. Her face is pinched in anger and her eyes narrow on her like prey.

I've never seen this demon show any bit of emotion, so it's jarring to see her challenge Seraphina like this.

"*You* no longer shall hold me back. I obtained vital information needed to save this realm, and I am going to use it, come the hells or high water. You are no longer mistress of The Keep."

"You dare challenge my authority?! Must I remind you; I built this Keep beside your *precious* Lilith," Kalinda responds with a curled lip.

"Watch me, Kalinda," Seraphina growls back.

Kalinda pins Seraphina with a glare for a long moment, her eyes searching Seraphina's before she settles, and backs away from the table, "As you wish, General," Kalinda says as she bows deeply.

"You can stay in The Keep. But you have no place at this table. You are to be sent to The Library; Mistress of Text," Seraphina says.

Kalinda's face is stoic as she nods deeply, accepting her terms.

I feel my eyebrow quirk as I observe their politics. I still am not well-versed in their methods, but it's unnerving to see this supposedly ancient demon switch so suddenly.

"The elf stays with me. She is under my watch. Whatever happens, if she is to be a nuisance, will be put on my shoulders. I take responsibility of her," Seraphina says, but her voice deepens to project to the rest of The Court.

"You wanted me to be Queen. And now I am. No longer shall I be under the thumb of The Court. All my endeavors will need no approval. I was chosen to lead this realm, and I will do so on my terms and *my* rules. If I am to save this realm, I'm doing it my way. Is that understood?" Seraphina adds as her head swivels to peer at all the women of The Court.

The mistresses bend at the waist in compliance, "Yes, Mistress," they call back in unison.

Seraphina flicks behind her, relieving the muzzle from my mouth, air rushes through my lungs as I take a deep gasp. The tension against my wrists lift and I stretch my hands out as I stand. Leaning over, I grab gently under the elf's thin elbow to help her to stand. She takes a quiet breath as she rubs at her wrists.

"Sorry about that," I whisper to her.

The elf's delicate neck is decorated with a purple sparked collar, same as the one around my own. Though, mine has lost some of its luster, probably alluding to the fact Seraphina is gaining her trust in me.

The ladies of The Court begin walking out the door, all except Selene. Kalinda lingers as the mistresses file out; her face tight in contempt before she nods at Seraphina. She, too, turns and leaves with the rest.

The large stone doors rumble closed against the ground as they leave, and Seraphina turns to us with a heavy sigh.

"Are you alright?" she asks as she walks up to the elf, her eyes downturned in concern as she places a hand on her shoulder.

The girl nods sheepishly as she continues to rub her wrists. "Y-yes, I'm fine," she says softly.

Seraphina kneels in front of her, "We need to give you a name. A *proper* name," she says with a kind smile.

The elf looks at Seraphina and returns her smile with a nervous one of her own, "I think I'd like that," she responds.

"How about... Xeneera?" Seraphina offers.

The elf girl's smile widens as she nods excitedly, "I love it."

Seraphina wraps her arms around the girl in a tight hug.

"It's been settled then. Welcome to Tantalia, Xeneera," Seraphina says as she stands and bows deeply to her.

Xeneera smiles and bows in return.

"Selene, get her cleaned up, and give her a room close to mine. Ward the doors so no one can come in or out, only us, and Xeneera," Seraphina says as she turns to Selene.

Selene smiles gratefully and nods, "As you wish, General."

Selene takes Xeneera from the room with Gideon following close behind.

As the door rumbles shut, Seraphina takes a few steps to her tall, black throne and falls into it.

Heavy is the head that wears the crown.

A deep-seated pang of sadness settles in my stomach as I watch her. Taking soft steps to the side of the throne, I kneel beside her and take her hand into my own.

"Are *you* alright?" I ask softly as I stroke her creamy skin.

Seraphina sighs as she nods, "That was... a lot," she admits quietly.

A somber glaze washes over her purple eyes as she watches my thumb graze her skin, "Even though I'm Queen now... it's not easy to command the people that were once your superiors. Especially hundreds of years your elder," she sighs.

A pit deepens in my chest as I listen to her. It's so hard to hear these beings I've thought were soul-less for so long, admit to such human emotions. Endearing, but a difficult thing to process.

Seeing her try to ease into this role she's been thrust into gives me a strange sense… of pride? Which doesn't make sense. I have nothing to be proud of, I'm not the demon's keeper.

But I am. I *am* proud of her. This is not an easy task, and she does everything in her power to do right by her people. Even going against The Court to get her goals accomplished.

It's very admirable and I find my feelings toward her deepening the more time I spend with her. A heated tug pulls hard against my chest as I look up at her face.

Seraphina's gaze comes to mine and the defeated glaze lifts as she smiles. "Come, I have a place I want to show you," she says as she stands.

And my heart beats a little faster as I realize I've let Asher into my own little safe haven.

CHAPTER 31

DEMON'S COVE

SERAPHINA

Asher and I checked in on Xeneera after we left The Court. She's settled into her new quarters with ease, and even in the few moments she's been here, she seemed much more at peace than when we found her in The Never Realm.

In the meantime, I had Selene bring her some more books from The Library and told her to bring her as much food as she asked for.

Eventually, Asher and I dressed in light tunics and breeches before I led him out of The Keep.

We took a long walk along the marbled path before we cut to a field off the main grounds.

The past few weeks have drained us immensely. I could feel his energy fading the longer we've had to subject ourselves to these perilous adventures. Even with feeding from him, there are other aspects I'm not able to fulfill with him alone. This was time for both of us to relax, at least a little.

Brilliant stars twinkle through the painted night sky. Shimmering curtains of purple, blue and green dance against the black backdrop.

The tall grasses sway in the smooth wind as we make our way to my special place. Cool breeze passes through my hair, and I look back at Asher, whose eyes drift around the wondrous night. Tiny pin pricks of blue sparkle every so often through the air and his eyes follow them in wonderment.

I could have flown us; I could have grafted us.

But I want a moment together that we could both enjoy. A moment just to slow down.

Plus, how could I miss this?

The human's curiosity as he takes in this mysterious place.

Luminescent butterflies float along the closed blooms of the flowers, and the tiny sparks of light whiz past us, looping around our bodies and dancing around our heads.

Asher jumps as one startles him, and I giggle in response.

"What are those things?" Asher asks softly as he continues walking, taking slow steps so as to not run into some on accident.

"Willows," I respond with a kind smile.

"I'm sorry?"

"Willows. They're spirits of succubus past. We demons may not have souls, but our magic that doesn't get returned to the earth lives as these little specks on the wind," I tell him as I come to a halt in the field. The air hits my palm as I hold my hand out, allowing a willow to fall softly into it.

It bounces off my skin before it soars away, picking up speed and disappearing into the night.

Asher watches in awe at the little light.

"We don't have anything like that back home," he whispers.

I smile in his direction before I continue walking. Wisteria flower petals mix with the swirling willows, and their dance lends to a whimsical charm. Like a rainfall of color, they float with the fragrant breeze; the one that seems to push us closer to the dull blue glow that comes from the side of the mountain ahead.

We approach the eerie hue, coming upon a large opening at the edge of the rocky cave mouth. The once dull blue is brilliant as we scale small boulders, descending lower into the earth, and we walk a short distance inside. Like light being pressed through bits of sea-glass, its illuminations consume the interior of the small space with twinkles of silver specs, and the glow shimmers off the damp ceiling as a small whirlpool swirls below us.

Warm, earthy steam replaces the night air as we step up to the pond nestled in this little cave. The cavern is delightfully heated, and I remind myself to come here more often.

"The Realm of Mages?" Asher asks curiously.

I laugh in response, "No, silly, that is in the other direction. This is my little getaway."

Wrapping my hand around his wrist, I pull him to the edge of the whirlpool, remembering the way this small haven used to melt all my stress away. A place just for me. And my heart beats a little faster as I realize I've let Asher into my own little safe haven.

Alongside the sound of the bubbling pool, drips echo against the slippery rock. Iridescent droplets fall from the spikes of stone that cling to the cave's ceiling. Wispy columns of steam swirl from the surface of the water, rising to the rock above to begin their cycle anew.

Asher's eyes gaze curiously into the pool, almost mesmerized at the sight.

"Demon's Cove," I tell him softly as I shed my light tunic, throwing it on the rocks. Soon, my flowy pants follow suit.

The glistening waters reflect in Asher's widened eyes as he watches me strip. My eyes trail down his tense body until it reaches the bulge pressed firm against his pants.

A smirk tugs at my lips as I dive into the pool. Heated liquid wraps me in its healing properties as I linger under the surface for just a moment. My wings tuck tight against my back as I come up for air, wiping my face and breathing a soft sigh as I look up at Asher.

His throat works in a gulp as he slowly bends over to remove his boots, placing them on the ledge. He reaches for the hem of his shirt, pulling it over his head and I watch as his glorious muscles ripple under his skin. His stomach is etched into perfect sections of hardened flesh that contort as the light from the pool wavers against them.

Soon, his hands grip at the band of his pants, lowering them slowly until they begin to fall, and he steps out of them. His cock hardens further as he looks down at me, but almost nervously, his hands scramble to cover himself.

The tang of blood coats my tongue as my fangs sink into my lower lip, my eyes stuck on the body of this beautiful beast.

Asher looks down into the water as he dips a toe in, easing himself in slowly. He hisses softly as he descends deeper, the sound losing itself amongst the bubbling.

"How is it warm?" he asks as he wades through the water to come closer to me. The glow from the pool bathes his body in ethereal illumination as he approaches, his hands sliding against the surface.

"It's a spring, the water is naturally warm," I shrug nonchalantly.

"Huh. So… there's no magic heating this water?"

"Nope. Just heat from the ground."

He nearly shrugs, as if that answer is good enough for him. Slowly, his expression changes and ease graces his face as the water climbs up his chest and to his neck. He sighs in content as he begins to lean back, dousing his feral strands of brown hair before he lifts his head and shakes the water from it.

I turn to swim to the other side of the pool, the swirling current expanding the leathery partitions of my wings as I make my way to the ledge on the other side. Turning around to face Asher, I open my wings wide enough to rise out of the water and above the rocky platform behind me. The damp ledge bites against my bottom wing talons as they pin into the stone, holding me up just enough to enjoy the water surrounding me. Water swirls around my legs as I kick my feet back and forth, soaking into the wondrous feeling of it.

"Why'd you bring me here?" Asher asks as his head swivels around to take in the cave walls.

My head tips back and I lock onto a point above me, watching as the glimmering veins shimmer against the ebony rock. Visions of the past work through my mind as I remember the importance of this little cave.

A heavy sighs pulls through my lungs, my head relaxing all the way back. "When I was younger, Lilith would work me into the ground. Nothing I ever did was good enough for her, training wise. And I just wanted to escape, to get away. And one day, when I was in a particularly harsh mood, I ran and I ran, until I found this cove," I explain.

The scent of dirt and sweat comes to the forefront of my memories. The sound of Lilith's yelling, the clash of our swords and the smell of burning air as she would throw lightning bolt after lightning bolt at me.

"At first I would just come sit here and enjoy the silence, watching the water spin. I'd let my mind get lost in something so simple as the water moving here all on its own. But one day, I got in and it felt like everything melted away. I would come here on hard days, and for just a few moments I felt at peace," I sigh softly.

Deep seeded inadequacy settles in my stomach as I reminisce the days when things were easy. It may have been hard to train under Lilith. But I wasn't crushed under the weight of the responsibility I deal with now.

The kingdom, the realm, and what feels like two different species of being, all lie on my wings.

As relaxing as this pool is, it feels like even that can't take this weight away.

My heart begins to ache as I think of how Lilith would handle everything; how she would take her duty in stride, and she never once complained.

I should be grateful for such an opportunity.

But I'm not. It's hard when you feel like it's an opportunity you shouldn't have in the first place.

There are some days that feel easier, that feel like I'm meant to be in this position, as if it was made for me.

There are other days I feel like I have no right to wear the crown or call myself Queen.

But I'm here now, and I must make do with what I've been given.

That's what Lilith would do. Or, at least what she attempted to instill in me.

Slowly, my focus comes back to the cave. Tilting my head forward, I look at Asher, who studies me carefully with a curious, green gaze. The ring of blue around his pupil seems to shine brighter in the azure glow of the cave.

It's amazing how fast he's learned here. He has fallen in step with our rounds and the warriors have expected him in trainings. Though he doesn't do much in trainings, I know they're aware of his purpose.

There is a silent confidence he beams at my back in The Pits, which in turn beams through me. It makes some of the heavier days a bit lighter.

The sight of this beast as he glides through the water causes my pulse to pick up. My breath catches as the glowing water reflects off of his flesh and I admire every inch of him.

Emerald eyes lock onto me in heated admiration, with warm water causing our flesh to infuse into one as he presses his body against mine. The jagged ledge at my lower back bites into the skin there.

His rough hand wraps gently around my cheek as he pulls me in to press his lips to mine. A kiss, so soft and sweet graces my lips and I feel the heaviness of his care as he holds me to him. He brushes wet strands of my hair behind my ear as his head tilts to deepen his affection. The dripping strands of his hair cause droplets of water to fall against my forearms as my arms come to rest around his neck, giving in to his embrace. I run my claws through his hair, slicking it back and gripping the back of his head as my chest heaves against his.

My nipples press against his hardened chest, brushing them softly and deepening the need for him, as I feel his thickening cock press against my stomach. A grin twists at the corner of my mouth before I slip my tongue through his lips.

But I have no desire to feed from him. I feel *full.* As if, for just a few minutes, I can exist here in his arms and wrapped around him without the need for his power.

I just want *him.*

The hand on my jaw runs down my throat, leaving a torrent of heated flutters in my stomach. Slowly, it slides down my collarbone, down my shoulder to grip under my armpit. The other hand comes to grab under the other side, and his strength lifts me onto the ledge with graceful ease.

His lips leave mine to press tiny kisses to my jaw. Soft and warm, they pepper my skin as he moves down my neck… my chest, slowly, making their way down to my breast to flick a velvet tongue over my nipple. A soft gasp sounds in the small cavern as I feel it, the sensation heightened by the steam in the air and the temperature of our bodies.

A thick hand palms at my other breast as he continues flicking the one in his mouth, his fingers pinching and rolling the small peak, eliciting a rush of ecstasy to course through me.

A groan crawls from deep within me as I give in further to this unfamiliar sensation.

"You're so responsive, angel…" he murmurs against my breast. His mouth vibrates against it from his words and my core pulses harder, begging for him to be inside of me.

The heavy weight of the world is lifted from my shoulders by the unfamiliar feeling, one that seeks to absorb my worries instead of my pleasure. The one that begs to make my strife disappear.

The rare feeling of being cared for.

Truly cared for.

Damp strands of hair run through my fingers as I grip at his scalp and look down at him, his eyes closed as he takes his time feasting on my flesh.

Soon, the hand on my breast runs down my chest, down my stomach. The heated flutters picking up pace and causing my stomach to flip as he presses his fingers against my slippery core.

His fingers rub soft circles with gentle pressure into my clit as his tongue continues flicking and sucking at my tit.

The cold, dripping ends of my wet hair brush against my spine as my head tosses back, eliciting a soft shiver from me as I attempt to process the menagerie of sensations flooding through me.

His fingers dip lower, pressing into me slowly as his thumb comes up to continue rubbing circles into the sensitive bundle of nerves.

Slowly, in and out of me his fingers pump, taking their time.

My pussy tightens around his fingers as I reach the edge, and the sensation fades, his hand leaving my center. The warm air of the cavern hits my nipple as he releases it, and his mouth finds its place against my lips. Slow and deliberate, he savors every part of me.

The weight of his body presses against me, pushing me back onto the stone. My wingtips detach from the ledge and expand to soften the fall.

His hardened body rises out of the water to hover just above me. His emerald eyes plunder every surface of my skin that pebbles with gooseflesh as the anticipation of his touch grows near. The blue glow from the cave hits the dips and curves of his hardened body; iridescent trails of water that run between the ridges of his muscles. My eyes trail his gorgeous form until they reach his cock that throbs for me.

My lower lip catches between my teeth as I nip down on it in glee. The prospect of him being inside of me makes my heart race with an urgent need for him.

My legs open under him, resting on his hips as he leans down between them. His rigid shaft finds its place between my soaked lips and glides against my clit in a maddening rush of pleasure.

His eyes look down to where we're connected, watching with a lost curiosity as his hips slowly rock against me. "Is this alright?" he pants softly as he comes to look at me in half-lidded desire.

"Yes, yes, it's perfect," I murmur. In a desperate attempt to feel every inch of his skin, I wrap my arms around his neck, bringing him closer to me as I latch on to his soft mouth. I take gentle licks of his lips to taste him once more.

His hips pull back just the slightest bit, letting the head of him slide through my center before he teases my entrance. A hiss pricks at the air surrounding us as he slips into me, inch by torturous inch. I nip on his lower lip, tugging on it as his jaw loosens and he gives in to my cunt.

As he presses deeper, I feel myself stretching around his thickness, and my throat sings with a fulfilled moan. He fills me in such a way that my thoughts vacate, I can't think, I can't speak. I can only feel how amazing *he* feels.

More of my moans spill into the air as he takes slow strokes in and out of me.

"This is the closest thing to the heavens I'll ever feel, Seraphina," he pants softly against my lips. His hips roll and glide against me, as if he's taking every second he can to memorize the way I feel.

I'm usually a rough rider, but I can't help but enjoy the way he's taking every bit of me right now.

How I'm not being used for pleasure.

I'm being *cared for* and dare I say, *loved.*

The thought causes my back to bow, the jagged rock pressing deeper into me as my tits rise to meet his face. My hips swirl to take him deeper, feel all of him that I can before his voice breaks through my pleasure.

"There's a good girl, angel, take what you need," he murmurs before my nipple is surrounded by warm, wet muscle once again.

"Asher," I pant into the air. The rapidly tangling knot in my tailbone tightens as I run with unexpected fervor to the edge of oblivion. The cliff is just out of reach. *Just* beyond the horizon.

"You're taking me so well, Seraphina. You feel so *fucking* good," he pants against my nipple. The vibrations from such a statement causes the feeling of him to heighten. His thickness, his depth, all of it causes my mind to flay as I process the immense pleasure.

"Come for me. I wanna feel you come for me. Show me what eternity feels like."

His words and the husky tone of his voice implodes my core and I dive off the edge. "Fuck!... Asher...! Fuck!" I pant as I feel my cunt tighten around him, my body plunging off the edge of the cliff to freefall into darkness. A visceral moan claws through the cavern as I descend farther and farther. My body shudders under his weight as I continue my fall.

"Gods above...!" I hear him groan through the void, my body tightens and my pussy flutters in waves as the sensation crashes over me again and again.

Asher's moans match mine as he dives into oblivion with me. His pleasure spills against my insides and the sensation drags me deeper into this moment with him.

He pumps into me a few more times before he slows. His hot breath grazes my skin as he pants into the crook of my neck. A hand strokes softly at my side as he presses languishing kisses into my flesh.

Our breaths mix as he relaxes against me. The feeling of his wet skin pressed against mine causes my breathing to slow, and I can't help the way my claws stroke softly into his back. Our breathing evens out slowly as we lay there together enjoying the way our skin sticks together. The sound of the water bubbling and the warm air flowing through my lungs fills my conscious as I soak in the feeling.

A strange emotion washes over me, one completely different from how it usually feels after sex.

Something much more... fulfilling.

I may not have been feasting on his pleasure, but this is the fullest I've felt in my entire life.

I can't help the way I feel in how he talks to her. I could burst through these cuffs and rip his throat out.

CHAPTER 32

INTENTIONS

ASHER

After Seraphina and I had laid in the cavern a little while longer, we came back to her bedroom.

Even though we spent that time in the cavern, I spent the rest of the night inside of her, taking every second of my time relishing her skin against mine. Her cunt wrapped around me and her claws sliced through my back.

This wasn't rough and aggressive like it usually was.

It was sweet, and soft. It was…

I have to admit, it was something I don't think I was even capable of understanding or feeling.

The way she fits around me, the way her skin feels under my fingertips. The way her scent drives me insane every time she's near. It's as if I can never get enough of her. It doesn't matter how many times I fill her, or how many times I feel her tighten around me.

With every press of my cock into her I need *more.*

I don't understand what sort of spell she may have me under. Part of me is fine with the experience. I don't mind feeling something this fulfilling, even if it is her doing. Or even if it isn't her doing and I'm just naturally experiencing this.

As crazy as that may sound.

This is something I don't think I could ever have in Vesperholm. Not with a human woman anyway.

Perhaps I could eventually… But…

The circumstances back home wouldn't allow for this kind of bond to be fostered.

And while I am keen on helping her people, I don't mind being here with Seraphina. I… I *like* being here with her.

I don't know if I could leave her side now even if I was allowed to.

Especially seeing her more human side. The way she took the elf child in, and her willingness to do things unconventionally. Her drive to fix this monumental problem that wracks the entire world we live in.

I would follow her to the ends of the earth, and I am still having a hard time with the idea that I would do that anyway. I shouldn't, and there is still a part of me that can't, not with my family still suffering back home.

But I would… and I would do it happily.

Seraphina and I checked on Xeneera this morning, who was settled into her new space, she had asked for some more books. She had apparently devoured the ones Seraphina had already given her. And Seraphina obliged.

We stopped by The Pits, and Seraphina gave Selene a rundown on how she wanted training to go. Of course, even in her absence, her warriors are her highest concern. Considering Seraphina and I were now going on another mission; back to the Realm of Mages.

Or *attempting* to go back to the Realm of Mages.

I knew she wouldn't drop the idea of returning to it. But when she would go back was uncertain.

Seraphina doesn't just throw away an option because it didn't work the first time.

That was evident with The Court.

She had us pack our bags, and we were grafting there today. Now that she knew where it was, it would make the trip a bit easier. And she was fairly confident she could get through the portal this time.

Why? I still don't know. Seraphina works how she does.

I didn't fight her on it, I don't feel like it was my position to say.

But I accompanied her anyway, whether she wanted me to or not.

Now, Seraphina and I linger at the outside of the cave we had found several weeks prior. Peering into the dark hole, she takes a deep breath before she steadies her shoulders, shakes out her wings, and advances forward.

My booted steps follow close behind as we splash through small puddles.

Seraphina makes no sound as we approach the archway, she doesn't even look back at me. So, I keep quiet, in case she has something on her mind that could dismantle this whole idea. I find myself scraping my pocket for my insignia, reminding myself that this is part of it all.

But the longer I linger on the insignia, the less weight the sentiment holds. I want to be able to remember why I follow her; to tell myself that I follow her to save my people.

But now, that feels like a lie, and that I follow her because I want to. Because I *need* to. I need to be with her. In my soul, it doesn't feel as if there is any other option.

My hand slides away from my pocket and I choose instead to focus on this demon I've decided to follow.

The blue glow of the runes beyond begin to shimmer through the darkness as we continue. The dripping water and eerie silence are the only thing to accompany our growing nerves.

The archway looks the same as it did when we arrived the first time, as if it hadn't tried to swallow us whole.

Seraphina loosens her wings and shakes out her shoulders before she takes a deep breath and kneels against the stone, placing her hands against the illuminated scratches.

A slew of murmured words in an ancient language begins blending with the sounds of the caves and the runes begin to glow brighter, its light damn-near blinding as the archway shimmers. A curtain of vibrant teal falls over the wall it rests against.

The colors swirl in a calm circle as it beckons us… no… *dares* us to enter.

Seraphina jumps to her feet in excitement as she claps, her tail swishing in glee as she turns around to look at me, "Yes! I did it!" She giggles.

My brow rises as I watch the portal, then bring my eyes back to her, "What'd you do differently?"

"As with my own powers, Asher-darling, I relayed my intentions," Seraphina nods confidently.

I watch her curiously for a moment before nodding as if I understand; I don't, "Okay…"

Seraphina rolls her eyes and grabs my arm, pulling me through the entry and landing on the other side.

"So, did you plan for this, or did you just expect them to greet us with a brilliant revelry?" I ask in annoyance as I try to shift my body weight against the cuffs that pin my arms over my head.

The metal is cutting off blood supply to my fingers and its rough edges nip into my skin.

I think I'm getting really tired of being restrained. There must be better methods of interrogation than tying me up.

"I didn't think they'd take us hostage," Seraphina grumbles from beside me. "But hey, we're here, and I do have a plan for that." She nods confidently.

Upon entering the portal, we were greeted by a group of menacing looking humans. All of whom presented their glowing sticks at us in threat.

Luckily, Seraphina had her wits about her and had them take us. I imagined fighting back would not prove to fare well for our endeavor.

They handcuffed us and threw us in this cell, and one could only hope they gave us a chance to talk.

"I'm beginning to think you don't have a plan at all and you're just winging it."

"Asher-darling, I'm always winging it, I'm a succubus," Seraphina says as she looks to me with a cheeky, fanged grin.

I stare at her as she shifts her wings against the brick that also pins her to the wall next to me. The talons at their tips make a sickening screech against it.

"What? I'm just trying to lighten the mood," she shrugs.

I release a sigh and jingle at the cuffs again.

Iron.

Which would usually be fine for me, I know how to escape iron cuffs. But these wizards put some kind of spell on them, not even allowing for a lock to hang from them.

"So, what is the Realm of Mages?" I ask.

"A pocket realm. Long ago, from my understanding at least, the humans learned how to wield magic. They were at odds with the other magical beings in the land, including us. So, they retreated to a pocket realm only accessed by those versed in ancient magic," Seraphina explains.

My brow furrows as I listen to her.

"Lilith, being the ever-brilliant ruler that she is, created a small portal to enter that realm. Over time, there was a treaty. Allowing the Mages to spell the entry for only those they saw fit to enter. I couldn't enter the first time because I hadn't been clear in my intentions. Therefore, the magic didn't allow me through."

What a peculiar concept. I had no idea magic was so… cognizant.

But I suppose it will make sense if it has the capabilities to do all that it can.

Seraphina jerks at her cuffs again before she gives up.

The large door across from us clangs and rattles before it swings open, revealing three different Mages.

An older man in the front with a long graying beard and a royal blue cloak. A woman about middle aged, with mahogany skin and black hair sprinkled with gray that drapes down her shoulders in long cords, her body sheathed in a red cloak. And a younger man, not much younger than me, with olive skin, frazzled dark brown hair, and rounded glasses. He appears much more nervous than the rest of them in his white cloak.

They take gliding steps into the space as the door slams behind them.

The older man looks between the both of us, his eyes sliding up and down my frame, before they land on Seraphina, "The treaty does not allow your kind here," he sneers.

I can't help the way I feel in how he talks to her. I could burst through these cuffs and rip his throat out. The rage in me gnaws at the boney enclosure of my chest, where the beast resides.

"I understand, but the portal allowed me through, and I need your help," Seraphina says gently.

The older man furrows his brow as he looks at the woman and younger man behind him.

They return his looks with apprehensive ones of their own.

"You? Need us?" He seems to laugh as he turns back to Sera.

"The Drannars are getting closer to war, and the power on our stone wavers every day we don't fix it. They had something of great importance to us, but it has been given to the Orcs. If the Orcs and Drannars team up to find the missing piece of the stone, they will take Tantalia *and* our power," Seraphina explains in desperation.

The older man's expression drops in concern, the thin skin of his face turning a slightly lighter shade as he looks back at his companions.

"How do I know you aren't weaving lies, demon?" the man asks as he comes to look at Seraphina again. The aged skin around his eyes crinkle in warning as he peers at her.

"It's true. We went to The Never Realm in search of The Caelestial Compendium," I add.

The three humans look at me, and their faces ashen of their color.

"T-the Compendium? The Orcs have The Compendium?" the woman asks with a worried slant to her features.

"Yes, do you know of it?" Seraphina responds.

"Our people helped Lilith write it during the treaty," the younger male responds.

My gaze slides to Seraphina, her eyes widening as it connects with mine.

"So, you know what's in The Compendium?" Seraphina asks.

"We aren't aware of what's in it, we are far too young. But we do know of its influence and power," the older male responds.

"So, you know how badly we need to return The Compendium to Tantalia?" Seraphina asks cautiously.

The older mage turns to look at his fellow wizards, and they return his look with furrowed, concerned brows as they nod.

"We do... We will help you. *But* only because we dislike the Drannars and Orcs more than we dislike *you*," the elder wizard responds, marking the end of his statement with a judgmental sweep of Seraphina.

Seraphina lets out a small sigh of relief as her head drops. "Thank you."

The older wizard brings his hands from inside of his cloak to reveal a long, twisted piece of wood, waving it at our cuffs. A metallic *tink* pings off the walls of the cell, followed by the clatter of chains and the rush of blood pumps through my fingers as my arms drop beside me.

"Aside from the obvious, why else did you come?" the woman asks.

"We need help getting to the Isle," Seraphina says as she shakes and adjusts her wings from where they were squished against the brick.

"Is there a reason you can't get there yourself?" the young male asks.

He seems to lean in as he speaks, his head tilts in curiosity as he looks at Seraphina like she's some goddess.

To me she is, but I don't like the way he looks at her.

I'm not sure why it makes my blood boil for him to look at her like this, even in admiration. But it does.

"Well yes, I don't know how to," Seraphina says as she bends her neck, allowing a crack to sound off in the chamber. "And potions… We need potions."

The older man quirks an eyebrow, "For the purpose…. of?"

"We can't kill too many guards, and I can't shift into an Orc, and neither can my companion. We have to be stealthy, and I have no idea what magic, if at all, they have on the Isle."

The Mage glares at Seraphina in distrust, "There isn't magic outside of this realm. Merely the magic in Tantalia, and the knowledge we have here."

The female witch leans in toward the elder Mage, "She brings up valid points, Bufort," the woman says quietly to him.

I try my hardest to stifle a laugh, inhaling a deep breath to steady myself and shaking my head to don a stone face.

Bufort.

The older man sighs. "We will allow you to stay here for the night, while we prepare your necessities. Potions take time and we need to gather the ingredients. I also need a list of the things you may require. My friends will take you to your quarters. Tyrick here, will return when you have decided what all you may need." Bufort sweeps his hand toward the younger mage and Tyrick gives a tense bow.

"I thank you again for your help and hospitality," Seraphina says with a deep bow.

Bufort nods in response, and behind him, the door opens with another symphony of clanging metal.

Bufort, Tyrick, and the witch in the red cloak file out of the room, with Seraphina and I following them.

Two guards in varying shades of dark brown leather armor stand on either side of the exit with our belongings.

The guard holding my pack hands it to me and I quickly throw it on my back, nodding to him in thanks.

The three Mages lead us down the dim, stony hallway. A sigh of relief rushes through me as I hear Seraphina from beside me, "Told you we'd be fine," she whispers as she nudges me in the arm.

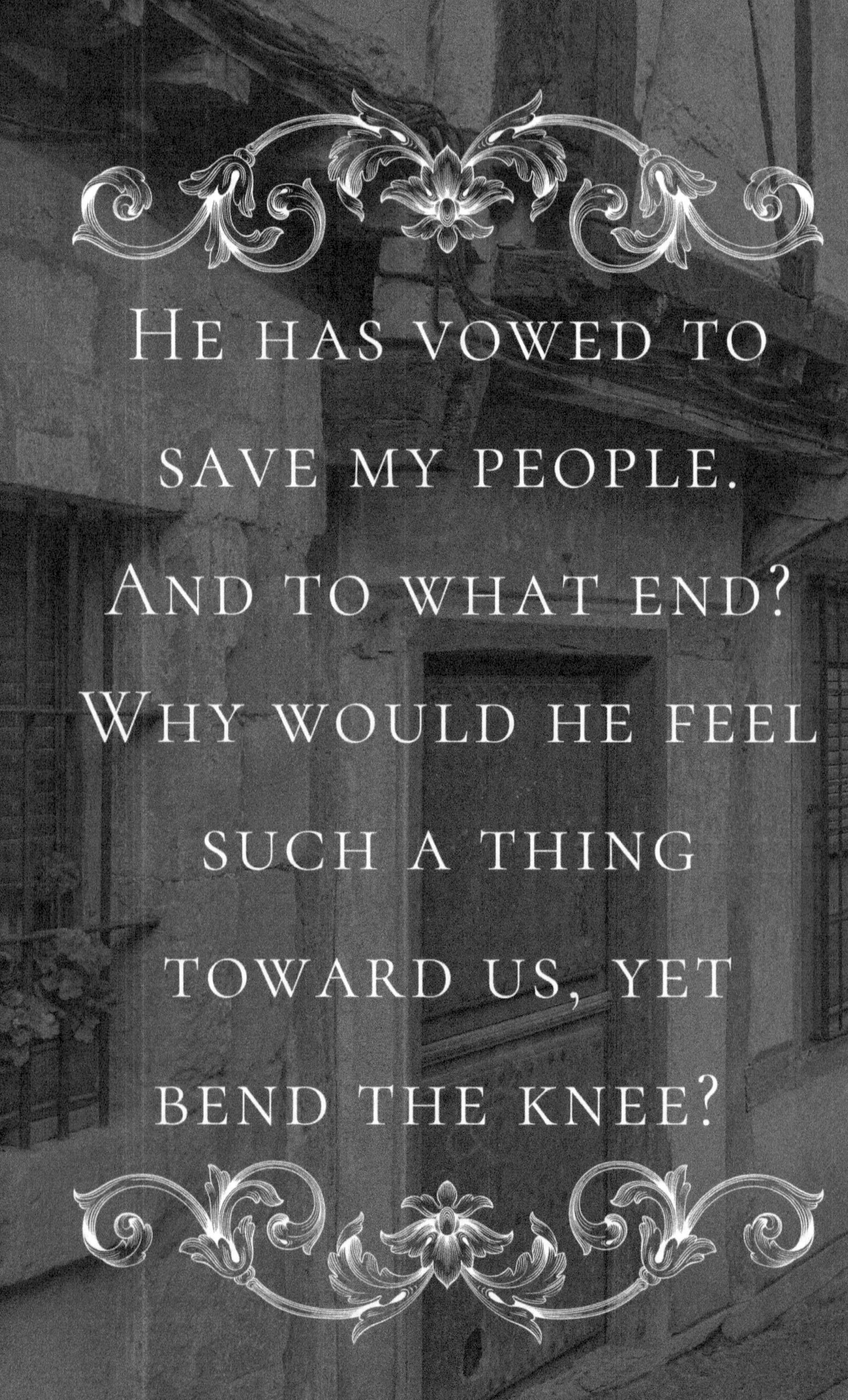

He has vowed to save my people. And to what end? Why would he feel such a thing toward us, yet bend the knee?

CHAPTER 33

KAITHOON

SERAPHINA

The Realm of Mages is nothing I expect it to be as we exit the cells and are led through the small city.

The looks we receive, however, *are* just what I had expected. I can't imagine the last time these people have seen a succubus.

And it shows.

The merchants on the streets selling their potions, cloaks and wands stop their pitches to gawk and stare at us.

Witch mothers hide their young children's faces as we pass.

I'm sure they all know of the treaty, but I can't remember the last time there was a demon in these lands.

Some shop owners quickly shut their doors.

Fair enough.

This little town seems like a Vesperholm mirror, before the Tantalia succs got to it.

And I can't help the small pang in my heart with what Asher may be feeling. I peer at him from the corner of my eye, and he holds his head high, not sparing a glance to the other magical humans in the area. Though the muscles in his neck are tight as his jaw clenches and the flesh against his cheek twitches in annoyance.

I'm so sorry, Asher-dear.

After a long trek through the streets, we come upon a large castle with another number of guards standing post outside of it. The exterior facade seems well kept, well-maintained. But the brick is old, and reeks of human influence.

Dismal. I surmise.

They lead us through the massive front doors and through a hall off the main foyer, depositing us into our quarters.

While the castle itself is made of brick, it seems as though they kept the original wooden structure. The walls in this room are made of such a thing, though it feels as if it should have been replaced with brick, it looks… unstable.

The room has only one bed, a small table with chairs, a desk in one corner and a hanging lantern in the other.

Nothing special, but it doesn't matter, we won't be here long anyway.

Asher slumps into the room, dropping his pack onto the ground next to our bed before he crashes onto the plush comforter that covers the mattress. His groan of relief fills the space as he relaxes.

"So, what is the plan now?" he sighs into the air.

My mind works for a moment, my claws scraping against my chin as my tail articulates slowly at my rump.

"At the very least, we need a map. From there we can figure out what other of things we may need. Potions. Weapons, if any. My magic will not work outside of here, so we have to be prepared," I tell him.

"Why doesn't your magic work outside of Tantalia and here? I thought you said you were magical beings?" Asher asks in confusion as he sits up on the bed.

"Only if there is magic in that realm. We wield it, we *are* magic's conduits. From my understanding, the connection to magic is weakened the farther you are from the source. And if there is no magic in the land, how am I to pull from an empty pot?" I explain as I pace, my claws gripping harder into my chin as I retreat further into thought.

"There is so much I don't know about magic," Asher sighs.

My body stills as I realize, he really *doesn't* know much about magic. His world is bare of it -- or at least bare of humans that know how to use it -- and from what I've seen in Vesperholm, bare of everything else.

I've had to skulk around on numerous occasions in search of him when I still saw him as a murderer. At the time, the idea that survival was all they were attempting, had not crossed my mind. I was merely fueled by rage and revenge.

But the idea that they must go through this world without magic, for a moment, scares even me.

Succubus are born with their affinities; we learn and live our life going through our world with magic. There's not been a time where I've been without it. I may not have been very good at using it. But I still had it. It's a feeling of power you can't get from anything else.

Not even seduction.

Since Vesperholm and Tantalia rest on the same realm, our magic bleeds into their land, at least a little. But with the magical humans retreating to their pocket realm, and the succubus guarded by their portals, there was no chance for them to learn.

"What was it like? Growing up there?" I ask softly as I turn to him.

Asher's face contorts in confusion and a sliver of disbelief as his eyes come to connect with mine, "Well… scary. When I was younger, the succubus had been taking men for a while. Only in small spurts -- singular men. The tale being you would steal them, use their seed and devour them whole. Which is why we were never able to see them again, the men stolen would never return. As the demons came to take more of our people, the population… fell," Asher says quietly as his eyes gaze at the floor. He runs his hands through his hair in frustration before leaning over to rest his elbows on his knees, his hands clasping in front of him.

"When I could hold a sword, I was trained in the hunter's gifts. But more men were taken a bit more sporadically. The town kept declining, until the main hunter houses retreated to the woods. They hid and then they all… gave up. No one wanted to figure it out, they just wanted to irradicate you. The brothers more well-versed in the hunter's gifts, would sleep with the sisters of other houses to supply the future generations with more than just one ability. It's gone slow. Especially with the amount of people taken versus the number of babies born," he continues.

My heart throbs in my chest. I had no idea the repercussions involved when we would take men. I was doing what I was told, following orders.

Even if I did so happily, they were still orders. I've claimed near hundreds of men from that town, with no thought on what it may have meant to them and how it could have affected them.

I was too busy caring about revenge. Caring about Lilith. Caring about The Legions.

The admission sends an arrow through me, knowing my people are the reason they've had to resort to such measures.

"After your Queen died, things got out of hand. The entire structure of our town collapsed. More Succubi came for our men. We had no one to provide us anything, so we would hunt for what we could. Because my family and I lived in the abandoned city, there was not much we could eat. Most days, it was rats. Sometimes father would be able to find us a deer and that would help us at least for a bit. But that was seldom. We did what we could with what we had," Asher finishes, his gaze unfocused on the ground in front of him. His hands grip tight against one another, trying hard to keep the memories of his past at bay.

I listen quietly, mulling over and weighing his words, his *reality*.

"I'm sorry," I whisper.

It's not much. It doesn't take back what we have done to each other for years.

But even though we hated the humans for what they were doing to our people, we never killed them. Lilith had forbidden it. She said they are not to be killed. No matter what, they'll be put somewhere. It doesn't matter where, but they are to live.

I never agreed with her. I never found her sentiment to make any kind of sense.

How did she not thirst for blood with the way they slaughtered us? How did she not rage against it? But she stayed true, to the very end.

The closer I get to Asher, and the closer The Fates push me into his palms, the more I find myself racked with guilt instead of rage. Empathy instead of revenge.

He has vowed to save my people. And to what end? Why would he feel such a thing toward us, yet bend the knee?

Surely, I can be capable of such accommodations.

His green eyes connect with mine as his head rises and he gives me a pained smile.

I take gentle steps to the bed, and he leans back enough to allow me to bend down between his knees. I place my hands against his thighs in comfort, offering an apologetic smile.

"We are going to save Tantalia, and Vesperholm," I tell him gently as I take his calloused hands into my own.

His grip tightens as I speak, his eyes flashing with confusion, hope, worry, and…

My lips curl in a smile as his expression softens.

His rough hand releases mine to grasp my chin, pulling me in close.

Heat rises between us and my heart pulses fire through my veins. My hands tighten where they've come to rest on his legs again. The sight of his tousled brown hair and his gentle expression urges me closer.

His lips just barely brush mine before a knock comes at the door.

"I am not spelled to do this; no. I am her Queen's Guard. I go where she goes."

CHAPTER 34

THE MAP

ASHER

My hand tightens for only a moment as an aggravated sigh eases from my throat. I press my forehead to Seraphina's in a silent "thank you" before pressing a soft kiss to her skin and she stands.

Seraphina saunters to the door with lethal grace, her tail flicking in annoyance or irritation, I'm unsure. But she opens the door a moment later, the nervous little mage in the white cloak almost trembling as he stands in the entry.

I stand from the bed to watch the event go down. Seraphina's wings tighten against her back as I see her look at the terrified wizard.

His amber eyes dart between Seraphina and me as he enters the room. Seraphina takes a step to the side to allow him entry, before she closes the door behind him.

"I've come to find out what supplies you'll be needing on your journey," he says softly.

Seraphina crosses her arms against her chest as she eyes the nervous mage with a cautionary gaze, "Tyrick… was it? What was the name of your female constituent?"

The young man's eyes widen as they look between us, clearing his throat as he shifts in place, "Retalnia. Applebaum."

Her eyebrow lifts as she observes him, "*Tyrick…* For now, we need a map," Seraphina says.

Tyrick nods, before his head swivels around the room, as if he's searching for something. His head lands on the small desk in the corner before he walks over to it, looking for a sheet of parchment.

He retrieves the item and places it on the small dining table in the room.

Tyrick reaches into his pocket to retrieve a crooked stick. The outside is smooth and almost silver, but the handle has been beefed up with a strip of leather. He takes the tip of his wand and presses it against the parchment.

"From land to water, and ocean to tree, show me the land they wish to see," he murmurs quietly as he closes his eyes.

Soon, a splat of ink hits the page, and the drop begins to roll along it, roaming around in haphazard lines as it begins etching out a map right before our eyes.

I glance to Seraphina who is too busy looking at her nails to worry about anything this little mage is doing. I, however, am absolutely entranced by this.

And while I do have hunter's gifts, I wouldn't say they're magic – they're more like a strength. But watching this mage do this makes me want to learn for myself.

I doubt Seraphina knows how to teach a human to wield magic from a wand. But perhaps I can ask this little guy later.

I hear a deep breath from Tyrick as the map finishes its scribbles and he grabs it before turning around to hand it to Seraphina with a shaky hand.

Seraphina takes the map from his fingers and walks to the bed to look at it, her hand waving him off as she zeroes in on this new plan.

"Wait, I had some questions," he says quickly. A bead of sweat rolls down his brow as he looks between us.

Seraphina turns around with an almost appalled expression, as if she can't believe he would even attempt to ask such a thing.

My brow rises as I face Tyrick, waiting to hear whatever he intends to learn.

His amber eyes dart to Seraphina before they land back on me. "How did you get here?" he asks gently.

My forehead tenses as I try to make sense of his question, "Well, we came through the portal. I thought that was pretty clear."

"No, no. I mean… How did *you* come to be here… with *her*?" he asks once more as his eyes shift to point to Seraphina.

Seraphina's head tilts as she watches him, his eyes twitching back and forth between the two of us as he waits for my answer.

"I am the Queen's Commander," I state plainly.

Tyrick's forehead creases, "Why? We know of what they have done to humans. Why are you her guard?"

Dozens of words work through my skull for a few moments, a menagerie of questions, but no clear answer.

"Because we are going to save our realms," I say softly.

My eyes drift to Seraphina, whose face softens at my response and her wings at her back relax just the smallest amount. The previously rigid flick to her tail turns elegant as it begins to sway behind her.

"Has she… spelled you to do this?" he asks cautiously as he sizes up Seraphina once more.

I give him a look of perplexion. "I am not spelled to do this; no. I am her Queen's Guard. I go where she goes."

Seraphina's lips twitch in a smile she attempts to fight as she stays her course on the young wizard. He has no idea that he threatens his life with his words.

He doesn't know what she's capable of, and I'm not entirely sure how far Seraphina is willing to go in this pocket realm, even when we need their help. But he walks a thin line.

I have to admit, being on the other side of this *is* splendid.

He watches us for a few moments before he nods and retreats from the room.

As the door shuts with a soft click, Seraphina turns to look at me, "That was strange."

"Indeed."

Very strange.

Though his questions have me pondering.

Yes, I want to save our realms. And sometimes, I feel like I don't truly have a choice in the matter.

But at the end of the day, I *want* to be by her side. And I don't know why I'm so enthralled by the idea of her mere presence.

I don't try to make sense of it. It just feels like something I have to do, whether I want to or not. But there have been numerous occasions recently where I've wanted to, no, *needed* to be with her.

After The Stone went down and she took the staff to the chest, it rocked everything that I thought I had known. And the small reality of her not being in my life, whether I understood my reaction or not, was one I cared not to witness.

To live without Seraphina now would be to exist without air. To exist without *reason.* It would make no sense, and I would surely perish.

Even still, I don't know what to make of it. Thinking any deeper about it causes my stomach to churn because I can't face the idea of what it might possibly mean.

That all this feeling *is* her doing, that I'm just a puppet on her string, waiting for her to cut the twine.

I would like, just for a while, to savor the idea of a life where I don't have to survive. I can thrive.

And if Seraphina has given me that chance, I'm going to take it.

Seraphina has taken a seat at the small table and is deep in thought as she surveys the map quietly.

I take steps over to her, leaning between her wings and looking over her head to the map below.

There are a variety of islands, labeled with small text. Drawings of different lands and areas highlight main points of interest.

I had no idea this world existed outside of Vesperholm. Until a few seconds ago, I merely thought it was just the few realms Seraphina spoke of, I was unaware of how much bigger the world was.

It makes me feel… small. So incredibly small.

And oblivious. There are entire other societies outside of Tantalia, Vesperholm and The Never Realm. To be honest, the realization is life changing in the strangest way.

Not to mention, it only puts into perspective the implications of the Drannars taking control of the stone and how much they would rule. The idea is frightening… terrifying even.

The most outspoken human would find it in their best interest to forge an alliance with the succubus. Especially when you've merely gotten a glimpse of what the Drannar are capable of and how they treat even their own people.

Imagine beings not of their kind? What would happen then? I've heard of their massacre; I saw their attack.

Every day I spend outside of Vesperholm feels not only hopeful for the idea I may be able to save my species but terrifying for the idea we may not be able to save the rest of the world.

My attention splits and I come back to look down at Seraphina, a sigh of grief escaping her, "We are going to need a lot of potions…"

His scent changes,
from piney woods
to something
more... divine.

CHAPTER 35

STRENGTH

SERAPHINA

The map is not shocking, but trying to figure out our trajectory is a little more daunting than I thought.

Tantalia exists as part of a land mass to the east, with Vesperholm south of us. Tantalia is protected and only accessed by portals.

The pocket realm exists southwest of Tantalia. Whereas The Never Realm rests across the Barren Gulf.

Further west from the Tantalia landmass, and far north of *Kaithoon* – I suppose is the name of this pocket realm – across the gulf, rests a long expanding forest called Castaway Grove.

Interesting name.

Small islands dot the waters, until it reaches a large island sur-rounded by dark seas.

Knogdagh Stronghold… Orxsile…

We are going to need a boat, and we are going to need potions for breathing underwater. But that's the very least of our problems.

Flying into Orxsile would be a foolish endeavor, not one I planned on taking anyway.

I will have to speak to the mages more on this, my knowledge of the island is far more limited than one would assume. Perhaps they could be made privy to sharing such knowledge.

"Potions?" Asher says from above me.

"Yes... many of them. We won't be able to do most of the things we would do in Tantalia, or The Never Realm. I will have to melee with anyone we encounter. Not to mention, flying is far too risky," I tell Asher absentmindedly, as my thoughts continue to work over the map.

There are so many risks involved in this idea, and part of me is wondering why I'm even allowed to do anything like this in the first place. But even if I was to be stopped, it would just make me want to do it more.

"So... What *will* we need?"

"Invisibility... water breathing... shapeshifting of some kind... and we need multiples as they usually have a time limit."

"*Greeeeaaaatt...*" Asher sighs. The floorboards alert his departure from my back, followed by the sound of the bed squeaking under his weight. "Do you think there will ever be a day where we aren't risking our lives in a suicide mission?"

"Perhaps. But not any time soon."

"Do you know anything about the Orcs?" Asher asks as I hear the thunk of wood.

My brow furrows in confusion as I turn around to observe the source of the noise. Asher relaxes on the small bed, flipping his favorite weapon in his hand. The dagger slides from his grasp as he flicks it above him, his palm steady and still. Waiting for it to ease from the wood, before it falls, finding its home back in his fingers.

He tends to carry that thing everywhere and I've noticed its handle is more intricately designed than the others he had with him when he arrived in Tantalia, but I've never taken a very close look at it.

"Why are you doing that?" I ask.

"It's fun, helps me stay sharp," he responds as he flicks the blade once more.

My eyes roll as I turn my attention back to the map.

I drag a sharp talon into the page with a small "X" as I mark a miniscule speck of land outside of Orxsile. The closest one to the fortress that would be a short swim and keep us obscured.

Though, the other tricky part comes in. Where we somehow breach this castle's defenses and get inside. Because I have no idea where I would even find this damn book.

The shapeshifting will help but I still don't know my way around the place.

I'll have to figure it out when we get there. Because at this point, I have no other option…

Damnit.

That stupid fucking phrase is awful. No wonder Asher raged at me when I'd say it.

"Have you ever interacted with Orcs?" Asher asks quietly.

"Personally, no. From my knowledge, they feast on succubus. We try to stay as far from them as we can, because they can be massive, and they have no self-control. Our magic helps us when we have it, but taking one on by yourself can prove to be fatal," I explain.

"As if I needed another reason to feel bad about killing your people," Asher grumbles.

"Vesperholm did it for self-defense… Orcs do it for fun," I sigh in response.

Asher is silent, but not without a loud *thunk* into the wood once more.

"Do you have anything to add?" I ask in annoyance as I peer at the map.

Castaway Grove is a long length of forest between the outside entry to the Realm of Mages, and the sea. A few days walk to the shore, considering we don't have Asher's precious friend.

I have spent my entire life between Tantalia and Vesperholm. Which means, I have no idea what other mythical beings could exist outside of this realm.

We have heard tales. Their legends or myths tucked away in our tomes. Sirens, dragons, dryads, unicorns, phoenixes. Anything *can* exist out there. What we don't know is *if* they do. And neither does Asher.

Going on foot appears to be our only option.

Unfortunate.

Asher lets go a loud sigh, the bed squeaking under him and the floorboards of the room wail once more as he approaches. He makes gentle movements so as to not hit my wings.

What a considerate beast.

He leans over my shoulder, and I inhale a deep breath of his scent.

Always pine and metal. I can't help the way my mouth waters as he leans farther above me. My eyes glance up to see him studying the map intensely.

His green eyes are so focused on the parchment and strands of his brown hair fall over his brow as it scrunches in concentration.

"Lots of woods… We're going to need to take two or three days to traverse the terrain. It'd be a bad idea to push it into one day. We'll need our strength," he echoes my thoughts as if he was reading them himself.

"Yes… yes, strength," I muse as I turn to look at him.

His scent seeps deeper into my being and causes my skin to prickle with hunger, but Asher pays me no mind.

"Asher-dear…" I lilt as I turn to brush my claws softly against his jaw.

His focus is still on the map until I drag a sharp tip against the skin, his eyes slowly come to meet mine as he is pulled from his thoughts.

The green orbs peer at me in question, until he looks deeper into my eyes.

My tongue falls from my mouth to drag up his throat, and his body quakes softly in response as his eyes flutter back.

"Sera, here? Now?" he groans.

"You said we need our strength," I coo seductively.

His scent changes, from piney woods to something more… divine. Spicy and masculine, like burnt embers of well-tooled leather. *Delicious.*

I glance to his leather breeches, a thick bulge pressing against the tough material as his body stills and he takes steady breaths in anticipation.

I stand from my chair, pressing a hand to his chest as I size him up with a seductive, hungry grin. I take steps toward him as he takes steps backward, until his knees hit the bed, and he falls onto it. His arms catch his torso as he sits up to look at me. Green eyes are wide with wonder as his throat works in a deep gulp.

I kneel between his thighs, nuzzling his firm cock through his pants with my face.

Asher breathes slowly as he watches me, his gaze mesmerized by the way I take control of him.

The leather of his armored breeches slides across my hands as I caress his thighs until purple glow consumes the material and they no longer cover his body. His cock, hard and pulsing, stands erect in front of me.

I swear drool drips off my fangs as my mouth opens, and my tongue ejects to slick my lower lip in unbridled desire. It wraps around the underside of him, the split caressing either side of his rigid length as I taste his skin.

A gasp sounds from his chest as I take the head of him between my lips. Precum coats my tongue, and I hum in delight at his taste. Peering up at him, I watch as his eyes roll back and I slide his cock deeper into my throat. My tongue presses against the underside of him to glide with every inch I take.

His hands dart out, wrapping around the base of my horns and gripping them tightly as I reach the hilt of him. My tongue splits at the bottom to wrap around his balls and squeeze them, my throat moving in waves against him.

He's not capable of moaning or groaning as I wrench the soul from him. Merely choked gasps that escape him as his hips buck softly against the back of my throat.

He glides against the roof of my mouth as I pull off from him, leaving a trail of my saliva down his balls as I separate myself. I grip my fingers around the wide base of him, taking soft kisses along his length before I peer back at him again.

I love watching the way he melts under my ministrations. It's almost as delicious as he is.

His chest heaves, and I feel the thrum of his pleasure course through my body and prickle against my skin as his balls tighten.

His hands grip tighter against my horns as he pushes his cock toward my face again, his gaze heavy with desire and focus as he watches every single move I make.

He enters my lips, and I take him down my throat once more, his groans picking up as he takes soft thrusts into my mouth.

His gentle thrusts lose precision as he approaches the cliff, his body shaking as he gets closer, and his head tosses back.

"Fuck… Gods… Sera, what are… fuck," he chokes out as his cock hardens further and jets of his pleasure splash against the back of my throat as he releases himself. The wrapped tension of his hands around my horns tightens almost painfully. His body damn near vibrates from the rumble that escapes his chest.

His thrusts slowly die and the grip on my horns loosens. Slowly, his hands slide through my hair, lingering on my cheek to stroke it gently before they fall onto the bed. Heavy pants fill the room as his body relaxes in a depleted heap of calm.

"Sera, what the fuck," he pants softly. Standing, I wipe the drool from my lips as I wave my hand over his lower half, clothing him. I watch him in delight as my hands go to my hips, satisfied with my feeding.

"What?" I smile devilishly.

"How am I supposed to keep my strength if you take it from me?" he continues his panting. His gaze is locked on the wood above as he regains his composure.

"Oh, you'll be fine," I wave him off as I walk back to the table, planting my hands against the wooden surface to glare at the map.

Feeding from Asher is so renewing, and I'm so glad he allows such delicacies, but he needs his strength as well.

"We'll need to discuss our methods with the mages," I murmur as I look over the plan.

Perhaps if I was embarking on this expedition alone, I would feel more apprehensive. And while I do feel some of it, having Asher at my side makes it a little better. Weeks ago, I could have taken him to these woods to rid him of his heartbeat. But his presence alone fills me with strength, his pleasure is just a fun snack. Even if it does *fulfill* me.

It's a different kind of a fill. An emotional one. Versus the physical fills I've come to be accustomed to, as a succubus.

I never thought a *human* could make me feel the things I'm feeling now.

I'd never been able to feel these things with any halflings, or even the humans I used to take from. And in all honesty, I never wanted this sort of bond with anyone. I was content going through my immortal life without someone. I didn't need another being to bring down what I could accomplish on my own.

But through this process, I have realized one thing.

I need Asher if I seek to fix my realm. Not for what he can provide, but for what his soul has to offer.

Courage.

While I am strong enough in my own right, I have my own misgivings. Asher stands by my side and has pulled me from ruts I may not have survived without him.

The room has gone suspiciously silent as I've retreated to my reflections, and I look toward the bed to find Asher passed out and snoozing peacefully against the mattress. I scoff as I walk to him. Picking up his massive legs, I slowly press him fully onto the sheets, scooting his body close to the wall that the bed is sitting against.

I smile as I come to lay beside him, nuzzling into his chest and inhaling the woody scent of this human.

Asher exhales a sleepy moan as his arms wrap around my waist, pulling me closer to his body.

My heart picks up as I sink against him, slowly falling asleep myself.

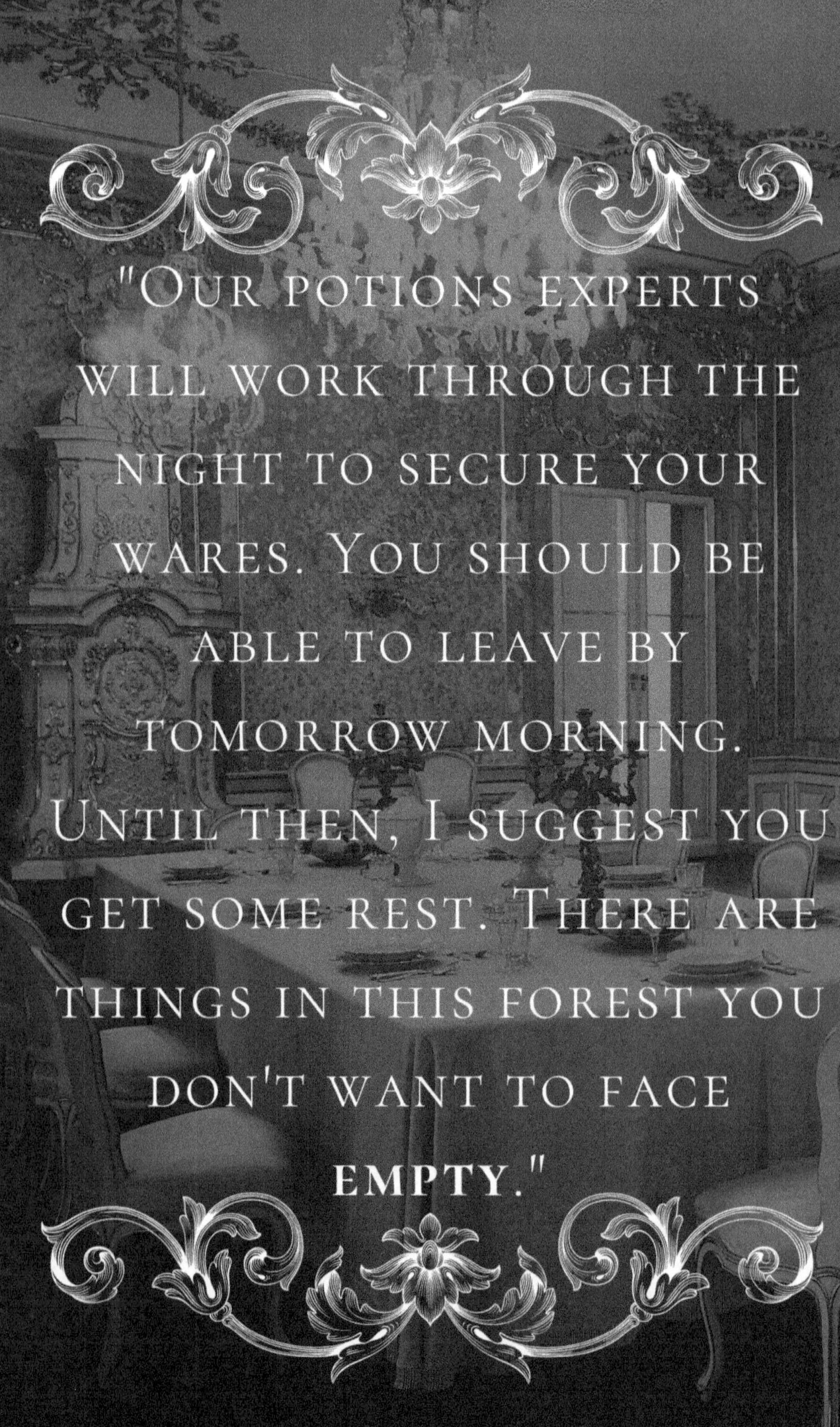

"Our potions experts will work through the night to secure your wares. You should be able to leave by tomorrow morning. Until then, I suggest you get some rest. There are things in this forest you don't want to face empty."

Chapter 36

The Dinner

Asher

"She is yours, Asher. And you are hers. Whether or not you choose to accept it." A disembodied voice breaks through my conscious.

My eyes open, and the area surrounding me is nothing but a black void. It feels like this void stretches for eons and I make to run, only to find I get nowhere, as if I'm running in place. A layer of black liquid sloshes against the hard ground, like I'm walking on a flooded floor.

"Who are you?!" I call through the expansive darkness.

"The key lies within you," the voice calls again.

I spin in place, searching, squinting to see if I can see anything, anyone.

"Show yourself!" I call back. My hand makes to grip at my dagger, only to find I'm weaponless and clothed in a bare tunic and breeches. My heart gallops in my chest as I frantically search for a way out.

Gods, where the fuck am I?

"I've made myself known. You choose not to answer," it says.

"Sounds like you're scared," I taunt.

"I have no such qualms. I am incapable of such."

A growl rumbles against my throat as I search.

-knock-

The sound shakes against the walls of the void.

"Better answer it," it drolls.

-knock-

It booms and echoes through the darkness.

"Better hurry."

-knock-

"Time is ticking."

-KNOCK!-

My eyes pop open, searching around me in panic. My breath comes in deep heaves as I rouse fitfully from my nightmare. Or whatever the fuck that was.

Sweat clings to my skin as I get a sense of where I am.

Pitch dark blackness surrounds us, and no candles are lit to illuminate the room.

Bed. Seraphina. Realm of Mages. Compendium.

I repeat as I take deep, calming breaths, feeling the air fill my chest before blowing it out.

The weight of Seraphina in my arms brings me back to the present, when another knock against the door tugs at my nerves. Seraphina doesn't stir as I slowly retrieve my arms and climb over her. The lantern in the corner illuminates to light the room in an orange, flickering glow and I pause in confusion as I look around the room in question.

This place is… something.

Stepping from the bed, I shake my dead arms out as I reach for the doorknob, slowly pulling it open. I peek my head around the corner to see the younger mage, Tyrick, standing sheepishly outside.

"The wizards request your presence for dinner to discuss your endeavors," he says gently.

In a half-awake daze, I nod mindlessly, "Yes, we'll uh… we'll be there in a moment," I respond gruffly. My voice still thick from sleep.

"I'll wait here to lead you to the dining room," he responds with a bow.

I go to close the door before something pricks my thoughts, "Hey, uh. Tyrick, right?"

Tyrick turns to me with a confused nod as I grab his attention.

"The lantern in the room. It was lit, earlier... When I woke up, it was out. Then when I got up to move, it just... lit up."

Tyrick gives a sideways smile, "The candles are spelled to relay the time outside. When it's dark, the candles go out if no one in the room is moving."

What the entire fuck.

"Oh... Uh... Thank you..." I give him a curt, confused nod before I slowly close the door, looking back at the sleeping beauty herself.

Her back slowly expands as she takes deep, slumbering breaths. Walking up to the bed, I rub softly at her shoulder, "Sera," I whisper.

She moans a sleepy sound as she stirs.

"Sera, the mages are requesting that we join them for dinner," I say as I nudge her shoulder softly once more.

"Mmmmmmmmmmmm," she hums again.

Ugh, gods dammit.

"Sera," I say a bit louder.

"Mmmm, Asher-darling," she sighs as she turns over. Her purple eyes hazy as she blinks slowly. Her gaze tries so hard to focus on me, "What time is it?" she asks as she takes a sleep-dazed look around the room.

"Apparently dinner time," I respond.

"Mmm, fine," Seraphina says as she slowly makes to stand, taking a large stretch as she sits up on the bed.

Her wings expand and knock into the wood walls as she eases the sleep from her bones.

"Are you ready, Asher-dear?" she muses sleepily as she yawns and looks to me with a contented smile. Her sleep-laden eyes threaten to close if I don't get her moving fast enough.

Is it always this hard to wake her up? My lords.

"As ready as I think I'll ever be," I grumble.

"Terrific." She smiles wider, "Come darling," she says as she walks past me, snatching the parchment from the table as she strides to the door.

Seraphina swings the door open to glare at the mage standing there, his eyes wide in trepidation as he waits for us.

"Ah, Mistress. The mages request you," he informs her.

"Splendid," she says as she walks from the room, her strong hand wrapped around my bicep as she guides me along.

Tyrick's eyes volley between her and I as he gives me a look of confusion and I look back at him with a small shrug.

Beats me, I'm just here for the ride.

The door shuts behind us before quick steps approach, the mage trying desperately to keep up and get in front of us.

He nudges past us, on a decorated wall of sorts, and continues to lead us to the dining area.

As we pass through this seemingly ancient castle, I try my best to keep my wits about me.

Even though they may have accepted us with crossed arms, I don't know if I can trust them completely. And I would sincerely hope that Seraphina has the same thoughts as well.

The brick that lines the walls of the castle are dark, chipped and worn away by time, with a dense scent of fragrant herbal smoke that feels like it chokes the air we breathe.

Different signets and crests are woven into banners that lay against the brick, and I try to take note of them all as we continue to make our way through the dark hallways.

Sconces blaze as we walk past, allowing only the dimmest amount of light to guide us.

Eventually, the dark hallway gives way to an expansive greeting hall. Tarnished silver armor rests on wooden stands and guards the stairwell that leads to the upper floor of the castle.

The nervous mage has not said anything, and Seraphina seems to be unimpressed by her surroundings as we continue traversing this unknown place.

Tyrick leads us to the stairwell, where we ascend up the shiny wooden steps that have been protected by an intricately designed carpet. Taking a right as we reach the first platform, we take another set of steps, into a separate hallway.

This one is not as narrow as the one our room is housed in, and the paintings on the walls are of different wizards and witches of ages past. In front of each portrait is also an expertly carved bust. Placed atop marble pedestals, almost as if to guard their own works.

Eventually, we reach a room off the hallway and are greeted by two servants who open the door for us to enter. The smoke smell isn't as strong in here, as it's been replaced by the scent of chicken, beef, and other various foodstuffs.

My mouth begins to water as I look over the stretched dining table that is framed by a variety of witches and wizards that stand to greet us as we enter.

"Announcing, Queen of Tantalia, Seraphina Moonsong and her Commander, Asher Blackwood," a deep voice calls through the room in a booming echo as we approach the table.

Some of the mages brows furrow in confusion as they watch us, their gazes slipping to one another before they come to rest on me.

Strange reaction to a human.

Seraphina holds her head high as she strides into the room, with me on her arm like a muscled accessory.

Tyrick gestures to one of the empty chairs in the room before he pulls it out, allowing Seraphina to sit in it. She nods to him in thanks as she places her rump in the seat, and he pushes her chair in.

I pull the chair out next to hers and sit as well, looking over the different faces in the room.

As Seraphina and I sit, the others follow suit. A symphony of wooden legs scrapes against the marbled floors as they settle at their placemats. Seraphina shifts uncomfortably in her seat, her wings opening and closing in an attempt to fit them in properly before she turns around.

Her claws sink into the decorative baubles on the top of the chair as her feet part on the floor. Bracing herself, she shoves it back, breaking the top of the chair off with a deafening crack. She holds the now dislocated piece of chair in her hands as she settles more comfortably in it, before tossing the large wooden piece to the floor behind her. The piece of splintered wood causes a loud crash to sound through the near silent room as it makes contact. Her wings relax and she leans against them as they pin into the stone behind her; steepling her hands in front of her mouth.

I take the chance to look around the table. Some jaws have gaped at her destruction, while other curious and almost fearful eyes dart from one another before they land on us.

Seraphina appears to pay them no mind as she looks over the food placed before us, her nostrils flaring and her eyebrow rising with a disgusted sneer before she ignores it.

Bufort, the older male wizard, sits at the head of the table, with the middle-aged witch, Retalnia, in the chair beside him.

"Welcome, Seraphina and Asher. I have brought the rest of the council to dine with us. As they all have a variety of knowledge to offer on your endeavors going forward," Bufort says to Seraphina.

"A toast! To our new… friends," he says with a slight grimace toward Seraphina. He raises his goblet in the air in a half-hearted toast.

The other mages mirror him, raising their goblets to us as well.

Seraphina nods appreciatively as they place their drinks back on the table.

"So, have you decided what route you plan to take?" Bufort asks as he begins cutting into his chicken.

I decide to dig in as well. I reach for my fork and knife beside the plate before Seraphina smiles charmingly at Bufort. Her hand gingerly comes to stop me as she begins speaking in a tensed and forcingly elegant timbre, "On foot, unfortunately, appears to be our best course of action.

An expedition of sorts that would take about three days' time from your exit portal to the shore."

My brow furrows as she stops me from eating, but I comply anyway.

Even though I'm very, *very* hungry.

"We will need a boat. As well as a list of potions, several vials of each, and I would like to have access to their production. A mirror shall be placed in our quarters for me to watch. I'm sure you can all oblige by those rules?" Seraphina asks kindly.

Bufort's eyes slide to one of the witches at the table, who returns his look with a prick of her brow.

This is going very oddly.

"Yes, that should be no problem at all. And the potions you require?" Bufort asks.

Tyrick stands next to Bufort with a piece of parchment in hand as a feather quill scribbles furiously against it.

"Water breathing, invisibility, and shapeshifting," Seraphina responds.

"A large order. What is your plan when you reach the shore?" he asks as he bites into his chicken.

"We'll abandon the boat on a nearby isle, then swim the rest of the way to the shore of the fortress." She leans back in her destroyed chair, her hands steepling in front of her as she kicks one leg over the other. The soft *tink* of her lower wing talons sound off in the room as they stick into the stone to prop her up.

"The fortress is usually unguarded from the outside. The inside, however, is a different story," a middle-aged wizard says from across the table. His beady blue eyes are framed in round glasses, and he wears fabrics of a vibrant royal blue. He runs his hands through his hair as he reaches behind his chair, retrieving a massive textbook.

The brown leather is torn and ripped in places. And there are indentations on its cover where gold leaf has flaked from its exterior.

He places the book on the table, and flips through it, "The Orcs are a brutal race of being, not needing magic because of their intense strength," he says as he peers intensely into the text.

My eyes slide to Seraphina, her features are relaxed in indifference as she watches the wizard.

"There is no magic on the Isle…" he says quietly, almost to himself as his eyes continue to scan the pages.

"Information on the internal structures is unknown, which means you're going in blind. The only transcribed text mentions their leader's quarters are at the very top, of the highest tower."

Great.

"Potions typically last for around ten to twenty minutes and are not able to be stacked. They can become a volatile mix when taken at different intervals or taken together, so plan your administrations wisely," A gray haired witch chimes in from her spot at the table, her eyes intent on her chicken as she severs another sliver from it.

I salivate as I watch her cut into the meat.

Seraphina better give me something if she's not letting me eat here.

"How long can we expect for our departure?" Seraphina asks.

"Our potions experts will work through the night to secure your wares. You should be able to leave by tomorrow morning. Until then, I suggest you get some rest. There are things in this forest you don't want to face *empty*," Bufort says with a gentle smirk toward me.

Pal, if I could, the plate would be empty.

"Splendid. Bring the mirror when you start our potions, the human and I must take our leave," Seraphina says as she quickly stands from her chair.

My eyes widen from the sudden announcement and I glance around the table of powerful witches and wizards, their own features almost sympathetic on my accord.

I push my chair from the table, and stand, giving them all a soft bow before Seraphina leads us from the dining room.

The guards standing by the door open it to allow us exit. The doors click softly behind us as they close while Seraphina and I make our way through the long hallway.

Her steps possess a vigor I wasn't expecting, and I take longer strides to keep up with her.

Once we reach the bottom of the grand stairwell and turn down the hallway to our room, I come beside her, "Was that strange?"

"Very," Seraphina murmurs quietly. Her features contort and shift as we pass the fired sconces.

"Why couldn't I eat the food?" I ask as we approach our door.

Seraphina is quiet as she surveys the wooden entry point, her eyes roam around its jam before she looks back and forth down the hallway.

She faces the door once more and places her hands against it. I hear a mumbling of words and the door shimmers with her signature purple glow before it slowly fades away. She opens the door before she quickly pulls me in and shuts it behind her. She speeds around the room, dragging her claws along its wooden walls. The sound is a sickening scratch as a small line of silver comes from the tips, allowing the walls to all shimmer with it before they too, slowly fall away.

Seraphina breathes a deep sigh before she settles and turns to face me, "The food was spelled, Asher. With what? I'm not sure, but they don't trust us," she responds as she crosses her arms.

My brow pinches in confusion as I look at her, "Spelled?"

"This room has been tampered with as well. I've protected us here for the time being. Regardless, we can't talk too much about the rifts in Tantalia, they're watching us," she says assuredly.

"Have you gone mad?" I ask. All of this is entirely too confusing.

Sure, the dinner was a tad bizarre, but they seemed keen on helping us. I can't imagine they would go to such lengths to thwart our plans.

"There was a scent on the food. Something vile. We have to take precautions while we still have magic. And I can't say I'm well versed in the ways of... non-magic living so I will allow you to take the lead.

This seems to be your level of expertise. And I can't exactly rely on your expertise if you're a fucking toad."

I ignore the toad comment as my heart flutters. Calling the shots here? I like the sound of that. I could even say it makes me a bit giddy, and I nod a tad more enthusiastically than I need to.

Seraphina offers an amused smile as she sits on the bed. "Come pet, we need to get our rest," she says.

Her hands graze her body, and in their wake, her armor disappears, clothing her body in her silky black nightgown.

My pulse picks up as I take in her tight body, my cock swelling in excitement as I think about being inside of her again.

"Not now, Asher-dear, I have to get what little rest I can before I have to watch the mages make the potions," she says as she lifts back the blankets on the bed, patting the space next to her for me to climb in first.

I make a grumbled noise of frustration as I walk to join her on the bed.

No food, no sex. What is this shit?

As I approach her with a pout, she places her hands gently on my chest.

"Oh, come on, you can't do that to me!" I tell her exasperatedly as I throw my hands out.

She lets a soft chuckle go, "You can sleep in your armor if you'd like."

"Fine," I grumble softly, allowing her magic to replace my armor with my soft night clothes.

I climb into the bed next to the wall and allow her to climb beside me.

Her face nuzzles into my chest as her wings tighten at her back for her comfortability.

I wrap my arms around her, and once more, I am lulled into a deep sleep by her potent floral scent and the warmth of her body.

Though, with every X he marks, the trees drip with the red sap. It's an odd sight. An eery one... but I do my best to ignore it.

As expected, I barely got any sleep last night.

The smaller mage, Tyrick, came a few hours later with a mirror which I sat in front of the entire night, watching intensely throughout their potion making process.

Cauldrons bubbled through the glass as they added various herbs and mythical proponents. Eye of newt, orcs blood, fish scales *and* tails. All the bits and pieces dissolved to become these liquids we'd end up ingesting.

The dinner had given me everything I needed to know about where they stood with us.

They were willing to help, but they didn't trust us.

Therefore, I was unwilling to bless them with our presence any longer than necessary.

I wouldn't put it past them to tamper with the ingredients and give us some sort of glowing eyes or turn us into beasts.

The entire night, I sat. The mages mixed their brews and bottled them carefully for our use.

All the while, I contemplated what the next few days would look like.

I could safely assume Asher is full and well on my side. Allowing him to take the lead would give him the confidence in helping me in the future. Not that I didn't expect him to anyway.

The forest is a dangerous place, especially one you know nothing about.

And while Asher is well-versed in the woods, we both are on equal footing; magically speaking, of course.

While I watched the mages concoct our potions, I took the liberty of gathering our weapons from afar; conjuring them before I ran out of magic to do such a thing.

When I move our clothes, or when I procure our armor, its usually hung on its own in its homing space.

The armoire in my room, for example.

Connected through intricately crafted intentional magic, the two things exchange places. That being said, I went through it piece by piece to gather everything we would need. My swords, our battle armor, and all of Asher's numerous daggers.

He always has his pretty one with him, but the others can change. I'd taken the liberty of supplying him with a few silver ones from Tantalia and had Reasha sharpen and balance them for his use.

At certain points of my conjuring, it took more time and was a bit more of a hassle, as it pulled a strain on my magic. But if I wasn't going to need it outside of this realm, I pushed it to its limits. By the time I was done, I was able to pack all of our necessities -- though it would be strange, actually having to change my clothes by hand.

An unfortunate circumstance for a monumental change.

I procured waist packs and other things he uses to carry his items. We would traverse the landscape in our armor, considering we can't full well pack those in sacks.

All in all, I had gotten everything we needed.

The next morning came and went in a blur. The mages gave us our potions and I held them all on a crossbody pack around my torso that they were kind enough to supply us with.

Asher seemed distant as we went through our motions and eventually said goodbye to the mages.

And now, Tyrick leads us to the outskirts of their town, where a marble platform rests deep in the woods; a clearing in the forest holds the lone archway. With the sun beaming down on it, lighting its various curves and shadows darkening the recessed areas, it beckons us to take the step onto the other side.

Beyond the portal is land as far as the eye can see.

With this place being heavily warded, I imagine it's just an illusion to guard the realm.

The marble platform glows with sporadically placed runes that are etched into the stone surrounding it, similar to the ones in the cave with a number of runes placed into the archway itself.

"Outside here, you are on your own. There is no magic, and I am forbidden to tell you about what creatures may lurk. When you get to the other side, there is no portal like this, there will only be a boulder to mark its spot. When you need to pass through here to get back to your lands, you merely knock three times against the boulder, and someone will retrieve you," Tyrick explains, his brow furrowed in concern as he watches us.

Asher's eyes narrow on the small mage in confusion, his head tilting as he observes him.

I seem to see what he sees, and I peer curiously at the wizard, "You don't feel the same as the elders, do you?"

His amber eyes widen in shock and surprise, "What makes you say that?"

"You don't seem as hesitant to help us as they are," I tell him.

"It's not that... I..." he admits softly as his gaze breaks away.

He sighs in frustration, "I find the succubus to be interesting creatures. I was raised to hate them. The treaty never allowed us to traverse the realms, and I want to see what else is out there," Tyrick says as he gazes at the portal behind us.

My eyebrow raises as I look behind me at the arch, surveying the graceful curves and elegant swoop of the stone. Turning my attention back to Tyrick, "If you would like, you are more than welcome to be the bridge of trust between our realms. There is much even I need to learn, and we could use anything right now."

While I don't think I can trust the other mages. This one seems to be privier to our efforts.

A wizard could be useful in these trying times.

Tyrick almost glows with the prospect, "I actually think I would like that. A lot."

"Splendid. Mull over it with your superiors. I'll have your answer when I return," I tell him with a soft bow.

"Thank you, I-I really appreciate it," he says as his cheeks tint a rosy, red color against his olive skin.

Fucking humans. I shake my head with a small smirk.

"Are you ready, Asher-dear?" I ask as I turn to Asher.

He has abandoned our conversation and has turned to the arch-way, his body still as he looks over it. My voice pulls him from his thoughts and his gaze connects with mine; his chest expanding as he takes a deep breath.

"Born ready," he says softly with a nod.

This portal dumps us in a clearing of Castaway Grove.
And not figuratively.

Since there is technically no access point, we basically fell from the sky.

Or at least it feels that way.

My massive pack of supplies crush me under its weight, and I lay there for a moment trying to recenter myself.

The mossy ground vibrates with a pained groan. Shifting my weight, I grind my head against the ground to spot the source, only to find Asher crushed under his own pack.

He looks as if he's taken a harder hit, as his face presses deep against the grass.

"You alright?" I ask.

A thumb weakly raises in the air, alluding to his condition.

"Great." I groan as I press against the ground to stand. Moss coddles my lower wingtips as I prick them into the earth, using the leverage to hoist myself vertically. As I set myself upright, my feet swing for the merest of moments before I plant them in the ground. Different points of my body prick with pain as I adjust myself and my pack before shaking my wings out. I look down at my chest, where the crossbody pack is secured, and unlatch the metal clasp. Glass vials clink against each other as I look over the wares and ensure their safety.

All good.

Looking to Asher, I watch as he slowly makes to stand as well, attempting to regain balance as, he too, adjusts his pack.

"That was shitty," he groans in annoyance as he stretches his neck from side to side.

I wiggle my wings to reset myself and inhale a heavy breath before surveying the area we've been dumped. The various latches and clasps securing things to my body knock into the plates of metal in my armor.

Fucking hells is that ever loud.

Vibrant green grass forms almost a perfect circle in the middle of these woods. When I turn around, an enormous, jagged boulder rests on the ground. Its rough surface decorated with moss, lichen and other leafy bits of overgrowth.

Approaching it, I see a small crest etched into its front. A cloak, like the ones worn by the mages is pressed into the stone with two wands crossed in front of it.

I reach into a pocket on my armored breeches, pulling out the parchment map and unfolding it. Color has developed since I last looked at it and there are more names on it.

Mage's magic may not work as quickly. I surmise.

On the map, outside of the Realm of Mages exit portal, rests a small circular portion in the woods, marked with the boulder I now stand in front of. With the name "Castaway Grove" written over the length of woods we must now traverse.

Studying the ink, I turn in the direction told on the map.

West.

I look to Asher, who punches his arms out to shake off the fall. His brow is pinched in irritation, and he seems a tad ornery. That's nothing new for Asher but something *feels* off.

"Where to?" he asks as he places his hands on his hips, looking around the thicket of trees surrounding this small, open patch of land.

I look to the stone and then directly in front of it, into the dark woods ahead.

"That way," I tell him as I nod to the forest ahead.

Asher nods before he walks to the tree line. His blade sings as he retrieves it from a sheath on his ribs and lumbering steps lead the way to a curtain of viney overhang that he grips and cuts through. Throwing the vegetation to the side, he steps over a moss-covered log and into the brush. He continues slicing his blade through numerous twigs, stems and vines as he surges in deeper. A few feet into the woods and he leans over to a tree beside us, slashing a large X into it before he moves on. The bark seeps with crimson drips of sap and I stare at it in shock.

Strange woods.

I push the instance out of my head as I follow Asher. My pack lifts slightly as I tighten my wings, not wanting them to get caught on the numerous hanging foliage we pass by. The air in the forest is thick, cool and incredibly damp. With the scent of moist dirt and leaves filling every pocket of space available as we press further in.

Asher continues with his methods. Chop, throw, mark an X. Though, with every X he marks, the trees drip with the red sap. It's an odd sight. An eerie one, but I do my best to ignore it.

He seems to be methodical in his ways, as he continues marking us through the woods. The only thing to keep us company is the scratch of metal into bark as we climb over multiple downed logs.

"Why are you slashing the trees?" I ask as I step through a small puddle on the ground.

"Gotta find our way back somehow," he says plainly as he cuts through another vine.

My eyes narrow on him as I look at his back. He's too… down. *Something is wrong.*

"What has you in a tizzy, Asher-dear?" I ask as I haul my foot over another downed tree along the ground.

"Nothing," he murmurs in response.

"Horrible liar, darling," I sing-song.

He sighs as he comes to a stop, his gaze fixed on the path ahead, "I keep having these dreams."

My eyebrow raises in curiosity as he speaks.

"It's nothing but a black void, and this voice speaks to me. There is no body. There is no being there that speaks. It seems to come from nothing. It tells me things I don't understand."

Interesting.

"It says that you're mine, and that I'm yours. And that some key lies within me. I don't *know* what any of it fucking means," he continues.

I sigh as he finishes. I don't know how I can point him in the right direction.

As much as I would like to.

"I'm sorry, Asher," I tell him softly.

"I want to help your people, Seraphina. I want to help my people. But this world… this world I previously thought was merely Vesperholm has expanded rapidly in front of me, and I don't know how to take it all in," he murmurs.

I suppose I never looked at it that way.

"Magic, a separate realm of magical humans, elves, orcs, all of it is so… so confusing and I feel like I'm just going through the motions all over again. I want to understand this place, and I want to be of use, but I feel like there is nothing I can do. The more I get answers, the more questions I have."

I step against a root as I come up behind him, wrapping my arms around his middle.

"We'll figure it out together, Asher-darling. There's much even I don't know. Like how to get through the woods without magic," I whisper to him.

His head turns to look at me over his shoulder with a small smile, "Okay… Okay, we will."

I return his smile with one of my own before I release him. He takes more steps forward, proceeding through the woods to slash another X through a tree when we hear a soft cry in the distance.

Asher turns to me with a confused tilt to his brow and I return it, shrugging.

His eyes gaze off as he leans his ear in the direction of the sound, waiting for it to happen again.

The crippled wail echoes through the trees and he waits for it to end before his puzzled gaze connects with mine, "A deer," he whispers.

"We have to help it," I tell him.

For what reason? I don't know. Something is surging me to find the small creature. Something I can't place.

Perhaps The Fates showing their hand once again.

"What? We don't have time, we have to get to the shore," he responds.

"I'm saving the deer, Asher," I say as I look up to scan the tree coverage. A small space rests between the large branches of the upper canopy, and I take the chance to spear through it. Small twigs catch and snap on my wings as I lunge into the sky.

Looking down into the woods, a few hundred feet from us, is a spot of white nestled in the deep green leaves.

My heart pounds as I tuck my wings, allowing my body to free fall through the air. The force of my fall snaps through a fallen trunk a few feet in front of Asher and he startles as I land.

"This way," I tell him as I lead the way through the dense brush. Slowly, we pass more downed and rotted trees and step over twigs, the sound of Asher's blade scratching through rough bark sounds off behind me every few feet until we approach a white bundle of fur against the ground. The pristine coat of a deer is stained with bright red blood, while flurries of white steam pour from its nostrils. A deep ache settles in my gut as I get sight of the lone being.

An *arrow* juts from the side of the creature's ribs.

An arrow? What could possibly be lurking out here with enough knowledge to have arrows?

I push the thoughts aside when twigs poke at my legs as I kneel into the ground, looking over the poor thing.

My brow furrows in sadness as I place my hands against its chest around the wound. In one swift motion I wrench the arrow shaft from its body and a frail cry echoes through the woods at the action.

Damp heat coats my hands as I scramble to cover the wound, more blood spilling onto the ground below.

A growl scrapes at my throat as I lean down, exhaling a meager cloud of black smoke over the animal. Its ribs rise and fall quickly as it inhales. The deer's breathing calms, and I spread my fingers to look between them. The gushing hole begins to patch, and I hold my hand on it just a bit longer until I begin to feel bits of fur prick under my palm.

The wound closes slowly, but the animal lays there, breathing in a more even rhythm.

"We've done all we can for now," I tell Asher as I stand. I look into the creature's eyes, who glisten in crimson as they peer back at me.

The corner of my mouth lifts in a small smile as I nod to the deer. "Let's go," I tell Asher, who silently watches from behind.

His eyes are wide, but he nods, taking steps to get in front of me to continue leading us through the forest.

I need to hear it again. I need to know who she belongs to; I need it **all**.

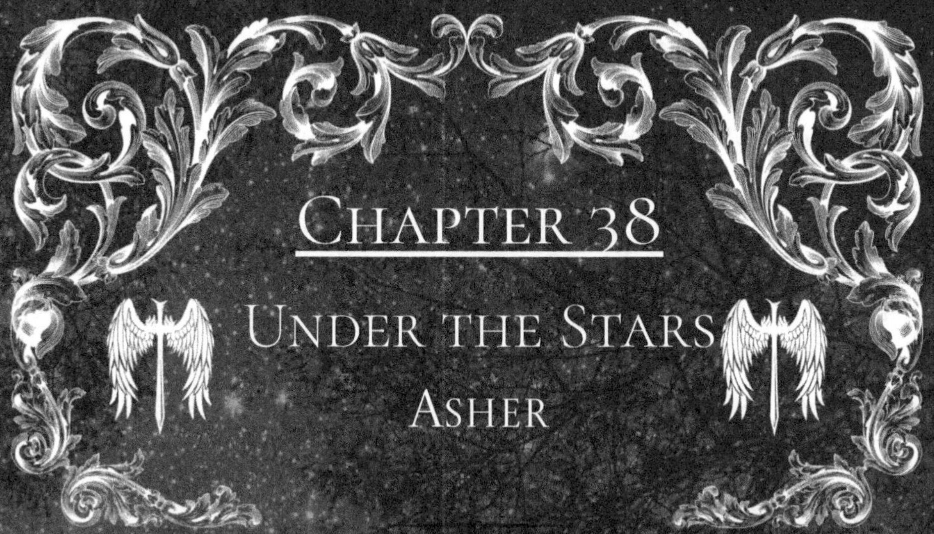

This forest is a nightmare to get through. Branches stick every which way. There are several trees collapsed one over the other. This is a much harder endeavor than moving through a forest in Vesperholm.

Every so often, I swear I can hear vines growing and wrapping around the trees we pass. Seraphina said there was no magic out here, but the energy in these woods is eerie. Not to mention, the trees have red sap. I don't think I've ever seen anything like that before.

It's a similar energy to the woods outside of The Catacombs.

Granted, I'm not well-versed in magic or its feelings, but still. It's not right here.

Eventually, we come upon a small clearing in the woods where the trees have given the earth room to breathe. The night has been descending on us for a while and the moon soon lit our way as it ascends high into the sky.

Seraphina takes the time to look for some food in the packs that I had her bring from Tantalia through her magic since *apparently,* I wasn't allowed to eat in the Realm of Mages.

She packed me some breads and cheeses that I couldn't wait to dig into, but first I have to figure out a small shelter for us.

The mages were kind enough to provide us some items for a makeshift lean to, so I got to work. Attaching the ropes to some of the trees and into the ground before I threw a swath of fabric over the top. It isn't much but we also need to be able to abandon it if we have to.

It is difficult getting the ropes up with only moonlight, but I get it done. My hands find their place on my hips as I stand back to admire my handy work. Seraphina and I decide that a fire isn't safe, especially when we don't know what lurks here. After a humble, quiet dinner, Seraphina and I take the time to lay in the clearing in front of our tent, watching the stars. We decide to rest on some of our extra clothes against the grass.

It looks a lot like Vesperholm before the clouds rolled in, and my chest pangs a deep-seated guilt. Once again, my hand drifts down to my pocket. My finger runs circles around the raised disk.

I find that it doesn't calm me as much as it did before. Not when I feel surer of my role in Tantalia.

I have been enjoying my time here with Seraphina. As much as I didn't want to when we first met, she has given me a feeling of fullness and accomplishment I wasn't able to find in Vesperholm. I worked so hard there to protect my people, and they disregarded my efforts at every turn.

But even still, I do miss home. I miss the sound of my father sharpening weapons, Cedric's groaning and checking in on my mother. I miss seeing the other houses and their people.

I wonder if my mother's had the child yet, and if it survived. I wonder if the Succubi have paused their kidnappings for the time being. I hadn't asked Seraphina. But we have been through so much peril, I forgot all about it.

Am I betraying my town because I've defected? Am I *bad* because I have found my place amongst these demons?

The voice that tries to deny my position here wants me to feel bad about my feelings toward Tantalia.

But my heart knows where I'm supposed to be. And it knows I need to be *here.*

There is so much more at stake here.

It feels as if we are so close to the end, that I can't help but charge forward.

There is also the feeling of peace with Sera. Her strength, her wisdom, even as young as a succubus as she may be.

The way her people look up to her causes it my heart to race, and soon, Seraphina's voice whispers through the dark night. "What are you thinking, Asher-dear?"

I sigh as my eyes connect to a bright beam of light far off in the night sky, "I miss Vesperholm," I admit softly.

"I would imagine," she responds.

"But I don't want to go home," I whisper.

The words spill out of me before I have a chance to think of them. And saying them out loud is scary. It's admitting to something I never thought I would in a million years.

The ground below shudders as Seraphina's head turns, with my own head falling lazily to find her gaze set on me.

Her hand comes to wrap around mine and the brush of her claws against my skin sets me ablaze.

"I like what I do here. I like being here with you. I feel as though this is where I've needed to be my entire life. And I don't know why," the words rush from my throat. Perhaps it's the dark night and not being able to truly see her that makes it easier to tell her these things.

But they are the truth. As much as my mind wants to reject them, my heart can't.

"Sometimes The Fates put us where we need to be, even when we don't want to be," she responds.

Her tone turns somber and the dull purple glow of her eyes in the night drifts to the hands between us. Her grip around my hand tightens.

The throne.

"Looks like we're in the same boat," I say lightheartedly as I grip her hand back.

Her eyes trail up my arm to connect with mine, "I'd say so," she whispers with a sideways smile.

The grass swooshes as she comes close, pressing her soft lips against mine in a tender kiss.

I may miss Vesperholm.

But her touch… her *lips*, is what really feels like home.

I lean in deeper, tasting all of her that I can, because it feels like the second I'm not, the harsh world crushes me again. And I want to live in this small moment with her. Just for a little while.

My hand comes to wrap around the back of her neck, pulling her in deeper as the heat between us rises.

Her claws come to stroke gently against my chin as she moans softly into our lips.

The hushed melody of her desire causes blood to rush through me, hardening me instantly.

My fingers tangle into the strands of her soft hair to pull her closer to me, in an attempt to get anything from her. Her body, her warmth, her touch, *anything* I can salvage.

Soon, my hand drifts lower, palming her beautiful breast with an eager grip. Her nipple hardens against it, and I shift my grip to run a thumb over the peak and she hums a delightfully submissive noise between us.

My throat releases a low groan as I feel her other hand grip at the bulge through my light night pants. The action causes my heart to drum hard against my chest, with vibrant fire pulsing through every portion of my body in anticipation.

My hand continues to slide down the fabric of her light tunic, taking care to feel every single part of her that I can.

I slip my hand under the hem of her shirt, caressing the soft skin of her stomach as my hand presses into the band of her night pants. Every touch and graze of her flesh against mine sends my breath thinning, my heart drumming and my thoughts fleeting. I slide my hand down further, relishing in the feeling of her skin as I reach her core. My fingers slide through her cunt, petting the wet slickness that coats her. A groan works its way through me at the thought I have this kind of influence on her; that I'm able to make her seep with desire like this. Without thought, my hips grind slowly against her side, searching for any amount of friction as I press my fingers deeper, rubbing the small bundle of nerves that make her quake.

She muffles her moan as I feel the moisture pooled there and I slip my tongue deeper into her mouth, pressing her to her back.

The warm, slick wetness covers my hand as I dip lower, pressing two fingers into her as I rub the heel of my hand against her clit.

Her hands wrap around my shoulders, her claws piercing through my night shirt and into my flesh as she bites her plump lower lip to stifle her perfect noises.

I work my fingers in and out of her, savoring the way her flesh grips around me.

Soon, I shift my movements, pressing a thumb into her clit, it glides easily up and down as her nails dig into the meat of my back. The warm drip of blood seeps through my tunic, and the pain pushes my desire further.

Have to be in her. Have to have her. Have to feel her. Need her. Now.

I remove my fingers as I lean down to kiss her and heavy breaths bleed into our kiss as I slowly pull her pants down, throwing them into the grass beside us. Mine follow shortly behind them.

My cock throbs a painful ache and I grip it, stroking myself a few times with my hand covered in her pleasure as I rest my forehead against hers. Our breaths exchange as I slide the head through her center.

Her body shudders upon my touch, and her moans try so, *so* hard to escape.

"I've missed this cunt, Seraphina. You keep so quiet for me." I praise as I press the head into her entrance.

If the world wasn't already plunged into darkness, it would be now, with the way the entire world fades when I'm inside of her.

The tight muscle wraps every inch of me in warmth as I press deeper and deeper, taking my time in how every corner of her feels. I want to memorize every ridge, every dip within her.

"Asher," she pants as her head presses back into the grass.

"It's okay, take your time, I'm right here," I whisper. As she bows against the grass, her neck is bared to me, showcasing her lavender-jasmine scent. It's all-consuming, it's maddening, it drives me deeper into her as I press soft kisses into the column of her throat. The vibrations of her groans that she tries to silence pulse against my lips.

She drives me fucking mad. Her scent, her taste, her cunt. All of it and I have to keep a leash on my restraint to not pound into her.

"Harder, p-please," Seraphina desperately pants as her hands come to wrap around my waist, attempting to press me in deeper.

"Shhhh, I want to savor this," I tell her as I plunge into her, closing my eyes as I memorize every portion of her body. Every curve, every swoop of her perfectly sculpted frame, I adhere it to my memory. I keep it locked away in a little book in my head so I never allow myself to forget the way she feels against me.

Wetness covers my thumb as I press into her clit once more, rubbing it as I pick up the pace and set a rhythm.

Her moans start to lose their quietness as I thrust into her. Her tits bounce against the fabric of her tunic and the sight drives me farther from my restraint.

My thrusts slow for a moment as I kiss softly into her plush lips, my hand leaving her core to lift her shirt.

I grasp a tit in my hand, compressing it to pull a hardened nipple into my mouth, as my thrusts pick up again.

Her strong legs wrap around my waist pulling me deeper, absorbing the pleasure and sensations I've subjected her to.

"Fuck, it's… Asher," she pants as she loses herself to the moment.

My name on her tongue is almost as divine as my cock on it. Urgency courses through me as she whimpers desperately for me. I've never seen her so submissive, and it causes my dominance to take precedent.

"Say my name again," I groan against her tit.

"Asher," she mewls.

The sound of her voice sends me into overdrive, my blood is fire as I soak in all of her, my thrusts picking up pace as I lose the frail hold I had on my leash.

"Louder. I want the leaves to tremble and the sky to fall. I need the heavens *and* the hells know who does this to you. I want your gods to know the way my name sounds on your tongue," I growl lowly, my eyes drifting to watch her face. Tension pulls at her features as she endures the pleasure coursing through her.

I need to hear it again. I need to know who she belongs to; I need it *all.*

"Asher!" she cries into the night. The tones pour into the dark as I bottom out, filling her to the hilt as I spill into her. I give her all the desire I can offer. Wings flap and the branches shake as her voice rocks against them in a melodic outpour of her pleasure. My body shudders and my vision sparks with purple stars as my cock twitches against her walls.

The feeling of her sliding against me makes me quake, but I keep thrusting. Releasing my hand from her breast, I keep her nipple in my mouth, moving my hand down to rub at her clit. Her body tensing as she gets closer and closer. "There's a good girl, come for me. You have more in you, and I *want* it. *Come* for me," I growl through my climax.

Her moans pierce the air as her body trembles against me, her cunt tightens around my length in hard waves. "Gods, you're like the light of the moon when you come, Seraphina." I urge her as I slow my thrusts in time with her orgasm; slowing down until her walls stop their movements. My hand comes up to stroke her hair, kissing into her damp neck as my hips roll slowly. I take my time wringing out every bit of her climax that I can.

Slowly, the world around me comes back, the trees and the leaves against them break through the darkness as I pant above her. My cock softening, I pull it out of her to feel the rush of my seed follow it.

I collapse next to her in the grass, my chest heaving as I come down from the intense summit that is Seraphina Moonsong.

I roll over to wrap an arm around her middle, her chest rising and falling as she catches her breath. Her arm drapes over my back and she brings me in closer, allowing me to rest against her warm body.

I nuzzle into her, and the sound of her breathing calms my soul. The gentle glow of her skin dulls as our breaths even out.

Eventually, the already dark night descends into inky black as my eyes close and I drift to sleep.

"Wʜᴀᴛ ᴡᴏᴜʟᴅ ʏᴏᴜ ʜᴀᴠᴇ ᴍᴇ ᴅᴏ ᴛʜᴇɴ?! Wᴇ ᴀʀᴇ ᴏɴ ᴀ ᴍɪssɪᴏɴ ᴛᴏ ʀᴇᴛʀɪᴇᴠᴇ sᴏᴍᴇᴛʜɪɴɢ ᴠᴀʟᴜᴀʙʟᴇ. Wᴇ ɴᴇᴇᴅ ᴛᴏ ɢᴇᴛ **ʜᴏᴍᴇ**."

CHAPTER 39

THE EYES IN THE TREE

Asher

The sun shines through a break in the trees above us, blasting against my eyelids as the birds begin their morning song.

I groan from the intrusion and roll over, finding it hard when I realize Seraphina has wrapped herself around me in the night.

Her arm weighs my stomach down from where it's draped across me. Her wing covers the both of us and her leg has flung itself over my hip.

Still weary, I settle into the feeling of her against me. Taking these small moments with her to be at peace.

Just a little while longer.

The sky is a brilliant blue this morning and the air is cool, lending soft flurries of steam to float into the air from my nose.

I watch those wisps for a while, until Seraphina stirs against me. A sleepy sigh comes from her as she nuzzles in closer. Her horn pokes into my cheek as she does and I let a soft chuckle go.

Her sleepy purple eyes blink as they glance up at me before she buries her face back into my side.

My laugh gets a tad louder as I press a kiss to her forehead, "Come on, we have to get going," I tell her softly.

We need all the daylight we can get, and with Seraphina not well versed in putting her clothes on herself, she needs her time.

I slowly move her arms from around me, standing from the damp grass and moving to the shelter we didn't use.

No regrets.

A smile tugs at my lips as I start deconstructing the lean to and pack it away.

The grass swooshes from behind me as Seraphina finally peels herself from the ground, her wings hitting some of the surrounding branches and shaking dew drops from the leaves as she stretches and yawns.

"Early bird gets to kill orcs," she mumbles.

Another laugh comes from me as I finish folding the piece of fabric and shove it into one of the packs.

I begin placing my armor on piece by piece, latching every buckle and strap. My eyes are glued to Seraphina as she gets going, stirring a warm pot of emotions in my chest.

I've been waking up to her for weeks, but there was always something happening.

And every quiet moment I spend with her is one I cherish.

I turn to look at Seraphina with a gentle smile and she returns it, before gliding her hands over her long tunic. Her strong legs are bare from her lack of pants.

I quirk an eyebrow in curiosity as I watch her, fastening some more of the buckles on my armor.

Her face contorts in annoyance before she groans, "Gods dammit," she huffs before she trudges over to our bags to put her armor on herself.

"I have no idea how you did this for so long," she grumbles as she begins pulling on bits and pieces of her fighting gear.

"Some of us don't have magical capabilities," I respond with a laugh as I slide my daggers into their sheathes.

"Wah, wah. Cry me a river, human," she teases.

A smile tugs at my lips as we go through the motions, as the back and forth of our quips warm through my soul.

Eventually, we pack everything away and have suited up for the day. Seraphina reaches for the map on her hip as she looks around again, nodding to a portion of the forest.

I nod in return and step through the grass, marking another tree before sliding through the thicket once more.

Seraphina and I haven't exchanged many words as we venture through the woods, mostly to keep any unwanted ears from hearing us, and just trying to get through these vines.

"Sera?" I ask softly as I scratch into another tree.

"Hm?" I hear from behind me as her boot roots into the ground behind me.

"Are the men from Vesperholm still being taken?"

There's silence that stretches for what feels like eternity as she delays her response, "Right now... no, we have not been taking more men from Vesperholm."

"When we return, to Tantalia... Do you think we could take one more? He could be of great use to us."

Her brow furrows in confusion as she looks at me.

"He is an alchemist, and if we could procure more potions, we wouldn't need to go to The Realm of Mages to help us," I say as I cut through a descending vine.

"If you can convince him to join our cause, perhaps," she responds.

A sliver of warmth courses through me as I slide my dagger through another tree.

But this one is different.

It gives way to flesh, and blood pours from the bark.

A screech wails through the leaves, causing birds to flitter away in its wake. I jump back, knocking into a tree behind me as I flip the dagger in my palm, lining my forearm and guarding my face.

Bright green eyes connect with mine in agony as a leafy figure steps from the bark. Taller than any being I've ever witnessed; its arms are sheathed in thick brown bark with green moss patched in small spots of growth.

The figure advances closer; its woody exterior creaks and groans as it moves, with bits of bark falling to the ground.

Seraphina backs away as she reaches for the swords strapped to her back. The metal singing from their scabbards and the distorted wails of the creature produce a cacophony of destruction against the shuddering leaves.

The ground feels as if it trembles, as vines slither against the rotted branches. The almost snake-like vegetation wraps slowly around my legs, and I furiously try to cut them away. A vine from above whips around my wrist, causing me to drop my weapon.

I grunt as I attempt to wrench my foot from this infernal trap.

I hear leaves flutter as vines descend from the surrounding trees to whip out and attach to Seraphina's wings. A cry pours from her throat as they snake around her middle, lifting her from the ground and dangling her in the air.

She growls and grunts as she thrashes against the restraints holding her. Her swords fall from her hands and make a sickening clatter against the forest floor.

"Ash-!!!" Seraphina attempts to say before a thick vine wraps around her mouth, muffling her.

I look for the green eyes among the bark and foliage, trying once more to pull myself from the thicket.

"A human..." the vibrant green being says as the wound in its stomach closes with leaves.

Flowers bloom around its forehead as it tilts its head in curiosity.

"And a demon..." it muses once more.

The thing gets closer, gripping a rough, wooden hand around my jaw. The hardness of it pinches into my jawbone with a primal strength as it glares at me with brilliant emerald irises, "So, it is *you* that has been marring *our* flesh," it says. Its voice breathes an ethereal lilt, like the sound of wind through the leaves.

I grunt as I attempt to snap my head away, but the strength this thing possesses has me solidly held in place.

"What are you talking about?" I grunt.

"You've been slicing through us for miles. For what *ungodsly* reason could you have, to do such an abhorrent task?" it asks.

"I-I didn't know you were 'things'! I was marking our trail back," I beg.

A flower raises against the being's forehead, as if alluding to a risen eyebrow, "Surely, there are other avenues that could have been taken."

"What would you have me do then?! We are on a mission to retrieve something valuable. We need to get *home.*"

The green eyes peer into my soul, searching for a long moment.

"You've come from Tantalia..." the being whispers.

Curiosity strikes before I register its words, and nod quickly, "Yes... Yes! Do you know it?" I ask desperately.

"Lilith is gone..." the being whispers again as it looks at Seraphina, who continues to thrash and kick at the viney restraints.

A thud shakes the ground as Seraphina's body falls from the sky, and a groan comes from her as she settles against it.

"Hey, what the f-" a vine comes around my mouth to hush me, holding me in place as the creature slithers against the ground. As if the earth has turned to waves, the creature easily slips through the thicket to Seraphina, giving me a good look at the rest of it.

No legs to speak of... No, just the mound of dirt that moves along the ground with it.

"Is it true? Has Lilith departed from this realm?" the thing asks. It looks between the both of us, and the expression shrouding them shows pain and sadness.

Seraphina groans as she stands, dusting herself off as she looks up at the being in annoyance. "Years ago, why do you care?" she growls.

The being tilts its head sympathetically as it gazes at Seraphina. "You look just like her..." it murmurs before it steels its spine and shakes it head clear. "Lilith gave us this forest. She made it a place for us to exist," the creature says as it looks toward the sky. "She has long since passed you say?"

"Yes. We are on a mission to find her book," Seraphina responds with her hands on her hips; clearly annoyed with this debacle.

"The Compendium," the being responds.

Seraphina rolls her eyes as she throws her hands in the air in frustration, "Yes, the fucking Compendium. Why do you all know about it but me?" she groans.

"We lived in Tantalia, long, long ago. Lilith would go to the forest to write in her tome. She wouldn't tell us its purpose. She merely said it would save the world one day. The forest was her place of comfort. When the crown got too heavy to wear, she would spend hours with us. When the Drannar invaded, they burned our wood, our trees, our *people*. So, she sent us away. The earth was paramount in her eyes to protect. We traveled far past the barriers, underground and sought refuge here. We have been here ever since."

Leaves shimmer against the back of the creature as I watch them. The features of Seraphina's face prick and twitch as she listens. Whatever energy is flowing between them is powerful, and I can feel her anger rise the longer she speaks with the creature.

"Great, what does that have to do with us?"

"If you are in search of The Caelestial Compendium, Tantalia must be in dire straits."

"It's apparently with the orcs. So, we are going to find it. How would you know about Tantalia by just looking at him?" Seraphina asks as she gestures to me.

"We are Dryads. We are the Earth. And as such, we are connected to its beings. It doesn't take much to extract your motives while you're in our grasp. And if a human is here *with* a demon after this many years, Tantalia suffers a greater loss than its queen." The being looks behind it, in my direction, but past me, into the woods beyond. "Dire…" it murmurs before it turns back to Seraphina. "We shall grant you safe passage through these woods. As you walk, we will mark your path."

Seraphina's eyebrow raises as she looks at the dryad, "Why would you do that?"

"Because Lilith granted us the same mercy."

Seraphina's face softens, and solemnly, she nods, "Thank you," she whispers.

The vines loosen from around me and I inhale a deep breath as I lean down to retrieve my blade. I wipe it off on my breeches before sheathing it back onto my ribs.

Seraphina's eyes seem to hold a storm of different emotions, and my chest pangs in response.

The being slides back to me, leaning into the tree, "My name is Junipher, a guardian dryad of Castaway Grove."

It backs up to the tree I had stabbed, blending into its facade. The only thing remaining is its eyes that peer through the wood.

"The vines will guide your way. Be safe, and do right by Lilith," Junipher murmurs, and with that her eyes disappear and there is nothing left in the wood but a small cut.

Seraphina trudges past me, murmuring words I can't understand, she follows the bright green vine that begins to trail through the woods.

In an attempt to catch up with her, I bound over some of the logs along the path.

Her wings are unbearably tense, and her movements are rigid as she continues her trek.

The energy pumping off her feels dark and I speed up to get closer.

"Are you okay?" I ask softly. A vine slithers around a tree that we pass, marking the path.

"How could she do this to me?" Seraphina mumbles to herself as she whips her hand at a hanging vine in front of us.

Her spiked armor rips at it as she walks by and her tail comes up to grip the emerald vegetation from her, tossing it to the side.

"Hey, are you good?" I ask as I reach to grab her arm.

Seraphina spins around to face me, her face streaked with silver tears and her purple gaze watery in furious pain, "How could she *do* this to me!?" she cries.

My eyes widen in shock as more tears run down her face.

"She set me up to fail! Turn after turn, I've hit dead end after dead end and *every* time someone knows something I *should* know! How could she not tell *me* about The Compendium!? How could she trust *me* to lead the kingdom and not give me the best chance to do so!? How… could she…" Seraphina's gaze drifts and her thoughts seem to run the longer she stares off.

"I… I don't know…" I murmur.

My heart breaks for her. I didn't realize she had been dealing with the information like this. But I can see why she would.

Lilith *was everything* to her.

"She knew about The Compendium. She knew where it was and what could be done with it yet never alluded to its existence! Then time and time again these… things! Allude to it! They know of it! Yet, our own people don't?!" she continues. Her feet pace and her hands gesture around her in frustration before she halts. Her hands clench at her sides, white consuming her knuckles as blood begins to drip through her fingers.

More silver streaks down her face, leaving a shimmering glow on her chest. Her eyes darken and she takes deep breaths, in and out as she attempts to settle herself.

"How… could… she…" Seraphina says once more before she collapses to her knees.

A wail sounds through the forest and amongst it, the flapping wings of birds vacating the trees.

Leaves fall around her as she trembles, her bloodied hands now clutched against her knees as her shoulders shake in silent sobs.

I stand cautiously by, watching her.

Her head tosses back, and her screech shakes the ground as a beam of brilliant purple light streams from her throat. It pierces the upper canopy to scorch some of the leaves in their wake before it breaks through the sky.

Her body shakes as she continues her sobs, and I make to dive for her waist. Wrapping my arms around her, I make a feeble attempt at calming her down.

"Sera, it's okay! I'm here!" I tell her, but the power coursing off of her is so strong, I doubt she can hear me over the roaring lightning.

The lightning dies slowly, until its nothing but sputtering sparks that erupt from her throat. As her neck loses strength, her head wobbles. With the whites of her eyes shining as they roll back in her head. She becomes dead weight against me as her body tilts and she begins falling to the side.

"Fuck," I grunt as I catch her. I lean her in the crook of my elbow, slapping softly at her cheek to rouse her. "Come on, wake up," I growl. My heart fractures with speed at her unconscious state, and a deep ache settles in the fissures created there. Fierce protectiveness courses through me, raging against my chest in an attempt to save her. I look over her body, taking account of her condition. Her chest rises and falls slowly, alluding to a blissful sleep and I breathe a sigh of relief knowing that she's at least unharmed.

My eyes track around the forest, looking deeper into the brush to follow the bright emerald vine that leads us to shore. My gaze settles back on her and I lean down to kiss her forehead as I rock her.

She's depleted and I realize I have to continue our journey with her on my back.

Taking another deep sigh and placing another kiss to her head, I cradle her close, "I can take it from here, angel," I murmur. I know she can't hear me, but just in case she can, I let her know that I'm here anyway.

Slowly, I haul her onto my back, resting her across my pack like a dead deer. I throw her intrusive wing behind me as it attempts to hang in front of my field of view and make sure she's secure before I press onward. And carefully, I follow the green vine that leads us to the shore.

I don't want to think she would keep something like this from me on purpose, and I want to be able to secure her memory, as good, in my head for as long as I can live.

CHAPTER 40

HIGHER CALLING

SERAPHINA

"*Your path was destined, Sera. I, alone, could not guide you.*" *A soft, ethereal voice echoes around me.*

The white stone beneath my feet is almost blinding as my eyes open.

"What are you on about?" I groan in response. My forehead throbs and my hand comes up to rub it as I gaze at these unfamiliar surroundings.

Tall pillars of ivory ascend into a milky white sky above. Looking ahead, ivory steps rise to a brilliant, marbled dais. Atop it, a black spiked throne, shrouded in a sheer onyx sheet.

"The Compendium was for you to seek. Not for me to tell."

No one sits the throne, but it sounds as if the voice comes from it.

"You were destined for this, Sera. You have to earn your place just as I had," the throne says.

A groan escapes me, "Let me out of here! I don't care anymore! I want to find this bullshit book and leave!" I call back.

Whispered sounds come from around me. Echoing in a deep, rolling grumble.

"Imperio destinatus. Nascimur ducere. Amissa anima sanguine mortis perfusa. Quaerite scientiam in fine."

"Urrrrggh, let me OUT!"

A heaving gasp clutches my chest, and I shoot out of my slumber. Frantically searching the area around me, I find Asher asleep with his

425

arm slung around my waist. The sky above is shielded by a swath of beige fabric.

Sighing, I take a moment to re-acquaint myself with this new place.

I don't remember falling asleep in a tent. Nor do I recognize the pattern of trees surrounding us.

Slowly, I pick up Asher's arm from my middle, gently placing it against him before I come to a stand. Pressing the fabric aside, I get a better view of the woods. The trees here are beginning to thin, with more bare ground in between them.

Meaning… *we're getting close to shore.*

I look to Asher in confusion; his chest rising and falling slowly as he slumbers.

How did we even get here?

I take notice of our small camp. Our armor has been situated next to our packs, and I have been dressed in my night clothes.

I creep up next to him, kneeling to his sleeping form as I rest a hand on his forehead.

Stupid human…

"Asher, dear," I whisper as I nudge his shoulder. He groans sleepily as he turns to where I was laying, only to be shocked awake when he finds my body gone.

He springs up, "SERA!" he calls as he looks frantically around, his body settling as his eyes land on me. A deep breath rattles through his chest as he looks at me cautiously.

"Are you okay?" he asks softly. His hands clench against the grass as he observes me.

"I am… but how did we get here?"

His face softens with palpable sadness as he watches me, "I carried you. I walked until the moon came up. You had passed out after whatever… thing you experienced, and I had to keep us going."

My heart pounds a little harder, with flutters consuming my belly at his action.

"I think we only have a little bit left until we get to the shore, hopefully the mages were able to secure a boat for us to depart," Asher responds.

I look through the thinning trees, the sunlight peaks through the branches as it gives way to the horizon beyond. Blue sky as far as the eye can see is just right through these woods. "At least it's a good day for travel," I murmur.

Asher stands from the small shelter, yawning and stretching against the dappled morning sun. I'm not sure if he noticed, but I surely did.

While he climbs out of the tent, it seems he has pitched one of his own.

"Have I ever told you how delicious you are?" I muse seductively with a fanged grin.

Asher looks at me in confusion as he yawns, and I nod down to his hardened cock in silent delight.

His head tilts and his eyes widen as he presses it down with his wrist, "It happens," he grumbles quickly.

I scoff as I stand. As much as I would like to taste him, we *do* have to get going.

A shame.

Slowly, we begin packing up for our last leg of the trip. The nerves in my chest begin to stir as I think about getting to the fortress.

According to Orc lore, they are ruthless beings of strength and power. Barbarians of a particularly brutal nature.

They're like gnats; serve no real purpose and live to cause annoyance. The thought is terrifying, but perhaps I will be able to take some… primalistic liberties when it comes to shapeshifting.

Eventually, we are able to pack everything, and the energy within me ratchets higher.

We proceed in silence through the forest. The only thing keeping us company is the sound of us moving through the wood, with vines and foliage moving out of our way to guide us.

After an hour or so, the trees thin to a large, rocky beach. The sun sits high in the sky, beaming its hot rays down on us and reflecting off the sparkling blue water that seems to stretch for miles and miles ahead.

The already pounding organ in my chest pounds even *harder*, as I look out at the skyline. Only the wisps of clouded black smoke seem to drift high on the horizon.

"At least they fulfilled the boat promise," Asher says as he points to a small rowboat attached to the ground on the shore.

This does nothing to calm my nerves. If anything, it makes my stomach churn, my throat close and my palms weep. But I'm sure that wasn't his intention either way.

"Let's get this over with," I grumble as I trudge through the sand to the boat.

I should be excited. I should be ready to get this leg over with, because it means we get closer to some answers.

But I'm not. Not with the amount of bullshit we've encountered and all the things I've learned over the past few days. The fact that Lilith kept something as vital as The Compendium from me. The fact everyone else knows what it is but *I*, the one she sought to train and mold, do not.

It shatters my heart and causes me to rage all at once, because I don't want to be angry at Lilith. I don't want to think she would keep something like this from me on purpose, and I want to be able to secure her memory, as good, in my head for as long as I can live.

But with what I've learned... with the beings I've encountered... It's so hard to imagine she didn't set me up to fail.

The fury rises higher and higher as we reach the small boat, a wooden dinghy of sorts. But, big enough to hold our gear and Asher and me.

Facing away from the boat, I lean back, reaching down to my underarms to detach the clasp of the straps of my pack. It drops into the dinghy with a sloshing thud as it bobs against the shoreline.

Asher slings his bag from his back and into the boat before settling on one of the wooden slats, "I'll row to the first island, you just tell me where to go," he says as he familiarizes himself with the movement of the oars.

Reaching into my side pocket, I fish out the map once more, looking over it to see what direction we *should* be going. It's hard to tell, because now, there aren't any discernible markings to lead us. But, with the number of islands speckled across the little strait, I imagine we should get there one way or another. We just need to find the closest one to the fortress that will allow us to get inside without being seen.

I look down to the wooden spike in the ground that holds the boat to the shore and kick it with my boot before throwing it in with us.

One foot hits the bottom of the boat, while the other pushes off the sand. With a gentle bat of my wings to propel us forward, the boat rocks, and we begin drifting away from the sandy edge of Castaway Grove.

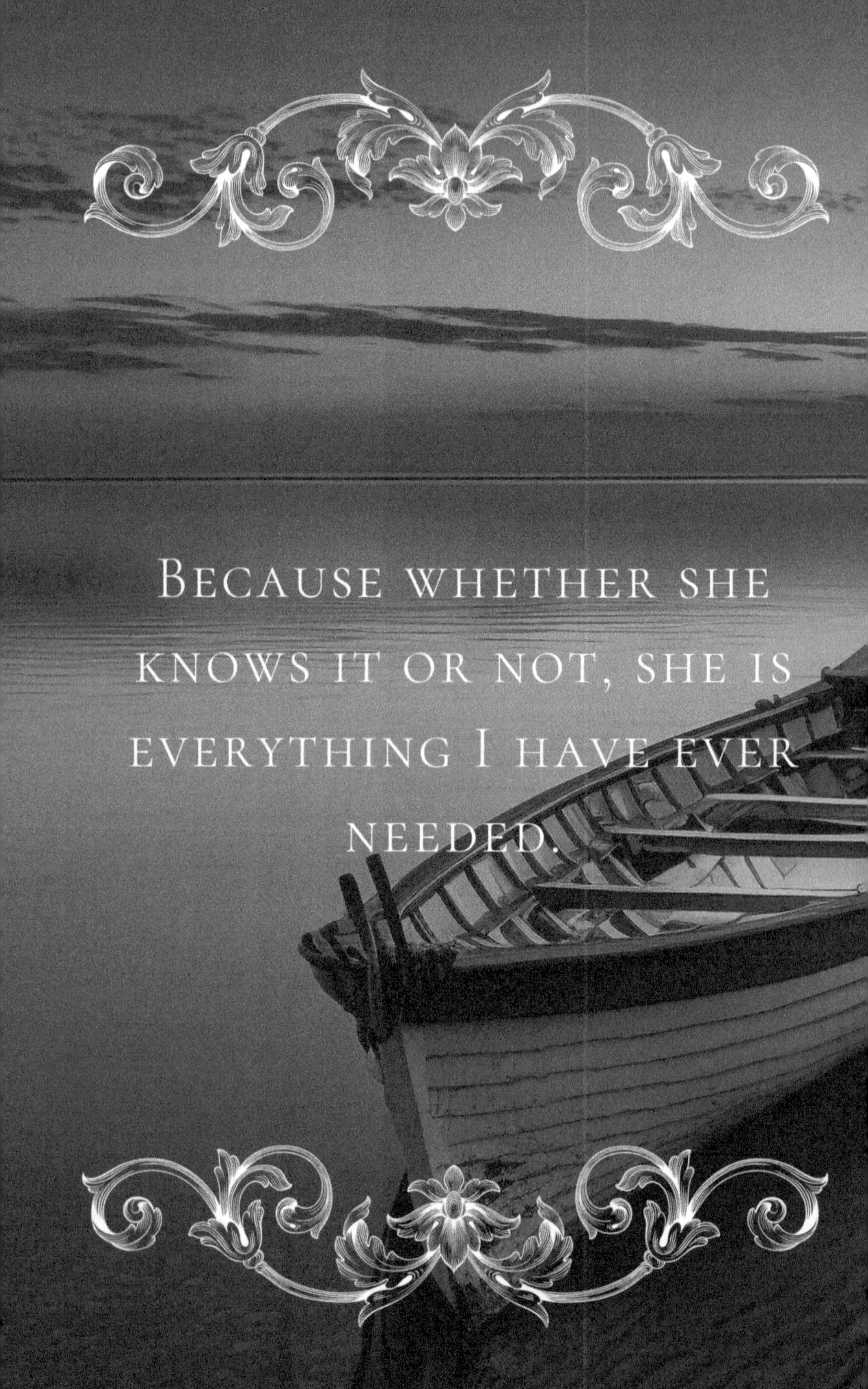

BECAUSE WHETHER SHE KNOWS IT OR NOT, SHE IS EVERYTHING I HAVE EVER NEEDED.

The heat from the water blasts up in our faces. I'm sincerely lucky I'm facing away from the sun that causes the immense heat, because it seems Seraphina is getting the brunt of it all as she stands with a foot on the sitting plank, looking out to the horizon for the island she picked for us. Her features are tight, and her eyes narrowed as she attempts to block out the bright sun.

She's been silent the entire journey through the forest this morning, and I've left her to her own devices. After her outburst, I find it best to let her work through whatever is plaguing her on her own. She's usually outspoken, so I imagine it'll come up when she wants it to.

It still doesn't stop the way I wish I could help her.

But I can't possibly begin to think how she may be feeling. Lilith has been her everything since the moment I met her, and the idea that Lilith may have set her on a path to failure… I can't think of how well I would be able to take that circumstance myself.

She has given anything and everything she has for her people. And for her to believe that Lilith, her idol, her mentor, put her in the line of fire… it has to sting.

But it still doesn't seem like those things are adding up, at least in my eyes.

But Seraphina takes things the way she's going to take them, and I imagine eventually, she'll figure it out.

Until then, I try to give her space to contemplate and be there for her when she decides she needs it.

Even now, as she guides us, she's silent, merely nodding in the direction I need to go. From time to time her tail dips into the water to steer us back on course.

Irritation and unease tugs at her facial features in small twitches, her mind working almost on a loop, if I were to guess.

"Asher-dear." Her voice finally breaks through the sound of the oar splashing against the waters.

I look up, meeting her face, only to find her gaze still on the ocean behind me.

"Do you really think I can be Queen?" she asks.

My brow furrows as absorb her question, "Of course."

"No, do you REALLY think I can be?" she asks again as she looks at me, her eyes are almost as watery as the sea we travel.

I don't realize the boat has come to a stop. *I've* stopped rowing as I connect with her troubled gaze.

"Seraphina…" I sigh.

She slowly removes her boot from the slat to sit down on it. Her hands curl in her lap and she picks at the skin around her claws.

"Lilith set me up to fail. Why did she keep this all from me?" Seraphina's voice sounds full of defeat. And with the slump of her shoulders, she *looks* full of defeat.

I reach forward, grasping her calloused hands into my own, "Sera, you have to be able to see what we're doing now."

Seraphina looks at me with a confused expression and a questioning tilt of her head.

"You have tried over and over, again and again. Gone against the rules of The Court, rescued an elf child. You got *into* the Realm of Mages, and we're halfway to Orxisle… You have done *so* much more in the time I've known you than I think I've ever done in my entire life," I attempt to assure her.

And the thought of all she has done, through all the setbacks and issues we've run into… a tug pulls at the depths of my being, urging more praise out of me.

"You fought the Drannar when they breached the portal, AND you took a staff to the chest and *lived.* Seraphina, you are the strongest being, human or otherwise, I have ever encountered in my entire life. And there is truly no one that could be a better Queen than you."

Her eyes sparkle with tears as they well, her gaze fierce as she connects with mine.

"But… why did she keep it all from me?" she asks. Her voice drips with raw pain.

A heavy sigh releases from my chest as my eyes drift to the wooden boat bottom, "I… I don't know, Sera. And I can't imagine how hard it is for you to learn all that you have recently. I know what Lilith meant to you. But we can't linger on that. We *have* to keep pushing forward."

"What if she didn't want me to be Queen? What if The Court is lying to me and throwing me on the stone to die in their stead?"

"Then they did. But it speaks volumes to your heart in your ability to step up. And it speaks volumes to *their* cowardice to throw you there in the first place. But you are the only one I've seen that can. And *will.*"

Her violet eyes drift away, lingering on the water beyond as her face tightens in a flurry of emotions.

Part of me feels like she doesn't want to accept this. It's all I can offer in this moment. But an even larger part of me knows she wouldn't let her people die this way.

"Okay… okay…" Seraphina says as she nods and sniffles. She takes a deep breath and steadies her shoulders as she wipes away a singular tear that escaped. Soon, she stands back on her perch, looking boldly to the skyline.

I don't know if what I said helped her, or if it even makes sense to her. But I hope with everything in me, that it is what she needs.

Because whether she knows it or not, she is everything *I* have ever needed.

But as I swim

frantically to meet

Asher, his

advancements have

stopped, and he begins

to sink as his body goes

limp.

CHAPTER 42

WEBBED HANDS AND DROWNED SONGS

SERAPHINA

Asher's words set my chest ablaze. The fervor in me rises, the closer we approach the tiny island I picked.

It can barely be called an island, if I'm to be honest. More like a patch of land in the ocean, but from here, I have a clear view of Orxisle. The ebony fortress, Knogdagh Stronghold, glows from within with a bright, clementine blaze.

The brick that makes its exterior seems as old as the water surrounding it. Cracked bricks and high walls surround it with no gate for entry. Tall outlook posts stand on every corner, though, they stand unguarded.

Orcs may be feral and strong. But they are also dumb as the brick of their keep.

This feels like a foolish endeavor. And in all honesty, it probably is. But right now, it is the only endeavor worth embarking on. At the end of the day, we need to get The Compendium and embarking on this mission is the only way.

Sand grinds against the bottom of the boat as we slide onto the isle. I take a soft bat at the air to lift me enough to propel me upwards and back, allowing my boots to land in the sand. Tugging on its bow, I haul Asher and our supplies to land.

Asher jumps out and helps push the boat the rest of the way onto the sand.

He goes through the bags a few times for any weapons he may have missed before he fishes out the fabric we've been using for our shelter, to cover the boat and our supplies.

I look to the fortress, my hands on my hips as my mind works over our best point of entry.

It's a moderate length of swimming and we'll have to go completely underwater to make it through undetected, but with the water breathing potions, it'll be a breeze. While there doesn't appear to be guards on the overlooks, we have to be careful. Succubus haven't ventured outside of Tantalia in centuries and seeing one now would surely cause suspicions to rise.

Asher seems to be doing the same. Though, hesitation pricks at his features as he looks over the ancient castle.

I look down to my crossbody bag at my chest and unclasp the metal piece holding it closed. Pulling out two vials of blue, I look over them. They're stamped with a wax seal with the initials "WB". A small sheet of parchment rests on the liner of the bag and shows the key for the vials.

Blue = Water-Breathing
Time: 10 Minutes
Green = Shapeshifting
Time: 20 Minutes
Red = Invisibility
Time: 5 Minutes

"I've never really taken potions before. And in all honesty, I don't even know if my magic allows water breathing without potions. Which means, I have no idea how this transformation works," I tell Asher as I throw him one of the vials.

A small hourglass rests inside of the pack and I remove it, looking over it carefully. I pull one of the small bits of twine from the inside, attaching it to one of the buckles on my armor. As I flip the hourglass, the sand doesn't fall through the narrow center, and I arch a brow in confusion.

Asher looks to me in trepidation as he uncorks the vial; I follow suit and hold it out to him in cheers.

"To fruitless endeavors," I tell him.

Asher nods with an apprehensive grimace, before we both knock the potions back.

It's oddly warm and tastes of sea water and fish guts.

The abhorrent concoction coats my tongue, and I damn near gag before swallowing it down entirely. A shiver runs through my body as it makes its way down my throat.

As I look down at the hourglass, I see small grains of sand begin to fall.

Fucking mages.

Asher and I look at each other in confusion for a moment or two, before I feel like the air begins to thin.

I feel like I can't take in anything, my lungs won't fill. Asher's hand comes to grip around his throat as he gapes at the air like a dying fish.

Fuck.

I look around quickly to make sure we have everything we need before running through the sand and diving into the water.

The warmth of the sea settles into my leather armor and feels as though it weighs me down, so I let it, allowing it to take me deeper before I gasp in the sea.

A feeling of relief runs through me as water fills my insides. Waves splash hard on the surface and a hoard of bubbles crash beside me as the black figure of Asher's body dives into the water.

I watch him for a few moments as he dives deeper. Seeing him gasp, his face is frantic, like he can't understand the idea of being able to breathe underwater.

"This way!" I try to yell through the briny curtain between us, but it just sounds like muffled noises.

Asher regains his composure and settles through inhaling water before he looks at me. His mouth moves but the only thing I can hear is the muffled rumble of his voice.

Great.

I roll my eyes as I swim toward him. Water tugs against my wings, hair and horns as I reach for his hand, pulling him in the direction of the fortress.

Asher gets the message, and I release his hand as he begins kicking through the water beside me.

My tail spins to help propel me, since our armor is not exactly made for swimming. And technically, neither am I. My different appendages push back against the current, making me work harder.

Small fish flitter past us and the depths below darkens as tips of long kelp reach for us, almost beckoning us to swim deeper into the sea with their slimy tendrils. The sun shines bright against the surface of the sea and the light filters through it in dappled specks of warbled glass.

It's a surreal feeling breathing underwater. One I don't think I enjoy. It's nothing that comes naturally and I would already love for this to be over.

Every so often, I look back to find Asher peering around at the little creatures that investigate us as we swim past them. And eventually a blurred dark mass begins to appear in the distance.

Orxisle.

I begin to swim faster, in order to get this over with. My eyes glance down at the hourglass that floats and bobs against my chest, watching the way the grains filter through the narrow center.

Half-life.

I turn around to make sure Asher is there with me, but my heart plummets into the depths below when I realize he isn't.

My eyes widen and I frantically swish back and forth to find him only to look down and see the outline of human hands reaching for me and small funnels of water rising in their wake.

No no nononononono fuck fuck fuck. FUCK!

A rumbled noise comes from my chest as I change trajectory, pinning my wings and kicking as fast as my feet will allow me.

I see a shimmer as filtered sunlight hits plates of slithering scales.

Gods DAMMIT! FUCKING SIRENS!

The counterpart to my own beings. I knew they existed, but I didn't know they'd be HERE.

I should have prepared for this. How could I bring a human into these waters when these beasts lurk in their depths?

Bloodthirsty creatures, hells bent on stealing men through their own methods of seduction.

The irony.

My heart clashes hard against the bones in my chest as I swim for Asher's outstretched hand. His body descends deeper and deeper as the sick beings drag him lower and *lower.*

I can't swim any faster. He gets closer *and* farther with every kick I take.

Eventually, I get close enough to see the fear on his face. His eyes are wide and his mouth is screaming for help. He kicks and punches at the toothy grins that bare against his leathers. Their blackened, webbed hands climb against his limbs as they attempt to take him farther. Their black hair is missing in clumps against their pale scalps.

Their ivory eyes are clouded, but I know they see it all. They peer at him in delightful contempt as they look to feast on him. Long, slender tongues swipe against the jagged, rotted rows of sharpened bone in their mouths.

I release a growl as I reach to my back for one of my swords. But my movements are slow with the weight of my waterlogged armor and the press of the ocean. The thought of not being able to fight these beasts with magic pricks in the back of my mind as I thrust the blade through the creature's chest. Everything moves in slow motion, even if my mind isn't and the realization is infuriating. My wrist twists the weapon in the siren's chest before yanking it out. Scraping bone vibrates through the metal and into the handle as it cuts against the creature's ribs.

A high-pitched screech claws at my ears, amplified by the ocean. I wince as I continue to kick them off him, trying to get him at least far enough away for him to swim to safety. Asher has secured one of his daggers and blood clouds the area from where he sliced at their hands along with the siren's massive bleeding wound from my sword.

More screeches sound off as they begin to retreat. Their quick tails shimmer sporadically in the glints of light and leave bubbly trails in their wake. The one I stabbed begins descending into the depths, blood pouring from its wound to disperse into darkness below.

I sheath my sword against my back as I look for Asher, who has begun swimming to the surface, the black mass of land just barely out of reach.

My eyes trail down to the hourglass to see the last few grains running through the center.

My already racing heart pounds deafeningly in my chest as I begin to feel my body fight for air.

Air… fuck!

But as I swim frantically to meet Asher, his advancements have stopped, and he begins to sink as his body goes limp.

The fear propels me through the water at breakneck speeds. The effort it takes to swim against the hunger for air saps anything I have but I can't let him die, I can't let him die. He can't die. Not like this. He *can't*.

After a moment of furious kicking, I crash into his body, dragging him to the surface as fast as physically possible. I inhale a deep gulp of air as hot sun hits my face. Asher is completely unconscious, and his body is deadweight against me.

The isle is just right there… Right there Asher, please. Hold on.

His drenched, armored body is immensely heavy with his lack of consciousness. I pull him through the sand to a secluded patch of beach beside the fortress. His armor clanks and splashes with a sickening drowned thud as I drop him to the ground. Crashing to my knees, I grip his head and hold him steady. My lips latch onto his, exhaling a breath of mist.

But it's weak. So, *so* weak. My powers are nothing by now, but I have to try in case there is something left.

Asher doesn't move for a long moment, and my panic rises the longer his chest doesn't.

I feel tears break against the drying salt water that tightens my face. My fists pound against the center of his ribs in a desperate attempt to make it move.

To make it rise. To do *anything.*

"Please, Asher, please, you can't!" I beg as I beat harder. The small thread in my chest that has been tethered to him since that moment in the alley feels as though it gets looser and looser.

I pound and pound into his bones. The squelch and clank of his dampened leather armor viciously taunt me as I beat against it. My throat tightens in agony as I try not to cry out.

My teeth bite hard into my lip as I stifle the immense tearing in my chest, while the irony tinge of blood coats my tongue as my fangs break through the skin. My heart roars against the pain deep within.

Not another one, please, not because of me, please don't steal another shred of my heart, I'm begging you. Please, Asher. I need you. Please. You can't go.

The crippling, familiar pang of failure, of letting another one fall at my hands, grasp at my heart. It holds it mercilessly in its palm, sinking its serrated claws into its mass, and I grip my throat in response, trying so hard to silence the throbbing defeat within.

A tortured breath rips through my throat as I attempt to hold myself together, while sobs wrack my shoulders uncontrollably. My head falls onto his chest, where the faint wood and metal scent bring me the smallest crumb of peace. My hands, shaking and clammy, grip with an immovable clasp around his arm.

The thread loosens… more and more…

"Please, don't go… please, Asher," I whimper against his armor. "Please…"

My breaths flee with the loosening tie. It feels as though I am drowning with him and my tears begin to pool on his chest.

Until that thread tightens. Slowly. So slowly does it tighten until it pulls with all its force against my heart and a burbled cough breaks through the sounds of the water lapping against the shore.

Asher's body shudders as water sloshes from his throat and he continues coughing. I quickly tug his arm to get him on his side, his coughs slowly becoming clearer the longer he expels the sea from his body.

He tries to inhale a shaky, ragged breath a few more times before his body relaxes on the sand. His chest slowly expands, and the fullness in my own returns the longer he breathes.

A deep, renewing breath courses through me, and I wrap a hand under his head to hold it up. Fullness returns to my chest; and relief, unlike anything I'd ever known, bathes me in its peaceful reprieve.

"Those… those things," he croaks through hazy eyes.

His hand comes up to rub against his head in pain as he attempts to regain himself.

"Sirens…" I respond softly as I wrap my other hand around his.

"I thought they were myth," Asher rasps.

"I didn't know they existed out here. I figured they were farther out. Not so close to…" My eyes trail up the cracked brick beside us before they land back on him.

"I heard music… and… I couldn't… I don't know what happened. I followed their song," he murmurs as his eyes gaze off at the sky.

I've never been in a land without magic. I've never fought without magic by my side.

And I almost lost Asher for it…

The fullness in my chest begins to squeeze, almost wrenching my own air from me. As if the feeling of inadequacy could get any worse.

How do I go without magic for merely a few days and Asher almost dies? *How* can I attempt to save my own fucking people?

The question that continues to plague me. The one that eats at me. It's devouring me in this moment and my shoulders slump as I come to rest my head against Asher's chest.

I don't want to make this about me right now. Because it isn't.

Asher is safe. He's *alive.*

But it's my fault I have to worry about this in the first place. How could I think to bring a human, so unfamiliar with life outside of his own walls, to accompany me on this journey? Was it selfishness? Was it possession?

"I would have come anyway, Sera," Asher croaks as I feel a hand stroke at my wet hair.

My concentration breaks as my head rises to meet his gaze, a kind smile against his face as he regains his strength.

"You're blaming yourself. Don't. I would have come if you pinned me to the cot," he says. His voice is raspy, his eyes kind, if not a bit pained, but through it all, he's genuine. I can feel the truth with every word he speaks, and it rushes through me in an unfamiliar warmth.

"But…"

"No. No buts. While I didn't sign up to be in Tantalia, I signed up to be your guard. And I meant it."

His hand moves from my hair to stroke at my cheek, the ring of blue around his pupil seems to glow against the green surrounding it.

"I…" The words get stuck in my throat.

From fear, from the failure of protecting him, from the tension in my neck… I don't know.

But they don't come out.
They can't.

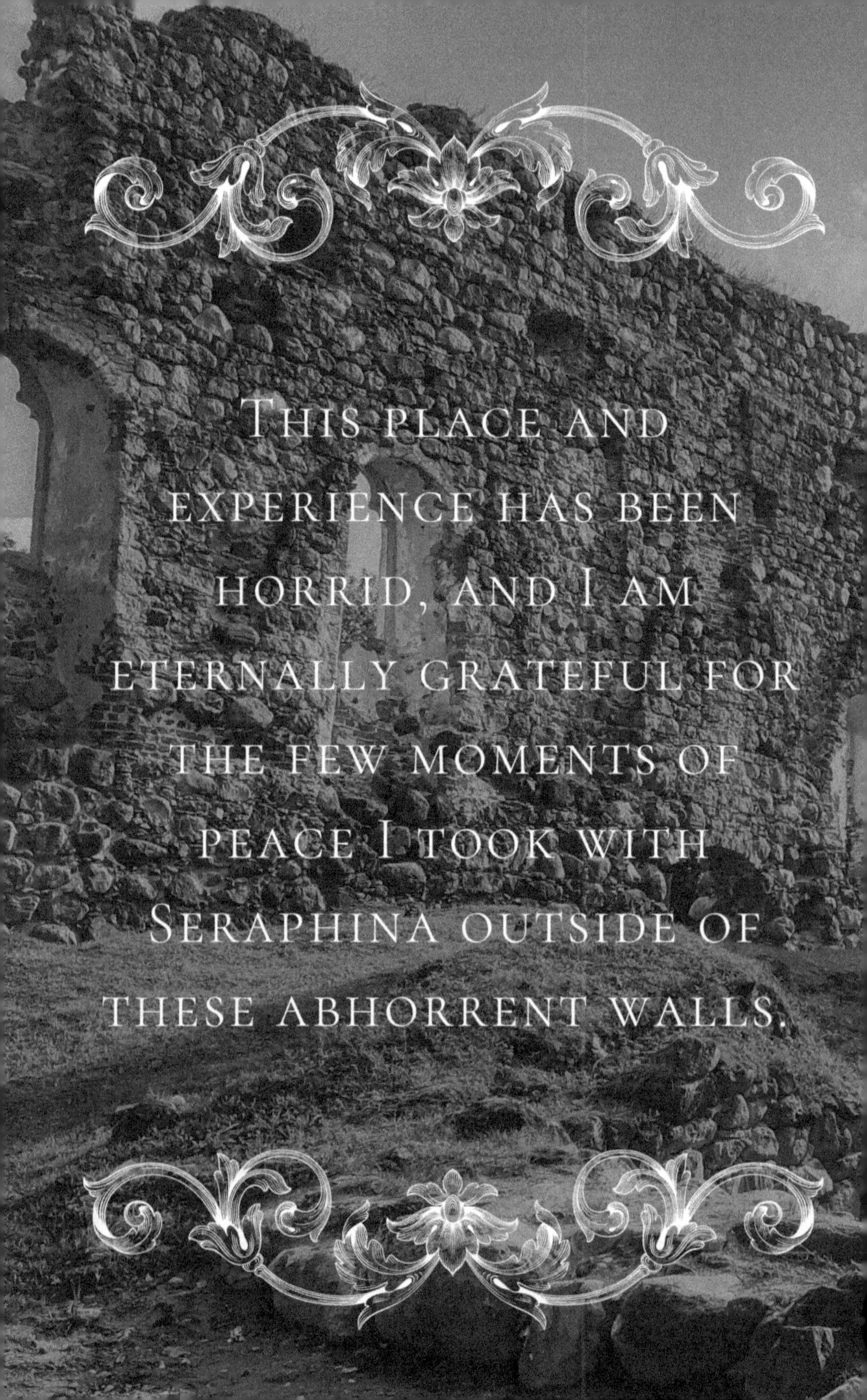

This place and experience has been horrid, and I am eternally grateful for the few moments of peace I took with Seraphina outside of these abhorrent walls.

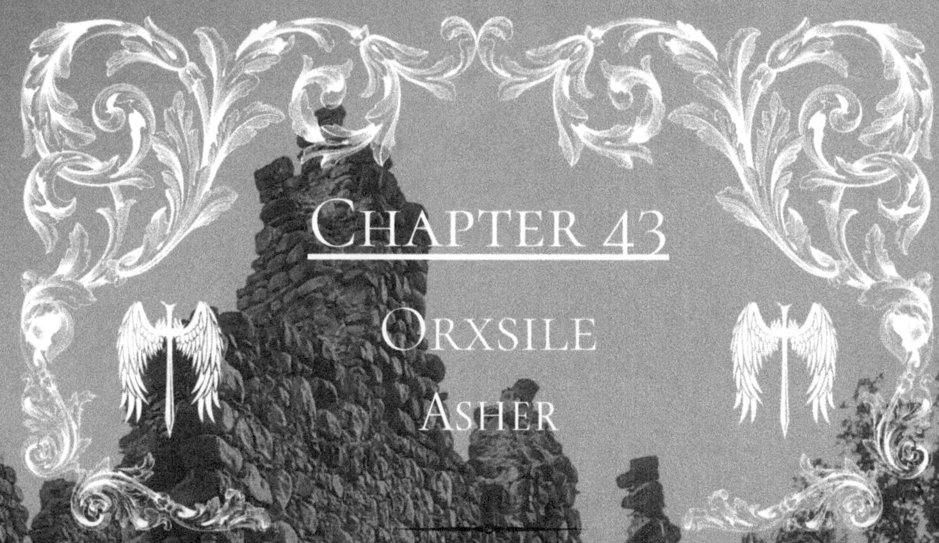

CHAPTER 43

ORXSILE

ASHER

It feels like my lungs are made of lead. And my body hurts… a lot.

Going from being able to breathe underwater to not, without a warning, is horrifying.

Drowning is not the way to go, I've decided.

But I can't linger on that, not when Seraphina is in "The Pits" of her inner thoughts.

A quiet murmur of words came against my mind as she sulked, as if I read the expression on her face, and I just couldn't ignore them.

I watch her for a moment, trying to get a grip on my breathing.

I wish more than ever her mist could work right now because I am in *pain*.

"When should we try to get inside?" I ask, my voice rough. The briny sea had burned my throat, and it feels like I'm talking through sandpaper.

Seraphina gazes at the brick wall beside us, then to the skyline. The sun is slowly starting to set, and she sighs as her eyes come to connect with mine in defeat.

"We should try to stay hidden for the night. We'll get a jump on it tomorrow. I don't know how your body will take a transformation like shape shifting after what just happened, we need to gather our strength in case something goes awry."

I nod softly before wrapping my hand against the back of her head, tangling her wet hair between my fingers. Slowly, I press her head against my chest, letting her rest on me.

The sound of Seraphina's breathing calms me as I gaze at the sky, watching the colors change the deeper the sun descends into the ocean. Every so often, a ragged cough interrupts our peace as I try to expel more water from my lungs.

I watch the colors of dusk fade, swirl, and change until the sun has departed, and the moon rises in the night. The stars that begin to speckle the blackened back drop above, twinkle in distant sporadic flashes of light.

The darkness is different here. It doesn't have the shroud of purple, blue and green like Tantalia does.

A deep part of my chest begins to ache because I never thought I would miss that wayward place so much.

Hells, I never thought I would *love* it to begin with.

Even with how similar this sky looks to Vesperholm before the succubus came... I would rather watch the curtains of color than this black abyss right now.

I peer down at Seraphina, whose shoulders rise and fall in slow movements. My hand brushes against her back slowly, savoring this small moment once again.

My heart swells with her presence, it feels full of these small moments we get to have. Even through the depths of peril, I take any moment I can to lay with her and breathe.

My gaze drifts back up to the sky, the stars twinkling in and out until the darkness of my dreams swallow the night whole.

One would think waking up to Seraphina would be wonderful *every* day. But today is not one of those days. With the sun rising behind the castle, I was not awoken by a bright light.

No, this was a horn tip to the cheek.

And by *gods* does that shit hurt.

The intrusion brings me out of my deep slumber and causes me to jump. Shudders slither through my body, against Seraphina's sleeping one and she groans in annoyance.

Her leg, arm and wing are wrapped tightly around me as she snuggles closer.

I sigh as I look down at her. Her hair is tangled and tight from the sea water. With her mouth agape in slumber, drool drips from her lips onto my armor.

I release a low chuckle, which causes her to stir a bit more as it jostles her body. "Come on, Sera… Early bird gets to kill the orcs," I whisper as I press a soft kiss to her forehead.

She groans in response, burying her head deeper into my armpit. "I don't want to," she grumbles.

"Well, *I* want to get back to Tantalia," I laugh as I slowly sit up, pressing her body up with me.

Seraphina slumps in on herself as she grumbles in annoyance. Her head lazily swings to glare at me in tired fury before she groans loudly.

My laugh breaks through the sound of the calm water lapping against the shore as I stand from the sand. I brush the grains off of my leathers as I stretch out my body. My arms and legs are a bit harder to move, as they have basically been in one position the whole night.

My hands find their place on my hips as I turn around to investigate the looming, black brick beside us.

"So… How do you think we're going to get in here?" I ask.

There doesn't seem to be an entry point, and the entire fortress is just that.

A fucking fortress.

It's surrounded on all sides by these enormous brick walls.

Seraphina is slow to rouse as she stands, brushing herself off and shaking out her arms before she jumps a few times to get her blood moving.

She tilts her head from side to side before she takes a deep breath, "Alright, give me a second," she grumbles as she continues waking up.

As she yawns and stretches one final time, her hand comes to her thigh to fish out the map.

Only to find it has entirely disintegrated.

Seraphina throws her head back in frustration as she lets the map fall to the sand, squishing it into bits with her boot.

"Looks like we're going in blind," she sighs as she looks around the massive wall.

"Weren't we already going in blind?" I ask with a quirked brow.

She groans, "I mean, yes. But I wanted to at least look at the stronghold so I could get a chance to *think* about something."

I start walking along the wall, searching for any small port of entry. Growing up in a bunker allows you to spot anything that may give you an advantage for small hiding spaces.

As I trudge through the sand, I catch a whiff of brimstone, coming from the back of the fortress. "This way," I murmur absentmindedly as I follow it.

We walk the entire length of the fortress wall, to the very back. A large metal grate seeps with the horrid odor and thick black sludge, which causes my stomach to churn the closer we get. It runs down the brick façade, into the sand, where it creates a small river of the muck that leads into the ocean. Murky black makes up the water behind the fortress and dead fish have lapped onto the shore to rot in the bright sun. Flies buzz around the stinking, rotting carcasses.

I grimace over the scene in disgust before I look to Seraphina and tilt my head in boredom, "Gods dammit."

"Welp. Let's get this over with," she sighs.

Seraphina walks to the metal grate, investigating it. Metal squeals as she tries to pry it from the wall with her claws, grunting as she fails several times over.

Of course.

I don't have time to be upset about the circumstance, as Seraphina thrusts her boot through the barred entry. The damp tunnel squeals with the sound of the metal bending as the gate gives way under her strength.

"What happened to stealth?" I ask.

"There's nothing stealthy about being a badass," Seraphina responds as she grips the now warped and split bars, bending them toward her to allow us inside.

I roll my eyes as she bends the bars of the grate from a mangled mess to a mouth of silver teeth that look to swallow us whole.

"Ladies first," Seraphina jokes as she gestures to the entry.

"Funny," I murmur as I stoop down to get a better view. The inside drips with unknown liquid, and farther down the tunnel, I see scurrying tails retreat.

"Where there's rats, there's food," I murmur to myself as I enter the hole.

It's not even big enough to crouch in. Which means we have to crawl.

The thought of having to be covered in whatever mythical muck is coating these walls, coupled with this abhorrent smell, causes bile to rise in my throat and a shallow gag tugs at my innards. I shake my head in disgust as I breathe through my mouth, shimmying through the tunnel.

I hear Seraphina's wingtips scratch against the stone as she climbs in behind me and we slowly make our way through. More rats appear the farther we get, and I follow their trail down the numerous splits and curves. The brimstone scent gets stronger the deeper we crawl. Which I honestly didn't even think was possible.

Eventually, we hit a large square metal gate that enters into this gods' forsaken hells hole.

Peering into the space, massive metal cauldrons burble in a large stone chamber, with an eerie glow.

I look around as much of the space as I can and find it to be void of guards.

Oh, thank fuck.

"No guards," I murmur to Seraphina, who responds with an annoyed huff.

I press hard against the metal bars, and the gate falls into the space with ease. My brows lift in surprise as I crawl from the tunnel and stand, shaking myself off and attempting futilely to rid my armor of the muck that clings to it.

A shiver runs through me as I flick the slime from my hands and wait for Seraphina to exit. Her wings spread wide as she comes out of the small space, flapping a few times to rid herself of her own mess.

"That was gross," she groans as bits of muck fling from her armor.

I look around the massive room, taking in the numerous cauldrons that bubble with various colors of a thick swirling goo. Seraphina approaches my side to peer at them, her brow furrowing in concern the longer she surveys them.

"What are they?" I ask.

There must be over fifty of these cauldrons in here. All with a number of different colors. The energy coursing out of this room is inherently sinister. And the thought of what they *could* be used for presses into my already churning gut.

"I… I don't know…" she responds.

I peer at the vats for a few moments longer before the small clink of glass shifts my focus. Seraphina is sifting through her little crossbody bag, retrieving two more vials. These ones hold a thick green sludge, like some of the contents of these vats.

Fucking hells.

This place and experience have been horrid, and I am eternally grateful for the few moments of peace I took with Seraphina outside of these walls.

Seraphina tosses me one of the vials as she continues looking in the little bag. "Okay, so… we have twenty minutes with these potions, we need to make the best of them because we only have one more pair of them," she says as she flicks the cork from her vial. A grimace contorts my face as I follow suit and the pungent stench of rubbish seeps from small open container.

"They couldn't make this any more appealing?" I ask as I bring the vial to my lips.

"Bottom's up," she says as she knocks back her potion.

An annoyed growl rumbles in my chest as I, too, toss back this terrifying green liquid. As I do, thick sludge paints every corner of my mouth with the sickening taste of rotten eggs. Shallow gags pulse against my throat as I try and work it down, trying so hard to think about literally anything else to keep my mind off this infernal situation.

The potion makes it down and my body shudders a visceral tremble in disgust.

I check in on Seraphina, whose face is twisted in the same sentiment. Her tongue smacking against the roof of her mouth as she attempts to decipher the taste.

For a few moments, it feels like nothing happens, with the sound of the vats burbling around us as we look at each other.

Until all at once, it does.

My arms slowly grow heavier and heavier as the goo begins to work its *magic*. My legs thicken and my body seems to widen to incomprehensible limits. Seraphina's body grows distant as I grow taller.

I look down at my hands that start to darken to a sickly green. The skin clinging to my frame scrapes and scratches against my armor as it begins roughening to a harsh leather.

My lower lip starts to hang as my jaw widens. Long, bony protrusions spear from my mouth to prick at my top lip.

Seraphina's body thickens as her skin deepens to the same green shade as mine. Her head grows thicker as she continues her transformation into a monster and the long, white strands of her hair shift into a deep black.

Her wings shrink more and more until they disappear.

Somehow our armor was included in this potion because they shifted with it.

Seraphina grimaces as she looks me up and down with her now dark eyes, "I like you better as a human," she says. But even her voice has changed, taking on a rugged, scratchy grunt more than her smooth, sultry lilt.

"Likewise, demon," I respond. My chest feels as if it rumbles from the depths of my being as the words quake out of my throat.

I shake my head of this experience before I begin to look around for an exit.

Across the other end of this room is a large metal door.

I capture Seraphina's attention before I nod in its direction. Lumbering down the row of cauldrons, my limbs feel like massive weights against my bones as my arms swing beside me.

Our eyes, however, keep investigating these damned vats.

I know absolutely nothing about all this stuff, but I can't imagine this can be for anything good. The thought makes my skin crawl, and I try to put it out of my mind as we approach the door, cracking it open to peer around the corner.

The other side of the door seems to be a long length of hallways, and we slowly traverse them. Passing cautiously by the other orcs every so often that seem to pay us no mind until we reach the large foyer.

If I thought the Drannar realm was bad, this is infinitely worse.

Tapestries have been ripped and torn, laying on the ground like makeshift rugs. Carcasses of large fish *and* sirens are strewn about the floor, half picked off and rotting with a putrid stench. Black and dried bits of muscle and flesh stick to the bones littering this hovel; with tails of sirens past hanging from the rafters. Wide fins of black scales are shriveled and dried, and long trails of old, browned blood streak the stone they rest against.

The inside of this "palace" reeks of rotting fish guts and horrible monster sweat, if I could put a name to it. If I grimace one more time, I fear my face will get stuck like that. But there is no other reaction to this place than abhorrent depravity.

Several large green beasts lounge around in massive wooden chairs, knocking their flagons of drink into each other's in cheers. Some are chewing on some of the spare bones from, what I imagine, are the sea creatures they have captured.

I look at Seraphina with a small nod of confidence, and she returns it. I take a deep breath and steel my spine as we pass them. Until one stops us, "Aye! Psylax needs bodies, 'o take care o' it," a massive pillar of green flesh yells in his rough accent from his spot at the table.

My eyes widen as I huff a grumbled sound in response.

"Where might 'e be?" I ask the creature, trying to copy their strange accent as much as I can to blend in.

The portly orc laughs a hearty chuckle, and his plump round belly jiggles in response, "Fuckin newbies, the towa!" he says as he takes a large gulp of his drink.

I turn to Seraphina, who looks down at the hourglass strapped to her chest, and her large green head nods in silent confirmation.

My eyes shift quickly around the large foyer, searching anywhere I can for a set of stairs. When I catch the cracked edge of a step in the corner of the room.

Where there are stairs, there is a tower.

We meander casually over to the stairs, where I look over my shoulder at the occupied monsters.

When the coast is clear, I take long strides up the narrow staircase.

Trying to make quick work of the distance, it goes around and around, over and over for what feels like… forever.

This body is a nightmare to move, and I feel like I'm heaving by the time Seraphina and I make it up to the top step, where a massive wooden door sits.

Pressing the panel open, it squeals on its hinges, and I peer around the corner to see a mammoth of an orc standing in front of a mirror. But instead of a reflection, it's a swirling pool of blue glow that is eerily similar to the mages' archway in the cave. The large orcs voice is deep and gruff as he talks to it, "We've not 'ad any demons 'ere, Turo," he says in the same accent as the beasts below.

"That doesn't matter, make sure The Compendium is with you. Or at the very least, guarded. My sources say they are on the hunt for it. And we cannot let them get their vile little claws on it," a smooth, yet obviously annoyed, voice says from the blue swirls.

"Relax, 'rutha'. The C'ompendium will 'e safe 'nd sound. But if it 'o *pleases* his majesty. I've two 'uards 'ere 'at'll 'o and retrieve it 'or me," Psylax – I'm assuming that's who this brute is – says as he gestures to us.

My eyes widen in terror as I realize he noticed our arrival. Though, I imagine the squealing door gave us away.

"It's in the dungeon with the other 'hit. Make 'aste, bodies," he cackles while a groan comes through the small portal.

"You left *The Caelestial Compendium* in the fucking dungeon?!" the mirror responds.

"It's been 'undreds a years! 'nd it 'eeds to be used? It was 'aking up space!"

"With Seraphina on the throne, she will stop at *nothing* to get this tome."

My heart pounds heavily against my chest at the mention of her.

How much do they fucking know? Where are they getting this information?

"'Eah, 'eah, 'ey're 'oin'," Psylax promises as he waves back at us again. I take that as our cue and usher Seraphina out the door, where we begin a hasty trek back down the hundreds of steps.

"Dragons are in tune with the world in a way you could never comprehend. I, even more so."

The discovery of the Orcs' connection to the elves was surprising. Not in them working together, no, we knew that much already. But a magic mirror? Where they can communicate with the Drannars? How *much* can they do through that? And how much magic is that thing able to take?

There is no magic in this land, the sea debacle told me as much.

But the idea of them having more access to The Never Realm than I thought makes everything so much more difficult. And terrifying.

Luckily, we found out where they were holding The Compendium.

The dungeon.

Quietly, Asher and I leave the steps of the tower. My eyes trail down to check the hourglass.

Half-life.

"We have to hurry," I whisper to Asher.

He nods before we descend the steps as quickly as possible.

Passing by multiple guards in the process, they pay us no mind as we traverse the tense fortress.

I have no idea where I'm going, but all I know is that dungeons are below.

We take several descending staircases until we meet two smaller orc pawns that guard a large metal door.

"'State your business," the one on the right grumbles.

Asher steps forward, "Psylax requests a relic from the chambers," he gruffly responds.

The two guards look at each other before they shrug, pressing the door open for us and standing aside.

We take confident steps into the damp, dark underground cavern before I peer at Asher with a soft sigh of relief; our steps echoing off of the high, stony walls.

"'Ave fun with the 'ragon," one says as the door slams shut behind us.

My brow furrows as I look quickly to Asher, "What the fuck did he say?"

Asher's eyes widen in confusion, "Dragon?! What fucking dragon?" he whispers.

I take a moment to study the door, immensely thankful that it has no window for us to be heard.

"I didn't know dragons were still alive, their myth expands time, and I thought they were gone! They haven't been seen in hundreds of years!" I whisper back as I turn to face the enormous cavern.

Gods, I should have read those fucking books like Lilith wanted me to.

Piles and piles of various golds and silvers are strewn about the dark space and piled in mountains on top of each other. Glints of millions of jewels reflect in a dusty haze against the slivers of light that come in from a small metal gate that rests along a top corner of the cavern.

Long stalactites grip the top of the high ceiling and slow drips sound off around us into small puddles formed in craters in the broken stone floor. Various thin bones rest along the ground, with long ashen streaks of what looks to be massive burn marks.

My eyes volley around the space, searching for any hint of this dragon the guards spoke of.

Hot steam blows through the space, cresting in and out against the cool, dank wetness like the waves of an ocean. The ground quakes beneath our feet as the sound of heavy, clanging metal echoes around us. The sound almost screams as it scrapes against the cavern floor.

"Whooooo daaaarreessssssss enterrrrrrrr The Dungeonnnnn of Knogdagh…?" a deep, rolling grumble says. The timbre makes my bones vibrate through my body and all the way to the tips my tusks.

Onyx scales glint in some of the small rays of light that seep into the space as a slender mass of *something* slithers slowly through the cavern. The clang of falling treasures shrieks against the other uneasy sounds of the cave as the thing moves. My eyes trail up the mass, following it until it widens, more and more until I can make out what it is.

The slithering mass is attached to the tall hindquarters of a massive, black dragon. As my eyes continue taking in the creature, I see the sharpened, keratinized spikes that jut tall all over its body.

"D-dragon," I whisper as I nudge Asher in the arm.

"I surely do see it," he responds quietly as we both begin to slowly crouch down.

"Hmmmmmmmm a mortaaaaal enters this realm… and a demon… how peculiaaaar…" the voice booms against the walls like thunder, shaking the very foundation of the stronghold.

Following the rest of the beast's body, I finally find the eyes of this massive creature.

Clouded white orbs catch my gaze, and my heart feels like it's seconds away from imploding as we stand in a stalemate with one another.

The large being serpentines its massive neck in our direction, and with it, the loud clanking of chains shudders through the air.

I look for the source of the abhorrent sound, to find the dragon's legs restrained. More metallic clangs sound off from above, and I look to its wings. They have been locked into a strange cage at the base, the strongest joint, not allowing for an escape.

Prisoner.

A sinking feeling captures my chest as I look back in the poor thing's eyes, "Y-you can see us? I-I mean *really* see us?" I call to it.

"Of courssse… Your shapeshiffffttinngggg does nothing to meeee," the being says as its head moves closer.

Holding my breath, I stand frozen against whatever it means to do to us. The area around its nostrils is cracked with graying shreds of skin, and its scales are marred by deep lashes that have scarred over.

A fierce looking opponent, it seems like every inch of this beast is covered in intimidating spikes.

The scent of brimstone fills the air as he huffs a hot breath in my face, blowing my hair back, "You've come looking for The Compendium," he says slowly.

My gaze slides to Asher, whose eyes are wide as they take in the dragon.

"Y-Yes, how did you know?" I respond quietly.

"You reek of demon… As does The Compendium," he pauses, his eyes narrow on me in inspection. "Your heart is rooted in this tome. Deeply woven into its pages."

I keep my eyes on the dragon as he speaks. His long, slender tongue slithers from his mouth to wipe a thick line of slime against the hundreds of sharpened bones that take residence inside of its massive, tapered jaw.

I make sure to not make any sharp movements, staying perfectly still as I ask, "So, The Compendium… it is here?"

"As here as it can be."

"Where is it?"

"Why should I allow you access to such power?"

Gods dammit.

I sigh softly, almost defeatedly, "I have to save my people. The Compendium is my only option. I've exhausted everything else," I admit.

The dragon tilts its head in curiosity as it eyes me, "You speak the truth, demon."

"I try to," I respond. My eyes trail back to the cage on his wings, "Why are your wings restrained?"

The dragon's eyes narrow on me, almost surprised by my question, "I am a prisoner."

"Why?" I ask. The sadness I begin to feel for this creature grows. Dragons are not meant to be kept in cages, at least the way legend told it.

"For being a dragon."

"How long have you been here?"

"Time is irrelevant when you've nowhere to go."

"Bu-"

"Long ago, the orcs invaded my homestead. Threatening to take my flock for their own selfish gain. In order to save my Queen, my eggs, and my brood, I sacrificed myself to their treasures. I bargained my life to protect their jewels," the dragon recounts as his gaze shifts to the metal grate above in longing. A deep ache seems to settle in his stony features.

"I have been here for more moons than I can count, but the thought of my mate, my eggs, and my brood kept safe, keep me alive and well," the dragon says as his gaze connects back with mine. "I'm sure you can empathize with my plight, *Seraphina Moonsong*."

My eyes widen as a crater blows through my chest, "H-How do you know my name? And how do you know what I've gone through?"

"Dragons are in tune with the world in a way you could never comprehend. I, even more so."

That's fair. Terrifying, but fair.

His gaze slides to Asher as his neck slithers in his direction. The dragon peers into Asher with a curious tilt of his head. Asher's skin begins to seep with his normal creamy tone as the shapeshifting wears off.

"And you. You have yet to face your own reality," the dragon says, blowing a burst of steam in his face.

Asher grimaces as he waves the steam away, "I don't know what you're talking about," he states as he folds his arms across his chest in annoyance.

"That the demon… is your mate."

Oh fuck me.

My eyes widen in incomprehensible limits as I glance at Asher. Violent pounding consumes my chest and I try with all of my might to think of a way to shift focus.

Now is not the time for life-altering secrets.

As Asher's tusks disappear and his body shrinks, his pale skin turns even paler. His green eyes dull as they widen in shock.

"The… the what? Is *what?*" Asher murmurs.

"Your meager bond reeks of confusion and peril," the dragon responds.

"B-bond? Wha-?"

I step in front of Asher, bringing the attention back to the task at hand, "What if we release you? Return you to your lands, will you tell us where The Compendium is?" I ask quickly. Glancing down to the hourglass on my chest, only a few grains of sand remain. We're running out of time and the ceiling shakes as I hear the rumbling steps of guards above. Pebbles fall from the ceiling to clatter against the floor as they approach.

The weight of my limbs decreases as my body shrinks, and my words become quicker as my tusks begin to fade away. Weight heaves against my back as my wings sprout and flap back into place.

The dragon is slow as he looks back to the grate, staring at it for a few moments longer than I would have liked before his ivory gaze connects with mine, "I will accept your bargain, demon. My only terms are that you do right by The Compendium. Use it for the good of your realm."

"Deal," I say quickly as shouts are heard from above and I look to Asher in fear.

Asher's gaze connects with mine in a hurricane of confusion, fear and damn-near madness.

We'll get back to that. I promise, Asher-dear.

"What is your name?" I ask the dragon as I come to look back at him.

"Oracle King of Infernal Summit, and Father of the Blaze, Kyraxes," the dragon says.

"Kyraxes, we're going to free you, do you think you could burst through this dungeon?"

"I can."

"Great, now where is The Compendium?"

Kyraxes' head swings to the corner of the cavern, huffing steam in its direction.

"Asher, go get the book, I'll get these chains off," I say as I run for Kyraxe's leg.

I hear Asher's boots pound against the cave floor as I look over the bindings surrounding the dragon's legs.

A massive metal cuff has been secured around both of Kyraxe's back ankles. Attached to it, is a long length of ovular rings of iron. The skin around his legs is bloody, ripped and rotted from the years he's been restrained here, causing a heavy pang of anger to prick at my chest.

I survey the bindings, trying to find the lock, before coming across a giant metal padlock. Using my thin, sharpened claw to press into the keyhole, I run the tip along the inside of it in a frantic haze until the lock pops open.

Quickly, I remove the lock from the giant cuff, throwing it to the side, and the deafening clank of metal shakes the ground as the cuff falls to the stone. I hear more precious metals clatter from across the room as Asher searches for The Compendium, and I crawl furiously over the hoard of treasures to reach his other leg. His massive, scaly body rises to allow me access, and he lifts his leg for me to help. I make quick work of the lock, and it clatters against the dozens of crowns and gold that take residence on the pile.

"Sorry about this," I say softly as I begin scaling the beast. My claws grip into his hard, armored body to reach his wings, looking over the barbaric contraption that keeps him here.

As I look over the numerous locks, a growl escapes my chest. Large plates of iron are pressed into the area of his back, not allowing for any kind of wing movement.

"Fucking bastards," I murmur as I go through and unlock every one, throwing them into the pile of treasure until the metal cage falls from his body. The impact of its fall causes gold and silver to fly through the air as it settles down to its new home. I look around for Asher, who runs at the pile with a large brown textbook clutched against his chest. The door to the cave swings open, and a hoard of giant orcs, led by Psylax, stand in the entrance.

"'UCCUBUS!" he bellows as the guards file into the room.

Asher clambers up the falling pile of treasure, and I settle in the space between Kyraxes wings, fixing myself amongst the numerous spikes along his spine.

The enormous beast begins moving from the mountain of gold, with his steps causing more treasure to fall and clang against one another. Asher's efforts are for naught as he ends up sliding back to the ground.

Kyraxes turns to the orcs, and the massive, calcified spikes in his mouth clack against each other when his jaw slacks. His bones vibrate against my legs as he prepares to set the threat ablaze. Brimstone and immense heat consume the air around us as he sets a jet of fired breath on the orcs in warning. Soon, his large legs pound into the stone as he takes a few more steps onto the ground, allowing Asher to climb him.

I lean down as Asher attempts to climb onto Kyraxes, reaching for his hand to haul him onto the dragon's back.

Asher pants as he tosses The Compendium to me, and I hold it tight to my chest while I grip at one of the spikes on Kyraxes to hold my seat.

Kyraxes fires another stream of fire at the orcs, who scream in agony as they are set ablaze.

I swear I feel a satisfied chuff vibrate against the dragon's bones as he takes his revenge.

"Hold tight," I feel, more than hear, from Kyraxes before his wings expand, beating in large sweeping bursts toward the ceiling. Another roar echoes in the cavern as he lets a blaze go, weakening the grate he means to burst through.

As we set for the sky, my stomach drops, and we are covered in brick and flame as we fly through the swirls of red and orange. Destroyed stone rains down my line of sight and an explosion rocks around us as Kyraxes breaks through the fortress, letting a deafening roar ring through the air.

Everything feels as if it flows in slow motion as we climb higher. Kyraxes body bobs up and down as his wings beat into the sky. I look down at the giant hole we've left in the bottom of the fortress; torches begin to blaze from below but shrink the higher we get.

Eventually, we climb high and far enough away from The Keep that Kyraxes can even out on the winds, and we soar away from Knogdagh Stronghold.

I take heaving breaths as the storm finally calms, and Kyraxes continues his flight path to a plume of black smoke in the distance. My heart still pounding from the rampant debacle we just barely escaped from.

As the dust settles, and I set my sights on the smoke beyond, Asher's chest rumbles with fury at my back.

"Mate?" I hear him growl.

Fuck.

Fuck all these gods damned riddles. They only seek to fuel the raging fire in my mind. I don't understand and I feel like I never will.

CHAPTER 45

MATE

ASHER

*M*ate? *Mate? Mate! Mate?! MATE! MATE?*

What the FUCK did that beast mean by bond?! *Mate?!*

My mind couldn't comprehend the simple word, and it took everything in me to focus on finding that damn book.

Seraphina couldn't have possibly known this whole time… could she? Is that what she's meant by fate? All this time? Has she been controlling me? Is that what mates do?

In Vesperholm, we don't have *mates.* Hells, we barely have *wives.* And now I'm faced with the idea that I have a *mate.*

The thoughts swirl in a sickening torrent of confusion, questions, and panic.

What does this mean? Am I never able to go back to Vesperholm? Do I have to stay in Tantalia forever?

I wouldn't mind, but that was before I knew I may *have* to stay there. I don't understand anything, and the thoughts beat harder and harder against my skull as I think about it.

My stomach churns from the flight of this dragon and the thoughts in my head, which cause me to lean over and heave my stomach --what little contents there are -- over the edge of Kyraxes.

Seraphina doesn't spare me a glance, and I imagine she won't. This is her modus operandi. This is just what she does.

She knows things and keeps them for me to figure out on my own.

It's not fair for her to keep something *this* big from me. Something I should be the one to KNOW if I'M supposed to be her fucking MATE!

The thoughts in my head turn from confusion to anger and rage at the idea that she keeps leaving me out of highly important information.

My hands grip tightly against the rugged spikes of this dragon's back as we approach a brilliant, orange glow that comes from the center of a giant crater across the sea.

My anger fades for just a moment as we take a wide circle around the black plumes of smoke that rise from the melted mountain, and a symphony of roars light up the air around it. Smaller burbling pools of melted rock dot the rest of the charred island, with some mid-sized dragons lounging by their lips. All of the other beasts are varying shades of color. Red, orange, black, blue.

Kyraxes body rumbles against my thighs as he gears up to return a roar of his own. The sound is absolutely deafening, and my hands clap over my ears in the process.

Several jets of fire shoot into the sky as the dragons celebrate the arrival of their long-lost King.

Kyraxes wings take wider sweeps to slow him down as we make to land. His feet slam into the jagged rocks, and a plethora of these massive, winged beasts stomp up to greet us.

Air blasts my face, as Seraphina bats into the sky to float down to the ground beside Kyraxes, clutching The Compendium tight to her chest.

My approach is slightly less subtle, as I swing a leg over to grab at the dragon's scales and slowly lower myself to the ground.

As Seraphina and I stand idly by, Kyraxes meets with a bright red dragon of a slightly smaller size. Not much smaller than him, but noticeably so.

It chuffs a deep sound from its ribcage as their spikes clack against each other. The large, crimson scales sparkle in the dying sun as its head nuzzles close into his neck.

Seraphina and I back away to give them room and a rainbow of different dragon's trudge down the mountain in booming steps.

Obsidian pebbles roll from the side of the barren, charred cliff as the rest of their hoard makes their way to greet us.

Two larger black dragons tackle Kyraxes and the earth quakes under their arrival. Roars and growls sound off as they wrestle each other into the ground.

The red dragon comes closer, its steps are not as heavy as Kyraxes' are and bows its head in gratitude, "Is it you who brought my mate to his homelands?" the dragon says with a feminine, kind timbre. Her eyes shine with an adoring golden glow.

Seraphina bows deeply before she nods, "We did. He helped us find something very important to us."

The features of the dragon's face soften as she tilts her head in thanks, "We are eternally grateful for his return. It has been too many moons since I have breathed in his essence," she says as she looks back at the tackled Kyraxes. Her head tilts in relief and longing, before turning her sights back on us and bowing her head. "I am Vizzuu, Queen of Infernal Summit and Mother of the Blaze."

"He didn't deserve to rot there. Dragons are meant to be in the sky, not in cages," Seraphina says solemnly.

"I wholeheartedly agree, demon."

Kyraxes is able to pull himself from the brawl against the mountain to take lumbering steps to his mate. He hauls a wing over her back to nuzzle her in close.

"You have done a great deed, Seraphina Moonsong. And the dragons of Infernal Summit are forever in your debt," Kyraxes chuffs with a heated burst of steam.

Seraphina's lips curve in an awkward smile of thanks, "I have only done what my mentor would have."

"You hold a deep fear, Seraphina. You shouldn't," Kyraxes says.

My brow rises at his statement, and I peer at Seraphina to gauge her reaction.

Her features prick with tension, but she nods sheepishly.

"You have much more to offer than even you know. Your heart is pure, and you will succeed in whatever endeavor you embark on. But you have to believe it yourself."

"But… how can you know that?"

"How do dragons know anything? How do demons exist? How do things come to be? Not everything needs a how. But need not forget your *why*, Seraphina. It will push you at every turn you encounter."

Seraphina's brow works as she weighs his statement, deciding to nod and accept his answer as that.

"And you, human," Kyraxes says as he turns to me.

My eyes widen as his focus shifts and his cloudy gaze pins into my soul, "Your confusion will only be worsened the longer you run away from your fate."

Fuck.

"I… I don't know what any of this means…" I say softly. The already pounding organ in my chest squeezes to near pain as I try to listen to him.

"You will. In due time. But this world works in strange and complicated ways, why make it that much harder on yourself?"

"Because… I don't understand any of it."

"Accept the words of The Fates, they know what you need. Even if you don't."

Fuck all these gods damned riddles. They only seek to fuel the raging fire in my mind. I don't understand and I feel like I never will.

I decide arguing with an oracle dragon king is not within my best interests, so I nod in return.

Kyraxe's head tilts, as if he's unconvinced by my response. "My brother, Xykes will return you to your homestead. If there is ever a need for us, I will know. I will call on the might of Infernal Summit and bring your enemy to heel. We are forever in your service, demon," Kyraxes says to Seraphina as an even larger black dragon lumbers his way to us. The ground clatters and shakes with his steps.

This dragon is nearly the size of the fortress we just escaped; his steps are slow as he approaches. The fearsome protrusions on his body reflect bits of dusk as the once bright sun shifts to deep oranges and reds. He bows deeply, lending a leg to allow us to climb.

Seraphina bows in thanks to the two dragons, "Your influence is not to be forgotten, and I hope we meet again, Kyraxes."

"We will, Seraphina. But it is not a question of *how*. It will be *why*," Kyraxes responds.

I mimic the revelry and bow in thanks, before following Seraphina to Xykes.

Her wings bat into the air to perch her on the dragons back, and I sigh as I claw my way up his body to find my spot behind her.

Kyraxes and Vizzuu send blazes of fire into the sky and Xykes roars into the air before he takes flight, and we fly back to Castaway Grove.

As the thoughts run through my head, a shining bright white light eases through the trees to the west of the boulder.

Chapter 46

Lilith
Seraphina

The tension between Asher and I is thick as Xykes flies over the ocean.

Sickeningly so.

Even through the beat of his wings and the roaring air around us, I can feel his energy shift against my wings. It radiates a rage unbound.

Small dots of land appear below us, as the trees of the grove come into sight. I hand Asher The Compendium before I jump and spread my wings, allowing the air to catch me. A tilt of my body causes me to drift on the winds, so I can fly near Xykes' massive, spiked head.

His dark eyes slide to me in annoyance as I come beside him, "What is it, demon?" he grumbles.

"I need you to land on the beach at Castaway Grove so I can grab our gear at a nearby island."

Xykes chuffs a heated breath in response before his eyes glide down to the land below and he surveys a spot for landing.

Like a falling star, I dive onto the island where we left our things. The sand blasts around my boots as I come to land and stalk toward the boat, keeping my head on a swivel, in case there are any stray beasts lurking about the thicket.

I find myself eternally grateful that our things have not been ravaged by some mystery creature and all our belongings are still intact.

Fucking sirens.

I grab the straps of my bag and fling them over my shoulders to secure them down at my armpits before I grab Asher's gear and lunge at the air, taking flight for the shore. Amongst the trees surrounding the area, Xykes has sat himself on the sandy bank, awaiting my arrival while Asher broods, deep in his thoughts along the creatures hardened back.

To see the dragon from this angle, especially against the trees of the grove, gives him a much larger, dominating presence.

The night has descended, and he stands like a scaly, menacing shadow. Taller than any building I've seen, aside from The Keep, his long spikes reflect in the moon and silhouette in the dark. His tail is crafted of sickeningly long and sharp spikes, producing a menacing weapon, with his unimaginably large wings resting around his body as he waits.

A magnificent beast.

I land in the sand next to Xykes, and he looks down at me with an annoyed huff, blowing hot air into my face before he nods at his back, "I've not got all night, demon," he rumbles.

I shake my head with an amused smile, and lunge for the sky, beating my wings once… twice… before I settle on the dragon's back with our gear in tow. The hardened scales hit into my rump as I take my seat.

I turn around to grab the book from Asher, his features are pulled together in thought as he mindlessly hands it over. His gaze won't meet mine and the energy that continues to pumps off him is intense.

I shove the book between my legs before I turn around to hand his bag to him. His knuckles whiten as he grips the straps and throws it on his shoulders, as if he is well-versed in the motion enough to do it without thought.

Xykes shoots for the sky once more to fly over the trees. The upper canopy shimmers and shakes against the heavy breadth of wind that knocks against them as he makes his way to the small clearing by the boulder.

A loud thud in the grass marks our arrival and the large beast shifts uncomfortably on the confined knoll.

Grabbing The Compendium, I clutch it tightly to my chest as I swing a leg over and jump to the ground. The grass cradles my boots as I steady myself and back up enough to give the being some space. Asher follows suit. He mindlessly slides down the dragon's scales to land in the grass beside me. His attention is finally pulled away as he gazes at the beast. Xykes meets our curious surveillance with a fearsome one of his own.

With the night falling upon us, small forest creatures make themselves known as the trees beyond Xykes titter with the sound of various bugs and critters that scurry in the underbrush.

The beasts dark, intimidating eyes meet mine in a look of boredom as I speak, "Thank you for returning us. If there is any use we can be to Infernal Summit, Tantalia offers it."

"A daring statement, demon," Xykes chuffs.

"Do you think there is a smaller dragon that could be of service to us? I wouldn't mind having wings," Asher says from beside me.

Xykes head serpentines slowly to Asher as he speaks before he tilts his head at the moon, "Perhaps, human. We shall see."

Asher nods with a small smile before he bows. The sound of his scales scrape together as Xykes turns to me, "Until next time, Seraphina Moonsong."

With that, he lunges, and his wings take a wide sweep that cause leaves and grass to flutter around us. My hair kicks up to furl around me as he beats into the sky and off into the moon.

I watch Xykes' large wings beat into the night until he is out of sight. My thoughts completely entranced by these massive creatures, before I turn around to face Asher.

His form is steady as he looks at the boulder. Almost frozen, if I were to put a name to it.

His hands clench at his sides with a crushing tightness as he stares.

A sigh releases from my chest as I realize what I may have to deal with now.

The heart pounding, blood pumping events from the last few days have worn off and crash into me at full speed. My body weakens as I take a deep breath, knowing The Compendium is in my hands now. But I'm still without my magic, and using what little of it I could, took an immense toll on me.

And there's no way Asher will allow a feeding right now.

Not with how pissed I imagine he is with me.

I was not exactly expecting to meet an oracle dragon on this trip, and I surely wasn't expecting him to scent what little bond there is between Asher and me.

Nor was I expecting said oracle dragon to reveal that sort of information to him.

I can't imagine what Asher is thinking with the way he's reacting. He was quiet at Infernal Summit, and his tense energy has only ratcheted up the closer we get to home.

Does he have a right? Perhaps. But I tried more than once to tell him.

He wouldn't listen, he wouldn't face his reactions or the things fueling and pushing the beast within him.

There must be some kind of cognizance, if your senses heighten and things happen to you that don't normally happen. While he is confused, I would hope humans know at least a little something about the concept of mates. Even if it isn't as powerful as it is with a magical being.

As the thoughts run through my head, a shining bright white light eases through the trees to the west of the boulder.

It beams like an opal and moves gracefully against the darkness. It almost floats along the brush.

My head tilts and I step in its direction as something deep within me pulls me closer and closer.

As I walk past Asher, he seems to catch the light, and he makes to fist his dagger. Lining his forearm with the blade, he steels himself against the threat he deems to annihilate, "Show yourself!" he calls to the darkness.

This being… it *belongs* to me.

I place my arm out against Asher's offense as I pass him in an attempt to take him off his guard.

"It's…" I murmur mindlessly as I take more steps to the edge of the trees.

Soft grass compresses under my boots and the sounds of the forest seemingly pound against my beating heart as I approach the tree line, and I peer deeper into the woods.

The shining light creeps closer, beaming brighter. Long protrusions, with no rhyme or reason in their shape, press through the branches as it exits the forest and bright crimson eyes meet my own. Bowing its head out of the trees, it grows nearer, until it stops right in front of me.

"The deer…" I whisper to myself as it comes from the trees.

The once dying animal has been renewed. With bright white fur that shimmers like stars in the night, and an unearthly glow that shrouds it in an ethereal beauty it didn't have when it was dying on that forest floor.

But also… it's grown?

In three days? Did my healing do this?

The bright red eyes of this creature meet mine in a show of gratitude before it leans forward on its front hooves. Its majestic antlers graze my chest as it offers itself to me.

My eyes widen as I take in this new discovery. Not only did I heal a dying creature with what little magic I had… it *transformed* it.

And everything in me is saying it wants to come with me.

It returns from its bow to nuzzle its wet, dimpled nose against my face in welcome. I can't help myself when I wrap my arms around its long neck and nuzzle into it. Its fur is warm and soft as I feel part of its soul connect to my chest, to burrow deep inside of me.

"Lilith…" I murmur softly.

"Seraphina, that is a male deer," I hear Asher say from behind me.

Fuck, he heard that?

As I look over my shoulder to meet his gaze, I see the purple glow in his eyes as his rage takes over. His face is solid with fury, but he doesn't realize what's happening to him.

I take a deep breath before I turn back to Lilith, nuzzling a comforting hug into the beast before I turn around to walk to the boulder. The soft press of grass behind me and the small thumps of hooves alerts me that Lilith's following me.

"I don't care. His name is Lilith," I retort.

Asher rolls his eyes in angst as he looks at the stoned entry point, surveying its exterior as he awaits my instruction.

My lungs fill with air as I gulp a deep breath and steady myself, "Place your hand on the boulder."

Asher's brow rises, and the purple in his eyes swirl as he presses his palm to the stone.

I throw an arm around Lilith and pull the deer closer before I knock against it three times, just as the little mage had told us.

It feels as if an eternity passes by with no answer. My brow furrows in confusion and my eyes slide back and forth against the forest behind Asher as we wait.

Suddenly the world shifts from under us, and I feel the powerful thrum of magic as we're deposited back into the Realm of Mages.

"WHAT KNOWLEDGE ARE
YOU HIDING, **MAGE**?"

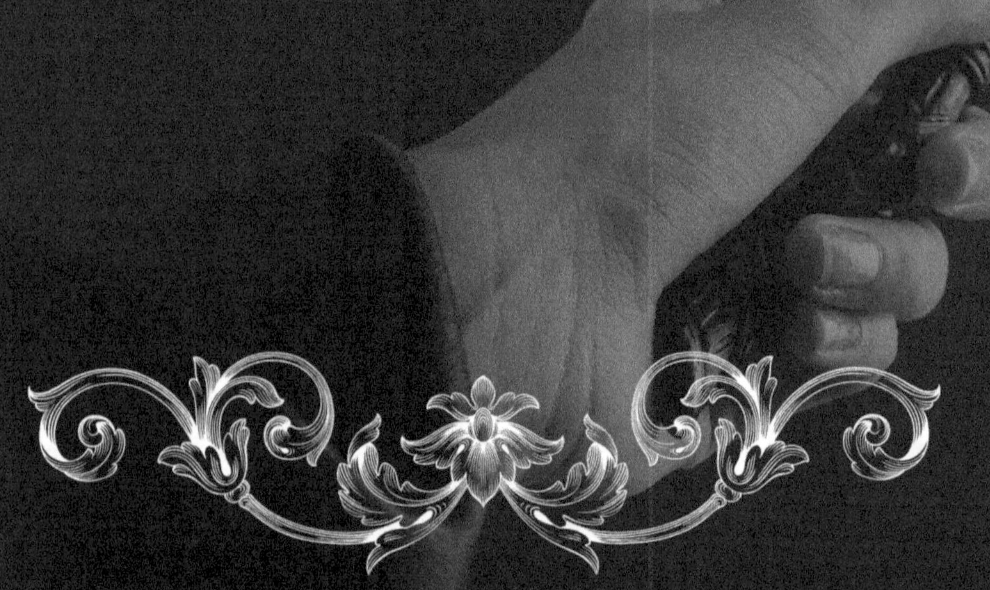

Chapter 47

The Mage
Seraphina

D irt and grass assault my skin as we barrel into Kaithoon. The gods forsaken portal throws us back into this place like we're fish out of water.

I swear, nothing has ever been this difficult when it comes to magic. How could these mages study magic for so long only for it work like shit?

A groan works through me as I come to stand, stretching out my limbs and wings, as my tail dusts off the earth that now sticks to various parts of my armor.

My veins feel like they vibrate and a hint of the meager energy of this land finally pulses through me. That electric trickle of magic pricks against my skin and I inhale deeply as it settles within my bones.

I can't help the way I jump and shoot lightning bolts into the air, and I cackle a hearty laugh as I let it course through me in joy. As I settle from my excitement, I look at Asher, who rolls his eyes as he dusts his armor of the debris stuck to it.

Lilith seems unphased by everything as he moves back and forth against the ground, nipping at the long blades.

I look around the small clearing to search for the being that brought us back, only to find the little mage, Tyrick, watching us with wide eyes. Though now, he doesn't seem as nervous and almost titters with glee.

"How did it go?" he asks curiously as his eyes shift to the now magical deer we've brought back with us, "Who is this?"

I wrap a happy arm around Lilith's back, barely interrupting his meal as I look at Tyrick with a grin, "This is Lilith."

Tyrick's brow furrows in confusion as he surveys the animal, "That… is… a male deer?"

"I am aware, yes."

Tyrick blinks a few times before he nods slowly, "Li…lith…"

His attention is broken when Asher begins speaking, the curious mage's head turns to Asher as he hears his shifted, deep voice, "We got the book, almost died to sirens, rode a dragon home, oh and Seraphina and I are mates. Whatever the fuck that means," Asher grumbles as he bends the fall from his neck.

Tyrick's golden eyes widen as he looks between the two of us, "M–mates? You've… you've been mated with a succubus?"

Asher's curiosity piques as he looks at the mage, his brow furrowing in anger. Within the blink of an eye, Asher turns and collides with him. His now clawed hands wrap around the mages throat as he leans in close to his face, "What knowledge are you hiding, *mage*?" he growls with venomous disdain. A snarl tugs at his lips to show the lengthened canines in his jaw, and the sheen of purple glows in warning as he peers into the little wizard's soul.

Tyrick yelps and clutches at Asher's grip, "V–very little! I just know it's only happened one other time! But the texts don't say anything more!" he chokes.

Asher's head tilts, his eyes narrowing before he throws the mage back, stalking off in the direction of the city.

Tyrick coughs and inhales a ragged breath as he looks at me with fearful eyes, "What did you do?"

"Nothing The Fates didn't decide for themselves," I sigh as I walk past him.

Lilith's soft steps follow, and Tyrick's heavy breathing becomes clearer the closer he gets to me.

"I don't know anything about demon mating protocol… Is that w-"

"Yes. He hasn't seemed to realize it himself, unfortunately. Even when he seems to switch so quickly with it," I respond.

Tyrick is silent for a moment as we make our way back to the city. "Will he be okay?"

"More than okay, I imagine. Mating bonds give traits to their weaker counterpart. Though, I've never seen it myself."

"Fascinating…" he murmurs from beside me.

I peer at Tyrick from the corner of my eye with a curious raise of my brow, "You are so enthralled by the idea of us. Why is that?"

Tyrick nervously glances away, "I've spent a lot of my time in the library. I came across texts of the succubus, and I've wanted to see them ever since. But every time it was mentioned, I was shunned. They threw me deeper into the ranks in an attempt to rid me of the idea, but it only became stronger. So, when you came to the realm with a human, I wanted so badly to go back with you. When you offered the chance, I ran to Bufort and Retalnia. It took some convincing, but they have allowed me such. If only to keep an eye on your endeavors."

My steps halt and apprehension pricks at my features as I peer to him, "So, you are to be a spy?"

His eyes widen and he fidgets where he stands, "That's what they expect of me… But I don't want to be a spy. I just want to learn."

My eyes narrow on him, gazing deep into the little man's soul, "You speak the truth," I whisper softly before I turn and continue onward. "Well, I have space for you. Though, you'll have to wear a collar to make sure you don't stab me in the back."

"I-I can do that. I want to see what this world has to offer," he responds sheepishly.

"You'll have to work for it."

"I can do that."

My mind works over these new beings I keep bringing into Tantalia. First Asher, then the elf child, now I come back with an ancient textbook, a human wizard and a fucking magic deer.

My eyes roll at my own actions as we finally reach city center, and head to the castle. The moon above us lights the cobblestone streets and it appears as if everyone has gone in for the night, save for the armored guards that stand watch outside of the castle's steps.

Asher is nowhere to be found, and I can only imagine he retreated to our room to ruminate on his circumstance.

As we take steps up the stairs, Lilith's hooves clap against them, and I remind myself that it's probably bad manners to bring a large, ethereal ungulate into a premises that I'm barely allowed to vacate.

I turn to Lilith and press my forehead to his nose, "Sorry, friend. I have to place you somewhere." Lilith nods softly as if he understands me and a smile tugs at my lips.

I look back to Tyrick, who stands on the top of the steps, "Is there anywhere I can place my horned companion?"

Tyrick's golden gaze turns to the sky as he thinks, "There is a stable for the horses, I can have the guards take your friend."

I nod and a guard comes beside Lilith, who chuffs an annoyed breath at him.

"Hey, it's alright, just follow them, they'll feed you and take care of you. I'll be back in the morning, I promise," I tell Lilith, and he chuffs another noise in annoyance before he follows the guard around the side of the castle.

I turn to follow Tyrick, who leads me to the dining room where Bufort and Retalnia stand by their table.

Their arms fold in their sleeves as they look over us, "Greetings, demon," Bufort calls. His voice scrapes against the ancient walls as we come closer.

"So, have you retrieved the text?" Retalnia asks.

"We have. We shall take our leave in the morning. It has been an eventful few days and I could use the rest."

"You intend to take our apprentice mage?" Bufort asks skeptically.

"I merely offered the option. The decision was his own."

"We have allowed him such. Though, we hope you do return him at some point."

My eyebrow rises against my forehead as I narrow my eyes on the elder wizard, "As you wish, *Bufort.*"

The two mages nod in my direction, bidding me farewell for the night.

I turn to Tyrick, "Make sure you have your belongings ready to go by sunrise. I will leave, with or without you."

Tyrick nods hastily before bowing, and I take my leave.

In order to stave the thoughts away, I ram every pulsing inch into her.

CHAPTER 48

THE BEAST

ASHER

I feel as if I've worn a path into the wood from my pacing. The split in my tongue has returned and I've nipped my lip several times with the irksome fangs in my mouth.

All the sounds around me are blaringly loud and I feel like I can see every speck of dust on *every single surface*.

This raging beast in my chest beats with urgency, *begging* me to take Seraphina.

I don't want to, I *can't*. Not with how seething I am with anger.

But even if I never want to see her, every time this monster rears its head, the one in my pants does as well. It only infuriates me further.

I need to be able to think about this situation and what being mates could possibly mean. What it means for me and my future in Tantalia. What it means for Seraphina and me.

Seraphina seems entirely unperturbed by this entire situation, and it causes blood to rush through my veins like lava. How can she continue to be so nonchalant about this? She seems to have sat herself with this reality in comfort.

Soon, the bedroom door creaks open, and the large wingtips of the demon I seek to mark, press through the frame. The sensuous curves of her tight body follow suit as she closes the door behind her.

Tension tugs at my nostrils as they flare, and her scent floods my being.

Her purple eyes watch me cautiously as she unlatches the straps of her pack and lets it crash to the wooden floor with a loud thud. She narrows her eyes and her head tilts as she takes slow steps to me.

A rough step meets her in the middle and her pulse pounds hard against my palm as I grip a hand around her throat. "Did you know?" I growl. Tension grips at my own throat as the words claw out in a graveled timbre.

Her eyes stay fixed on my face, "I did."

"Why didn't you tell me?"

"I tried to, Asher," she chokes. Her full lips part in an attempt to take in more air. But the action causes a pang of lust to pulse through me. The sight of her lips parted and my cock isn't between them…

A shame.

I search her purple eyes as I tighten my grip, "How long have you known?"

"The alley," she hoarsely responds.

My eyebrows furrow in heated rage, my nostrils tighten as my lips curl in a snarl. The timeline of it all whirling through my head has my eyes volleying about the ground as I recall all the events leading up to now. The reason she showed up at the portal that day, the reason she was so hells bent on finding me in Vesperholm and bringing me back. Making me her Queen's Guard instead of throwing me to The Catacombs.

This entire time… *she's known.* And she *kept* it from me.

My rage ratchets higher and higher the longer I hold her here. And it only causes *me* to harden further and I connect with her desired purple irises.

Her eyes sparkle with knowing, her nostrils flaring as they glance down to my groin. "Asher-darling, I am rather hungry. Your anger only fans my flames," she says as her claws scrape gently against my jaw.

"Your hunger is of no consequence to me. You hid things. You *lied* to me, Seraphina."

"I hid nothing. I am not at liberty to reveal secrets that are not mine."

A rumble in my chest bounces off my ribcage as it crawls from my throat and my eyes volley against hers furiously.

Take her. Claim her. She is yours. Take her. Satiate the one within.

My lips crash into hers in ravenous hunger, and my pulse picks up as I pull her body against mine.

She hums a satisfied moan against my lips as the heel of her hand presses against my aching cock.

With a groan, the urgency heightens, fueling every fiber of my body into mind-numbing need. I turn her around, pressing hard into the space between her wings to shove her against the small wooden table.

A resounding *riiiip* courses through the room as I tear her breeches from her. The scent of her arousal fills my nostrils, and a feral growl claws its way from my insides as I retrieve my cock from my breeches.

Hard and aching, I wrap my fist around it, pumping it a few times before rubbing it through her pooled center. My mind flays at the wet delicacy that seeks to swallow my cock whole.

Her wings tighten at her spine as she feels me and her tail takes gentle strokes up and down my chest.

Groans fill the room as I fight the screaming in my head.

Claim her!

STOP! YOU'RE MAD AT HER!

No, CLAIM HER! TAKE HER!

She LIED TO YOU! STOP THIS!

To stave the thoughts away, I ram every pulsing inch into her.

The thoughts flee as I bottom out and soak in the feeling of her cunt. The way it molds to me in decadent warmth causes the screaming to reside for only a moment.

"Gods, Seraphina," I grunt as my hands come to grip her generous hips. As if I lose control, my thrusts pound into her with reckless abandon. The sound of her flesh slapping against my leather breeches only fuels my depth into her further.

Her moans fill the room with ethereal tones as I continue to take out my punishment on her.

I lean down between her wings, wrapping her long, white hair around my fist to pull her back against my chest. With my hips still pistoning in and out of her, I taunt the demon that tortures me. "See, what happens when you make me angry? See what you do to me, *angel*?" I groan as I bite down on the tender flesh of her neck. The sweet flood of her blood on my tongue makes my eyes roll. Delicious in every language. The one I know and the one I wish to learn if it means understanding the way her body speaks to me. Every lick, every touch, every single thrust into her is sustenance for this beast that screeches her name and begs to imprint her being on my soul.

A pull tugs hard against the beast inside. Her moans get stronger, and her body vibrates as she feeds off me. My pleasure, my anger, every bit of emotion I'm pressing into her right now. Her tail wraps around my back to pull me in deeper.

"I need to make you angry more often," she pants as her eyes begin to roll back.

"No, no, you're going to look at me when I fill you. Your eyes stay on *me* when I fuck this little cunt," I tell her as my hand lets go of her hair to wrap around her throat, pressing her head back far enough for me to peer into her eyes. The bright purple is hazy, and her mind is a puddle of ecstasy as I continue my untethered thrusts into her.

"There she is... There's my *sweet angel*. You're my good girl, aren't you, *Seraphina*? Do you like the way I fuck you into submission for your lies? Do you enjoy the way my cock fills you for your betrayal? Is this deep enough for you now, *Mistress*?" I taunt in frustration. The hues of her eyes swirl like a magic portal, they suck me deeper and deeper into her vortex. "Have any more *secrets* to reveal? Any more knowledge to share to before I fuck your brains out?" I growl as I lose myself in her eyes.

For a moment, human Asher takes hold and attempts to gain control. *Attempts.*

Until a thrum of *something* pricks against my veins as the power exchange shifts, and I begin *taking* from her, my strength increasing with every thrust.

The beast rears its ugly head and the tension in me fills to the brim until that knot of pleasure tangles tighter and tighter in my spine. The edge approaches and I take one more thrust into her before I pump her full of my seed. Burning, rabid power pulses through my veins, it speeds through me and causes the rage I'm experiencing to climb higher and higher. I release a feral groan into the air as I feel my seed coat her insides and rub against me... against *her.*

More. More. I need more. I need it **all.**

The voice that screeches in my head consumes everything in me and I grab at her shoulder, hauling her from the table and pulling myself out to spin her around and press her to her knees. Her chest heaves as she looks up at me with wanton eyes.

The sight drives me wild, and I fist my cock to pump it a few times. My hand slides back and forth with ease as cum drips from the tip and I press it to her lips, "Clean up the fucking mess you've made," I growl.

A devilish grin adorns her face as her mouth opens and her tongue falls from it. The halves wrap around my cock like a muscled vortex before she takes it into her mouth, her eyes not leaving mine as she does. The moist warmth surrounding me causes my head to toss back as my hands go to her horns, gripping them to thrust into her throat and make her take every inch. I lean down to wrap my hand around her neck as I keep a hand on her horn, tightening my grip when I feel myself swell her throat. It compresses around me in mind-numbing pleasure. Groans leave me in a lust filled haze as I relish in the feel of her, if only to satiate the screaming inside.

Aftershocks of my climax rock through my body as I siphon more and more of her power and pleasure from her, the feeling of feeding from her so inherently addicting I almost forget why I'm so mad.

Almost.

The thought of her secrets… they pulse through me faster and I pull my cock from her throat before yanking her back up by the hardened spikes in her scalp to throw her on the bed. Her wings splay to catch her fall as she lands against the mattress.

Until he chooses to accept the bond, the traits will overpower him.

CHAPTER 49

DEPLETED

SERAPHINA

The taste of Asher and me on his cock sends my heart into a gallop, and I don't have time to relish in it before I'm tugged by my horns to the bed. I was able to siphon a little bit of the anger from him before he shifted his energy and began to siphon it from *me*.

He prowls to the bed, his gaze precise as his purple eyes darken in primal, lustful vengeance.

I grin, taunting the beast within, "Come on, Asher-dear, that can't be all of it."

He snarls as his hand grips my throat again, pressing me into the mattress. My legs open wide under his body, beckoning him to claim me further.

"Haven't you had enough?" he growls. His purple gaze catches my cunt, lingering there as he admires the way his seed drips from my core. He runs his fingers through my center, pressing his fingers against my clit. The action causes a shudder to roll through my body in ecstasy as he collects some of himself and me on his fingers and brings them up to his mouth. The separated muscle that has become his tongue swirls around his fingers, lapping them clean. His gaze latched onto mine as he does. "Your lies are *delicious*, Seraphina," he growls.

My eyes slide down his body. His muscles have increased in mass and he's even maybe a few inches taller. They slide down his precisely etched abs, his lower stomach, to see his cock twitch in anticipation.

His own gaze has traveled down to my aching cunt, dripping with his lust, and his breath catches for the barest of moments before he thrusts every solid inch back into me.

The stretch of him causes my eyes to roll, the pressure and depth of him is all-consuming and the sharp claws of his lust latch deep into my power for him to steal.

He leans in close to my ear, his voice gravelly and deep as he bottoms out again, "You're going to take... every single inch," his hips thrusting with every word before he pauses. "Because you have *everything* I want. And I'm going to take all of it with every single press of my cock into that *needy* cunt. *You* are going to give *me. Everything.*" He punctuates the last words with a sharp flick of his tongue before it slides from between his teeth, split down the middle and slender on both ends. Damp warmth caresses my skin as he glides it against the side of my face. Even now he extracts my power with every lick he takes of me.

The depth and thickness of his *punishment* stretches me to delicious limits. Even as I attempt to feed from him, that thin string that connects us pulls taut, not allowing me such pleasantries. The corded attachment glows red in my mind, spearing straight toward the black wall in the abyss.

The pleasure coursing through me is insurmountable, and my body tightens as he siphons my power from me with every pound of his hips. The promise he keeps rings true as he bottoms out in each thrust. His skin shimmers from the exchange. Feral and untamed, he continues his movements, with no rhyme or reason.

But they feel so good and my back bows against the bed as my claws dig into the mattress, shredding through the delicate material. Pleasure unlike anything I've ever known surges through every portion of my body, running through my veins to seep into his. "Oh *gods*," I grit through my teeth.

A strong hand grips my jaw, forcing me to look into the darkened purple hue that has consumed his eyes. A heavy hand splays against my lower stomach, pressing against the bulge there as his cock seemingly thickens within me, stretching me more and more. The Asher I know is gone. This beast has replaced him. His deep, thunderous growl trembles against his chest as he speaks, "Your gods have abandoned you, Seraphina. Only *I* shall be your salvation." Even as he speaks, the hair falling over his brow in desperation begins to shift colors. From normal chestnut brown to a deep and inky black.

His words take the last bit of power from me as the electrifying feeling of my climax shoots through my tailbone and through every part of my body. My cunt tightens around him in a last-ditch effort to retrieve any bit of my strength that I can. Slamming straight into the expanding darkness of my orgasm, I moan an ethereal scream into the night as I give in to him.

"When you meet your gods at the gates of eternity, tell them *I* sent you. Tell them *I* was the one who made you call for your eternal damnation like this. Tell them *I* brought down the Queen of Bloodshed with a simple." He slams into me. "Thrust." Again. "Of my cock." Another. His voice rumbles through his chest, graveled and husky. His hand slides down my jaw to wrap around my neck and squeeze as he finishes thrusting through my orgasm.

Soon, his movements slow, and he looks down at my plump, aching cunt. His chest expands as his eyes focus on it. Small scratches scrape against my neck as his claws retract, his eyes swirl with emerald and the fangs peeking from his lips slowly retreat. Even his hair begins to lighten as his breaths work through him.

His now green eyes begin to roll back as his body wavers and thin breaths escape his parted lips.

Uh oh.

Quickly, I graft to the other side of the room, giving him space for his body to collapse against the mattress. He crashes in a limp heap and I watch him for a few moments longer to make sure he's breathing.

A *hmph* comes from me as I shimmy a hand over my lower half to sheathe my legs in my night pants.

If he doesn't get control of this beast, it'll eat him whole. He may now know we are mates, but his anger comes from the confusion of it all.

Fucking me will solve nothing, it will only feed his anger. And there is still only so much I *can* tell him.

Demon mating bonds are rare. They happen, but infrequently. I've personally not known anyone that had such a bond. But there are books, and I remember Lilith throwing them at me *constantly* to make me read up on it. But the books don't relay the specifics of completing the bond. They don't relay *how* to get a grip on this thing within him.

The things I do know are what I told Tyrick earlier.

Of course, when Asher's eyes first turned purple in The Catacombs, I was so fascinated. I'd never seen the transformation take place. Of course, it's dependent on the species bonded and their traits given to one another. I imagine that is why there is so little information on it to begin with. Too many variables to have concrete knowledge.

Until *he* chooses to accept the bond, the traits will overpower him. They beg and scream to be let out and complete the bond. But because he hasn't. It feasts on his rage; lying dormant until the energy is there to be let out.

With him giving in to his emotions, he wracked his body out. Feasting too hard and too fast with no way to control it. Humans *can* learn how to wield magic, but because he doesn't know how, it just tears him apart. As with most of everything, you have to be willing to take what is thrown at you.

He is not willing. Not right now.

I suppose this is as much a learning experience for him as it is for me. However, with The Compendium now in our possession... I fear there are more pressing matters to attend to.

I glance to the passed-out Asher. His back rises and falls in a smooth rhythm as he slumbers. Flicking a hand at him, I sigh as my magic replaces his armor with light sleeping clothes.

I'll teach him about the mating bond eventually -- what little I do know at least.

To an extent, we're both going into this blind.

The drain wracked on me, however, begins to seep into my bones and I take a wide stretch and a yawn. The leathery space between my wing bones shiver as I shake off the tension. My feet make soft pats against the floor as I walk to the bed, waving my hands over my body to shed my top armor and drape my torso in a soft nightshirt. A sigh leaves my body as I savor the feeling of my magic.

Missed that.

I press Asher's body further onto the bed, making sure to face him near the wall. I don't want to crowd his space with how volatile he is right now.

I climb into the covers next to him and pull the blankets over us before sleep takes me.

A knock raps at the wooden door to our chambers, which pulls me reluctantly out of my deep sleep.

Usually, Asher is the one to answer the door, but it seems as though he is still recovering from the surge of power that he took on.

With a grumble and a huff, I peel myself from the mattress to open the door with blurry eyes and find Tyrick standing with a massive pack full of papers and books.

My tired brow scrunches as I look at him, "Tyrick, what time is it?"

"Sunrise."

I observe his emotions for a moment and realize how excited he is to get out of here.

These mortals are so easily entertained. It has begun to be an endearing quality. Such mundane things for their short lives.

"I'll wake Asher. If you could, please go tell Lilith I'm coming to get him. We'll say goodbye to Bufort and Retalnia and be on our way."

Tyrick nods a tad more enthusiastically than I think I've seen in the few moments I've spent with him, and he rushes down the hall.

I groan as I close the door and turn to look at Asher.

Still asleep.

I take a moment to make sure everything is ready for our departure. Waving my hands over my body, I sheath myself in my armor and take a second to do the same to Asher while he continues to rest.

I check our bags and double check to make sure The Compendium is safe and sound.

Crouching down, I haul the straps onto my back before re-attaching them at my pits. Shifting the weight around to make sure it feels right, I look over at Asher. He still lays on the bed in a slumbering heap.

I step over to him and nudge his shoulder. He doesn't so much as budge.

An exasperated groan comes from me as I realize he may be out for the next few days from the surge on his body.

I finish getting our things and bring the packs out of the castle, where Tyrick waits with Lilith, Bufort, and Retalnia.

I drop Asher's pack to the ground before I walk over to Lilith and nuzzle his nose, "Sorry friend, you're going to have to carry my mate. He's down for the count."

Lilith snorts and bobs his head up and down in disapproval before I chuckle and press a kiss to his wet nose.

I turn to Tyrick, and the elder mages, "Asher had… a reckoning last night. He's currently incapacitated. I have to go retrieve him, I just needed to bring the gear out here first."

The mages nod in confused understanding, their expressions twisting in a menagerie of different emotions before I make my way back to the room.

Asher still slumbers peacefully against the mattress, and I take one last sweep around the room, pulling down the magic I had placed when we settled in. I sigh as I walk to the bed and look at the heap of meat that I now have to sling over my shoulder.

I sit on the bed, facing the door, and flare my wings wide to give him space and turn around to grab his hands. Pulling him toward me, I wrap his arms around my shoulders like a giant dead weight pack.

A grunt rumbles against my throat as I shift him, which is infinitely more difficult than when he's awake.

Of course I've done this before, but I had the leverage of flying to do such a thing.

After situating him on my back, I lumber back down to the mages in the front of the castle, whose eyes turn wide with shock as they see me carrying the passed-out hunter on my back.

I roll my eyes and sigh as I pass them before depositing Asher onto Lilith's back, "I know what it looks like, but I promise I did nothing to him. He just is dealing with some… things and he dealt with them in a way he didn't know he couldn't handle."

Bufort and Retalnia look at each other with skepticism before they look to Tyrick.

"Oh, calm down. Your little mage will be fine. The worst that will happen is he participates in an orgy," I say as I wave a hand toward them.

Bufort's jaw drops and Retalnia giggles as Tyrick's bronzy skin deepens with a tint of red. His throat works in a gulp as he leads the way to the portal to Tantalia.

"Until next time, wizards!" I call over my shoulder as I follow Tyrick with Lilith clopping by my side.

"THE FATES WILL AWAIT YOUR COMPLIANCE."

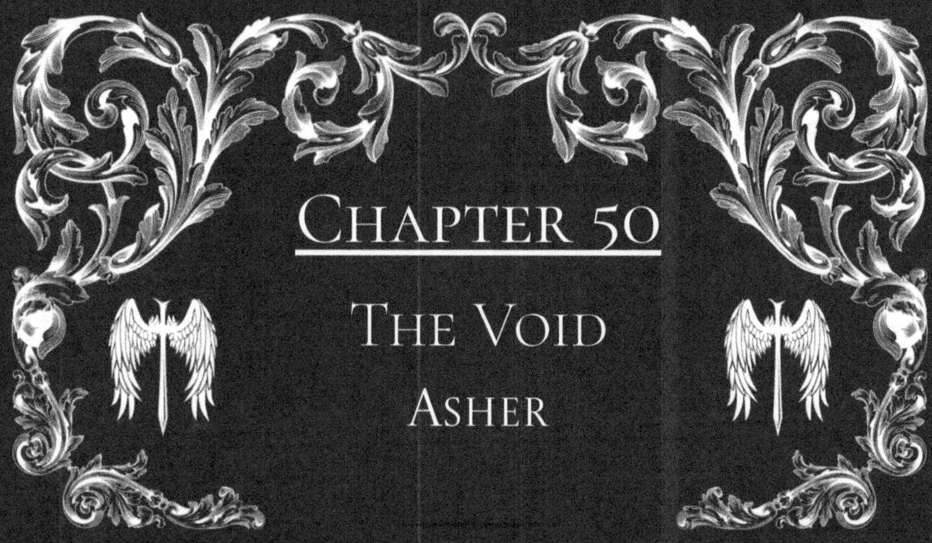

CHAPTER 50

THE VOID

ASHER

My groan reverberates against the black walls surrounding me as my eyes open.

The tension in my body is at an all-time high and I have no idea where the fuck I am.

Until the realization hits me…

Fucking hells I'm in this gods' forsaken dream realm.

I release a growl as I come to stand. The ground below is solid but covered in at least an inch of liquid that sloshes against my boots.

"WHY HAVE YOU BROUGHT ME HERE AGAIN!?" I call into the darkness. My head swivels to see if there is anything, anyone I can spot.

Nothing. Same as last time.

"I've done no such thing," that same voice responds. It's not quite human. Not quite demon… Not even quite… worldly.

"Ugh, you again."

"And I will return until you surrender."

"Surrender fucking what?! Every time I feel like I get a singular grasp on this fucking place, it comes crumbling down with one more fork in the road! I don't know how much longer I can take this!"

"The Fates will await your compliance."

My loud groan echoes in the void, "Stop this! I don't know anything! Why won't any of you tell me anything!?"

A red glowing light appears from afar, not round. Not square.

No, it's long.

My brow furrows in angered curiosity as I walk slowly toward it. The sloshing from my boots echoing through this hellscape is the only thing my mind can process. That and this new light.

As I get closer to the light, it gets farther, and I begin to run.

My chest beats like a thousand stallions and my breaths come and go in quick waves of panic.

I sprint, and sprint, and the light falls farther away. But I keep running.

I can't stop running.

"Brick and stone shall forge the way, open the door and show us the cave."

Chapter 51

The Mistress and The Mage

Seraphina

Tyrick, Lilith, Asher, and I make it to the outskirts of Kaithoon, where we walk down a brick path in the forest.

The thrum of magic through my veins increases the closer we get to the portal. While there is magic here, it's not *my* magic.

Tyrick has been quiet on our walk, and I have retreated deep into my mind, looking over at Asher every so often.

Lilith seems unperturbed by the sack of meat he carries, but I imagine there's not much the being *can't* carry now that it's magical.

"What should I call you?" Tyrick asks after a long while.

Tension pulls between my brows as I look over at him.

What a random thing to ask after these many days.

"Mistress is fine. I will introduce you to the others when we get there," I respond as we continue our journey through the woods.

After a short time, we come to the outside of the large archway that is carved into the side of the mountain.

the portal to Tantalia.

"What… what happened to him?" Tyrick asks nervously.

I peer at the mage from the corner of my eye to see him surveying Asher with a cautious nip at his lower lip and a furrowed brow.

I give him a smirk and a scoff before I release a sigh, "The mating process is fickle. He has yet to accept the terms, and he rages against the beast that wishes to complete the bond."

Tyrick looks at me as if he hasn't a singular clue what I mean.

I imagine it's because he truly doesn't.

"While I've never seen the mating process in my kind or mortals, I've read some things about it. Forced upon me by my now-deceased mentor. Texts would explain the compliance of The Fates. While fate may guide us, we are still beings of free-will. We can't be *forced* to accept a bond just because it *is.* Until recently, Asher had no idea the bond even existed. When he found out, the little monster inside of him raged, fucked me to the edge of insanity and the power he siphoned from me was too much," I explain with a mere shrug.

Tyrick pauses in his steps, his jaw slacking and his eyes widening as he looks over the sleeping hunter.

I notice his halt and turn to look at him with a perplexed brow, tilting my head. "Are you alright, little mage?"

He's silent for a long moment before he shakes his head to bring his focus back on me, gaining his bearings of the information I've just bestowed upon him.

"That's… that's a thing? That can happen?" Tyrick asks.

"I suppose. He's not versed in any form of magic, so the power he took from me was too great. It shut his body down and now he needs to recuperate. As I'm sure you understand, magic cannot be wielded without a conduit, because we succubus *are* conduits, it passes through us. You, as mages, have your fancy little sticks and words. Asher-dear, has nothing, and no knowledge of such. So, it shut him down." I shrug.

Tyrick's eyes volley back and forth between the dead weight of Asher draped across Lilith and me for a long moment before he approaches the portal.

My eyes roll in my head as I come to stand next to him.

Silly humans.

He surveys the portal before his voice breaks through the silence, "So… who opens it?"

Thoughts run through my head. Because who actually *does* open the portal? In all honesty, I have no clue. I suppose either one of us *could* potentially open it, considering it enters Tantalia.

But I personally don't feel like using any of my renewed magic, so I peer at Tyrick from the corner of my eye.

I lay a hard slap against his pack, and he jolts forward as he's pulled from his observation.

"You're up, little mage," I say as I place my hands on my hips.

Tyrick looks at me with wide eyes and nods softly, taking a deep gulp before he fishes his wand from the pocket against his ribs.

He takes a steady breath as he presses his wand against the stone wall, shaking out his shoulders to steel himself, "Brick and stone shall forge the way, open the door and show us the cave."

My eyebrow quirks as the portal warps and warbles. A faint purple glow slowly illuminates and as it spins, it brightens more.

He opens his eyes and gazes at it in wonder, "I did it…" he whispers to himself.

Huh?

"Did you think you couldn't?" I ask.

"Well, I'm not a very strong wizard. There's a lot I can't do yet."

I give him a laugh as Lilith walks through the portal, "We'll change that, mage." I follow Lilith into the glowing curtain, where the dripping echo of the cave and the heavy thrum of my magic pulses through me.

After we came back into Tantalia, I paraded us to the Court of Mistresses.

The other mistresses were shocked to find another purple collared human and mythical deer following me. I even called Mistress Kalinda in to rub it in her face.

"Seraphina, what is the meaning of this!?" my mother asks from beside the table.

I release the straps of my pack to let it fall to the marbled stone floor. Crouching down, I ruffle through the menagerie of clothes and items, before retrieving the hunk of leather and parchment that has caused me so much strife.

Standing, I slam it on the ebony table before crossing my arms and glaring at Mistress Kalinda. Her eyes fall to the textbook, staring at it for a moment before a small muscle twitches in her cheek. A moment later, her eyes slide up to meet mine.

Her brow dares to rise, "You've found the tome."

"I have."

"How fortuitous," she says through grit teeth.

"Yes. Indeed."

"And the *human*?" Kalinda asks as she nods to the trembling young wizard behind me.

"He wanted to come, so I let him. I figure he could be of use."

"Is there a way we could get you to *stop* bringing humans here?"

"Fat chance."

Her lips curl in a sneer as her eyes glance at Tyrick, "Boy," she calls to him.

His eyes widen to saucers as he stares at her, my wings lift and he ducks under one to stand beside me, "Y-yes Mistress?"

"Your name."

"Tyrick... Tyrick Claud. Apprentice Wizard to the Mage Realm, Kaithoon."

"Kaithoon..." Mistress Kalinda sneers.

Tyrick nods sheepishly.

"There is another thing," I offer to the mistresses.

The women turn to me with curious gazes.

"When Asher and I snuck into Knogdagh, we entered the fortress through tunnels and into a… room."

Foreheads wrinkle with tension as the words soak in.

"Cauldrons full of liquid, similar to that in the catacombs."

The mistresses exchange glances before they come to look at me. My mother speaks up, "What do you think it is?"

Tension pulls at my eyebrows as I look down at The Compendium, "I… I don't know, but whatever it is feels sinister. I don't know what they're planning. But the Orcs have a direct contact with Bruthar through a mirror in Psylax's chambers. They can't see anything. They can only hear. But they are more involved with each other than I thought. And Bruthar is looking for The Compendium."

The air turns thick as the energy of the combined succubi power heightens. Their fears rise as their wings tense along their spines and tails flick nervously behind them.

"This…" Selene murmurs, her eyes gaze at the table below as she braces herself against it.

"Is an unfortunate but well-relayed message, Seraphina," Mistress Kalinda says with a curt nod.

"Have you known?" I ask Kalinda.

I may hate her for her lack of intervention, but she is the only mistress that has stood the test of time against all the others. Perhaps her wisdom could be of use to me as much as I may hate it.

"Of course, we all know the Orcs and the Drannars have been allies for centuries. The mirror however…"

"Why can't *you* fix The Stone?" I ask.

I've asked her before. I've asked several times… But it doesn't make sense for her to be here as long as Lilith and not be able to do something like fix The Stone. Surely there is something she can do. Her uselessness aside.

"When Lilith first invoked the stone's powers and its wards, she forbade me from such a gathering. Spells of such strength can cause interferences when a party is present but not involved. I did not want the burden of the stones invocations, so Lilith took it upon herself to invoke it after the massacre."

"What is that thing you said about the Queen holding the power?" I ask as I remember her words to me months ago.

"The Queen is the power of The Stone."

"But what does that mean?"

"I imagine you'll find the answer in The Compendium. It is all that Lilith told me of such."

I groan as my hands slap against the table in frustration. Why does no one have *answers?!* And why am I the one asking all the questions!?

The history of Tantalia is long, there have been things picked and thrown at us that have been *thought* as important.

But the more I learn, the more I realize Lilith kept so much from us.

Why? For someone who loved her people as much as she did, *why* would she keep so much from us?

Sighing, my eyes connect with the book below, glaring at it as if it's the problem.

Technically, it is.

"Seraphina, do *you* even know anything about The Compendium?" Selene's voice breaks through my wallowing.

"I don't. But apparently every other being outside of here *does*."

Shifting sounds off around me before Learra speaks, "How can they possibly know about The Compendium when even we haven't the barest clue?"

"I don't KNOW! And it tore me apart trying to get to the bottom of it. But every being I encountered, either knew of Lilith or her fucking book. But *we* have it now, and *we* will never let it be forgotten ever again."

"Lilith was secretive when it came to The Compendium. The only beings she sought for help was the Mages of Kaithoon, during the treaty. I only know because this was her other reasoning for going there -- aside from the treaty itself. She was still young and wanted to learn how to wield her magic better. The humans had been practicing before she arrived and she spent time there learning," Kalinda recounts, her gaze drifting off as she recalls Lilith's actions.

"We are taught of the treaty and the importance of a book like The Compendium. But humans are short lived, and so the knowledge of its contents were lost to time. Before Seraphina arrived, we were unaware of Lilith's passing, or that The Compendium was in the Orc's possession. Kaithoon is locked away. The elders want nothing to do with the world outside of it," Tyrick chimes in.

Dead end after dead end and *I'm* the one that has to figure it all out.

I wish Lilith would have left me something, ANYTHING that would make a lick of sense.

None of her methods made sense. It would be fitting for them to continue years after her departure.

I groan as I plop into my throne. My hand grips my chin in thought as my claws brace into the leather armrest.

Heavy is the head that wears the crown. An adage older than time, I imagine. And frustrating to boot.

"Where is Asher?" Selene asks as she looks around the room.

"He's off sleeping. He's dealing with the whole mate thing," I say absentmindedly as I wave a hand in her direction.

My mind is still stuck on the entire idea that Lilith didn't tell *our* people about the Compendium.

"So, he's realized it?" Selene asks.

"More like an Oracle Dragon told him."

Lilith was methodical, even with her almost riddlish way of relaying information. As if she knew things we didn't. She always did. But would she keep something like this from everyone for no reason?

"I'm sorry… A what…?"

"We saved a fucking dragon king, who scented our bond. Or what little bond there *is* and told him."

What did Lilith know that allowed her to share this secret with beings outside of Tantalia?

"What does that have to do with why he's not here?"

I groan as her incessant questions break through my thoughts.

"The fucking beast in him raged against his non-compliance and he fucked me of all my power until his body couldn't handle it and he shut down."

Unless…

"I have to go," I tell The Court as I stand, grabbing the book and walking around the table.

"Tyrick, grab my pack, we're going to The Library."

Tyrick sputters as the soft clop of Lilith's hooves echo through The Court.

"What about the deer?!" I hear Selene's voice from behind me.

"His name is Lilith!" I call back as Tyrick and I take our leave.

"Outside of Onyx Citadel... Well. That's a different story."

CHAPTER 52

THE WAR OF THREE HEARTS

ASHER

I've run for hours… Days… I don't even fucking know anymore.

The glowing red light never gets closer.

I decide at one point to sit and stare at it.

I can't leave this fucking place, and part of me is angry that Seraphina put me here.

It's like her to do something like this. Leave me in the pits of my own mind to figure my shit out.

It causes the rage to rock through me once more.

But the red glow keeps me… Stable… Calm.

The voice hasn't returned. It hasn't said anything else. I've just been here thinking of everything in this stupid void.

This "mating bond." And the fact that Sera didn't tell me anything about it. Getting home to save my people. Saving Tantalia. My brothers. Everything. I can't make left or right of anything.

And eventually the frustration gives way and tears stream down my face as I sob into the arms crossed over my bent knees while I sit in this black liquid.

I don't understand. I just don't.

I want to save my people. I want to help Tantalia, and I want to make the world a better place, even if I was a murderer at one point. I was misguided. I was wrong. At the end of the day, I was wrong. And I'm trying to fix it, so desperately am I trying. But I don't know anything.

Why does everything have to be so difficult? Why do any of these things need to happen at all? Why couldn't we all just play nice with each other?

I wouldn't be stuck in this void with no answers and a million questions.

"You have a strong soul, Asher Blackwood," the voice comes again.

"Please just let me go…" I murmur against the cloth of my breeches.

"The Fates have placed you with a strong ally. It would be in your best interest to see this bond through."

"Or what!?" I cry into the void as my arms leave my knees. I stand from the inch of water on the ground, and it sloshes against my rage. My arms rise as I scan around the void, yelling into nothing. "You're going to lock me away again!? You're going to keep me here forever?! Do your fucking worst! It can't be anything more than what this fucking place is!"

As if the air is sucked straight from my chest, my body courses with red hot fire. My heart surging almost to the point of failure as my limbs are pulled taut by shadows.

All at once, visions of blood, war. Yelling. Screaming.

The scent of brimstone. Massive beasts of tooth and claw with pointed ears charge against the meadow.

Seraphina's screams… Her blood curdling screams…

Gideon yells. Selene's ethereal screech. The beat of wings and the groans of dying men.

Metal clashes. A rainbow of lightning that devours the air.

Chaos. Roars. The sound of dragon wings beating with vigor as bursts of fire singe the bloodied air. The ground rumbles beneath me.

"Time is ticking."

Fire. Metal.

"You're running out."

Blood. So… So much blood.

Sunlight.

Bright… beaming, sunlight.

The fresh scent of wisteria flower.

The soft sheets of Seraphina's bed.

Though they're drenched in my sweat and absent of the demon. My chest heaves with deep breaths as I finally leave that void. That dark hellscape.

A shiver runs through me as I remind myself how grateful I am to be here in this bed.

I survey my immediate surroundings. There is no sign of Seraphina anywhere. No tethers. But a pressure wraps around my neck, and I catch the dull glow of my collar from the corner of my eye.

I don't remember *anything.* I don't remember anything after that night with Seraphina. And for now, whatever beast took over me is gone.

The lingering frustration of everything still pricks at my skin, but I'm not as angry as I was.

I have no idea how much time has passed. But apparently enough for me to be back in Tantalia and in Seraphina's bed.

It appears I've been cleaned and reclothed in better nightwear. Comfortable, considering the last few days have been spent sleeping on the ground and going through disgusting tunnels.

I lay in that bed for a long while, gazing out the window, in the same way Seraphina did those weeks ago.

Contemplating *everything.*

On top of saving, basically the entire world, I now have to worry about being a mate to this being I barely know.

But in the same breath, maybe that's why it feels like I can't ever be without her again.

I thought it was just the way it felt to truly care for someone that cared for you. I've never experienced this feeling before.

Watching Seraphina take the staff to the chest. Saving her life on several occasions. Her sheer *presence.* The sight of her makes my heart implode, wrenching the air from my chest. Breathless, she is… Truly.

Her strength, her vigor, her drive. All of her is something I would give my everything to.

Is that what a mate is? Is there more to it?

I admire her. I'd throw down my dagger and relinquish any ounce of freedom I have if it meant I could serve at her side forever.

But... how could she have *kept* this from me? Is this *my* fault for not listening closer to her words?

My eyes linger around the room, looking for my armor. I find it laying over the armchair, and for a moment, I contemplate retrieving my insignia...

But I can't.

It doesn't hold the same sentiment it once did. Not when I'd sacrifice my life for this demon.

The questions and conflicting emotions swirl and taunt me until the bedroom door creaks open. The little elf child, Xeneera, walks in with a tray of food.

"Xeneera... Good to see you, friend," I say as I sit up against the pillows.

My body feels inherently stiff, probably from laying here for so long and whatever else it took to get me here.

"Seraphina wanted me to bring you some food. She's with... Tyrick? I think that's his name. In The Library. She sent a lady with your food to bring to you," she says softly as she places the tray on my lap.

Warm breads and meats cover the plate in a medley of seasonings and spices. My mouth waters at the sight and it takes everything in me not to attack it.

Taking my time, eating the food, Xeneera comes to sit on the bed in front of me, peering at me as I eat.

The action is curious, and I look up at her in question, "Is something wrong?"

"I've never really... seen a human before," she says.

The admission is shocking. I suppose hard to register for me, because she has seen me before. But I know what she means.

"Never?" I ask as I take another bite of my meal.

"There aren't humans in The Never Realm. Only elves."

That makes sense. I don't even know why I asked.

"What was it like there?" I ask.

One would think it'd be a good time to get information from her. But I don't find my question to be one of prying. It's more bare curiosity than anything. I don't know if I have it in me right now to do any snooping.

Her crimson gaze turns sad as it drifts to the hands in her lap that tighten around each other.

A braided crown of white hair encircles her head, with the rest flowing down her back. The bits that hang free, curtain around her face, her body now clothed in some of the same black armor as the other mistresses. Though hers has a bit more modesty to it.

"I was forced into working in the library. I suppose I didn't mind. My mother and father were bookkeepers, and I just so happened to be next in line. There are much worse places for a Drannar to end up. The mines digging for silver. The forges creating staffs. Floor cleaners. I find myself to be luckier than most. I lived in the castle, but *living* I think is a tad generous," she says with a curt laugh. She's silent for a moment before she sighs.

"Outside of Onyx Citadel... Well. That's a different story. The lands and markets are just people surviving. Trading different staffs for some hint of magic. But there isn't enough there. Bruthar has sapped anything he could and hoards it all for his army. He thinks they need it for whenever the succubus want to attack."

Attack? Is there something *I'm* missing?

"Who is Bruthar?" I ask gently.

"Bruthar is The King of The Never Realm. Almost as ancient as time himself," she responds quietly.

As if this world couldn't get any more fucking confusing. My jaw slacks as I listen to her story and visions of this horrid place brew in my mind.

"After the War of Three Hearts, the portals to Tantalia were guarded so heavily that it locked the power off from our realms. Bruthar had guards sap what they could from the wards to claim for himself. Powerful elves have tried all they could to imbue the staffs for his army."

War of Three Hearts?

"What do you mean, War of Three Hearts? Was there another war after The Jilted Massacre?" I ask.

"Jilted Massacre? I'm not sure what you're referring to," Xeneera says as she looks to me in question.

"The… the war where the Drannars came and slaughtered the succubus in the thousands," I say softly.

Xeneera's brows furrow in concern, "Slaughtered? N-no… The books… the texts… They say the Drannars liberated the succubus from their cruel leaders?"

Fuck.

I groan, placing the tray next to me on the bed before I run my hands over my face in confusion, "I don't think I know enough about this information to tell you everything."

Xeneera's features tighten in a variety of emotions. Ones I'm not sure she knows how to handle.

Me too, kid.

"Maybe we should go find them. I think Sera will have more answers for you than I will."

Xeneera stares off at the floor before she nods absently. She stands, her head droops as she walks to the door.

I breathe a heavy sigh as I come to stand, taking a big stretch before I follow her. I decide to go in my nightclothes, because in all honesty, I really don't feel like changing.

I don't know how much of this place she has seen and the thought of her walking past the tapestries may cause more questions than answers. But I think they're important.

They were for me, at least.

She opens the door, and we leave the room, starting down the hundreds of steps.

Xeneera is silent as she looks around the halls, her eyes dart to the succubus who scurry through The Keep doing their duties in their different colored cloaks and their different baskets of items.

Eventually, we reach the area I worried about and Xeneera freezes as her eyes catch the woven fabric.

"Have you seen these yet?" I ask quietly.

"No… I haven't really left my room since I got here, I just… I just wanted to take time to myself before venturing out…" She responds mindlessly as she shakes her head. "What is this?" she whispers.

I sigh as I turn to face it, looking over the same threads that had *me* question everything.

"The Jilted Massacre," I respond solemnly.

"This… this can't be… real… this can't be true?"

"It's what has been taught here for thousands of years, to my under-standing."

Her eyes frantically search the cloth, fear tugging at the muscles of her blue-gray skin.

"I'm so sorry you had to learn this way," I tell her as I place a hand to her shoulder.

A tear runs down her cheek as she continues walking down the tapestries, surveying every single one in paralyzed horror.

I can see why. The tapestries leave no detail behind. Blood and gore are weaved into vivid displays of war.

I can't imagine it would be easy to see my people taking part in something like this either.

"I… *my* people did this?" she asks as she turns to me.

The red of her irises is glazed with shiny tears. The pain and sadness in her eyes spears straight through my soul.

"I…" an exasperated sigh comes from me as I softly grab her shoulder and lead her down the hallway, into The Library.

"The Jilted Massacre is being taught in The Never Realm as 'The War of Three Hearts.'"

CHAPTER 53

A BLIND WORLD

SERAPHINA

After my thoughts took hold of me in The Court of Mistresses, I brought my new little friend, Tyrick, down to The Library. Along with Lilith, who has taken residence next to me on the hard stone ground and rests in silence.

I should open The Compendium. I *should*. But, I can't.

Knowing all that I went through for it, and the emotions behind its unveiling, my heart can't take it.

Not right now.

Tyrick seems well versed in looking for information. He has a passion for knowledge, is what I've surmised. So, I figure he may have some insight in what we could look for next.

He was a bit shocked to learn he had to listen to the books, as apparently, they're titled in his little wizard realm. But once he got the hang of it – and stopped screaming – he seemed to figure it out just fine.

The thoughts in The Court lead me to the idea of fates. Lilith made sure to engrain in us the importance of their words. The importance of their guidance. What if there was something she knew about that we didn't?

Obviously, she did, considering she hid The Compendium from us. But… something, maybe even fate itself told me to keep looking.

I searched the aisles of The Library for anything. Anything that could point me in SOME direction. Any direction at this point. I don't care.

I found a tome that screamed something about "The Inevitables" that kept yelling repeatedly about The Fates. It was deep, *deep*, in The Library. A dark portion covered in webs and dust that no one seemed to travel to. Its voice silenced where no one could look upon it.

Even now as I read over this book, it merely tells me about The Celestials and that they are the gods of our realms. I never knew we had "gods". Yes, we say that, but only because that's what we considered fate to be. We never praised anything or relented to them. We merely listened to their warnings.

But this book… it tells legend of the celestial beings -- Death, Time, Love, and Chaos.

The Inevitabilities of life.

This seems insanely important information to be privy of, why wouldn't Lilith teach this? Why wasn't this something she taught us?

We all *know* these things exist, of course. But them being separate *gods* of a celestial plane is an entirely different story.

It's all so absolutely infuriating and soon, a loud *whap* echoes in the desolate library as I slam the book shut.

Tyrick jolts in his seat as my action startles him. He peers cautiously at me from the book he was engrossed in.

"This is convoluted. All of it," I groan as my head falls against the dusty brown tome.

The door to The Library shudders open, and my focus turns to find Asher, still in his night clothes, being led to me by Xeneera.

My heart flutters for the barest of moments before I realize there are tears streaming down her cheeks. Rabid anger rises in me, as I only assume Asher snapped at her in a fit of rage.

Growling, I graft in front of him, gripping the air beside his head as a glowing purple lead extends from my hand to tighten his collar against his windpipe, "What did you fucking do to her?" I grit.

Asher's eyes go through a circle of emotions; surprise, anger, rage, and realization as he scratches futilely against his collar.

"The truth, Seraphina," he chokes out. A small jab, no doubt. But *that* isn't what he means to say.

"What *truth*?!"

"The Jilted Massacre is being taught in The Never Realm as 'The War of Three Hearts.' The Drannars think that *they* saved Tantalia," he rasps quickly through his compressed vocal cords.

Tension pulls my brows together as the words and their weight sink into me. Slowly, my hand restraining him loosens, and the purple tether spins back into my wrist. Asher coughs as his windpipe is released and he takes heaving breaths. As I turn to Xeneera, I see the pure sadness that shrouds her features.

"Is it true? Did we?" she asks solemnly.

My lips thin as I gaze down at her in sympathy. Kneeling in front of her, I put a hand on her shoulder, "What all do you know, little one?"

More tears stream down her face and she tries to wipe them away as she gazes off beside me, "W-we were taught, that The War of Three Hearts was a liberation of your people. That we freed the Succubus from their overlords, but we were pushed out, locked away. We were locked out of the magic, and we have to stack up our army for when you guys planned to attack."

Son of a bitch.

That scheming little elf man…

I sigh deeply as I come to gaze in her sad little eyes, "Xeneera. We have no plans to attack the elves. Hundreds of years ago, the elves *slaughtered* my people, in the thousands. Lilith locked the wards and invoked ancient, powerful magic, sealing the elves off from us and locking them away so that they couldn't hurt anyone else… Lilith was *there,* she recounted the story many times because *she* was one of the hearts. She erased the third heart from existence."

Xeneera's glazed eyes spill over with more tears, her face contorts in pain as she comes to wrap her arms around my neck, before she sobs deeply into my shoulder.

My gaze turns to Asher, whose face has turned solemn and his lips thin as he nods in comfort.

This little girl has been lied to her entire life, and her people are part of the problem.

I nod back to him in thanks for bringing her to me. As I imagine, having this conversation with him right now would be difficult.

"You did nothing wrong, Xeneera. You were merely born to a cruel leader," I whisper as I place soothing strokes against her back. Her shoulders tremble with grief and her grip on me tightens.

"But my people did. I'm *one* of them," her watery voice muffles against my neck.

"You aren't your people. You are *you.*"

The statement is true. But it hits deeper for me than it should.

I am not my people. I am Seraphina. Queen of Tantalia, Mistress of Bloodshed, General of the Night's Legions and Angel of Death.

Lilith was her people; it was the ones around her. She lived for her people.

And I am not Lilith.

Lilith would not want me to be her. She never instilled that in me.

She always wanted me to be me. And I am *me.* I will *always* be *me.*

And I am going to live for *my world.*

My grip around her tightens as I bring her in closer.

We have all done terrible things to each other. Back and forth, for hundreds of years. Humans killing succs. Succs stealing humans. Succs killing elves. Elves killing succs. The list goes on and on.

A truly… truly blind world.

But I'm going to be the one to change it, because I'm the only one who can.

And I'll start with the small elf girl in my arms.

Did I want to talk to
Cedric?
Yes, of course.

Did I want to talk to
Cedric right this
moment?
No.

CHAPTER 54

THE BEAST AND THE BROTHER

ASHER

While Seraphina and I did sleep in the same bed that night, it was nothing like it used to be.

Our backs were turned to each other as we gave each other space. We muttered not a word to one another. She seemed deep in thought from her encounter with Xeneera in The Library.

It was… solemn. To say the least.

She may have been beside me, but she felt miles away. And part of me doesn't know whose fault it is.

Is it hers for not telling me? Is it mine for being so angry?

It's hard to think about it even now, when Seraphina has gathered the High Mistresses around the table in The Court. The Compendium placed in front of her and her hands pressed into the ebony stone as she glares at this thing she's gone to war with.

The ladies stand silently around the table, their hands clasped in front of them as they wait for her to speak.

"Selene. The warriors," Seraphina finally says, her eyes still locked on the book.

"They've… declined in your absence," Selene responds sheepishly. Her cheeks flush as she knows what's to come next with such an admission.

A low groan comes from Seraphina as her head drops completely. "Learra. The crops."

"While you were gone, there was a surge. Right before you arrived, actually."

Seraphina's head shoots up as her sights set on Learra, "I'm sorry?"

"For a moment or so, the crops burst to life, the magic was heavier, *thicker*. The wards had their glamour back for a moment, even if toward the end of your leave, they weakened with more Drannars breaching the defenses. But then, it disappeared. We have placed more warriors in the farmlands and the meadow to keep them at bay."

I watch Seraphina's back, her tail flicks and twitches in angst as she glares at the farmer, "Is there… a reason… that I wasn't made privy to THIS VALUABLE INFORMATION?" she growls as the air thins and lightning begins to snap and pop her feet.

"We assumed it was something *you* had done!"

Seraphina takes a deep inhale, and her lightning slowly dies as her head rises and she adjusts her shoulders.

Her wings begin to tighten at her spine, "Selene, warrior training will fall on Gideon and Asher until further notice. I need you for the Compendium. Learra, administer duties to who you see fit, I need you as well."

Selene and Learra nod in compliance before their gazes drop to the table.

My eyebrow raises in annoyance. Part of this just feels like a way for her to push me further to the wayside. But at the same time, she really does need to look at The Compendium. And I need to check on Cedric.

"I'll do it," my voice echoes through The Court and the mistresses all turn to me in confusion as they hear my voice.

I suppose they aren't used to hearing a human speak out of turn. But it doesn't matter, I need to get out of here. I need to think of what needs to happen next.

Seraphina continues staring down at The Compendium for a few moments longer before she looks up at everyone.

"This text… I have gone through a lot to get it. Asher and I, *both* went through a lot for it. *I* personally, learned a lot not only about myself, but about our departed matriarch. There is much that Lilith has not divulged to us. So, if there is anything you may have received from Lilith or remember of her teachings, it would be imperative to come forth with it. We have no idea what things she may have told us all separately, considering the things she has done outside of our realm."

Seraphina's voice is deep, strong, *commanding*. Whatever shift she may have gone through with all of this has seemed to fill her with strength.

I know Seraphina is strong. I know what she's capable of, but sometimes I feel like even *she* is not aware of what she can do.

Perhaps it was her meeting with Xeneera, or maybe she feels as if things can start being put into motion with the finding of The Compendium. But she seems to be taking this deer by the antlers and driving it into the mud.

Part of me wants to be turned on by it, but I'm still stuck on my own problems.

I turn to Gideon, who listens silently to the women and nod in signal.

Gideon glances sideways at me before he nods in response.

"Gideon and I will go now, General," I tell the room.

Seraphina doesn't so much as look at me as she waves a hand in my direction, grafting Gideon and I down to The Pits.

While I have no singular idea how to train several magical, winged halflings, I am well-versed in hand-to-hand combat and fighting against succubus.

Is that what these men need? More than likely not. But I do have an army at my disposal, willing to risk anything and everything for their land.

That thought in and of itself is something I never imagined I'd be able to witness. Especially after years in Vesperholm of trying to get people to do *anything* of note.

Gideon and I stand in the dirt arena, waiting for the next group of soldiers to come in when he turns to me, "So, we haven't had the chance to talk about anything that happened while you were gone. And things were... tense between you and Seraphina."

I sigh as I look to the dust below me, kicking at it as I cross my arms against my chest, "I found something out, and I'm not sure how to take it," I admit to him.

"Like?"

Another sigh leaves me as I recount all the instances over the past few days. When I sit down to think about it, it's insane to realize it only happened in a matter of days.

"Well... Aside from the dragons, the tree spirits, the magic deer and an entire realm of magical humans; I found out Seraphina is my *mate.*"

Saying it out loud causes my heart to race and a tug at this thing in my chest.

"What?" Gideon asks as he turns to me with shocked eyes. "A fucking mate? What does that even mean?"

"I don't know! We haven't even had the chance to really talk about it. She's pushed herself into this Compendium shit and fixing The Stone, and I was passed out and locked away in some hellscape for who knows how long."

Gideon stands frozen, gazing at me with wide, unbelievable eyes.

"As if I thought this place couldn't get any weirder..." he murmurs. "So, what happens now with this whole mate thing?"

"I don't... I don't know. There is this beast that comes out anytime I'm angry. It rages against my insides and just throws itself at her. It begs to fuck her for whatever reason. I don't even understand any of it. It just *happens* and I have no control over myself when it *does* happen. The last time it happened I felt like I took every ounce of power from her, and I could *feel* it… I could *taste* her power," I explain as I turn to him, almost in desperation. I search his face for any kind of sign that I'm not the only one that has ever experienced this before.

His brows lift against his forehead as he looks at me, "A beast?"

Fuck.

I groan a frustrated hum as I run my hands through my hair. "I… Yes."

"That's… interesting."

I take a deep breath, realizing I'm the only one of the two of us experiencing this madness, "And then I passed out, and the next thing I knew I was waking up in Seraphina's bed." I throw my hands out in defeat before they slap limply against my legs.

"Hm. That explains the weird tension between you two."

You're telling me.

Soon, we hear a murmur of voices come from beside the opening where the warriors enter. Their boots lazily drag against the dirt as they come to the center, swinging their swords, stretching out their necks and wings as they prepare for the training.

Giant masses of muscled meat are in The Pits today, at least a hundred of them.

Lunae Legion.

One of which… is my dearest brother.

Fucking hells.

I groan as I realize there is a chance for this day to get worse.

Did I want to talk to Cedric? Yes, of course.

Did I want to talk to Cedric right this moment? No. I figured I had at least a few days to even think about what I could say to him.

But of course.

He catches Gideon and I at the front of the arena, without the mistresses, and his brow furrows in anger. A snarl tugging at his lips as he glares at us.

He's put on an insane amount of muscle since I've seen him last. He's even grown a beard to give him a fiercer presence.

I have to say, at least he's being useful here. In Vesperholm, he just seemed to be deadweight.

Part of me is proud of him. Even if he's livid with me.

Gideon leans over to whisper, "Heads up. He's been *extra* feral while you've been gone."

I sigh as I come to rub at the muscle between my eyebrows, "Wonderful…"

The winged men get in their ranks and look to Gideon and I in waiting.

I step up and dig deep to project my voice, "General Moonsong, and Mistress of Law, Selene, will be preoccupied with endeavors concerning the safety and longevity of Tantalia!" I call over them.

They all exchange glances, as if they can't believe two meager humans could think to lead them.

In their defense, I agree. They're larger, stronger and faster than Gideon and I combined. But at the very least I can instill some level of discipline in them. That much I should be capable of.

"In their absence, Gideon Shadowfang and I will be leading trainings!"

Several groans sound off as they hear the news of their new leadership.

"I know! Look, I don't know nearly as much as you guys do," I start with a sigh.

A defeated, exasperated sigh.

Because in all honesty, I don't know as much as them.

Hells, I barely know anything now.

But I suppose that is the best I can do right now, *is* honesty.

"I *do* know what General Moonsong wants from her Legions. And I know what she looks for. I can't teach you anything new. I can't teach you to wield your magic or use your wings. But I can teach you discipline. I can teach you how to be aware of your surroundings, I can teach you how to save yourself and the people around you when push comes to shove."

Some of the warriors begin to murmur amongst each other as they look to one another in confusion.

"I want to build a rapport with all of you. Because as it sits, I may be here for a lot longer than I thought. And if I am to trust my life in your hands, I want to be able to hold yours in mine."

I have no idea what I'm saying. It feels like it spills out of me.

But I mean every word of it. And some of it feels like something that could be productive, mentally for me while Seraphina and I work through this new reality. And if I planned on probably staying in Tantalia to begin with, perhaps being mates just pushed me farther to this side.

A few warriors begin to cheer and the rest of them follow suit. The arena begins to roar with manly applause as they listen to the end of my statement.

My eyes widen and I peer at Gideon with a small sliver of hope and shock.

"Looks like they're ready for you, friend," he says with a proud smile.

I look back to the men, fishing my Blackwood dagger from my thigh to raise above my head, "To Tantalia!" I call to them all.

"TO TANTALIA!" they cry in unison as they thrust their swords to the sky.

I decide not to do training today. Gideon and I spend the time getting to know all the warriors. I ask them what they like, and the things they enjoy doing when they aren't training. Some like to lay in the meadow. Some like to fly around the lands in their free time. I learned they play little strategy games with pieces of wood they've carved out. They keep themselves busy, but regardless, they seem like they love their land, and they love what they do.

One by one, Gideon and I learn about every one, until the very last warrior comes to stand in front of us. Gideon slaps my shoulder as he retreats, leaving me to face Cedric by myself. His boots scrape against the dirt sounding off from behind as I lock eyes with the irritated glare of Cedric.

His green eyes are familiar. And even through our strife, I miss him. I miss *seeing* him. Aside from Gideon and Gnox, he is all I have of home right now.

His jaw is sheathed in a thick, brown beard, and he glares at me in seething contempt.

"You've put on muscle. It seems like you're doing well here. They put you in Lunae." I compliment him.

His eyebrow rises in skepticism, "You're going to get bigger when all you do is train, shit, and eat."

Alright then.

"Why are you still so mad at me?" I ask exasperatedly.

The lingering anger from the past few days, pricks against my skin, all because I don't understand any of his reactions. And I can't imagine I was that awful of a brother.

"You keep climbing the ranks. And now you *lead* us. It's laughable."

My brow furrows in annoyance, "How did you know about Alden?"

"You learn a lot down here."

"Why didn't you try to do anything about it when you found out?"

"What do you think I was going to do? And by the looks of it, you haven't done anything either. You parade yourself around as this fucking *messiah,* and yet our brother rots in those fucking vats," Cedric says as his voice tenses, his lip curling in a snarl.

"What would you have me do, Cedric!? I was offered a deal. A deal that saved your fucking life!"

"Saved my life?!" he guffaws. "It's admirable the lengths you go to in order to come out on top, when *you* are the reason we rot here." He shakes his head. "If you were so keen on saving lives, rescue Alden! Take him back to fucking Vesperholm! I don't know, something! You apparently have the answers to everything and yet you don't have the answer to this?!" He makes a display of calling to the empty arena, swinging his arm out to me as he yells. "Hey, everyone! Asher has no fucking clue what he's DOING!" He turns and his gaze lands back on me in fury, "So much for a *messiah,* Asher Blackwood."

A growl rumbles in my chest as he taunts me. He knows how to press my buttons, and this time is no different, "I don't FUCKING KNOW ANYTHING HERE, CEDRIC! Every single second I spend here gets more and more confusing! I saw *dragons.* I saw humans that wield fucking magic! There are ORCS out there! There is an entire world we don't know even exists! And you're worried about me leading you!?" My finger points in the direction of the Kaithoon Portal, spearing into his gaze with anger at his ignorance.

"I don't give a shit what happens out there! Our family is rotting away in Vesperholm, and our brother is held in a fucking vat of bullshit!" He yells as he points in the direction of The Catacombs, leaning in close to my face.

I step back, trying to take a deep breath before I run my hands through my hair. Defeat tugs at my insides at the constant bickering, and soon my arms flop to my sides, "Cedric, I *want* to help you. I want to help Alden. I want to help everyone that I can. But I... I can only do so much," I sigh. The weight of everything begins to settle on my chest and the prospect of failure bears down with it.

"Oh, so now he understands the problem! Terrific! Now you can solve everything!"

Anger rises, and I feel my senses heighten. The colors turn vivid, even in the dulling sun of the day. The sounds are sharper, and scrape against my ear drums, even if the only thing I can hear right now is the rabid pounding of my heart in my chest. The lengthening of my teeth as they stab at my lower lip, coating my tongue in a wash of blood. "Shut UP!" I growl as I lob a fist into his hairy jaw.

There is a lot of power in what you can provide, especially if your worth is on the line.

CHAPTER 55

WORTH

SERAPHINA

I have bid the other mistresses I didn't need back to their sectors and kept the necessary compatriots with me.

I sent Tyrick to The Library – with a succubus of course – to scout out more information. Possibly more things on Celestials and their history.

Now, I hold Selene, Learra, and Xeneera in The Court with me.

A deep breath courses through me as I lock my gaze on The Compendium.

The Caelestial Compendium.

"It'll be alright, Phinney. Mother knew what she was doing." Selene's voice is soft as she places a hand on my shoulder in solidarity.

I glance at her as my head tilts, and I give her a small nod in hope.

The tome comes back into the view as I face off against it, peering over its cover.

Simple brown leather covers the wooden boards that secure its brittle parchments. While slashes, marks and even splatters of black blood decorate the outside.

A shiver runs through me, and murmurs of whispers begin to sing to me the longer I look at it. There is no title, there are no words. And there doesn't seem as if there ever *were* any words on it. The murmurs become louder the longer it sits closed, but I can't understand an ounce of it. It's almost like music.

I throw the cover of the text open and am met with silence.

There is nothing inherently strong about the book. No strong thrum of magic, no surge of power.

Not that other books *do* have that. But I would have assumed a book as powerful as this to have *something.*

The first page is blank, and I turn the next one to find a number of symbols.

Triangles, circles. Almost like runes, but much more primal.

I look to Selene, who furrows her brow at me, "What is it?"

"It's all in symbols," I murmur as I look back down at the book.

I start flipping through it and find hundreds of pages of just *symbols.* There are no words in here. Not even any that I personally know. The thought is defeating, but there is a reason Lilith wrote this.

She *meant* for someone to look for this book.

The purple gem of my amulet begins pulsing against my chest. Vivid violet beams through the space as I flip through the pages. My brow furrows in confusion as I look down at it.

"Is that Mother's amulet?" Selene asks.

"Yes. I took it from her when I found her in Vesperholm."

Selene peers curiously at it, narrowing her eyes in study. "Does it always do that?"

"Sometimes. It pulses. It vibrates. Much more so when Asher and I are… entangled."

Selene weighs my words for a long time before her gaze trails off and she shakes her head at the thought.

"Mother was always very strange when I was growing up. She kept me away long after I could hold a sword. She would train me when she could in a private area of The Keep."

Selene was born after the massacre. Not too long after, in fact.

But from my knowledge, she was carried by Lilith herself, to term. A rare circumstance for demons.

"As far back as I can remember, she was nervous. You all know Lilith, the Queen. But Lilith, my mother, tried all she could to keep me safe. She would tell me tales of my father. How strong and admirable, he was. Her amulet would glow and pulse when she did. But I never knew what it meant..." She trails off as her attention is pulled away. Her head tilts in the direction of the window behind her as her face tightens in concern. It's as if she's listening to something.

Lilith was never that way with me. In fact, she thrust me into everything that she could. There was always a look in Lilith's eyes when she gazed at me, sometimes with the pulse of her gem.

She told me always, *"To be Queen is to die for your people."*

It was the reason I was so hesitant to take the throne. I don't want to die for my people. As much as I love them, I enjoy living. But I wouldn't throw an unworthy demon on the throne for the fuck of it.

I never knew if Lilith was trying to instill that idea in me, or if she had to remind herself. But most of her teachings were rooted in sitting on the throne.

I was taken from The Pits when I showed an advanced nature in my bloodshed. I was taken under Lilith's wing, but she had come around to the nursery more when I was there, and my mother seemed keen on letting me be taught by Lilith.

I was just happy to learn under our matriarch, to be seen for my bloodthirsty ways, to eradicate the threats that deemed to eradicate us.

I was the one who stole most of the men from Vesperholm. I had the fervor and drive for such things.

I was moved up in rank, quickly spearing into Lunae, and then Stella to become General. My thirst for vengeance and my hate for the humans was so inherently palpable, I imagine that's why she was so keen on my ascension.

Her gem pulses and vibrates in tune with my running mind. But my thoughts are interrupted by the rabid panting of Selene's dog, who has been grafted into the room. Selene turns to him as he bends over and takes heaving breaths, "What is it, dear? I heard your call," I hear her murmur as she approaches him to place a hand on his back.

"The Blackwood Brothers…. They're alone in The Pits," he pants quickly. His brown hair is sweaty and mussed against his forehead.

"What about the warriors?" I ask as I close The Compendium.

"Lunae Legion came in today but we didn't train them. Asher wanted to get to know them. When it came to Cedric, I left. I stayed outside of the arena to make sure everything was okay, but it turned… quickly," he continues.

Selene looks to me in confusion and I offer a growl, "Selene, secure The Compendium. It goes to no one. I'll be back."

Selene nods as she helps Gideon stand back up, and she grips his jaw in her hands as she strokes his hair in comfort. I pass them, striding to the balconied courtyard and onto the baluster. My foot dangles over the edge before I lean forward, and my wings expand for air to fill the spaces.

A few hard wing beats in the direction of The Pits and a few banking turns take me to the arena, where I flap to hover above it. Small clouds of dirt rise from the ground as the brothers squabble. Fists spear back and forth as their hands pull and tug at the straps of their armor to hold each other in place for more punches.

I position myself in the middle of The Pits, before my wings wrap around me and I force my body into a spin. As my speed picks up, I corkscrew fall into the dirt, feet first. Sand and pebbles fly from my boots as I land in a crouch and look to the skirmish.

The boom of my arrival does nothing for the warring brothers, as their fists pound into each other's faces.

I watch the scramble to try and spot Asher, when I catch the purple sheen of his eyes. Fear grips my innards as I realize Cedric is in grave danger. Asher would never be able to forgive himself if he did something to his brother.

A growl crawls from my chest as I graft to their position, placing myself in the middle of them. My arm extends to hold Cedric at bay, as Asher is blown back into the dirt from my arrival. A lightning lead spears from my wrist, into Asher's collar, to whip him against the wall on the other side of The Pits.

The crackling purple tether wraps around his thrashing body before it streaks out against the stone like a web to pin him in place.

He roars, "LET ME GO! I'VE HAD IT WITH THIS!!" His voice is deep and booming, causing birds to flitter from the trees beside The Pits as he pants heavily against the web of lightning. His hair haphazardly sticks every which way on his scalp and his eyes flare with bright purple.

His skin is marred with dark, blue bruising and his cheek drips with blood. His lips lift in a snarl to bare his fangs at Cedric. As if he could catch my scent, his eyes search the arena frantically before landing on me. His nostrils flare as he catches sight of me. "Mate." I hear him growl, low and hungry.

My hand splays at Cedric, and my lightning reaches for his collar, pulling him to the ground on his knees and securing his arms behind his back as he catches his breath. His eyebrow and lip are split; dripping with blood that soak into the hair on his face.

He spits, and the ground stains beside him before he looks at Asher with a satisfied grin. "Looks like the *good boy* had his master come save him once again," he laughs as his emerald eyes turn to me in smug challenge.

"What is the meaning of this!?" I growl to Cedric.

"Your little lap dog thinks he's hot shit and I told him he isn't," Cedric pants with a shrug. He spits another mouthful of blood into the dirt before he slides his tongue across his split lip.

I roll my eyes, "Aren't you supposed to be brothers?"

He laughs a sarcastic chuckle. "We were, before you promoted him to cunt-stuffer," he says as his eyes glimmer with taunt.

I've not interacted with Cedric; I've merely commanded his superiors, heard of his progress. And Asher doesn't talk much about his family. But whatever strife they have *certainly* does not involve me.

His immaturity for this situation has my gaze shifting to Asher, who pants with his gaze locked on me. His mind has left him and the only thing controlling him is the beast inside. His eyes zero in on me, his features pinched in rabid focus, and he damn near nips at the air to be let go.

"What's his deal?" Cedric asks.

My brows tense as I look at him in surprised confusion, "I'm sure you know. Aren't you the cause of all of this?"

"No, the eyes. The teeth. This isn't a hunter gift."

"Ah yes. We're mates," I state matter-of-factly as I watch Asher rage against his cage.

If I release him, I'm sure to get fucked of my power and then I'm out of a General for the next three days. That can't happen right now, even if I would like it to.

Cedric has gone quiet, and I peer at him from the corner of my eye, "M-mates?"

"Correct."

"What do you mean? Like… married? You got married? Betrothed?" he asks desperately.

"Mmmmm… Not quite. I know you humans aren't well-versed on the idea of *mates*. But in the magical realm, mates are… cosmic pairings, if you will. Pre-destined lovers that are determined by The Fates."

"What does that have to do with the teeth and the eyes?" he asks as he stares off at Asher.

I roll my eyes and pinch my brow as I reiterate this information to yet *another* clueless human, "Mating bonds give traits to the weaker party to ensure their survival. Because Asher is the weaker species, his senses increase, and he becomes stronger. His eyes see better, his ears hear better, his features become sharper. But because he hasn't *accepted* the bond, the beast inside him increases with his rage. He can't control this shift. So, it tries to come out in times of stress to complete the bond."

"Aren't you already technically bonded if you're mates?"

"He has to accept it. The monster that takes residence within him won't be satisfied until he surrenders."

Cedric blinks, staring blankly at me, "None of that makes sense."

"Magic doesn't make sense. It's just what happens."

Cedric peers at Asher, who has finally passed out against the web of lightning with his hands, feet and head slumped. His chest rises and falls slowly with his even breaths.

"So, what is *your* issue?" I ask as I look down at Cedric.

Cedric gazes away as he registers my question, sighing in annoyance before he unfolds his legs from under him to plop into the sand. "Why the fuck do you care? You don't have to give a shit about me because your mate is my brother."

My brow rises at such an odd statement, "Because I am the Queen, it's my duty to care about all who inhabit my realm -- including more unsavory characters such as yourself."

His green eyes meet mine in annoyance, "Gee, thanks. That's reassuring."

"I'm not here to give you reassurance."

"Again... Why do you care?" he huffs.

"It seems as if something is eating at you. Asher doesn't talk much about you, but he asked for your release. You must mean a lot for him to call for your freedom. Or I suppose, lack thereof at this point. And while I don't care if you're my mate's brother, you are my soldier. And I do care deeply for those that fight for our realm."

Cedric looks to me in confused thought as he listens, his gaze tracking beyond the arena. The day has departed and the skies behind the arena walls have turned to a fiery orange and red as the sun continues to set.

He takes a long while to answer, before his gaze shifts hesitantly at the dirt below, "Back in Vesperholm... I was forced to carry the line.

As if the weight of our entire family rested on *my* shoulders," he starts, and his brow furrows in frustration. "The eldest brothers back home are to bed the sisters from other houses. But when push came to shove, I..." he inhales a deep breath, shaking his head. "I couldn't... I could never give them what they needed."

The muscles in my forehead pull together as I listen, and I take a moment to sit in the dirt with him. While I've had to deal with Asher and his confusion with this situation, I've not taken the chance to ever get to know Cedric.

He was thrust into this magical realm the same as Asher, and he's only had the warriors with him.

While I'm sure he's learned a lot, the warriors aren't exactly, "emotional."

"Then Alden... when Alden was taken... everything came apart," he says softly, his gaze locked on to a small rock before him.

He sniffles once as tears begin streaking down his face to land in the dust below.

"Father never cared about our feelings, he never cared about what mattered to us. It was always the family; it was the lineage and the gifts. My worth was in what I could provide to the family, and I *couldn't.* Asher always did, he always *could.*"

Sadness pangs deep in my belly, and my heart breaks for him. There is a lot of power in what you can provide, especially if your worth is on the line. I know I can relate.

For his small clan to not deem him worthy for what he couldn't provide, has to be hard. Asher, I imagine, was also unaware.

For Cedric to be down here, and watch his brother only become more powerful for what he can provide... for him to fall into another pattern of unworthiness because he can't... It's...

"I'm sorry," I whisper.

"I don't hate Asher for being important. I think... I think I hate myself, because I'm not," he admits softly, his watery gaze tracks to the spent Asher. "But we're hunters. All we know is carnage. So, it felt like my only reaction was to rage against the thing I hated. Against the thing I wanted to be, but couldn't."

"You're always important in Tantalia, dear friend," I tell him as I place a hand on his knee.

"It doesn't feel that way. And watching Asher lead us after wholly being absent for as long as he was… It *stung*. Watching the way the warriors *cheered* for him," he sighs as he shakes his head. The tension he's held in his neck releases and his head falls as more tears hit the dust to create a small crater of sadness.

The moon rises above him in the sky, shining a light down on us.

"I don't even know why I'm telling you this," he sniffles as he shakes his head once more. He brings his head up to fix his gaze on a point across the arena and stiffens his features to don a strong face.

"While succubus *can* be physical feeders, we can be emotional ones as well. Sometimes it can bring about a feeling of trust."

Cedric's face meets mine in a contortion of disgust, "Are you *feeding* off of me right now?" he asks as his eyes skeptically track up and down my body.

"You wish. But no. Whatever you're saying is completely under your own admission," I tell him with a shrug.

His gaze trails off, as if he doesn't believe me.

"Is there a way I could make you feel as if you're more important?" I ask softly.

His gaze refocuses and he looks up to the sky, his eyes locking onto the painted curtains that shimmer overhead, "I don't know. But this conversation is a start."

I smile as I grasp his shoulder, rocking him in comfort. In the process, I release his bindings and allow his hands to go free.

He sighs a deep breath of relief as he brings his arms in front of him, rubbing his wrists out, "Thank you," he says gratefully.

I nod in return, "Hopefully Asher will feel the same."

Cedric steadies his gaze on Asher, his mouth thinning as he observes him, "I've never seen him that angry. He doesn't usually *get* angry."

I track his gaze, watching the sleeping form of my mate. Things have been so askew since we returned from Kaithoon. I am saddened by the fact it's partially my fault. And soon, remorse settles in my belly. Right next to the pain of his distance.

"It'll be alright in the end," I whisper.

Cedric stands, brushing the dust off of his breeches before he stretches his arms out. He offers a hand to help me up.

I grip his calloused palm, pulling myself up to dust myself off, "Thank you." I give him a kind smile. A smile that tells him he can come to me if he needs help.

Whether he understood the small gesture, I don't know. But I tried anyway.

"Thank *you*," he responds before he walks out of the arena and to the barracks.

I turn my attention back to Asher and walk slowly over to him before I sit on the ground in front of him.

The bright, crackling lightning snaps and pops as it illuminates the area between us.

And I watch him.

Wait for him.

Long for him.

"This isn't just your land, or my land anymore. If you're the Queen and I am to be your mate... Seraphina, this is **our** land. **We** make the rules here."

CHAPTER 56

GIVING IN

ASHER

R ousing from my sleep, water sloshes against my limbs. My back feels as if it's cradled by puffy clouds covered in water. But I know exactly where I am… This place has become a familiar type of hell.

A groan burbles in my throat as I open my eyes, and I look up above me; into the void.

"Please… why am I here again?" I murmur as I close my eyes.

I don't even bother getting up. I just lie there, depleted. I didn't even take anything this time.

"Your confusion will be your downfall," a deep, unfamiliar voice murmurs.

"You're new."

"To you."

My eyes blink open, and I search the darkness for anyone.

The red glowing light has returned, but there is a faint shape to it this time.

My brow furrows as I make to stand, walking slowly toward the light.

It doesn't get farther, and as I come closer, it seems as if the bright red glow is caused by a brilliant ruby.

"You must look within, for the answers you seek, Little Blackwood," the voice calls. This one is soft, feminine.

I peer around the void, confusion plastered against my forehead before I set my sights on the light.

"What if I can't find them?" I ask softly, taking steps toward it.

"You will. It is your fate."

As I get closer, the illumination reaches for me. It beckons me. Promises of a life without peril. Promises of a love that can fuel the world itself. Promises of peace, and solidarity. The promises it speaks are warm to the touch. I make to wrap my fingers around the ruby and…

A deep breath courses through my lungs as my eyes pop open and my head scans my immediate area. My arms can't move, but my hands wiggle from where they stick out against the crackling purple lights that streak in haphazard lines that hold me against the wall.

As I move, the brick façade of the arena scrapes and bites into my armor.

The last thing I remember is watching Seraphina talk to Cedric. Watching her be anywhere near him made the anger course through me at a rate I'd never felt before.

I had no wits about me, there was only marking, claiming. The usual bout of rage when this happens. But eventually it took over and I descended into that dream realm.

As I get a grip on where I am, I see that night has cloaked Tantalia in the signature-colored curtain. The moon half full rises high above the arena, bathing the area in a hazy iridescent glow.

I catch the wingtips of Seraphina as she watches me from below. Her purple eyes swirl in melancholy, and the moon light reflects off her armor as her tail scrapes against the sand where it flicks slowly behind her.

Her tortured gaze connects with mine. The heaviness of her despair fills the air and pulls me down with her. "You feel so far away," she murmurs. Longing replaces her melancholy, and her eyes beg for the promise of a future where we come out on top together.

I've missed those eyes. Those beautiful, vexing eyes…

I watch her… study her. *Admire* her. "I'm right here, Sera. I never left."

Seraphina's face doesn't twitch with tension, it doesn't change, she merely observes, "I wanted to tell you about being mates, Asher. But it's something you must figure out on your own…"

"How am I supposed to know what that is? I'm not from here, and I have no idea what mates are. It seems unfair to let me figure out something that I would never know about."

Seraphina's gaze travels to the ground in front of her, "I understand. I think we were just… living by the rules of our own lands."

I watch as her wings droop. The claws of her lower wingtips leave small trails in the sand as they scrape against it. They go limp and splay around her hips like a flowing gown of leather and bone.

"I think… I think if this is going to work… *truly* work… We need to create our own rules."

Her brow works as she continues staring at the ground, weighing my words carefully, "What do you mean?"

"This isn't just your land, or my land anymore. If you're the Queen and I am to be your mate… Seraphina, this is *our* land. *We* make the rules here."

"But The Fates is not a rule we can change."

My lips thin in thought as I remember the words spoken to me in that dream realm. "Perhaps not. But we can change how we communicate with each other. We can make rules on how things are done here."

There is a lot we need to learn about each other. Even if it feels like I've known her forever. In reality, we *don't* know each other.

The feeling of a mate, if that's what this feeling *has* been, is just as confusing as the concept itself.

I hadn't known what it meant. But if my gifts were nothing to her, perhaps that should have been my first clue.

Is it wrong to be angry at her for not telling me? I'm not sure. And I don't know if I ever will know. But I don't think I will be able to dwell on that any longer. Not when we're faced with such dire circumstance. The Drannars and their intrusions, the cauldrons of Knogdagh, and the Orcs working with them. Every day here feels like a day closer to certain death.

Seraphina's gaze softens and settles on mine before she gives me an apologetic smile, "I'm sorry that I didn't tell you, Asher."

"I'm sorry I was upset about it all. It's confusing being here."

Seraphina gives me a sideways smile as she stands. Her fingers wave against the air to release me from the wall and the lightning slowly retreats. It weaves back into itself and as the tension holding my body loosens, it lets me free for my feet to hit the ground.

I take a good look at this breathtaking demon I have been tagged with. Her power, her leadership. The way her entire realm bends to her every word and whim.

What makes *me* so worthy of such a being? What have I done to deserve someone as incredible as her?

What can I offer that she doesn't have herself?

She has given me a new life, a new purpose, a new meaning. Being with Seraphina has changed *everything* about my life. And the memory of struggle is something that feels so distant, even if it wasn't.

My slow steps eat the distance between us, and she meets me halfway. The light of the moon shines down on us, bathing us in its sheer, silver light. Bathes her in the light I wish she could see in herself. An ethereal goddess that has ravaged my soul with the intent on conquering.

And by the gods, she has. And I will let her if it means I can continue to look in her eyes for all of eternity. If it means I can hold her against me when the world turns to dust and the sun darkens to obsidian.

"To Tantalia," I tell her softly, as I take her hand in my own. Rubbing a thumb over her calloused knuckles, I look down into those purple eyes; the vexing orbs that drive my pulse higher, and my soul into bliss.

They shine with admiration, with hope, with *love.*

My heart pounds deep in my chest, hard and fast as my mind swirls with so many questions. The tug deep within pulling with a fervency.

Is that what this feeling is? Love? Like life without her would be void of meaning? Like the thought of going a day without seeing her face would drive me to the edge of a cliff?

Would I have fallen for her without these fates she speaks of? Would I be here without them? Are we destined for more together? Or is this our future? I don't know... I imagine, eventually, I will.

But what I do know now, is this feeling in my chest, the one that has wracked against me for so long and caused me so much strife. The bone deep warmth that presses through me whenever I scent her... whenever I see her...

My focus leaves my thoughts, peering at her hopeful expression, her sweet smile and her apologetic eyes that shine through her thick lashes. I roam my gaze over every part of her face, because if I miss one singular detail, how will I ever be able to love her in my memories?

This is love...

Intense, fiery love for this Queen.

"To Tantalia," Seraphina whispers back. Rising on her toes, she releases my hand to caress my jaw. The rush of her skin against mine, and the feeling of her lips as she pulls me into a deep kiss, sends me straight into the abyss.

I missed the feeling of loving her, of touching her and just *being* with her.

My darling angel, Seraphina.

It feels like the only touch we've had recently was one of another purpose.

Power, feeding, anger.

But the way she touches me now... the way she melts into me *is* love.

The moonlight shifts against my closed eyelids, and the dirt under my boots turns steady as the air around us warms and the arena is replaced with marble.

My eyes slowly open and the tall posters of Seraphina's bedroom come into view as her sheer canopy curtains sway in the breeze from her window.

"Are you sure you want me? This? After everything I've done?" I ask softly as I bring a hand to her chin, stroking the flesh of it with my thumb.

"All I want right now is *you*, Asher," Seraphina responds. Her eyes show an unrelenting conviction as her hands trail down her body to rid it of her armor.

Her skin glistens from the dull light that shines from outside. The ethereal glow hits her curves from behind, creating a devastating silhouette in the night. With her spired, curving horns mimicking the swoops of her wide hips and tight waist.

The spaded tail behind her swishes elegantly in anticipation as she gazes at me in heated adoration. Her wingtips rise above her head in a show of seductive dominance.

A mirrored vision of that night in the alley comes in to my mind. Though instead of fear, there is only love.

The sight of her makes blood rush straight to my cock. Any thoughts I have are silenced by the pounding organ in my chest that begs for her.

Her clawed hands rest softly against my chest as my armor seemingly evaporates and the warm air of her quarters hits my skin. The tense material that restrained my groin releases, allowing my cock to harden further while her soft skinned stomach presses against it.

Her eyes glance down to my groin as her hand glides down my chest and talons graze over my abs, down my pelvis, eliciting a shiver from me when she wraps her hand around my cock.

I release a small gasp through the silence as I continue looking in her eyes, absorbing the feeling of her touch. The haze of her dulls the world around me. The air becomes thinner, and the room burns with desire. The same as the burning in her eyes.

I slide my hand against her neck, reaching for the nape and tangling my fingers through her hair to angle her head back. Her skin beckons me further as my other hand slides down her side, gripping tight at her hip to hold her against me. My tongue slides from my lips to press into hers as I bring her mouth to mine. Her lips part and her tongue caresses mine in a delicious dance as the halves split.

The taste of her sets my insides ablaze, burning with unhinged need for her flesh.

Her hand moves back and forth along my cock, gripping and stroking every inch of me as her other hand rubs small circles on the head with her thumb. The pad of her finger slipping over it as I drip with precum.

Groans meld into where our lips meet, the feeling so entrancing that I can't think, I can only feel what her fingers are doing to me.

"Sera…" I pant between us, groaning as I buck into her hands.

Seraphina giggles before she slithers her tongue from my mouth. Her gaze locks with mine before she slides down my body. Her tongue leaves a trail of fire in its wake as she drags it against my skin. Lower and lower she goes, until she's on her knees in front of me.

A shiver wracks through me as her tongue wraps around the base of my cock, allowing it to corkscrew around my length as she travels to the tip. The slender ends of the forked muscle tickle against the head as she leans her head back and opens her mouth. Her tongue splits once more to wrap around my balls, squeezing them softly as her lip brushes the underside of me.

Watching her causes me to pulse and throb harder. There is no singular way I would *ever* experience this in Vesperholm.

The corners of her mouth lift in a devilish grin as she releases my balls, kissing her way up my shaft before taking the head in her mouth. The moist warmth of the inside of her cheeks has my head tossing back for reprieve and my hand wrapping the back of her neck. I cradle her head as she takes every inch of me into her throat and I press my hips deeper for more. "Angel… angel please…" I beg in a breathless plea. My knees wobble as I fight the sensation to fall from the way her lips suction around me.

Fuck, I can't take this.

I remove my hand from her neck to wrap around her horns, pulling her to a stand. The plush give of her breasts does nothing to soothe the ache of my cock as I grip them in my hands. The hardened peak of her nipples press into my palm and I push her to the bed.

She complies, backing up with my movements and climbing onto the plush comforter. She perches herself in the middle on her knees and gazes at me, her eyes dark with desire as she brings her clawed hands up to play with her nipples.

A fanged bite sinks into her lower lip as she watches me. I haven't even realized my hand has gone down to my cock, stroking it with the loss of her touch.

"How do you want me?" she purrs seductively.

There are so many ways I could take her… But there's only one that matters to me right now though.

"Lay on your back," I rasp as my eyes roam her decadent frame.

Her wings expand and swish gently, blowing a fragranced burst of lavender-jasmine air in my direction, "As you wish," she responds as she falls sideways on the bed, her head crashing to the pillow and her legs spread as she waits for me. One of her hands has traveled down her body to slide through her core.

As I watch her, I climb onto the bed, crawling in between her legs as the mattress cradles my knees.

The glistening sheen of her cunt calls my name; it damn-near *sings* with how it pools for me.

I can't help the groan that escapes me as I continue stroking myself, watching the way her slender fingers swirl around her clit.

My eyes travel up every inch of her body, memorizing every dip and curve of her tight frame. The way her stomach flattens and the swoop of her waist as it tapers in from her hips. The mountainous curvature of her tits.

Stroking myself one more time, I lean my hips in to press the head into her. My hands go to grip under her knees and hold her open for me.

The feeling of her rich, soaked core causes a ripple of pleasure to rock through my spine. Her hand begins to leave when I grab at her wrist, keeping her there, "I didn't say you could stop," I warn her with a devious grin.

Her fangs gleam in the moonlight as she grins at me, "Yes Asher-dear," she moans. Fingers part her core, opening herself wider for me. She envelops every inch of me as I press deeper and deeper, taking every second to feel *every* bit of her.

I've felt her before, in more ways than one. But giving in to the idea of her being my mate, and sitting with the fact that this is mine for all time…

I groan as my head tosses back; my eyes clench shut as I descend balls deep into her.

Her moans enter my consciousness, and her fingers rub against the sides of me as she pleasures herself.

I pant as I look down again, slowly rocking in and out of her. My cock comes out covered in her wetness and it causes my thrusts to pick up. I lean down in between her legs, my fingers gripping onto the tendons in the pit of her knees as I try to contain myself.

Her lips brush against mine as I lean in close. The tips of her claws prick my neck as her hands come up to my jaw, pulling me in.

"I've missed you, Seraphina. I've missed this perfect cunt… your perfect lips, your body… fuck I've missed this," I pant softly. "My mate… my *love*," I whisper. Tender kisses join us together and I rock in and out of her in slow pumps. Her lips against mine sets ablaze a fire inside of me I didn't think would ever be lit.

Soft moans seep down my throat as I press all the way into her, holding myself in to let her clench around me, "Angel..." I pant into her, nipping at her lower lip before my head drops into her shoulder.

"Asher-darling," she moans back as she caresses my head and shoulders. The skin of my chest presses against her tits, and the sensation pulls me deeper. I roll my hips into her, giving in to the sound of my name and the breathy pleas she makes of it. The way she calls for me like a prayer, like a salvation.

"You... this... you feel so fucking good," I pant, my hips slowing to absorb every point of contact I make with her.

My head departs her shoulder to wrap my hand around her chin, holding her in place to look in her eyes. The hazy lust shrouding them sends jolts of pleasure through me in sporadic bursts that are in time with my thrusts.

I feel the strong muscles of her thighs as they grip around my waist, her arms tightening around me, and before I can think, the air of the bedroom at my back is replaced by her bedding. The room spins as she appears on top of me.

Her chest rises and she looks down at me with devilish eyes. My eyes widen as I take in every single inch of her, her skin, her tits, her *everything*. Her cunt at this angle is divine, paired with seeing all of her makes my heart pound with a fervency.

Her hips swirl, and my hands go straight to them, gripping into her flesh as her hands steady her against my chest.

The pillow cradles my neck as my head presses back further. The feeling of her cunt flays my mind and the longer she rides me, the more loss of sense I get. I'm at the mercy of her cunt, and I wouldn't have it any other way.

"You were right, Asher-darling," she moans as she glances down at me.

"About what?" I manage to pant. Her words barely break through the pleasure, but I can't ignore the sound of her voice when I'm inside of her.

Her torso lowers, and her breasts press against my chest. Her breath grazes my neck as she licks across it and the action sends heated shivers through me. My hands tighten on her hips in a desperate plea for more.

"You are my salvation. And I would surrender the Legion's… all of Tantalia, and my standing as General… just to worship you for eternity," she whispers.

My heart fills at her words, and I bring my hand to her jaw, positioning her head above me. "*You* are my eternity, Seraphina," I return.

Her hips swirl and move on me, the pleasure becoming insurmountable the longer she rides me. Soon, I glide one of my hands up the length of her body, lingering on her waist before it moves higher. I take a soft pinch at her nipple before I wrap my hand around the back of her neck, pulling her lips into mine. I kiss her slow and deep, sliding my tongue across her lips, her tongue, spearing into her mouth for every bit of her taste. Her body against mine is greater than the sun on my skin, greater than any chance we have at peace.

Greater than anything I have ever known.

"Sera… I-… Fuck I'm gonna-" I groan as my climax sneaks up on me, filling her with every ounce of my release that I can.

Her moans slither down my throat as she feels me, her hips pressing deep to take all of me that she can. She grinds deeper and deeper, letting me finish my hard pulses within her.

Her hips lift slowly, and I watch as she removes me. My cock falls onto my stomach for her to grind her drenched core against the underside of it.

My eyes roll back as I lose myself entirely.

Her moans are the only thing I can hear as she uses me for her pleasure. The thought of her using my cum and my cock to finish herself, in turn finishes me and my hands grip for purchase against the sheets. My back bowing as I hear her moans get louder, "Seraphina," I groan.

"Asher-darling," she returns. Her moans pitch and she deepens her grind.

"Take what you need, angel. Be a good girl and come for me. I wanna watch you fall," I pant.

Her eyes connect with mine, struggling to retain some level of clarity as the thoughts flee her skull and the pleasure consumes her. Her moan comes out as a breathy plea, "Asher."

"I'm right here, my love. Come for me. Let go. I'll catch you."

And I mean every word.

"It's so much, Asher. I-I can't," she moans, shaking her head as she moves faster against me.

I wrap my arms around her back, bringing her flush against me. I position my hips just enough to press back into her. The feel of her slickness wrapping around me sends a groan through the air as I pump in and out of her, grinding my pelvis against her clit to send her further into oblivion.

"You're taking me so well. Come all over me… you can come for me."

My words tip her over the edge and her body tightens as she cries out. Her cunt tightens around me and I groan at the pleasure coursing through her body. It vibrates through my soul and my heart sings with the feel of her surrender.

"That's it. I've got you, my love," I groan as she rides herself through her orgasm. "There's a good girl, angel… such a good fucking girl. You come like a goddess."

Soon, her movements slow, and she lays limp against my body. Her back rises and falls in quick bursts as she catches her breath.

My arms loosen and I bring a hand up to stroke through her hair as I press soft kisses to her damp forehead.

I never thought it'd be like this. And I never thought we'd get here. With her loving me, and me loving her. Fated mates aside.

But here we are. The ascent of our love spears me on its point, and I can't let this go. I can't let *her* go. And I'd slaughter any human, demon or elf that attempted to rid her of her breath.

I bring the awareness back to my body, and to the points of contact I make against her. To the fact that I could stay like this forever, and I would have lived a full life.

The feeling of her relaxing on top of me, and her cunt still wrapped around me causes my breathing and heart to slow.

"I love you, Seraphina," I whisper into the dark.

There is no response as her back rises and falls slowly.

But the gem around her throat beams ever brighter.

"Anyone else like to
take a trip to Infernal
Summit?"

CHAPTER 57

THE INNER COURT

SERAPHINA

A momentous thing is happening this morning.

I've brought my "Inner Court", to *The* Court today.

I have brilliant minds from all corners of our world as we know it in my realm. I'd be foolish not to take advantage of their knowledge.

Now we sit at the onyx meeting space we've frequented as of late. Lilith has taken residence on the ground behind my seat, where he rests quietly.

While one would assume I'd keep the large mammal in the stables with Gnox, he likes to be beside me. And sometimes Lilith does actually sleep in the stables. But during the day, he follows me around. Today is certainly no exception.

To the left of me, Asher sits with his hands clasped against the table, his brow furrowed in thought as he waits for me to address everyone.

On the other side of me, Selene sits with her dog next to her.

Tyrick sits next to Asher with a stack of textbooks from Kaithoon and books from The Library placed in front of him.

Xeneera is next to Gideon.

Xeneera has assimilated well here. After her discovery, she's tried to find ways she can be helpful around The Keep. Sometimes she'll help the cooks in the kitchen, sometimes she'll come down to research with Tyrick. Most of the time, I find her in the forges with Reasha.

She seems to have a zeal to her now that she didn't before. Perhaps it was the newfound knowledge she gained or a new outlook on life.

It can be renewing for such a young being.

Tyrick has also been doing quite well. He has given me more information on The Inevitables, or at least in their wisdom. They were to guide the mortals and beings of this world to live a rounded, balanced life.

I suppose that makes sense. Death is inevitable, something we all need to be aware of. Though us demons are immortal, we can be killed. Mortals obviously are well versed in their demise and short times on this earth. If Love is inevitable, something you can't escape, I suppose that would make sense for fated mates. If Chaos is inevitable, how are we to learn how to use our free-will? If Time is inevitable, how do we know when to exist? How does the sun rise? Where does it fall?

All of these questions lead my attention back to the tome before me. The book that has plagued my little brain lays unassuming on the table.

Taunting me.

The frayed leather cover has become a staple in my thoughts, and I rage at the sight of it.

All the things we had gone through for this damn book… all of it… for it to be unreadable.

I had taken some time to leaf through it one night after Asher had fallen asleep, looking over all the symbols by the light of the moon. It felt like Lilith was shining down and guiding me.

But in the same breath, I felt lost. There was a feeling of despair as I gazed over the lines and curves of the various symbols. They were almost as primal as cave drawings, if I were to put a name to them.

That is when the idea came to me to bring all these minds together to make some sort of headway on this.

Everyone at the table seems to be waiting with bated breath as I stare down at it. I gather my thoughts before I press my hands against the table to rise from my seat.

"This book..." I start low and irritated, my gaze burrowing deeper on the tome as I inhale a deep breath.

I shake my head, steel my spine, tighten my wings, and peer at everyone as my hands clasp behind my back.

"The book is written in symbols that are unreadable. There is no one in the kingdom who knows what it means. I've gone through each of the eldest mistresses. Even Kalinda. None of them understand the writing. They've never seen anything like it." A sigh creeps from my lips as I glance at Selene.

I slide the book to her, flipping open to a random page, "Do *you* understand *any* of this?"

Selene raises an eyebrow before she looks down at the text. Her eyes slide around the page as she studies the symbols, "I... I don't... Mother never used this kind of writing before." Her voice is low and contemplative as she begins leafing through some of the pages sporadically.

A growl rumbles in my chest, "Ever?"

"No... No, not that I can tell," she says, her brow furrows deeper as she looks at it.

"Are we sure this is The Compendium? What if you got the wrong book?"

I hadn't thought of that possibility. And I think if I had to linger on it, I may burn Tantalia to the ground.

I sigh, "I sincerely hope it is. But Kyraxes said The Compendium was there, and he showed us where it is."

Selene looks up at me in confusion, "Kyraxes?"

"The oracle dragon king."

Selene's eyebrow raises, "Couldn't you ask... the oracle?"

My thoughts stir, "Perhaps I could."

I should have asked the dragon about the book at the time, but the night was turning quick, and we needed to get home.

I honestly hadn't thought about it, I had no idea the book was unreadable. He knew it belonged to a demon, and he knew the power it possessed. But did he know it was unreadable? And did he know who it belonged to?

The longer I mull over the idea, the more questions I have and the urge to leave rises exponentially.

I peer at Asher, who's sat quietly in his spot the entire time. His head rests in his hand as he listens to the conversation with an unfocused gaze.

His green eyes connect with mine as he realizes the lull in conversation, and he gazes around the table. Noticing the eyes are on him, his brow furrows in confusion and he turns to me with a look of boredom, "Seraphina, we just got back. What about The Legions?"

I wave a hand in his direction, "We know where we're going this time, and we have Tyrick," I say with a smile as I gesture to the small mage.

Tyrick's golden eyes widen as he gazes at me like a spooked deer, "M-me?"

"You said you wanted to see the world, little mage. How do you feel about dragons?" I ask with a devilish grin.

Tyrick's throat bobs in a gulp, and he nods slowly.

"Anyone else like to take a trip to Infernal Summit?" I say to the rest of the table.

Everyone looks to me with a variety of emotions.

Selene's face crinkles with a nervous smile, but her dog would probably be wagging his tail if he had one.

Xeneera gives me a sideways smile and my gaze lands on Asher, who sighs and throws his hands lazily in the air as he sits back, "I guess we're taking a trip."

The next morning rolls around, and I've instructed all the necessary people to converge at the meadow.

Warm sunshine beams down on us, wishing us farewell as the air blows a decadent breeze. On either side of my head, braids have been weaved into my hair and flow in long snakes down my back.

I had my armor reshined and my swords sharpened. With my corset tightened around my body with a comfortable tension. It reminds me of a journey, of discovery, and it causes the blood in my body to rush through me as we face this new prospect ahead of us.

I called off training for the next few days and I've left the kingdom under my mother's thumb in my absence.

With everyone important enough to lead without me now coming *with* me, she is the only one left behind that I can trust.

Everyone gathers in the meadow with their packs. There shouldn't be as many trials and tribulations this time around, we are merely going for a chat. But knowing how things go with us, it's always good to be prepared. I had people bring their weapons just in case.

Selene has supplied her dog with a new bow and a quiver of silver tipped arrows.

I've had Asher's blades resharpened from the miles of trees he had chopped through.

Xeneera, however…

I turn to face the elf with a kind smile, "Are you sure you'll be okay without a weapon, little one?" I ask as I place a hand on her shoulder. Her long, white hair is braided on either side of her neck, and a long black cloak covers the leather armor I supplied her with.

Her crimson eyes come to meet mine and she nods sheepishly as her lips thin, "Yes, I'll be okay…"

I give her a small smile and nod before I turn to Tyrick, who seems to shift excitedly with his large pack and my brow raises in amusement. "Are *you* ready, little mage?" I ask with a sly smile.

He nods excitedly, "Very much so."

I give a soft chuckle and roll my eyes before I come to face Asher. His eyes are fixed on the path beyond, his leather armor pristine as he stands there like he's ready to conquer the world. The hardened stance of his body as he looks to the journey ahead sends heated shivers through my body.

A man who looks like he's been crafted to lead. A man *I* crafted to lead.

My mate.

The bond between us has grown stronger. Though, something is missing. I don't know what goes into the completion of a bond like this. Or if we may have already completed it.

The books I read never stated specifically what needed to be done for the bond to enter completion. It relied on the pairs and their needs. Not to mention how infrequently bonds like this happen.

I only ever remember Lilith telling me to remember the feeling, the way it tugs in your chest, and that you couldn't hurt the being, even if you so badly wanted to.

"To live without your mate is to die with them." Those were the words she always spoke of fated mates. Her eyes would fade to that of deep, painful longing. But I never knew Lilith to have a mate, she lived long enough to have one. I had suspected the male in the tapestries, though she always shut it down when I'd ask. She had wanted nothing to do with that human for one reason or another. Perhaps it was the reason she had us take men from Vesperholm. I don't know.

But that was Lilith.

I shake my head of the thoughts and memories before I turn to my own mate. His thick hands are clenched in a tight grip by his sides and his back expands in deep breaths.

Asher turns around and his jade eyes come to meet mine as his lips soften with a sweet smile. "Are *you* ready, Seraphina?" he asks gently.

My lips curve in an adoring smile and I look over the valley ahead of us, "As ready as I'll ever be."

Save Tantalia.
Save Vesperholm.
Cause no harm.
Save my people.
Save **our** people.

CHAPTER 58

NO FOUL INTENTIONS

ASHER

The idea of going out to Infernal Summit so soon after returning to Tantalia, is a bit of a set back. But if it helps Seraphina get the answers she's looking for, fine.

I felt it was time I could use to get to know The Legions. In the same breath, I would like to ask Kyraxes for a dragon again. I'm not exactly fond of having the guards fly me or graft me up to Celestial Keep.

The farther we get through this entire process, the more haphazard everything becomes. But I suppose when you're dealing with magic, it's going to be that way.

As I've given in more to this "mating bond," there is this thing that tugs deep at my soul. It's hard to recognize what it is. Perhaps it's part of it. But it's also terrifying in the way it pulls me and binds me to Sera. But this wall blocks us, as if I pull the small twine holding us together to follow it into black brick.

I wouldn't mind bringing the wall down and seeing what is on the other side. But I have no idea how I would get through such a barrier to begin with.

I shake my head of the thoughts as I look over the valley to The Portal to Kaithoon. This land that I was terrified of, only a few months ago, has become so familiar.

It feels like *home*.

I can't pinpoint why.

"So, how is this happening?" Gideon asks as he stretches his arms out.

He has been overly excited to see dragons. Probably because he knows that they won't eat him. If only he could imagine the feeling of possibly being devoured by one of those creatures, he wouldn't be so keen.

Seraphina's gaze settles on the valley and her tail flicks slowly behind her in thought. Her armor shines in the sun and she stands as if she commands the sky itself.

I find my jaw slacking as I get lost in the sight of her.

Gods, she is magnificent. *How did I get so lucky?*

My heart flutters in my chest before her voice breaks through and she turns around to address us, paying my gawking no singular mind. "We'll graft to the cave. Tyrick will get us inside the portal and from there we'll traverse to the exit to Castaway Grove," Seraphina says.

Peering around at the patrons gathered, there are a lot of differing energies.

Tyrick appears nervous at the mention of Kaithoon, but nods softly, "Alright… alright I can do that."

Selene merely shrugs, seemingly unaffected by the entire situation.

Seraphina grabs my hand, and reaches for Xeneera's, who peers at it nervously before her chest expands in a deep breath and takes it.

Lilith appears, nudging Seraphina in the shoulder, causing her and I to wobble.

She looks to her ivory friend with a sad smile, "I'm sorry, Lilith. Go to Stella Legion, they'll take care of you while I'm gone. I can't bring you to Infernal Summit."

Lilith huffs a breath of annoyance before he begins trotting off to the stables.

Seraphina watches him leave, before she eyes Selene from across her.

Selene gives her a ready nod before she wraps her arm around Gideon's bicep and reaches for Tyrick's hand.

Gideon leans forward to glare at their joined hands and growls, "Any farther and you won't even realize your death."

Tyrick's eyes widen as he looks at Gideon in terror, "O-okay… Noted?"

I roll my eyes, "Gideon, leave the wizard alone."

"If he touches any other part of her, I swear to the gods, he'll wake up without his di-"

I don't hear what he says next as the world shifts around us. The warm Tantalia air is replaced with cool, wet, earthy scent and dripping echoes as we appear outside of the Kaithoon portal. Boots land on the stone and ring off in a symphony of different weights as we all settle toward the archway.

The portal looks the same as it did the last time Seraphina and I entered it. Though now the normally stoned wall begins to swirl with vibrant azul the closer Tyrick gets to it.

Seraphina, Xeneera, and I are a few feet behind the rest of the group, staring at the portal.

The six of us stand rigid as we look over this new development. Three of them haven't seen it, while the other three have never seen it do *this*. "Is it supposed to do that?" Seraphina asks.

Tyrick looks over the swirling blue curtain carefully. He reaches hesitantly into the vortex and his hand melts into the space. Closing his eyes before his brow furrows. "I'm not… sure… But it is the mages' magic."

My eyes meet Seraphina's, who shrugs in confusion as she glances at me.

Tyrick takes steps away from the wall to shake his head before he turns to us all with a heaving breath, "Alright, because this pocket realm has been closed off from anyone with foul intentions, we need to lock hands. As we cross through the portal, you need to relay your intentions to this realm. It *will* lock you out if you aren't pure in what your goals are here."

Selene looks at Seraphina with a bored scrunch of her brow, "Is this wizard serious?"

Seraphina sighs before she nods, "Entirely. It was the only way I was able to get in before."

Selene groans as she looks at Gideon, "Darling, I need you to clear that pretty little head of yours and think only about how much you want to love on the dragons with no foul intentions."

Gideon nods as he gazes lovingly at her.

Do they have a mating bond too? Would he know if he did?

It's hard to believe they don't with how things have unfolded for them. But Gideon is also Gideon and could just be attached to this demon for one reason or another.

I shake the thought out of my head as I replace the annoying chatter with pure intentions.

Save Tantalia. Save Vesperholm. Cause no harm. Save our *people.*

As I repeat the mantra in my head, the small metal insignia in my pocket feels as if it burns. As if it curses me for calling this place my home, and these demons my people.

I press the insignia's presence out of my skull, choosing instead to focus on the task at hand.

Xeneera looks nervously over the portal as she takes a deep breath, closing her eyes. Her forehead tenses in concentration as she begins her own process.

Eventually, we all lock hands, with Tyrick in the lead.

Selene follows him, with the order going, Gideon, me, Seraphina, and Xeneera.

Tyrick looks over us all, "Alright, are you all ready?"

Heads bob as we nod in confirmation.

He turns back to the portal, taking one last deep breath before he presses his hand into the wall. He begins sinking through and steps into it, guiding the rest of us along with him.

Soon, all of us have made it through, and are greeted by several large guards, led by Bufort and Retalnia.

"I love you,
Queenslayer."

CHAPTER 59

MISTRESS AND QUEENSLAYER

SERAPHINA

You'd think if a bunch of wizards knew we were allies, they wouldn't be so quick to smite our little group.

Of course, I had underestimated the grudge these elderly mages held.

There's a *treaty* for a reason. But my gods.

The ground below scratches into my knees and the bones of my wings prick into my elbows from my arms tightened in magical cuffs behind my back. They didn't even bother taking us to a cell this time. They just restrained us outside the portal. It was as if they had a window to see who was coming, and were already here to take us.

They secured *all* of us as soon as we came in, even the little mage.

"If we knew your departure would end up bringing more vagrants to our realm, we wouldn't have let you leave," Bufort scoffs as he walks lazily along the line of us.

"Grand Master, we are merely passing through. We are going to talk to someone," he states nervously.

Bufort halts in his tracks as he stops in front of Asher, his form slowly turns to peer at Tyrick. His steps are precise and calculated, trying to allude to some level of dominance over us. But this man doesn't scare me in the slightest. He doesn't know what I'm capable of only because I've allowed him those pleasantries and I need his realm. He approaches Tyrick, turning on a heel to face him and glare daggers into the innocent mage.

"*Someone,* Tyrick? You know better than to withhold information from us," Bufort says gently to the trembling wizard.

Oh, that bastard definitely sent Tyrick to spy on us. That asshole.

"It's… it's very important for the demon's mission in their realm. He may have information that could be pivotal to the efforts in Tantalia."

Bufort's eyes narrow and he crouches to be eye-level with the small mage, "He?"

"Y-Yes… he…" Tyrick says as he gulps.

I roll my eyes before sighing over this ridiculous situation.

"Is there a reason you needed to bring two more demons and a *Drannar* to our realm?" he asks. His head tilts slowly in Xeneera's direction before he scales his eyes up and down her in utter disgust.

She doesn't notice the action as her head stays bowed, looking into the dirt submissively.

"She was rescued from The Never Realm by Seraphina. She is not of any consequence," Tyrick responds. He's attempting to inject some level of confidence into his tone.

He is failing.

Bufort looks Xeneera up and down one more time with a foul grimace and a shudder of disgust before he turns back to Tyrick, "How should *you* know? You've been gone but a fortnight. Has your allegiance strayed so far in such little time?"

"We're going to see the Oracle King Kyraxes on Infernal Summit," Asher calls from where he kneels. As I glance at him, he has not even turned his head in the direction of the mage. He seems just as fed up with all of this as I am as his head leans to the side, and he boringly glares at something in distance.

I imagine with how often he's been restrained he's used to the sort of punishment.

Bufort's eyes leave Tyrick as his head slides down to Asher in amusement, "So, the *human* wants to be of service now? Has Tantalia gotten to your bones yet, son?"

"Don't call me son. I'm tired of you looking down on us because of whatever ancient gripe you hold," Asher snips.

Ooooo, feisty Asher-dear. I like this.

Bufort rises from his position in front of Tyrick to lazily walk over to Asher, before he peers down at him with a sarcastic smile, "And what are *you* going to do about it? You not only have no magic, but you are also *restrained*."

Asher rolls his eyes, "I don't give a shit. You've insulted my mate, my brother, and my family. We have shown you nothing but kindness and you continue to impede our mission at every turn. It's childish."

Family?

Asher's simple words threaten to burst my heart.

"Perhaps you're all here to infiltrate our realm. How are we to know she hasn't spelled you to do all her dirty work?"

"I do all her dirty work. And I do it with *pleasure*," Asher challenges with a sly grin and a taunting glance. Choosing to keep his head forward instead of allowing Bufort the pleasure of looking at his face.

"Disgusting," Bufort sneers at Asher, "You'd betray your realm for filth like that?"

"Call my mate filth again, and you'll taste the inside of your skull. It would be within your best interest to hold your fucking tongue in my presence," Asher growls as his sly grin is replaced with cold fury. Purple shines in his eyes as his muscles expand. I can smell his shift and my heart plummets.

"Or what?" Bufort challenges as he crouches down in front of Asher, gripping tightly at his cheeks to pull him close. My eyes volley between the two as the energy between them climbs in an instant.

Fuck, fuck, fuck, fuck.

Asher stills for a moment, his eyes steady against Bufort's and his body tenses as he prepares to retaliate.

He's going to fuck up this truce.

"Asher…" I warn low, threading bits of ethereal control through my voice.

Asher's eyes widen as his neck tightens. He grits his teeth while he fights my command of him. Slow, heavy breaths expand his chest as his nostrils flare and I see the sharp point of fangs peek through his lips. But he can't go after this mage as much as I would like him to.

A rumble crawls from Asher's chest as he growls at the mage and I release him, his body jolting forward from the loss of my control.

His head turns to me slowly in contained rage, and I plead desperately through my eyes for peace.

"Tyrick. You're to meet with me, while your… *friends* wait at the exit portal. You will be escorted by guards to the archway and watched until your departure," Bufort finally says before he waves his wand at us.

Blood rushes through my hands as my cuffs are released and we're all able to stand.

The sound of clanking weapons against leathered breeches closes in around us as the large guards circle us. One by one they yank us by our elbow to lead us through town.

The long walk is unbearable as I wish we could have flown out there. But of course, one more notch in the rope.

If I thought the people of Kaithoon were afraid of us before… The majority rush in their shops and houses; with shouts of panic being heard from inside as they set their eyes on Selene, Xeneera, and me.

What absolutely vile creatures.

They know nothing of us and yet cower before us. Normally, this would be welcomed by me.

But not when we're merely passing through. There is nothing here for us but a gate.

Of course, the townsfolk only see us for what they know of our legend.

Blood thirsty. Men snatchers. Killers.

The list goes on.

It doesn't matter. They hold no candle to me in any form.

Eventually, we make it to the outskirts of the city, standing in front of the archway to Castaway Grove. The guards that surround us have been quiet, save the sound of their annoyingly loud, clanking armor. I take a moment to glance at Asher, whose face is contorted in angered annoyance. I can still scent his shift and see the slight glimmer of purple in his irises.

I place myself in front of him and take his face in my hands as I tempt his gaze onto me. "You need to calm down. You couldn't go after the mage. They are a necessary evil, even if we don't want them to be," I whisper. My eyes slide to the guards around us to make sure they don't make any moves.

Small swirls of purple mix with the green in his eyes as his upper lip thickens from the tips of his fangs that continue to peek from under it, "How could you let them talk about you like that? About *us* like that?" he growls, the timbre in his voice descending to feral depths.

"Because they're uneducated. They're foolish. I can handle my own, and they know nothing of our purpose. But we are going to need the mages. They have magic that we don't, and eventually we are going to have to see them again if Tyrick is to be a part of us."

Asher growls, his lip lifting in a snarl as his eyes predatorily slide around the small group. They linger on some of the guards with murderous rage.

"It will be okay, darling. There are more important things to set your sights on than a few measly mages."

His eyes land back on me, and he brings a hand to my jaw, his clawed thumb strokes at my cheek. The purple streaks inside retreat slowly, and his eyes clench shut as he takes a steeling breath.

"They called you filth, Seraphina," he murmurs.

"It doesn't bother me. They don't know the words they speak," I assure him.

Weight settles on my shoulder as he drops his head into the crook of my neck, stroking the side of my cheek softly. He breathes a tortured sigh, "It bothers *me*."

My chest throbs from his insistent protection and my stomach flutters when his head rises; his gorgeously sad eyes meeting my own.

"I know, my darling. But I can handle it. It'll be alright." I give him a sweet smile, and he returns a hesitant one of his own with a small tug at the corner of his lip.

He presses his forehead against mine as his eyes shut, "I love you, Mistress."

His admission sends wonderous butterflies through my belly. My chest threatens to implode with the emotions that restrain my heart at the mercy of this man.

"You have yielded for him, Seraphina." A distant ethereal voice echoes in my mind.

I have… And I will yield for Asher until the heavens fall. Until the sun singes the earth to ash, and the moon is swallowed by the sea.

Only ever for Asher.

"Right… as all things should be." The voice responds.

Through all the strife, and the things we have done to and for each other. For all the trials we have gone through.

For *this*. For *love*.

A soft smile forms against my lips, "I love *you*, Queenslayer."

He gives me a smirk as his eyes open, "I suppose I have brought this Queen down, haven't I?"

"To the depths, my dear."

He gives me a chuckle before he presses his lips to mine. Gentle strokes are felt up and down my braids as he pulls me close. Taking one last lick across my lips, he releases me, and I turn to our troupe.

Xeneera has been eerily silent. Her head bowed, and her hands clasped in front of her as she ignores the commotion.

My heart aches for her. She's barely a hundred, which is a young adult for an elf. But her experience outside of her lands has been full of unpleasantries. I truly hope when we get back to Tantalia I can get her back into The Pits to learn. I want to give her the strength that Lilith gave me. But without the expectation of sitting my chair.

MY chair…

I shake the thought from my head and turn to watch Selene and Gideon. They share passionate looks with each other as his hand caresses her jaw and he looks down in her eyes. Her hands grip the sides of his armor as she gazes adoringly at him and a smile tugs on my lips as I watch.

Good for you, Selene.

She deserves love. More than I feel I do.

Soon, I catch sight of the colored cloaks that are making their way toward us. Tyrick, Bufort and Retalnia slowly approach with Tyrick leading the crew; a nervous veil shrouding his features.

Tyrick takes his spot amongst our group as his head hangs. I take a tentative look over the mages.

Retalina has an indifferent gaze set upon her features. And yet, Bufort has a cocky air of confidence wafting around him.

"When you return to Kaithoon, you are to be led straight through. There will be no stops, we will not house you or your *kin*. The patrons of this town are already uneasy with such endeavors. I trust you would agree with this arrangement?" Bufort says with a smug smile.

I roll my eyes, "Sure thing… Bufort."

A snicker sounds from Asher as I turn to the portal, and the others follow close behind.

As my foot hits the stone of the marbled platform, I hear Bufort's voice call to us one last time, "Be careful out there, demon."

That earns one more eye roll from me as I slide through, only to be thrown onto the ground of the other side.

594

If I accepted the bond,
isn't that all it takes?

CHAPTER 60

FALLING

ASHER

*F**uck this portal. Exponentially.*

My time in the magical realms has been one of learning, of course.

And in that time, I have learned that this portal is dreadful.

There's no reason there shouldn't be an actual area to step out to. Why must we all fall from the sky one body on another as if being dumped from a bag?

It's ridiculous.

Eventually, the mass of bodies stops falling and I'm able to roll out from under the pile to catch my breath. My muscles twitch and prick as I inhale and stand. Dirt and grass sticks into my leathers and I frustratedly dust them all off.

"Insanity," I grumble as I stretch out and readjust my pack.

Everyone falling on you with all their gear is a nightmare that I hope to never live again. It's right up there next to that hellscape dream realm I was constantly thrust in to and the tunnels of Knogdagh.

Everyone finally rises from their fall. But not without a cacophony of pained groans and rattling weapons against leather. They all take a moment to survey the outside of the portal before we all turn to the small open space of trees nestled in the dense foliage on the outskirts of the forest.

These guys are so lucky. They didn't have to walk this ridiculous trail over several days.

Seraphina's voice carries over us as she walks to the tree line, turning around to face the rest of us as she props a leg on a log. "This is Castaway Grove. The last time I was here, we met a dryad named Junipher, who said she knew of Lilith. They were cast away during the Jilted Massacre."

Selene's head tilts as she listens, "Mother made this forest?"

"I suppose she did. They said the Drannars attacked the tree spirits in Tantalia during the massacre and she cast them outside of the realm. This is where they came for safety."

My gaze slides to Xeneera beside me, who looks nervously into the woods, her features deepening in sadness as she learns more of the injustices her people had served.

My hand makes to grip her shoulder in comfort, because I was there once.

"It'll be alright. We're making it better together now," I remind her.

Xeneera's red eyes slowly meet mine, glossy with tears as she nods gently, "Yes… yes we are."

Empathy pulls my lips into a smile before I turn to Seraphina.

"There is also no magic here. So, good luck using it," she states matter-of-factly.

Selene scoffs and crosses her arms in annoyance before Gideon raises his hand, "But Mistress, Selene is right here."

Selene blushes before she nudges Gideon playfully. A sly grin spreads across his face as he catches her nudge and pulls her in close.

My eyes roll as I walk to the tree line next to Seraphina, "Alright love birds, enough bullshit, time is of the essence."

With that, I step through the thicket and follow the green vine that takes us to Castaway Beach.

It feels as if there isn't enough time to get through this forest, even with the trail being laid for us.

It doesn't help that Gideon keeps asking a menagerie of dumb questions to keep spirits high.

I tuned him out hours ago and have been ruminating on my own.

Everything jumbles together in my head in a flurry of words.

The mate's thing, this damn book, the cavernous rift that has grown between Cedric and I, saving Tantalia. All of it.

I still don't understand what mates mean entirely. Even if I feel as if I've accepted it, there is something missing. I've admitted I love her. I know that the world would cease to be without her. And yet when I tempt a tug on that little thread, it pulls me straight into brick. When I feel like it should lead me straight into her.

I feel happy with Seraphina, and I would smite anything that tried to do her any wrong. But there is a gap in my soul that I'm not able to pinpoint and it pulls at me.

If I accepted the bond, isn't that all it takes? Is that what that voice talked about with surrendering? Because I feel as if I had already done that.

At least emotionally.

But the beast that pulls at me when I anger is still there. It still makes its appearance. It presses me to protect her or fuck her.

There is no in between.

If I accepted it, wouldn't the beast be kept away? With it baring its teeth, that means there's something I haven't done yet. And I'm frustrated with the absurdity of it all. I don't like not being in control of myself and with this monster inside, I lose all sense of control. I'm at the mercy of what *it* wants.

It's maddening.

The other thought is this book. We thought it would be the end all, be all and everything would be fixed. This book was supposed to save this realm.

But of course, there had to be another catch.

One thing after the next -- it seems like the universe keeps telling us to stop trying. But we can't.

I know I would never be able to get Seraphina to stop. That'd be a futile undertaking.

Seraphina's soft voice comes from beside me as we continue walking through the woods. Her hand wraps around my forearm as she catches up with me.

The rest of the group are in conversations of their own behind us as we continue leading the way.

"You've been rather quiet, Asher-darling."

I give her a small, thin lipped smile before nodding, "Just in my head."

"Care to let me in?" she asks with a kind smile.

My lip tilts in amusement as I peek at her from the corner of my eye, "Everything is just a lot... *all* the time."

Seraphina sighs as she steps over a giant root in the ground, "It is…"

"I still don't understand the mates' thing. Or why I transform when I'm angry."

"Ahhh… yes… I suppose that information would be important for you to know," she says nervously.

I look to her as I halt, "So, you *know* why I've been angry? Why haven't you told me?"

She puts her hands up at the shoulder, her brows raising as she surrenders, "I didn't find a place I could interject it, otherwise I *would* have. And I have no problem telling you *now* if you would like to listen."

My eyes narrow on her before I continue the trek forward, "Go on."

"Magical mating bonds, at least from what I do know, give the weaker species traits of the stronger species for better survival. But because you haven't accepted the bond, you don't have control over it. It's just an anger response to the thing inside that seeks to complete the bond."

Gods damnit. That's… interesting… and scary all at once.

Is that why I could see and hear better? And the fangs and claws?

I've got to admit, that is nice. Especially as a hunter. But even still, it's a maddening thing to learn.

"How have we not completed the bond yet? What do you mean?"

Seraphina sighs again, "There is a ritual… but there is no information on it. Too many variables between pairs and their needs to pinpoint something of note. There has never really been *mates* among our kind. Not usually. But we are taught certain aspects of it in case The Fates decided us worthy of such a thing."

"So, we aren't fully bonded yet?"

"No… no, not yet," Seraphina admits.

"And I have no control over this beast inside of me until the bond is complete?"

"This appears to be the case, yes. Especially with your anger so easily triggered, there is something we are missing about this entire situation."

Great. Just like I assumed.

Two steps forward, ten steps back.

I have to admit, it is much more infuriating than I could have ever imagined.

"Perhaps we could ask Kyraxes if he knows anything about the bond," Seraphina suggests in comfort.

The idea is good, and I don't know why we keep forgetting we have an oracle dragon on our side. It gives me a little bit more hope for our future as we continue through the forest.

"I talked to Cedric the night that you two had your skirmish," Seraphina says as she dips under a hanging vine.

My lip contorts in a grimace as I glance at her. "Terrific."

She places a gentle hand against my elbow, "There is more to his *own* anger than you think."

My eyes narrow as they shift focus to all of her and I halt on the path again. "What are you saying?"

Seraphina sighs before she grasps my chin in her hands, "Asher-darling. There are many more things wrong with this world than a tiff with the only brother you can speak to. Make amends while you have the time. Because I never got to say goodbye to my dear Velaria."

A sadness swirls at her irises as I watch the thoughts in her mind drift. Her focus draws on me with a pained smile before she stands on her tiptoes to press a gentle kiss to my lips, her bright eyes caring as she strokes my jaw with her clawed hand.

I return her smile with a skeptical one of my own.

The sight of Cedric taunting *my* Seraphina during my bout of rage, it flashes through my mind, and I feel like I see red. The fact he was so close to her when I couldn't be. The way he continues to cause problems. Perhaps another time I'd hear her out. But not now. Not after he pissed on my territory.

Gideon's voice breaks my focus as it breaks through the trees, "Hey, so are there any rules for these dragons when we go to see them?"

Seraphina and I turn to Gideon, who has now secured Selene on his shoulders as he walks through the forest.

"Is there a reason you aren't walking?" Seraphina asks Selene with a bored sigh.

"I didn't want to get my boots dirty," Selene shrugs as she tugs at the dark brown strands of Gideon's hair and kicks her feet lazily on either side of his shoulders.

Seraphina rolls her eyes as she perches her hands on her hips, "As far as we know, no. However, Kyraxes, will know things you don't. So, prepare for whatever things he might say."

Xeneera's brow furrows in concern as she looks to Seraphina, "Is he… are they going to attack me because of…?" she asks nervously.

My eyes slide to Seraphina as Xeneera awaits her answer. Her face contorts in an empathic sadness for the little elf girl, and she approaches her, kneeling to grasp her hands in her own.

Seraphina's tail takes gentle swishes behind her as she speaks, "Xeneera, you are not your people. Just as I am not *my* people. It's *what* we do with our time here, not *who* gave it to us."

Xeneera steels her gaze as she looks at Seraphina, nodding in understanding.

"Kyraxes will see the pureness of your heart, not the darkness it came from."

Xeneera smiles at that and nods once more before Seraphina stands and comes to lead the rest of the group with me.

She strides past me with a soft pat against my chest as she burrows deeper through the forest. Her sights set on the trail beyond.

I make to follow her, my eyes locked onto her strong wings and her tail that slowly swipes at some of the twigs in my way as she walks.

Her strength, loyalty and power are so inherently ferocious that I can't help but admire every aspect of her. Her leadership, her willingness to do the unthinkable, even when faced with defeat after defeat. She has grit and passion unlike anything I've ever seen in her fight for her family, and her realm.

While the mate's thing may have me in a tizzy, there is one thing I am sure of.

I am desperately in love with this demon.

"I... NEED. YOU."

CHAPTER 61

THE HUNTER AND THE DEMON

SERAPHINA

After several hours of trekking, we've finally made it to Cast-away Beach.

However, by the time our feet hit the sand, the moon is high in the sky, leaving us to rest on the shore for the night before we set off for Infernal Summit in the morning.

We all relieve ourselves of our packs and sit down with a sigh of relaxation against the trees.

The gentle waves of the water crest in and out against the shoreline, lapping at the sand in calming splashes. The sound presses me to gaze out at the moonlit waters. Rough bark scrapes against my wings and back as I settle against a tree off the edge of the forest, but at least the sand cradles my rump nicely.

Moon beams dance on the surface of the sea beyond as it continues rising in the night.

Every shine of the moon brings me back to Lilith. *She* was Queen of the Night. She was the moon to me. My heart sinks into my stomach as I watch it glow from afar.

And I desperately hope that it's her glow that shines down on us now.

I would hope she would approve of my actions since her death. I would hope even now she would be proud of me. I would hope that she would love to see me in her seat, even if I didn't want to see myself on it.

The relaxing splashes settle my being and will me into calm, and soon my eyes slowly begin to blink shut. The night fades away until strong arms come to cradle me in their warmth.

The oak and iron scent of Asher's hair floods my senses, and his arm wraps around my middle in protective longing. His face nuzzles deep into my chest as we relax against the sand.

"Hello, Asher-dear," I coo softly as I run my clawed hands through the soft strands.

He mumbles something unintelligible as he swings a leg over mine, bringing me closer to his body.

The feeling settles my being and wanes my worries, allowing me to meld into him.

"Sera…" he whispers.

"Hm, Asher-love?" I murmur back as I coil a lock of his hair around my talon. I watch the way the strands circle the sharpened claw, getting lost in this feeling of bliss for a few moments.

"I… I think I need you."

My brow furrows as I look down at him, "Right now?"

My eyes track to the others, who have laid themselves against the trees or their packs, with soft breathing pulsing through the leaves as they relax. Selene and Gideon are cuddled on one another, with Selene laying on the mountainous Gideon like a massive flesh bed.

Tyrick has set himself against his pack and covered his body with his cloak, turning over to give us his back while Xeneera has curled into a ball deeper in the forest.

Asher shifts in the sand, and it brings my attention back to him as he sits up to look at me, "I… need. *You.*"

His brilliant jade eyes swirl with a menagerie of emotions, a plethora of feelings.

All of them *begging* for me.

What would possess him to claim me at such a time? Who knows.

But I *do* know that he speaks a deep truth. I can feel his words seep into me. They cause a rush of desire to pulse through me, spearing straight to my core.

Asher stands from the sand, dusting himself off before he offers me a hand. My palm slides into his and urgency hits me all at once. His eyes glide around our friends, who are all slowly falling asleep.

He guides me down the beach, into a small area of thinned out trees. Every so often, he looks back at our friends to make sure no one is following us.

His strength tugs me into the forest before he presses my back against the tree. Flutters are set ablaze low in my belly and my heart beats rapidly in my chest.

Soft lips latch onto mine in hungry desire as his hands slide down my armor. When they find my hips, he grips tightly and pulls me flush against him. His scent changes; from oak and iron to burnt embers and spice. It causes the pulses in my core to increase even more.

"I have to have you, I couldn't wait, I'm so sorry," he murmurs into the kiss, his tongue slipping across my lips to request him entry.

"What are you sorry for?" I murmur against his lips as my arms wrap around his neck.

"It's inopportune. But the way you've fought for us. The way you *lead* us. It's so fucking electrifying; I thought about it the entire way here." His voice rumbles against my lips as he presses harder against me. His cock is stiff under his breeches, and it shows me how badly he really *does* need me right now.

Cool air hits my lips as he pulls away, and his hair scratches at my forehead as he leans in to rest it against mine. One of his hands slides up my body to rest against the tree above my head, bracing himself against it, his other hand stroking with restraint on my side. Soft pants blend into the small space between us as he steadies himself.

"Seraphina, I know that this mate's thing has been difficult for me. But if this is what it feels like to be bound to you, I never want it to end," he says softly. Falling bark slides past my line of sight as his hand comes from the tree to caress my cheek. His eyes meet mine in fierce longing; sheer admiration and relentless passion all swirl together in the brilliant emerald hues.

"Where is this coming from?" I ask as I grip tighter at the hardened armor on his sides.

This morning, he seemed so in his head. So for him to need me like this, *now*, causes curiosity to tingle at my skin.

He sighs as his eyes drift to my neck, his knuckles brushing against the soft skin there. "In the forest, when you calmed Xeneera's broken heart. The way you keep forging a path that no one else dared to walk and the way you took the punches from Bufort all in the name of protecting Tantalia. You do so much for us and everyone else all the time. It just pulls me in deeper and deeper. And whether I wanted to accept it in the beginning or not, you *saved* me, my love."

My heart swells at the way he views me, the way he puts me on a pedestal I don't feel I deserve. I'm just doing right by Lilith and Velaria, everything else is just to try and save the ones worth saving.

But the energy that pumps off him… the love that thickens the air around us. That much is there. *That* much is real.

And I can't help the way I lean into him, kissing him tenderly as I wrap myself around him.

Asher gives in, devouring my mouth in tender licks and kisses as his strong hands leave my hips to grasp under my thighs and pin me against the tree.

His mouth travels down my jaw until he reaches my neck, peppering soft kisses into the delicate flesh as he rubs himself against me. His hardened cock against my clothed center causes slickness to dampen my core and my breath lightens.

The friction builds and causes sparks of desire to skitter through my blood the longer he stays outside of me.

Unwrapping my legs from his waist, I make quick work of removing our breeches. Granted, it is a tad harder to remove leather armored clothing, but I try to work as fast as I can.

His cock stands hard and ready for me, pressing against my lower stomach as he wraps me in his arms. The warmth of his skin causes the hair on my body to rise in anticipation.

He lifts me with ease, pressing me back against the tree where I feel his cock tease my dripping entrance.

The sensation causes my thoughts to evaporate as I savor way he opens me with his thickness.

The rough bark scratches against the base of my wings as he presses me deeper, using the tree as leverage to release one of my thighs and grab his cock to rub against my clit.

The pleasure bursts through my body as he slides against it with ease. A stifled moan fights against the lip I have clenched between my teeth.

"There she is… there's those fucking moans, Sera," he murmurs. His lips meet mine, swallowing every one of my desperate sounds.

My head tilts back as I try to regain sense of where I am, but all I can feel is the head of him against me.

"Gods…" he groans as he presses his cock to my entrance, slowly pushing himself in.

My breath hitches, feeling him everywhere, all at once. His thickness stretches me more and more, with my thoughts descending into a realm of ecstasy I've never stepped foot in.

Every inch of him stretches me farther and my claws grip above my head, spearing into the wood to hold me in place.

Soon, he's pressed himself to the hilt and every portion of him seems to fill every single portion of me.

"Asher," I pant softly as I adjust to him.

"I've got you, angel. You're doing so good for me," he whispers as his cock slides in and out of me.

I try so hard to keep my moans down and quiet, but I can't. Not with the way he feels right now.

Something about this is different. Everything else didn't have nearly as much passion as this. Not even when he accepted the idea of being mates.

This is a *primal* sort of love. Something that would stand the test of time.

His teeth sink into my neck as his hands grip tight into the flesh of my thighs, almost holding on for dear life as he presses in and out of me in deliberate strokes.

His groans grow louder as he loses himself and soon, his thrusts pick up. He slides through me as if it's the last time he'll ever touch me again.

Every press of his fingers and lips against me begs me to fall apart in his grasp. Begs me to surrender to his soul.

"My Queen. My Mistress. My *love*," he pants almost to himself.

My moans begin to echo through the forest as he claims every part of me and I let go. The bark of the tree scratches against my wings as he thrusts, sending small shoots of delicious pain through me in time with his movements.

"Seraphina, your moans… Gods, your *fucking* moans… Give them all to me," he pants as his head leans into my neck. The hot, damp press of his skin against mine sends fire through my veins and my cunt tightens around him. The pleasure in me rises to insane heights as it reaches the edge.

I unlatch my hands from the bark to wrap myself tightly around his body as he continues thrusting up into me, holding on for dear life as my orgasm crashes through me and stars blast against my clenched eyelids in brilliant rays of light.

A scream shudders through me as he pounds harder and deeper, his grunts turning primal as I feel him spill into me.

Rumbles vibrate my nipples against the inside of my armor as he growls and continues to press every ounce of himself into me, relishing in the way it coats him.

Wobbly steps carry us to the beach before he kneels and rests my back on the sand.

His chest rises from mine and he looks down at me. The moon shines on the small drips of sweat on his brow, alluding to his efforts. His calloused hands run down the soft skin of my thighs, pressing into the skin there to open me wide for him. Taking slow, precise strokes into me, his eyes travel to where we're joined, and he seems to glow with pride.

My chest rises and falls in calculated succession and I take in his slow pace, feeling every single piece of him he offers me.

"This is mine…" Asher murmurs almost to himself as he watches our union.

"All yours," I manage to murmur as I try to get a grip on the intense sensation coursing through me. His cock shoots pleasure wave after pleasure wave into my veins and my body can barely contain it.

His eyes flick to mine as he hears my voice, a devilish grin wiping over his features as he pins his stare into me.

"*All* mine," he growls as he leans down between my legs, still pressing himself in and out of me in torturously slow strokes. He caresses my cheek in gentle brushes as he gazes into my eyes. A palpable tenderness swirls in the emerald pools of his.

I writhe under him, swirling my hips to match his languid movements.

"I needed this," he whispers against my lips. "I needed you."

"I needed you too," I whisper back as I rest my arms around his neck, soft breaths cresting in and out of my chest as I come down from my climax.

His body begins laying deeper onto me, his cock still held within as he holds me in his arms.

"No… I needed you. My whole life, I think I've needed *you*. You are everything I have ever needed. Everything that I didn't even *know* I wanted." The kisses on my lips trail down my chin, down my jaw before they press softly into my neck as he speaks, his breath warm against my skin as he slows his thrusts to a halt.

My brow furrows as I run my hands through his hair, listening to his softened voice.

"There was always something missing… There was a piece of me lost somewhere in the world. I just didn't know that that piece was you."

My heart threatens to burst, the emotion behind this and the fact he's still held himself inside of me as he admits these things to me.

"There is no corner of this world I wouldn't follow you to. There is no place on this earth that I'd go without you. And my heart would cease to beat if you were to leave this land behind."

A purple glow shines bright between us, as the gem on my amulet begins to illuminate. The metal at its back heats fervently as he speaks.

"Seraphina, in this life and every life onward, I am yours. At your feet. At your side. And in your corner. I yield to the being you are, and the being you will become. I yield to everything you've ever been, and I will yield until the breath leaves my chest, and my heart pounds no more. I'd forgo my realm, my weapons, and my very freedom just to sit at your feet. Just to breathe your air. I am yours in mind, body, and soul, my love. For all of eternity," he says softly as he leans back up to connect his eyes with mine. His thumb slides back and forth against my cheek as the emerald pools shine with promise, with strength and with pure determination. "I love you, Seraphina Moonsong," he whispers.

My lips part on a breathless gasp as my eyes search the depths of his soul, and even now… every word he says, he says with every ounce of truth he possesses.

"And I yield to you. To your love, to your care. To your soul and your heart. To your strength and your courage, and to your kindness. The Legion's would dissolve, and I'd throw my crown in the sea and let Tantalia burn to ash, if it meant I could feel your embrace for all of my eternity. I give you all that I can offer, in mind, in body, in spirit, and I relinquish my being to yours… To you, Asher Blackwood. To *us*," I respond.

As our words finish, power surges through me, and heated strength warms every inch of my skin. As if my magic has surfaced, it presses against my veins in a violent rush of energy. That meager thread of connection between us pulls taut against my chest, thickening into a rope of pure, undying emotion. Sadness, pain, happiness, love, indifference. All of them visceral and raw against my insides.

A gasp erupts from my throat as my back bows against the sand, Asher's body straightens from mine before it curves back, and a brilliant purple light beams from the amulet to spear into his chest. He bends back, his arms gripping the air at his sides as if an invisible restraint has held him hostage. And a loud, pained groan exits his throat.

The longer the power courses through me, the more precise I feel its trajectory.

Pinning right through the crystal and into Asher, his body glows in magenta shimmer. Bright crimson begins to shine from the tree line, bursting forth through the dark and into Asher's back, coursing through his chest to meet my own light. It mixes in a majestic shade of mauve. An orb of power and light dances between us as it continues to course through our bodies.

His memories, his light, his dark. His emotions, his thoughts, they explode through my head in sporadic visions of a life I've never lived. Visions of Vesperholm, rats, potions, people I've never met, places I've never been. Treehouses. Empty cities. Destroyed shops. Rusted weapons. Dirt walls and a fired hearth.

All through the eyes of this mate of mine.

The brilliant light between us slowly shrinks before it swallows itself and bursts forth in a heavy sweep of rippling waves across the land, as far as the eye can see. My body relaxes as the power surging through me cools through my blood.

My chest heaves in deep breaths as I settle my gaze on Asher. His eyes are wide and glazed over as they connect with mine.

The blue ring around his pupil has transformed, turning bright purple against the vibrant green. It shines with a mesmerizing contrast of color, as his hair shimmers between silver and deep onyx in waves before it all darkens with the night.

Of *us*.

"The… the bond…" he pants.

"The bond, Asher-dear," I say with a soft smile.

But now, I feel whole. I feel complete. I feel like everything I've ever known has come together into this one moment with Seraphina.

Chapter 62

The Dagger

Asher

This *feeling* that runs through my veins… It's unlike anything I've ever felt before. It's as if I've tapped into a power I never knew to exist. With the rage, the power was there, but I had no leash on it. There was no control, and it felt like I was at the whim of some other *thing*. When I first had sex with Seraphina, it was just a small sliver of whatever is pumping through my veins right now. Even though it slowly fades away as I come down from this feeling of her.

With this it's *pure* strength. I have my wits about me and there is no rage in sight.

Even though, now, the power is dull. I can't imagine what it would be like to be in a realm of actual magic. I suppose I'll find out.

The feeling that overtook me during the bonding that just happened, it threatened to break me in half. It tore into my being at an inconceivable rate.

And with it, the monster inside was vanquished. I felt it die; with its bones and pieces within, it weaved into my soul, becoming one.

The beast that had been pulling at my soul for so long grew and burst through my chest, until I could barely hold on to the land of the living.

But now, I feel *whole*. I feel complete. I feel like everything I've ever known has come together into this one moment with Seraphina.

As I pull out of the frenzy in my mind, my gaze connects with Seraphina's bright purple one. She stares deep into my soul, as if everything I've ever done has risen to this point in a grand symphony of unity.

"Asher-dear," I hear.

But Seraphina's lips don't move.

My forehead tenses as I peer closer at her.

"What is he doing?"

Her lips stay still, and her head tilts in curiosity.

"Seraphina… why can I hear you in my head?" I ask in a soft murmur.

"What?" she asks with a shock of tension that contorts her features.

"You… you said Asher-dear. But your lips didn't move."

Her forehead creases as her eyes narrow on me in concentration, *"You can hear me?"*

I release a yelp that echoes through the night, as her voice enters my brain again. My body scrambles through the sand as I jump back, "I can *hear* your thoughts!"

Seraphina flashes a devilish, fanged grin as she tilts her head and narrows her eyes again, *"Asher-dear, please be careful. You don't want to get sand on your cock."*

I look down to realize I'm still naked from our tryst on the beach, and my hands furiously move to cover myself up, "Stop that!"

Seraphina lets out a hearty laugh as she comes to stand, skipping merrily over to the edge of the beach to retrieve our clothing.

She tosses my leather breeches to me as I cover myself but another yelp rings through the air as a spear of heat scorches my skin. The leather breeches fall from my grasp and into the sand, where small clouds of smoke slowly rise from the folds.

"What the fuck…" I murmur as I kick the material around.

The black wisps billow from in between the leathers as it flips over itself, to reveal my dagger. Intense heat and the scent of burned meat fill the air as the metal blade and decorative handle glow in a heated crimson.

Seraphina has pulled her breeches back on and saunters over to me. Her head tilts as she investigates the plumes of smoke. "What's going on?"

"My dagger... it's–" I explain as I hover my hand above the blade. It has burned a hole through my breeches, and I sigh as I realize I'll have one less sheath to secure it to.

Great.

"It's fine, Asher-dear, your armor has plenty of pockets," Seraphina waves off.

"Stop listening to my head!" I groan.

Seraphina leans over to grab my dagger; the metal continues its glow as her hand sizzles against it.

"Sera, you're going to burn yourself!" I say as I reach for the blade.

She stops me, waving a finger in my direction, and rips the dagger out of my reach. "Asher-darling, a little hot metal is nothing. Calm yourself."

I roll my eyes as I grab my breeches and wave them out in the air.

As I pull them on, a gaping hole is revealed. Burned and crisped on the side of my thigh where my dagger usually lays.

I groan as I look back at Seraphina, crossing my arms against my chest.

Her eyes slide slowly back and forth along the handle and hilt of my dagger intensely, holding it close to her eyes in the moonlight. "Where did you get this?" she asks quietly.

"It was given to me by my father. It's The Blackwood Dagger."

Her eyes stay focused on the weapon, grazing over it several more times, "This handle... it was made in Tantalia."

My brow furrows in confusion, and my lips tense as I look at her, "What the fuck are you talking about?"

"These designs, this metal. It's from Tantalia. Where did your father get this?"

"It's just a dagger that has been passed down through our generations. It's the only weapon that can kill a succubus with just a cut."

Seraphina's hands quickly retreat from the blade, as if the heat had finally got her, – though, I know it didn't – and a small hiss sparkles from the sand as it falls to the ground.

"We have to have the elders look at it when we get back to Tantalia," she mutters absentmindedly as she begins to walk to the rest of our sleeping group.

I watch the blade for a moment before I reach down to grab it. The metal handle is still hot as I bounce it from hand to hand, and I run to toss it into the ocean. A loud, burbling sizzle sounds off as it sinks into the black water against the shoreline.

Even from the few feet away that I am, the ruby on its hilt beams a brilliant red against the shallow edge of the beach, somewhat pulsing as it awaits me.

My brow furrows and I make my way to the shoreline. I wave my hand through the water, tapping gently against the once hot metal, to make sure the heat has been extinguished enough for me to take hold of it.

When I find the coast to be clear, I pull it from the water, looking over the things even *I* might have missed.

There's not much I imagine I would have missed with this blade. It's been with me for as long as I could hold a weapon. It was one of the first things that solidified my hunter status in Vesperholm. And even looking at it now, there is nothing that sticks out to me as odd or different. It's just a series of swirls and patterns that seem to collide with one another.

I study the blade for a moment longer before I go to sheath it in a separate pocket on my body, and I walk down the beach to meet up with Seraphina and the others.

The rest have fallen asleep, and Seraphina has gotten comfortable against the tree where I initially cuddled with her. Her arms open to welcome me and a smile spreads across my face as I come to meet her.

I nuzzle into her body, sinking deep into the feel of her against me. I throw my arm and leg around her as I pull her in close, relaxing against the leather bodice of her armor. Her heart beats slowly, and it calms every beat in mine.

I inhale her glorious scent but there's something different about it, triggering something much more primal in me.

But I don't have time to mull over it, because soon her wings wrap us in a warm, intimate cocoon and we fall asleep against the beach.

The next morning, a fervent heat beats down on us as the sun rises high in the sky.

A rough noise escapes me as I turn over against Seraphina and hide my face from the light.

I always try to take these small moments with Seraphina as much as I can. Even more so, with how full my heart feels with her. And as much as I would like to now, something else has thrown a crater into that path.

A tight grip wraps around my ankles, yanking me from Seraphina's grasp to drag me across the sand.

I release an annoyed groan as I kick against the strength hauling me away from my beloved. I turn over and see the being who decided to ruin my quiet morning.

Gideon.

"What the hell is your problem?!" I shout as he finally releases my legs.

"You guys said we're going to see dragons. You just *expect* me not to be excited on dragon day?"

I roll my eyes as I stand, brushing the sand from my body and stretching the sleep off of my bones.

Gideon's eyes connect with the giant burnt hole in my breeches and his brow furrows in question, "The fuck happened to your pants?"

I look down with a sigh, dusting some more of the caught sand from the hole, "Long story."

His eyes turn away from me to beam at the tree line. The dark blue glistens with excitement as Selene comes toward us.

Her smile is kind and sleepy as she approaches but slowly changes to a grimace the closer she gets. She creeps up to me with a curious expression, her nose sniffing furiously over my body.

"Something… happened… Why do you smell like that? And why is your hair black?" Selene asks as she comes to stand beside Gideon with an arm around his waist.

"Nothing. Probably just forest smell," I lie as I look to the tree line.

Xeneera and Tyrick are stretching and yawning as they begin to wake for the day.

"No, no, no. I know forest scent… This isn't that."

Her eyes narrow on me, surveying me.

"You've completed the bond," she says with wide eyes.

Gods damnit.

"How can you tell that from just a scent?" I groan.

"There is a scent when there is a close connection between beings. Usually you scent of wood and metal. This is like the wood has been lit on fire and someone threw flowers on it."

I roll my eyes as I wave her off, "Absurd. We need to get going."

Seraphina trots to us with a smile. Her body is loose and relaxed as she approaches, and it makes my heart pound with an urgency.

Even *her* scent from this far away drives me insane. And upon seeing her, I can't help the way my cock begins to throb.

Fucking hells. Please, not right now.

"Awe. You don't want a little morning tryst on the beach, Asher-darling?" I hear Seraphina's voice as it threads through my thoughts.

I peer into her eyes, and decide to play her little game, *"How's it feel?"*

"Not as good as when your cock is inside of me, but I'll take it." Her voice is sweet and taunting, like beautiful music against the inside of my skull. Her gorgeous eyes glimmer with challenge.

I groan an exasperated noise as Tyrick and Xeneera come to meet the rest of us. They've secured their packs and Xeneera looks entirely too exhausted to be awake right now. Tyrick has his hands on his hips as he looks out to the expanding sea before us.

"So, how is this going to work? There's no boat and only two of you can fly to the summit," Tyrick asks.

Seraphina turns in the direction of the columns of smoke in the distance, and her wings make small, twitching movements as she stands silently for a moment in thought.

I try to zero in on her, seeing if I can listen to anything in her mind, but it's been blocked. As if I try to approach it and there's a black wall there instead of her mind.

"Nice try, Asher-darling. You have to learn how to ward your thoughts."

Her voice breaks through my mind with ease and I groan as I try and push her voice away, to no avail.

She stares off a little while longer before she turns around to us, "I will fly to Infernal Summit on my own. Once I'm there, I will send a dragon to secure the rest of you."

"Why not you and Selene?" Tyrick asks.

This earns a small growl from Gideon as he glares daggers at the small wizard.

"If something happens, there will be no one here to protect you from the mythical creatures lurking about these woods."

Shoulders shrug as they accept Seraphina's reasoning. Her steps squish in the wet sand as she comes to me and presses a soft kiss to my lips, "I'll be back soon, Asher-dear," she whispers.

The idea of not being by her side aches. It's a *deep* sensation I've never experienced.

I want to be glued to her. I want to be in her skin at this moment, and that's the only thing that feels out of my control.

But I nod anyway, even though it pains me to see her fly so far without me.

She strokes my jaw with a soft caress before she lunges into the sky. Flying far, far away, to the plumes of black smoke in the distance.

"THESE... THESE SYMBOLS
ARE NOT OF THIS LAND."

Chapter 63

Unintelligible Truths

Seraphina

The air this morning is magnificent as it whips at my braids. Cool wind blares against my eardrums as I speed my way to the summit.

I must be as fast as I can, because the way it feels to be away from Asher right now, is abhorrent. Like a chunk of my chest has been ripped clean out.

And as much as I would like to enjoy the sky right now. There is something much more prevalent squealing through my mind.

This meager bond that kept pricking and pulling at a black wall had given way to a burst of brilliant light and energy. My own being threaded through his in a tangled web of light and dark.

The feeling of this energy combination is so foreign. It feels as if there is another being's soul in my chest, and it is *powerful.*

More so than I could ever conceive.

There is nothing that Asher and I can't accomplish together and that is something I feel *deep* within me.

I had never been one for romantic love. It was not something I ever lingered on or wished for. The halflings disgusted me. The humans in Vesperholm even more so. There was no one I ever had my eye on in that sense. And I was perfectly fine with that life.

But Asher… whether The Fates had made this connection more than what it really is or not, I'm unsure. I do know how it feels to be loved by him. To be cared for in a way that I never thought I needed.

I suppose it would make sense. If I can't care for myself when the whole world crashes down upon me, how can I even imagine taking care of that world that threatens to crush *me*?

I had no idea the implications of such care until I met Asher. There are so many times where I don't know if I could have carried the weight of it all until he picked up my head and held me by the waist to drag me through it. He has replenished a strength in me I had no idea was empty. I always thought I could do it on my own and that I would be able to do the things I needed to without the impact of a romantic partner. Of course, those things are foreign in Tantalia. We merely fuck and take. There isn't really a such thing as *partners*.

But I am happy I found out. Because this feeling of love with him… I don't think I would trade it for anything else in this world.

On the other side of the coin, though, there is the matter of his dagger.

The handle is so intricately designed, and it's *silver*. The same metal we use in our weapons.

I have no idea where he could have gotten something like this.

Perhaps it was stolen off a succubus years ago. But there is something inherently regal about that blade.

If it did belong to a succubus, why would it have the power to kill *any* of us with such ease?

I should have taken a better look at the damn thing before all of this. He always has it on him and is constantly playing with it.

The thoughts run through my head, until the powerful scent of dragon leather and scorched rock break through the rabble.

My gaze sets forth on the glowing mountain in the distance.

Taking a hard bank, I make to land. Roars tremble into the air, and jets of the dragons fired breath beams up at me in hello.

I decide to have a little fun as I approach, and weave back and forth through the blaze as the dragons of Infernal Summit greet me with a brilliant revelry of fire and smoke.

Brimstone fills my nostrils and heat licks at my wings as I bank in and out of their hellos, before my boots plant into the blackened rock below.

Kyraxes' deafening steps pound against the landscape as he approaches.

Small dragons fly around his head as he lumbers down the mountain.

"Seraphina Moonsong. At last, we meet again," his deep voice shakes the earth as his clouded eyes meet mine.

"My friends are on the beach across the ocean, is there a way you can send a dragon to retrieve them?" I ask quickly before we get into specifics. My vision drifts to one of the small brownish dragons that circle his head, "Who are these little guys?"

One zooms around my head, and its wings flutter furiously as it hovers in front of me. It blows a huff of steam in my face that scents of rotted meat and dragon flame.

I cough as I wave the smoke away, watching as the little creature swirls and dives around the sky.

"Right before I was taken from my land, Vizzuu had laid eggs. I had not had the pleasure of fertilizing them before I was captured. When I returned, I was able to fulfill my duties, and they hatched." Kyraxes clouded gaze sets on the three flying dragons around him and his leathered lips pull in a small smile as he watches them fly.

His eyes come back to me, narrowing as he inhales a gust of air from me.

"You've completed the bond."

My eyes widen and I give a nervous smile, "We have."

"That is what The Fates have asked of you. Among other things."

Don't remind me.

I nod softly before Vizzuu joins us, her golden eyes are bright as she gets wind of me, "Seraphina, a pleasure to see you on our lands again."

I bow in hello, "The pleasure is mine, Vizzuu. From one Queen to another."

Vizzuu's head tilts in admiration as Kyraxes' voice breaks through our greeting, "I shall send Xykes for them."

I give him a nod in thanks. "I appreciate your gratitude, friend."

Kyraxes' head turns slowly to the flaming mountain. The ground trembles as his ribs vibrate, and his jaw unhinges for him to release a deafening roar into the sky. The air itself feels like it quakes with the timbre, and I feel it through every bone in my body.

For a moment, nothing happens. Then a flash of black bursts from the glowing crater behind Kyraxes. Large globs of bright orange, burning rock flings from the mass as it ascends higher and higher. The splatters fall through the air and splat onto the mountain or into the water with a sizzling hiss.

Xykes banks hard toward us to land on the ground beside Kyraxes with a quaking thud.

My body wobbles as I try to stay standing and the intimidating dragon looks down at me with boredom, "So, it is the demon that has called for our aid. As expected."

"My friends are on Castaway Beach. The majority of them are unable to fly over the ocean and it would take too much time to have them all come one by one."

Xykes huffs an annoyed noise before he trudges for the shore. His stomps cause the earth to tremble under my feet, and his tail barely misses me as his body turns. He lunges for the air and the torrent of wind from his wings blows black dust, pebbles and sand around us in a hurricane of volcanic debris.

I wave the dust from my face as I watch him beat through the sky. Soon, my gaze comes to meet Kyraxes. And the weight of this mission comes hurtling back down onto me.

His gaze is steady and sure as he takes a moment to look over me. "You've come about The Compendium."

Damnit.

"I have… I can't read it."

Kyraxes tilts his head in curiosity as he looks down at me, waiting for me to unsheathe the tome.

I unlatch the clasps of my straps, allowing the pack to fall to the ground behind me. I crouch to ruffle through the clothing items and other bits and pieces I've brought with me before pulling out the book.

I wish I could be here on other circumstances and not to ask for more help.

But here I am.

I linger on the sight of it before I stand, sighing as I open the textbook. Flipping to a page with a majority of the symbols, I hold it out for him to see.

Kyraxes gets closer, peering into the pages with narrowed eyes for a long moment.

"These… these symbols are not of this land," he huffs. His voice his deeper than normal, shocked if anything.

"I know. But where could they have come from?"

"No… No, I don't think you understand. They do not come from *any* of the realms. Land, nor sea. These are Celestial symbols."

My brow furrows as I look to him, "They are?"

Kyraxes leans back to look into the sky, his gaze steady on the blanket of blue above us. He's silent, his head tilting as if listening to something.

"Celestial symbols are runes of an ancient, powerful race of beings. Only able to be written by the beings themselves. They are not of this land, as they've come from far beyond. *They* are The Fates. Whoever wrote this text, imbued it with magic that only *you* can read when you have become worthy of reading it."

My eyes widen and I feel like a crater has lodged itself in my chest. That book I read in the library.

The Inevitables.

Kyraxes gaze meets mine again, "They are who speak to us, who *guide* us. They are the ones responsible for this endeavor you've been cast upon."

"But-"

"The Fates are a fickle thing. They only reveal their identities to those worthy enough to know of them, should they so choose to do so. With a power such as theirs, their truths must be hidden. The other beings of this world are greedy. They would take the power of The Fates if they knew how. I, myself have only faced one of them. A dastardly thing, he is."

My mind runs and runs in circles as I try to grasp the idea of actual *beings* playing puppet master with the people of our land. My confused gaze lands on the parchment below, and almost wobbles as I try to make sense of it.

I was under the impression that they were just gods. Ethereal orbs of light in the sky.

Not actual *beings* on this earth.

Kyraxes' voice breaks through my puzzle work, "When I stated before that your heart is rooted in this tome, I thought you were the one who had written it. Your being is heavily threaded into its work. *You* are heavily embedded into it."

The rapid beating of my heart increases. I feel as if sweat drips from my brow and my hair as I stare down at the book.

Pieces of this story begin pulling together, and my eyes lock onto the symbols below as the bigger picture forms in front of my eyes. I thought… I thought maybe The Fates were speaking through Lilith into this book… that they used her as a conduit for their teachings… but.

My hands shake and my throat threatens to seal as I look up at Kyraxes. My vision tunnels, and the only sight I can register is the gravely deep and serious haze of his clouded eyes. My voice softens, pressing with all its might against my tight neck to escape, "But Lilith wrote this book."

"Then Lilith… was a Celestial. A Celestial that wrote this book for *you*."

"Xykes! Great to see you again, friend!"

Chapter 64

Fallen

Asher

Gideon has attempted to wrestle me into the sand several times. While the others have merely stood back and watched.

It started with a grab to the neck and escalated from there.

One would assume that growing up with brothers meant I was used to this, but we weren't really a rowdy bunch of brothers. Not like Gideon and the rest of the Shadowfangs.

They would always play fight with one another and in some ways, I believe it was how they bonded.

That was not the case for us Blackwoods.

So, every time we get a moment of silence, Gideon decides he wants to wrestle. Unfortunately, because of his size, he's usually a harder opponent to fight against.

But with the bond completed, it seems as though I may have the upper hand in strength when I'm able to get my arms around his middle from behind. Gripping with all my might to bow backward, I send him tumbling over my shoulder and into the sand. As I release his body, I flip over and scramble on my hands and knees to back away and stand before he has a chance to retaliate.

I settle my movements when I realize he's been outmatched. His groan muffles against the grains and Gideon spits some of the sand out of his mouth as he lays uselessly against the ground. I dust off my hands in victory.

"Enough, Gideon, you need your strength in case the dragons decide to make you their dinner."

Gideon groans again in response before a tremble shakes the ocean beside us.

Briny water sprays the group of us as Xykes makes his landing on the shallow shoreline.

A grin spreads across my face as I realize they sent the *big boy*.

Stalking through the sand, I pass the shocked faces and frozen forms of Selene, Tyrick, and Xeneera as they stare at the giant reptilian beast.

Gideon looks up from the sand as I walk past him, his eyes locked onto Xykes in wonder.

"Xykes! Great to see you again, friend!" I call to him as I rest my hands on my hips.

Xykes' amber eyes meet mine and he chuffs a rough noise, "I wish I could return the sentiment, human," he grumbles.

I give him a sarcastic laugh as I pat his scaly leg, "I missed you too."

His leg pulls away from my touch, almost in disgust, and he rolls a wing from his back to allow the others to walk along it.

My mouth drops in shock as I watch, "You didn't do that for me last time!"

Xykes large head serpentines to hover in front of me. A smirk tugs at the leathery corners of his mouth, revealing the massive, sharpened teeth in his jaw, "You didn't ask."

I roll my eyes as I face the rest of our group, "Friends! This is Xykes. He is Kyraxes brother. He'll be taking us to Infernal Summit."

Selene stares at the beast for a moment before she shrugs, lunging for the sky to settle herself between a set of spikes on Xykes back.

Tyrick begins to make his way to Xykes before he's thrown to the side by Gideon's barreling form that races for the dragon's wing. He runs up the scale covered bone to settle himself behind Selene on Xykes' back. Selene leans into his touch as he wraps his arms tight around her middle and nuzzles her neck.

My eyes roll as I watch Tyrick climb next. He slowly traverses the dragon wing like a breathing balance beam, with his arms out to steady himself.

I turn to see Xeneera looking over the beast with big, wide eyes and her body shaking furiously.

"That's a very… very large dragon…" she murmurs mindlessly.

I give her a small smile before I offer her a hand. She eyes it for a moment before her gaze falls back on Xykes. Her throat works in a gulp as she takes my hand, and I guide her up the wing. I follow soon after and sit myself behind Xeneera.

"Hold tight," Xykes rumbles to us. A powerful lunge jostles us against one another as he takes flight.

The glowing crater of Infernal Summit lingers in the distance, the billowing black smoke marking its spot in the ocean.

As I look down at the obsidian ground below, Seraphina has sat herself crisscrossed, The Compendium open in front of her as she looks over it.

Xykes turns through the air to land on the ground, causing us to wobble against his spiny back.

His massive wing flaps send large breadths of air swirling, blowing dust and rock away in his wake. Soon, he settles on the land and slides a wing out to let us off. Selene stands against a spike, flapping her wings once to propel her from the dragon's back and onto the ground. Gideon slides down the wing like a carefree child, with Tyrick and Xeneera following close behind.

I take the other route of swinging a leg over and scaling the massive beast's body.

I find my way quickly to Seraphina, who looks over her tome with a furrowed brow.

Tense and troubled energy shrouds her the closer I get, and I reach out into the black void of the bond to touch a sliver of her thoughts. But I can't.

It's been walled off.

Concern pulls at my forehead as I come to her side, sitting next to her in the dirt as Gideon, Selene and the rest go to introduce themselves to the dragons.

She doesn't seem to notice me as her gaze stays connected to the ancient parchment.

The leather of her armored breeches slides against my palm as I wrap a hand around her thigh, letting her know I'm there. Her clawed hand slowly comes to wrap around my own, gripping it tightly as she continues her steady gaze on the book below, "Lilith… she was… a Celestial." Her voice is quiet, pained.

I feel confusion pull at my face as she speaks, "A… a what? What is that?"

"Apparently a race of beings not from this land… at all. They don't even belong on this earth. But they *walk* this land, Asher. She was from the *sky*."

What in the fuck?

"That too, was my thought," Seraphina responds.

An annoyed huff comes from me as she speaks. So, *I* can't be let in, but *she* can.

Irritating, but not the time for these things.

"What does this mean?" I ask as I look over the symbols in the books.

"Kyraxes can't read the symbols. He is not versed in this language. But he said that *I* am woven into this book." She shakes her head in defeat. "I don't understand, this book was written way before I was even conceived. But she wrote this for me, Asher," Seraphina says, almost desperately as her eyes come to meet mine. Grief and sheer sadness swirls amongst the pinky purple hues.

The trembling of her emotions rock through the bond, shaking that rope that binds us and my heart squeezes at the intensity.

I may not be able to hear her thoughts, but I surely can *feel* them.

My arms wrap around her, bringing her in close. As she leans into me her head falls into my shoulder and she closes the book softly with a ruffled pat of brittle parchment.

"What do we do now?" I ask quietly. The soft strands of her hair soothe my own nerves as I run my hands down her braids.

"We try to secure some dragons for Tantalia, we let the others learn what they'd like, and then we leave… Our journey here was for naught," she sighs with a heaving sadness.

My brow furrows as I listen to her, "That's not entirely true. We learned something here. Even if it wasn't what we were looking for. It's just another fork in the road, but I'm ready for whatever path we take, Seraphina. We'll get there."

Seraphina tilts her head to look at me with a small, defeated smile and I take the moment to look at her. Really look at her, that is.

Her brilliant purple eyes. Her high cheekbones. Her ferocity. Her fervor. Her passion and her unwillingness to relent. My heart swells and my soul beams with pride for this magnificent Queen of mine.

Seraphina's smile widens before she wraps her arms around me in a tight hug. Her body slowly shifts to press herself into my lap, wrapping her legs around my waist before she tightens her grip around me even more. Her breath warms my neck as she nuzzles into it and her horn bumps my cheek as her chest expands and she inhales a deep gust of me. "I love you, Asher-darling," she whispers softly.

My hands drift to her lower back, pulling her in close, "I love you more, angel."

"Asher Blackwood.
Fitting that you
would succumb to
bonding with a demon."

CHAPTER 65

THE DRAGONS AND THE COURT

SERAPHINA

*L*ove…

Undying, unrelenting love. This is an emotion I never wanted.

It's a bright light I never expected and my courage shoots through the air with his strength guiding me.

I never thought love would feel like this. Nor would I ever imagine Asher being my true love and mate.

But he is here. And I'm beside myself with the way it feels to be in his arms. To be *his*.

I had relinquished my control to The Fates early on, even if I hadn't wanted to in the beginning. I had surrendered to him in every way that I could.

But Asher had to make the decision on his own, and when he finally surrendered…

Well.

I lean back to look into his purple ringed jade eyes, relishing in the feeling of this man becoming a part of me. Something deep and inherently familiar about his soul taking residence in my chest rings through me as I press a gentle kiss to his lips, running my hands through his now onyx hair.

I feel him harden beneath me and a giggle threads between us as I lean back again, a nervous grin plastered along his face as pink tinges his cheeks. "Sorry, it's a hard thing to control around you."

Warmth runs through me in little trickles and I press another kiss to his lips before I release myself from his body. I shimmy from his lap and onto the ground, placing The Compendium into my pack before securing it on my spine.

Asher stands before he reaches down to help me up. His calloused palms feel like home as I slide my hand into his.

We walk hand in hand toward the others who have gathered around Kyraxes, who currently peers down at Tyrick. His rumbling voice causes vibrations to run through me as we approach, and we caught the last bit of his wisdom. "Your thirst for knowledge is immense, little wizard. You must believe in your ability to learn. It will take you farther than you think," Kyraxes finishes.

Tyrick looks like he'll soil his pants as the dragon stares at him, and he nods slowly, "Thank you, Kyraxes… I will try."

Tyrick bows before the large, imposing dragon serpentines his spiked head to Xeneera. She stares up at the creature with eyes wide in wonder… *and* fear.

"You… you are *very* special," Kyraxes says slowly as his eyes narrow on her.

"I-I am?" she murmurs in disbelief.

"You have potential you have not accessed and power you don't know exists." His eyes close for a moment and his head tilts as if he's listening to something we can't hear. "*Strong* power you must be willing to use for good. Your heart is bright, and you will have the opportunity to be the change you wish to seek. I suggest you take it when the moment presents itself." His eyes slowly open, and his clouded hues lock onto Xeneera.

Xeneera seems bewildered by the information presented and her face softens.

Me too, kid.

His gaze shifts down the line to land on Asher.

"Asher *Blackwood*. Fitting that you would succumb to bonding with a demon."

Asher's head tilts in curiosity, "What do you mean?"

"The truth will come to light when the time is right."

He sighs, almost defeatedly, "When will the time be right?"

Kyraxes looks toward the setting sun, watching the sky swirl into decadently soft reds, pinks and orange. His gaze steady on the horizon before he turns to face Asher, "You will know, dear friend."

Asher nods, before he looks up at Kyraxes with a hopeful smile, "Do you think I could bring a dragon back with me to Tantalia?"

Kyraxes lets out a chuckle. "Your persistence is admirable, human. Xykes told me of your request at last we met. I shall supply you with your own dragon. Only for the will of your spirit. I know you would be a wonderful rider for our volunteer."

Asher's body tenses in excitement as Kyraxes swings his head to the summit. The ground rumbles as his jaw slacks and he sends a high-pitched screech into the air.

A dragon nearly a quarter of Kyraxes' size crawls from the crater's edge, sliding down the rocky cliff on its belly.

Asher's head tilts as he looks over the curious creature, "What is it doing?"

Kyraxes turns to Asher with a small smirk, "That is Vylai. She is a peculiar thing. She came to us many years ago when her flock had pushed her away. The Blaze of Infernal Summit took her in, and she has been a part of our clan ever since."

Vylai barrels down the mountain, bounding to Asher in pure excitement. She crashes into him in a flurry of bright, white fuzz and pins his arms and legs against the ground as she pants a heavy, excited breath in his face.

This little creature is surely different.

She isn't scaly or prickly like the others; her body is covered in plush ivory fur with small spots of ice blue that blend in circular patterns around her.

"I am SO EXCITED TO GO ON THIS JOURNEY WITH YOU, HUMAN!" she bellows to him.

Her eyes are a brilliant teal and keratinized spikes jut from the fluff on her head.

She's not thick and robust like the other scaled creatures, she seems to have a much more slender frame.

Kyraxes' voice breaks through my observation. "When I offered the idea of aiding the demons to the brood, Vylai was the only one who spoke up."

"Yep, yep, yep! I wanted to see the world! I wanted to be of service! Oh, how I wish you would have come sooner! I asked every day when you would return and I'm so happy to finally be of use!"

The little dragon has enough energy to fuel an entire town. I've never seen so much energy come from *anyone* let alone *these* creatures in the time I've spent with them.

Asher's face contorts in discomfort as Vylai pins him, "Can… can I have my limbs back, please?"

Vylai jumps back and sits on her rump in front of him, nodding voraciously. "Oh! Yes! I'm so sorry! Are you to be my rider? This is so wonderful! I can't wait to see your land! Are there other dragons? Do you have fish? Those are my favorite things!"

Asher stands from the ground, dusting the black dust from his armor. Vylai dives to his leg to inspect the giant hole in his breeches, "Did someone burn you? Why is there a hole in your scales?" Her head tilting in curious observation.

Asher's eyes meet mine in a widened cry for help, and I give him an amused smile.

I approach Vylai slowly, reaching a hand out to touch her nose, "Nice to meet you, Vylai. I'm Seraphina."

Vylai shoves her snout into my hand, and the strength from her excitement shoves me back, "Hello, hello, HELLO! It's so wonderful to meet you! You have wings, too! How amazing!"

A laugh crawls from my chest at the playful creature. The muscles in my face start to hurt from smiling at the thought of how much fun she will have with Asher. Even if he finds her to be a tad overbearing, I think it'll be good for him. I know he's not been happy about having the guards fly him up to The Keep. But we'll have to build a new enclosure for her. Unless, of course, she wants to roam the lands.

I shake my head as I come from my thoughts, looking to Kyraxes who has now turned his attention on Gideon, who damn near shakes with excitement.

"What about me!?" he asks quickly. He clasps his hands at his chin as his eyes glow with unbridled anticipation.

The temperament of this large man is so bizarre, but I do find him to be funny.

Kyraxes' gaze settles on Gideon, his eyes narrowing as he inspects him, "You are a peculiar little thing, aren't you?"

Gideon's head tilts as his brow clenches in confusion, "I guess? Is there anything else?"

"That is all."

His mouth opens in a gape and Asher cackles hysterically next to him before slapping the massive man on the back, "Better luck next time, friend."

As the day turns to night and the moon rises in the sky, I look toward the orb of hope. My mind goes back to last night when Asher relinquished himself to me.

The thought causes a pleasured shiver to run through my body as I remember the way it felt to thread together.

"The night grows near, Seraphina. It is time you take your leave," Kyraxes says as he matches my gaze at the moon.

I nod absentmindedly, my eyes stuck on the light beyond, "Yes."

"Xykes will take your flightless friends. I imagine this would be good practice for Vylai and Asher."

Vylai bounds about Asher in pure excitement, "THIS IS GOING TO BE SO MUCH FUN!" she yells as her massive, furry body circles in jumping ivory arches.

Asher sighs as he watches the beast, but the tug in my heart tells me this *is* going to be fun.

"Thank you, rider. I'm lucky to have you."

We say goodbye to the dragons of The Blaze. Xykes returns from the volcano to carry Gideon, Tyrick and Xeneera back to the clearing by the boulder, while Seraphina and Selene fly next to him. We make sure to go as far east as we can, so we aren't spotted by the stronghold.

I, however, ride Vylai back to the clearing. Rather quickly, in fact.

I thought that it was going to be easy, considering how often I ride Gnox. In my head, it was going to be the same concept.

I was gravely mistaken, and was rudely awakened by the swirling, diving, and twirling dragon that may not have the wits about her to realize she has a rider now.

Because she is much smaller than Kyraxes or Xykes, the feeling of riding her is much more visceral. My stomach churns *violently* the longer she plays around in the air.

Every so often she'll level out and give me a chance to breathe, but that doesn't last very long before she starts corkscrewing and I have to grip onto her horns and fur for dear life.

I'm sincerely hoping Seraphina can supply me with a saddle.

But I have no time to think as Vylai dives to the empty field holding the boulder at unparalleled speed.

I almost think we're going to crash, and my stomach falls into my ass. A feral screech echoes through the air as I try with all my might to hold my seat. She slows at the last second, hovering *just* above the ground before gently landing us in the grass.

My stomach rolls and bounces around in my body as I fall from her side and onto the ground. The cool, dewy blades do nothing to quell the war raging in my belly. Slowly, I roll onto my hands and knees before I crawl to the edge of the forest. Heaving what little contents there were in my stomach onto the tree line, I constantly gag until my insides threaten to follow the emptiness.

Sweat beads against my forehead and I groan as I topple over onto the ground, curling up in a ball. Heavy breaths cool down the air around my face as I try and regain myself.

Vylai slowly approaches, her wet nose nudges my shoulder softly, "Are you okay, rider?" she whispers.

My breaths are shallow as I slide my head against the ground to look at her.

Her bright sapphire eyes are concerned, and her head tilts as she watches me.

A tug of guilt pulls at my sore insides, and I nod slowly, "Yes… Yes, I'm alright. Just not used to riding like that."

A frown tugs at her large mouth, "I'm so sorry. I was so excited to see everything out here. I'll be calmer next time." She nods understandingly.

Her head droops as she realizes her excitement may have gotten the best of her and I sigh in remorse.

Fuck.

Slowly, I make to stand, wobbling as I push down the pain of my retching. Taking a few steeling breaths, I attempt to settle myself. I wipe the sweat from my brow before I take tentative steps to her, placing a hand on her snout, "It's alright. I understand."

Her eyes come to meet mine and she shows a shadow of a smile, "Thank you, rider. I'm lucky to have you."

My heart squeezes and I realize I may have been too hard on her in our first moments together.

I need to love her like I love Gnox.

"I'm lucky to have you, Vylai."

Her long, slender, feathery tail sways behind her in excitement as her eyes seemingly melt with happiness and she nuzzles her large head into my chest, knocking me back gently.

I wrap my arms around her, giving her a sweet hug, when we're interrupted by the landing thuds of Seraphina and Selene.

Seraphina stretches her wings to shake off the flight before she looks up into the night sky, "The others are running behind. Xykes is not particularly quick." She starts walking toward Vylai and me, watching us almost admirably.

I release Vylai and pat her on the head before I turn to Seraphina, "It's alright. Vylai and I were having a moment."

The excited beast sits her rump against the ground behind me before she rests her head on top of mine. She wiggles back and forth, which in turn causes my body to serpentine under her. It's as if she's playing with the feeling of my body movements.

"Vylai, do you think you could handle a saddle?" I ask from under her.

Her jaw jostles my head as she speaks, "A sad… ulll? What is that?"

I laugh as I come out from beneath her. I circle her slowly, looking over her small frame and the abundance of plush fur that covers her, trying to figure out what kind of apparatus would allow such a thing.

"Well, it's like a seat. It would help me hold on to you a bit better."

Vylai tilts her head in thought before she nods excitedly, "If it helps you, I'm all for it!"

I give her a laugh as I come to pat her back, and Seraphina smiles at us lovingly, "I knew you would like her."

I send Seraphina a playful glare, "Just a learning curve."

Selene surveys the area around the boulder before she calls to us, "So, there is no portal, how are we supposed to get back?"

Seraphina turns to Selene as Xykes begins to circle overhead, "We have to knock on the boulder, but we can't go back until we have everyone."

The fury of his flaps, even from his incredible height, sends the grass shimmering around us and the leaves swirling into the air like small green tornados.

"Well, obviously. I imagine Gideon would lose his mind if I wasn't here when he landed," Selene says with a dismissive wave of her hand.

Seraphina rolls her eyes as Vylai begins frolicking in the grass around us, soaking in the night air and dancing with the leaves.

"Are you and Gideon mates, Selene?" I ask as she watches Xykes prepare to land.

"Us? No, no!" she laughs. "He's just a smitten little beast, and I'm more than happy to oblige. I enjoy his company," she says with a dreamy smile and a soft shrug.

That easy, huh?

I watch Vylai bound around the grass for a moment before Seraphina's sensuous voice pulls my attention away, "So, how was the ride? I felt your heaving," she laughs softly as she comes to press her body against mine, wrapping her arms around my neck.

I tighten my hands on her hips and pull her close before I sigh, pressing my head into the crook of her neck, "It was very… something," I respond as I stroke the ends of her braids that flow down her back.

Seraphina laughs. "You'll get there. She's just excited."

Her scent, floral and irresistable, eases through my blood, and my soul begins to drift on a sea of bliss as I inhale her. I feel her heart beating against my chest in time with mine and the synchrony of it all melds me to her. "Me too, Seraphina… Me too."

I'M NOT HERE. I'M NOT IN MY HEAD ANYMORE. THIS BODY IS FOR NAUGHT, AS I GIVE IN TO THIS TORRENT OF RAGE THAT THREATENS TO DEVOUR ME.

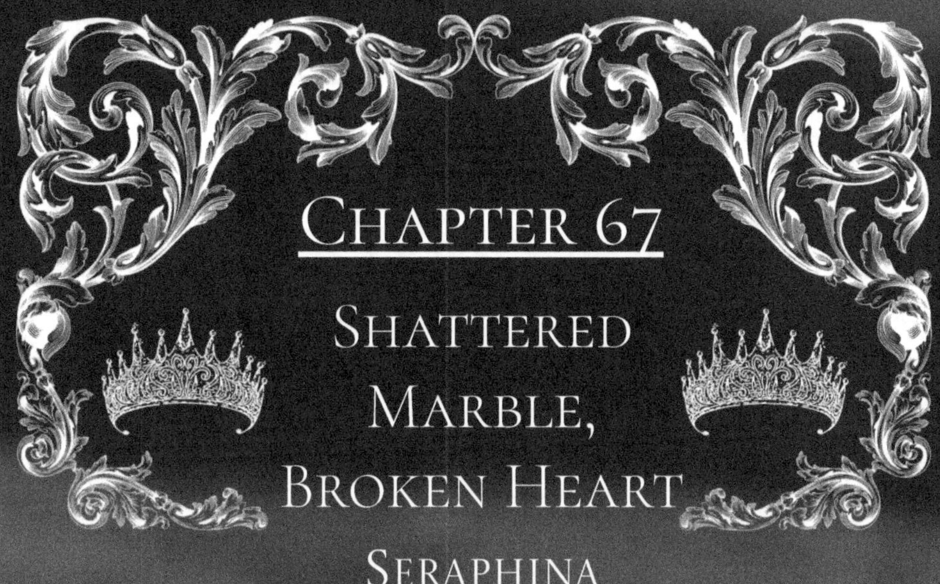

CHAPTER 67

SHATTERED MARBLE, BROKEN HEART

SERAPHINA

Seven days later

After we made it back through the portal to Kaithoon, the mages were not happy with the fact we had brought a dragon with us.

Tough shit.

Once we had our magic back, Selene and I grafted Tyrick, Xeneera and Gideon to the cave portal. Asher rode Vylai through the sky so the patrons of the city weren't alerted by a giant, white creature trotting through their *quaint* little town.

Eventually, we made it back to Tantalia, where I let Vylai roam the lands while the rest of us retreated to our chambers.

With Asher finally accepting our bond, he spent several hours merely claiming me. His deep and husky voice breathed and groaned about how much he loved me. How the world would stop its motion, and the seas would dry without me.

Through all our bonding, I am plagued with the need to shift our focus, considering the things we had learned at Infernal Summit.

We had gone there with the intent of Kyraxes being able to read The Compendium, only to find out that Lilith was apparently a "Celestial" and not even a being of this world. And not only that, but she was a

Celestial that walked this earth. Who else could be part of this race of beings? Do they walk among us? How would we even know who they are?

My mind spun with these questions, and I only fell deeper into this hole. The idea that she wrote this book, specifically for me in a language I couldn't even understand, and that I had to be worthy enough to read it, set my mind ablaze in a fury of lightninged smoke.

It makes no sense; none of it does.

How am I not worthy yet? After all this time? After she had spent so many years training me and teaching me? How… HOW am I still unworthy of this information? What do I have to do to prove this? And how will I know when I have? Is there something else I have to do for the text to be legible? Am I going to have to find someone else to confirm my worthiness?

My chest aches and the deep feeling of sadness settles in my gut with the idea that this was all a horrible game.

Then, there's the matter of Asher's dagger and the unknown reason he has a fucking demon weapon.

Eventually, we would get to that, but I needed to talk to the mistresses to see if they know about Lilith's origins.

Which is why, early this morning I called all the mistresses to The Court. They all sit here; waiting with bated breath and their mythical eyes all on me.

My hands clasp behind my back so tightly that my claws prick into the meat of my skin as I look over them all.

Someone has not been very forthcoming with their information on Lilith.

Will I get to the bottom of it? At this rate, I have no fucking clue.

But I surely can try.

"I have learned *troubling* things about Lilith during my travels to Infernal Summit."

My mother eyes me with a confused brow, while Selene stands beside me in calm knowing.

She, herself was not even aware of her mother's status as a Celestial. And even then, does that mean that technically Selene is a Celestial?

And more so… what the *fuck* IS a Celestial?! Where do they even come from if they are not from here? There is more to this world than what is outside the boundaries of the sky? The thought is sickening and causes my stomach to churn violently.

Taking a deep breath from the bile that threatens to make an appearance, I shake my head and look around at the women surrounding the table.

Looking down the line, Learra seems intrigued by this statement. Reasha, the weaponsmith, is stone faced as she looks at me; the rest of the nobles having varying degrees of shock, confusion and intrigue painted on their faces.

"The oracle dragon, Kyraxes, informed me that the symbols of The Compendium are not of this world. He *also* informed me that Lilith was a Celestial."

The women of The Court exchange looks of utter confusion, their brows scrunched, and their heads tilted as they look back at me.

"What… what does that mean?" Learra asks.

"Kyraxes told me that Celestials are an ethereal race of beings that essentially *are* The Fates."

Gasps sound from around the room, "The Fates are… *things?* They're actual beings?" my mother asks.

I nod as my arms cross my chest and I bring a hand to my chin in thought.

I turn to face the large marble statue of Lilith that looks over the mountain of Celestial Keep.

My eyes take in the various lines and curves of the stoned guardian and my heart shatters into tiny pieces at the sight of her. All over again, I realize how much my dear mentor kept from me.

"They are..." I murmur.

Turning back to The Court, I press my hands against the stone table as my head droops. My unbound, white hair curtains around me, hiding my face from the others as my heart speeds with a fury and my chest tightens with the depth of my breathing.

The thoughts that course through me seem to accelerate the longer I look down at pale ivory lines that run through the surface.

The day Lilith made me General.

"Mistress of Bloodshed. Angel of Death." Her voice had declared. Her eyes shone with an esteemed level of pride I'd never seen before.

The years I spent in The Pits torturing myself through maneuvers and training. In The Library, with her teachings on what now appears to be useless information; *"You must learn to accept the things you don't know. There is more to this world than bloodshed and war. It's all in the books, Seraphina."*

Her words to me that day in Vesperholm; *"Something very special is here, and we are going to find it."*

Day in and day out. She *knew* that The Compendium existed out there. She *knew* that I was to find it one day. She *knew*. Every. Single. Thing.

Under her palm and her thumb. Constantly teaching me of my purpose and my duty.

For *what?*

The way she expected me to stare down at this table in utter loss and confusion.

She *knew* what she was doing. She *knew* that I would be here, suffering without her.

Lilith spent hours with me every single day, telling me of my potential, telling me of what I was to accomplish.

Day after *day*, she told me I'd be Queen one day. I ignored every ounce of it. I refused to believe her.

Yet, she kept *so* much from me. She kept almost *everything* from me, yet expected *me* to take up her throne. To rule in her stead.

The air thins as the energy of my fury begins to rise. Charges of rage spear through the air as it climbs. The sunlight from the windows turn to shadows as dark clouds slowly begin to shroud The Keep.

"Get out," I murmur. The blood running through my body causes my hearing to muffle as all I begin to see is *red*.

"Seraphina, isn't there more to discuss he-" I hear Reasha attempt to ask.

"I said… Get. *Out,*" I murmur once more.

Static clings to the surfaces as my lightning begins to crackle at my boots. Then a boom of lightning strikes the side of The Keep.

The ladies all begin to move, soft scuffles sounding off from around the room. The stone doors rumble open to allow the ladies exit before the walls quake with their closure.

My shoulders begin to tense. My wings, more so as they tighten hard against my spine.

Slowly, I raise my head and turn to face the statue of Lilith once more, standing against it. The large, carved wings that relax against her figure feel like the most repulsive sight I've ever laid eyes on. They sear into my gaze and scorch the insides of me.

Wind begins to blow outside, and with it, sprinkles of rain that hit Lilith's statue, dripping slowly over the marble.

"*You* set me up to fail. *You* knew every move you'd make. You *knew* what you did. At every single turn and every single thought. *You* did this to me. And for WHAT, LILITH!? WHY!?" I yell at the silent figure.

But she's frozen in time. Frozen here, with her back to me.

"WHY DID YOU DO THIS TO ME, LILITH!?" I screech. Rage rips through my chest, through my *being* and tears me apart as I challenge her statue.

But it stands firm, watching over the lands below.

Heated tears stream down my face, and thunder booms against the sky, shaking the window frames and the open window panes. The rain tilts and beats against the sky in massive droplets as the clouds descend further and drape The Keep into inky black.

My sharp claws stab into my skin, where my hands ball into fists at my sides. Warm blood pools against my palm, before it oozes from between my fingers, rolling down my knuckles to hit the floor.

I feel my wings expand, stretching to their limits. My tail whips furiously against the lightning kicking up against me. The purple sparks that lick my boots and legs are violently illuminated against the darkness the clouds brought in with them. They cast vibrant shadows off the white figure I've settled my strife on.

"YOU *KNEW*, LILITH! YOU *KNEW* WHAT YOU WERE DO-ING! YOU TOLD ME I WAS TO TAKE YOUR THRONE! YOU TOLD ME I WAS TO BE QUEEN!!! AND YET YOU GAVE ME *NO* DIRECTION! YOU *LIED* TO ME! YOU DECEIVED *ME*, LILITH! HOW *COULD* YOU!?" My voice feels distant, it doesn't feel like my own. I don't even feel as if I'm in this vessel that I must call a body.

Sparks whizz around the room as wind kicks up against the lightning at my feet. Rain pours outside against the thunder that rocks the air around The Keep, drenching Lilith in its wake. Small pools of water collect on the marble floor, reflecting Lilith's stone face in it.

And as I catch sight of her closed eyes, calm and peaceful, the dam… *breaks.*

I hear a screech bounce off the other stone guardians in The Court. I *hear it…*

But…

I'm not here. I'm not in my head anymore. This body is for naught, as I give in to this torrent of rage that threatens to devour me.

I don't realize my movements as my hand rises to Lilith's statue. I don't realize the sobs that crush my being, that cause me to shake uncontrollably as I take aim between the wings of this stoned beast that has betrayed me at every turn.

Immense, dark power pricks against my bloodied palm, expanding further and further, until it hits a hard wall.

"I *LOVED* YOU, LILITH!!!" is all I hear, followed by the crash of stone against stone and the shattering of tiny bits of marble against the ground.

Rocky dust circulates into the wind that swirls around me, as the head of Lilith's statue rolls toward me.

The relaxed face and closed eyes of the severed head stare back at me.

My heart pounds, and more sobs consume every ounce of me as my hand drops to my side. The ground below crashes hard into my knees as I surrender.

"I yield, Lilith… I *yield*… is this what you've wanted?! My surrender? Did you want me to yield to your games?! Because I surrender! I yield to this torment you've set upon me!" I cry. My throat scratches and aches from where the words crawl through me.

My neck cranes back as heated tears run down my cheeks, my throat, and neck. Trailing down, farther and farther to cover my chest in coolness as the wind swirling around me whips against it.

I don't recognize the familiar smoked and woody scent that breaks through the rage, through the pain. I don't realize that the lightning and wind have died and that the air has stilled around me or that the rain outside has stopped.

I don't react when strong arms wrap around me in a futile attempt to calm me down.

I don't listen when Asher's voice desperately tries to break through the rabble.

I don't think when I fall into his chest, and the sobs devour me.

I don't look at the stone head of Lilith, from where it lays separated from her shattered statue on the floor of The Court of Mistresses.

I can't.

My strong Queen has fallen and she's taken my soul with her.

Even through her strife, I would gladly let her.

I would always let her.

Even if it killed me.

Chapter 68

Helpless

Asher

To find Seraphina drowning in her tears beside the destroyed figure sent arrows through my body, through my soul. I felt her pain deep within me, and I tried all I could to be the anchor for her to grieve safely.

I tried… but even then, I felt like I failed.

I don't know what happened.

I was down in the stables with Gnox, I wanted to catch up on some time with him while Seraphina addressed her court.

She assured me I wasn't needed, and I wanted to make sure he knew I still loved him with how long I've been gone. I had also fed Lilith while I was there; he huffed and trotted around his stable in evident agitation as harsh winds and rain kicked up across Tantalia. Booming thunder rocked the air around us, and that wasn't normal for here. Not at all. There haven't been many times, if at all, that I had seen it rain here.

But soon, an agonizing pit cleaved through my chest. I felt it tearing my soul into two and *knew* it wasn't my doing.

I *knew* it wasn't me. But I did know *who* it was.

I felt the way that rope in my soul tightened to immeasurable limits, threatening to snap and I knew that something… something was very, *very* wrong.

I called Vylai to the stables, with the specific call we created that would travel through the valley, and she came with a quickness to fly me to Celestial Keep. When we reached the courtyard balcony, I merely found a blur of wind and purple lightning encircling my dear mate. Her head thrown back in despair as the statue of her mentor laid crumbled against the floor in front of her. Rushing inside, I dove to her to hold her tight until the winds died, and Seraphina collapsed in a puddle of her tears.

I then brought her to our room.

I called for Selene to help change her clothes with her magic, because I didn't want to disturb her, and I was afraid that the movement involved in changing her clothes by hand would be too much. That was when Selene informed me of what happened.

Seraphina had asked all the women to leave after she told them about Lilith being a Celestial. Selene stayed outside of the door and listened to her friend's turmoil. She knew she couldn't help her. She felt just as helpless and confused, she had admitted, to knowing her mother was essentially a god amongst demons.

She didn't know where it left her, and she didn't know what it meant other than she didn't feel the same as Seraphina because there hadn't been as much pressure on her to take the throne.

She said she was lucky I came, because I was going to be the only one that could help her. It was one of the gifts of mates, she informed me.

Now, as Seraphina sleeps in her bed, I'm just grateful I was able to be there for her when I could.

She has been sleeping for a long while and I've sat by her bed, watching her to make sure I'm here when she awakes, in case something happens.

I wish I knew *anything* at this point. I feel like there is nothing I *can* do but be here for her.

The idea of finding out your mentor -- and basically your idol -- potentially lied to you your entire life by hiding her true identity and then expecting you to clean up her mess after she dies is a lot to handle.

I don't blame Seraphina for her reaction, not in the slightest.

Seraphina's emotions can be particularly volatile, and I would expect nothing less in this instance, especially when faced with the knowledge she now holds.

But it doesn't make it any easier when all I would like to do is help her. I can be here. I can love her. I can tell her everything she is capable of and what she can do. But her own self-worth is rooted in what Lilith made her to be.

What do you do when that self-worth feels like a lie? Or even worse, just a test you keep *failing?*

I don't think Seraphina has failed, not even a little bit. But she looks at herself through Lilith's eyes. And what happens when that vision feels like a mockery?

How do you take that? How *can* you take that?

Seraphina's chest rises and falls slowly as she rests. The moonlight that sneaks through her open window bathes her sleeping body in an ethereal glow.

I can't help but admire her beauty and I'm happy for the calm and peace she finds in sleep.

I am happy that for just a few moments she's not plagued by her thoughts and "*misgivings* ", as she would probably call them.

A sleepy groan sounds in the room as her forehead scrunches softly in confusion.

Her body stirs as she slowly wakes; her eyes sleepily roaming the area from where she has huddled herself in her blankets.

Soon, her gaze grows distant as she stares off into the darkness.

"I broke the statue..." she admits quietly. But her voice holds no remorse.

That confirms at least one of my suspicions, but I keep quiet in case she says anything else.

"I... I couldn't..." she murmurs as her attention continues drifting farther and farther away. Her eyes clench shut as she takes a deep breath.

"I couldn't stop," she whispers as her eyes open and silver tears begin streaming down her face.

Her focus comes back to me, her gaze and features etched in pain and sorrow.

I feel her pain through the thread that holds us together. Viscerally, in fact, as if *I* was the one who broke the statue.

I press myself out of the chair I sit in, dropping to my knees before slowly approaching the bed. I shuffle against the stone until I reach her side.

My hands creep under the blankets to find hers, as they've tangled themselves in the sheets. "I am *so* sorry for what you're going through, my love," I whisper as I peer into her eyes. Her normally strong grip is absent as I wrap my hand around hers.

Her eyes almost plead with me, *beg* me to take this pain and confusion away as her hand stays limp in my own. And my heart threatens to rip into pieces as I realize I *can't*. I would love to do everything I can to soothe her. To make her happy. But I am at a loss, which causes the strife I feel beside her to increase even more.

"She's made a mockery of me. She's made me a failure, Asher."

A sigh escapes my throat as I look at her, "Seraphina... You are anything *but* a failure. You are the *Queen* of Tantalia. You can't let the what ifs of Lilith's actions dictate today or tomorrow. You *have* to keep moving forward."

Seraphina goes silent, her gaze breaking away once again as she hears me, "I can't... I just... can't."

I sigh as I rest my chin on the bed beside her, bringing my hand out from the blanket to stroke her hair.

"I know you can, Sera. I know that doesn't mean anything. But Lilith doesn't define everything you've done since her death."

"But everything I've *ever* done has always been for Lilith. In Lilith's name. In her memory. What do I do now that I know it's a fucking lie? A fucking ploy for her to laugh at me from the beyond?"

"We don't even know if that was her intention. I don't know anything about Lilith, but she doesn't seem like the type to humiliate you in this way."

"We apparently don't even know Lilith. She was a cosmic creature." Seraphina's face begins to tense in annoyance, and I feel her anger slowly ratcheting up the longer I try and convince her of this separate ideology.

In an attempt to de-escalate, I shift focus. "What do you need from me?" I ask gently. I try to connect with her lost gaze, try anything I can to make her feel better. Anything at all.

"Just go…" she murmurs.

The admission hurts far more than I think even she knows.

If she feels it, I don't think she cares right now.

But I understand. As much as I don't want to understand, I do.

I nod as I lean forward. Pressing a kiss to her forehead, I linger on her skin much longer than I should. I don't want to leave her… not here, not like this. But she's made it clear what she needs. And I would give her the moon on a string and paint the sky with my own tears to see her smile. I stand and stroke her hair once more, "I love you, Seraphina."

"I love you too, Asher," she murmurs back.

I sigh as I turn around to head for the door.

Taking one last look at her before I leave, I find more silver tears streaking down her face and her gaze lost to the darkness.

I roam The Keep for a long while, taking in the tapestries and the various statues of the old succubus. I look over their forms and just explore. There is no one else out. No one except Mistress Kalinda who roams the halls listlessly.

"Human... Interesting to see you out and about without your master," she lilts in a tauntingly.

She stops me on the way back up the stairs, her eyes narrow in observation.

I've never had the chance to talk to her on my own, so I take this opportunity to ask her about the things going on around here.

"I know Seraphina won't ask you... but what does it mean to be a Celestial?"

My question seems to catch her off guard, but her face remains stony, her brow twitching the merest amount as she pins me with her icy stare. "A Celestial, you say?"

I nod in confirmation.

"I personally have never heard of such a thing. But it must be important enough to cause Seraphina to destroy the statue of our dear Queen."

My brow works as I take in her words *and* her energy.

She's inherently dark. I suppose I'd never had the chance to pick up on it when we were in The Court of Mistresses with her. But alone, here with her, it's oddly unnerving.

"I suppose you heard about that, huh?"

"I did. I took the pieces to our stonemasons for repair."

I gaze at one of the statues in the foyer below, but my focus pulls away from the stone guardian as she speaks, "I know it seems as if I am a hindrance to the strength of Tantalia. But no one wants to see Tantalia succeed more than I do. This is my *home.* I have been here longer than anyone else, and all I want is for the borders to be secured and our livelihood to not be affected by the Drannars any longer." Her brow furrows as she looks at me and her words hold immense weight as she speaks.

"But why didn't you do anything when the time came? Why did Seraphina have to be the one to step up?"

She talks a big game, but she couldn't do what she needed to when the time came, so it feels like her little pity party is all for show.

"The day she passed away, Lilith knew she was going to die. She hadn't told Seraphina. She merely said she was on a quest and that it would be her last. She knew that Seraphina was to take the throne. And she knew Seraphina was averse to the idea. But there was no one else that Lilith wanted on the throne more than Seraphina. Who am I to deny my departed Queen's final wish?"

Lilith knew she was going to die...? Was this mentioned before? Has Seraphina learned of any of this?

My thoughts take me farther and farther away, and Mistress Kalinda has gone quiet as she watches me, her face a mask of indifference.

"I merely was doing what I was ordered to do."

My gaze connects with hers, searching her cold eyes for a long while before I nod slowly, "Thank you."

Mistress Kalinda bows deeply before her long, ivory cloak billows around her as she glides away.

I turn back to the stairs, climbing each one with what feels like a lead covered foot.

Lilith knew she was going to die...

Which means... she *knew* she was going to die by *my* hand... she had said it that day in the alley. She had been looking for me.

Why else would she have given up her fight against me so easily? Why did she not attempt any of their tricks? She merely played cat and mouse with me before I struck her.

The instance was strange, but I hadn't known who she was at the time. How could I with how little I'd known about them?

The more we learn about Lilith, the more confusing this all *does* seem.

Why would she bring Seraphina with her on that trip? Seraphina herself said that Lilith had only mentioned they were looking for something there.

Was it me? How long have *I* been on Lilith's map?

The thoughts propel me faster and faster up the stairs. I have to tell Seraphina. I *need* to tell her.

Eventually, I make it back to our bedroom and find her asleep. I decide to let her rest and tell her in the morning. Perhaps the sleep will allow her to calm down enough to hear me out.

I think she could handle learning these things. But with Seraphina you truly never know.

The sun wakes me up bright and early the next morning. Primality grips me by my throat as I inhale a large gust of Seraphina's scent, and I pull her closer to me.

Though it is difficult to spoon her this way with her wings and tail, I try to make do.

Seraphina slowly stirs and groans a sleepy noise as she begins to wake with me.

I linger in silence with her for a long moment until her breathing changes from rhythmic sleeping to a calculated movement of inhales and exhales.

"Seraphina..." I whisper as I rub a hand over her silk covered stomach.

Seraphina doesn't answer me. She doesn't even flinch.

"I... I learned something last night," I tell her.

My hope is that this information helps her work through whatever strife she may be experiencing.

But I am met with silence. Long, deepening silence.

"Mistress Kalinda... she gave me information about the day Li-"

"Don't." Her voice is gravely serious, raspy even.

"But Seraphina I think it's important for you to kn-"

"DON'T!" She yells. She jolts up against the sheets, holding them to her bare chest as she glares at me. Her lips bared in a half sneer, half snarl.

The purple of her eyes swirl with pain and grief and her neck tightens as she bites back the tears.

"I–"

"*I* do not care, Asher. Do *not* mention her in my presence. She is dead to me. Literally and figuratively."

My heart sinks as I let a sigh go and nod slowly, "Is there anything I can do to make this easier on you?"

"Leave me be," she snips as she wraps the blanket around her and lays back in the bed.

"But I want to help," I plead.

"I don't need help. I need time." Her voice is rough, terse and short.

And usually that is what she needs. And if I plan on rooting my life here in Tantalia while still giving her space… I suppose I should tie up my life in Vesperholm for the time being.

Maybe she will be able to process without me in her immediate area, because it feels like it's all I can do right now.

A small sigh releases from my throat as I rise from the bed. Going around the room, I gather my things and slowly I pull them on before latching the pieces of my armor on. I take a deep breath as I work myself up to telling her. "Seraphina. I'm going to go to Vesperholm. I think I need to say goodbye to my family."

"A guard will escort you. I'll be waiting for your return," she responds curtly.

Ow.

"Can I take Cedric with me?"

"Whatever you need, it's yours, Asher. But if you don't return, I *will* find you."

I nod solemnly, though she doesn't see it as her back continues to face me. Every second spent gearing up to walk away from her, is another chip knocked off my heart.

I don't want to leave her here by herself, and I don't *want* to be away from her. And I don't want to make my trip in Vesperholm long, I need to get in, tell my parents, and leave. That's it. They can't convince me to stay.

Not anymore.

As I finish securing the last of my buckles along my armor, I pack a few things in my bag before I make my way to the door.

As my hand rests against the handle, I glance over my shoulder at my mate.

My *love* and my entire heart.

My strong Queen has fallen, and she's taken my soul with her.

Even through her strife, I would gladly let her.

I would *always* let her. Even if it killed me.

And the sight of her now *does* kill me.

Dark circles have formed under her eyes against her pale skin. She looks drained; sapped of any life she once had. Even though her skin is already pale, it seems almost blue in the light of the day. She hasn't requested food or even a feeding from me.

Though I can't blame her. Not with the things she's going through.

I throw one last effort at her, in hopes she knows she hasn't pushed me away. "I love you, Seraphina."

"I love you too, Asher-dear," she murmurs. The sound of her voice spears me through the chest, and it hurts then when I feel how much love she has for me as I leave the room.

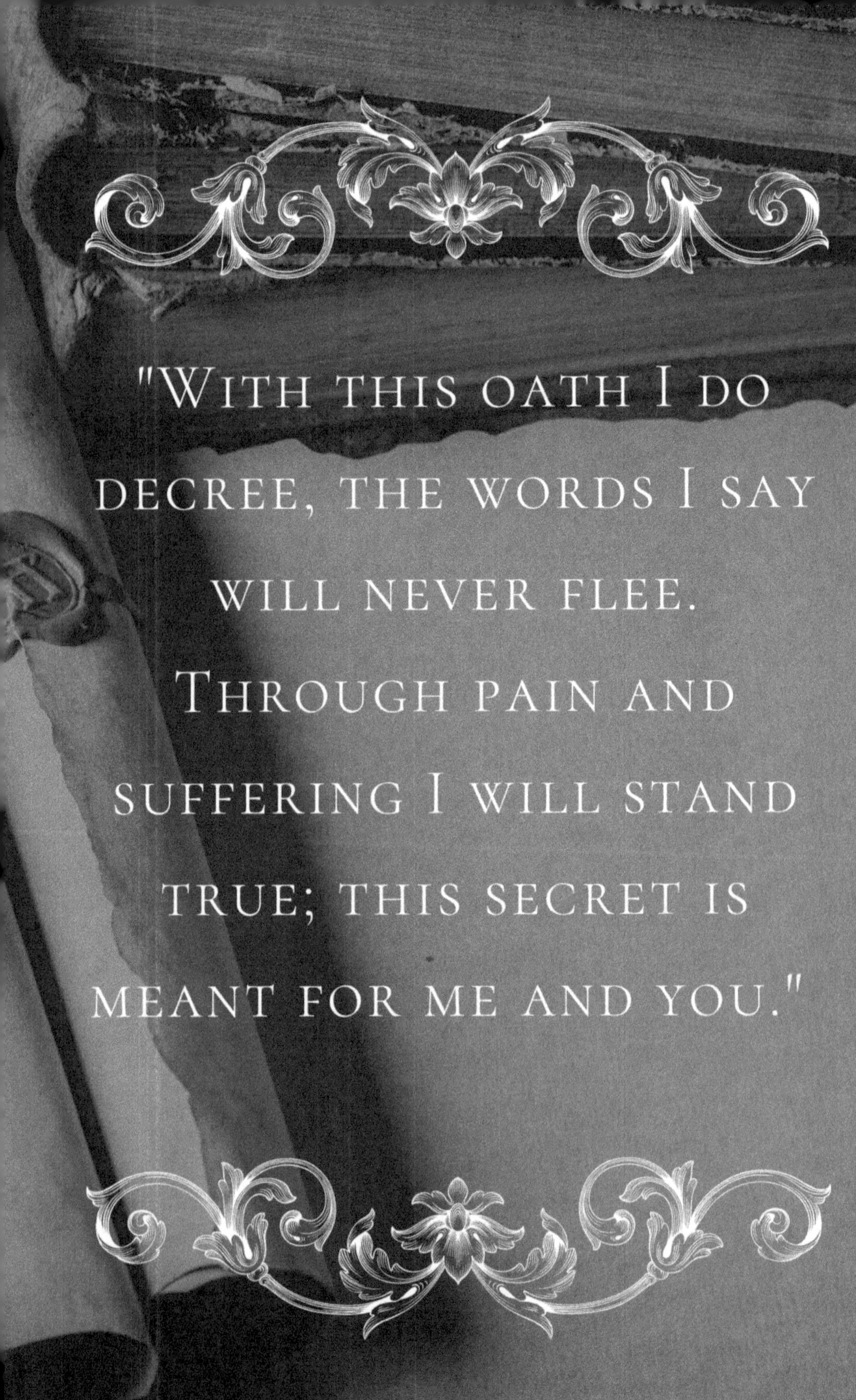
"With this oath I do decree, the words I say will never flee. Through pain and suffering I will stand true; this secret is meant for me and you."

CHAPTER 69

THE WORDS LEFT UNSPOKEN

SERAPHINA

This bed feels like a prison of my own design and before long, I get restless.

I have felt weaker as of late, ever since we returned from Infernal Summit. It felt as if my power didn't regenerate fully when we entered Tantalia, and it has continued to dwindle through my anger.

Perhaps it's the constant strain that my rage is taking out on my powers. The expulsion of such power can be detrimental to the wellbeing of even the strongest demons.

While still, something... *something* feels off. I have felt a drain on my power before, but not like this.

This feels deeper and it sends pangs of worry through me. Along with a coarse grating of curiosity that pumps through my blood, and I decide that I may need to go to the Mistress of Bloods for evaluation. Perhaps there is a tonic that could allow me to sleep for the next several hours and allow me to forget about the atrocities of Lilith's actions.

I toss the sheets of my bed back before standing and swiping my claws through my hair. I take a deep breath to settle myself and make sure my nightgown is at least presentable.

There is only one succubus I can go to that I can trust to be seen by.

A Queen showing up in The Infirmary is bad news for her people, especially in midst of rising tensions. So, I have to make sure I am undetected.

Zephyra is the only one I can trust for such things.

There is the smallest, irking feeling inside that something is much more awry than I anticipate, but I squash it as I close my eyes and breath deep.

Envisioning her quarters and her door, I zero in on Zephyra's space.

Soon, the world tilts around me, and my body is blown by a gust of cooler air. As I open my eyes, I come face to face with the large wooden panel that guards Zephyra's room. The hallways surrounding her quarters is absent of any demon and I stand alone for this task.

I steel myself and take a solid knock against the wooden entry.

A few moments pass before the door slowly opens, and Zephyra takes a perplexed look at me, "Mistress, what are you doing here?" she asks.

She is half dressed in her white gowns and cloak, customary for infirmary workers.

I push past her to rush to the middle of her room and the intensity of what could be wrong begins to race through my mind. This feeling is different, it's stronger, and it doesn't feel like the normal drain on my power. It causes my pulse to ratchet higher and I find myself pacing the floor.

Her head tilts in curiosity as she closes the door and turns to face me, wrapping her arms tight around her middle, "What can I do for you?"

My teeth nibble on the inside of my lip for a moment as I mull over my reasoning. My eyes dart around the room to search for anything that can ground me before I finally halt and settle my sights on her. Zephyra is a Lunarflame, a smaller noble house in Tantalia, and her eyes are bright purple, with a rounded chin and short white hair, like Velaria's. My chest clenches at the similar bob that sways around her jaw.

I shake my head of the thoughts, steeling myself with a deep breath, "I think my anger is draining me of my power. My strength comes from my feedings on Asher, but he has returned to Vesperholm to talk with his family. Is there anything you can do for me?"

Zephyra's eyebrow rises against her forehead, and she nods slowly. "Yes, of course. Come. Sit on the bed," she says as she gestures to the black blankets that lay neatly arranged on her mattress.

It feels like I move to the bed quicker than intend to as my nerves take hold and I place myself on the edge. Zephyra takes a tentative look over me as she approaches, almost fearful of my reasoning for being here. Soon, her gaze turns focused as she begins to examine me.

I hold a hand up, stopping her before she gets too far. "Zephyra, it is imperative that this encounter stays between us. The people cannot think their Queen is weak in times such as this. It is why I didn't go directly to The Infirmary."

Zephyra dips her head in confirmation, "Understood, Your Grace."

I give her a nod in return and swing my legs onto the platform to settle myself back. I shimmy my shoulders and wings as I will myself to relax, and my eyes drift shut. Her energy climbs as her hands hover over my body. A heated shroud of prickles envelops me, sinking into my bones and working its way through my blood.

The sensation lasts for only a few seconds before I hear a small gasp, and the heated shroud melts from my being almost as soon as it began. "Seraphina…" she murmurs quietly.

My eyes open and I catch her gaze. Her eyes are wide, glazed over and locked on my stomach. Her lips part in shock as her eyes begin to dart shallowly about my middle.

Tension squeezes my forehead as I watch her, and I press myself up on the bed. "What? What is it?"

Zephyra shakes her head, and her eyes track slowly up my body to land on my face, her focus coming back to stare into the depths of my being. Surprise, shock and *fear* lace her features. "You… Seraphina. You are with *child*," she whispers.

I…

"What… what do you mean?"

"Your womb. It… it has no vacancy. There is *life* within you. *That* is what is draining your power," Zephyra explains.

My eyes gaze off to stone floor below. The pounding of blood through my ears dances with the thoughts threatening to tear me in half.

A child… Here? In these times of peril? I…

"Seraphina, that is not all."

My eyes snap to her, "What do you mean 'that is not all'? Get on with it!" I demand.

Zephyra is not moved by my reaction, she merely takes a deep breath, "Twins, Seraphina. Two take residence in your belly."

The muscles in my jaw release, and my mouth opens as my sight hazes. "I must go." My body moves, but my thoughts are gone, there is only one action.

As I reach the door, I take a moment to turn back to Zephyra, leveling her with an icy gaze. "This goes to your grave, Zephyra. Or I will take it there with you."

Zephyra nods hastily in response, before I continue my journey to my next destination.

As the world shifts, the dark surrounds me and the distant shriek of baby halflings wails from the other side of the wall. The Pod Room is a large chamber; protected by thick, black brick, and holds small cradles, each covered in a dome of glass. Inside are small babies in various stages of incubation. Some are merely orbs of light. Some are barely formed, and some are ready to emerge. With scrunched, pudgy faces, tiny horn nubs and thin little tails. Sconces of blue fire are placed on the walls, lending a calming glow to the warmed space. This chamber is kept heated to mimic the bellies of demon mothers.

The foundations of the little silver cradles are short tree trunks, corded with thick roots that burrow into the ground, pulsing and glowing with vivid differentiating colors. Green, yellow, orange, red, purple, blue.

An elder succubus approaches as my eyes swipe around the chamber. The distant echo of my past screeches at me in retaliation as I steel my spine. A deep breath settles me just enough as I face the demon. A soft smile tugs at her cheeks, "Your Grace, what a lovely surprise," she says sweetly.

I give her a curt smile before I sigh. The gravity of my intentions in this space settles deep into my bones, and a rush of guilt trembles up my spine. "I wish it was."

The demon tilts her head as she looks at me. While most demons don't age, she has the merest evidence of wrinkles, and her hair is pulled into a bun high on the back of her head. Her lavender eyes are kind and she's a small, portly woman, draped in The Pods periwinkle cloaks.

I take her hands in mine, almost desperately, as I search her eyes, "Mistress, I need you to swear on your life, and the lives of these kin, that you will keep safe the words I am about to tell you."

She nods slowly, curious and confused. "Whatever you need. I am forever at your service."

The delicate skin of her hand slides against my fingers as I turn her palm over. Taking one of my claws, I slice through her flesh and her blood pools in the center as I do the same to one of my hands.

I slide my palm into hers and the energies of our power begin to intertwine, dancing a horrific tango. My throat tightens and my voice wobbles as I recite the binding spell. "With this oath I do decree, the words I say will never flee. Through pain and suffering I will stand true; this secret is meant for me and you."

The elder repeats my words, her tone strong and pure.

It gives me just the smallest amount of solace as my free hand drifts to my stomach.

Purple light shimmers against our skin, and a surge of energy pulses through me, binding her word to mine.

"Mistress, I... I need a pod. Two, in fact."

The feel of the words on my tongue is bitter. Sour even. In any other circumstance, I wouldn't question carrying the babies. But with my life hanging in the balance, and a target on my spine, I can't risk their lives for my pride.

I could never risk them.

The elder demon's eyes widen before they drift to my stomach, "Seraphina, you are with *child?*"

I nod hesitantly. The lump in my throat tightens to near pain as I speak and tears well in my eyes before I take another steeling breath. I take both of her hands in mine in a near death grip, a near plea for protection for my babies. "They need to be kept away from the others, only to be cared for by you. They cannot be known; they *must* be hidden. It is imperative they are kept in secret. If anyone found out about their existence, they would perish, they are the new heirs to the throne. Which means they are a *target* now, Mistress."

Her gaze is considerate, thoughtful as she adheres to my words, nodding slowly, "Yes... yes, of course. Follow me."

Her tight grip wraps around my hand before she leads me through the rows of pods. Along one of the back walls in the corner, she looks over a blank space before placing her hand against it. Her eyes close and soon a powerful thrum vibrates the foundation of the chamber. Brick gives way to dirt as a rectangular entry is carved away.

With one mighty push against the falling dirt wall, it hollows, and a small holding space is created inside. It's a small room, merely big enough for two pods.

I watch as the elder demon gets to work crafting the new cradles for my babies. The wood she conjures from the ground and the vines that begin to hollow against the exterior form into delicately crafted pods.

These babies would be a dream in a life I'd like to live. A world where Asher and I can raise them together, where we can train them in whatever they choose. In a world where the wards are secure and the Drannars aren't threatening to destroy us.

But this world is not that dream… and I am fully awake.

My hands tremble and my breaths begin to move shallowly through me as I continue watching her set up the pods.

A few moments pass, and two small, silver cradles have been constructed within the space.

The plush, purple velvet lining pulls tautly against my heart.

How I wish that could be me.

How I wish *I* could be the one to offer this solace.

My teeth catch my lip as the sinking feeling of abandoning them creeps into my being. It tears through every bit of me, and I don't try to push it away.

I deserve to have it tear me apart.

"Are you ready, Your Majesty?" the elder demon asks gently.

I spend a few moments staring at the cradles before my hand flicks at the air, conjuring a piece of parchment.

I press the paper against the dirt wall, with rocks and sand falling to my feet before I slide my talon along it in neat rows. Swirls of purple light dance across the page as my thoughts are etched into it.

The thought of doing this makes everything weigh heavy. Heavier than it's been in any of the trials I have gone through so far. Including taking the crown.

I can't stop the tears that begin to flow freely against my cheeks, and I can't stop the pain coursing through my blood.

So, I don't. I let my tears speak for me as the words splatter the page, and I let my heart fall apart.

I fold the parchment before I turn to hand it to the mistress, my hand shaking beyond my control. "If something happens, I need this to go to my mate and commander, Asher Blackwood. He is the only one allowed to have the knowledge of these kin."

She nods as her fingers gingerly grip the paper. But my hand tightens against it, and she pulls it away.

As I watch her pocket the note, I wipe the sadness from my skin and press my wings against the wall. "I'm ready now."

The demon approaches with a remorseful smile and my eyes close as I wait.

"You may feel a slight pinch, darling. I'm so sorry," the mistress says gently.

I connect with the wall, digging my fingers into the rock and gripping against it for strength, because it feels as if I have nothing left. Sand falls to the ground as my body pins to it.

A strong pulse begins to course through my center, and my belly heats. My groan is muffled in the small room as a strong tug is felt in my stomach, as if a ball of energy is being ripped through my skin.

A nip is felt as my teeth sink into my lip to stifle my pain, and my nails grip a stray root in the dirt wall. The irony tinge of blood coats my tongue as my fangs break skin.

The fraying bits of sand and rock between my fingers ground me, and the pulsing stops for a moment.

I take a few deep breaths, before another surge of pulsing rocks through me, and the second orb is pulled free.

As my power slowly climbs higher, my eyes flutter open. One of the pods have been sealed and inside is a glowing purple orb with a red center. It's different from any other pod baby I've ever witnessed.

The mistress holds the other orb of light in her palm before she places it in the cradle beside it, and a glass dome slides closed to seal it with a hissing lock. The small ball of light glows green with a purple center. Soon, the thick, corded veins along the trunks begin to pulse, and the colors fill them as their respective hues shift with each throb.

I approach the cradles, standing in the middle of them as my hands graze over the glass. Weakness pulls at my torso, bringing my knees into the dirt and my wings toss over the glass domes. Buried roots eat into my knees and the rocks pinch at the skin there. My tail wraps around my hips in a futile attempt to calm me.

My head hangs as I brace myself on either side and heated sobs break through me. Flooding every bit of my being. I've walled off my pain from Asher... he doesn't deserve to feel this sorrow, it isn't his burden to carry.

Tears stream down my cheeks, cooling through the heat that has risen on my cheeks.

"They will be safe here. No harm will come to them here." But the voice telling me this is not my own.

"I have yielded, and it has not been enough," I whisper back as the tears pool below me.

The voice is silent as the tears flow from my face.

"When... when will my sacrifice be enough? When will I be worthy of peace? I have given my all, to have it crushed beneath my circumstance... Why? What have I done?" I murmur. I don't know if I'm speaking to myself, or if I'm speaking to The Fates.

Regardless, no one responds. Nothing has come to save me from myself.

Soon the pool forms into a salted mirror, and I catch a glimpse of myself in it.

Dark circles have formed beneath my eyes, and the image of a girl lost stares back at me.

As if I feel the heavy glare of the gods at my back, I realize then that nothing will come to save me.

Because I have to save myself. I have to yield to my own pain, or it will eat *me* alive.

As I stare at the image of myself in the salted mirror, strength courses through me, when I know I've done what is best for my babies.

I may not be able to save myself quite yet, but at the very end of it all, at least I saved them. I saved the small pieces of my heart I've been forced to stash away.

I stare at my image for a moment longer before I breathe deep and settle my nerves.

Standing, I lean over and place a singular kiss to the each of the domes. "You will be safe here. I will make sure of it."

The orbs pulse within, and the metal back of my amulet burns against my skin.

I will my spine to stiffen before I turn to the mistress. Her hands are pressed into the sleeves of her cloak as she watches me.

When Asher returns, I will bring him here and show him what we've done. He can't go without the knowledge of his babies. He needs to know their protection is paramount in the days to come.

But everyone else... I lock gazes with the demon, staring deep into her lavender eyes and willing every amount of strength that I have into my voice. "No one is to know."

Her voice doesn't echo in here, like it does in the large chamber beside us. It's quiet, almost muffled against the dirt walls, as she responds, "No one will know."

But all of it, I wouldn't change anything.

I got to meet Seraphina.
I get to love her.

And I get to be here with her.

CHAPTER 70

HOME
ASHER

I haven't talked to Cedric since our fight in The Pits.

And as much as I really don't want to talk to him, I don't think I can go back to Vesperholm without him. I think I also need to talk to Gideon.

Soon after I leave our bedroom, I make my way to Selene and Gideon's, knocking softly against the large wooden door.

A few moments pass before Gideon answers the door, sans clothing, his cock out for the world to see. I shield my eyes as I yelp, turning my head away, "Gideon! Put some fucking clothes on!"

"Asher, it's a cock. You've seen one before," he groans.

"I don't want to see YOURS!"

Gideon scoffs before the door clicks shut and I can turn back to it with a heavy breath of relief.

A few *more* moments pass, and Gideon returns to open the door, wearing forest green night breeches.

"Thank you," I sigh.

He rolls his eyes, "Okay, so what is so important that you had to interrupt my morning romp with Selene?"

"I'm going to Vesperholm. I'm going to tell my family I'm staying here with Seraphina and that I'm safe."

Gideon's face slacks in concern and he looks back into the room before he steps out into the hall, closing the door behind him, "You… you're going to Vesperholm?"

"I'll be coming back. But I'm asking if you wanted to go with me."

Gideon's face works for a while, his gaze trailing away as he thinks, "No… no. I'll have you send a letter to my family. I'll face them when things are better."

That's not entirely surprising. Gideon has been incredibly attached to Selene since the moment he met her.

"Are you sure?"

"Yes. I don't want to go home right now. I don't want to leave Selene."

There it is.

"Alright then."

"Let me go write the letter," Gideon says as he opens the bedroom door.

I nod to him, and he disappears. He emerges a few moments later with a rolled piece of parchment, and hands it to me. "This needs to go to Finnley. I don't think my father could handle reading it."

I nod in understanding as I take it, placing it in my waist pack before I open my arms. Gideon eyes me for a second before he wraps his arms around me in a crushing hug and a heavy pat to my back, "To Tantalia, brother," he whispers.

My chest pulses with a heavy breath as I squeeze harder against him, "To Tantalia."

Gideon releases me, and I give him one final shove in the shoulder before I make my way back down to the large greeting atrium at the front of The Keep. When I reach the landing platform outside, I whistle for Vylai.

The sky around Tantalia has descended into darkness. It hasn't stopped raining since Seraphina retreated to her room. It flies against the blackened clouds at an angle, and you can't even see the ground below. It's just varying shades of dark gray that topple one over the other.

Soon, the bright white fur of Vylai breaks through the cloud coverage and she lands on the platform.

When we returned from Kaithoon, Seraphina had taken the time to have the leather smiths work on a saddle for her. They needed to make some strange adjustments considering it was for a dragon body. But it has worked well so far.

Of course, the leather is a deep onyx that contrasts starkly against her shimmering white fur.

It wraps in a large harness against her chest and under her front legs to sit pertly on her back.

Instead of a bridle, she wears a snout apparatus that allows her to speak but still gives me some level of control. I took some time after the fittings to get a feel for it and I have been taking time here and there to gain my bearings with this new method of movement.

As Vylai lands on the platform, her fur drips with small beads of water that she shakes haphazardly off of her body and wings. She looks to me with a sad tilt to her head, "Where is your mate, friend?" she asks softly.

I sigh as I come to rub Vylai's snout, "She'll not be joining us. I'm returning to my realm to tell my family I'm staying here in Tantalia."

"You seem upset about that," Vylai says as her frown deepens and her curious head tilts even more.

"I am. Things are… fickle, right now," I tell her as my gaze glides to the clouds beyond.

"Can I accompany you to your home?" she asks.

I sigh as I weigh her question. Of course I would love to bring her along, but I have no idea what my people would do to her. And I don't think I could live with her dying by my people's hands. "I don't think that's a good idea. My people are unkind toward different creatures. And they've never seen a dragon before. I think it best you stay here."

Vylai nods sadly before she shifts for me to mount her. Her long talons clack against the stone platform as she readies herself for flight.

I pull on the saddle horn to haul myself up and sling my leg over her. Steadying my feet in the stirrups, I whistle hard against the blowing wind. She lunges through the dark clouds and the rain licks against my skin as we fly through the black puffs. It's hard to see where the fuck we are, so I lean forward to get as close to Vylai's ears as I can, "Take me to the barracks!" I yell over the roaring wind.

The reigns tug against my hands as Vylai nods, and she takes a hard bank to the bottom of The Keep where the barracks rest.

As we descend through the cloud coverage, the barracks come into view, and I see the lands of Tantalia. It seems as though the people of this realm are still going about their daily duties. They're all shrouded in varying shades of magical glow to keep the rain from hitting them.

Though, it pains me to see no one in The Pits. It should be Gideon and me, or Seraphina and Selene down below training The Legions.

I'm pulled from my sadness as my stomach drops and Vylai lands on the ground beside the barracks.

I climb off of Vylai, giving her a pat on the head for her good work and tell her to wait while I take a moment to say hi to Gnox. I've made the last-minute decision to ride him through the portal and back home.

He seems excited by the prospect and bucks his head in confirmation.

A shadow of a smile tugs at my lips. At least someone is excited, because I particularly, am not.

I walk around the stable to head for The Barracks, looking around at the different buildings to see which one Cedric could be in, but I have no idea.

A few large soldiers in Lunae Legion cloaks lounge around some of the buildings, soaking up the rain for whatever strange reason.

As I approach, they all stand to address me before kneeling, "Commander!" they all shout in unison.

My brow furrows as I look at them. It would be nice to appreciate this sort of greeting, but right now it feels wrong.

"I'm looking for Cedric. Has anyone seen him?"

The warriors stand and the blond haired one to the right nods, "He's inside. Should I get him?"

"Please, if you could."

The soldier nods and retreats to one of the barracks behind him, calling for Cedric.

Patiently, I wait. The nerves in my chest rise the longer I stand here mulling over the things that could happen.

Will we fight again? Will he taunt me? Will we get nowhere, when we need to be going somewhere together?

I don't know if Cedric would want to stay here, but I really, really hope he does.

He deserves to have a place he can thrive as much as I have. Even if the reason for our ascensions has been against our will, I wouldn't change a single moment if it got me into Seraphina's arms.

Soon, voices are heard from one of the buildings and Cedric comes back with the soldier. His bearded face has a shadow of a smile as he approaches me.

"Asher," he says curtly with a bow.

"Cedric," I sigh in relief.

He has continued to put on muscle and his beard is even longer now. He also wears the same cloaks as some of the higher-ranking Lunae warriors. And I can't help the way my heart beams with pride for him

Well done, Ceddy.

I connect with his gaze and take a steeling breath, hoping that what I'm about to say doesn't anger him and that he understands. His familiar green eyes are curious, and he waits patiently for me to speak.

"I'm… I'm going back to Vesperholm," I start.

His brow furrows in wild confusion, "What do you me–"

"No, no. I'm going to tell father that I won't be returning home, that I've chosen to stay here. And I wanted you to come with me. I wanted to give you the chance to stay or go."

Cedric's face contorts in a series of differing emotions and his thoughts seem to run wild the longer he stares at me. Until he finally speaks, and nods in slow understanding. "Okay."

"Okay…" I say hesitantly as I watch him in mild skepticism.

He hasn't been this calm around me in ages. But maybe that talk with Seraphina *did* get through to him.

I'll have to ask her what she said to him when I return.

"I'll grab the guards and have them take us to The Portal," he says.

I nod in return. There is a beaming glimmer of hope that shines in my chest at how well the interaction has gone so far. I can't remember the last time Cedric and I spoke this well.

"I'm going to get Gnox, I'll meet you over there."

Cedric nods and I run to the stables. Gnox hasn't been ridden in a long while and I can tell he's itching to get out.

Vylai stands next to the stables, nipping at the water that comes down from the sky. She catches sight of me and her face perks up as her tail wags and the rain is forgotten. "Rider! You've returned!" she says excitedly.

I give her a small smile, "I'll be leaving now. Please keep an eye on Seraphina for me, the best that you can."

Vylai nods excitedly, "Yes, of course! Anything for you, rider!"

I wrap my arms around her in a grateful hug and she nuzzles against me to wrap her tail around us. "Be safe, rider. I'll miss you."

Her words send a spear through me, and I grip her tighter. "I'll miss you, Vylai."

I release her from the hug, and she nods one more time before she lunges for the sky. Dipping and twirling, she disappears into the clouds.

I was hesitant to have her at first, but, she has quickly grown on me and I'm more and more appreciative of her and her light every single day.

I enter the stable and begin tacking up Gnox, petting and stroking him sadly as I realize I'm leaving Tantalia for the first time since I was stolen.

As I place his purple saddle pad on his back, and pull his saddle from its stand, I remember every moment of my journey here so far.

The way I wanted to ruin them from the inside.

When the saddle settles easily on his back, I remember how much guilt I felt when I caught sight of the tapestries for the first time.

Looping the buckle around his chest to fasten it, I remember The Library and the talking books there.

Tightening the strap, I remember watching the soldiers in The Pits and our daily rounds in the meadow.

As I move to attach his bridle, I remember The Catacombs... the dreaded Catacombs.

But all of it, I wouldn't change anything.

I got to meet Seraphina. I get to love her. And I get to be here with her.

I shake my head of the memories as I finish tacking Gnox up, and then mount him. Clicking him out of the stables, we round the back to meet Cedric at the barracks with two large guards.

They lead us around The Barracks, past several massive, armored buildings, before we reach a large set of black metal doors at the bottom of The Keep.

I have never seen this area before.

The one time I had been through it, I was blacked out.

The entry is shielded by large guards that stand outside it. As we approach, the guards call to one another, and the doors screech open in the horrific symphony of metal against stone.

Cedric grabs Gnox's reigns to lead him through the doors and into the chamber. The Portal Room is a massive space, and eerily dark. With high walls and even more guards, a white stone path leads you straight to The Portal. The massive structure is crafted in a circle with more onyx bricks that make up the walls surrounding us. The Portal itself shimmers vibrantly and bathes the dark area in deep shades of amethyst light, that beckons us as we walk up to it.

The thought of leaving, and the thought of telling my parents that I won't be coming back causes my stomach to plummet, and I look down at Cedric in fear. My hands grip hard on the saddle horn, as if bracing myself. He looks up at me with a reassuring nod before he leads us to the glowing purple vortex. The silence in the chamber makes Gnox's clops sound just as loud as the pounding in my chest.

"When you see us approach, let no one else through. Only Cedric and I," I tell the guards that stand near the colors, before my gaze shifts back to Cedric, "If he so chooses to return."

Cedric gives me a ghost of a smile before he nods, and the two of us step through the vivid purple curtain, only to be greeted by the bright sunlight heating Vesperholm on the other side.

My chest begins to heave with feral breaths as crimson consumes my vision all over again.

CHAPTER 71

LEATHER TOMES AND LIGHTNING BOLTS

SERAPHINA

After I leave The Pods, I make my way back to The Keep. Where I spend a few minutes pacing my room. My power returning gives me the energy to think about the things that I have tried to push away from the past few days. Soon, my rage returns and anger rushes through me. The audacity of that man to bring up Lilith in my presence after everything I've experienced recently with her.

I love Asher. I do… and part of me knows he's just trying to help, but I *can't* right now.

But I also can't stop researching all together, no matter how sad I am.

As if the anger fuels the rampant flurry of questions in my skull, I trudge down to The Library.

I don't feel like conversing with anyone. I don't go searching for Xeneera, Tyrick, or Selene and her dog when I leave my room. I don't say hello to anyone as I traverse The Keep. I don't acknowledge anyone's presence as they stop and bow as I pass them.

And when I reach The Library, I tell everyone inside to vacate.

All the demons inside shuffle out with a quickness, leaving the door to rumble shut behind them.

I needed to find something, *anything* on Celestials.

But the *rage* that begins to course through me here… it prods and pokes at my insides and my heart drums violently against my chest.

The memories of *her* teaching me in this room.

Her voice almost bounces off the high ceiling and the bookcases that surround me. "*You'll find your place here. Your purpose is in the books as much as it is on the battlefield.*"

This is what Lilith wanted. She sent me on this goose chase. *She* brought me here day after day.

For what… *why?*

The longer I stare at the vacant spines of the books, the louder their murmurs become.

The rambling words mesh and cause me to seethe with rabid fury.

The angrier I get; the less control I have on the barely secured restraint I have.

My chest begins to heave with feral breaths as crimson consumes my vision all over again.

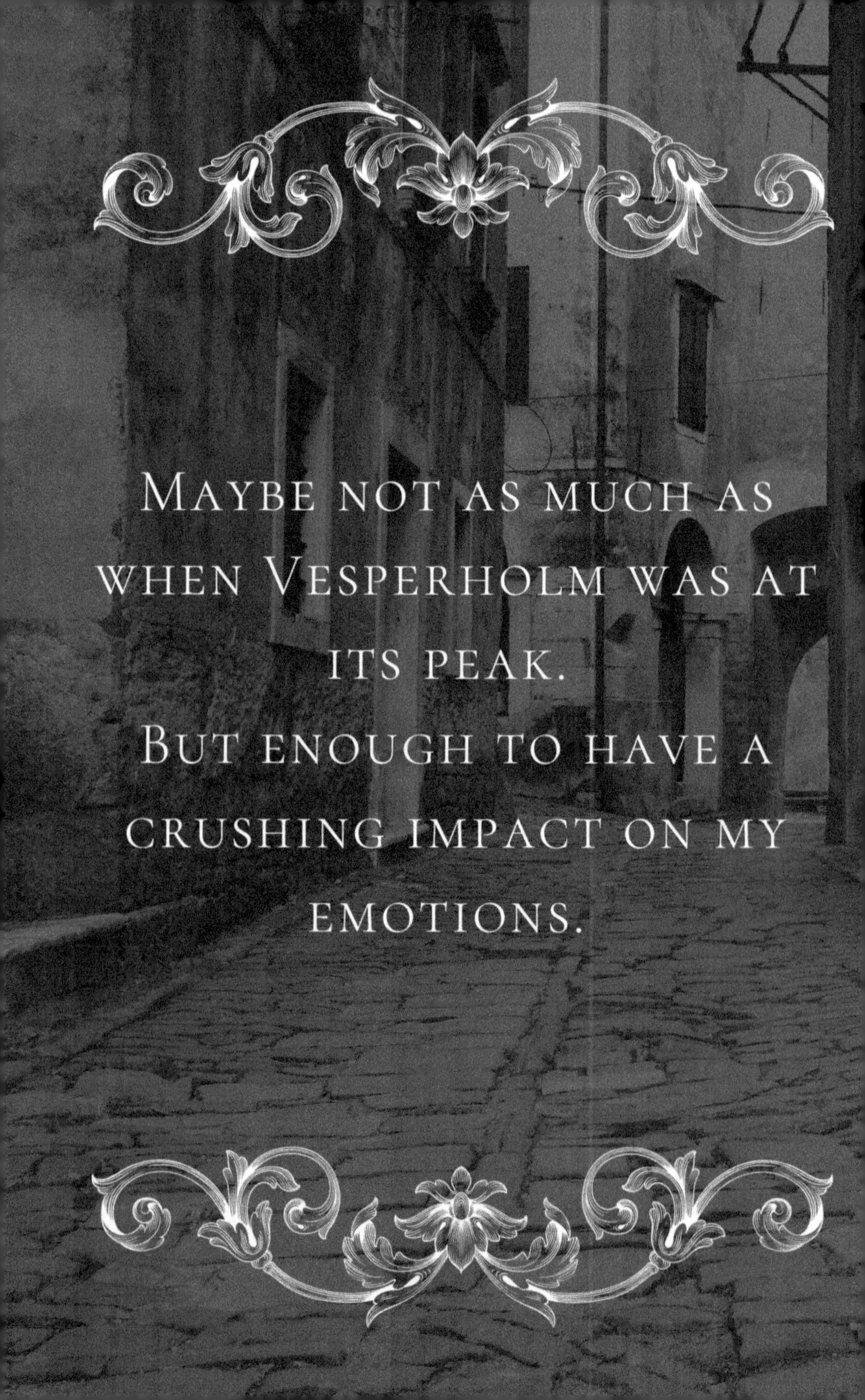

Maybe not as much as when Vesperholm was at its peak.

But enough to have a crushing impact on my emotions.

Chapter 72

Vesperholm

Asher

Cedric and I look at each other as we enter Vesperholm; shocked to find the bright sun heating our faces as we leave the cold and wet land of Tantalia behind.

As if night had turned into day, birds chirp their songs. Little animals scurry around outside of the portal yet run into the woods at our arrival.

Even the grass around the trees seems to have gained some of their vibrancy back.

"What… what happened?" Cedric asks.

I survey the land a little longer; truly astonished at how much has changed in our absence.

I am happy for our people, but it hurts that it only got better *after* we left. It makes it seem as if our presence in this space was not even needed, which sends a poisoned spear deep into my soul.

I shake my head as I turn to face Cedric, "Seraphina said they had stopped retrieving men from Vesperholm."

Cedric is silent as he looks over the stark differences made in our land in such a short amount of time.

"Do you wanna hop on? It'll be quicker that way," I ask. Cedric's attention is reluctantly pulled back to me and he nods.

I offer him a hand and pull him onto the back of Gnox, where he sits behind the saddle.

Gnox takes a slow trot through the thick brush, taking care now that he knows there's two of us on him.

As we look around, parts of the woods have been abandoned, as if Shadowfang have left their hideouts.

Some of the stray members of Shadowfang come from their houses in the trunks to gawk at us as we pass by, and I take the moment to stop, "Where is Finnley?" I ask an older gentleman that stayed behind.

The man stands with his mouth agape, "The… the city," he murmurs as he points in the direction of City Center.

I imagine seeing two humans, clad in black, demonic armor atop an onyx steed, is a sight to behold.

Especially when both are from the strongest house in the Realm.

I nod in thanks and click Gnox farther into the forest. The abandoned hideouts have been left to rot with some of their entry doors missing.

Cedric and I say nothing to each other as we continue through the forest and reach the outskirts of East Territory. But I don't think we need to say much. I can feel his body tense against my back the closer we get to The City.

The grass around the forest has turned a light green, as if it has just started growing back. Short blades of new growth peak through the browned, dead earth. And there are even more people peddling around the area, setting up some areas for farming.

The pain that begins to course through me is visceral, and the energy of Cedric at my back seems to match my own. I am happy for them and the fact they have been able to start their world anew. This is what I had wanted in the first place, wasn't it?

But the fact I had to leave my world behind for such a thing to happen… It hurts a lot more than I expected.

"They… didn't really need us, did they?" I hear Cedric murmur from behind me.

"No… No, I guess they didn't," I respond solemnly.

As we pass by North Territory, there are several people outside and along the road to the mansion, helping rebuild the Bloodreign Estate.

People are cleaning its exterior and pulling weeds from around the property, and I take a left to head into South Territory.

As we approach City Center, it seems to be bustling with activity.

Maybe not as much as when Vesperholm was at its peak. But enough to have a crushing impact on my emotions.

Finnley and his father are standing outside of a shop, replacing some of the crushed windows and sweeping up some of the debris in front of it.

They turn to me with wide eyes before they start calling people out into the street. Others begin filing into the street from their shops and some of the surrounding homes that were once abandoned.

A menagerie of children come with them, proving how much they were able to accomplish in this time.

I hear the steady breathing of Cedric behind me.

Even the air of the city is clearer as the once blazing pit of fire that burned the succubus bodies has gone dark.

There is no scent of rot and decay, or smoke.

No, it's fresh air now.

Finnley approaches us with wide eyes, "You've… you've returned," he says almost in disbelief. His eyes roam our bodies, lingering on the harsh plates of armor that line our shoulders and chests.

I nod curtly, "I have. It seems you all have done well with yourselves here."

Finnley glances behind him before he returns his gaze to us. Gnox's hooves clack against the cobblestone road as he shifts back and forth against it.

"Shortly after you were taken, the Succubus stopped coming. After we realized the coast might be clear, people started venturing out. A few months passed and we started rebuilding."

I suppose all of that makes sense.

But it doesn't lessen the pain. Not at all.

"I see that."

"Where is Gideon? Is he alright?" Finnley asks nervously.

My heart gallops against my ribcage. Every single hard pulse sends a wave of nausea through me as I reach into my waist pack, slowly unclasping it to pull out the parchment letter. The small scroll makes a quiet scraping noise as I shake uncontrollably; slowly handing it to Finnley, who eyes it in confusion as he takes it.

He unrolls the parchment and his eyes scan over it, his brow slowly tensing in anger as he reaches the bottom of the letter, "What… what the fuck does this mean?"

Air fills my lungs as I take a deep, steadying breath, trying my best to stave away the panic inside, "The same thing it'll mean for me when I go to see my father." I can't beat around the bush with an admission like this one. I have to shoot straight in case they try to talk me out of it. And I imagine that's the same reason Gideon didn't come.

"You both are going back?" he asks as his eyes volley between Cedric and I.

I glance at Cedric over my shoulder who meets my gaze with a confirmation of his own before we both nod at Finnley.

"H-… How could you all abandon your people like this?" Finnley asks. His face twists in disgust as he looks over the both of us, backing away as if he can't stand even being in our proximity.

The way his eyes slide up and down us, as if he's never seen us before.

"Because there are worse things out in this world than the Succubus. And we're going to fix it." I fix my shoulders and carry myself just a tad higher.

I have let them walk over me for years, and even now when our efforts are the reason they stand in the open, they try to trample me.

But not anymore.

They don't get to chastise my accomplishments when they've been *carried* out of their cowardice on *my* back.

"How the fuck would you know?"

"Because I've seen it, Finnley. And they'll come for you all next if we aren't fucking ready."

"You idiots have just been placed under their bullshit spells and have been sent to finish us."

"We're Blackwoods. We don't need to be under a spell to do the right fucking thing. When Vesperholm is out of the woods, you'll have us to thank for it."

His words send anger coursing through me, and I kick Gnox in the side to gallop him away from the situation.

I know now what I'm walking in to.

The biggest fight I think I've fought thus far.

And it only gets more apparent the closer we get to the once abandoned forge of our home, to find my father and mother inside with a small baby boy.

The parchment before me has a singular drawing -- a very **important** drawing.

CHAPTER 73

BLOODIED PARCHMENT

SERAPHINA

Papers flutter to the ground from where they float in the air. The sound of the parchments scrape against the stone as they land and it causes awareness to surge through me, bringing me back to my destruction.

The last of the bookcases have fallen, and the floor is littered with destroyed tomes.

The winds had picked up, lightning crackled through the chamber, and rage gripped me by my throat. It threw me deep into the pits of rage. And I brought every last shelf in here down with me. I tore through them all. Ripped them apart and left their souls in pieces just as Lilith had done to me.

Extinguished candle smoke lingers in the large, darkened library to mix with the old parchment that has been torn from the books.

The speaking books have ceased their ramblings, as all of their pages lay scattered across The Library.

Torn leather, strings from their bindings, and small panels of wood lie naked on the stone without their skins. They create a portrait of the destruction that *I* wrought.

Me.

The blackened room slowly descends on me, as if the walls are closing in. It presses deep against me as my chest heaves.

My eyes settle on some of the papers around me, looking over them all as my anger slowly wanes away.

The realization of my actions slowly seeps into me, and a shallow retch tugs at my throat as bile rises.

I've destroyed our history.

I've wrecked our ages.

And it was *Lilith's* fault.

It was *Lilith's* doing.

She favored the knowledge of our world. Yet, she kept the knowledge worth knowing all to herself.

How could one be so keen on saving her people, yet keep the way to save them away from the ones who could?

How…?!

Over and over my eyes scan the papers; until one catches my attention.

My anger is forgotten as I focus on it and the etches against it become clearer. I scramble desperately to it, pressing away half-destroyed textbooks in the process. I ignore the harsh scrape of my knees against stone as I reach for the paper.

The parchment before me has a singular drawing -- a very *important* drawing.

This… this is why I couldn't find something. It's a *picture.* It's not *words.*

On the sheet, is my amulet, wrapped around the hilt of a dagger.

But not just *any* dagger.

Asher's dagger.

With a primal drawing of Lilith and the faceless human beside it.

But I don't have time to put any of the pieces together when a crushing blow knocks against my skull and the world around me fades into black.

"You're a **monster**."

CHAPTER 74

REUNION

ASHER

———◆———

The already squeezing pain in my heart increases and my throat tightens almost to a seal. My soul desperately screams for air. But it can't. Not as I watch my father through the window of our repaired forge. My hand drifts to my pocket, where I rub the small metal disk. I remind myself of my purpose, and my duty.

I *am* here for the good of my people.

But at the end of it all, my allegiance is to my mate.

And I would sooner abandon my family than abandon my love.

The small baby in my mother's arms stirs softly and my father leans in to press and play with the little boy's face.

I haven't seen him smile in years… I didn't think my parents would be so content in our absence.

"They…" I hear Cedric as his breath presses against my ear.

"Yes… yes they did."

I click Gnox to our once dilapidated stable. It too, has been repaired and the two horses inside seem much more content with their surroundings.

Cedric's horse, however, begins to whinny as she sets her eyes on him.

Cedric leaps from the back of Gnox to run to his horse, throwing his arms tightly around her large white neck, "Rosey girl. Hey, hey.

I missed you," I hear him murmur as I bring Gnox inside the stable, jumping off and letting him mingle.

He takes a moment to trot around the open space, saying his hellos to his long-lost friends.

I'm not sure how much he missed them, but they were always here together, and I wonder if they had ever noticed his absence.

They must have with how excited they appear to see him.

Cedric gives Rose a kiss on the nose and pats her head as he walks to me, and we both make our way to the entrance of our shop.

I look to him in disappointment, and he gives me a thin-lipped smile before he nods in solidarity. The small gesture steels me just enough. And together, we press open the door.

"Shops closed today, fr-" my father's once gruff voice has turned light as he looks to the people entering his shop.

My eyes swivel around the space, taking in all the changes that have been made. The tables have been reset, and the walls are lined with different tools. There aren't as many axes, daggers and swords. Instead, he's traded them for different tilling and farming items. Hoes, shovels, and rakes to help bring their town back to glory. There are some metal bits and bridle pieces for horse tack, as well.

Dust and webs have been swept away, and the shop no longer reeks of earthy mold.

My gaze settles on him, and I don a gentle half-smile. His weathered face drops, alongside my mother's, whose features turn in shocked happiness as she tries to hold back her tears.

My father quickly stands, his eyes wide as he stumbles to us. He looks us up and down before wrapping his arms around the both of us in a crushing hug. His hearty chest rumbles as sobs escape him. "Boys… boys you're home, I thought- *we* thought you were gone. We thought you had died saving us."

We wrap our arms around him and heat begins to seep down my cheeks when tears break through my fear. Not just from this reunion, but from his admission and from the painful truth I must share with him.

"We're alright," I whisper softly to him as he loosens the strong hold he has on us. His thick, worn hands wipe a few of the tears from his aged face as he peers at both of us. His head tilts in observation as he looks in my eyes and he narrows his eyes. Deciding to ignore what he sees there, he shakes his head, "You boys have packed on some muscle," he laughs as he slaps us on the shoulders.

I nod nervously as he goes to sit back in his chair beside the table. "Come! You have to meet our new little warrior! He'll be a fine killer one day. We named him after the founding Blackwood. Broward," he says as he slaps the table in welcome.

I glance to Cedric, who shakes his head solemnly before I settle my gaze on my father, "We uhm… we aren't staying. We came back to tell you… something," I say nervously. My mother wipes tears from her eyes as she watches us, her arms bouncing the little bundle she holds.

My father's brow furrows in confusion, "Back?" He finally catches sight of our clothing.

His eyes linger on the metal plates and the blackened leather, and his features begin to contort in denial.

I inhale a deep breath, allowing him to look over us for a moment longer.

If he puts the pieces together himself, maybe it'll be easier to tell him.

Knock the arrow.

"Cedric and I are safe. We have been aiding the efforts in Tantalia, and… we are going to be staying in The Realm of the Succubus… We are staying in Tantalia."

Let it fly.

I don't think I've ever seen my father's eyes grow this wide before. And while I have seen him speechless, I don't think I've seen him *this* speechless.

"We have found Alden… He is safe as well. But he is… incapacitated."

"W-what?" he responds in shock. His jowls and eyebrows slack
as his eyes dart between the two of us.

"Cedric and I have found our purpose and our life in Tantalia.
And we will not be returning to Vesperholm."

"How… how could you do this to us?" my mother's watery voice
asks.

"My mate…" I sigh softly as I look down to the newly refurbished
floor. "I have been mated to a succubus. She is the Queen of their
realm. And I have indebted my life to her and all that she does."

"Mate? You've sunk your cock into a demon, boy?!" my father
growls as he comes to a stand once more. He braces a hand on the
table as he rises to his full height.

Rage pricks against me as I attempt to hold onto my restraint, and
I catch Cedric's face drop from the corner of my eye as he senses
whatever is about to happen.

"I have. She has become… my entire world," I say in an attempt
to hold my anger at bay.

My father grimaces, a snarl tugging at his lip, "You would
abandon us for her filth? You'd give your soul to them willingly?
You are a Blackwood! We do not bend to the wills of their games!"

His words spear through me, sending my vision into a fiery red.
"Hold your fucking tongue. You may be my father, but I will not
allow you to deface my mate. She has played no games with me."

"Father?" he scoffs, "No son of *mine* would *ever* give his life to a
demon."

"You're wrong. She has given me more purpose than I have
ever had here in Vesperholm. I am the Commander of the Nights
Legions. A *mate* to their Queen. What did you give me for my work
here? A fucking kick in the ass."

"You may have been the strongest here, but not strong enough to fall victim to their tricks."

"She did no such thing. Everything I've ever done for her was of my own volition."

My muscles expand the higher my rage gets, and I let it. I let it show what I've become under her care. I feel the prick of my teeth as they lengthen from my jaw. The room becomes clearer, and I can hear someone brushing shattered glass away from the street outside of the shop. I can hear a fly buzz in the corner of the room.

"She's changed you," Rowan says as he narrows his eyes on me, his head tilting to follow my increased height.

"Surely has, *Rowan*. And I would let her change every part of me if it meant I could bury myself in her demon *cunt* every night," I growl in response. My voice shudders in my chest as it descends deeper and *deeper*.

My father's face contorts in disgust, "You're a *monster*."

"Perhaps I am. But I'll be the monster that saved Vesperholm."

"You disgust me, Asher."

"Splendid."

Rowan's eyes shift to Cedric as he gestures to him, "And you?! Have you fallen prey to the vile beasts as well?"

My eyes slide to Cedric, whose nostrils flare with the change in focus, "Your audacity is admirable, father. I was given a chance to be worth something that didn't involve me shoving my cock in someone I didn't give a shit about." His own lip snarls as he takes an up and down sweep of Rowan.

"So, you're going with him? To live amongst the *demons*?"

"That's exactly what I'm doing. Because I'm *living* there. I'm not just surviving and fucking sisters."

Usually, my rage would have swallowed me whole by now, but *I* am in control. It *is* me who calls the shots.

A twisted grin contorts my lips as my gaze meets Rowan's, my head tilting in crazed challenge. "It appears your precious Broward can do your dirty work now, Rowan. I'm sure he'll have more than enough fun training his life away to slaughter the only beings that can save you from the threats you aren't aware of."

Rowan's lip twists in disgust before he grits through his teeth, "Relinquish your blade. The Blackwood Dagger should belong to just that. A Blackwood."

A growl rumbles from my chest as I move, my hand twitching as it roams to the handle of my dagger.

After all I had done, after everything I did for them. After sacrificing my life for their safety, throwing myself into Tantalia for the comfort they sit in now.

This is the thanks I get… *this* is the revelry I've been given.

Stripped of my name, stripped of my weapon, and stripped of my standing.

Even in Tantalia as I work to save our people, I am disowned. But I don't want to be part of a race of beings that seek to maim the one I love.

My hand wraps around the handle of my dagger, the ruby of its hilt burns into my palm, as if warning me. And I hesitate; for only a moment.

This dagger has been the grounding force for everything I've done since I've received it. The only thing that has reminded me of who I am. The one thing that has stayed constant in my life, and alluded to any level of influence I may have on a future I can't control.

But at the end of the day, hunters of Vesperholm can't come through The Portal, I'll make damn sure of it. And there is no succubus I'd use it on.

The metal sings from its sheath, and I hold it up to him to see. "You can thank me later, Rowan." I flick it into the wood at his feet with a deafening thunk, "I don't need it anyway."

With that, I turn away from the people I called my family, from the place I called my home, with Cedric on my heels.

We make our way back to the paddock, where I breathe deep, pressing the anger away enough to shrink my body and climb onto Gnox as Cedric tacks up Rose.

"Are you alright?" Cedric asks softly. The sounds of his tacking gear ring through my skull as I try to contain the rage pulsing within.

I look out at the street, watching the happy children play with each other. At the women baking breads, and the men selling tools.

"I'll be fine," I respond gruffly.

Cedric mounts Rose and I hear the soft crunch of hay before he approaches, and they stand at the ready beside me.

As I click Gnox out of the stable, I fish my hand into my pocket, pulling out my Blackwood Insignia.

Holding it in my palm, I stare at it for a moment longer. The familiar etches in the metal that once brought me peace and purpose stare back at me. It merely sings a song of betrayal, of abandonment, and disappointment.

A heartbroken sigh escapes me the same time as a single tear does.

I toss it onto the cobblestone, and it *tinks* a hollow sound as it hits ground.

Gnox makes a point to plant a hoof onto it before we make our way back to East Territory.

Back to Tantalia.

CHAPTER 75

DISCONNECT

SERAPHINA

*B*lackness… dull, expanding blackness.

A nervous, unfamiliar voice, "Are you sure this was the right course of action?"

A smooth response, "It is all part of the plan. Patience."

Nervous, "Her people will come looking for her. They fight until the bitter end for their queen."

Smooth, "All in due time, Percy. We have what we need for now. It is all a waiting game."

Nervous, "But… but the-"

Smooth, "Silence."

Dull… expanding… blackness.

"CATCH ME IF YOU CAN,
ASHER BLACKWOOD."

CHAPTER 76

WRATH

ASHER

Rage consumed my insides the entire way back to The Portal, even when we entered.

Rage. Pure, unrelenting -- until we touched foot on the grounds of Tantalia. Where prickles of darkness replace the rage and my skin crawls at the sensation… The energy…

Something is wrong.

Something is very, very, *very* wrong.

I feel it as soon as we step through The Portal.

The normally strong thrum of magic has dulled, and it didn't take much for us to walk through the vortex.

There is no tug at my chest when I enter this realm. The energy of my mate is completely absent. As we exit the portal Chambers, I notice the weather in Tantalia. The air is clear, and the sky bright. The storm had disappeared.

But there was darkness, *somewhere.*

Seraphina…

Cedric looks to me as he notices my state. "It'll be alright, Asher. We're better off here."

"No… No, something is awry. There is something wrong," I murmur mindlessly.

I attempt to climb that rope in my chest. And I climb for a long time, a much longer time than I have ever needed to, even before our bond was in place.

When I reach its end, there is… a wall. A thick, black expanding wall that I *know* Seraphina did not put there. "Seraphina is in trouble."

Quickly, I kick Gnox through Tantalia at breakneck speed until a blur of black shoots down to the ground before us. Gnox rears and whinnies from the intrusion; spooking at the visitor.

Heaving breaths escape the black figure as she comes to a stand before us. Her face is pinched in fear and panic, frantically attempting to get my attention as she locks gazes with me.

Selene.

My voice deepens to an immeasurable timbre, shaking the ground as I connect with her frantic eyes, "Where is she!?" I bellow.

"She… Seraphina… she's gone," Selene says through heavy pants, her eyes are apologetic. As if she's trying to plead with me for forgiveness.

I don't even know what happens next.

I don't know how I made it to The Library.

I don't know what sight I beheld when I walked into that pitch black room of destroyed books and shelves.

I don't know what I thought when I saw the lock of her hair dripped in blood on the floor. Or the crushing pain in my back as brand-new appendages began to force themselves through my skin; cracking and splintering with a violent whip at the air.

I can't feel the way my throat forces out my cries for my love, "WHERE IS SHE?! WHERE IS MY MATE?! WHERE IS SERAPHINA?!"

I don't know why the lightning lapped at my boots as it prickled and sparked around me. I don't know why the wind swirled, causing papers to swim in the air.

I don't hear the bellows of my cries as they shake The Keep and the domed skylight threatens to burst.

And I don't know what happened when I read the small sheet of parchment stabbed into the stone with a small dagger.

> *"Catch me if you can, Asher Blackwood."*

All I knew, all I felt now; was blood-boiling wrath.

And the hells hath no fury like the wrath of a scorned Asher Black-wood without his mate.

"IT'S NOTHING PERSONAL, DARLING."

CHAPTER 6 ½

VELARIA

The energy in The Court today was high.

Very high.

I know that Seraphina is averse to the throne. Lilith was her everything and Seraphina has this notion that her seat must not be vacated. The thought is unfortunate because I always felt that Seraphina was destined for so much more than war and The Pits.

It keeps me company as I take the time to grab some food and head back to my room to plan out tomorrow. There is a group of younglings that have grown enough to be sent to Cometa Legion. And while I am so sad to see them go, I'm so excited for their growth.

Raising the kin has always been a deep setting in my heart. Watching them grow from the pods to little babies. To the warriors they'll become. It's a fulfilling role and I am so happy to be where I am.

As I enter my room, the curtains of my window sway with the wind.

My forehead tenses as I look toward it in confusion. I never open my windows. Not to mention… there is a very *dark* energy in here.

I kick the door closed behind me as I walk with my small tray of food in hand.

When a clawed hand wraps around my mouth, a twisting feeling pulls at the blood in my veins, and I halt. The tray in my hand clatters to the floor and I watch my meal spill over the marble below. The only thing I can move is my eyes, my limbs incapable of action… As if I've been frozen by something.

Or more like *someone.*

The hand runs across my face to grip a handful of my hair in their fist, wrenching my head back to bare my throat.

A cool, soft voice brushes against my ear, "It's nothing personal, darling."

But it's… familiar… I *know* this voice.

Though, I don't have time to remember who it belongs to. Because the warmth of my blood running down my chest has stilled my thoughts as searing pain slices through the delicate flesh of my neck.

That's the last thing I remember as I watch my body fall to the floor below me, my head dropping and rolling in the opposite direction.

That, and the raven flying out the window before darkness closed in around me.

THE END
OF BOOK ONE

Yes, that is the end of Book One.

Have fun losing your mind until Book Two.
And whoever you think it is,
it's not.

For more updates and sneak
peeks
be sure to scan the QR code
for links to my socials!

Acknowledgements

Firstly, I need to thank Hailey-Bug.

This book had been one of my earliest ideas after Elevated Ambitions, and I was afraid to write it because of what it was. But I had locked it away in "The Vault" (which if you don't know, The Vault is the little storage facility in my brain where I keep thought of book ideas, or started books that haven't entirely come all the way to fruition yet) and she encouraged me to bring it out.

I had a vague idea on the story but I didn't know where it would go. However, I am so so so thankful she pushed me, because this story has been so amazing to work on, and it has given me so many artistic liberties that I wasn't able to take with EA. She read it from its baby days, to now, and I am so thankful for her. She is one of the first strangers that read EA and has pushed me constantly with her love and support. This book wouldn't have happened when it did without her, and she held space for me to create in a place I didn't know I could create in. I found my love of fantasy with this book, and it's because of her that I was able to find it. Thank you so much Buggy. <3

Secondly, to my wonderful husband; this book was initially an idea I had when I had first started Elevated Ambitions. I was going over ideas with him, as he is my muse and this book was born. He's given me my pen name, titles for books and so many ideas and the idea was that I wanted us to write a book together.

However, it became this parallel of us as this book continued to go on. Trials and tribulations with the loving bits and pieces in between.

Thank you my love for always supporting me, for giving me space to create, for making the gears in my brain turn and thank you for holding me together through it all. I am so happy to grow and share this life with you, you are everything and more to me, my sweet love.

To Anna; there are so many days where everything felt worthless. Where writing felt like a pipe dream and I wanted to give up. You carried me through those dark days. You threw me over your shoulder and said, "Nope, come on. We have shit to do, let's go." Whether it was sitting in silence on facetime for hours while we poured our souls into our work, or just making sure I stayed the course, your very presence in my life has been a grounding force. Thank you so much for being my friend, and thank you for suffering with me. And also putting up with my endless yapping over this series. I love you and may our page reads be plentiful and our readers satisfied.

To Kiarah; MOTHERRRRR! Thank you for all you've done for this book. BETA reading and trying to decipher all the bits and pieces of this story. Thank you for being brutally honest and telling me what works and what doesn't. I know that if there is something that needs to be said, I can always count on you to be like, "Nah ah. Delete it." Thank you for being an amazing handler and taking the time to learn me. There are not many people that can learn the things they have about me, continue to stay AND love and understand me. Thank you for being a true friend and helping me trust people again. I know it can be difficult to be friends with me sometimes and figure out my weird way of interacting, but I appreciate the effort you have put into our friendship. Thank you for being you, and loving me the way you do. I love you so much.

To Paige; thanks for bringing the vibes baby. I love you!

To Kaylah; My chaotic, unhinged twin. I'm obsessed with you and our conversations and reels. They truly bring me out of some dark places and I'm so blessed to call you my friend. Your hype and energy is everything I need and more, and I'm so lucky to have met you. I loved you since your first TikTok I saw and I love all your content and YOU now! Thank you for proofreading this book, and reading it through its different stages. You're an amazing hype man and I can't wait to meet you in real life.

To AAron and Jax; yall are truly incredible. The amount of times you guys read this book is so admirable and I am so appreciative of the time you guys have given it. It means more to me than you could possibly know and yall are always so ready all the time. I can not wait to give you guys Book 2. You guys have been with me early on and I hope to have you guys with me for many many more. Truly, truly, MVPs of my ARC team for REAL! I love yall.

To Mega-Tron (Megan) and Lindsey; you guys gave me the vision of something I hadn't seen before, and its because of you both that this cover was given the face it deserves to succeed. I can not even begin to express my gratitude for pushing me in the direction of a book cover designer (Shout out Dragana, an absolute wonder to work with and I'm over the moon to have met her; she did her thang with this cover!) when I was hell bent on trying to do it myself. It's hard to let go of an idea that you are so connected to, but I am so SO glad they showed me what it could be. I will never ever forget it for the rest of my life, because it was needed, it was necessary. They are also awesome for listening to me yap and just being there through this process. Thank yall so much for your friendship.

To Alida, Benny-Boy, Morgan and Marissa; I love yall so damn much. Your support and constant cheering is more love than I could ever imagine possible from new friends. Your infectious joy for my work keeps me going. I am so lucky to have met you guys, and I am so lucky to share this space with you. You guys make the hard days so worth it, and I need to meet all of you one day, someway somehow, I'll make it happen. Come hell or high water. Thank you so much for being here. And thank you so much for being my cheerleaders. You guys are amazing!

I have poured a considerable amount of brain power into this book. I wouldn't say time, it doesn't take me long to get the end result. But the brain power involved is insane, and when I feel iffy about something, they are always there to hear me out and see what else can be done differently. I love all of these people so much, and I hope you're ready for the work that is about to come up with book 2, because we all know that is going to be one heck of a ride.

And to you; the reader. For making it for through, or caring enough to read the acknowledgements, and make it to the end of this book, THANK YOU. I love writing, I love telling stories, but what are stories without readers? What are worlds with no patrons? Empty. Without you, this endeavor would be nothing more than a pipe dream for me to live out my insanity. I thank you, for taking a chance on an indie writing her first fantasy, her second book, and for giving me the chance to dream. And allowing me to dream big. Thank you.

There is no possible way I could have done this without any of these people. There is so much work that goes into being an indie author that most people don't see. And these people have seen it, and I appreciate them. I appreciate you, and I appreciate all the readers to come.

Because without you, a dream is just a dream. It's every one of the people in the process that turn that dream into reality.

I love you guys, and I'll see you in Book 2.

Until next time, my darling readers.

About the
Author
Aurora Steinhart

While Aurora is merely an alias, the face behind the name has enjoyed writing and reading for as long as she could remember.

An army wife, and a life-long Alaskan, she has spent her life baking, cooking, and reading. Her life-long passions.

Being an army wife means keeping busy with hobbies, which has resulted in a menagerie of different past times.

She has tried her hand at drawing, makeup, reading, weightlifting, crossfit, cross-stitch, diamond art, video games, content creation (Tik-Tok, Youtube, Twitch), and now being an author. Her motivation changing day by day as she gets struck by whatever idea sucked her in.

When she's not writing, she's spending time with her husband, 2 kids, 3 cats and 2 dogs.

www.ingramcontent.com/pod-product-compliance
Lightning Source LLC
Chambersburg PA
CBHW070257310726
48976CB00005B/1466